CRITICAL TAX THEORY: AN INTRODUCTION

Tax law is political. This book highlights and explains the major themes and method-ologies of a group of scholars who challenge the traditional claim that tax law is neutral and unbiased. The contributors to this volume include pioneers in the field of critical tax theory, as well as key thinkers who have sustained and expanded the investigation into why the tax laws are the way they are and what impact tax laws have on historically disempowered groups. This volume, assembled by two law professors who work in the field, is an accessible introduction to this new and growing body of scholarship. It is a resource not only for scholars and students in the fields of taxation and economics, but also for those who engage with critical race theory, feminist legal theory, queer theory, class-based analysis, and social justice generally. Tax is the one area of law that affects everyone in our society, and this book is crucial to understanding its impact.

Anthony C. Infanti is a Professor of Law at the University of Pittsburgh School of Law. His work focuses on sexual orientation and the law, paying particular attention to the application of the tax laws to lesbians and gay men. Widely considered one of the leading critical tax scholars in the United States, Infanti's scholarly articles have appeared (or will soon appear) in, among others, the *Buffalo Law Review*, the *Santa Clara Law Review*, the *Harvard BlackLetter Law Journal*, *Unbound: The Harvard Journal of the Legal Left*, the *Michigan Journal of Gender and Law*, the *Virginia Tax Review*, the *Florida Tax Review*, and the *Tax Lawyer*. He is also the author of *Everyday Law for Gays and Lesbians (and Those Who Care About Them)* (2007). Infanti is the past recipient of an Excellence in Teaching Award from the graduating students of the University of Pittsburgh School of Law, where he is the chief faculty editor for the *Pittsburgh Tax Review*. He is an elected member of the American Law Institute.

Bridget J. Crawford is a Professor of Law at Pace University School of Law. Prior to joining the Pace faculty, Crawford practiced law for more than six years at Milbank, Tweed, Hadley & McCloy LLP in New York City. Crawford's current scholarship focuses on the intersection of gender and tax policy. She has won numerous prizes for teaching, scholarship, and service to the legal community. Crawford is an elected member of the American Law Institute and the American College of Trust and Estate Counsel.

Critical Tax Theory

AN INTRODUCTION

Edited by

Anthony C. Infanti
University of Pittsburgh School of Law

Bridget J. Crawford
Pace University School of Law

CAMBRIDGE
UNIVERSITY PRESS

CAMBRIDGE UNIVERSITY PRESS
Cambridge, New York, Melbourne, Madrid, Cape Town, Singapore, São Paulo, Delhi

Cambridge University Press
32 Avenue of the Americas, New York, NY 10013-2473, USA

www.cambridge.org
Information on this title: www.cambridge.org/9780521734929

First published 2009

Printed in the United States of America

A catalog record for this publication is available from the British Library.

Library of Congress Cataloging in Publication data

Critical tax theory : an introduction / edited by Anthony C. Infanti,
Bridget J. Crawford.
   p.   cm.
Includes bibliographical references and index.
ISBN 978-0-521-51136-0 (hardback) – ISBN 978-0-521-73492-9 (pbk.)
1. Taxation – Law and legislation – United States.   2. Taxation – Social aspects –
United States.   3. Income tax – Law and legislation – United States.   4. Tax
administration and procedure – United States.   5. Fiscal policy – United States.
I. Infanti, Anthony C., 1968–   II. Crawford, Bridget J.   III. Title.
KF6289.C75   2009
343.7304 – dc22   2008054004

ISBN   978-0-521-51136-0 hardback
ISBN   978-0-521-73492-9 paperback

For our students, past, present, and future

and

For Hien – ACI
For the Janes – BJC

Contents

List of Illustrations

List of Tables

List of Contributors

Alice G. Abreu is the James E. Beasley Professor of Law at Temple University's Beasley College of Law.

Anne L. Alstott is the Manley O. Hudson Professor of Law at Harvard Law School.

Taunya Lovell Banks is the Jacob A. France Professor of Equality Jurisprudence and the Francis & Harriet Iglehart Research Professor of Law at the University of Maryland School of Law.

Grace Blumberg is a Professor at the UCLA School of Law.

David A. Brennen is a Professor at the University of Georgia School of Law.

Dorothy A. Brown is a Professor at Emory University School of Law.

Karen B. Brown is the Donald Phillip Rothschild Research Professor of Law at the George Washington University Law School.

Sande L. Buhai is a Clinical Professor of Law and the Director of the Public Interest Law Department at Loyola Law School–Los Angeles.

Patricia A. Cain is the Inez Mabie Distinguished Professor of Law at Santa Clara University Law School.

Pamela Johnston Conover is the Burton Craige Professor of Political Science at the University of North Carolina at Chapel Hill.

Bridget J. Crawford is a Professor and Associate Dean for Research and Faculty Development at Pace University School of Law.

Joseph M. Dodge is the Stearns Weaver Miller Weissler Alhadeff & Sitterson Professor of Law at the Florida State University College of Law.

David G. Duff is an Associate Professor at the University of Toronto Faculty of Law.

Mary Louise Fellows is the Everett Fraser Professor of Law at the University of Minnesota Law School.

Wendy C. Gerzog is a Professor at the University of Baltimore School of Law.

Gwen Thayer Handelman is a Scholar in Residence at Nova Southeastern University's Shepard Broad Law Center.

Wilton B. Hyman is an Associate Professor at the New England School of Law.

Anthony C. Infanti is a Professor at the University of Pittsburgh School of Law.

Carolyn C. Jones is the Dean and the F. Wendell Miller Professor of Law at the University of Iowa College of Law.

Lily Kahng is an Associate Professor at the Seattle University School of Law.

Nancy J. Knauer is the Peter J. Liacouras Professor of Law at Temple University's Beasley College of Law.

Marjorie E. Kornhauser is a Professor at the Sandra Day O'Connor College of Law at Arizona State University.

Francine J. Lipman is a Professor at Chapman University School of Law.

Michael A. Livingston is a Professor at Rutgers School of Law–Camden.

David Lowery is a Professor in the Department of Public Administration in the School of Behavioral and Social Sciences at the University of Leiden.

Edward J. McCaffery is the Robert C. Packard Trustee Chair in Law and Professor of Law, Economics, and Political Science at the University of Southern California's Gould School of Law.

Beverly I. Moran is a Professor of Law and a Professor of Sociology at Vanderbilt University.

Lisa C. Philipps is an Associate Professor at York University's Osgoode Hall Law School.

Daniel M. Schneider is a Professor at Northern Illinois University Law School.

Theodore P. Seto is a Professor at Loyola Law School–Los Angeles.

Nancy C. Staudt is the Class of 1940 Research Professor of Law at Northwestern University School of Law.

Miranda Stewart is an Associate Professor and Co-Director of the Taxation Studies Program at the University of Melbourne Law School.

William J. Turnier is the Willie Person Mangum Professor of Law at the University of North Carolina School of Law.

Mylinh Uy received a J.D. in 2004 from the UC Davis School of Law.

Dennis J. Ventry, Jr. is an Acting Professor at the UC Davis School of Law.

Amy L. Wax is the Robert Mundheim Professor of Law at the University of Pennsylvania Law School.

William Whitford is a Professor Emeritus at the University of Wisconsin Law School.

Lawrence Zelenak is the Pamela B. Gann Professor of Law at the Duke University School of Law.

List of Common Abbreviations

ABA American Bar Association
ADA Americans with Disabilities Act
ALI American Law Institute
BWTC Basic World Tax Code
Code Internal Revenue Code
CTC Child tax credit
DOMA Defense of Marriage Act
EITC Earned income tax credit
GAO General Accounting Office
HITC Household income tax credit
IMF International Monetary Fund
IRS Internal Revenue Service
ITA Income Tax Act (Canada)
ITIN Individual taxpayer identification number
NSFH National Survey of Families and Households
OECD Organization for Economic Co-Operation and Development
QTIP Qualified terminable interest property
SIPP Survey of Income and Program Participation
SSA Social Security Administration
SSN Social Security number
TANF Temporary Assistance to Needy Families
TIN Taxpayer identification number (whether ITIN or SSN)
VAT Value added tax
WOC Work opportunity credit

Introduction

Tax law is political. That is a fundamental assumption of critical tax theory. Critical tax scholars ask why the tax laws are the way they are and what impact tax laws have on historically disempowered groups, such as people of color; women of all colors; lesbian, gay, bisexual, and transgendered individuals; low-income and poor individuals; the disabled; and nontraditional families. Far from being an organized "movement,"[1] however, critical tax theory is a label that applies loosely to the work presented in this volume.

Though working mostly independently of one another, these scholars have all been influenced by the seismic intellectual shifts in the legal academy that occurred from the 1970s through the 1990s, namely, the critical legal studies movement and its progeny – critical race theory, feminist legal theory, and queer theory. Scholars working in those fields encouraged investigation into the law's unrevealed biases. They sought to demonstrate how accepted understandings of the law are constructed and contingent. They inspired both their contemporaries and those who work in their wake – including critical tax theorists – to question aspects of the law that might otherwise seem normal, natural, or plainly incontestable.

In the last fifteen years, there has emerged a small but steady stream of scholarship that, taken together, constitutes an incipient body of "critical tax scholarship." Specialty law reviews and journals have played a key role in bringing this new generation of critical analysis to the marketplace of ideas. This book, however, is the first to present critical tax scholarship as a distinct mode of inquiry. When viewed as a whole, it becomes clear that all critical tax scholarship shares one or more of the following goals: (1) to uncover bias in the tax laws; (2) to explore and expose how the tax laws both reflect and construct social meaning; and (3) to educate nontax scholars and lawyers about the interconnectedness of taxation, social justice, and progressive political movements. Critical tax scholars employ a variety of methods to achieve these goals. Among other methods, the contributions to this book demonstrate how critical tax scholars bring "outsider" perspectives to the study of tax law; use historical material, contemporary case studies, and personal or

---

[1] *See* Anthony C. Infanti, *A Tax Crit Identity Crisis? Or Tax Expenditure Analysis, Deconstruction, and the Rethinking of a Collective Identity*, 26 WHITTIER L. REV. 707, 711 n.11 (2005) (briefly discussing the question of whether critical tax theory qualifies as a "movement" within the meaning[s] of the term put forward by sociologists).

fictional narratives to illustrate the practical impact of the tax laws on individuals and groups; interpret social science and economic data to show how the tax laws impact groups differently; and explore the interconnectedness of tax laws with economic forces such as the labor market (especially as it impacts women) and international financial and political development.

Students, teachers, researchers, and scholars of tax law and policy can use this book in a variety of ways. It may accompany traditional classroom instruction or serve as an overview for those who want an accessible introduction to this new and growing area of tax scholarship. It can serve as a resource for tax scholars who are curious about, or seek to refute, critical tax scholars' assertion that the tax laws – whether intentionally or unintentionally – reflect and even reify discrimination based on race, gender, sexual orientation, class, disability, or family structure. Substantively, this book fills a noticeable gap in traditional approaches to the research, study, and teaching of tax law and policy. By organizing and presenting excerpts from critical tax scholarship, this book demonstrates that a complete study of tax law and policy requires an understanding of the historical, social, political, and cultural contexts in which the tax laws operate.

This book will interest students and scholars in the allied fields of critical race theory, feminist legal theory, queer theory, class-based analysis, and social justice generally. Tax is the one area of law that truly affects everyone in our society – at some point in our lives, we all directly or indirectly pay taxes of one sort or another, whether income, payroll, sales, property, excise, or transfer taxes. Yet, those interested in social justice generally overlook tax as an area of inquiry, probably deterred by its reputation as an arcane area of the law. By presenting critical tax scholarship in a format that is accessible to both the novice and the expert, we hope to help those working in allied fields to extend their theoretical inquiry to an area of law that might otherwise seem impenetrable to the nonexpert.

The ideas and arguments presented in this book are general enough for both students in an introductory tax course as well as experts in the field. It is our hope that this book will serve as a primary reference for students, teachers, researchers, and scholars of tax law and policy who want to understand, elaborate on, or respond to existing critical tax scholarship.

This book organizes representative samples of critical tax scholarship by general themes – historical perspectives on taxation, the goals of tax policy, the practical application of critical tax theory, race, gender, sexual orientation, the family, class, and disability. We also include a chapter on global critical perspectives on taxation and a chapter that presents arguments by scholars whose assessments of critical tax theory have not been entirely (or, in some cases, at all) positive. The chapters and the organization of articles within them do not follow a neat, chronological order. This is because critical tax theory has not developed along a linear path. Rather, it is a method of inquiry that scholars have begun to apply, in approximately the last fifteen years, to a broad range of tax laws. No substantive area or line of inquiry has been exhausted yet. Furthermore, articles placed in one chapter might just as well have been included in one or more other chapters because critical tax scholars often address the effects of multiple forms of subordination at the same time. This overlap stems from the fact that different forms of subordination are not akin to parallel lines moving in the same direction along separate tracks; instead, the different lines of subordination examined by critical tax scholars often cross one another to create an interlocking pattern of subordination. Yet, despite bringing multiple perspectives and methodologies to diverse issues, critical tax scholars are unified by their unwavering commitment to examining the impact of the tax laws on historically subordinated groups.

For the most part, the selections speak for themselves. Brief introductions to each chapter provide any necessary background and draw out the common themes in the selections in that chapter. To make this book accessible to all readers, we have significantly pared down each of the included excerpts. We have chosen not to indicate where cuts have been made to the works, and we have deleted all nonessential footnotes. Except when correcting typographical errors in the original texts and making minor changes to create a uniform style for the book, we have reflected any changes in brackets. None of these changes affect the substance of the contributions; they are all intended merely to preserve the flow of the text.

This book should pleasantly surprise those who assume that tax is a dry and boring field. Even those familiar with tax scholarship may be surprised at the insights that critical tax theory can bring to a familiar subject. For those already writing in the critical tax field, it is our hope that this book will stimulate further research and provide encouragement to continue what can seem – even to a tax scholar – a lonely project.

Critical tax theory enhances our understanding of the substantive tax law as well as its historical, social, political, and cultural contexts and consequences. This book does not claim that critical tax theory is the only way (or even the best way) to approach tax law. It is a lens that one can pick up and put down, but it is a lens that is never far from our own eyes. We invite you to look through that lens and see the tax law differently.

January 2009

Anthony C. Infanti
Bridget J. Crawford

CHAPTER 1. FOUNDATIONS OF CRITICAL TAX THEORY

Grace Blumberg is the original critical tax theorist. Many scholars and commentators before Blumberg critiqued U.S. tax law and policy, but Blumberg was the first to offer a systemic analysis of the tax law's negative impact on a disempowered group – in this case, women. Writing in 1971, Blumberg called the tax disincentives against women's paid labor "an instrument of social control." Blumberg pointed at the Code as inappropriately influencing women's career choices: "If the right to work is understood as a fundamental individual right, every individual should be afforded a neutral context in which to make a decision about work." Blumberg's scholarship is especially remarkable when placed in its historical context.

In the year that Blumberg's article was published, sex equality gained its first jurisprudential foothold when the U.S. Supreme Court decided *Reed v. Reed*,[1] the first important gender discrimination case. In *Reed*, the Court invalidated a state statutory preference for a male administrator of an intestate estate. Two years later, in *Frontiero v. Richardson*,[2] the Court held that it was unconstitutional to require a female member of the military to prove dependency of her spouse in order to obtain certain benefits, when a male member of the military was not required to do so. Finally in *Craig v. Boren*,[3] the Supreme Court articulated its "intermediate" scrutiny standard to be applied in gender discrimination cases, when it invalidated state liquor laws that treated women as a class differently from men as a class. Blumberg's cogent critique of the tax laws was ahead of its time.

In the 1970s, at the same time that feminist lawyers and their allies brought constitutional challenges to laws that discriminated on the basis of sex, young people were protesting in record numbers against the war in Vietnam and in favor of civil rights. As some of those young activists moved into the legal academy, legal scholarship experienced the first rumblings of the intellectual revolution that came to be known as the critical legal studies (CLS) movement. The "crits," as they were called, asserted the indeterminacy of legal rights and drew attention to the ways people in power use the legal system to reinforce the power they already have.

---

[1] 404 U.S. 71 (1971).
[2] 411 U.S. 677 (1973).
[3] 429 U.S. 190, 197 (1976).

What scholars now call critical race theory, feminist legal theory, and queer theory represents the second generation of critical scholarship. In response to perceived gaps in CLS analysis, different clusters of scholars began to use race, gender, and sexual orientation as lenses through which they could complicate the CLS analysis and explore the law's limitations. For example, "intersectional" scholars apply insights grounded in the perspective of those who are multiply disadvantaged (e.g., along lines of race *and* gender or race *and* sexual orientation).

As so many of the contributors to this volume acknowledge in their work, critical tax scholarship owes intellectual debts to all of these movements as well as to the specific scholarship of Grace Blumberg. Her article was the first to show how ripe the Code is for critical analysis.

Sexism in the Code: A Comparative Study of Income Taxation of Working Wives and Mothers

GRACE BLUMBERG[1]

Close scrutiny of the Code reveals a strong pattern of work disincentive for married women and inequitable treatment of the two-earner family. The observation that American working wives are predominantly secondary family earners is not intended to express a social ideal. It merely reflects a contemporary social reality. Women workers generally earn substantially less than their male counterparts. Working wives earn less than their employed husbands. The American wife's working career is likely to be broken by child bearing and -rearing. Unless prompted by economic necessity, her return to work is generally considered discretionary. Even when she is earning a substantial salary, her husband is unlikely to view his employment as discretionary. Thus, the American working wife should properly be understood as a secondary family earner for the purpose of determining the work disincentive effect of various Code provisions.

UNITED STATES TAXATION OF WORKING WIVES AND MOTHERS

Prior to 1948, taxation was individual. Joint returns were authorized but seldom used because the aggregate family income was taxed as though it were the income of a single taxpayer. Since each individual taxpayer was taxed at progressive rates, a tax benefit would result from shifting earned and unearned income among family members. (Earned income is the fruit of personal effort and labor, e.g., salary; unearned income arises from the ownership of property, e.g., rent and dividends.) Thus, a husband with taxable earned income of $8,000 would secure a tax advantage by shifting $4,000 to his wife. Because of the progressive nature of income tax rates, each would pay less than one-half of the tax that the husband would have paid on the entire amount. The Supreme Court initially disapproved such shifting of earned income, but later created a serious problem when it allowed shifting in community property states where each spouse has a vested right in all property and income acquired during the marriage. In *Poe v. Seaborn*,[2] the Court construed the Code provision levying income tax on "the net income of every individual"[3] to allow each

---

[1] Reprinted by permission from 21 *Buffalo Law Review* 49 (1971).
[2] 282 U.S. 101 (1930).
[3] I.R.C. § 1(a) (1954).

spouse to file a separate return and pay tax on one-half of all community income. Since spouses in common law states do not have a vested interest in all property acquired by the other during marriage, they were denied the benefit of income splitting of earned income.

While *Seaborn* was clearly an improvident decision which could have been remedied by a legislative enactment requiring that earned income be taxable to the earner, all countries employing individual rather than aggregate taxation have had to contend with the persistent problem of unearned income shifting. A husband who owns two properties yielding $8,000 annual income can always transfer one of them to his wife; each spouse is then taxable on $4,000. Pre-1948 law, therefore, tended to impose higher taxes on earned family income in common law states than in community property states and to generally tax earned family income more heavily than unearned family income when the family receiving unearned income distributed the income-producing property among its members.

In 1948, Congress faced the choice of legislatively repealing the community property–common law distinction created by *Seaborn* or enacting the benefit of *Seaborn* for residents of common law states. It chose the latter course and in so doing created a serious disincentive for married women who wish to work as well as a disproportionately high tax liability for single people.

The new system was based on two separable elements, aggregation and income splitting. Under present law spouses may file a joint return in which they aggregate income, exemptions, and deductions. Total taxable income is split in half; from 1948 to 1970, the half figure was taxed at the individual rate and then multiplied by two. If a husband was the sole family earner with $20,000 taxable income, his income was taxed as though he were two individuals each earning $10,000. A couple in which each spouse earned $10,000 thus received the same tax treatment as a couple in which the sole family earner made $20,000 and theoretically (but not effectively) received the same tax treatment as two unrelated individuals each earning $10,000.

Aggregation

Aggregation of spousal income, as opposed to individual taxation of each spouse's income, is based on the indisputable economic unity of the family. Since resources are generally pooled by spouses, their ability to pay taxes is best measured in terms of family rather than individual income. Aggregation creates, however, a strong work disincentive for potential or actual secondary family earners. The secondary earner's first dollar of income is effectively taxed at the primary earner's highest or "marginal" rate. Assume that a husband earns $12,000 taxable income. At 1970 rates, he is taxed 14% of his first thousand dollars of taxable income, 15% of the second thousand, 16% of the third thousand, and so forth. His final or twelfth thousand is taxed at 22%. Any dollar that he earns in excess of $12,000 will be taxed at 25%, his marginal rate. If his wife decides to work, her very first dollar will be taxed at her husband's marginal rate. As the husband's income increases, so will his marginal rate and the wife's work disincentive. Filing separate returns is not an economically practical solution. While the wife's effective rate would be lower, the family would pay a larger total tax unless both spouses have equivalent individual incomes, in which case filing separate returns would yield no benefit or loss.

Employee's Cost of Earning Income and Earned Income Allowances

Congress has the "power to lay and collect taxes on income, from whatever source derived."[4] In relation to income taxation, the least contested definition of income is "the money value of the net accretion to one's economic power between two points of time."[5] Taxable income is, thus, generally understood as net rather than gross income. Allowance for the cost of earning income may even be constitutionally required. Although the Code presently contains some provision for an employee's cost of earning income and the special expenses incurred by working women, the deductions are narrowly drawn and of little general applicability.

The Code draws a sharp distinction between businessmen and employees. A businessman deducts all his "ordinary and necessary business expenses" from gross receipts in order to determine his adjusted gross income; he then deducts personal exemptions and the optional standard deduction (or itemized deductions) to reach his taxable income. An employee, on the other hand, can deduct only four types of expenses from gross income: expenses reimbursed by his employer, expenses for business travel away from home, transportation expenses incurred in the course of employment, and expenses incurred as an outside salesman. With regard to other deductible employment expenses, the employee must choose between itemizing them or taking the optional standard deduction.

The optional standard deduction should not be understood as a substitute for an earned income allowance: it is available to all taxpayers regardless of whether they have earned income; it is effectively taken away from a working woman when she marries even though she continues to work; and it is available to a businessman after he has deducted all his deductible costs of earning income.

Deductible employee expenses are relatively few: limited child-care deductions, educational expenses necessary to maintain present employment, employment agency fees, labor union dues, employee's short-life tools, and uniforms so long as they are not suitable for general wear. Nondeductible items include commuting expenses, the cost of an employee's lunches, clothing necessary for work but suitable for general wear, and all housekeeping and most child-care costs incurred by working wives. An employee who does not incur large deductible expenses which are strictly personal in nature, that is, unrelated to the fact of his employment, is likely to be better off with the optional standard deduction which can, thus, best be understood as a compensatory exemption for taxpayers who do not incur certain personal expenses (the deductibility of which is open to serious question).

Since the ability to pay taxes is a primary factor in distribution of the tax burden, it would seem that an employee's cost of earning income should be excluded from his taxable income in order to put him on a par with recipients of unearned income. Other nations have come to this conclusion and allow an earned income credit or

---

[4] U.S. Const. amend. XVI.

[5] Edwin R.A. Seligman, *Income Tax, in* 7 Encyclopedia of the Social Sciences 628 (1932).

deduction for wage earners. There is [a] fourfold argument in favor of an earned income allowance for working wives and mothers. First, since most families have at least one earner, failure to provide an earned income allowance for the first family earner distributes a burden, albeit inequitable, equally among families. Since, however, most families do not have two earners, such families bear an extra burden. Secondly, the working wife is likely to incur more employment-related expenses than the primary earner. In addition to normal commuting, clothing, and lunch costs, she is also likely to incur housekeeping and child-care expenses. Thirdly, since the wife's first dollar is effectively taxed at her husband's marginal rate, she has less disposable income with which to defray her cost of earning income. Finally, providing the wife with an earned income allowance would tend to mitigate the work disincentive of income aggregation. Thus, if the revenue cost of an earned income allowance for all workers is judged to be excessive, consideration should still be given to earned income allowances for working wives and mothers.

Deduction of Child-Care Expenses

In 1954, the House Ways and Means Committee recommended that a deduction be allowed to widows and widowers with young children for child-care expenses incurred for the purpose of enabling the parent to pursue gainful employment. The Senate Finance Committee liberalized the bill to include expenses paid by working women and widowers for the care of any dependent physically or mentally incapable of caring for himself.

As passed, the Act allowed gainfully employed widows, widowers, and women to deduct up to $600 for expenses actually incurred for the care of children under the age of twelve and other dependents incapable of caring for themselves. The Act contained no general maximum income limitation beyond which the deduction could not be claimed. But married women with husbands capable of self-support were subject to a special provision allowing a deduction only if the couple filed a joint return and if the total adjusted gross family income did not exceed $5,100.

[In 1971,] § 214 allows a deduction for expenses paid during the taxable year for the care of certain dependents (a son, stepson, daughter, or stepdaughter of a taxpayer under the age of thirteen and any dependent not physically or mentally capable of caring for himself) while the taxpayer is gainfully employed or seeking gainful employment.

Deduction for the care of one child may not exceed $600; deduction for the care of two or more children may not exceed $900. Persons eligible to claim the deduction are all women, widowers, divorced or legally separated husbands, and husbands with incapacitated or institutionalized wives. Single men are not eligible.

In the case of working wives, and husbands with incapacitated wives, the spouses must file a joint return and the amount of deductible expense is reduced by the amount that adjusted gross income exceeds $6,000. This limitation does not apply to a working wife whose husband is incapable of self-support because of a mental or physical defect or to a working husband with an incapacitated wife who has been institutionalized for ninety days or more. A woman is not married, that is, not subject to the income limitation, if she is legally separated or divorced, or has been deserted by her husband and has secured a judicial support order against him.

While the provision was not intended to cover all costs of maintaining a child (e.g., food, clothing, education), when those costs are an inseparable part of child care, they are deductible. Therefore, the full amount paid to a nursery school is deductible even though the fee effectively covers lunch, education, and recreation as well as care, that is, babysitting. There is no requirement that care be the least expensive available. When a maid is hired to perform housework as well as child care, a reasonable allocation should be made.

The Conceptual Basis for § 214 and the Family Income Limitation for Working Mothers

The House Ways and Means Committee initially reported:

> Your committee has added this deduction to the code because it recognizes that a widow or widower [not yet liberalized by the Senate to include working wives] with young children must incur these expenses in order to earn a livelihood and that they, therefore, are comparable to an employee's business expenses.[6]

The Committee's explanation leads to two different conclusions depending on the meaning one gives to "livelihood." If it is understood to signify the pursuit of income through gainful employment, all persons who necessarily incur such expenses ought to be allowed this deduction as a cost of earning income. If, on the other hand, "livelihood" is intended to mean the pursuit of income for the purpose of basic family subsistence, then it is arguable that a family in which one parent can earn and the other parent can stay home to care for children should not be eligible for the deduction unless the earned income of both is absolutely necessary for family survival. The latter interpretation would seem to be the operative one in view of the Senate's subsequent expansion of coverage to low-income, two-earner couples.

> It is recognized that in many low-income families, the earnings of the mother are essential for the maintenance of minimum living standards, even where the father is also employed, and that in such situations the requirement of providing child care may be just as pressing as in the case of a widowed or divorced mother.[7]

Such a reading is not, however, consonant with the economic policy expressed in other Code provisions or the American spirit of wealth acquisition. The Code does not require that a businessman show that he is economically constrained to pursue his business as a prerequisite for deduction of business expenses. Our society does not encourage individuals or families to view mere subsistence as an ultimate economic goal. While the low-income, two-earner provision might be understood as an exercise of congressional grace for the benefit of low-income families, the entire section does not lend support to such a reading. There is no income limitation on single-parent earners. Thus, the widowed business executive

[6] H.R. Rep. No. 83-1337 (1954), *as reprinted in* 1954 U.S.C.C.A.N. 4019, 4055.
[7] S. Rep. No. 83-1622 (1954), *as reprinted in* 1954 U.S.C.C.A.N. 4621, 4666.

with $10,000 unearned income from securities and $25,000 earned income from employment is eligible for the deduction as is the divorcée with $10,000 in alimony and $10,000 in salary. The deduction is, therefore, granted not because they need it but because it is expected that they will work and because child care is effectively a "business expense."

The basis for the distinction between single parents and couples thus emerges: a single parent will or should work; a married mother with a husband capable of support will not or should not work unless her income is absolutely necessary to provide for basic family needs. While this consideration was not articulated in the congressional reports, it is frequently mentioned by tax policy writers.

Whether § 214(a) is understood to confer a benefit on certain taxpayers or to register congressional recognition of child care as a "business expense," the equal protection guarantee requires that it be made available to all gainfully employed persons who incur child-care expenses unless a rational distinction related to the furtherance of legitimate legislative concerns can be made between the benefited group, sole household heads, and the denied group, working couples. Since there is no income limitation on single heads, the distinction is not based on ability to pay taxes. Nor is it based on the taxpayer's demonstrated need to seek employment. The distinction appears to be merely a reflection of congressional feeling that mothers should generally stay at home. Since infringement of the right to work is not a legitimate legislative goal, there would appear to be no constitutionally valid basis for the distinction between sole heads and married women.

DOES UNFAVORABLE TAXATION OF WORKING WIVES ACTUALLY CREATE A WORK DISINCENTIVE?

The argument that unfavorable taxation of working wives is likely to create a work disincentive is not equivalent to the assertion that taxation does, in fact, deter wives from seeking gainful employment. Commentators often conclude that taxation of working wives, while inequitable, does not deter them from working. Reference to the increased proportion of married women in the labor force would seem to support their position. The statistics do not show, however, what the rate of increase might have been in a more neutral tax context.

Commentators gather further support from British and American research which indicates that factors other than money play the most important role in work motivation. Studies involving the work motivation of male professionals and executives are frequently cited. Such research should probably not be used to measure the effect of tax disincentive on wives.

Firstly, male executives are likely to work for different reasons or, more precisely, to feel comfortable articulating certain nonmonetary motivations. A male executive or professional says that he likes the power, prestige, or sense of identity that he obtains from work. While the same factors may motivate a wife to work, she generally does not feel comfortable expressing them. A desire for power and prestige is unfeminine. She is supposed to find her identity at home and she is expected to enjoy staying at home. She says, therefore, that she works primarily to supplement family income. If she is not substantially adding to family income, she ought not, by her own articulated criterion, be working. Any wife contemplating work or actually working will compare her disposable income (after taxation without exemptions at her husband's marginal rate) with the additional expenses incurred because of her daily departure from the home. If the difference is not great (and under our present system of taxation and prevalent pattern of wage discrimination, it is not likely to be), the wife may well stop working regardless of the unarticulated nonmonetary benefits that she and her family derive from her work.

Secondly, the male executive is the primary family earner. He and his family expect him to be employed. Even if he can choose between early retirement and continued employment, he is likely to opt for a continuation of his life pattern. Unlike the wife, he has no reentry problem. Between his first job and his final retirement, it is unlikely that a male will ever consider the possibility of not working. His wife's initial employment is likely, however, to have been terminated by marriage or child bearing. Her reentry into the labor market is generally the result of a considered and often discretionary choice.

Thirdly, the studies involved general tax increases. The larger resultant tax burden did not imply any societal judgments regarding the desirability of the taxpayer's gainful employment. But the disincentive provisions not only reflect national policy; they also express it normatively. The married woman who is instructed to claim "0" exemptions, informed that child-care expenses are disallowed because her family is not poor, and taxed at her husband's marginal rate is effectively told that her proper place is the home.

If the right to work is understood as a fundamental individual right, every individual should be afforded a neutral context in which to make a decision about work. The pattern of work disincentive embodied in the Code is entirely inconsistent with the principle of sexual equality enunciated in title VII and further expanded by the federal and state judiciaries. The aggregation of spousal income should be abandoned in favor of individual taxation for all wage earners; the § 214 income limitation for working couples should be abolished; and an earned income allowance for secondary family earners should be enacted.

CHAPTER 2. HISTORICAL PERSPECTIVES ON TAXATION

When studying the evolution of tax law and policy, students and scholars typically study official records – decisions by judges, rulings and publications by administrative agencies, statements by elected officials, and legislative histories. These are the traditional tools for uncovering the "history" of taxation, and yet the story these official records tell is incomplete. The contributors to this chapter seek to fill the gaps in our understanding of the social and political meaning of taxation in everyday life. Historical perspectives on the Code yield multiple implications for our understanding of the tax system.

In her article *Dollars and Selves: Women's Tax Criticism and Resistance in the 1870s*, Carolyn Jones examines nineteenth-century news articles to explain how proponents of woman suffrage linked their claims to the right of women to vote with the unfairness of the tax system. As Jones explains, suffrage advocates used tax protests to draw attention to women's lack of power in the public sphere. Through these tax protests, women made claims both about their economic rights and their right to participate in public life. The very meaning of taxation, Jones reminds us, is historically contingent.

In her second contribution, *Split Income and Separate Spheres: Tax Law and Gender Roles in the 1940s*, Jones again looks beyond court cases and policy statements to reveal a rich history of an "official" tax story. Jones carefully studies newspaper articles, advertisements, and letters written by citizens to their elected representatives to understand the tremendous role that war, gender, and property rights played in the development in 1948 of the joint income tax return. She urges the reader to analyze the relationship between tax law and everyday "culture."

In *The Rhetoric of the Anti-Progressive Income Tax Movement: A Typical Male Reaction*, Marjorie Kornhauser focuses on a distinct break with the past – the sustained attack in recent decades on the idea of a progressive income tax. Kornhauser critically examines the seemingly rational and semiscientific terms that scholars use to make the case against progressivity. Through her article's provocative title, Kornhauser draws the reader's attention to the role of rhetoric in any written or verbal communication, including descriptions of tax policy and, more particularly, the case against progressivity. Lawyers and economists make broad claims about the incompatibility of a progressive system with individual liberties. Kornhauser inverts these claims to suggest that tax progressivity is a foundational element of a just society. She uses relational feminism as a lens for illuminating that interconnectedness and mutual responsibility are not incompatible with property rights and individual freedoms.

Dollars and Selves: Women's Tax Criticism and Resistance in the 1870s

CAROLYN C. JONES[1]

> It is true that most people will when I talk of our claim on the ground of human rights, blink like owls in the daylight; but they understand me at once, when I speak of my right to look after the dollars which I have paid as a tax. In short, they understand the worth of my dollars, and my right to look after them, but do not understand what above all I hold of worth – my personal self and my right to represent it.
>
> – Mary Eastman, 1877[2]

Although women's history scholars have mentioned tax protests and refusals to pay in the woman suffrage movement, relatively little analysis has been devoted to these issues. Key to understanding both the dollars and the selves taxation arguments is an appreciation of the centrality of metaphor.

By trying to use familiar historical narratives of the Revolutionary era [e.g., no taxation without representation] as vehicles to explain or reveal something of women's tax protests and resistance in the 1870s, woman suffragists used a metaphor that was generative of later policy decisions and adverse consequences for the women's movement. The selves arguments were bottomed on metaphoric employment of taxation outside its familiar context of governmental exactions. In writings from the 1870s, taxation was critical to an understanding of gender within society. The selves taxation arguments used by woman suffragists in the 1870s were an attempt both to set forth a meaning for "taxation," an important symbol in American political life, and to use "taxation" to "limit and contain the metaphoric possibilities" of other cultural constructs.

One particularly important construct to the analysis of both types of taxation arguments is another metaphor – the doctrine of separate spheres and the closely connected public–private distinction. The notion that men and women occupied different "spheres and destinies" was both a traditional and dynamic notion in the nineteenth century. The domestic sphere to which women were consigned was seen by some in that period as prescriptive and limiting.

---

[1] Reprinted by permission from 1994 *University of Illinois Law Review* 265.
[2] *Annual Meeting Massachusetts Woman Suffrage Association*, 8 WOMAN's J. 48 (1877).

Equalitarian arguments for women's rights attempted to lift certain confining aspects of the separate spheres ideology. These strategies tried to portray women as equal, not separate or different from men. Suffragists, however, also used separate spheres thinking as a positive argument for their cause. Building on women's culture and friendships fostered by segregation, woman suffragists argued that women would bring different and valuable perspectives to public life. Women in the nineteenth century maintained a high degree of separate religious activism. The home in the Victorian age continued to be seen as the repository for civic virtue and religious morality, qualities seen as absent from the male worlds of government and market.

THE *WOMAN'S JOURNAL*: ITS POTENTIAL AND LIMITATIONS AS DATABASE

This article uses the suffrage newspaper *Woman's Journal* during the 1870s in its analysis of taxation issues in the suffrage movement. The *Woman's Journal* was the most prominent of the suffrage newspapers during the 1870s and enjoyed the longest life, lasting until 1920, the year that the Nineteenth Amendment was adopted. On its masthead, the *Journal* proclaimed that it was "devoted to the interests of Woman, to her educational, industrial, legal and political equality, and especially to her right of Suffrage."[3] The newspaper targeted conservative, middle-class, professional men and women, providing a counterpoint at its inception in 1870 to [Elizabeth Cady] Stanton and [Susan B.] Anthony's *Revolution*, a more radical publication that met its demise that same year. The *Woman's Journal* had a distinctly New England focus, featuring lengthy discussions of developments in New England legislatures, particularly that of Massachusetts. Although the *Journal* received missives from editors or correspondents as far west as California, the center of gravity was in Boston. As a weekly paper with at least eight pages in each issue, the *Journal* could, and did, address the issues of taxation and women's rights repeatedly and in detail. The *Journal*'s national circulation reached women who could not or would not attend women's rights conventions and meetings. Its intensive focus upon New England and the middle class and the somewhat conservative nature of its editors and audience made the *Journal* unrepresentative of all of the factions of the movement. The extensive concern with taxation, particularly with local property taxation, may have reflected the regional and class concerns of the editors and readership.

DOLLARS ARGUMENTS FOR SUFFRAGE

The models for woman suffragists in the 1870s were Revolutionary tax resisters and contemporary women and a man who refused to pay taxes. Prior to the 1870s, there had been instances of refusal to pay taxes because women could not vote. Lucy Stone, leader of the American Woman Suffrage Association in the 1870s

---

[3] Susan S. Huxman, *The Woman's Journal, 1870–1890: The Torchbearer for Suffrage, in* A VOICE OF THEIR OWN: THE WOMAN SUFFRAGE PRESS, 1840–1910, at 88 (Martha M. Solomon ed., 1991).

and editor of *Woman's Journal*, had experience as a tax resister in the 1850s. Her refusal to pay taxes resulted in a foreclosure sale at which some of her household goods were auctioned. None of the tax resisting or protesting forebears received the national prominence that the Smith sisters achieved in the 1870s.

The Smith sisters, Abby and Julia, were in their seventies when their involvement in the woman suffrage movement began, prompted by what the two perceived as the inefficiency and injustice of the tax system. The Smith sisters were probably the wealthiest women in Glastonbury, Connecticut, and certainly among the most well off in that community as a whole. Abby and Julia were the survivors of a family of five sisters. They had inherited considerable property from their father, an unsuccessful Congregational clergyman turned successful lawyer, and their mother, a wealthy woman in her own right. In June 1869, the overseer of highways asked the Smiths to pay their $18 assessment early and they obliged, only to be billed for the assessment again in October. The overseer contended he could do nothing about the situation. Angry about this situation, Julia and Abby attended a suffrage convention.

In 1872 the Glastonbury tax collector notified the sisters that their town tax had been increased by $100. The Smiths believed that the only taxpayers given higher tax bills were women taxpayers. Although the sisters paid the 1872 tax, their sense of indignation heightened and they refused to pay their November 1873 tax installment. On January 1, 1874, the tax collector attached the Smiths' cows, and sold them at auction to satisfy the unpaid tax liability. The foreclosure purchaser for six of the seven cows was an agent for the Smiths. The elements of the Smiths' story – two elderly unmarried women, their refusal to pay taxes, and the sale of the cows at the auction elicited great interest in newspapers and among suffrage groups. The cows became famous at the Union Bazaar. Souvenir bouquets were made from the hair of Alderney cows into the forms of jasmine and buttercups, and tied with black ribbon bearing the legend "Taxation without representation."

The Smiths continued in their refusal to pay taxes. In June 1874, the town collector auctioned eleven acres of meadow land to a neighboring farmer at a price which the Smiths contended was less than 10% of its value. The Smiths resorted to the legal system to contest this auction primarily on grounds that the collector had illegally auctioned land before selling their remaining personalty – their furniture, cows, and hay. This claim prevailed; the town won a reversal on appeal. The appeal was set aside in 1876 by the court of equity in Hartford.

In April that year, the tax collector again auctioned three Alderneys, in addition to bank stock. The Smiths bought back two of the cows. Two more cows were auctioned off in September 1877. Throughout the period from 1873 to 1878, the Smiths publicized their tax resistance and appeared before local, state, and national suffrage meetings and congressional and legislative hearings. The *Woman's Journal* covered their story heavily, reprinting correspondence from the sisters, and editorializing about their plight. Their tax resistance effectively ended with Abby's death at age eighty-one on July 23, 1878. In the spring of 1879, Julia married for the first time at age seventy-seven. Her husband, retired Judge Amos A. Parker, paid taxes on the Smith property. Julia reimbursed him with gifts of money. Julia died March 6, 1886, asking to be buried between two of her sisters. Her tombstone bore her birth name only.

To the north in Worcester, Massachusetts, was a contingent of suffrage tax resisters during the 1870s consisting of Mrs. Marietta Flagg, Stephen and Abby Kelley Foster, and Sarah Wall. Abby Kelley became an antislavery agent in 1839. Kelley linked the causes of slaves and women. She married Stephen S. Foster, a fellow abolitionist in 1845, and both continued their reform work. The Fosters' tax resistance apparently began with Stephen Foster's announcement at a meeting of the Massachusetts Woman Suffrage Association that he would refuse to pay taxes until his wife and sister could vote. The Fosters' tax strike was compared to their civil disobedience years earlier in aiding fugitive slaves.

The Fosters' home was sold, but they retained possession during the redemption period. Meanwhile, the Fosters' case stayed in the public eye at suffrage conventions, legislative hearings, and Fourth of July celebrations.

The recounting above is[,] of necessity and design, not a complete representation of all "events" of the Smith and Worcester tax resistance. Even the characterization of their activities as tax resistance implies some ideological dimension beyond a mere failure to pay taxes. The "events" in Glastonbury and Worcester were subject to varying interpretations. Some in those towns alleged that the Smiths and others were wealthy women shirking their obligations to their communities as a whole.

At times, supporters made great and obvious attempts to draw parallels between women tax resisters of the 1870s and their predecessors a century earlier. T. W. Higginson rebutted arguments that the American Revolution was fought to secure local, not personal, representation. This use of familiar historic narratives as vehicles to explain or reveal something of the nature of woman suffragist tax resistance is the process of metaphor – the use of a familiar concept to display, primarily, the similarity between the familiar vehicle and a subject dissimilar from the vehicle.

Rather than portraying the Smiths or Fosters as comic crackpots or selfish skinflints, the writers in *Woman's Journal*, including the Smiths and Fosters themselves, fundamentally adopt a tragic romantic myth of civil disobedience or continuation of revolution. In the tales of tax resistance, the strength to oppose the tax collector is found in religious or republican virtue. The vulnerability of the home and the existence of a moral basis for opposition to the government implicate the ideology of separate spheres in ways that both attack and reinforce it.

Although traditional narratives of tragic romance stress the hero's strength, aspects of the tax refusal narratives focused upon the vulnerabilities of the resisters. At one level, the tax resistance of the Smiths, Fosters, and others provided a sharp illustration of the artificiality of a separate, protected "woman's" sphere. Women taxpayers were indeed subject to law. Women tax protesters who worked off their road taxes were making the point that government's exactions could force women out of their homes and out of traditional types of work for Anglo-American women. The story about the sale of Lucy Stone's household furnishings at the foreclosure sale after her refusal to pay taxes provided another illustration of government power over the woman's sphere of home and children. The Smith sisters seemed to be aware of the powerful and repugnant nature of such events. A court eventually held one foreclosure sale of land by the Glastonbury tax collector to be illegal because the tax collector should have taken personal property to pay taxes before taking real estate. The Smiths' insistence that their furniture, hay, or other personalty be taken first could have merely been the available legal ploy to defeat foreclosure. Alternatively, it could have been a strategic statement about government power and the assailability of the home.

The ultimate lack of protection for woman's sphere also emerged as a theme in the Foster tax resistance case. The vivid demonstration of the subjection of woman's sphere – the home – to government power was in part an argument for suffrage. If the home was not truly separate from the public–governmental sphere, the separate spheres construct was illusory, women were as subject to governmental authority as men, and therefore, women should be equally represented.

By aligning themselves with tax resisters and civil disobedients of the Revolutionary era, woman suffragists repeated the common slogan "no taxation without representation." Although this may have been true of spoken tax protests, once "taxation without representation" became active tax resistance or civil disobedience, the narrative and metaphoric patterns associated with that type of story and its element of higher law meant that religious imagery became an important component of discourse. Here the separate spheres ideology's celebration of women's greater moral and religious virtue became significant.

Civil disobedience results from refusal to submit to the demands of public law because it conflicts with the dictates of a higher law. Woman suffragists in the 1870s often invoked Christian and republican principles as justification both for suffrage and for refusal to pay taxes. Women could be seen as the special guardians of both types of principles.

The tax resisters' adherence to their personal or private visions of "right" caused them to refuse to submit to existing public law. The religious and republican heritage maintained particularly by women in their separate sphere had the potential to remake the public sphere of politics, again demonstrating the interdependence of public and private spheres. Tax resistance was not merely a justice or equality argument for suffrage; it also partook substantially from expediency – the gains to be made from the differences between men and women. The Smiths, Fosters, and their cohorts chose to occupy the territory of religious and patriotic martyrdom. It was a concept particularly well suited to women.

In making dollars arguments, woman suffragists employed historical, metaphoric, and mythic patterns to assert similarities between woman suffrage tax resisters and martyrs or heroes of the American Revolution. Because of the pervasive background metaphor of separate spheres, however, women's vulnerability to public authority and their essential moral and religious virtues came to be emphasized. Separate spheres were also the focus of a collection of writings in the *Woman's Journal* that dealt not with taxation as an actual governmental coercive exaction, but rather used "taxation" as an image to convey greater truths about women's lives.

TAXATION REDEFINED: ARGUMENTS ABOUT SELF

Traditionally, taxation is conceived as the taking of money or property by the government by use of law. Although most of the tax suffrage discussion focused upon this brand of coercive governmental taking, suffragists writing for the *Woman's*

Journal displayed a more catholic notion of taxation – one that perceived that coercive societal action against women was not just limited to government, but extended in a continuum to increasingly "private" transactions. Some of these women saw the unfairness of their wages in relation to men's. The market, they said, exacted a tax – in the form of lower wages – from them because they were women. At the evening session of the 1874 Anti-Tax Convention in Worcester, Massachusetts, Mary Cobell spoke and an account appeared in the *Woman's Journal*:

> She said she had heard much about the taxation of women, but one thing she had not heard, and that was the tax on sex. In the difference in remuneration of men and women in different positions in life, she had calculated that she had paid for being a woman at least $10 a month. She had taught schools successfully where young men had received $30 per month, and been obliged to receive $20, if she would keep it as well.[4]

By conceiving of the lower wages paid to women in relation to the male wage as a "tax on sex," suffragist commentators implied that the reigning liberal vision of the market was inaccurate. First, the imputed "tax" on women suggested a governmental role in the marketplace – certainly it did in the hiring of schoolteachers, a major occupation of women in the 1870s. More importantly, the "tax" label implied coercive elements in the "free" market, elements that limited a woman's ability to bargain for wages in a way that a man was not constrained. In exposing a structural bias against women in the marketplace, a bias expressed in the governmental sector by taxation without provision of women's suffrage, these women writing in the 1870s used an expansive notion of taxation to bridge the public governmental and public–private market spheres.

Taxation holds within it the notion of taking valuable things. In characterizing pay inequity as a tax on sex, suffragists were arguing that employers were taking women's services without paying adequately. Those using the concept of "social taxation" saw clubs, churches, and polite society extracting time and wastefully inefficient amounts of money from women. Although the writers in the *Woman's Journal* did not quantify the amount of tax extracted through pay inequities, social obligations, and housework, they were convinced that what was taken was both valuable and significant.

The expanded notion of taxation also refuted the idea that American life was divided into separate spheres – one public and one private. By arguing that one word applied to both "public" and "private" transactions, the *Woman's Journal* authors highlighted similarities that undermined prevailing notions of social organization. Taxation is coercive. It entails an exercise of power over a subject. This is an accepted notion with respect to governmental taxation. It should be less applicable to government in its role as license-giver or benefit-conferrer. Suffragists who attacked the regulation of prostitution objected, in part, because women who were sometimes forced into that profession were required to pay "taxes" or fees that were not levied against their male clients. An unfair license regime operating in

---

[4] *Report of the Anti-Tax Convention in Worcester*, 5 Woman's J. 52 (1872).

a realm in which suffragists saw women degraded and victimized was labeled as a "tax" – a coercive appellation, not as the voluntary purchase of a governmental privilege.

Market transactions were sometimes characterized as private because they were regarded as nongovernmental. They were, for purposes of gender relations, however, seen as public, as distinct from the private domestic sphere occupied by women. The market was theoretically typified by voluntary transactions entered into by willing participants, each bargaining for his own economic interests. Presumed equality of bargaining power was attacked by the use of the word taxation to characterize market transactions. If women systematically received less than men for the same work, the market was less free than it was said to be. A coercive distorting force was present in market transactions, making the market less distinct from the state and its powers.

Churches, clubs, and relations among neighbors were public in the sense that they were external to the family and home. Such groups could, in theory, be viewed as private because they were outside the competitive public sphere of the market and more characterized by affection and altruism, the hallmarks of the domestic sphere. The idea of social taxation attacked this premise as well. If donations or gifts were demanded, not freely given, and enforced with social sanctions, coercive methods usually associated with government could be said to be at work here. The "private" world of community social relations was not distinguishable from government in this respect.

The family clearly was assigned to the private sphere. Family relationships were supposed to be based upon love and altruism. If housework was taxation – coercive exaction of a woman's time – the special identity of the private sphere was less obvious. Rather than protecting women, the home seemed to replicate the constraining patterns of government, market, and polite society.

The use of *taxation* to signify various types of economic disadvantage experienced by women had the potential to deconstruct the separate public and private spheres, and, indeed, to demonstrate society's exactions across spectral gradations from government to family. It also suggested, however, that taxation was not beyond the intellectual and experiential grasp of the *Woman's Journal* readers. This was a crucial point for woman suffragists who valued an educated electorate. If housework was an example of inequitable taxation, understanding more "difficult" concepts of public finance was not only feasible, but quite likely. The epistemological and metaphoric move from familiar to unfamiliar was a strategy endorsed in the *Woman's Journal*.

"Taxation" in these articles functioned as a metaphor for various types of oppression experienced by women in their dealings with the government, employers, community, social groups, and the family. For suffragists in the 1870s, taxation described features of the social system that took valuable things and time from women without affording them the opportunities or rights they demanded.

An understanding of the woman suffrage movement in the 1870s requires that both dollars and selves arguments be kept in focus. Both arguments could have been fashioned as a basis for universal woman suffrage. The dollars argument and the tax resistance incident to it, however, used historical metaphor and a narrow definition of taxpayer in ways that were quite consistent with limited woman suffrage. Although the selves arguments with the redefinition of taxation could have resonated with women with very different life experiences and social statuses, the illustrations given appealed primarily to the experiences of middle-class women – the readership of the *Woman's Journal*. The role that taxation arguments played in the woman suffrage movement of the 1870s cannot be understood without considering how race, ethnicity, and class figured in the case for woman suffrage.

PROPERTY AND PARTIALITY: ETHNICITY, RACE, CLASS, AND LIMITED SUFFRAGE

Taxation was in the forefront in the 1870s as men of the era debated public policy. Federal taxes such as the tariff, the Civil War income tax, and alcohol and tobacco taxes were the subjects of intense discussion and violent disagreement. At the state and local levels, men debated the allocation of the tax burden. At farmers' club meetings, critics protested against heavier state and local taxation of real property in comparison with more lightly taxed personal property. Higher corporate and railroad taxes were called for and there was support for state income taxes. During this period, the term *taxpayer* assumed a new descriptive role as committees with memberships numbering in the teens or hundreds were mobilized for political action.

Just like the men in the taxpayers' committees, middle- and upper-class woman suffragists sought to use their ownership of property and payment of direct taxes to distinguish themselves from the lower classes, particularly from the lower-class men who had gained the franchise. The distinction drawn was not only economic, however; it had very strong nativist and racist elements.

The tax protests, refusals to pay, and tax rhetoric of the woman suffrage movement, while recognizing the universality of the incidence of taxation upon women of all classes, tended to focus upon property taxation. Distinctions between property taxpayers and nonproperty taxpayers were initially economic, but a tendency to view recent immigrants and African-Americans as almost uniformly of the lower economic classes provided a more emphasized racial and ethnic dimension. Woman suffragists did not make the metaphoric connection to the American Revolution an occasion to argue unambiguously for universal woman suffrage. Rather, the cleavage drawn between native-born property-holding women and the foreign-born or those facing economic struggles tended to narrow the broadest metaphoric implications of "no taxation without representation" and to accentuate what are now taken to be less attractive aspects of republicanism, particularly its emphasis on self-reliance and property ownership. The Boston Tea Party, Revolutionary mottos, and the legitimacy associated with them were appropriated by one group of women to the exclusion of American women who arrived more recently or were poorer.

The second cultural metaphor, the doctrine of separate spheres, gave women an entry, although again a narrow one, into political life in the 1870s. The separate spheres arguments took at least three forms. The first type of argument posited that educational issues already formed a part of woman's sphere. Granting her the vote in local and school elections would, in substance, augment a woman's ability to act competently within the sphere of particular interest to her. A second argument used separate sphere language, but expanded the meaning of home to justify woman municipal suffrage.

An expanded notion of motherhood including public motherhood redefined woman's role while conserving the ideology of separate spheres. There is no necessary reason why public motherhood would be confined to the municipality, but if a woman's own family was to be her highest priority, charitable or public motherhood may have been appropriately confined geographically. Finally, separate spheres arguments for municipal or school suffrage sometimes harkened back to the ideal of republican motherhood from early in the nineteenth century. Republican motherhood recognized both the confines of woman's sphere and its impact and contribution to public life through mothering. By giving women a more direct stake in local government, it was hoped that they would more adequately meet the expectations of them as republican mothers and wives.

CONCLUSION

Some of the more important developments in American law in the 1870s focused upon the mutability of the term taxation. Legally significant attempts to control the meaning of taxation were not limited to treatise writers and lawyers of the time. Woman suffragists found in taxation a "cultural symbol"[5] – a powerful metaphor for their condition in American society in the 1870s. Their efforts to alter law and language provide valuable insight into metaphoric strategies and limitations in legal discourse. Tax protests, work in payment of taxes, and refusals to pay tax were ways of drawing attention to disenfranchised taxpaying women. The dollars arguments of the era's woman suffragists were historical metaphors, patterning the actions of the Smith sisters or the Fosters into familiar narratives of Revolutionary tax resistance and that famous motto: "no taxation without representation." Supporters drew parallels between the stories of refusals to pay by woman suffragists and the Revolutionary pattern. Certain variations were, however, attributable to the predominance of women as civil disobedients. The women were seen as more vulnerable protesters, but ones in tune with higher law because of their segregation in woman's sphere, a place where republican principles were still observed and cherished.

The taxation arguments of the woman suffrage movement were also about self "Taxation" proved to be an interesting metaphor for the disadvantages women experienced in their dealings with government, the market, civil society, and their husbands and families. Redefining taxation and arguing its applicability to the whole spectrum of women's experience tended to undermine the very powerful metaphor of separate spheres.

The taxation metaphor suggested the acceptability of partial suffrage for women. In fact, these more narrow aspects of historical metaphor triumphed as school suffrage was given, often, to tax-paying women. The dollars arguments tended to reinforce the middle- and upper-class orientation of the woman suffrage movement.

[5] Joan W. Scott, Gender and the Politics of History 43–44 (1988)

Split Income and Separate Spheres: Tax Law and Gender Roles in the 1940s

CAROLYN C. JONES[1]

PERCEPTIONS OF WOMEN'S ROLES DURING THE 1940s

In the 1940s, there was considerable conflict and concern about the role of women in society. During the previous decade, the Depression combined with traditional views of gender roles to create a variety of disincentives or barriers to the employment of women. While the phenomenon of working single women seemed to be accepted, Americans were not convinced that women could or should combine careers with marriage and family.

America's involvement in World War II created tension between perceptions of traditional roles for women and ideas about their contributions to society. The wartime diversion of 12,000,000 men into the military service converged with a period of high industrial production and with business and government requirements to create an unprecedented demand for labor. Women constituted the largest reserve of potential workers. As a result, America's participation in World War II caused a dramatic increase in the employment of women outside the home. One of the most notable trends was the increase in the employment of married women. By the war's end, 23% of married women were employed. Women perceived as making a real contribution to the war effort were usually doing what had traditionally been men's work in factories and on farms. These new factory and farmworkers were celebrated as patriotic citizens, but they were not insulated from tensions created by traditional visions of gender roles. This tension was manifested in efforts to characterize the new women's work as domestic work, in hostility to women workers, in wage disparities, and in the continuing message that the new work was "for the duration" only.[2]

Voluntary or not, over 2,000,000 women left the labor force by 1946. The decline in employment was most marked in heavy industrial jobs, first opened to women during the war. Part of the decline in the female workforce is attributable to a greater emphasis upon the home as the center of women's lives. "Social stability had replaced military victory as the national goal and women were needed as wives and mothers rather than as workers."[3] The homemaker and mother again

---

[1] Reprinted by permission from 6 *Law and History Review* 259 (1988).
[2] KAREN ANDERSON, WARTIME WOMEN 6, 48, 59–62 (1981).
[3] SUSAN HARTMANN, THE HOME FRONT AND BEYOND: AMERICAN WOMEN IN THE 1940's, at 25 (1982).

became the prototype of American women. For women, the employment downturn was compounded by hiring preferences for returning veterans, discriminatory reclassification of jobs, and union failures to protect women's seniority.

The end of the war eliminated an impetus for unconventional behavior. New prosperity and a "return" to family-centered norms meant that more women married and had more children than previously. A woman's contribution to society after the war was thought generally to be as a wife and mother.

INCOME SPLITTING AND GENDER ROLES

Tax-law decision makers – Congress, judges, and administrators – were also concerned with questions about the value of the various types of work that women did. They were obviously affected by prevailing views about women and their work, but they were also concerned about maintaining the revenue-producing capabilities of the tax system. The incentives for tax savings through income splitting were fairly substantial and varied according to income bracket. The benefits of income splitting were relatively small for those with net incomes of $5,000 and below. The savings increased in total dollars with net income, but the percentage of savings declined once the top marginal rates were reached.

With such high stakes, the Bureau of Internal Revenue and the courts attempted to confine the benefits of income splitting to atypical arrangements. Two of the most prominent income-splitting devices, the community-property system and husband–wife partnerships, illustrate this point. The community-property system was until the late 1930s, a system of property used in a relatively small number of states and regarded as strange or foreign. Husband–wife partnerships were recognized when the wife was an active participant in the business or contributed her own capital to it. Significant business activity by a woman was thought to be unusual. The allowance of income splitting in these exceptional cases would not, policy makers thought, do great harm to the treasury of the United States.

The Spread of Community Property

In general, under a community-property regime, a husband and wife each have an equal, undivided interest in income earned by a spouse, unearned income from community property, and in other community property acquired during their marriage. Some states also treat income from separate property as community income. If a couple lived in a community-property state and only one of them produced taxable income, federal recognition of that state's law allowed an equal division of income between husband and wife. This income-splitting opportunity meant that the aggregate community income was often subjected to lower marginal rates than if that income had been earned by an unmarried taxpayer in a community-property state or by one spouse in a common-law state. The certainty of favorable tax treatment in community-property states plus the mixed success of such devices as family partnerships and family trusts for income-splitting taxpayers in common-law states led some of the latter states to conversion to or consideration of a community-property regime. The pressure toward community property became greater as tax rates began to increase at the end of the 1930s.

In 1939, Oklahoma became the first state to convert to a community property regime. In 1945, the Territory of Hawaii adopted a community-property system, and in 1947, Nebraska, Michigan, and Pennsylvania switched from their traditional common-law systems. By so doing, it was estimated that these states saved their citizens substantial amounts in federal taxes.

There seems to have been a general awareness of the favored tax status of couples in states with this system, and an underlying tone of resentment in accounts written about it. For example, George Werning of Newhall, Iowa, wrote to his Senator, Bourke B. Hickenlooper: "I wish you would do all you can to enact a law, so that husband and wife can split their income and thereby reducing their income tax. It isn't right that some states are able to do so and others are not. For instance Calif. has that law. I have a brother-in-law there that has much larger net income than I have and yet we have to pay more income taxes than they do."[4] Magazines such as *American Magazine, Business Week, Collier's, Fortune, Nation's Business, Newsweek, Saturday Evening Post, Time,* and *U.S. News & World Report* carried articles explaining the tax benefits of a community-property system and emphasizing the point with illustrations and maps.

The puzzle is why, with such incentives in tax dollars, more states did not convert to community property. Colorado, Illinois, Indiana, Kansas, Massachusetts, New Jersey, New York, South Dakota, and Wyoming apparently considered conversion, but either rejected the switch or marked time until Congress acted in 1948. The reluctance to convert can be explained by at least two reasons, both of which suggest that common-law and community-property regimes were not seen as equivalent systems, which tends to undermine the argument of unfairness so often advanced by those seeking a federal solution to the different treatment of couples in community-property and common-law states. The first reason for the failure of more states to switch to a community-property system was a hostility toward a wife's present interest in community earnings and property, which were usually thought of as being the product of the husband's labors. The second reason, no doubt related to the first, was the legal difficulty in engrafting an often brief community-property statute onto a legal system rooted in common-law principles.

The spread of community-property laws during the period from 1939 to 1947 is testimony to the efficacy of the federal tax incentive for readjustment of economic power between spouses. Because the new popularity of community property was apparently based only upon the possibility of tax savings, the new community-property states and territory did away with their community-property systems shortly after Congress adopted the voluntary joint return and gave the tax benefits of income splitting without requiring the wealthier spouse to give assets or legal rights in property or earnings to the other spouse. Without more deep-seated

---

[4] Letter from George Werning to Bourke B. Hickenlooper (Jan. 6, 1948) (available in "Tax, Income, 1948," Bourke B. Hickenlooper Papers, Herbert Hoover Presidential Library, West Branch, Iowa).

commitment to economic equalization of husbands and wives, the tax-generated community-property reforms of the 1940s could not survive the removal of that stimulus. The clear perception during the heyday of the new community-property states was that the passage of a community-property regime would involve a transfer of power from men to women.

A Proliferation of Husband–Wife Partnerships

If a taxpaying couple lived in one of the community-property states, their marriage automatically created a partnership that would be recognized for tax purposes and would allow each marital partner to report half of the community income whether that income resulted from labor or from capital. In common-law states, many couples formed business partnerships in order to achieve the same tax advantages. The Bureau of Internal Revenue and the courts were called upon to assess the validity of a number of these husband–wife partnerships. While some fortunate taxpayers did achieve the desired income-splitting results by avoiding audit or defeating Bureau objections, the methodology used by the administrative and judicial decision makers was quite different from that used in evaluating community-property partnerships.

The ability to split income in a community-property state was determined by the community-property statutes and without regard to the behavior of particular couples. The focus in common-law states was quite the reverse. The fact that a spousal partnership was recognized under state law was of little relevance in the determination of tax consequences. The notion of control has been critical in tax jurisprudence. In a number of cases, a grantor's retention of the income-producing property or continued possession of important powers over the income or property could mean that the grantor, rather than the income recipient, would be viewed as the appropriate taxpayer. The machinations of the market were not assumed to be present in the context of family partnerships. The courts returned to concepts of control in deciding whether such partnerships should be recognized for tax purposes.

The courts, Treasury, and popular press were often reluctant to concede that husband–wife partnerships should be given tax effect because of stereotypical notions of family relationships as hierarchical, and because of tendencies to view "men's work" as contributing more to a business enterprise than "women's work." Almost every factor used by the courts in deciding the tax validity of a husband–wife partnership carried with it these notions of control and valuation of a woman's business contribution. These factors included service by the new partner (typically the wife), including participation in management, the source of capital contributed to the business, and the use of partnership earnings by the partner. Each of these factors was thought to indicate whether control of the business had remained with the donor or whether it had come to be shared by husband and wife.

Often the result of a partnership case depended upon whether a wife had rendered "vital services" to the business. If the wife wished to be a partner, she usually had to contribute capital or vital services to the business in order to gain tax-recognized income-splitting benefits. If there is a theme to most of the unsuccessful partnership cases[,] it is the failure of the wife to provide services that would be characterized as "vital" or "manlike." The wife performed no service for the business in approximately half of the unsuccessful cases.

The partnership cases and rulings from the 1940s are evidence of the two-sphere construct of the world used so often and so long in structuring our world view. Domestic-sphere work was not seen as relevant to or contributing to the business. It was just this sort of view that had animated wartime propaganda portraying housewives as failing to contribute sufficiently to the war effort. While the War Manpower Commission ordered that women with dependent children should not be encouraged to join the paid labor force, other housewives were viewed by planners and propagandists as underemployed or unemployed, and were urged to do their part by taking paying jobs. A 1944 Maxwell House Coffee advertisement implored: "Lets Work – Not Wait – For Victory! Uncle Sam needs womanpower! Trained women workers are already employed – millions more are needed. That leaves just you, Mrs. Housewife. So, for America's sake, go to work, get a job, and *stick to it*, until Victory comes!"[5] The negative message, of course, is that housewives were "waiting" for victory and doing nothing to assist in the war effort. The italicized *stick to it* also suggests that housewives, even if employed, were not particularly reliable workers.

If the wives in the unsuccessful court cases rendered services to the business it was often clerical assistance. Clerical work was seen as a "wifely and motherly function" – one that could not really entitle a woman to status as a partner.[6] The view that the contributions made by clerical workers to business were not adequate to qualify such workers as partners is reminiscent of the failure to commend these workers' wartime efforts. Even though clerical workers were working outside the home providing needed services, they did not receive the level of "commendation" afforded Rosie the Riveter.

THE ADOPTION OF THE JOINT RETURN – A RETURN TO "NORMALCY"

Pressures for tax reduction had been building after the war; Republicans proved successful in the elections of 1946 partly because of their tax program. Across-the-board tax reductions were attempted twice in 1947 only to be vetoed successfully by President Truman. In 1948, [Harold] Knutson, [Republican chairman of the House Ways and Means Committee,] introduced a new bill that increased personal exemptions, added an exemption for the blind and elderly, and, most significantly, allowed income splitting through the joint return. Truman vetoed the measure. The idea had sufficient Congressional support, however, and the veto was overridden.

The joint return was attractive for several reasons. The Senate Finance Committee report summarized these reasons as a desire for geographic equalization, "forestalling" the "impetuous enactment of community-property legislation by States that have long used the common law"; reduction of incentives to create

---

[5] Saturday Evening Post, March 25, 1944, at 51.
[6] Hartmann, *supra* note 3, at 18.

trusts, joint tenancies, and family partnerships; and reduction of administrative difficulties resulting from income splitting.[7]

Concerns about the administrability of the tax system became more pressing during the 1940s with the emergence of the income tax as a mass tax. In 1940, approximately 7,000,000 Americans paid income taxes. By 1945, that number had risen to 42,000,000. Increased governmental responsibility for the economy, welfare programs, and America's expanded role on the world scene after World War II meant that the tax would not return to prewar levels.

Yet income-splitting measures in existence before 1948 were not all administratively burdensome. The recognition of community property as an income-splitting device produced relatively few administrative difficulties. Senators from community-property states did not hesitate to point out that the "inequities" could be remedied if only those in common-law states would be willing to accord wives more legal rights by adopting a community-property system. Yet the spread of the community-property system was unacceptable to many of those in common-law states. Even the continuation of community property in some of the new community-property states was objectionable to some who looked to the federal government as a means of obtaining tax reduction without changing the legal rights between spouses.

The choice of the income-splitting joint return was neither obvious nor inevitable. It was more expensive than allowing the states to adopt community-property legislation. While it possessed the virtue of ease of administration, it also was viewed as a way of conserving traditional gender roles and power relationships. These conservative ideas about family relationships were a major theme in the tax-law decisions of the 1940s and in writings for and by the general public. The pervasive discussion of gender roles and relationships that surrounded these decisions – decisions that continue to shape the structure of tax law in the 1980s – should be exposed and thought of in terms that go beyond definitions of income, assertions about political credit, and concerns about administrability. While these concepts are important in understanding the tax-law decisions of the 1940s, they focus on too narrow a range of tax-law decision makers. Newspaper and magazine columnists, editorial writers, and citizens writing to senators and to local papers are individuals who also impact upon tax law, yet are often ignored in legal scholarship. The writings of these people make it clear that these tax-law decisions are cultural artifacts – understood as a part of a larger societal structure and, simultaneously, revealing of that culture. By providing a more distant vantage point, the passage of time has made more apparent the connection between these choices about income splitting and postwar American society. There is, however, no reason to assume that the connection between tax law and more general "culture" was unique to the 1940s and to income-splitting issues. For historians and legal scholars, the challenge is to expose and analyze that connection.

---

[7] S. Rep. No. 80-1013, at 26 (1948).

The Rhetoric of the Anti-Progressive Income Tax Movement: A Typical Male Reaction

MARJORIE E. KORNHAUSER[1]

This title is not exactly true; it's not exactly false either. It contains a truth that has been shaped by my preferences (or, if you wish, my biases, philosophy, or prejudices) and by my desire to grab the reader's attention and force him (and I mean him) to reach a specific conclusion. It is, in short, rhetoric. In that respect it is not unlike many of the arguments now popularly raised against the progressive income tax. My argument differs from many others in its open acknowledgment of the use of rhetoric.

The progressive income tax is currently under siege. This is a new phenomenon: new not in the fact of the opposition itself, but in the extent of the opposition. In 1913, the general public, economists, and politicians argued about the exact schedule of rates and exemptions, but the *idea* of graduated or progressive rates was accepted with surprising ease and generally has remained unquestioned ever since. The economic and political consensus about progressivity began to fall apart sometime in the 1970s. Two alternatives to progressivity gained strength: a modified flat or proportionate income tax and an expenditure- or consumption-based tax. An expenditure-based tax proved politically unacceptable but the (modified) flat tax alternative gained strength and culminated in the Tax Reform Act of 1986. The drastic erosion of support for progressivity spurred the writing of this article. Before we consent to this erosion we should reevaluate the arguments upon which it is based.

Neoconservative philosophy, with its belief in the primacy of individual rights, both leads to and is supported by the belief in the efficacy of the market as the means to achieve each person's rights and satisfactions most fully. The "science" of economics thus easily becomes a tool of this particular vision of society. Because it is a "science," however, its use as a tool – its rhetoric – tends to be masked.

Rhetoric has a bad reputation these days, and with some reason. The term "rhetoric" can be used – and indeed often is used – in its negative sense, to mean insincere or flowery language used to mislead and emotionally sway an audience. But rhetoric need not have this pejorative connotation. Virtually all speech and

[1] Reprinted by permission from 86 *Michigan Law Review* 465 (1987).

writing must use rhetoric because the purpose of language is communication. Rhetoric is the study of "how people persuade," discovering good reasons for conclusions or beliefs.

Because the underlying assumptions of much of the current progressive tax debate are unstated – indeed unnoticed – by many of the speakers and audience, the debate tends to be rhetorical in the pejorative sense. It hides the underlying premises which give the arguments their force; it confuses rather than illuminates.

THE CLASSIC ARGUMENTS AGAINST PROGRESSIVITY
AND THEIR REBUTTALS

The current attack on progressivity stems from the classic arguments against it. First, critics claim that progressivity fails Adam Smith's criterion of simplicity. Second, progressivity has been called a "politically irresponsible formula,"[2] because it leads to the majority's irresponsibly voting higher taxes for the minority, or "soaking the rich." Progressivity is politically irresponsible in another manner: it leads to rhetorical posturing that often confuses or contradicts reality. For example, Congress votes for high nominal rates but at the same time passes exclusions, credits, and deductions which effectively flatten the rates by narrowing the tax base of the wealthier taxpayers. The appearance is that of a highly progressive system, but the reality is otherwise: the rich don't get soaked because they have umbrellas in the form of tax preferences or shelters. Thus, the argument continues, the inevitable political posturing surrounding progressivity is itself an argument against progressive rates: a degressive tax is actually more progressive than a system with *nominally* high rates but low *effective* rates due to credits, deductions, and exclusions. The third major criticism of the progressive tax is that it is economically inefficient: marginal tax rates are disincentives to work and/or invest, and therefore they reduce society's productivity. However, proponents of this objection may be confusing the effect of graduated rates with the effect of high tax rates generally.

In addition to these specific objections, critics reject the major justifications of progressivity as either invalid or too vague to be useful. Specifically, the benefit and marginal utility (or sacrifice) theories are rejected as invalid; theories of equality are rejected as too vague and personal. A less frequently used justification for the progressive income tax is discussed just as summarily. Some proponents argue that progressive taxation can help achieve our social, economic, and political goals. By reducing economic inequality, progressivity helps provide political stability (by insuring against revolution), secure democratic institutions (hungry people don't care much about freedom of speech), and ensure that political power does not concentrate in the hands of a wealthy few. The rebuttals to this rationale range from ignoring it to denying its effectiveness.

---

[2] Walter J. Blum & Harry Kalven, Jr., *The Uneasy Case for Progressive Taxation*, 19 U. Chi. L. Rev. 417, 435 (1952).

ECONOMIC OBJECTIONS TO PROGRESSIVITY

Because the popular press and political rhetoric tend to link unrelated issues (e.g., simplicity and proportionality) the first step in analyzing economic objections to the progressive income tax is to separate out those objections which relate specifically to progressivity. Some economic criticisms of the present system may be accurate but do not really criticize *progressivity*, whereas other complaints do treat progressivity but also apply to many other forms of taxation. For example, progressive taxes have been criticized for creating a drag on the economy, but this can generally be said of all taxes.

Some of the objections to progressivity are, in reality, objections to high rates of tax. To the extent that there is a correlation between taxes and savings, low rates seem to be an important factor. A flat but high rate of tax (e.g., 60%) should depress savings (if at all) as much as, if not more than, a graduated tax with the highest marginal rate equal to the flat rate of 60%. Similarly, if the highest marginal rate is low enough, then the graduation of the rates should be insignificant.

Nevertheless, economics and economic arguments play an increasingly important role in tax policy. [Some economists argue that] increased economic growth achieved through the private market is the best way to help everyone: increased growth enlarges the economic pie so that everyone – including the poor – gets a larger slice.

There are several problems with this theory. First is the empirical question: does the wealth, in fact, "trickle down"? It is far from clear that an increased pie benefits everyone. The gap between rich and poor is widening. This does not necessarily mean that the poor get no benefit from a bigger pie; it may just be minimal when compared to the benefit those in the upper incomes receive. Furthermore, some people may not be affected by the larger pie – they may get the same size slice or no slice at all.

More importantly, even if the (relatively) poor do get a larger slice, there are questions of equity and fairness about the resultant distribution which economic efficiency does not address. Pie (especially apple) may be greatly desired by the American public, but a bigger one is not necessarily a better one. As the private market has shown, quality as well as quantity determine the price a consumer is willing to pay for a good. From a societal standpoint, "quality" includes non-"economic" values such as fairness: traditional tax reform goals include fairness and simplicity as well as economic efficiency. A comprehensive tax theory should deal explicitly with the tradeoffs among objectives. The "bigger pie" theory fails to do this.

Another problem with the efficient private market view is its idealized concept of the private market. Although in *theory* the market always achieves efficiency, in *actuality* there are market failures. These failures may be due to a variety of factors, such as imperfect information, free rider problems, and administrability difficulties. Consequently, and perhaps paradoxically, true economic efficiency may be impossible without state intervention.

Justification for a tax system based on economic efficiency ultimately depends on normative judgments about the distribution of goods, and theories of public choice. The flat tax movement relies on a contractarian minimal state view of government emphasizing "procedural (or process) justice and private property rights."[3] This approach, with its reliance on voluntary exchange, is seen as more appropriate for a society of free people than theories of end-state (or distributive) justice. To the extent that progressive taxation is justified by an appeal to redistributive justice, it is seen as violative of the liberal rule of law.

Although tax systems need not, and I believe should not, be designed primarily to accomplish specific economic or social goals, the choice of a system inevitably has social, economic, and political effects. The choice must be a normative one.

While the inevitability of normative decisions is recognized in many economic and philosophic discussions, it is generally missed at the popular and political level of debates. In fact, much of the current flat tax reform rhetoric obscures the inevitability of normative choices through its linkage of the flat rate issue to separate issues such as fairness, comprehensiveness, and rate reduction and by its emphasis on economic efficiency and growth as objective goods. This is not surprising; economic analysis has had a "long tradition" of obscuring the normative underpinnings of economic theories of tax.[4] It lends a patina of neutrality, because economics – particularly neoclassical economics – is viewed by many noneconomists (and even by some economists) as a "science," and therefore as factual and objective. Economics is indeed a science, but not in the way we understood "science" in high school, not in the way we as laypeople wish it to be: it is not absolute, totally demonstrable, truth; it is, as all human knowledge is, fallible, tentative, and evolving. Nevertheless, the appearance of neutrality and truth is reinforced by the language of economics, the dazzling statistical displays economists produce, and finally by the willingness (even eagerness) of the public (and some economists) to accept the first two on a surface level.

In actuality, however, economics – like all scholarly fields – is a literary endeavor and amply employs rhetoric, metaphors, analogies, and so forth. What is perhaps different about economics is the resistance people display to this notion. The very words used are metaphors – demand curve, production functions, invisible hand – but because economists use the words so frequently, they and their audiences lose sight of the fact that the words remain metaphors even in their "scientific" usage.

The problem, then, with the use of neoclassical economics to support a flat limited tax is that its conclusions are viewed as hard objective facts – facts which, moreover, are the only possible relevant, valid facts, produced by a methodology which is the only relevant, valid methodology. However, the "facts" are not as determinative nor the methodology as exclusive as they claim to be. Because the ascendant theory of economics is premised on private property and market exchange, its assumptions (overt and implicit), as well as the very language of much of its theory, reflect these values. The economic arguments are not neutral and must be evaluated through examination of their underlying premises.

---

[3] James A. Dorn, *Introduction: The Principles and Politics of Tax Reform*, 5 Cato J. 361, 368 (1985).

[4] Richard E. Wagner, *Normative and Positive Foundations of Tax Reform*, 5 Cato J. 385, 392 (1985). [This discussion draws much from Deirdre N. McCloskey, The Rhetoric of Economics (1985). – Eds.]

PHILOSOPHICAL PREMISES AND PROGRESSIVE TAXATION

The Premises of Neoclassical Economics and Neoconservative Philosophy

Both neoclassical economics and neoconservative philosophy are founded on a belief in the primacy of the individual and the satisfaction of his interests. Liberty of individual action and choice is essential because without it individuals cannot achieve their interests. The free private market is the best mechanism to achieve the highest level of satisfaction because individuals themselves are best situated to make choices for themselves and the market allows them to do so in a way that respects autonomy: because the market is based on explicit or implicit consent, this concept of economic efficiency is congruent with its underlying normative value of liberty. Because the market is efficient, most activities should occur in the private market. When government must step in, it should mimic the private market as much as possible. This view inevitably leads to a limited government which raises what little revenue it needs through a flat tax, preferably consumption-based.

This Neo view of individuals and society is anchored in a belief in the total sanctity of private property. What gives people this ultimate right to property? Most proponents derive it from John Locke's theory of a person's natural right to his body, his labor, the fruits of his labor, and any property with which he has commingled his labor. Locke, however, attached an important proviso to the right to property: one is entitled to the property so long as his appropriation does not disadvantage the next person. That is, enough of good X must remain after an appropriation so that others may also appropriate it. Most resources today obviously are not (and have not been for many years) so abundant that this proviso can be met.

Alternative Visions

Neoclassical economic methodology and its underlying neoconservative philosophy see "the history of all hitherto existing society [as] the history of interactions among selfish individuals."[5] Certainly, selfishness is a human characteristic and much of history can be read as a playing-out of this trait. But selfishness is not the only human trait, and history is not solely the recitation of centuries of acts of selfishness. If we view people and history through a lens of selfishness, then perhaps we see more of it than is really there. There are numerous documented examples of actions which are exactly the opposite of selfish – true "heroic" acts to help others without regard for self – as well as many other acts which are, if not exactly unselfish, at least not purely selfish. These include the acts of Mother Theresa, Albert Schweitzer, Martin Luther King, freedom riders, Peace Corp volunteers, missionaries, Andrew Carnegie medal winners, and ordinary people who helped Jews in Nazi Europe. These people, and many others like them, prove daily that the history of humankind cannot be called simply a history of the interactions of selfish individuals. Through a different lens we might view people and history

[5] McCloskey, *supra* note 4, at 25.

as the interactions of economic classes, or as the struggle for a kingdom of God on earth, or as the cooperative efforts of people to enrich their lives and those of their fellow humans.

Certain philosophies, or just plain outlooks on life, see people and society not solely in terms of their individual rights and entitlements but also – or even primarily – in terms of people's needs and obligations to others as well as themselves. Many religious visions, for example, prescribe a life in which individuals help others, are connected to others, and as a community move toward a just society. Both religious and secular utopias throughout the ages, from early Christianity to hippie communes of the sixties, also have had strong communal goals. True, many have failed, but their values persist as each generation reincarnates them in different forms. Various political theories also include communal aspects. Historically, socialism and communism come to mind; more currently, other communal visions of humanity have gained prominence: republicanism, the Critical Legal Studies movement (CLS), and feminism. These theories differ, but according to each, a sense of connectedness with and obligation to others is an intrinsic part of the nature of the individual. Such a view of humanity naturally supports a redistributive progressive income tax. While each vision is supported by a rich body of literature, I shall only briefly describe one – feminism – to illustrate the strength of the alternatives to the Neo view. I have chosen feminism because in its loosest form, the form I shall describe, it is less a theory than a way of knowing and of being, experienced by a large segment of the world's population.

As an attitude, feminism provides a flexibility that is compatible with the idea of a variety of connections to others. Feminism – as a way of knowing, as an attitude, as a view about human nature – remains receptive to diversity and change.

A major work on the feminine vision is Carol Gilligan's *In a Different Voice: Psychological Theory and Women's Development.* She notes, as other feminists have, that the modern paradigm of humanity is in actuality only a paradigm of *man*: man as a being who is essentially individualistic and autonomous. Consequently, moral problems, problems of justice and fairness, are seen as formal, universal, and abstract. Problems are defined in terms of conflicting rights and rules. Under this paradigm, the highest stage of morality and justice is that position at which rights and rules are universally defined and weighted, and decisions are made impartially on the basis of these abstract rules without regard to context. Studies show that women consistently fail to reach this stage; they are mired in a "lower" stage. Gilligan and other feminist writers posit that rather than being a lower level of morality, this is a *different* view of reality and morality. Women see themselves and the world with different eyes and, therefore, they speak with a different voice. Women perceive themselves, and thus the world, in terms of caring for others, in terms of responsibility to others, in terms of connectedness to others, whereas men perceive themselves and the world in terms of separateness, autonomy, and universal rules and rights.

The fact that women see the world as one of interrelatedness, of the interconnectedness of people, as a "web of relationships," is not a denial of the self. Rather, it is a realization that the self is not immured in a nonpermeable plastic bubble. The self is created, maintained, and enhanced through connections with others.

At its most mature level this view means being responsible not only to yourself but to others. Being responsible to yourself *includes* being responsible for others. Thus, the "male" distinction between self-interest and altruism is a false one which disappears. Responsibility in this sense goes beyond the conventional meaning of making and adhering to a commitment; it means being aware and responsive to others.

Thus, there are "two voices, two ways of speaking. One voice speaks about equality, reciprocity, fairness, rights; one voice speaks about connection, not hurting, care, and response.... [T]hese voices are in tension with each other."[6] Responsiveness to others is "proactive" in the "female" voice, reactive in the "male." For the female voice, being receptive to others and caring for others involves initiating action, not merely responding. More importantly, caring is a constitutive act of the self: we become more fully ourselves by caring for others. The male voice, in contrast, sees caring almost as a defensive act to protect the self: we "care" about others so that they will care about us and our rights, so that we may remain our independent selves. Male "caring" is self-referential; it emerges from a need for reciprocal caring by the other in order to protect the self. It is tit-for-tat: I will care for you, so that you will care for me.

However, even under the feminine vision that we care best for ourselves when we also care for others, we cannot care for everyone to the same degree. Such an ideal is unrealistic. To erect such an ideal would be an invitation to ignore the goal in despair of ever achieving it, even in those instances when it is obtainable. Moreover, such a demanding ideal, even if achievable, might lead to a deconstruction of the self. Whereas caring should be a constitutive act, caring about everyone equally would leave no time to care about oneself. This would lead to self-effacement. Therefore, there must be some limits on caring. Even within the limits of care there must be different levels so that our responsiveness and obligations to our friends, for example, are different than our responsiveness and obligations to acquaintances or strangers. Yet we cannot even exclude the stranger that we meet completely from our care. S/he is connected to us, not just as a fellow human, but potentially as a future spouse, a child's spouse, a dearest friend, a valued employee; every current stranger is perhaps a person who will one day be within the inner circle of caring. Thus, in *direct* contact with a stranger, we must be responsive to her needs.

We also must maintain a minimal, less burdensome connectedness to the non-proximate stranger. At this minimal level of care, I need make no great sacrifices to help the unmet others. Moreover, I need respond only to those others' most urgent and basic demands. The basic needs of any person go beyond those of bare survival to include attainment of the preconditions of liberty that allow us to be free, voluntary agents working toward self-fulfillment. These conditions include education and some level of personal safety and comfort. Only when a person has these basics is she able to work toward her potential and self-fulfillment. The minimal level of care, then, requires that I help others attain these basics so that

---

[6] Carol Gilligan, In a Different Voice: Psychological Theory and Women's Development 37–38 (1982).

they have an *opportunity* to achieve self-fulfillment just as I do. Because it involves a *minimal* level of responsibility, my obligation to help others attain this state of opportunity does not require that I give up my own opportunity, nor even that I constrain it very much. It does require that as my discretionary income grows, I contribute money at a greater rate than previously to help others. This is not an unduly burdensome obligation. It denies me no freedom of action. I can still choose when, where, and how much to work. I am still rewarded for my efforts. The income contribution required of me will not be so large as to unduly handicap my own attempts at self-fulfillment. As my income grows, it is easier for me to contribute more without impinging on my ability to reach my own goals. My minimal obligation to others requires that I contribute that nonintrusive amount. Thus, a progressive income tax rate satisfies my obligation to myself and others. It is not a redistribution of wealth, merely a paying of my "just debts" to others.

The "male" and "female" voices, of course, do not belong exclusively to males and females, respectively. In fact, by the time people are adults, most use both voices. However, approximately 70% of those who use both focus on one voice, using the other minimally. As their labels imply, the female voice is predominantly the domain of women and the male voice belongs to males. The male voice traditionally is the dominant, valued one. It informs our view of the law as a domain of rules, rights, and blind justice: we are autonomous, independent beings and the law as fashioned by men helps maintain that separateness. It constructs barriers between "my" property and "yours"; "my" rights and "yours." The female voice emphasizes our relatedness to others. It builds bridges rather than barriers. In this sense, the feminist vision is aligned with other communitarian visions such as classical republicanism, whereas the male vision more closely follows the pluralistic, individualist, liberal theory of today.

The female voice not only fits reality but is the best interpretation of reality in that it "fits" what we see. Even on casual observation people display much behavior that does not appear to fit the Neo view that all action is determined by self-interest. Nonselfish altruistic behavior does not "fit" the Neo theory of people. The Neos attempt to explain away these discrepancies, and to achieve "fit" in either of two ways. One Neo approach to altruism acknowledges the existence of altruistic behavior but confines it to the private sphere of life. The other Neo approach to altruism is to define away the behavior. Both approaches fail to achieve a satisfactory "fit."

The first approach dichotomizes human behavior. People are assumed to be self-interested in the marketplace but altruistic (or at least not totally self-interested) at the hearth. It is natural and proper to care for and share with others – but only within the family circle or small voluntary groups. There is no place for duty to others in the marketplace or the political forum. In those fora, *man* is a separate individual whose rights and self-interests are paramount.

This view is arbitrary at best. How can people have one nature in private and a totally different one in public? Perhaps, as the group gets larger and our participation in it less direct or less voluntary, our relationships with and responsibilities to others in the group are altered, but the connection is not severed. How, indeed, can we separate public from private?

Many of the distinctions we make between private and public areas are artificial and based on exploitation. Under the first Neo approach, "economic man" is self-interested, self-reliant, and individualistic in the marketplace but caring and sharing within the family. Yet even if we accept this dichotomized description, the self-reliant individual is made possible in part by the fact that he has depended on a wife who supplied daily physical and psychological maintenance, cared for the children, and generally provided services that might otherwise cost money in the private or public sector.

When women enter the workforce, they continue to provide caring and support, but doing so becomes more difficult. Thus, the lament in two-career families that what the couple needs is a "wife." Sometimes it becomes impossible for the family to meet all of its needs. Collective responsibility in the form of some government obligation may then be necessary. This collective responsibility is not necessarily inconsistent with individualism. Individualism presupposes that the government will create or preserve those elementary conditions which allow persons to pursue their own self-interest.

CONCLUSION

The anti-progressive tax movement claims that the progressive income tax is too complex, economically inefficient, and unfair because it unjustly takes private property which belongs to the individual. These arguments are not only over-stated, but premised on an atomistic view of humanity which many people do not share and which does not explain the totality of human behavior. Other views of humanity, such as the feminist vision, see people as interrelated and therefore support and even mandate some progressivity.

Progressivity is not necessarily adverse to the Neo view that the amount of tax paid should reflect the benefits received. Governmental benefits and income show some positive correlation. That we cannot determine the precise degree of this correlation does not mean we should abandon graduation. If benefits and income do correlate, a flat tax is clearly erroneous. Where is the merit in choosing a clear error over an approximation at truth? Simply because we cannot attain perfection does not mean we should do nothing. The second-best option is that which does the least harm. Overtaxing those who can more easily afford it is more desirable than overtaxing those less able to bear the burden.

The preconditions of freedom are not merely physical. They include those conditions – such as education, security of person, and property – necessary to enable individuals to be free agents who make voluntary choices. If individualism and individual development require that these basic preconditions be met, then a person's rights in any excess property may be constrained by a duty to provide these to others. A progressive tax is one way to reflect this.

A redistributive progressive tax can help provide another precondition of free-dom: stability of a democratic form of government. Although a democracy does not need an *equal* distribution of wealth, a wide gap between the wealthy few and a large dispossessed or marginal class is destabilizing. Moreover, a healthy middle class (defined only as an income level between poor and rich) also increases stability by increasing citizens' vested interests in the continuance of the government.

When the organization is as large and diverse as our country is, and when individualism is emphasized, the danger always exists that the pressures of individualism and diversity which pull against organization will overcome the weak center (the state) which holds things together. Some force must counteract this. The only force powerful enough to do so is a sense of community, a sense that we are all connected to each other, that we acknowledge our fates are somehow tied together.

CHAPTER 3. THE GOALS OF TAX POLICY

Critical tax scholars face a high hurdle to gaining entry into – and thus influence on – mainstream tax policy debates. The hurdle is the conventional wisdom that tax policy is a neutral terrain on which experts engage in technical, quasi-scientific debates about the optimally efficient distribution of the tax burden. For those who accept this conventional wisdom, emotionally and ideologically charged topics – such as race, ethnicity, gender, sexual orientation, class, and disability – simply have no place in tax policy discussions. These topics are best discussed – and social problems related to them are best resolved – outside of the tax realm.

In their contributions to this chapter, Dorothy Brown, Lisa Philipps, and Nancy Staudt reexamine different aspects of this conventional wisdom and undermine it in ways that may help critical tax scholars to gain entry into (and influence on) mainstream tax policy discussions. First, in *Racial Equality in the Twenty-First Century: What's Tax Policy Got to Do with It?*, Brown questions the notion that the U.S. tax system is neutral with regard to race. In the excerpted portion of her article, Brown explores how the federal government, on the one hand, subsidizes employers who engage in race discrimination by allowing them to deduct employment discrimination damage awards, but, on the other hand, adds to the injuries suffered by the victims of employment discrimination by requiring them to pay tax on those same awards. Brown proposes several changes to the tax laws that would rectify this problem and discourage employers from discriminating on the basis of race.

Then, in *Discursive Deficits: A Feminist Perspective on the Power of Technical Knowledge in Fiscal Law and Policy*, Philipps demonstrates that this conventional wisdom is not unique to the United States. Philipps takes on the technical, quasi-scientific aura of tax policy debates and explores how technical discourses effectively mask the normative frameworks that underpin them. Philipps exposes how experts can manipulate those discourses to promote certain ends through their choices of assumptions to make, questions to ask, and evidence to be considered relevant – all while professing neutrality and objectivity and denying that they promote any given end at all. Philipps undertakes this exploration with respect to two different examples: (1) the debate about the Canadian budget deficit and (2) the judicial treatment of two different feminist challenges to the Canadian income tax. Only the latter example is excerpted here. The excerpt both uncovers this masking effect in operation and discusses the potential for, and limits of, feminist appropriation of technical discourse in fiscal reform efforts.

Striking a similar chord in *The Hidden Costs of the Progressivity Debate*, Nancy Staudt looks below the surface of a remarkable consensus among participants in the debate over the progressivity of the federal income tax to expose the normative framework underpinning it. As Staudt explains, tax policy theorists have coalesced around the idea that the poor should have no income tax liability at all. Staudt then questions (and offers some answers) why the theories commonly used to justify imposing different tax burdens on taxpayers with different incomes are never taken to their logical conclusion – a conclusion that might require a positive right to income for the poor, not an exemption from tax. Staudt goes on to explore how mainstream tax theorists contribute to the social marginalization of the poor by sending the message that the poor, in contrast to the relatively wealthy (who, given the consensus about the tax treatment of the poor, are the inevitable and exclusive subject of progressivity debates), are excluded from not only paying taxes but also from fulfilling other social obligations. Staudt concludes by considering potential changes to the tax laws that would encourage the poor to (1) contribute services to community organizations (thus acknowledging both the value of their contribution to society and the multiplicity of ways in which they can contribute to society) and (2) obtain the education necessary to participate in a liberal democracy.

This chapter closes with cautionary notes for critical tax scholars and those interested in critical tax theory. In *Tax ~~Equity~~*, Anthony Infanti warns critical tax scholars to be cautious when engaging in tax policy debates that use frameworks or terminology developed by and for mainstream tax scholars. He considers – and, through a series of examples omitted from the excerpt, illustrates – how the core tax policy concept of "equity" (i.e., tax fairness) quietly closes the door to critical contributions to tax policy debates through an unbending focusing on economic differences between individuals – and a concomitant disregard of all other types of difference (e.g., of race, ethnicity, gender, sexual orientation, and physical ability). Due to its focus on "objective" and "neutral" economic factors, tax equity is cloaked with an aura of scientificity that legitimizes its co-opting, neutralizing, or diminishing of the ideas put forward by critical tax scholars. Infanti concludes with a discussion of how this concept of tax equity serves only to entrench the power of the dominant group in society and calls on both mainstream and critical tax scholars to develop competing – and more inclusive – concepts of what makes a tax fair.

In *Tax Policy and Feminism: Competing Goals and Institutional Choices*, Anne Alstott highlights the fact that, notwithstanding the umbrella moniker, "critical tax theory" is far from monolithic; rather, as emphasized in the Introduction to this book, critical tax theory is a group of – sometimes competing, sometimes harmonious – perspectives on how the tax laws affect traditionally subordinated groups. Alstott makes this point by demonstrating how different feminist goals can collide or coincide in different feminist tax proposals. Her excerpted discussion of feminist proposals to reform Social Security – to use Alstott's words – "illustrate[s] particularly clearly the tradeoffs among competing goals."

In addition, Alstott cautions critical tax scholars to bear in mind the limited ability of the tax laws to influence social behavior when formulating their tax policy proposals. In a portion of her article not included here, Alstott explores the similar limits that exist in other areas of the law and considers how coordination between different areas of the law might better advance feminist objectives.

Racial Equality in the Twenty-First Century: What's Tax Policy Got to Do with It?

DOROTHY A. BROWN[1]

In 1976, Supreme Court Justice Byron White recognized that tax statutes may have a disparate impact based upon race. You may ask how this is possible given that the Code is race-neutral on its face. There is nothing in the Code that explicitly says blacks pay more, whites pay less. This is still America – isn't it? I submit, because this is America, one could intuitively expect to observe racial disparities in the implementation of our federal tax laws, which date back to the Sixteenth Amendment and the Revenue Act of 1913.

CURRENT TAX POLICY AND RACE DISCRIMINATION IN THE LABOR MARKET

My charge was to suggest a change in the Code that would work toward the goal of achieving racial equity in the twenty-first century. I believe there is no greater culprit that prevents the achievement of racial equality in this country than the systemic racism found throughout the paid labor market. My proposal therefore will be to use the federal tax laws to disrupt the wage discrimination faced by workers of color.

I would like to begin by giving you some background statistical information that I suspect is all too familiar. For 1995, the Census Bureau reported median weekly earnings for white males, of $566, for black males $411, for black females $355, for Hispanic males $350, for Hispanic females $305. The unemployment rate for whites was 4.9% for 1995, for blacks was 10.4%, for Hispanics 9.3%.

Class action lawsuits alleging job discrimination more than doubled between 1993 and 1997. A July 1998 *New York Times* article reveals that under welfare reform for the first time in the history of our country, there will be more minorities on welfare than whites because employers are preferring to hire white welfare recipients over welfare recipients of color.

Employment discrimination, while an evil in its own right, leads to more serious consequences. Wealth has been described as "one indicator of material disparity that captures the historical legacy of low wages, personal and organizational discrimination, and institutionalized racism. One road to wealth is long-term steady

[1] Reprinted by permission from 21 *University of Arkansas Little Rock Law Review* 759 (1999).

employment in the kinds of work organizations that offer job-sponsored benefits and retirement packages."[2] Similarly, the lack of those employment opportunities over the long term "result[s] in less savings, less investments, and less transfers to succeeding generations. Over time, less income can result in vast differences in asset accumulation."[3]

In 1993, white households had median measured net worth of $45,740 while black households had median measured net worth of $4,418. In the highest income level, the median net worth of whites was $123,350 and of blacks was $45,023. In the lowest income level, the median net worth of whites was $7,605, compared with $250 for blacks.

How do the federal tax laws exacerbate societal racism that is reflected in the paid labor market? This section will describe the tax treatment of deductions under § 162 of the Code. [First,] with limited exceptions, employers can deduct all wages under § 162(a)(1) provided they are ordinary, necessary, reasonable, for services rendered, and incurred in a trade or business.

Second, although the Supreme Court in 1958 announced a "public policy" limitation on deductions under § 162 of the Code, "if allowance of the deduction would frustrate sharply defined national or state policies . . . evidenced by some governmental declaration thereof,"[4] Congress limited the instances in which courts could apply the public policy doctrine. The 1969 Congressional amendments limited the applicability of the public policy doctrine to the following: (i) a certain portion of punitive damages in antitrust awards; (ii) of fines or penalties paid to a government for the violation of any law; (iii) or for illegal bribes or kickbacks. Further, Treasury Regulations under § 162 provide that "[a] deduction for an expense . . . which would otherwise be allowable under § 162 shall not be denied on the grounds that allowance of such deduction would frustrate a sharply defined public policy."[5] Therefore, it is well settled that courts are unable to apply the public policy doctrine to any situation not already proscribed by Congress in § 162.

Third, it is generally accepted that employment discrimination awards are deductible by the discriminator under § 162, regardless of whether the damage awards are compensatory or punitive.

With respect to the income side, the recipients of employment discrimination awards are held to have received taxable income regardless of whether the damage awards are compensatory or punitive. Further, wages received by employees who were discriminated against on the basis of race will constitute taxable income. Discriminators can deduct their wage expenses and the discriminated against are taxed upon those wages.

Well, what does this all mean and what changes would I make to federal tax law? What this means is that the federal government[,] by allowing deductions for wages paid in a racially discriminatory manner and allowing deductions for actual damage awards, is subsidizing the race discriminator. By taxing the award to the

---

[2] *See* Melvin Oliver & Thomas Shapiro, Black Wealth/White Wealth: A New Perspective on Racial Inequality 112 (1995).

[3] *See* Michael Sherraden, Assets and the Poor: A New American Welfare Policy 131 (1991).

[4] *See* Tank Truck Rentals v. United States, 356 U.S. 30, 33–34 (1958).

[5] Treas. Reg. § 1.162-1(a).

recipient the federal government is adding insult to injury. If we lived in a society truly committed to racial equality, our current tax law policies in this area would change.

REVAMPING THE FEDERAL TAX LAWS TO DISCOURAGE LABOR FORCE DISCRIMINATION

How would I change the Code to discourage employers from discriminating on the basis of race? First, I would prohibit the deduction by employers for the punitive and/or compensatory damage awards made in race discrimination cases. Second, I would enact the proposal of Professor Karen Brown of George Washington University "to exclude from taxation all components of job bias awards" from the income of the person who has been discriminated against. [See Chapter 6.] Third, I would prohibit the deduction by employers of wages for *ALL* workers whenever the employer lost a race-based employment discrimination lawsuit or settled a race-based employment discrimination lawsuit, with respect to any of its workers. Fourth, and finally, I would exclude from income the wages received by employees who were discriminated against on the basis of race.

I would define race discrimination to include all instances where damages were paid pursuant to a judgment against an employer who was found to have discriminated against an employee on the basis of race as well as damages paid in settlement of a lawsuit. We must remember that federal tax laws are widely believed to encourage behavior through allowing deductions and credits and discourage behavior by denying deductions or imposing penalties. Why shouldn't federal tax laws be designed to discourage race-based employment discrimination? For as long as we have had federal tax laws they have subsidized race discriminators by allowing them complete deductions.

When Congress codified the public [policy] doctrine in 1969, it observed that to allow certain deductions would frustrate sharply defined national or state policies. As a result, the public policy doctrine was enacted to prevent a tax deduction from reducing the "sting" of a penalty intended to punish the wrongdoer. Similarly here, denying wage deductions to employers who discriminate on the basis of race as well as denying the deduction for the judgment or settlement amount will penalize the employer. By denying the deductions, the "sting" of the penalty will not be reduced. The race discriminator will be punished in civil court and will be punished again through the operation of the federal tax laws. If eliminating discrimination on the basis of race is a clearly defined national policy, this proposal must be adopted.

All other similarly situated employers who do not discriminate on the basis of race will be able to take wage deductions. To the extent the company were publicly held, one might expect shareholders to sell shares in Company A, a race discriminator, not allowed to deduct wages[,] and instead to purchase stock in Company B, a non–race discriminator, allowed to deduct wages paid to their employees. The race discriminator becomes an economic outcast and must change practices if [it is] to continue operating competitively.

With respect to the employees who receive damage awards or settle lawsuits alleging race discrimination, those awards should be excluded from taxable income in order to compensate the victims for the harms suffered. The exclusion should provide an additional incentive to the employees to file suit against their employers. In addition wages paid while the taxpayer was being discriminated against should also be excluded for similar reasons. Assuming most of their taxable income comes from wages, and withholding taxes were deducted, they should receive a refund of all taxes withheld for the years in question. In order for the pervasiveness of racism to be eliminated, it must be fought on several fronts.

This proposal seeks to move the employment playing field from an overwhelmingly white, male field, to a more inclusive one. Who would my proposal not affect? Nonprofits and governmental agencies because they are not motivated by tax considerations. I leave, for another day, solutions to address those entities.

If my proposals were enacted, one would expect to see a significant diminishing of race-based employment discrimination. People of color would earn as much as whites. We would expect to see wealth in households of color increase over time. We might even see more families of color in marriage bonus households, because either wives or husbands of color would earn sufficient amounts to become the sole wage earner.

CONCLUSION

Although the federal tax laws did not cause societal racism, they are operating to exacerbate that racism by permitting employers who discriminate on the basis of race to deduct their discriminatory damage awards as well as deducting their discriminatory wages. The federal tax laws' role in reinforcing societal racism must be explored, written about, challenged, and ultimately eliminated.

Discursive Deficits: A Feminist Perspective on the Power of Technical Knowledge in Fiscal Law and Policy

LISA C. PHILIPPS[1]

No great powers of observation are needed to notice that both tax law and fiscal policy formation are dominated by a relatively small and elite group of experts. Nor would many dispute the inaccessibility of the technical language in which these issues are often discussed. In this paper, I focus on the way these technical discourses tend to deny the normative content of tax law and policy, and thus to deflect political challenges to the prevailing fiscal order. In this manner, technical discourses work to protect the interests of the relatively wealthy and powerful, and to sustain and legitimate the economic marginalization of women and other subordinated groups.

THE TECHNICAL IN TAX LAW

What is a technical discourse? The term has several layers of meaning, as it is used in this paper. Tax law is technical in the dictionary sense that it is a specialized field of knowledge, with its own language, involving a terminology and grammatical style that is not readily accessible to persons without specialized training. This inaccessibility is not merely a function of complexity or excessive detail. Indeed, bits of jargon and special terms can be used to bestow authority on even the most superficial or oversimplified analyses.

In addition, tax law is affiliated with certain other discourses that are technical in the same sense of being specialized fields of knowledge: economics, accounting, public finance theory, traditional tax policy analysis. Aspects of these discourses have been imported into, and internalized within[,] tax law, though judges in tax cases are quick to assert that such external knowledges always remain subject to any overriding legal principles. I think this is an example of the phenomenon observed by [Carol] Smart, in which law "sets itself above"[2] other, nonlegal discourses, while simultaneously incorporating selected aspects of those discourses for its own purposes. Smart argues that this allows law to extend its reach and maintain its power in modern society by allying itself with those knowledges that are important to what Foucault has termed the "disciplining of the social body."[3]

---

[1] Reprinted by permission from 11 *Canadian Journal of Law and Society* 141 (Spring 1996).

[2] Carol Smart, FEMINISM AND THE POWER OF LAW 10 (1989).

[3] *Id.* at 17.

There is a further dimension to the term "technical," one which goes beyond mere specialized knowledge. It also implies a form of knowledge which is *scientific* in nature, and this claim to scientificity is central to the power of technical discourses. The relationship between the technical and the scientific is not as straightforward as it first appears. Certainly, both are concerned with method and systematicity. But the strong association of these terms is primarily due to the fact that both refer in somewhat different ways to superior forms of knowledge; the former quite explicitly in terms of expertise, the latter more obliquely through the claim to objectivity and pure truth. The construction of the technical discourses in and around tax law as scientific feeds into a powerful ideology in our culture about the nature of truth and knowledge.

FEMINIST CHALLENGES TO FISCAL DISCOURSE

The question raised in this part is how feminists can best engage with technical discourses in the effort to obtain reforms to the tax system and the larger fiscal order. At one level, this is simply a new version of an old problem for feminists: the need to expose the contingent nature of seemingly objective and universal concepts, rules, and social arrangements. The tax system poses a distinct challenge, however, because of the extraordinary degree to which it is dominated by expert knowledge. Tax law's association with other technical discourses, such as economics and accounting, strengthens its claim to scientificity. This inhibits critical conversation about tax laws by those defined as nonexperts (including, sometimes, judges), and tends to delegitimize overtly value-based critiques of taxation.

The centrality of experiential knowledge to much feminist theorizing makes it appear less objective than the kinds of abstract quantitative reasoning traditionally employed within discourses like accounting and economics. Additionally, feminist challenges to the tax system often have to do with the treatment of women's caregiving work, with all its bodily, emotive, and expressive associations. Because it is constructed as the epitome of rational, economic legislation, tax law seems particularly resistant to any form of challenge which appears to be perspectival or personal. I do not suggest this is the only factor working against feminist challenges to fiscal policy. Rather, technical discourses complement other layers of politics.

The judicial treatment of feminist arguments in the *Symes*[4] and *Thibaudeau*[5] cases helps to illustrate these difficulties. These cases also raise some hard questions about when and how fiscal feminists draw upon technical discourses to advance their own arguments. While these discursive strategies have some liberatory potential, there are also risks associated with "putting the new wine of critical theory into the old bottles of patriarchal linguistic categories."[6] A brief summary of the cases is in order.

Beth Symes, a partner in a law firm, argued that the cost of hiring a nanny to care for her young daughters should be fully deductible as a business expense,

---

[4] Symes v. Canada, [1993] 4 S.C.R. 695 (Can.).

[5] Thibaudeau v. Canada, [1995] 2 S.C.R. 627 (Can.).

[6] Sue Curry Jansen, *Gender and the Information Society: A Socially Structured Silence*, 39 J. Comm. 196, 198 (1989).

either on a proper interpretation of the [Income Tax Act (ITA)], or pursuant to the equality rights provision in § 15 of the Charter of Rights and Freedoms [(Charter)]. The core of her argument was that Revenue Canada's construction of child-care expenses as personal rather than business-related is gender-biased; it reflects a world view in which women and their domestic activities are seen as private and separate from the public sphere of commerce, and in effect perpetuates women's exclusion from the business world. At trial, Cullen J. agreed with Symes, holding the nanny's salary to be fully deductible. His decision was reversed by the Federal Court of Appeal. The Supreme Court of Canada dismissed Symes's appeal, holding that Revenue Canada's denial of the deduction was justified under the terms of the statute, and that there was no violation of Symes's sex equality rights. The majority was comprised of the seven men on the Court – the two women dissented.

Shortly after the Supreme Court's decision in *Symes*, the Federal Court of Appeal ruled in favor of another woman, Suzanne Thibaudeau, who challenged the taxation of her child-support payments. The Court accepted Thibaudeau's argument that the ITA discriminated against her as a separated custodial parent by requiring her to include child support in income while allowing a deduction to her former husband. Writing for the majority, Hugessen J.A. held that the inclusion requirement discriminated on the basis of family status, which he identified as a ground analogous to those enumerated in § 15 of the Charter. Hugessen rejected the argument that the provisions discriminated on the basis of sex, however, despite the fact that virtually all persons paying tax on child support are women, and despite broad evidence of women's postdivorce poverty relative to men.

The government appealed the *Thibaudeau* case to the Supreme Court of Canada and won. As in *Symes*, the majority rejected the equality challenge, holding that the impugned provisions imposed no burden on Thibaudeau. Two factors were central to this decision. First, the majority chose to focus on the aggregate impact of the inclusion/deduction system on the (ex-)couple, reasoning that the tax system actually confers a benefit by allowing the parents to split their incomes and reduce the net tax burden on their combined incomes. In response to the argument that in practice the custodial family often derives no benefit from this tax subsidy and is sometimes prejudiced by the inclusion requirement, the majority turned to the family law system. Any such inequality between the ex-spouses is caused not by the tax system, they said, but by the failure of family law processes to ensure an adequate level of support. Once again, the Court split along gender lines. The two women Justices, McLachlin and L'Heureux-Dubé, would have struck down the inclusion requirement on the view that it discriminates against the custodial parent.

These two Supreme Court decisions have attracted a number of academic commentaries. My purpose here is to make a few points about the role of technical discourses in these cases and the way such discourses both advanced and thwarted feminist arguments. In both cases, statistical and social science evidence was introduced to advance arguments for a feminist, or at least a more gender-neutral tax law. In *Symes*, the taxpayer brought in a feminist sociologist to testify to the increasing role of women in the paid labor market, and the barriers posed to women due to their primary caregiving responsibilities. In *Thibaudeau*, the parties and intervenors submitted studies on the financial impact of the taxation of child support on men and women across income brackets.

These strategies are attractive because they can confer additional authority on feminist arguments. They may allow us to capitalize on the positive, democratic potential of scientific and technical knowledge, that is, its appeal to a rational order superior to entrenched traditions or prejudices. Didi Herman has remarked upon the judicial tendency to rely on sociological evidence to support innovative and progressive interpretations of the law and to reject earlier interpretations as the product of uninformed biases. It is also true that the choice of discursive strategy in any context is constrained in part by the existing framework of debate. In many cases, feminists have little choice but to respond to the technical arguments held up to justify the status quo. However, it is important to recognize the potential pitfalls in trying to beat tax law at its own technical game, and the subtle ways in which technical discourses may undermine feminist politics even as they advance the immediate interests of particular women.

First, we must be conscious that feminist social science or other expertise is not entering a vacuum when it is presented in tax cases. Besides having to contend with the political predispositions of individual judges, it is up against other technical knowledge systems like economics and traditional tax policy analysis. The gendered assumptions of these other discourses have already been deeply internalized within the jurisprudence and provisions of tax law. An example of the influence of extra-legal knowledge can be seen in the *Thibaudeau* case, in the majority's reliance upon a traditional economic concept of the family unit. Mainstream economic theory has tended to reduce heterosexual family groupings to their male breadwinners, presuming that an increase in men's welfare benefits all members of the household. Even in more reflective theories which recognize that families are comprised of individuals, men are generally assumed to pool their incomes with women and children, who are assumed to be earning less market income.

As many critical scholars have exposed, this image of the heteropatriarchal family is founded on assumptions which may be accurate for some but which grossly distort the experience of many. The assumption of a male breadwinner, for example, does not reflect the realities of many working-class women and women of color, whose waged work has been critical to the survival of their families. Further, in families where men are the primary earners, economic theory exaggerates the degree to which intrafamily relations are characterized by altruism and equal sharing. Indeed, central to the feminist arguments in *Thibaudeau* was the reality of economic inequality within heterosexual marriages – the fact that women frequently do not benefit equally from market incomes received by men, and that men do not necessarily share their incomes willingly, especially following separation.

Despite the evidence offered to them, the majority judges in *Thibaudeau* were unable or unwilling to see any problem with treating the heterosexual family as a unified economic entity. They concluded the deduction/inclusion system is not burdensome for women, and in fact generally confers a benefit, because it allows for co-operative income splitting which increases the resources available to support the children. The statistical and social science evidence, cited abundantly by the two women Justices in dissent, indicated that in almost 30 percent of cases there is no potential for income splitting at all, because the woman is earning as much or more income than her former husband, and consequently is not in a lower tax bracket. They also cited evidence that family courts often have not adequately accounted for the tax implications of support, and noted that, in any event, the great bulk of support arrangements are negotiated in private, without court supervision, and often without lawyers or tax advice. In addition, the clear evidence that women's standard of living declines relative to men's following divorce suggests that the sense of sharing and mutual obligation assumed by the majority is not a reality for many people.

Perhaps most striking is that the majority did not discuss the social science evidence submitted by the taxpayer or the intervenors, even to indicate why they rejected it. This ability to silently disqualify feminist expertise is a particular concern given that judges are often asked to choose between two or more expert opinions, potentially advantaging whatever appears on a superficial level to be the best science. It seems likely that courts will very often find studies which proceed from dominant assumptions to be more objective and authoritative. Moreover, corporate and state interests have far greater resources than women's groups or anti-poverty organizations to produce technically sophisticated-looking research. There is likely to be a hierarchy of technical discourses, in other words, in which expert evidence perceived as feminist will often be seen as less objective.

Perhaps the best evidence of technical knowledge exercising power in *Thibaudeau*, however, is the special deference accorded to tax law and traditional tax policy concepts by the majority. While being careful to state that tax legislation is not *exempt* from Charter review, they emphasized the importance of not interfering unduly with the government's fiscal priorities. Gonthier J. argued most strongly for this deferential approach, pointing to the ITA's "special nature,"[7] and admonishing the taxpayer as follows:

> [O]ne should not confuse the concept of fiscal equity, which is concerned with the best distribution of the tax burden in light of the need for revenue, the taxpayers' ability to pay and the economic and social policies of the government, with the concept of the right to equality, which ... means that a member of a group shall not be disadvantaged on account of an irrelevant personal characteristic shared by that group.[8]

These statements appeal to the notion that tax law has its own internal logic and imperatives that operate beyond the reach of politics. Fiscal policy is constructed as something governed by a higher authority of objectively determined criteria which even the Court is less than fully qualified to review. Reframing the issue as one of fiscal equity removes it neatly from the sphere of equality discourse into the expert language of tax policy. Gonthier's distinction is nonsensical, of course, because notions of fiscal equity rely on precisely the same ideologically charged standards and beliefs as equality rights doctrine. Indeed, the political contingency of tax interpretation is demonstrated by the majority's invocation of the so-called postdivorce family unit in *Thibaudeau*. Again, however, arguments

---

[7] *Thibaudeau*, [1995] 2 S.C.R. at 675.
[8] *Id.* at 676.

that are perceived as feminist or otherwise politicized may be effectively disqualified when tax law is constructed as a specialized body of knowledge.

One response to these difficulties is simply to accept them. Feminists must always contend with more powerful, masculinist discourses in the courts, in academe, in the popular media, and in policy-making processes. If greater use of empirical data and expert languages can narrow the odds against us by creating a more authoritative feminist discourse, some would argue this is enough. It is significant, for instance, that both Symes and Thibaudeau managed to convince one court on the way up, as well as both women judges on the Supreme Court of Canada, in the process generating a body of dissenting jurisprudence that may show the way forward in future cases. And the political controversy and lobbying activities generated by Thibaudeau's case undoubtedly were a major influence in the government's decision to propose the repeal of the inclusion/deduction rules in its 1996 budget. It is entirely possible that the marshaling of technical discourses in support of Thibaudeau's position played some role in bringing about progressive change. Even if this is so, however, a couple of potential problems remain.

There is a risk that addressing problems of sexism and other social biases with scientific research may encourage the same kind of depoliticization that occurs when such research is used to support dominant ideological positions. The basic political and moral questions being raised by feminists may be translated into technical matters for specialists to debate. A different but related problem is that the subtle normative thrust of expert discourses may operate at cross-purposes with the feminist political aims they were invoked to serve. The *Symes* case provides an example.

In the successful litigation at the trial level, Cullen J. picked up on the evidence given by the feminist sociologist, making it a central part of his reasons. It is worth quoting him at some length:

> [T]he plaintiff exercised good business and commercial judgment in deciding to dedicate part of her resources from the law practice to the provision of child care. This decision was acceptable according to business principles which include the development of intellectual capital, the improvement of productivity, the provision of services to clients and making available the resource which she sells, namely her time.... Further, [the expert] evidence supports the notion that the availability of child care increases productivity by enhancing the peace of mind of employees. Enhancing productivity... is totally in keeping with well established business practices. Moreover, [the expert] evidence indicates that the absence of child care is a barrier to women's participation in the economy... and therefore lowering the barrier by arriving at a satisfactory means of dealing with the costs of child care would make good business sense.[9]

While this line of reasoning helped support a decision in favor of Symes, it is important to reflect on the larger implications of framing the issue of child care in these terms. For most of the above passage, Cullen distances himself from the feminist political arguments in favor of state-subsidized child care. He does refer to the barriers to women's participation in paid labor, but quickly translates this back into a question of "good business sense," rather than sexual equality.

[9] Symes v. The Queen, [1989] 89 D.T.C. 5249 (Can. Tax Ct.).

Moreover, the passage is far removed from any sense that child-care work is itself a socially and economically valuable activity, or that it would be a good idea to distribute that work more equally between men and women. Framing the issue in these narrow economistic terms also leaves the class and racial politics of the private model of child-care services completely unproblematized. Audrey Macklin has detailed the vulnerability of immigrant women, particularly women of color, to economic, physical, and sexual exploitation as domestic workers. Nor does the decision address in any way the situation of the vast majority of women who do not earn business income, and their lack of access to affordable child care. Does this judgment introduce a feminist discourse into the field, or does it translate the feminist political challenge into a technical question that fundamentally endorses existing economic relations and their attendant inequalities?

One may argue that these problems simply reflect the limits of equality rights litigation, with its inevitable focus on a narrow legal issue. It is notable, however, that the economic discourse used by Cullen is so well suited to the task of placing the larger political issues aside. One may also argue that the business woman and the domestic worker have a common political interest in any change that attaches greater economic importance to women's work. However, the language of the Tax Court decision by no means encourages this connection, with its tight focus on the efficient generation of profit in the paid economy.

I do not wish to suggest that feminists should reject science out of hand as a way of knowing and changing the world. A technical rendering of the child-care issue in terms of human capital and productivity does after all capture some part of some women's experience. What is needed, however, is to revise the concept of science and objectivity to recognize the locatedness and partiality of all knowledge.

I have several suggestions as to how this challenge might be taken up in the fiscal policy field. First, those working for change need to be alert to the contradictions of technical discourse and the ways it may undermine political struggles around deficits and taxation even while supporting immediate law reform struggles. Second, it would be useful, I think, to push the technical discourses themselves in a more radical direction whenever possible. In *Symes*, for example, it might have been possible to draw on the work of feminist political economists to talk about the productive value of child-care labor itself, and the way women's caregiving work subsidizes profitability in the public economy. This would be an alternative means of challenging the construction of women's family responsibilities as private and noneconomic, in a way that permits a more radical critique of the division of labor and its effects on different groups of women. In other words, it is worth considering how to challenge the gender, class, and other biases within technical discourses, when we are deploying them to achieve progressive change in the law. Finally, it is critical in my view to resist the technocratic ideology of value-neutrality, and to keep the political and moral issues that are at stake in the foreground of any analysis. While it may be necessary and worthwhile to counter arguments justifying the current fiscal system on their own terms, it is equally important to expose the partiality and contingency of technical renderings of fiscal policy and to insist on democratic discussion of the political merits.

The Hidden Costs of the Progressivity Debate

NANCY C. STAUDT[1]

Progressive taxation – taxing high-income individuals at a proportionally higher level than low-income individuals – has sparked more than a century of controversy. Those who support progressive taxation have heralded it as a policy that promotes the greatest good for the greatest number in society, protects traditional democratic values, reflects the communitarian worldview of women who see themselves as responsible for the well-being of all individuals, and reveals the "aesthetic judgment" that income inequality is "distinctly evil or unlovely."[2] At the same time, critics have condemned progressive income taxation as social policy that amounts to theft and involuntary servitude, reflects the democratic process gone awry, penalizes hardworking individuals, and produces economic waste throughout society. Theorists in almost every discipline have entered the progressivity debate, proposing a variety of different tax rates in order to disburse the costs of public goods and services.

Despite their contending viewpoints, theorists on both sides of the debate have reached surprising consensus on the proper treatment of the truly poor. Both sides agree that legislators and policy makers must avoid imposing tax costs on individuals living at or below subsistence levels of income. This agreement is notable in light of the widespread perception that advocates of progressivity worry about the poor while its detractors worry about the wealthy.

In fact, all tax theorists have divided society into two groups – relatively wealthy individuals who pay taxes and poor individuals who are excluded from the face of the laws entirely. Of course, if the goal of tax policy is to distribute the costs of public goods, then offering an exemption to the poor might seem desirable and perhaps even an obvious policy choice, given that the poor have little or no income. While the practical difficulty of collecting the tax explains why theorists have advocated an exemption, it does not explain why they have failed to explore any positive rights beyond an exemption or, indeed, any responsibility the poor might have to society despite their lack of income.

---

[1] Reprinted by permission from 50 *Vanderbilt Law Review* 919 (1997).
[2] HENRY SIMONS, PERSONAL INCOME TAXATION: THE DEFINITION OF INCOME AS A PROBLEM OF FISCAL POLICY 18–19 (1938).

THE MISSING DEBATE OVER POSITIVE RIGHTS

Traditional tax theorists implicitly agree that individuals at subsistence levels of income should have, at the minimum, the privilege or the negative right to be free from coercive interference by the government, at least with regard to taxation. It is surprising that theorists have not explored more thoroughly any positive rights the poor might have in light of their underlying principles and ethical mandates. Many of the theories, taken to their own logical conclusion, could justify a positive right to income. If traditional tax theorists have purposefully failed to consider the positive rights of the poor, the obvious question is – why? One reason might be related to the notion that tax policy involves the imposition of *liabilities*, not the award of *rights*. The question of positive rights, therefore, should be left to the welfare debate which largely takes place outside of the federal taxation context. A second reason for tax theorists' neglect of positive rights could be related to the existence of the deductions, credits, and exemptions that arguably protect any positive rights the poor might have. In short, because the political process has addressed satisfactorily the question of the poor's positive rights, traditional tax theorists have focused only on the relatively wealthy. Finally, tax theorists might argue that they have not ignored positive rights, but they have pursued an alternative strategy altogether for assuring economic security. Rather than specific subsidies that ensure a minimum income for the poor, theorists have focused on the possibility of using the Code as a means for promoting market growth and productivity. The benefits of market growth are assumed to trickle down to the poor and are often assumed to provide benefits far greater than any direct subsidy ever could.

THE MISSING DEBATE OVER RESPONSIBILITIES

Although traditional tax theorists appear to assume that the poor have at least some minimal rights with regard to the state, no theorist has ever considered the possibility that the poor might also have responsibilities. While tax theorists' failure to investigate rights imposes obvious and hidden costs upon the poor, the problems associated with their failure to explore a poor individual's positive obligation to the state is much more subtle. At first cut, it might appear that in more thoroughly addressing individual rights we can only advantage the poor while addressing responsibilities can only produce further marginalization. When the effects of tax theorists' failure to consider a poor individual's responsibility to the state are analyzed closely, however, it becomes clear that this oversight has seriously disadvantaged the poor. Accordingly, I argue that tax theorists must recognize the possibility that all citizens, wealthy and poor, are capable of contributing to the greater social good.

Early social contract theorists and utilitarian theorists explicitly addressed a relatively wealthy citizen's obligation and responsibility to the greater social good. The contemporary debate on distributive justice, however, has focused on individual rights which, in turn, has led traditional tax theorists to center their discussion on taxpayer rights and entitlements before considering the individual's obligation to the state. Focusing primarily on rights in the taxation context is particularly surprising in light of the fact that the laws raise obvious and fundamental questions with regard to a citizen's responsibility to the public good.

Countless theorists have lamented society's preoccupation with rights, arguing that "it is the responsibilities of a citizen that provide[] a bridge between selfish, rights-bearing individuals and their community."[3] Rights talk, it is argued, "promotes unrealistic expectations, heightens social conflict, and inhibits dialogue that might lead toward consensus, accommodation, or at least the discovery of common ground."[4] Moreover, many political and moral theorists have forcefully argued that the very notion of citizenship is intimately linked with both individual entitlement and obligation to a community. The political theorist T. H. Marshall, for example, contended that by guaranteeing civil, political, and social rights to all, the state ensures that every member is able to participate in and enjoy the common life of society. Withholding these rights ultimately marginalizes individuals in the community. At the same time, theorists have argued that the inability to fulfill community obligations or to maintain some level of civic virtue is as much of an obstacle to full membership in society as is the lack of equal rights. Accordingly, I seek to refocus tax theorists on the importance of individual fulfillment of social obligation and at the same time expand the discussion to include both the wealthy and the poor.

It is obvious that by contributing money to the fisc, taxpayers fulfill an obligation to the community. Paying taxes, however, does not only impose a burden. Taxpayers share in the benefits of an organized society as well as the provision of public goods and services that could not be obtained in the private market.

Moreover, by paying taxes, the relatively wealthy seem to attain a privileged status in contemporary political and legal debates. The idea that an individual's social standing improves upon the payment of taxes is likely to be met with suspicion, perhaps even laughter, by contemporary tax theorists. Understanding the social value of paying taxes, however, is key to understanding fully why traditional tax theory has contributed to the marginalization of the poor.

First, consider the fact that tax policy debates have generally privileged the interests of the relatively wealthy. In the 1996 presidential election, both candidates focused on tax issues that could only be of importance to middle- and upper-class individuals. Bill Clinton and Bob Dole, for example, both proposed tax reform that would enable individuals to set aside a greater percentage of income in tax-free retirement funds. Dole also advocated a decrease in the marginal tax rates in general and the capital gains rates in particular.

Perhaps more disturbing than devising tax legislation tailored to the interests of the relatively wealthy is the fact that society itself accords more respect to taxpayers than nontaxpayers in the public debates. The discourse related to the distribution of welfare benefits easily demonstrates this point. This dialogue views taxpayers as hardworking and disciplined individuals who unfortunately must provide economic assistance to the deviant and lazy welfare recipients. Not only does the

---

[3] Suzanna Sherry, *Responsible Republicanism*, 62 U. CHI. L. REV. 130, 132 (1995).

[4] MARY ANN GLENDON, RIGHTS TALK: THE IMPOVERISHMENT OF POLITICAL DISCOURSE 14 (1991).

welfare rhetoric paint relatively wealthy taxpayers as humanitarians who must save the poor from themselves, but welfare legislation also often more explicitly addresses the interests of taxpayers than the needs of the poor.

In advocating an exclusion from the tax laws and from all other social obligations, traditional tax theory, therefore, has worked to marginalize the poor in both the social policy-making process and in society-at-large. This exclusion and marginalization, in turn, works to curb the poor's interest and commitment to broader social and political issues. Rather than participating in the political process by expressing their own ideas and viewpoints, the poor often remain outside public debate even in circumstances under which they could easily make their views more widely known. The demographic characteristics of those who vote reflect the political apathy of poor individuals. Only 8% of voters come from families with income under $15,000, though these same families represent 23% of the population. Conversely, families with income above $15,000 make up 78% of the population but represent 92% of the voters. Commentators have argued that this political indifference is directly linked to the manner in which social policy, and tax policy in particular, tends to address the interests of the relatively wealthy rather than the concerns of those living in poverty.

Of course traditional tax theorists may not have entirely neglected the poor, but may have intended to impose *negative* rather than *positive* responsibilities (i.e., self-restraint vs. positive activities). Indeed, just as many other public policy areas rely on self-restraint, successful tax policy also relies upon the poor to meet their negative responsibility to society. If poor individuals avoid demanding excessive benefits under the Code, for example, they will avoid imposing inefficient costs upon society and infringing upon the property rights of the relatively wealthy. That traditional tax theorists have raised these concerns for over a century implies that they have sought to impose just this type of negative responsibility upon the poor. While all citizens have certain negative obligations to society, the notion that the poor must privilege the rights and interests of the relatively wealthy is precisely the notion that has led to the deep bias against the poor in taxation debates as well as their cultural marginalization and political apathy. It leaves the poor in the disadvantaged position of patiently and quietly waiting for the wealthy to decide their social and economic fate. To ensure the poor are meaningfully included in society, tax policy must more explicitly address both negative and positive responsibilities.

Recognizing that the poor have some positive responsibility to the greater social good does not necessarily lead to the conclusion that the state should coerce the poor to contribute their labor in order to attain full citizenship. A number of possibilities exist for enabling even the poorest and most disadvantaged individuals to contribute on a voluntary basis to society. Consider market participation. Judith Shklar has argued that American citizens have found the marketplace to be an important aspect of citizenship. The right to earn a living wage has been integrally linked with independence, freedom, and status. Market participation has also been viewed as a social and cultural obligation. Many theorists have argued that individuals have a duty to avoid dependence as well as a positive duty to contribute as much as possible to the productive output of society. In short, earning a wage is widely viewed as "a necessary quality of genuine, democratic citizenship."[5]

Political and economic theorists have begun to recognize the possibility of using the Code to encourage poor individuals to undertake this social duty. The notion that one has an obligation to work in the waged labor market is reflected in the [earned income tax credit (EITC)]. The credit is available to those individuals who work in the waged labor market, indicating that the right to the credit is integrally tied to the responsibility to work. In this sense, the EITC could be viewed as a tax provision that imposes a positive duty upon poor individuals and thus embraces a policy that seeks to ensure the cultural and social integration of the poor into society as valuable citizens. Indeed, advocates of the policy have applauded the EITC for just this reason.

Although the adoption of the EITC represents an important advance with regard to recognizing the rights and obligations of the poor, the provision does nothing to ensure that the poor actually have the opportunity to participate in the market economy. Indeed, as Ann Alstott has noted, the program creates unambiguous work *disincentives* for some individuals. Moreover, the EITC ignores the fact that many individuals are unable to participate in the market because of personal responsibilities in the private sphere, lack of education and training, and the general lack of employment opportunities. In short, tax theorists have made the market economy, the sphere in which the poor are least successful, the only site where the poor can satisfy their positive responsibility to the greater social good. Without ensuring universal work opportunities, the exclusive focus on the market imposes a threshold to citizenship that is virtually impossible for some individuals to meet. It also ignores a variety of other approaches that tax theorists could use to facilitate the satisfaction of one's responsibility to the state.

Theorists could easily devise a variant of the market-oriented approach to promote meaningful participation in political and social institutions for those who are unable to work in the waged labor market and who have no ability to pay income taxes. Indeed many political and moral theorists have argued that the responsibilities and virtues of citizenship are found outside the context of the market. Michael Walzer has argued, for example, that a democracy is not necessarily achieved when all citizens work in the market for a wage. The "civility that makes democratic politics possible," Walzer argues, "can only be learned in the associational networks" of society.[6] Mary Ann Glendon further argues that it is in community organizations that "human character, competence, and capacity for citizenship are formed."[7] In lieu of market participation, therefore, theorists could explore the possibility of tying a tax credit to one's participation in voluntary organizations found throughout civil society such as a church, union, ethnic association, environmental group, or any other socially worthwhile organization.

Giving recognition to one's contribution to community organizations is not entirely unfamiliar to traditional tax theorists. The Code currently recognizes the

---

[5] JUDITH N. SHKLAR, AMERICAN CITIZENSHIP: THE QUEST FOR INCLUSION 92–93 (1991).

[6] Michael Walzer, *The Civil Society Argument, in* DIMENSIONS OF RADICAL DEMOCRACY: PLURALISM, CITIZENSHIP AND COMMUNITY 89, 104 (Chantal Mouffe ed., 1992).

[7] GLENDON, *supra* note 4, at 106.

importance of individual participation in community-centered activities. Section 170 of the Code, for example, permits a taxpayer to deduct monies donated to a charitable organization. This charitable deduction, in effect, conveys Walzer's and Glendon's notion that an individual who has voluntarily contributed to a community organization has satisfied at least part of her responsibility to the greater good. By allowing the taxpayer to deduct charitable contributions, the legislature recognizes that one's social responsibility can be satisfied either by giving to a worthwhile community organization or by giving directly to the government coffers.

While § 170 is valuable for its nonmarket focus, the poor are unable to contribute income to a community organization just as they are unable to carry the burden of income taxation. That only monetary contributions are tax-deductible, however, reinforces the idea that the Code is set up to enable the relatively wealthy to meet their social responsibilities. Congress, however, could expand upon the current approach. It could maintain § 170, giving a deduction to the wealthy, and at the same time amend the provision to provide a "charitable service credit" that gives a payment to individuals donating services and not income.

A charitable service credit could simply work as an incentive for individuals to participate in social and political institutions and at the same time give public recognition to their labor as socially valuable. Accordingly, theorists exploring the possibility of a charitable service credit need not be concerned with the actual value of the work or the possibility that the federal government will be a public employer. The credit should be a small, almost symbolic, payment subject to the same limitations imposed on the EITC. Moreover, if charitable service is widely perceived to be a valuable contribution to society as Walzer and Glendon suggest it is, a small payment would not necessarily offset the gain that inures to society due to the increased levels of community involvement. The combination of a charitable service credit and the EITC would convey to the poor that they too have the option to satisfy their obligation to society in a variety of ways.

Tax theorists could also explore the relationship between education and one's responsibility to participate in a liberal democracy. Countless theorists have argued that in order to participate effectively, citizens must engage in reasonable public discourse. Such discourse, however, is not simply the willingness to make one's views known but also includes "the willingness to listen seriously to a range of views which, given the diversity of liberal societies will include ideas the listener is bound to find strange and even obnoxious."[8] Moreover, theorists have argued that publicly and freely discussing political issues does not entail excessive demands on the state but rather a reasonable and conscientious debate about one's preferences and needs. The place to learn the virtue of "public reasonableness," according to many political theorists, is through a system of education.

Tax theorists, however, have failed to explore the possibility of using the Code to encourage individuals to meet their social obligation to becoming responsible and deliberative citizens. Under the current Code, education costs are deductible only

---

[8] WILLIAM A. GALSTON, LIBERAL PURPOSES: GOODS, VIRTUES, AND DIVERSITY IN THE LIBERAL STATE 227 (1991).

if they are associated with the taxpayers' market employment. The deductibility of employment-related expenses does nothing for individuals who are unable to participate in the market. Moreover, the current tax subsidy entirely ignores the notion that education is important for reasons far beyond the market.

If tax theorists and policy makers were committed to the notion that market activities along with participation in the political process as well-educated citizens were important to society-at-large, the tax laws could easily accommodate and encourage these activities. Educational tax incentives, for example, could be devised in an effort to push individuals to seek the education necessary to learn the virtue of public reasonableness. A credit, for example, could be offered in an effort to reflect the societal value of an individual's time and energy devoted to educational activities. Indeed, by recognizing the value – and the responsibility – of education, tax theorists would enable both wealthy and poor individuals to satisfy their obligation to the public good.

Tax ~~Equity~~

ANTHONY C. INFANTI[1]

Each year when I teach federal income tax, one of the topics that I reflexively cover with my students in the first or second class is the triad of tax policy concerns – efficiency, equity, and administrability – that will inform many of our discussions during the semester. Whether the topic is an objective test for deducting the cost of work-related clothing or the propriety of taxing capital gains at preferential rates, I have found that introducing students to the notion that we should strive for a tax system that (1) minimizes interference with economic decision making, (2) is fair, and (3) is easy to administer and comply with, helps them to see tax not as a dry and arcane subject, but as one that involves the balancing of important policy considerations that have a real, everyday impact on all of our lives. Evidence that others share in the belief that it is important to introduce these tax policy concerns to students early on in their tax education can be found in the large number of basic income tax textbooks that begin with a discussion of them.

Tax equity, the topic of this article, has influenced not only classroom debate, but also political debates and, to a lesser extent, judicial application of the tax laws. In academic circles, however, tax equity has engendered significant controversy. For decades, commentators have debated the choice of progressivity (as opposed to proportionality or regressivity) as the most appropriate means of achieving "vertical" equity in the income tax (i.e., of differentiating the tax burdens imposed on taxpayers with unequal incomes). Of late, "horizontal" equity – the intuitively appealing notion that taxpayers with equal incomes should be treated equally – has also come under fire for, among other things, its lack of independent significance. Some commentators have taken aim at both horizontal *and* vertical equity, arguing that they lack independent normative content and contribute nothing beyond conceptual confusion to the tax policy debate.

Yet, despite these critiques, all mention of horizontal and vertical equity has far from disappeared from the pages of law reviews. Both "mainstream" and critical tax scholars have embraced horizontal and vertical equity in their contributions to the tax policy literature; indeed, there has been some debate about whether critical tax theory raises issues of horizontal as opposed to vertical equity. There has even been speculation that some of the misunderstanding between these two groups of tax

---

[1] Reprinted by permission from 55 *Buffalo Law Review* 1191 (2008).

scholars stems from a failure to see critical contributions in the same tax equity light. As it turns out, however, the problem is not that "mainstream" and critical tax scholars are talking past each other, but that critical tax scholars attempt to frame their discussions in tax equity terms at all.

Approaching the concept of tax equity itself from a critical perspective, the basic thesis of this article is that the extant critiques of that concept miss the mark in an important respect. Far from lacking normative content, tax equity abounds with it. For example, as defined and applied for purposes of income tax policy analysis, tax equity is solely concerned with the fair treatment of individuals who either have the same or different incomes. This represents a normative choice to consider economic differences – and *only* economic differences – in determining the fairness of a tax whose larger purpose is to allocate the burden of funding our government and of paying for public services. Through this insidious homogenization of the population, tax equity performs a sanitizing and a screening function; in other words, it effectively forecloses consideration of noneconomic forms of difference (e.g., of race, ethnicity, gender, sexual orientation, or physical ability) when determining the appropriate allocation of societal burdens, even though these other forms of difference have served, and continue to serve, as the basis for invidious discrimination that already imposes heavy burdens on its victims. Put differently, and a bit more bluntly, tax equity, with its ostensible concern for fairness, is often the most logical avenue for introducing critical concerns into tax policy debates; however, the concept is defined in such a way as to bar entry to precisely these types of concerns. It should come as no surprise, then, that "mainstream" tax scholars tend to be so resistant – and, at times, openly hostile – to critical contributions to tax policy debates.

MUSINGS ON THE MEANING OF EQUITY

Discussions of tax equity are typically phrased in terms of one or both of its two subtypes: horizontal equity and vertical equity. When applied to the income tax, horizontal equity is conventionally defined as treating taxpayers with equal incomes equally, and vertical equity is conventionally defined as an appropriate differentiation in the tax burden imposed on taxpayers with unequal incomes. On its face, then, tax equity appears to take into consideration both sameness *and* difference when determining a fair allocation of the overall income tax burden. But, as the saying goes, appearances can be deceiving. Even though the heuristics of horizontal and vertical equity do direct the attention of those concerned with fairness toward the proper treatment of taxpayers who are similarly situated *and* those who are differently situated, there is only *one* type of sameness or difference that counts in these explorations of tax equity: sameness or difference of *income*. In other words, for purposes of determining the fairness of the income tax, the concept of tax equity presupposes homogeneity in the population along all lines except one: income. This supposition is, of course, wholly groundless – but, as we will see, it is far from harmless.

In reality, people are also grouped and divided along lines other than income. Race, ethnicity, gender, sexual orientation, and disability are just a few of the notable additional lines along which such groupings and divisions (often invidiously) occur in everyday life. Yet, horizontal and vertical equity efface these lines of similarity and difference. They transform three-dimensional, flesh and blood individuals into two-dimensional accounting statements, reducing them to no more than the sum of their transactions in the economic marketplace. Horizontal and vertical equity take race, ethnicity, gender, sexual orientation, disability, and other characteristics into account only if, and to the extent that, they happen to have an impact on economic income – all other effects are simply ignored. By assuming a far more homogeneous population than the one that actually exists, horizontal and vertical equity screen from the tax policy debate many issues relating to race, ethnicity, gender, sexual orientation, and disability, and they tend to transmute any remaining issues into ones of economic class. This is a powerful rhetorical move that simultaneously sanitizes the debate over tax fairness – cleansing it of uncomfortable discussions of racism, sexism, heterosexism, and disability discrimination – and allows that debate to be easily manipulated in favor of those with wealth and power.

THE HEGEMONIC QUALITY OF TAX EQUITY

The concept of tax equity is part of the "entire system of values, attitudes, beliefs, morality, etc. that is in one way or another supportive of the established order."[2] Cloaked in a mantle of positive connotations, tax equity is viewed as an indisputable good: "Equity is good. No one argues that an equitable state is morally or functionally flawed."[3] Even when not stated quite so forthrightly, we often see equity described as one of the hallmarks of a "good" tax system or of "good" tax policy. Equity has thus become part of our tax "common sense"; it seems nearly "unchallengeable, [a] part of the natural order of things."[4] In fact, the concept is so fundamental to our "worldview" of tax that many of our basic tax textbooks begin by introducing (indoctrinating?) law students to the desirability of striving for an "equitable" tax system.

To achieve this ideological hegemony, the dominant group (i.e., economically privileged, able-bodied, straight, white males) has had to make sacrifices; however, those sacrifices have occurred only at the margins. In particular, our tax system has consistently – albeit controversially – embraced the idea that the income tax burden ought to be progressive in nature, meaning that the amount of tax paid should increase as a taxpayer's income increases. The visible face of progressivity in our income tax system is the graduated rate structure, which, with nominal rates proceeding in five steps from 10% to 35%, appears to exact an increasing proportion of an individual's income as that income rises. But, again, appearances may be deceiving. As commentators have noted, "there are a number of reasons why nominal rate structures may not reflect the actual distribution of the tax burden," not the least of which is tinkering by Congress with the tax base "to exclude

---

[2] CARL BOGGS, GRAMSCI'S MARXISM 39 (1976).
[3] Samuel A. Donaldson, *The Easy Case Against Tax Simplification*, 22 VA. TAX REV. 645, 739–40 (2003).
[4] BOGGS, *supra* note 2, at 39.

many items included in most economic definitions of income."[5] Although it can be difficult to determine whether the tax burden is progressive in practice and not just in appearance, it has been said that "[m]ost analysts believe the effective federal income tax rate structure is progressive, although not as progressive as the nominal rate structure."[6] Furthermore, when other sources of federal revenue are also taken into account, a noticeable shift occurred between 1969 and 1983 away from more progressive forms of taxation (e.g., the income tax and the estate and gift taxes) and toward more regressive forms of taxation (e.g., payroll taxes). Indeed, a recent study that covered individual and corporate income taxes, estate and gift taxes, and payroll taxes documented a striking decline in the overall progressivity of the federal tax system at the highest income levels between 1960 and 2004.

In return for what has turned out to be a small (and decreasing) economic sacrifice, the dominant group has obtained control over the flow of ideas in tax policy debates. With this control, they are able, with the help of intellectuals, to channel the tax policy discourse in a direction that helps to obtain the consent of other groups to their own subordination. To this end, the dominant group has taken a concept (i.e., equity) that, at least in the abstract, cannot help but evoke positive feelings and has made it even more appealing to academics by nearly eliminating its one potentially objectionable aspect: its inherent subjectivity. The entire idea of what counts as an "equitable" tax system has been constructed on and around "neutral" and "objective" economic factors. Though cynics might be wary that equity is open to manipulation because it is an "empty idea,"[7] the tax version of equity seems to have allayed these concerns through its reliance on purely "neutral" and "objective" economic factors. Notwithstanding any leeway that persists with regard to the choice of relevant economic factors to include in the tax equity formula, this version of equity ("Equity 2.0"?) undoubtedly benefits from an aura of scientificity.

This scientificity also furnishes ready and plausible reasons to academics for *not* addressing concerns associated with race, ethnicity, gender, sexual orientation, disability, and other axes of subordination in the tax arena. In practice, it works even more effectively by rendering any mention of these subjects in a tax context immediately suspect. To use the cover of "neutrality" and "objectivity" to create a presumption that such discussion is irrelevant or improper serves only to advance the ideological hegemony of the dominant group. This presumption makes it easier to co-opt, neutralize, or diminish the alternative or oppositional ideas put forward by critical scholars – many of which were shaped by this specific hegemony to begin with. In short, the presumption works to both solidify and obscure the dominant group's control over subordinated groups.

The influence of this construction of tax equity is also felt beyond the confines of legal academia. By isolating economic factors as the sole permissible topic for discussion, the dominant group has shifted the political debate over taxation away

---

[5] Joseph Bankman & Thomas Griffith, *Social Welfare and the Rate Structure: A New Look at Progressive Taxation*, 75 CAL. L. REV. 1909, 1909 (1987).

[6] *Id.* at 1910.

[7] Peter Westen, *The Empty Idea of Equality*, 95 HARV. L. REV. 537 (1982).

from the potentially difficult topics of race, gender, sexual orientation, disability, and other forms of invidious discrimination and toward a topic that it can easily manipulate and turn to its own advantage – economic class.

After more than six years of the Bush Administration's championing tax cuts that greatly benefit the wealthy, we now have at our disposal a veritable bounty of examples of rhetoric that seeks to justify these tax cuts by exploiting the unbending focus on the economic dimension of individuals in political discussions of tax fairness. Thus, we are told that (1) "every American who pays income taxes"[8] should benefit from tax reductions – even though that group includes the economically privileged and excludes those among the working poor who do not pay income taxes, but who do pay payroll taxes; (2) conversely, providing tax relief to those too poor to pay income taxes (but who pay other taxes) is equivalent to sending them a welfare check; (3) "the American people should keep more of their own money"[9] – which plays into the misleading "everyday libertarian" notion that "all taxation takes what belongs to us; what we are fundamentally entitled to is our pretax incomes";[10] (4) eliminating the estate tax makes the tax laws fairer for small businesses and family farms – which contributes to the impression that the estate tax applies to a broad spectrum of taxpayers across a range of wealth levels when, in fact, it only applies to a tiny (and currently decreasing) fraction of wealthy decedents' estates, an impression that is designed to help foment "grassroots" support for elimination of the despised "death tax"; and (5) merely mentioning the possibility of raising taxes on the wealthy is labeled "class warfare" – which effectively paints those at the bottom of the economic ladder (as well as those who advocate on their behalf) as violent aggressors. Of course, I could go on, but I think that I have made my point that, as expected, the dominant group's construction of the concept of tax equity influences not only legal academic, but also everyday political debates about what constitutes "fair" treatment of taxpayers.

Overall, the concept of tax equity has a particularly hegemonic quality. Despite a series of otherwise devastating critiques, tax academics still turn to the concept in a casual, almost offhand manner for help in grappling with questions of tax fairness. Many of us also teach our students to think of the Code in tax equity terms from the earliest days of their introduction to the tax laws. The concept's seemingly universal appeal has even lulled critical tax scholars into framing their tax policy analyses in tax equity terms. Yet, notwithstanding its natural appeal, tax equity is far from a benign metric for gauging the fairness of our tax system. Rather, it insidiously shapes our thinking about tax fairness by tacitly singling out economic factors – to the exclusion of all others, no matter how relevant or worthy of discussion they may be. By packaging this very partial version of fairness in a way that gives it universal appeal, the dominant group has quite effectively been able to maintain its power and privilege by avoiding discussions that could result in "radical" proposals that might actually deliver on the promise of fairness in taxation to a much broader swath of society.

---

[8] Remarks on Signing the Tax Increase Prevention and Reconciliation Act of 2005, 42 WEEKLY COMP. PRES. DOC. 943, 944 (May 17, 2006).

[9] *Id.* at 945.

[10] LIAM MURPHY & THOMAS NAGEL, THE MYTH OF OWNERSHIP: TAXES AND JUSTICE 35 (2002).

Tax Policy and Feminism: Competing Goals and Institutional Choices

ANNE L. ALSTOTT[1]

Despite the dramatic increase in women's labor market participation in recent decades, women continue to perform a disproportionate share of "family labor," or the unpaid work of caring for children and other family members. Feminists have long been concerned that the gendered division of family labor reduces women's wages, contributes to the high and disproportionate rate of poverty among single mothers, limits married women's autonomy within the marital household, and circumscribes women's life choices and social and economic power.

Although many feminists agree that legal reform should address the economic and social consequences of the gendered division of family labor, they differ significantly in their objectives and policy prescriptions. Feminists may seek to increase women's autonomy, economic well-being, power, or happiness. Feminist policy prescriptions also differ, although they tend to pursue one of three main goals. Some feminists advocate *equal treatment*, or the application of the same legal rules to men and women, in order to eliminate legal biases that discourage women's market work and reinforce traditional gender roles. Others favor policies that would not only eliminate legal biases but affirmatively *encourage women's market work* in order to change gender roles and enhance women's economic self-sufficiency. A third group argues that instead of trying to change women's behavior, public policy should provide additional income transfers and other *assistance to caregivers* in order to directly improve their economic security and social status.

This article argues that tax policy can make an important contribution to a feminist legal agenda, but that some prior scholarship has overlooked the normative and institutional complexity of translating feminist goals into concrete policy prescriptions. Tax policy is a major form of economic regulation, with a significant financial impact on many women and families, and a number of scholars have recommended tax law changes intended, at least in part, to improve women's lives by changing the economic incentives and rewards for women's market work and family labor. The major proposals include the adoption of individual (rather than joint) filing of income tax returns by married couples; a special, low tax rate schedule for married women; family allowances; an expanded dependent care tax credit; and reforms in the Social Security payroll tax and benefits rules.

[1] Reprinted by permission from 96 *Columbia Law Review* 2001 (1996).

This article suggests that tax law changes, particularly in combination with other legal reforms, could improve the economic well-being of families with children or help ease women's labor force participation. This article also shows, however, that feminist arguments for these tax proposals have overlooked important conflicts among feminist goals and have overstated the capacity of incremental financial incentives and entitlements to change gender roles and improve women's economic well-being and power within the family. A closer analysis suggests four principal conclusions:

First, any feminist tax proposal incorporates normative judgments about the best way to help women, and none of these norms are uncontroversial, even among feminists. This article considers three feminist goals that tax policy proposals might serve – achieving equal treatment, encouraging women's market work, and assisting caregivers – and shows how each proposal faces difficult but inevitable tradeoffs among them. A better understanding of these competing goals highlights some striking – but often unacknowledged – tensions in conventional arguments for these tax proposals. For example, feminist arguments for "tax neutrality" or eliminating "biases" in taxation are really claims about the goal of equal treatment, which is enormously contested in feminist theory. Further, taking seriously the feminist goal of assisting caregivers poses a fundamental challenge to individual filing and other prominent feminist tax proposals that focus primarily on reducing tax rates on women's market earnings.

Second, proponents of tax law reforms have tended to overstate the impact of incremental tax incentives and income transfers on women's (and men's) attitudes and behavior. Tax law changes can supplement family incomes and modestly increase women's labor force participation, but these limited achievements – although they may be well worth having – do not necessarily advance more ambitious feminist goals. Despite proponents' claims, it is extremely difficult to use tax law rules to change the division of family labor within the household, to improve women's economic well-being, or to increase women's financial power within the family. This constraint is not unique to tax law, but instead reflects the limited capacity of legal rules governing financial entitlements to change deeply entrenched social norms about gender roles.

Third, a better understanding of these issues suggests that some tax law reforms are better able to achieve their underlying goals than are others. Although individual filing is a standard feminist prescription for tax law reform, a closer look suggests that some key feminist arguments for individual filing are weaker than proponents have recognized. Arguments for market work tax incentives for wives also rely on some particularly contingent empirical assumptions about the effects of incentives on behavior. In contrast, the feminist case for family allowances is somewhat stronger than typically portrayed, and an expanded dependent care tax credit could both facilitate women's market work and modestly assist some caregivers.

Finally, a crucial but often overlooked question is whether tax policy is likely to be more or less effective in achieving feminist goals than alternative changes in other legal regimes, including family law, welfare policy, and labor market regulation. A comparison of institutional capabilities suggests that tax policy has comparative advantages over other legal measures but also notable weaknesses, and that other legal regimes face similar constraints in using financial incentives and entitlements to change attitudes and behavior. The analysis also suggests, however, that coordination between tax rules and other legal rules could draw on the diverse strengths of different legal regimes to expand the institutional options for feminist legal reform.

FEMINIST PROPOSALS FOR SOCIAL SECURITY REFORM

Social Security provides cash benefits upon retirement to covered workers and their dependents. Workers become eligible for Social Security coverage by working in covered employment for a minimum period and by paying Social Security payroll (FICA) taxes on wages. Social Security benefits are calculated based on lifetime earnings, but the formula for determining Social Security benefits is progressive, so that Social Security benefits replace a higher proportion of total wages for low earners than for high earners. Social Security also provides an additional "spousal benefit" equal to 50% of the benefit the covered worker would receive if single. A spouse who is covered independently under the system through her own FICA contributions does not receive both the 50% spousal benefit and her own independent benefit, but instead receives the larger of the two amounts. One consequence of the spousal benefit rules is that a single-earner couple can receive larger total Social Security benefits than a two-earner couple with the same total earnings and payroll tax contributions.

As a group, women receive larger Social Security benefits relative to their payroll tax contributions than do men. Women are the principal recipients of spousal benefits and thus by definition receive benefits that exceed those to which wives would be entitled based on their own contributions. Women also typically live longer than men and so collect benefits longer. In addition, because women tend to earn less than men, they gain more from the progressivity of the benefit formula. At the same time, however, elderly women's average Social Security benefits are smaller than elderly men's, and elderly women remain significantly poorer than elderly men, due to their dependence on husbands' incomes, their longer lives, and their lower lifetime earnings.

Equal Treatment and the Spousal Benefit Rules

One feminist critique of Social Security is that the system discourages married women's market work. Married women must pay Social Security payroll taxes on their full earnings, but the spousal benefit rules mean that many working wives receive no additional benefit for the payroll taxes they pay. If a wife's earnings are low enough relative to her husband's, she will in the end collect only the spousal benefit, which she could claim even if she had never worked outside the home.

This argument is reminiscent of the equal treatment argument for individual filing. If we recognize that women are more likely than men to be secondary workers, then the current system is biased against wives' market work. For primary workers, the Social Security payroll tax is offset, at least in part, by an expectation of future benefits, which are positively correlated with earnings. For secondary workers who are likely to receive the spousal benefit, however, the situation is quite different: for them, the payroll tax is a true tax, because it confers no incremental future benefits.

The goal of equal treatment suggests repealing the spousal benefit entirely, so that primary and secondary workers would receive an equal benefit from their payroll tax contributions. The revenue saved through repeal of the spousal benefit could be used to reduce payroll taxes or increase benefits across the board. The dilemma, of course, is that equal treatment would help some women but hurt others. By definition, repealing the spousal benefit would reduce Social Security benefits for many wives, particularly full-time caregivers and those with low earnings. Without spousal benefits, a married woman would receive as much as (but no more than) a single woman with the same earnings history. The resulting redistribution of Social Security benefits could reduce benefits for many wives, particularly those with low market earnings or an intermittent or nonexistent work history.

Thus, there is a tension between achieving equal treatment in Social Security and assisting caregivers (if we assume, realistically, that many homemakers are also caregivers and that caregiving work tends to reduce many women's lifetime earnings). This tension may recede a bit with time because younger generations of women tend to have consistently higher rates of labor force participation than older generations had. Even younger generations of women, however, do not duplicate men's patterns of market work: women continue to encounter significant disruptions in their work patterns during childbearing years, and women's lifetime earnings still are lower than men's.

Repealing the spousal benefit might encourage women's market work, which could in turn increase women's Social Security benefits. Although repeal of the spousal benefit creates a potential work incentive because it restores the connection between women's payroll tax contributions and their ultimate benefits, the practical significance of that work incentive is hard to gauge. Social Security provides only a deferred reward for women's market work. Women may fail to respond to market work incentives in Social Security if they misunderstand the terms of the program, discount the availability of Social Security benefits due to widely publicized financial stresses on the system, or "myopically" discount their future well-being.

Assisting Caregivers Through Homemakers' Credits

A second feminist critique of Social Security is that it does too little to assist caregivers. Although the spousal benefit rules are intended to ensure coverage for women in "traditional" families, critics point out that spousal benefits are derived from husbands' coverage and thus provide limited benefits for divorced or never married women and women married to low earners. Some scholars propose replacing the spousal benefit with a system of "homemakers' credits," which would provide independent Social Security earnings credits for women (or men) primarily engaged in family labor. Homemakers' credits would essentially impute to the caregiver a deemed earnings amount, which would be added to her lifetime Social Security earnings record. Repealing the spousal benefit would ensure that each worker received benefits based on her own earnings record, while the additional homemakers' credits would ensure that caregivers would be protected. Unlike the spousal benefit, homemakers' credits would be fully independent of marital status, and thus equally available to married, divorced, and never married women.

Proposals for homemakers' credits raise a host of serious difficulties, however. First, the proposal only reshapes rather than removes the conflict – created by the spousal benefit – between equal treatment and assisting caregivers. Repeal of the spousal benefit would eliminate the secondary-earner bias that current law creates, so that working wives would no longer pay payroll taxes without receiving additional benefits. Homemakers' credits, however, would recreate an incentive for wives to stay out of the labor force by awarding a new class of benefits that are not paid for (in the financial sense anyway). Second, critics point out that the credits would help only those women who can afford to be full-time housewives and would provide no benefit for women who work in the market while also performing significant family labor. While women who work in the market would pay payroll taxes beginning with the very first dollar of their earnings, housewives would earn Social Security credit without making any contribution at all. Although the current spousal benefit has somewhat the same effect – by definition, it provides "unearned" benefits to wives – the spousal benefit is available both to (low-earning) working wives and to homemakers. Third, homemakers' credits create a host of administrative difficulties, including identifying women and men engaged in family labor and valuing family labor for purposes of imputing earnings credits. Finally, it is not clear that homemakers' credits would effect any dramatic improvement in homemakers' retirement security, at least if the change is close to revenue neutral. One empirical simulation found that the distribution of the benefits of homemakers' credits would differ little from that of spousal benefits, unless family labor were valued highly enough to increase the aggregate benefits available to women.

Earnings Sharing: Another Compromise Solution

Another popular Social Security reform proposal is earnings sharing, which seeks a compromise between the goals of equal treatment and assisting caregivers by removing the worst distortionary effects of spousal benefits while maintaining or improving Social Security coverage for women engaged in family labor. Although earnings sharing proposals differ in important details, in general they would repeal the spousal benefit and provide that a husband and wife would each receive Social Security credit for half of the couple's combined earnings, regardless of the distribution of earnings between spouses. For example, suppose that in 1996 a husband earns $100,000 and his wife is a full-time housewife. For 1996, the Social Security system would record $50,000 of earnings credits for each spouse. If the husband earns $60,000 and the wife earns $40,000, again each spouse would receive $50,000 in earnings credits.

Earnings sharing implements a "partnership" model of marriage, treating each spouse as making an equal economic contribution, whether through market work or family labor. Proponents point to three advantages of this model. First, earnings sharing would improve the situation of two-earner couples. Under earnings sharing, couples with equal aggregate incomes would receive equal total benefits; that change would tend to benefit two-earner couples, who can receive smaller benefits than single-earner couples under current law. Second, earnings sharing would eliminate the secondary-earner bias that the current spousal benefit rules create: both spouses would earn incremental credits for their work, although credits would be shared fifty-fifty with the other spouse. Finally, earnings sharing could help divorced women by creating "portable" earnings credits that could ensure some independent Social Security coverage for divorced women not now entitled to coverage.

Although earnings sharing is an attractive compromise, it is not a panacea. Without a politically difficult increase in aggregate Social Security expenditures, larger benefits for some groups must come at the expense of others. The major tradeoff is that earnings sharing plans that are roughly revenue neutral would reduce benefits for single-earner couples and survivors (usually widows) of such couples or for other couples in which the wife does not have a significant work history. Even if these benefit reductions were seen as acceptable in the long run as the price of change, the question of transition is a difficult one. As always, the tradeoff is between protecting expectations under the old regime and slowing the evolution to a new system, but Social Security changes are particularly sensitive because they can disappoint very long term expectations (and a sense of entitlement), and have a serious impact on elderly persons' economic security.

All of these proposals are enormously complex, due to the intricate structure of Social Security and the fact that the effects of any particular reform depend critically on the details of financing, benefit levels, and transition rules. Although a full evaluation of these proposals is beyond the scope of this article, this discussion illustrates the potential tensions among the three feminist goals and the tradeoffs inherent in a compromise approach.

CONCLUSION

This article argues that tax policy can take important steps toward increasing or reforming income support for women and families and easing the way for women's labor market participation, but that the task of designing effective feminist tax policies is significantly more complex than some proponents have understood. Like any feminist legal reform, feminist tax proposals face difficult tradeoffs among competing goals, and no solution will be uniformly acceptable to all. Feminist tax proposals also encounter the inherent difficulty of using incremental changes in financial incentives and entitlements to influence patterns of behavior that reflect deep-seated attitudes about gender roles.

This article suggests that a better understanding of the normative and empirical complexity of policy design can enhance the feminist case for legal reform. A more informed awareness of competing feminist goals, of the differences among seemingly similar tax policies, and of the diverse capabilities of tax and nontax legal reforms, allows feminists to make careful and informed choices about how best to implement a particular set of goals. Given the reality of scarce resources and the difficulty of marshaling political support for feminist legal reform, we can ultimately do the most for women by concentrating on what tax law reforms really can accomplish. A nuanced and realistic appraisal of the capabilities of feminist tax and transfer policies can focus attention and resources in ways that maximize the potential impact and can prevent feminists from settling for overly simple proposals that promise much but deliver relatively little.

Moving from theory to practice, the articles in this chapter represent applications of critical tax theory to the nuts and bolts of making, interpreting, and working with the law. In the first piece, *A Legislator Named Sue: Re-Imagining the Income Tax*, Marjorie Kornhauser imagines a tax system designed and implemented by women. She suggests that female legislators would be guided by an "ethic of care" to change the definition of income, modify the tax base, and create new deductions for workforce reentry costs and child-care expenses. Tax expenditures, in Kornhauser's estimation, likely would be favored in a female-designed tax system in order to benefit dependents and families.

Turning to those who interpret the laws, Daniel Schneider undertakes an empirical study in *Using the Social Background Model to Explain Who Wins Federal Appellate Tax Decisions: Do Less Traditional Judges Favor the Taxpayer?* In his study, Schneider identifies race, gender, educational status, and other social factors as statistically relevant to the outcome of appellate decisions in tax cases. He hypothesizes that some judges' awareness of racial bias in the Code may account for some pro-taxpayer results. Schneider's work also suggests that Marjorie Kornhauser's instincts are correct: women do appear to approach the tax laws differently than men do.

In *Tax Protest, "A Homosexual," and Frivolity: A Deconstructionist Meditation*, Anthony Infanti then explores the collision of traditional judges with nontraditional taxpayers. In his essay, Infanti tells the story of Robert Mueller, a gay man who spent more than a decade protesting the discriminatory treatment of gays and lesbians under the Code. As a result of his tax protest, Mueller was jailed for more than a year and then was twice pursued by the IRS for taxes and penalties. Infanti questions the Seventh Circuit's labeling of Mueller's claims as "frivolous," in light of earlier lesbian and gay rights decisions from the European Court of Human Rights, the United Nations Human Rights Commission, and even the U.S. Supreme Court. Infanti argues that, by slamming the courthouse door shut on Mueller's claims, the Seventh Circuit directly contributes to the forcible closeting of lesbian and gay issues in tax.

Next, in *Sisters in Law: Gender and the Interpretation of Tax Statutes*, Gwen Thayer Handelman shifts the focus from the courts to the tax lawyers who interpret the Code daily. Spurred by the different reactions of men and women to an earlier article on the interpretation of tax statutes, Handelman reflects on how her femaleness has influenced her approach to statutory interpretation. Drawing on the work of Carol Gilligan and Deborah Tannen, Handelman suggests a paradigm for statutory interpretation that is informed by empathy and a sense of connectedness to lawmakers. Such attitudes, Handelman acknowledges, may be especially difficult for men, who generally prefer autonomous gamesmanship to deference and respect.

In *Deconstructing the Duty to the Tax System: Unfettering Zealous Advocacy on Behalf of Lesbian and Gay Taxpayers*, Anthony Infanti continues with the focus on the tax lawyer as interpreter of the tax laws. He shows how the conventional (i.e., heteronormative) view of a tax lawyer's dual duties to both her client and the tax system when interpreting gray areas of the tax laws can cause the lawyer to become an unwitting accomplice to the federal government's invidious discrimination against lesbian and gay taxpayers. At the same time, the conventional view of the duty to the tax system can cause the tax lawyer to act contrary to the interests of the tax system itself, eroding the very integrity of the tax system that this duty is supposed to protect. Infanti suggests that, because the scales of justice are so unfairly tipped against gay and lesbian taxpayers, lawyers can act zealously on behalf of their clients and still fulfill their duty to the tax system. He urges lawyers to speak out, litigate, and perhaps even engage in more "radical" activism in order to educate people about the discrimination that lesbian and gay taxpayers face.

A Legislator Named Sue: Re-Imagining the Income Tax

MARJORIE E. KORNHAUSER[1]

When America's Founding Fathers gathered to establish the legal framework for the new republic, Abigail Adams wrote to her husband John Adams asking him to "remember the ladies."[2] For countless generations lawmaking had occurred this way; when the vote was called, the answering voices were always male. Women were heard only indirectly through the men. Centuries later, a few of those voices are finally female. Now that a woman can directly influence legislation, the question is whether her voice makes a difference. The answer is yes. Studies indicate that women legislators, regardless of whether they are feminists, act differently from male ones, and this difference affects the legislative process as well as policy outcomes. As a consequence, the presence of female legislators makes a difference not only for women, but for men as well.

That the mere existence of women legislators would make such a difference should not be surprising. The force of gender is both everywhere and nowhere. It is everywhere, affecting how people dress, walk, talk, work, and play; how people structure society; and how they think about themselves and about others. It is also nowhere, however, because much of gendered behavior is invisible. It is hidden behind the guise of universality imposed by male dominance, which is one of the few consistent manifestations of gender throughout recorded history.

Tax laws are no different. The Code, for example, as part of the codified federal laws, incorporates § 1, Title 1 of the United States Code, which states "He includes she." Although the Code generally avoids this obviously gendered language through its use of the unisex "taxpayer," there are still many substantively gendered aspects of the tax laws. This is not surprising since for many years most taxpayers were men. Even today males carry more weight as taxpayers by the mere fact that they earn more than women, far outnumber women as legislators generally, and fill many more seats on congressional tax committees in particular.

This essay explores a simple proposition: a change in the gender composition of the people who make the tax laws would change the content of those laws. To put it in legal terms, envision if you will, a world in which 1 U.S.C § 1 says

---

[1] Reprinted by permission from 5 *Journal of Gender, Race, and Justice* 289 (2002).
[2] Letter from Abigail Adams to John Adams (Mar. 31, 1776), *quoted in* THE OXFORD DICTIONARY OF QUOTATIONS 1 (4th ed. 1992).

"she shall include he." In other words, envision a world in which women, not men, hold the power. Power in this context does not mean mere physical power (such as the ability of one person to pummel another) or interpersonal power (such as one spouse may hold in a marriage) but structural power.

This essay takes a practical approach rather than a theoretical one. It is based on empirical evidence showing that the presence of women – regardless of their political party, age, class, race, ethnicity, or attitude toward feminism – affects both the legislative process and policy outcome. Specifically, women are more likely to be concerned with certain issues – not just women's issues but social issues generally such as health education and welfare. They are also more likely to put such issues into a broader cultural context, and are more likely to want the government to play a larger role in these areas. For example, one study found that male legislators viewed criminals as autonomous individuals who choose crime, whereas female legislators placed the criminal in the context of access to education or economic prospects. The manner in which the legislators conceptualized the problem affected how they conceptualized solutions. Since the men defined the issue more narrowly than the women, they focused on narrower policy issues than the women.

Since these findings are consistent with a broad-based web or ethic of care philosophy or outlook often identified with cultural or difference feminist theory, this essay assumes that a majority-women Congress would reflect this perspective. Consequently, it is this web of care perspective that is meant when the essay refers to a female or feminist Congress. It is also to note that a web or ethic of care perspective, as used here, does not reduce to gender essentialism, a frequent criticism of feminist scholarship. One can believe that there is a common, invariable, or "essential" thread binding all women without denying that there is also diversity among women. People can, and do, differ as to what that common thread is. This essay pragmatically assumes that a broad ethic of care outlook captures an aspect of womanhood, however small or undefinable, that is familiar to most if not all women regardless of other important aspects of their identity.

The possible changes a female-controlled Congress, operating under a web of care philosophy, might make to the income tax are both large and small. Such a Congress might alter general policy in areas such as the proper tax base, the appropriate rate structure, and the uses of tax expenditures as well as specific tax provisions such as capital gains preferences or child-care expenses.

RISK AVERSION AND CAPITAL GAINS

Congress currently "spends" vast amounts of money by reducing the income tax rates on capital gains. Yet, the pressure on Congress to further reduce these rates is constant. This preferred tax rate, in the form of both deductions and exclusions, does not affect all taxpayers equally because not all taxpayers can take equal advantage of it. The poor, for example, hold fewer capital assets than the rich and therefore have little opportunity to use the preference. Similarly, scholars such as Beverly Moran and Bill Whitford have found a racial bias, arguing that the capital gains preference treats blacks less favorably than whites, since the former invest in capital assets less than the latter [see Chapter 5].

Although there are many justifications for a capital gains preference, a major premise for this favorable treatment is that it promotes economic growth through the encouragement of risk-taking. Economic risk-taking may often be desirable, but preservation of capital and less speculative investments also have their roles in the economy. The assumption that riskier investments are more productive, per se, than more conservative ones, is not even necessarily true. Nevertheless, there is a long tradition of a capital gains preference and a strong movement to either increase it or eliminate the taxation of capital gains entirely.

One possible explanation for this strong preference for risky investments via the capital gains preference, despite their mixed benefits, may be the existence of a general preference for risky behavior. Certainly, many people are risk-takers, as the popularity of lotteries and gambling attest[s]. Nevertheless, a preference for or against risk is a complicated phenomenon.

One of many variables that affect a person's attitude toward risk is gender. Empirical studies during the past two decades indicate that girls and women generally are more risk averse than males. One reason why gender affects attitudes toward risk-taking, according to some research, is that risk-taking plays an important part in defining one's self and an individual's autonomy. Consequently, if women generally define themselves by their connectedness with others and by their ethic of care, they may value behaviors that minimize risk and ensure minimum social welfare. Men, on the other hand, who tend to view the world more individualistically, would value risk-taking more highly as an expression of their individuality. Thus, it is not surprising that the United States, founded on male principles of individual liberty, highly values risk. Given the male attitude toward risk as well as its role in the political and popular cultures of this country, it is not surprising that a male-dominated Congress has enacted tax laws that encourage risk-taking, such as found in the capital gains provisions.

A female-dominated Congress, with a greater risk aversion, might not enact a capital gains preference (or might narrow it) because it overencourages risk-taking behavior that would no longer be so desirable. Such a Congress would more easily recognize the downsides of capital gains as well as other conventional reasons to eliminate the preference, such as the complexity it causes and the fact that capital gains already have the advantage of deferral because they are not recognized until "realized." Rather than encouraging risky behavior, a female-dominated Congress might enact more preferences for behaviors and investments that minimize risk in order to provide minimum social welfare so essential to a web of care philosophy.

THE TAX BASE

Almost anything can be, and has been, taxed. The selection of the tax base (i.e., the object of the tax) reflects not just a need for revenue or the ease of administration but also values of society, as interpreted by the legislature. Consider, for example, Britain's seventeenth-century tax on bachelors or Russia's seventeenth-century tax on beards. These taxes not only raised revenue, but perhaps more importantly, furthered policy goals of the government. Similarly, the United States's enactment of an income tax at the turn of the twentieth century reflected a policy choice to make the tax system fairer. Specifically, it accomplished this by choosing the income tax, which was based more on an ability to pay than the then current system of excise taxes, the primary method of taxation then in use. Today, many politicians, economists, and tax theorists are urging that the current income tax base (taxable income) be replaced with a consumption-based tax.

The debate about whether income or consumption is a better tax base is a complicated one involving many factors regarding equity, economic efficiency, and administrative practicality. There is already a very rich literature devoted to the subject. The goal here is merely to raise the question of whether a female Congress would decide the issue differently than a male one. The answer is not clear; there are factors that argue in either direction. On balance, however, a female Congress might be more supportive of an income tax than a male Congress. Economic efficiency and growth, primary arguments for a consumption tax, fit squarely within the dominant individualistic tradition associated with males. On the other hand, the ability to pay argument traditionally associated with the income tax, as well as its broader base, seems better suited to fulfilling an ethic of care.

The most obvious reason for favoring an income tax is that consumption taxes are regressive. Taxes based on consumption place a greater burden on the poor and middle classes who spend a greater portion of their income and wealth while decreasing the burden on the rich who can save large amounts of income and reduce their tax burden. This result is contrary to a web of care philosophy with its concern for the social welfare.

The issue of income versus consumption base, however, is complicated by the fact that earned income, the primary source of most people's income, is very fragile. The production of earned income depends on the taxpayer being able to work. Therefore, people who must work for their income are at a great disadvantage compared to those who live off their investments. The latter can earn income even if they are old, sick, or disabled whereas the former cannot. Investors, in contrast, receive income from their investments regardless of their personal health. This logic has been the rationale behind the earned income preference that has existed throughout most of the history of the U.S. income tax. Although there is currently no across the board preference for earned income, there are particular preferences, for example, the earned income credit and pensions. Both an ethic of care philosophy and its related risk aversion would thus seemingly favor an earned income preference.

BASIC CONCEPTS

At the most fundamental level, a female Congress might redefine basic concepts such as gross income (the first step in the computation of tax liability) and taxable income (the actual base of the tax). The current definitions have different effects on different classes of taxpayers. Consider gross income, a tax concept that is less inclusive than the economic definition of income. The Code currently excludes certain items that an ethic of care Congress would also exclude such as scholarships, foster care payments, and welfare transfer payments. A female Congress, however, intent on improving social welfare, would broaden certain exclusions, narrow others that predominantly aid wealthier taxpayers who have a better ability to pay taxes, and even create new exclusions. For example, it might broaden exclusions for educational assistance, minimize the exclusions for gifts and the imputed income from the rental value of home ownership, and create a new exclusion for some portion of alimony.

TAXPAYER LIABILITY

A female-controlled Congress operating under a web of care philosophy might treat certain issues regarding taxpayer liability differently. The most obvious issue is the treatment of joint and several liability created by the filing of a joint tax return. Although recent changes in the law make it easier for "innocent spouses" to obtain relief, and for certain taxpayers to be liable solely for an amount of tax allocable to them if filing singly, this area remains problematic. A female-controlled Congress might switch to the individual as the taxable unit, thereby eliminating joint returns and its concomitant liability as a problem.

Another problem of taxpayer liability arises for many conscientious objectors to war. These taxpayers would like to pay their income taxes but do not want any of their tax money to pay for military expenses. Consequently, they do not pay all or a portion of their taxes because to do so would violate their consciences. As a result, they are liable not just for their taxes but additional interest and penalties. In every Congress since 1972, a "peace tax" bill has been proposed which would allow these taxpayers to satisfy both their legal and moral obligations. Under the bill, conscientious objectors would pay the entire amount of their tax liability, but no part of it would be used for military purposes. A female Congress might be more receptive to this bill than past and current Congresses because an ethic of care would be more sympathetic to calls of conscience and to the greater context of the issue.

TAX EXPENDITURES

Congress can spend money one of two ways: through direct expenditures such as a school lunch program for poor children, or through tax expenditures such as oil depletion which allows certain taxpayers to pay less than the normal amount of tax. The current Code is riddled with tax expenditures aimed at both corporate and individual taxpayers alike.

Tax expenditures are a cumbersome method for benefiting poor and middle-class taxpayers, a group of particular interest under a Code motivated by an ethic of care. Poorer taxpayers, including a disproportionate number of women, either cannot take advantage of the tax expenditures, or get fewer benefits from them than wealthier taxpayers. Even when a tax expenditure is limited to lower bracket taxpayers through mechanisms such as refundable credits (e.g., the earned income credit) or phaseouts of benefits as income increases, tax expenditures are a clumsy mechanism. They complicate the Code, are often difficult to understand, and never even reach people with no tax liability unless they are refundable – which creates a whole other set of problems. Consequently, a female Congress would prefer direct expenditures to tax expenditures whenever possible. When and if a female Congress did use tax expenditures, the ones it enacted might be different because they would reflect an ethic of care philosophy.

The Code already contains many provisions that promote social policy concerns. For example, several provisions are intended to benefit dependents, who are primarily children. These provisions include tax credits such as § 21 "Expenses for household and dependent care services necessary for gainful employment"; § 22 "Credit for the elderly and the permanently and totally disabled"; § 23 "Adoption expenses"; § 24 "Child tax credit"; § 25A education credits; § 32 the refundable "earned income credit"; § 44 "Expenditures to provide access to disabled individuals"; and of course, § 151 the general deduction for dependents. The 2001 tax act liberalized many provisions dealing with dependents such as making the child tax credit partially refundable. Despite the large number of provisions dealing with dependents, many people believe that these preferences are inadequate either because they do not provide sufficient aid or because the aid provided is poorly targeted. The newly amended § 24 child tax credit illustrates both these deficiencies. Although it is more helpful to a low-income taxpayer than a deduction, the amount of the credit ($600 through 2004) is so small that it comes nowhere near the actual amount needed to raise a child. Even though it is now partially refundable – unlike most credits – the partial nature of the refund means that some poor taxpayers will get no (or very little) help from it. Furthermore, the credit does not necessarily accomplish its nominal goal of helping children since there is no requirement that the money actually be spent on the child.

A Congress based on a web of care philosophy would undoubtedly support dependent care more generously and universally than it currently does. Moreover, it would be more likely to provide this support through direct expenditures because there would be less political opposition. Finally, if Congress were to provide the support through the tax laws, it might redesign the tax expenditures to achieve their goals more accurately. Thus, for example, if the purpose of a tax expenditure were to aid children, it might target specific activities such as child care that would actually benefit them. This is in contrast to some current tax expenditures (such as [the] § 24 child tax credit) that do not necessarily reach the targeted goal since taxpayers claiming the credit need not actually use the saved taxes on children at all.

CONCLUSION

Although the income tax laws are written in gender-neutral language, they have, generally, been written by and for men. Consequently, legislators have, for the most part, considered and enacted tax legislation based on a narrow perspective that concentrates on individualism, economic growth, and the necessary risky behavior needed to achieve both. As a result, the income tax laws often have not well served the needs of particular groups of taxpayers, such as women and the poor nor adequately reflected the priorities of men and women with an ethic of care perspective. There are, however, other ways to conceptualize income tax that better meet those needs and concerns.

This essay invented a fictional female-controlled Congress as one method of re-imagining the income tax. Although this fictional device is contrived, it is grounded in both theory and practice. Empirical evidence that the behavior of actual women legislators reflects broad social and welfare concerns is consistent with a broad-based feminist theory associated with an ethic of care. This perspective would affect both process and policy outcomes regarding tax legislation in areas ranging from broad policy issues such as the rate structure to specific provisions such as those dealing with child-care expenses.

The cumulative effect of these changes would be significant, although any one particular change might not be. In fact, most, if not all, of the changes enacted by an ethic of care Congress would reflect a change in emphasis rather than innovations. They are best characterized as differences in degree, not in kind, with roots in current ideas, if not current practices that are not unique to an ethic of care. All the changes would expand or strengthen existing policies and practices that further this viewpoint. These changes would cover areas traditionally thought of as women's issues such as dependent care health and medical expenses. They would also involve other issues not traditionally women's issues such as the capital gains preference, an earned income preference, support for progressive rates, and support for an income tax base rather than a consumption base.

The total effect of these changes would be more radical than the sum of its parts. They would transform the Code in two ways. The first transformation would be a substantive one reflecting a shift in priorities. From the establishment of a peace tax fund to increased support for progressivity and expanded aid for basic human needs, the tax laws would better implement a vision of the dignity and interdependence of individuals. The second change would be a structural one. An ethic of care Congress could help simplify the tax laws, a basic but elusive goal of tax reform, by replacing many tax expenditures with direct expenditures. It would use more direct expenditures both because they are a better vehicle for executing its social policies and because such a Congress would have the political will to enact them. Thus, by using direct expenditures, an ethic of care Congress would not only strengthen and broaden support for social welfare programs, it also could eliminate the complex tax provisions that currently deal with these issues in a less successful manner. Such a streamlined code, stripped of many tax expenditures, would be a simpler and fairer tax, a goal that even the current Congress aspires to – at least in theory.

Using the Social Background Model to Explain Who Wins Federal Appellate Tax Decisions: Do Less Traditional Judges Favor the Taxpayer?

DANIEL M. SCHNEIDER[1]

Legal research examining how judges decide cases has begun to complement political science literature about the effects of judges' social backgrounds on their decisions in various areas of the law. However, very little systematic research has been conducted with respect to tax litigation, and almost none has analyzed whether or how a judge's social background influences the outcome of tax litigation. This [article] applies social science techniques to a data set of recent federal appellate tax cases compiled for this paper to study the connection between outcomes of tax litigation and the social backgrounds of the deciding judges.

This article tests two hypotheses about appellate-level tax decisions: (1) the social background of judges influences who wins cases; and (2) judges with less traditional social backgrounds – judges without elite educations, or who were women or not white – are likelier to decide in the taxpayer's favor than are judges with more traditional social backgrounds.

The first hypothesis is borne out by the evidence: many aspects of judges' social backgrounds are associated with who won the cases in this data set. The second thesis is also sustained by the evidence: social background factors of a "less traditional judge" are associated with pro-taxpayer outcomes.

THE LITERATURE

One characterization of judicial decision making is that judges engage in traditional legal reasoning, applying the law to the facts, and, implicitly, that any judge should arrive at the same result if presented with the same law and factual situation. Others have suggested that the factors leading parties to settle or litigate "are solely economic, including the expected costs to parties of favorable or adverse decisions, the information that parties possess about the likelihood of success at trial, and the direct costs of litigation and settlement."[2] So long as the first interpretation is correct, the litigants should not have to take account of the judge as an individual

---

[1] Reprinted by permission from 25 *Virginia Tax Review* 201 (2005).
[2] George L. Priest & Benjamin Klein, *The Selection of Disputes for Litigation*, 13 J. LEGAL STUD. 1, 4 (1984).

at all, but to the extent it is not borne out empirically, some effort to determine what else guides a judge's decision making is useful.

Political science suggests that judges may rely on much more than the "law" in deciding cases. One theory, the "attitudinal model," suggests that "[Supreme Court] justices base their decisions on the merits on the facts of the case juxtaposed against their personal policy preferences."[3] Thus, two judges might decide the same case differently because one is a liberal Democrat and the other a conservative Republican.

This article's approach relies more generally on judges' social backgrounds, suggesting that "judges' personal traits . . . educational training, and . . . pre-judicial activities can help explain court decisions."[4] In theory, if one assumes that both parties in an appellate case are more likely to have tenable positions, one might expect more readily to observe the influences of the judges' social backgrounds on the verdict. If both sides can muster plausible legal arguments, then perhaps law matters less and a judge's background matters more in the decision, more than even the judge's policy preferences.

Results derived from the social background model have been mixed. Some literature, especially earlier articles, examines background factors such as gender, race, education, professional experience before ascending to the bench, political affiliation, and the judge's seniority on the bench when the decision was rendered, often in isolation from one another. This literature suggests that sometimes social background variables matter, and sometimes they do not. Recently, however, more robust research has appeared which analyzes the impact of multiple background factors on judges' decisions. The articles analyzing multiple background factors simultaneously conclude that social background has some effect on outcome. The results of this later research were not so weak that one would infer that social background never mattered when explaining how judges decide cases, but neither were the results so strong as to suggest that another model (e.g., legal reasoning) never mattered.

No model is free from doubt or criticism, but good models should explain why things happen. Maybe judges do use traditional methods of legal reasoning; maybe they are influenced by deeply held and inflexible beliefs. The legal reasoning and other models are theoretically at odds with one another. Searching for the best model by filtering a representative group of cases through the lens of judges' social backgrounds lies at the heart of this article.

DATA

The data set includes 10% of all federal tax decisions rendered by the federal circuit courts during a recent five-year period. Only decisions by the Federal Circuit, an

---

[3] Jeffrey A. Segal & Harold J. Spaeth, The Supreme Court and the Attitudinal Model Revisited 312 (2002).

[4] James J. Brudney et al., *Judicial Hostility Toward Labor Unions? Applying the Social Background Model to a Celebrated Concern*, 60 Ohio St. L.J. 1675, 1682 (1999).

appellate court of more limited appellate jurisdiction, were excluded. The data set includes both published and unpublished opinions. The data set includes cases decided between 1996 [and] 2000, the most recent five-year period for which cases were available when the research began. Every tenth case was included in the data set.

The data set contains a separate entry for each judge who participated in a sampled case, not just a single entry per case. Thus, a case decided by a three-judge panel would be represented by three entries. Treating each participating judge's decision as a unit of analysis is theoretically consistent with the social background model: if how a judge votes might reflect his background, then a judge voting for the government should do so whether he is writing for the majority, concurrence, or dissent, agreeing with one of these written opinions, or even just agreeing with a per curiam decision.

STATISTICALLY SIGNIFICANT PATTERNS

Patterns of correlation between two variables, for example, between gender and eliteness of education or gender and outcome, are most meaningful when they are statistically significant or when they approach statistical significance because only then are they unlikely to be results of chance occurrences. Patterns from the data set that were statistically significant or approached statistical significance appeared in various aspects of the relationship between the judges' background and the way they decided cases.

The most interesting pattern that emerged that was statistically significant or that even approached statistical significance was between the party for whom a judge had decided and race. Black judges and, to a lesser extent, white judges decided proportionately more cases in the taxpayer's favor than did Asian and Latino judges.

Statistically significant results also emerged when comparing different substantive areas of tax law. Taxpayers tended to win decisions involving trusts and estates or individual tax matters, while the government tended to win cases involving procedure or criminal law questions. Cases were more likely to be reported if they involved trusts and estates and less likely to be reported if they were about procedure or crime.

LOGISTIC REGRESSIONS – PREDICTING WHO WILL WIN

Logistic regressions permit the association of independent and dependent variables. The effect of each independent variable may be isolated while controlling for the influence of other independent variables and while measuring the magnitude of the influence. In this appellate court data set, if a judge being a woman correlates with the taxpayer winning in a statistically significant manner or in a manner approaching statistical significance, then it may be inferred that a way of predicting who will win these cases is by asking whether the judge is a woman.

Education

The eliteness of someone's education has been seen as a signal of socioeconomic background, and the signaling effect is stronger for undergraduate than for legal education. In the appellate case data set, many of the statistically significant associations (or those approaching statistical significance) of education with a decision in the taxpayer's favor were for educations at nonelite institutions. The only association of a nonelite college education with a decision in the taxpayer's favor was for female judges. More correlations appeared for judges who had not attended elite law schools.

What can be said of the apparent association of nonelite education with pro-taxpayer decisions? On the one hand, the association of elite educations with pro-government decisions would seem to conform to the perception that liberal judges favor government regulation. If their elite educations reflect the fact that they grew up under better economic circumstances or that they studied under liberal teachers, liberal judges might be expected to equate decisions for the government with the liberal desire to extend government regulation. On the other hand, tying a blue-collar background to education at nonelite institutions is more consistent with the other associations found in this data set, that less traditional judges were associated with decisions in the taxpayer's favor.

Race

In a manner that is either statistically significant or approaches statistical significance, several logistic regressions associated black judges with decisions favorable to the taxpayer. This was true whether the black judges were women, appointees of Democratic Presidents, had not come from private practice, had no stated religious background, or were Protestant. Race was also associated with decisions in the taxpayer's favor for all other ethnic categories when judges did not have elite law school educations.

Two points can be made about the correlations between race and outcome. First, the correlation between a judge being black and a decision in the taxpayer's favor was statistically significant. Second, among the black judges, a slight majority had no stated religion, slightly less than half were Protestant, and the remaining 5% were Catholic. In the predictive statistics, all of the black judges except for those who were Catholic were associated with pro-taxpayer decisions. While there is no necessary connection between descriptive and predictive statistics, the two sets of statistics underscore the importance of race, specifically when a judge was black, in this data set.

What could lead to correlations between a judge being black and a decision in the taxpayer's favor? At first glance, answers might lie outside taxation; in criminal law, black judges have sometimes been shown to be more sympathetic to black defendants. Likewise, correlations between black judges and pro-union decisions in labor law might be explained by black workers' recent identification with unions, notwithstanding the earlier history of union racism. However, logically such situations provide weak analogies to tax. A stronger anchor may lie in recent research about the bias of the Code against blacks. That research suggests that, for example, white taxpayers may benefit more from the home mortgage interest deduction than black taxpayers, because whites more frequently own homes upon which they can borrow and then deduct interest payments, and therefore the correlation between black judges and pro-taxpayer decisions might reflect the judges' perception that the Code is biased against blacks.

Gender

Several logistic regressions also correlated a judge being a woman with decisions in a taxpayer's favor in a statistically significant manner or in a manner approaching statistical significance. Such was the case when female judges were black, had not gone to elite colleges or to elite law schools, and when they were more senior. The only other association of gender with decisions in a taxpayer's favor was for male judges who had not gone to elite law schools. Male judges without elite law school educations were associated with decisions in the taxpayer's favor, but this might be explained by the lack of an elite education rather than gender.

One starting point for assessing the effect of gender on a judge's decision is Professor Carol Gilligan's suggestion that women speak in a "different voice," one that is more oriented to the community than is the masculine orientation toward rules. The connection between community and decisions in favor of the taxpayer seems strained, however, and so that assertion does not fit the current results well. Pro-taxpayer decisions seem no more bound to community orientation or to a rules-bound approach than do pro-government decisions. Nor do arguments about a feminist approach to tax seem pertinent in explaining why a judge being a woman correlates with decisions on behalf of the taxpayer.

Another possibility is the suggestion that until the number of women in deliberative bodies reaches a critical mass, they might act differently than they would as part of a critical mass. Unlike trial decisions, either by a district court or a Tax Court judge (other than those decisions, relatively few, that are reviewed by the Tax Court), appellate cases are ordinarily decided by panels of three judges, creating opportunities for women to act together. However, although correlations between these factors in the appellate study might be explained by the critical mass theory, the strength of comparable associations between gender and outcomes in the trial court data set (where judges usually made decisions alone) suggest that something else is at work.

CONCLUSION

Literature suggests that judges' social backgrounds might influence their decisions. Most of the tax cases in this data set followed a similar pattern: they were usually appeals brought by taxpayers; the judges presiding over the cases were largely white men; and the taxpayers usually lost. If one focuses solely on the judge's race, from most likely to decide in the taxpayer's favor to the least likely, the order is: black, then white, then Latino, and finally Asian. Since the taxpayers usually lose, there are two possible reasons: that frequently unrepresented taxpayers are bringing specious claims and the courts rightly weed them out; or that the courts are generally hostile to taxpayer arguments and even if there are differences among judges, by and large they favor the government. The predictive statistics also suggest that the nonelite education of a judge, especially in law school, may be correlated to a decision in the taxpayer's favor. The same was true of black judges, women judges, and judges appointed by Democratic Presidents.

The data offer evidence that judges' social backgrounds have some effect on the party for whom they decide tax cases. Extrapolating from this data, one can begin to analyze how social background might influence judges' decisions. One unifying feature of those background factors that seem to influence judges to decide cases more frequently [for] taxpayers is that they all generally depart demographically from "traditional" judges.

Tax Protest, "A Homosexual," and Frivolity: A Deconstructionist Meditation

ANTHONY C. INFANTI[1]

TAX PROTEST

The words "tax protester" conjure the image of a crackpot, deadbeat, or charlatan. So tainted is the label that Congress has prohibited the IRS from referring to anyone as an "illegal tax protester" or "any similar designation."[2] As explained by the Treasury Inspector General for Tax Administration, who is charged with monitoring compliance with this prohibition, "the Congress had concerns that some taxpayers were being permanently labeled and stigmatized by the [illegal tax protester] designation."[3]

That a stigma is attached to the "tax protester" label may seem odd, given that tax revolts and rebellions have played an important role in the history of the United States. The Boston Tea Party, Shays' Rebellion, the Whiskey Rebellion, and Fries' Rebellion were all tax protests. Indeed, the Boston Tea Party and its protest of "taxation without representation" have become iconic symbols in the United States. Yet, despite the storied role of tax rebellion in U.S. history, it seems that the phrase "tax protester" has come to be associated with an assortment of crackpots, deadbeats, and charlatans who wish to tap into this nostalgia in order to legitimize (i) their assault on government and its ability to impose taxes, (ii) their desire simply to avoid parting with their money, or (iii) their exploitation of individuals who fall into one or both of the latter two groups.

However, not all tax protesters can be characterized as crackpots, deadbeats, or charlatans. There are others who do not readily come to mind when you hear or read the words "tax protester," but who clearly fall within the ambit of that term. What these individuals have in common, and what distinguishes them from the crackpots, the deadbeats, and the charlatans, is that they acknowledge the legitimacy of the taxes (particularly the income tax) enacted by Congress.

---

[1] Reprinted by permission from 24 *St. Louis University Public Law Review* 21 (2005).

[2] Internal Revenue Service Restructuring and Reform Act of 1998, Pub. L. No. 105-206, § 3707, 112 Stat. 685, 778 (1998).

[3] TREASURY INSPECTOR GEN. FOR TAX ADMIN., DEP'T OF TREASURY, FISCAL YEAR 2004 STATUTORY AUDIT OF COMPLIANCE WITH LEGAL GUIDELINES PROHIBITING THE USE OF ILLEGAL TAX PROTESTER AND SIMILAR DESIGNATIONS 1 (2004).

Some of these people use the tax system as a vehicle for nontax protest. Most prominently, this group includes pacifists who, for religious, moral, or ethical reasons, do not wish to support war – either directly (through military service) or indirectly (through financial support).

Other individuals acknowledge the legitimacy of the tax laws, but protest their application to a specific group. They seek to highlight and to remedy wrongful discrimination codified in the Code by Congress. The story of Robert Mueller is the story of just such a tax protester. With this background (and hopefully with an open and untainted mind), we can now proceed to consider the story of the tax trials and tribulations (and incarceration) of Robert Mueller, "a homosexual."

"A [THE] HOMOSEXUAL"

From 1975 until 1982, Robert Mueller was "in a traditional heterosexual marriage which allowed the filing of joint returns and other benefits."[4] After that marriage ended in divorce, Mueller "decided to stop hiding his homosexuality."[5] A few years later, angered by the fact that he could not receive the same tax benefits in a same-sex relationship as he could while married to his wife, Mueller ceased filing tax returns and paying taxes as a protest against being limited to filing a tax return as "single," no matter what his actual relationship status. In 1989, Mueller entered into a relationship with Todd Bates that continued throughout the remaining years of this tax protest.

Mueller continued his protest for a decade; he did not file a tax return again until 1996. In 1996, the IRS finally caught up with Mueller and charged him with three counts of willful failure to file an income tax return. In a trial before a magistrate judge in 1997, Mueller was convicted on all three counts "and sentenced to a total of thirteen months' imprisonment and one year of supervised release."[6]

Mueller I

In 1998, the IRS then pursued Mueller for the taxes that he owed for the years 1986 through 1995. In its notice of deficiency, the IRS alleged that Mueller owed more than $249,000 in taxes and over $69,000 in penalties (with, of course, interest – compounded daily). Mueller promptly contested the asserted deficiency in Tax Court.

During the course of this first of two Tax Court cases in which he represented himself, Mueller made a general attack on the marital classifications in the Code. In the course of a very short trial, most of which consisted of a give and take concerning the admissibility of exhibits into evidence, Judge Laro made it abundantly clear that he was not receptive to Mueller's challenge to the tax laws. He told Mueller that the "Court only interprets existing law," and admonished him not

---

[4] Petitioner's Brief at 4, Mueller v. Comm'r, 79 T.C.M. (CCH) 1887 (2000) (No. 15289-98).
[5] Id.
[6] United States v. Mueller, 2001-1 U.S. Tax Cas. (CCH) ¶ 50,205, at 87,342 (7th Cir. 2000).

to make arguments about changing the law "because, frankly, it's not anything I can relate to."[7] Unsurprisingly, Judge Laro issued an opinion sustaining the IRS's proposed deficiencies and penalties. In his opinion, Judge Laro immediately desexualized Mueller's challenge to the Code's discrimination against gay and lesbian couples:

> Petitioner's sole claim in this case is that he should be accorded married, rather than single, filing status on his tax returns for the years 1989 to 1995. Petitioner does not claim to have ever been married. Rather petitioner argues that he had an "economic partnership" with his *roommate* and that he was unconstitutionally denied the opportunity to file a joint tax return with him in recognition of such partnership.[8]

The purposefulness of this desexualization was made clear later in the opinion when Judge Laro stated that "[p]etitioner claims discrimination not as a homosexual but as a person who shares assets and income with someone who is not his legal spouse. Petitioner therefore places himself in a class that includes nonmarried couples of the opposite sex, family members, and friends."[9] Having desexualized the issue presented to the court, Judge Laro quite easily dismissed what he interpreted as a new gloss on an old equal protection challenge to the marital classifications in the Code.

While taking the gay issue off of the table may have made Judge Laro feel more comfortable and may have allowed him more easily to render his decision in favor of the IRS, Judge Laro engaged in a far less than charitable reading of the record in Mueller's case. In fact, the record is replete with references to the Code's discriminatory treatment of gay and lesbian couples – as well as to Mueller's self-described "civil disobedience" to bring this issue to light so that it might be addressed in the appropriate forum. In closing, Judge Laro made a nod to these references and told Mueller that if he wished to petition for redress of any discrimination in the Code against gays and lesbians, such a petition would have to be addressed to Congress.

The Seventh Circuit Court of Appeals affirmed Judge Laro's decision in an unpublished order. The Seventh Circuit reiterated its decision in previous cases that the marital classifications in the Code do not violate the Constitution, and it declined to address Mueller's challenge to the federal Defense of Marriage Act (DOMA) because that law "was not in effect during the 10-year period for which Mueller was assessed deficiencies."[10] The Seventh Circuit also indicated that Mueller had not rebutted the presumption of correctness enjoyed by the IRS's notice of deficiency; his evidence "discussing the status of homosexuals in various countries . . . did not establish that the Commissioner erred in computing the deficiencies."[11]

---

[7] Transcript of Trial at 41, *Mueller* (No. 15289-98).

[8] *Mueller*, 79 T.C.M. (CCH) at 1888 (emphasis added).

[9] *Id.* at 1889.

[10] Mueller v. Comm'r, 2001-1 U.S. Tax Cas. (CCH) ¶ 50,391, at 87,901 (7th Cir. 2001).

[11] *Id.*

Mueller II

In 1996, Mueller changed his method of protest. In that year, he did file a tax return – a return that he had completed jointly with his partner, Todd Bates. On the return, Mueller listed his name first and Bates's name second, striking out the word "spouse" where it appeared in the label block of the return. Mueller marked filing status 2 ("Married filing joint return"), but "struck out the word 'Married' on that line so that it read 'filing joint return' instead of 'Married filing joint return.'"[12] Mueller claimed an exemption for a "spouse" on line 6b of the return, and claimed a standard deduction "based upon his claimed filing status of 'filing joint return.'"[13] Mueller also used the married filing jointly tax rate schedule. He had Bates sign the return on the line below his name, but again struck out the word "spouse" in the signature block.

In its notice of deficiency, the IRS asserted a deficiency of $8,712 in tax. This deficiency was due to (i) the reclassification of certain wage income as self-employment income (with a resulting liability for self-employment tax), (ii) the determination that Mueller was only entitled to the standard deduction for singles, and (iii) the determination that Mueller was required to use the tax table for singles in computing his tax. Mueller's tax had been reduced by filing jointly because Bates was unemployed in 1996. Had they been allowed to file a joint return, they would have benefited from a marriage "bonus," saving $1,897 in additional taxes.

Having learned from his prior experience in the Tax Court (where Judge Laro misconstrued the argument that he was making), Mueller was much more specific, careful, and direct in fashioning the question that he wished the court to address in this case. In contesting the deficiency proposed by the IRS, Mueller made a direct challenge to the constitutionality of DOMA, which was in force during his 1996 taxable year.

Mueller's second Tax Court case was heard by Special Trial Judge Pajak, who, at least at trial, proved more sympathetic to Mueller's cause than Judge Laro had been. Nevertheless, Judge Pajak ultimately sustained the IRS's proposed deficiency. Judge Pajak's thinking was foreshadowed by the comments that followed his statement at trial in support of Mueller's cause: "I think there's merit in it [i.e., Mueller's case], but I think you're in the wrong forum. This is a statutory court. We can only do what the laws say we can do."[14] In his opinion, Judge Pajak held that DOMA was irrelevant to Mueller's case. In 1996, no state recognized same-sex marriage. As a result, Mueller was unable to marry Bates before the close of his 1996 taxable year. Because Mueller was not married to Bates at any time during 1996, DOMA's redefinition of marriage as a union between a man and a woman "effected no change in the law otherwise applicable in this case."[15]

Then, completely ignoring the fact that he was actually incorporating DOMA-type discrimination into the Code by relying on state law to define "marriage," Judge Pajak quickly concluded that Mueller's federal tax filing status for 1996

---

[12] Mueller v. Comm'r, 82 T.C.M. (CCH) 764, 765 (2001).

[13] Id.

[14] Transcript of Trial at 12, Mueller v. Comm'r, 82 T.C.M. (CCH) 764 (2001) (No. 4743-00).

[15] Mueller, 82 T.C.M. (CCH) at 766.

was single, and he reaffirmed Judge Laro's earlier conclusion that the marital classifications in the Code do not violate the Constitution.

The Seventh Circuit again affirmed the Tax Court's decision in an unpublished order. The Seventh Circuit concluded its order with the following warning: "We remind Mr. Mueller once again that despite his personal dissatisfaction with the current tax laws, he does not have license to ignore them. We also warn Mr. Mueller that if he continues to file frivolous tax appeals, he faces the possibility of sanctions."[16]

FRIVOLITY

Frivolous? The Seventh Circuit's intent in choosing this rather harsh and derogatory label is unmistakable. Although the word "frivolous" enjoys more than one meaning, its meaning is clear when used as a legal term of art: "Lacking a legal basis or legal merit; not serious; not reasonably purposeful."[17] By ostensibly labeling Mueller's arguments in both of his Tax Court cases "frivolous," the Seventh Circuit tainted Mueller's protest. They branded Mueller as some sort of a crackpot whose arguments are not even worth considering. This allowed the court to shove Mueller back into the closet and slam the door shut on him. The sound of the slamming door can be heard in the threat to impose sanctions on Mueller – a threat that effectively forecloses the possibility of any future challenges by Mueller to the constitutionality of the Code's discrimination against gay and lesbian couples.

The violent imagery of Mueller being shoved into the closet and having the door slammed shut on him is actually quite apposite here, because the word "frivolous" etymologically implies the application of force. It has been suggested that the word "frivolous" was probably borrowed from the Latin word *frivolus* (meaning silly, empty, or trifling). The Latin *frivolus*, in turn, is a diminutive of a lost adjective *frivos* (meaning broken or crumbled), which was derived from the verb *friare* (meaning to break, rub away, or crumble).

By labeling Mueller's arguments "frivolous," the Seventh Circuit applied force to those arguments, attempting to crumble them in their hands. At the same time, the court clearly attempted to break Mueller's spirit, to discourage and dishearten him, to dissuade him from making future challenges to the constitutionality of the discrimination against gay and lesbian couples that Congress has embedded in the Code. In applying this force to crumble and to break, the court attempted to rub away, to erase the specter of Mueller (both past and present) from their consciousness, because they did not want to be reminded of Mueller or of the arguments that he was making. They justified this erasure – the effacing of their very discussion of Mueller's case from the official public record – by stating that his arguments were not even worth taking the time to consider. But, despite the court's best efforts, a trace of Mueller remains: a record where we can bear witness again to Mueller's efforts to raise awareness of a wrong and to have that wrong rectified by the government that committed it.

---

[16] Mueller v. Comm'r, 2002-2 U.S. Tax Cas. (CCH) ¶ 50,505, at 85,112 (7th Cir. 2002).
[17] BLACK'S LAW DICTIONARY 677 (7th ed. 1999).

This application of force by the court is designed to banish gays and lesbians to the closet, to make them invisible, to silence them, which is by no means an anomaly in tax. A concerted, forcible silencing of gay and lesbian dissent manifests itself in the microcosm of Mueller's case. After I spent a day in the Tax Court public files room reading through the records of Mueller's two Tax Court cases, I was able to see a common thread running through his submissions to the court: Mueller felt that a wrong was being done to gays and lesbians, and he wanted to bring that wrong to the attention of the appropriate authorities so that it could be rectified.

Mueller had thought about going to Congress, but, given its overt hostility toward gay and lesbian couples, he knew that it would not be receptive to his arguments. He asked the IRS to recognize his relationship with Bates, but was told that if he wanted to be a test case he would need to get into the court system and seek change there. In his criminal tax case, Mueller pressed his claim that the discrimination against gays and lesbians in the Code violated a number of rights guaranteed to him by the U.S. Constitution. However, the Department of Justice attorneys who were prosecuting him argued that a criminal trial was not the appropriate forum for his protest; they contended that Mueller should seek the relief that he desired in a civil tax case. When Mueller finally made it into the Tax Court, he was met with varying levels of receptivity to his arguments, but, in the end, Mueller was told by two different judges that civil court was not the right forum for his protest either and that he should petition Congress for redress – the same Congress that he had earlier concluded it would be pointless to approach. Then, to make sure that Mueller could in no way misunderstand his being rebuffed, the Seventh Circuit labeled his arguments frivolous and told him not to darken its door again.

THE FRIVOLITY OF "FRIVOLOUSNESS"

In his submissions, Mueller repeatedly claimed that the Code's discriminatory treatment of gay and lesbian couples constitutes a violation of human rights. However, none of the courts that heard Mueller's tax cases ever addressed this issue. Nonetheless, we will briefly explore the treatment of sexual orientation discrimination as a human-rights issue because it is an integral part of the progressive force that opposes and resists the reactionary force that Congress, the IRS, the Tax Court, and the Seventh Circuit all brought to bear against Mueller.

Both the [European Court of Human Rights (ECHR)] and the [United Nations] Human Rights Committee have strong records of acknowledging and rectifying sexual orientation discrimination as a human rights matter. Importantly, a number of these decisions directly address the issue of according legal recognition to same-sex couples. In *Romer* [*v. Evans*][18] and *Lawrence* [*v. Texas*],[19] the U.S. Supreme Court also acknowledged and rectified sexual orientation discrimination as a constitutional matter. In *Lawrence*, the Court even referred, explicitly or implicitly, to decisions of the ECHR and the Human Rights Committee in reaching its own

[18] Romer v. Evans, 517 U.S. 620 (1996).
[19] Lawrence v. Texas, 539 U.S. 558 (2003).

decision. In the wake of *Lawrence*, many opponents of same-sex marriage now fear (and many proponents of same-sex marriage now hope) that one of the Court's next steps in the gay rights area will be to strike down prohibitions against same-sex marriage. These fears (and hopes) are stoked by the growing recognition that excluding same-sex couples from the benefits and protections associated with marriage is unjustified and unjustifiable. Court decisions in Hawaii, Alaska, Vermont, Massachusetts, and Washington have all found that prohibitions against same-sex marriage violate their state constitutions. To rectify this discrimination, Hawaii permits same-sex couples to register as reciprocal beneficiaries, Vermont allows same-sex couples to enter into civil unions, and Massachusetts permits same-sex couples to marry. In addition, the California and New Jersey legislatures have each enacted statutes allowing same-sex couples to register as domestic partners.

These decisions and developments, many of which occurred before the Seventh Circuit issued either of its opinions in Mueller's civil tax cases, undermine the Seventh Circuit's bald assertion that Mueller's arguments were "frivolous." With courts at the international, national, and state levels recognizing and rectifying instances of what can only be described as pervasive sexual orientation discrimination, how can it be meritless to ask a court to recognize and rectify the sexual orientation discrimination that exists in the federal tax laws?

Sisters in Law: Gender and the Interpretation of Tax Statutes

GWEN THAYER HANDELMAN[1]

There is both obvious and not-so-obvious diversity in the legal profession, even behind the apparent homogeneity of the upper-middle-class mainstream legal elite. The differences play themselves out not only in our substantive conclusions as lawyers but also in the way we reason, not only in our policy judgments but also in our methodology. My particular concern in this essay is how these differences manifest themselves in the central task of tax lawyering: statutory construction.

In *Zen and the Art of Statutory Construction*,[2] pursuant to the view that only politically authorized decision makers legitimately can define the scope of legal rights and duties, I proposed that lawyers approach statutory interpretation as an attempt to adopt the perspective of the historic drafter(s). I was startled by the fervor with which several colleagues disputed that it was even possible, let alone appropriate, for interpreters to set aside their preconceptions and assume another's standpoint. I began to detect that women, who uniformly failed to object to the propriety or feasibility of the methodology, were more comfortable with my proposal than men. Quite technical in portions and interspersed with mathematical equations, *Zen* does not look much like "women's work." Nevertheless, I had to consider that somehow I brought my womanhood into my professional undertakings, that my work is that of "a lawyer and a woman,"[3] although I have never before formally addressed "women's issues" or referred to feminist scholars.

In this paper, I begin to crystallize my thoughts on why men and women might approach the reading of tax statutes differently. I can see that my prescription in *Zen* of diligent attention to and identification with the historic drafter may reflect my social-psychological orientation as a woman and may actually tend to offend male values. Of course, my work also reflects other determinants of identity, for example a place of relative privilege in American society, notwithstanding my gender, that may influence me to reside greater trust in that society and recognize, because of the greater benefits I have enjoyed, greater social obligation than others less privileged. Nevertheless, the influence of gender appears to be powerful, and I

---

[1] Reprinted by permission from 3 *UCLA Women's Law Journal* 39 (1993).

[2] Gwen T. Handelman, *Zen and the Art of Statutory Construction: A Tax Lawyer's Account of Enlightenment*, 40 DePaul L. Rev. 611 (1991).

[3] Karen Gross, *Foreword: She's My Lawyer and She's a Woman*, 35 N.Y.L. Sch. L. Rev. 293, 294 (1990)

am hopeful that the recognition of gender differences in approaches to tax practice can inform the effort to define ethically responsible tax advice.

THE NATURE OF GENDER DIFFERENCES

The publication a few years ago of Carol Gilligan's *In a Different Voice* familiarized a broad readership with the hypothesis that there are two fundamentally divergent social-psychological orientations, allocated roughly along gender lines. Her thesis is that divergent social orientations result in distinctive approaches to moral reasoning: defining moral problems either in terms of rights and rules or as issues of care and responsibility. Deborah Tannen has explored the hypothesis that, depending upon orientation, communication is seen as a means to achieve either power or solidarity. There follows a summary description of the constellation of characteristics associated with men and women that I have derived from these authors and employed to assess the influence of gender on my approach to the interpretation of tax statutes.

The orientation associated with maleness is individualistic and hierarchical, emphasizing separateness. Males thus focus on achieving autonomy, differentiating themselves from others, and negotiating status. Gilligan's studies show that men tend to perceive intimacy as dangerous. The desire for personal distance leads to abstraction of human relationships and away from empathy. Men seek to achieve gratification through dominance, and strive "to gain control over the sources and objects of pleasure in order to shore up the possibilities for happiness against the risk of disappointment and loss."[4]

Morality is equated with observing the autonomous bounds of others and a Golden Rule of not doing unto others what you would not want to have done to you. It is a morality of one-on-one (*mano a mano?*) respect determined from the perspective of the moral actor rather than the other immediately concerned, let alone that of those not immediately represented for whom the action or inaction may have consequences.

The orientation associated with femaleness emphasizes commonalities and sustaining connections, defining the self in relation to others. Establishing their gender identity with reference to commonalities shared with their mothers, girls have "a basis for 'empathy' built into their primary definition of self."[5] Those focused on living life in relationships attempt to achieve gratification by trying to please others rather than by trying to dominate others. Gilligan's studies show that women tend to fear isolation. They are reluctant to differentiate themselves in any way that will risk dislike, because likability is essential to maintaining connection with others. Women perceive that aggression is tied to "the fracture of human connection," and thus pursue "activities of care" that "make the social world safe, by avoiding isolation and preventing aggression rather than seeking rules to limit its extent."[6]

For those focused on connection, responsibility to others becomes the central moral dictate, and visions of right and wrong are particularized and contextualized,

---

[4] Carol Gilligan, In a Different Voice: Psychological Theory and Women's Development 46 (1982).
[5] *Id.* at 8.
[6] *Id.* at 43.

rather than abstract. The "capacity 'to understand what someone else is experiencing' is the prerequisite for a moral response."[7] Moral problems arise "from conflicting responsibilities rather than from competing rights" and require for their resolution "a mode of thinking that is contextual and narrative rather than formal and abstract."[8] Deborah Tannen has authored several sociolinguistic analyses of conversational style. According to Tannen, men employ conversation to negotiate status. There are only two choices: one is in a position of either superiority or inferiority in relation to others, one-up or one-down. For women, "the community is the source of power," and "[t]he symmetry of connection is what creates community."[9] Women seek connection through conversation and tend to look for agreement, while men struggle to identify a unique point of view. Tannen recognizes that both sexes use conversation to achieve power and solidarity, but asserts that they "place different relative weights on status versus connection,"[10] and demonstrate distinctive manners of achieving dominance or connection in conversation.

SOCIAL PSYCHOLOGICAL ORIENTATION AND TAX LAW

That writings on gender differences in moral reasoning and conversational styles could instruct the methodology of tax lawyers seems a preposterous proposition initially but is almost obvious upon reflection. Moral judgments underlie any system of taxation, and an individual's response to the tax system has moral implications as well. Different ethical traditions answer differently questions of whether a moral obligation to pay (or refuse to pay) taxes exists and, if so, the basis of such an obligation, the content of any attendant conditions, and who is to judge whether the conditions have been satisfied.

Carol Gilligan suggests that gender influences one's receptivity to particular ethical perspectives and raises for tax lawyers the issue of how, if professional judgments reflect one's values at all, they may be colored by gender. Deborah Tannen's work suggests that gender differences affect individual styles of communication, ways of hearing and responding to others. Viewed as a mode of communication, statutes must be interpreted, and methods of resolving statutory ambiguity may vary with conversational style. Then, differences in social orientation could produce not only divergent philosophical and political values, but different approaches to statutory interpretation, and potentially different understandings.

FEMININE ZEN

To ascertain the legislatively authorized meaning of statutes, *Zen* advocates methodology that I would describe as practical reasoning if the term had not already been appropriated. It might also be called "women's intuition." The prescribed method reflects modes of relating to a problem that have been described

---

[7] *Id.* at 57 (quoting study subject "Claire").

[8] *Id.* at 19.

[9] DEBORAH TANNEN, YOU JUST DON'T UNDERSTAND: WOMEN AND MEN IN CONVERSATION 29, 173 (1990).

[10] *Id.* at 71.

as characteristically female: contextual, particular, personal. The technique relies on the characteristically feminine skills of attentiveness and empathy, based on the simple proposition that attentiveness plus empathy will yield understanding.

Zen describes statutes as a form of communication, noting that the word "communication" is derived from the same stem as community, referring to commonness, and analogizes interpreting statutes to conversing with the drafters conceptualized as individuals who actually existed and acted purposively. Personifying and situating the drafters in their historical context and employing empathy to connect with them contrasts sharply with abstraction of the drafting process and "legislative intent" in the standard literature on statutory interpretation.

I had thought that reminding lawyers that real people, with real intentions, not constructs of "legislative intent," were behind statutes, would clarify the potential for communication between drafter and audience. I had repeatedly been startled by the vehemence with which writers of various leanings dispute the relevance and/or reliability of reconstructions of intended meaning (the historic message) inferred from the context in which legislation was enacted.

I did not appreciate that reinjecting the real, historic, human players into the process of statutory interpretation would not cause all the pieces of a model of statutory construction to fit into place because my view of how conversation is conducted and my assessment of what it accomplishes may be peculiarly feminine. My account of statutory interpretation as conversation may resonate with women's experience but is the stuff of fantasy (or nightmare) to men. The nature of the male orientation and its position of dominance in American society make it more difficult for men to recognize a reality other than their own.

The prerequisite attentiveness to the thinking of the author of legislation inherent in my conception of civic responsibility reflects a female orientation. For me, personifying the drafter is comfortable, facilitating a sense of connection. From the male perspective, it is acknowledging the intolerable: that we are governed by people, not laws. This seemed to me a simple, obvious "reality" since, notwithstanding the example of the tablets on Sinai, laws do not spring fully formed into existence. For men, maintaining that disembodied texts, rather than people, have authority, may preserve the capacity for obedience to law without triggering their resistance to personal submission. Male "reality" allows for compliance with rules without the need to acknowledge assumption of a one-down position vis-à-vis another in a hierarchy.

In sum, *Zen*'s approach to statutory interpretation requires interpreters to engage in conduct that may be extremely emotionally difficult for men:

1. Admit that they are not in possession of important information and attend to another who is. This requires the interpreter to assume what men would perceive as a one-down status.
2. Empathize, that is, break down barriers between themselves and others and confront their essential commonality. This may threaten male identity by opening up the possibility that they are like their mothers from whom, in Freudian terms, they have so desperately striven to achieve separation as prerequisite to establishment of their masculinity (or, in feminist terms, to

assure that they are not relegated to a status of permanent inferiority in the society).

3. Acknowledge that their autonomy to assert their independent judgment is subject to the condition that they empower the government by providing information (through disclosure). Status in the male system is gained by telling others what to do and lost by obedience. The requisite attitude in such an environment is vigilance against attempts to bend their will. Cooperation is risky, and may not be recognizable as distinguishable from submission.

There is always potential for misunderstanding in cross-cultural exchanges, but at least if we understand that we misunderstand each other, we can move toward understanding and dialogue. It appears to me that men are being deliberately uncooperative in their approach to statutory interpretation, still playing "King of the Hill." Directly addressing each other would be confrontational, necessitating a contest to determine their respective positions in a hierarchy: who is to be "one-up" and who "one-down."

This may be reflected in the American Bar Association's formulation of the approach to understanding the tax laws as predicting how a court would decide or Treasury's prescription to pursue "the same analysis that a court would be expected to follow."[11] These may be efforts to articulate a way to achieve a common understanding of the requirements of the internal revenue laws with reference to an authorized decision maker without demanding of the interpreter the personal deference, attentiveness, and empathy that my formulation entails. The lawyer is asked to parallel judicial decision making, act in concert with, not as follower of, the politically authorized decision maker. Therefore, male resistance to direction and attempts to control them may not be triggered. Still, even these formulations seem to require the "impossible," that the interpreter identify with the perspective of another.

An issue for the tax system is whether it is important for tax practitioners to acknowledge that they do not get to make law unless they are hired into public service for that purpose. I have my doubts as to the efficacy of avoiding the issue in addressing the current crisis in compliance. After all, the Code's notoriously odd syntax is peculiarly nonconfrontational and may indeed result from sensitivity to the need for delicacy. The central command of the income tax laws is phrased in the passive voice: tax "is imposed" on "taxable income," and the rest is definitions. Further, the language of the Code is notoriously impersonal. The technical terminology may helpfully camouflage its human source to deflect resistance. However, the very features of federal tax statutes that may serve to accommodate an ethic of autonomy – the stilted and impersonal tone, the passive voice construction, the technical and precise terminology – may also be alienating. There may be need instead to accommodate in the substantive tax law and the standards of tax practice those oriented toward connection.

---

[11] Treas. Reg. § 1.6661-3(b)(3) (1985) (superseded by Treas. Reg. § 1.6662-4(d)(3), which deletes this phrase but leaves the interpretive approach intact).

Deconstructing the Duty to the Tax System: Unfettering Zealous Advocacy on Behalf of Lesbian and Gay Taxpayers

ANTHONY C. INFANTI[1]

When we think about where a lawyer's loyalty lies, our thoughts most naturally turn to her client. However, a lawyer also sometimes owes a duty to others that trumps her duty to her client. For example, a lawyer is ethically prohibited from counseling her client to engage in criminal or fraudulent conduct. Moreover, a lawyer owes a duty of candor to a court, arbitrator, administrative agency, or any "other body acting in an adjudicative capacity," even if the information that must be revealed is otherwise subject to the duty to maintain client confidences.[2]

Likewise, it is generally acknowledged that a tax lawyer owes a similar special duty to the tax system that may conflict with and constrain the duty that she owes to her clients. There is some intuitive appeal to the notion that a tax lawyer must balance the duty to her client against a countervailing duty to the tax system. From the start, the taxpayer has a decided advantage over the government in tax matters merely by dint of the ability to self-assess her rightful share of the overall tax burden. Under our self-assessment system, the taxpayer has the advantage of: (1) being the only party with full knowledge of the relevant facts; (2) maintaining a great deal of control over whether – and, if so, how – those facts are shared with the government; and (3) knowing that the government lacks the resources to audit compliance with the tax laws in all but a small handful of cases. This combination of advantages creates an incentive for taxpayers either to avoid reporting questionable transactions at all or, if they must, to report them in a way that will not draw the attention of the IRS. To superimpose unbridled loyalty to the client over these already hefty advantages would only seem to foster abuse of the tax system that will undermine its integrity and, eventually, erode its viability as a means of collecting the revenue upon which the functioning of our government depends.

Unfortunately, however, intuitive appeal often leads to unthinking application. Thus, a tax lawyer might be tempted to apply this conventional conceptualization of the duty to the tax system to the unconventional advice that she provides to her lesbian and gay clients. Having been crafted with only heterosexuals in mind, the conventional conceptualization of the duty to the tax system reflects

---

[1] Reprinted by permission from 61 *The Tax Lawyer* 407 (2008).
[2] MODEL RULES OF PROF'L CONDUCT R. 1.0(m).

heterosexual taxpayers' considerable tactical advantages over the IRS and posits a nearly constant tension between that duty and the tax lawyer's duty of zealous advocacy. In contrast, the alternative view that I lay out in this article delineates a duty to the tax system that exists in harmony with, rather than opposition to, the duty of zealous advocacy. This alternative view allows a tax lawyer simultaneously to protect her lesbian and gay clients from harm and to discharge her obligation to safeguard the integrity of the tax system by actively preventing its abuse by an overreaching federal government.

THE DUTY TO THE TAX SYSTEM: THE HETERONORMATIVE VIEW

A common – and plausible – justification for imposing a duty to the tax system on tax lawyers relies upon the realities of the tax compliance and enforcement process: The duty to the tax system serves to level the playing field between two unequally matched adversaries. It requires the tax lawyer, who is representing the relatively more powerful player in this match-up (i.e., the taxpayer), to take account of the interests of the less powerful player (i.e., the government) whenever she exercises discretion, as she inevitably does, in settling on the appropriate tax characterization of a transaction.

At first blush, this analogy may seem counterfactual. After all, aren't taxpayers, their tax lawyers, and the government all working toward the same end – namely, to determine the "correct" tax treatment of items reflected on the taxpayer's return? In theory, the answer to this question should be "yes." In reality, however, the organized bar has staunchly defended the view that the relationship between taxpayers and the IRS is adversarial – and not cooperative – in nature. Taxpayers reify this putative adversarial relationship and signal the start of the game whenever they attempt to press their superior starting position to maximum advantage. The only reason for taxpayers to play this game is that they "fear scrutiny by the [IRS]."[3] This fear of scrutiny indicates that they are taking their tax reporting position based on a belief that the IRS will not discover the transaction rather than on a good faith belief in its merits. This is counter to their duty as taxpayers to fairly make their tax situation known to the IRS under the self-assessment system.

The duty to the tax system intervenes to remind tax lawyers that: (1) tax compliance is not supposed to be a zero-sum game; and (2) they, like all lawyers, have an ethical duty not to undermine the integrity of the legal system of which they form a part. Given the realities of the tax compliance and enforcement process, it might therefore be more accurate to say that, when the tax lawyer enters gray areas of tax characterization, she is asked to privilege her duty to the tax system over her duty of zealous advocacy in an attempt to right the relationship between the taxpayer and the IRS. Viewed in this light, the duty to the tax system serves as a check on the more powerful party (here, the taxpayer) in order to prevent her from riding roughshod over the less powerful party (here, the IRS) to the great detriment of the tax system – and, vicariously, other taxpayers.

---

[3] Richard Lavoie, *Making a List and Checking It Twice: Must Tax Attorneys Divulge Who's Naughty and Nice?*, 38 U.C. Davis L. Rev. 141, 199 (2004).

Where the application of the tax laws is clear, the tax lawyer can discharge both her duty to the tax system and the duty to her client simply by advising the taxpayer to pay the "correct" amount of tax. More commonly, however, the "correct" amount of tax is unclear and striking the balance becomes difficult because the tax lawyer's duties to the tax system and to her client conflict with each other. As a result, a tax lawyer does not ordinarily experience these two duties as a harmonious whole; rather, she experiences them as opposing forces that pull her in two entirely different directions, one client-regarding and the other public-regarding.

THE DUTY TO THE TAX SYSTEM: A LESBIAN AND GAY PERSPECTIVE

A lesbian and gay perspective on the conventional conceptualization of the duty to the tax system seemingly requires a trip through the looking glass. For lesbians and gay men, each of the key features of the conventional view of the relationship between taxpayers and the IRS that underpins the duty to the tax system is turned squarely on its head. This reversal stems from the unique position that lesbians and gay men occupy as the only victims of both *overt* and *covert* invidious discrimination in the application of the tax laws.

Overt Invidious Discrimination in the Application of the Tax Laws

Overtly, Congress engaged in invidious discrimination against lesbians and gay men when it enacted the Defense of Marriage Act (DOMA). The federal government treats same-sex and different-sex relationships differently for tax purposes, even when state governments – the traditional arbiters of marital status for federal tax purposes – place those relationships on the same legal plane. For example, it is clear that DOMA prohibits same-sex couples who have married in Massachusetts from checking the "Married filing jointly" box under "Filing Status" on their federal income tax returns. It is equally clear that same-sex couples cannot claim the benefit of nonrecognition treatment for transfers between spouses under the income tax or the benefit of the gift and estate tax marital deductions, which, when taken together, allow spouses to transfer property within the couple tax-free.

Covert Invidious Discrimination in the Application of the Tax Laws

In many important areas, however, the tax treatment of same-sex couples has been left quite murky. Two factors contribute greatly to this murkiness. First, DOMA only tells same-sex couples that they may not look to the rules applicable to married couples for guidance; it says absolutely nothing about how the Code should be applied to them. Second, after the enactment of DOMA, Congress and the IRS have utterly failed to provide meaningful guidance on how the Code should be applied to same-sex couples, sometimes even in the face of direct pleas for such guidance from conscientious taxpayers. The void created by the federal government's studied silence regarding the tax treatment of same-sex couples did not last long – it quickly swelled with some profoundly troubling tax issues. One of the starkest illustrations of this phenomenon concerns the tax treatment of same-sex couples who pool their financial resources.

Contending with the murkiness. Regardless of the extent to which they pool their resources, different-sex married couples are treated as a single economic unit for tax purposes and transfers within that unit are wholly disregarded. In contrast, same-sex couples who have married or entered into a civil union or domestic partnership are nonetheless treated as two separate, "single" economic units, even if they actually pool all of their economic resources. This means that, far from being disregarded, transactions within a same-sex couple can have serious tax consequences.

Because transactions within a same-sex couple are *not* disregarded for federal tax purposes, a same-sex couple must annually calculate and document their respective contributions to the economic pool and determine the amount, if any, of the net transfer from the higher-earning partner to the lower-earning partner that results from differing contributions to the pool (the net interspousal transfer). Same-sex couples are faced with a whole spectrum of possible combinations of characterizations for a single year's net interspousal transfer, with widely varying tax consequences. At one end of this spectrum, we find the most benign characterizations; for example, the same-sex couple might take the position that the net interspousal transfer constitutes a support payment. This is beneficial because the lower-earning partner could exclude the support payment from her gross income and the support payment would not be taxable for gift tax purposes. This benign characterization is roughly equivalent to the treatment that is afforded to different-sex married couples, for whom net interspousal transfers are essentially disregarded. At the other end of the spectrum, we find the most punitive of characterizations; for example, the IRS might assert that the net interspousal transfer should "be characterized as income to both partners for income tax purposes and as a taxable gift from the higher-earning partner to the lower-earning partner for gift tax purposes. Consequently, a portion of the income of the higher-earning partner might be subject to triple taxation."[4] In between these two ends of the spectrum are combinations of characterizations that might be considered merely malignant, because they involve some form of double (rather than triple) taxation of the couple.

Contending with so-called guidance. In the rare instance when the federal government does speak, it is not necessarily to illuminate the "correct" answer for same-sex couples. A telling example is found in recent guidance on the federal tax treatment of same-sex couples registered as domestic partners in California. The extension of community property laws to domestic partners naturally raised the question whether the IRS would allow domestic partners to split their earned income for federal tax purposes, as do married different-sex couples subject to California's community property laws. An answer to this question was sought

---

[4] Anthony C. Infanti, *The Internal Revenue Code as Sodomy Statute*, 44 Santa Clara L. Rev. 763, 788 (2004).

some seventeen months before registered domestic partners would have had to file their first federal income tax returns with respect to a taxable year in which they would be covered by California's community property laws. Despite the pressing need for public guidance on this issue, the Treasury Department and the IRS remained silent for more than fifteen months. Finally, the Chief Counsel's Office issued a memorandum in which it opined that California registered domestic partners must each report their earned income separately. This opinion came late – only a few short weeks before the April 15 deadline for filing federal income tax returns.

Commentators roundly criticized this "guidance" for being "unpersuasive, historically inaccurate, and ultimately indefensible."[5] Given this harsh criticism, one can only surmise that this guidance was driven more by ideology than by objective legal analysis aimed at ascertaining the correct application of the tax laws to the earned income of California registered domestic partners.

Contending with impossible burdens. In its interactions with lesbian and gay taxpayers, the IRS has also taken advantage of the nearly impossible burden placed on same-sex couples to document whether, and if so, to what extent, they pool their finances. Pat Cain provides evidence of this behavior in a series of narratives included in a piece that she contributed to a symposium on the estate tax [see Chapter 7]. Cain obtained these narratives "from lawyers and accountants who have represented gay and lesbian clients in estate tax audits."[6]

Summarizing Our Predicament

The relationship between lesbian and gay taxpayers and the IRS looks nothing like the (now, clearly) heteronormative view of the taxpayer–IRS relationship that underpins the conventional conceptualization of the duty to the tax system. Far from finding themselves in a presumptively cooperative relationship, lesbian and gay taxpayers must contend with a federal government that has already declared itself openly hostile to them. In addition, far from having the upper hand in this relationship, lesbian and gay taxpayers find themselves constantly on the defensive. Furthermore, their only protection from an empowered and overreaching federal government is not really a form of protection at all, but just additional punishment: Lesbians and gay men can most effectively counteract the IRS's advantages by retreating into the closet; that is, by effacing all references to their relationship from their tax returns and playing the audit lottery. As a result, what heterosexual taxpayers experience as a distinct tactical advantage in their dealings with the IRS, lesbian and gay taxpayers experience as a self-inflicted form of punishment that merely substitutes for a more humiliating, publicly inflicted punishment.

Now, just imagine, what would happen if a tax lawyer who scrupulously fulfills her duty to the tax system when representing conventional (i.e., heterosexual)

---

[5] Dennis J. Ventry, Jr., *No Income Splitting for Domestic Partners: How the IRS Erred*, 110 TAX NOTES 1221, 1221 (2006).

[6] Patricia A. Cain, *Death Taxes: A Critique from the Margin*, 48 CLEV. ST. L. REV. 677, 696 (2000).

taxpayers were to decide that she must do likewise in her representation of lesbian and gay taxpayers. In all likelihood, this tax lawyer would quickly encounter the conflicting pull between her duty to the tax system and her duty of zealous advocacy, if only because the woefully inadequate level of guidance from Congress and the IRS on the tax treatment of same-sex couples causes so many transactions entered into by these couples to fall into the "gray zone." To resolve doubts in favor of the IRS in this enlarged gray area would risk doing serious harm to the tax lawyer's lesbian and gay clients. In this regard, let us return to the example of characterizing a same-sex couple's net interspousal transfer. On any scale of "questionable" positions, the least questionable (and, from the perspective of strictly applying the conventional conceptualization of the duty to the tax system, the most acceptable) positions will tend to be those involving at least double, if not triple, taxation of a same-sex couple's income. On this same scale, the most questionable positions will tend to be those involving any characterization that results in a single level of taxation and, therefore, places the same-sex couple's tax treatment on a par with that of a different-sex married couple. In this context, resolving doubts in favor of the IRS makes the tax lawyer nothing less than an accessory to invidious discrimination.

SEEING THE DUTY TO THE TAX SYSTEM IN A DIFFERENT LIGHT

The conventional conceptualization of the duty to the tax system harms not only lesbians and gay men but also the tax system itself. A tax lawyer who adheres to the conventional conceptualization of the duty to the tax system in the representation of lesbian and gay clients may harm her clients by facilitating the federal government's immoral (if not illegal) invidious discrimination against them. At the same time, by dint of her role as accessory to this discriminatory treatment, the tax lawyer acts contrary to the interests of the tax system itself, eroding the very integrity that discharging her duty to the tax system is supposed to protect and preserve.

The dual harm (i.e., to the client and to the tax system) wreaked by the reflexive application of the conventional conceptualization of the duty to the tax system reveals the possibility that there may be more of an alignment than an opposition of a tax lawyer's client-regarding and public-regarding duties in the context of representing lesbian and gay taxpayers. In this context, it becomes possible to imagine an alternative conceptualization of the duty to the tax system – one which exists in harmony with, rather than in opposition to, the duty of zealous advocacy.

To begin the process of restoring the integrity of the tax system for the benefit of all of us will require tax lawyers to counter the federal government's use of the tax laws as a tool for invidious discrimination against lesbians and gay men. In other words, a tax lawyer who truly wishes to strive for the fair, honest, and upright application of the tax laws will refuse to be made an accomplice to the government's invidious discrimination against her lesbian and gay clients. In the many areas where the law is unclear, she will resolve any and all doubts in favor of her clients, adopting whatever tax characterization does her clients the least harm possible, and she will encourage her clients to take full advantage of the audit lottery in doing so. She will help her clients to challenge the constitutionality of the government's discriminatory application of the tax laws as well as the soundness of ideologically driven misinterpretations of those laws. She will use every procedural device and failing of the system to her clients' advantage in an effort to prevent the IRS from profiting from its own tactical advantages vis-à-vis lesbian and gay taxpayers. In short, to discharge her duty to the tax system and contribute to restoring the integrity of that system, the tax lawyer will treat the IRS as a real adversary at every stage of representation (i.e., from early tax planning to return preparation to audit and finally on to litigation), and, accordingly, she will zealously advocate on behalf of her lesbian and gay clients from the start to the finish of the representation.

CHAPTER 5. RACE AND TAXATION

The one area of critical tax theory that most obviously faces the hurdle of the myth of the "neutrality" of the tax laws is the intersection of race and taxation. Mainstream tax scholars are wont to point out that the tax laws are, on their face, race neutral. After all, we do not have one rate schedule for whites, another for African Americans, a third for Latina/os, and so on. The contributions to this chapter illustrate the fallacy of this myth of "neutrality," underscore the importance of viewing tax through the lens of race, and, at the same time, nicely illustrate the influence that critical race theory and its methodologies have had on critical tax scholars writing in the area of race and taxation.

Deftly using the narrative voice in *Tax Counts: Bringing Money-Law to LatCrit*, Alice Abreu opens the chapter with "a lesson from Cuba" and an accompanying call to scholars interested in social justice to heed the importance of tax (and "money-law" more generally) as a site for battling subordination. Given her own experience, Abreu urges Latina/os to embrace the study of tax and to enter the tax field because of the diverse perspective that they can bring to this area of the law. To illustrate her point, Abreu identifies how her being Cuban and her immigrant background have shaped her general perspective on tax law and her specific scholarly contributions to the field.

Eschewing the controversial technique of personal narrative, the chapter's remaining contributors turn to statistics, social science research, and conventional legal analysis to explore the tax system through the lens of race. In *A Black Critique of the Internal Revenue Code*, Beverly Moran and William Whitford test the hypothesis of critical race theorists that racial subordination is a structural feature of American society to determine whether the facially neutral tax laws systematically favor whites over blacks. In testing this hypothesis, Moran and Whitford consider whether a number of deviations from an "ideal" income tax have a disparate impact on the basis of race. We have included here only their examination of tax benefits granted to wealth and wealth transfers; in the full article, they also discuss tax benefits relating to home ownership and employee benefits as well as the marriage penalty. Interestingly, Moran and Whitford adopt the metaphor of the "Black Congress" – that is, a Congress that is oriented to the interests of blacks as a group – to consider what changes it might recommend to these various departures from an "ideal" income tax in light of their findings.

Also searching for racial subordination embedded in a facially neutral income tax, in *The Marriage Bonus/Penalty in Black and White*, Dorothy Brown uses census data to explain how (1) married black couples are more likely to pay a marriage penalty than married white couples and (2) married white couples are more likely to benefit from the marriage bonus than married black couples. Furthermore, recurring to the theme that critical tax theory is far from monolithic, Brown highlights the gender essentialism in discussions of the tax laws' impact on women, which often assume that women are invariably the secondary earner in married couples. Brown warns against assuming that the experience of all women is the same, because data indicate that black women may actually be the primary earners in many black married couples.

Mylinh Uy carries this line of inquiry – and a similar caution against essentialism – to the impact of the tax laws on Asian Americans in *Tax and Race: The Impact on Asian Americans*. Uy scrutinizes the empirical literature to show how (1) it comes up short in painting an accurate picture of the economic life of Asian Americans and (2) many Asian Americans may be disparately impacted by the tax laws in much the same way as African Americans. In doing so, Uy shows how lumping many different groups together under the rubric "Asian American" masks the difficult economic situation of a number of ethnic groups. At the same time, Uy works to break down the black–white binary in the tax literature (i.e., the tendency to equate issues of race with the experience of African Americans). Taking up calls from the likes of Moran, Whitford, and Brown, Uy enriches the dialogue about race and taxation by adding the perspective of Asian Americans to the mix.

David Brennen carries the inquiry further and warns against another type of myopia. In *Race and Equality Across the Law School Curriculum: The Law of Tax Exemption*, Brennen explores the relevance of race to the area of the law of tax-exempt organizations. At times borrowing Moran and Whitford's metaphor of the Black Congress, Brennen discusses how neutral rules applicable to tax-exempt organizations can look different when viewed through the lens of race and how some rules that are designed to battle race discrimination clearly lack the insights that a victim of discrimination might provide. Throughout this discussion, Brennen highlights the importance of a critical perspective to the taxation of entities as well as the taxation of individuals.

The chapter closes with a second piece by Dorothy Brown. In *Race and Class Matters in Tax Policy*, Brown embraces Derrick Bell's interest convergence theory. Brown explains how the earned income tax credit (EITC) has come to be viewed as "welfare." As a result, EITC recipients have come to be perceived as undeserving and black – a perception that generates opposition to a program that, in fact, helps to lift many working families out of poverty. Brown uses empirical data to show that, contrary to this general perception, the primary beneficiaries of the EITC are white. She argues that once the EITC is properly "raced" – that is, once it is shown primarily to benefit whites – opposition to the EITC will recede and efforts to reduce the burdens imposed on EITC claimants will finally move forward.

Tax Counts: Bringing Money-Law to LatCrit

ALICE G. ABREU[1]

Tax and business law have generally remained outside the LatCrit enterprise, and that is too bad. The problem may be that tax and business law seem to be ultimately about money, and worrying about money appears so crass – so alien to the issues of antisubordination and social justice that have occupied center stage in LatCrit discourse. Those of us who labor in areas of the law concerned with the distribution, protection, and multiplication of money might therefore seem unlikely contributors to the LatCrit enterprise.

Although money-law is often seen as involving what Fidel Castro dubbed *preocupaciones burgesas*, of import only to those who have money and thus have reason to care about its protection and multiplication, such a view is shortsighted. A study of the ways in which the law entrenches the distribution of money and enhances its multiplication should be within the purview of all scholars who care about antisubordination, because the law can entrench and abet the absence of money and thus contribute to continued subordination. As I will demonstrate, tax systems can do precisely that.

MONEY, THE SECOND GENERATION

My claim is that the concern about money and economic well-being is not just a *preocupación burgesa* but is, at bottom, a concern about human rights. Social, economic, and cultural rights may be referred to as second-generation human rights, but the important thing is that they are acknowledged to be human rights.

A study of how the design of a tax system affects economic well-being is central to this analysis, particularly in the United States, where so much of our social and economic policy is effectuated through the tax system rather than through direct expenditure programs. Although tax systems operate less directly than civil rights systems in determining the well-being of an individual or group, an individual or group which is taxed disproportionately suffers an injury that is not unlike the injury suffered by an individual or group denied access to employment. Indeed, because tax systems often act invisibly, they may be even more dangerous than

[1] Reprinted by permission from 78 *Denver University Law Review* 575 (2001).

systems that act overtly and thus invite more immediate scrutiny and resistance. In sum, tax should count in the critical enterprise.

DISTRIBUTIONAL EQUITY

Tax systems are the primary means by which democratic governments redistribute wealth. It is neither an accident nor a coincidence that some of the most respected legal philosophers of our time use the tax system as a vehicle for developing and articulating views about justice.

That tax is at the heart of inquiries about the meaning of justice is not surprising. In developing a tax system, a society must work out the relationship between the private and the public. A society must ask itself how much each individual is going to be asked to contribute to the common good, and in working out the answer to that question it must grapple with fundamental values. It should come as no surprise, then, that tax systems reflect the values of the societies that create them.

Lesson from Cuba

A story, both true and recent, will help to illustrate not only why I think all of us should care about taxes but also why it is that I, a Cuban refugee, do. While visiting Cuban friends in Miami, I was asked where I had boarded my Philadelphia dog. I explained that the vet had recommended a new place, ingeniously designated a "pet resort," and I recounted the experience of registering my dog there. As I explained, I had been asked how many times I wanted the "play technician" to visit my dog – for an additional fee, which would vary with the number of play sessions I ordered, a play technician would amuse my dog. As I suspect I was intended to, I ordered more play sessions than was fiscally prudent because I felt guilty about leaving my dog at the kennel. As I told this story in Miami one of my listeners shook his head and said: "Sometimes I think that what this country needs is a good dose of Fidel Castro."

Although I knew that the observation was not an endorsement of Fidel's economic philosophy, I nevertheless found the observation startling. The speaker had used Fidel to express what I consider to be a laudatory sentiment – a condemnation of the conspicuous consumption so prevalent in contemporary American society – but in my circle of Cuban refugee friends and relatives, I had never before heard Fidel's name used to express anything other than contempt, derision, and hatred. The statement got my attention.

As I considered the differences between Fidel's reaction to the problems of income inequality and wanton consumption among Cuba's upper class during the 1950s and the reaction of American tax scholars to rampant consumerism in American society, I was struck by both the differences and the parallels. The gulf that separated the haves and the have-nots in the Cuba of the 1950s was probably no bigger than that which separates those in the top and bottom of the income distribution in twenty-first century America. The great sugar plantation owners and rum and tobacco scions of the old Cuba were easily as disparate from the *campesinos* who worked in the fields as the Wall Street barons, corporate executives, and dot.com *wunderkinds* of today are from the inner-city project residents and single welfare mothers who seem to be an intractable part of urban life in the United States today. Absence of inequality does not distinguish one place from the other.

Nevertheless, the two places differ dramatically in the governmental response to inequality and its consumerist manifestations. Castro's answer was to nationalize industries and strip property owners of their holdings without compensation, while jailing or executing all who disagreed with his tactics or ideas. By contrast, in the United States consumerism and the paucity of individual savings have become fodder for a national debate. That debate has focused not on outlawing private property or market transactions, but on using the tax system to even the playing field and provide a disincentive for engaging in wanton consumption. Thus, the Cornell economist Robert Frank has written an entire book on the runaway train of conspicuous consumption and has advocated the use of the tax system to slow it down, and the pages of law journals are filled with debate over the merits of a consumption tax. Scholarly literature debating the merits of progressive taxation also abounds.

As I reflected on my Cuban friend's backhanded compliment to Fidel Castro's policy objectives, I also realized that the observation provided a window into what attracts me to the study of tax policy. For me, tax policy is interesting and important because it reflects and implements our values. Tax policy determines the distribution of the tax burden, and that affects the distribution of income and, ultimately, the distribution of wealth. However, unlike Fidel Castro's policies, tax policy in this country functions through the democratic process, flawed and imperfect though it is, and respects human rights.

The beauty of tax is that a tax system that develops through the exercise of the democratic process can serve the redistributive objectives of leaders like Fidel Castro, who captivated the American left because of his egalitarian rhetoric, but can do so without obliterating civil and political rights. Tax policy allows us to distinguish between the redistributive goals of Fidel Castro, many of which were commendable, and his means for achieving them, which were almost universally reprehensible. Of course, a tax system cannot carry the weight of all of a government's policies, and how the government spends the money it collects is crucially important to the well-being of its citizens. My point is not that tax systems are everything, but only that they are an important component of social policy, one that too often is relegated to outsider status in critical discourse.

The brief exchange that began with a query about my dog allowed me to come to a more nuanced understanding of both Fidel and his *revolución* on the one hand, and the near-canonization of him so prevalent within the American left on the other. For me, commendable ends do not justify repressive means, and Fidel is guilty of having sacrificed the means to the end. By contrast, tax systems offer the promise of achieving egalitarian ends through democratic means.

The Promise of Tax Systems

A tax system that results from the exercise of the democratic process offers the promise of justice in both the means and the ends. A study of tax systems ought therefore to be the province of any progressive enterprise. By studying tax systems, we can learn about the connection between the operation of the system and the distribution of income. We can also discover how the design of a given tax system reflects the allocation of power, and its converse, subordination, in the society to which it applies.

THE ALLOCATION OF POWER IN TAX SYSTEM DESIGN

Taxes, like the coins in which they are ultimately paid, have two sides. On one side is the burden they impose. That side is easy to see and is shared by all tax systems, but the other side of tax systems is harder to see. On that other side is the empowerment that tax systems can provide.

Tax systems can empower individuals in at least two ways. First, they can give individuals the power to alter the amount of their tax liability by altering their behavior. For example, a tax system that provides a deduction for home mortgage interest but not for rent gives taxpayers the ability to alter (reduce) their tax liability by buying a house which they finance with a loan secured by a mortgage. By encouraging taxpayers to behave in ways that affect the size of their tax bills, the tax system empowers them. A taxpayer who can say to herself, "I've bought a house and now my taxes will be lower," feels in control of her tax destiny because she has taken an affirmative action that affects her tax liability. Of course, the taxpayer who cannot afford the down payment on a house and must continue to rent will not enjoy that feeling of mastery, but more about that later. The point is not that the tax system empowers everyone, but that in providing for different tax consequences for different behavior, it empowers *some* people.

Empowerment is not a necessary attribute of a tax system. Tax systems do not have to be designed in a way that empowers anyone. Consider a system that provides only a "standard" deduction of the same size available to everyone. Taxpayer behavior would not affect tax liability under such a system and taxpayers would therefore lack the power that the current system gives some of them. Thus, when we adopt a tax system that empowers, we are faced with deciding whom to empower.

Second, tax systems can be designed to give individuals the power to shift the economic burden of the tax. For example, a system that taxes the sale of an item gives the seller, who has the obligation to remit the amount of the tax, the ability to shift the economic burden of the tax to the buyer. The seller can effect such a shift by charging a given amount for the item and having the tax apply to that. In effect, the seller is simply collecting the tax, and it is the consumer who is bearing the economic burden of it. The design of the tax – a tax on sales – gives the seller the power to shift the economic burden of the tax to the consumer. Choosing a different method of taxation would change this allocation of power.

A review of the current federal income tax system reveals that the system grants many choices, but it generally grants those choices to people who possess material wealth. It therefore distributes choices progressively, just as it distributes burdens. A comparison of the way the two most significant federal tax systems, the federal income tax and the federal employment (Social Security) tax system, allocate choices will illustrate the ways in which the allocation of power in tax system design implicates values.

Under the income tax system, the wealthier an individual is, the greater the number of choices she has. Not only do those with less wealth have fewer choices under that system, they also have a greater proportion of their wealth subject to tax under the other system, one that provides virtually no opportunity for the exercise of taxpayer choice – the Social Security tax system. Indeed, studies have shown that "lower- and middle-income Americans now pay more social [security] taxes than they pay in federal income taxes."[2]

By contrast to the federal income tax system, the Social Security tax system provides little opportunity for the exercise of choice. The mere receipt of compensation for personal services generates the liability for the tax. No deductions and very few exclusions exist regardless of what the taxpayer does. For most taxpayers, the only choice the system provides is not to work. Why is it that the tax that imposes the greatest burden on low- and middle-income Americans is also the tax with the smallest opportunity for the exercise of choice? It is because of the value we, as a society, place on material capital.

Taken as a whole, the federal tax system provides for the exercise of choice in proportion to wealth. This exercise of choice turns a seemingly progressive system, like the income tax system, into one in which the outward appearance of progressivity can be overturned "by the voluntary actions of individual persons over time" and in which the connectedness wrought by the objective of progressivity is undercut by the disconnected manner in which each choice is exercised.[3] Moreover, because bestowing the power to choose in proportion to wealth is itself anti-egalitarian, possession of the power can overturn the egalitarian objective even if that power is not used. The rich can buy houses, invest in tax-advantaged financial instruments, and get paid in stock options that generate no current income or employment tax liability, but the working poor have none of those choices. By distributing the power to choose in proportion to wealth, the federal tax system contributes to the subordination of poor people, particularly poor working people.

TAX FOR EVERYONE

Critical scholars have begun to apply the tools of critical analysis to the current tax system and in so doing have provided us with much food for thought. But those efforts have met with substantial resistance from within the tax academic community, and much work remains to be done. Word of that work needs to spread beyond the ranks of tax scholars.

Latina/o scholars have much to contribute to this critical enterprise. Not only do we have a perspective traditionally underrepresented in tax policy debates, but the diversity in our community cannot help but enrich those debates. For example, Alfonso Morales has advanced our understanding of tax compliance behavior based on his field study of recent immigrants from Mexico, which demonstrated the complexity of tax compliance decisions and the influence of what Morales terms "supply-side" considerations in tax avoidance behavior. Following are other

---

[2] Chris R. Edwards, *Typical American Family Pays 40 Percent of Income in Taxes*, 66 TAX NOTES 735, 735 (1995).

[3] ROBERT NOZICK, ANARCHY, STATE, AND UTOPIA 164 (1974).

examples of the ways in which a Latina/o perspective can affect tax policy debates. I confess that my thinking in this area is embryonic, but I offer it because it has the potential to prompt others to add their voices and thus enrich the discourse, and to underscore the importance of tax to the LatCrit enterprise.

Citizenship

For some portions of our community, citizenship matters, and citizenship matters a lot in some areas of taxation. My own interest in the taxation of individuals who renounce U.S. citizenship to save taxes – tax-motivated expatriation, as it has come to be known – grew out of the very personal way in which I value my U.S. citizenship. That personal connection caused me to think about it often and led to interesting discussions whenever I taught the subject in my course on International Tax. It is not surprising that when Congress proposed significant changes in this area, writing about it was easy. I do not think that it is mere coincidence that I was the first scholar to publish a law review article on the subject, and I wonder whether it is mere coincidence that the second such article by an academic was also written by a Cuban. That we take differing positions is further evidence of the diverse ways in which Latina/os can enrich the debate, even in what seems like a technical area of the law.

Residence

My connection to my citizenship has also made me interested in the ways in which the tax system discriminates against individuals who have resident status for tax purposes (and are therefore subject to the full force of U.S. taxing jurisdiction even though they cannot vote and often do not enjoy resident status for immigration purposes), and who are sometimes treated more harshly than citizens. Although my work in this area has barely begun and its fruits will have implications far beyond the Latina/o community, my interest in undertaking it is undoubtedly colored by my family's experience, for a time, as tax-paying but non-voting U.S. residents.

Culture

My perspective as a Latina and my understanding of Latina/o culture has also been useful in helping to understand the administration of the tax laws. During a discussion of the IRS's treatment of immigrants who claim the earned income tax credit at an [American Bar Association (ABA)] Tax Section meeting several years ago, I was struck by the way in which cultural assumptions informed, or, more accurately, misinformed, the IRS's interpretation of actions by members of some immigrant groups. The discussion centered on the problem of grandparents, aunts, and uncles who claimed that certain children were their dependents even though the adults' relationship to the children did not fit the definition of dependent established for that purpose in the Code. The underlying assumption seemed to be that the individuals in question were either stupid or dishonest. To me, however, an alternative explanation for the difficulty was at least plausible: a difference in the cultural assumptions about who was "family."

In Latino culture, extended families are common and the bonds between generations are often strong. It is not uncommon for multiple generations to share a dwelling, which makes it harder to sort the familial relationships into the more atomistic and money-based categories of Anglo culture, which the Code reflects. Such a difference in cultural perspective could explain the behavior the IRS was seeing and could allow for more thoughtful responses to the communication problem it posed. My participation in that discussion did not lead to a new legislative initiative and was less than a drop in the bucket of solutions to administrative problems in the tax system. I was speaking to but a handful of individuals who are part of a system that consists of thousands. Nevertheless, what I was able to do in the context of that handful of individuals illustrates the changes that can occur as more of us who can bring a different cultural perspective develop the technical expertise and the clout to move in those circles.

I could not have made a difference in that context had I not first mastered the technical aspects of the tax law. But I was able to offer something beyond technical mastery: a different cultural perspective that technical mastery alone cannot supply. Others can make similar contributions, and every little bit will help.

CONCLUSION

The paucity of current work on the impact of the tax system on the Latina/o community leads me to conclude by again urging that more of us need to become engaged in this work. We need more Latina/o tax teachers who cannot only serve as role models, but who can also eloquently state, by their presence, that this is a field open to all. As a community, we also have to be willing to embrace tax and other business subjects so that our students do not feel they have to suppress any interest or passion they may have for them. We have to nurture our students' interest in these subjects by making the subjects ours.

Nurturing more minority tax lawyers is crucial to the critical enterprise for another reason. Even if the study of tax systems could not offer insights important to the LatCrit antisubordination project and even if the experience of Latina/os could not enhance tax policy discourse, it would be important for Latina/os to become tax lawyers. By being at the table, I believe that I help to earn respect for Latinas and Latinos. By being a walking billboard for the intellectual diversity of Latinas and Latinos, I think I advance the cause of inclusion and empowerment generally.

If we are to make a difference, if we are to achieve for ourselves the kind of self-actualization to which I think we all aspire, our presence must be felt in every facet of life. For those of us who are lawyers, that means in every facet of law, including the money-law areas traditionally closed to us and often alien to our lives. In other words, tax counts, and all of money-law should become a vibrant part of the critical enterprise. Tax should not be just for tax people anymore.

A Black Critique of the Internal Revenue Code

BEVERLY I. MORAN AND WILLIAM WHITFORD[1]

This article raises the question of whether the Code systematically favors whites over blacks. In recent years a small number of scholars in the legal academy have become known as critical race theorists. One main thrust of critical race theory is a belief that racial subordination is everywhere, a structural aspect of all parts of American society. If this part of critical race theory has merit, then every important American institution should reflect racial subordination, even such a seemingly neutral institution as the American tax system.

Discrimination connotes that persons who are similarly situated except for race are not treated similarly. This definition presupposes, however, some standard for determining when people are similarly situated. In the context of the Code, every-day tax policy analysis provides us a ready tool for this analysis. In *Commissioner v. Glenshaw Glass*, the Supreme Court defined income as "all accessions to wealth, clearly realized, and over which the taxpayers have complete dominion."[2] Since then generations of tax scholars have used this definition to craft a conception of a comprehensive income tax base. Our standard for when persons are similarly situated, therefore, is when they have the same income, and we too use the *Glenshaw Glass* definition of income.

Of course, many provisions of the Code deviate from the ideal of taxing all income in the comprehensive income tax base. Sometimes the Code compromises the ideal in order to achieve a more administratively practical rule. More often, Congress has decided to encourage particular lifestyles or behaviors by holding out tax benefits as an incentive.

Our hypothesis is that deviations from the ideal of a comprehensive income tax systematically favor whites over blacks. While many studies about the impact of tax law rely on data from returns, we were unable to do so because tax returns are not coded by race. In the absence of tax return data, we have turned to social science studies of the lifestyles and behaviors of whites and blacks. This evidence will enable us to estimate what proportion of each group is seemingly eligible for various tax benefits. We define as a tax benefit any opportunity for deductions or

---

[1] Reprinted by permission from 1996 *Wisconsin Law Review* 751. Copyright 1996 by The Board of Regents of the University of Wisconsin System; Reprinted by permission of the Wisconsin Law Review.

[2] 348 U.S. 431 (1955).

exclusions from income that deviate from the ideal of a comprehensive income tax base, or opportunities to postpone reporting income to a time later than when it should be reported according to the ideal of the comprehensive tax base. Our evidence about the availability of these tax benefits to whites and blacks comes both from existing social science studies conducted for other purposes and from our own analysis of some important demographic databases.

THE SIGNIFICANCE OF OUR WORK

For the most part we reserve our conclusions until we have presented the data. But we must address preliminarily the potential significance of a finding of systematic racial subordination in the Code. If these findings have no significance, then there is no point to conducting our study.

First, we want to make clear that we are not asking a question about discriminatory intent. We do not hypothesize that members of Congress set out to harm blacks through the Code. Nonetheless, in America a gap exists between blacks and most lawmakers because many whites and blacks do not interact in any meaningful way. Legislators are affected by this social segregation. Black life remains largely unknown to most of the white world, and to most white legislators. Hence legislators are largely unaware of the Code's impact on blacks. We believe that this ignorance is one of the reasons for structural racial subordination in America.

Second, although we cannot possibly come to a definitive conclusion about the entire Code, we will present evidence suggesting that certain provisions benefit whites more than blacks. If the Code as a whole reflects racial subordination, we believe such a finding has value as social science. It would offer support for the basic substantive theory of critical race theory – that racial subordination is everywhere.

However, as lawyers concerned with racial justice in America, we also believe that if the Code systematically subordinates black interests, then Congress should change it. To develop possible changes, we have invented a metaphor of a Black Congress that is exclusively oriented to the interests of blacks as a group. We will suggest changes in the Code that such a Congress might consider. Because no change should be enacted without consideration of the Code as a whole, and because we studied a limited number of provisions, we make no final recommendations. Our suggestions should not only stimulate interest in possible reforms, but also illustrate how the actual Congress, largely unaware of black lifestyles, might have created a Code that systematically subordinates black interests.

WEALTH

Tax Benefits

We looked at four code sections that protect wealth, both while the original owner holds it and when the original owner passes it on to other people, usually younger family members. These four provisions are the § 1014 basis adjustment, the § 1 reduced rate for capital gains income, the § 102 exclusion for gifts, and the § 1015 gift basis. In addition, we considered two unwritten rules that work to benefit wealth – the realization requirement and tax-free financing.

Each of these sections and rules allow[s] taxpayers with wealth to avoid income taxes that would be due under the *Glenshaw Glass* goal of taxing all "accessions to wealth, clearly realized, and over which the taxpayers have complete dominion." These provisions are relevant to our topic of black/white differences in tax benefits for two reasons. First, on average blacks own less assets than whites. Second, to maximize the tax benefits of many of these provisions an individual needs not only to own property, but to own the right types of property. As we will show, the small percentage of blacks who do own assets are likely to own the wrong type of assets to maximize tax benefits.

Realization and refinancing. When a taxpayer earns a salary, his increase in wealth is immediately subject to tax. In contrast, when many assets appreciate in value in their owners' hands, the increased value is not immediately taxed. A nonstatutory rule called "realization" determines the time of taxation. A multitude of rules determine[s] when realization occurs with respect to different assets. For example, interest on bank accounts is realized when it accrues and is immediately taxed. But appreciation in the value of stock, real estate, and many other assets is not deemed to be realized until there is a "sale or exchange."

The realization requirement often permits taxpayers to delay paying the tax on an accession to wealth. Delayed taxation is usually advantageous to a taxpayer because he can then invest the resources that would otherwise have gone to taxes. Further, if realization occurs only after a sale or exchange, the taxpayer has considerable control over the timing of taxation, and can plan to realize the accession to wealth in a year in which he has little other income, or even an excess of realized losses, thereby avoiding taxation at higher rates or altogether.

From the taxpayer's perspective, one problem with the realization requirement is that, in order to obtain its benefits, the taxpayer must often hold onto his property. Fortunately for those with assets to spare, the Code provides several ways around this limitation. Most importantly, the taxpayer can exploit the principle that borrowed monies are not income because the corresponding obligation to repay means there is no accession to wealth. Taxpayers with appreciated property can borrow against that appreciation without having a realization event. By using the borrowed funds, wealthy taxpayers can enjoy property appreciation without a corresponding tax cost.

Section 1014 basis adjustment. When a taxpayer owns the type of property for which appreciation in value is not recognized in the year in which it occurs, the taxpayer can avoid liability for the appreciation altogether by owning the property until death. Section 1014 provides that the heir of property acquires a basis in the inherited property equal to its fair market value at the time of the decedent's death. Any previously untaxed (because "unrealized") appreciation in the value of the property escapes tax altogether. This is true even if the decedent enjoyed the benefit of that appreciation by, for example, using the property as collateral for a loan.

In order for a taxpayer to obtain § 1014's benefits, the type of property involved is crucial. First, § 1014 only benefits property that has appreciated in value. Property that has declined in value receives a stepped-down basis on the owner's death, and thus nobody takes a deduction for the lost value. Second, even if the property appreciates, § 1014 only benefits those who inherit property with unrealized gains. Bank accounts can appreciate as they accumulate interest but that interest is realized and taxed each year. When the heirs receive the contents of those already-taxed accounts, there is no built in – yet untaxed – gain for § 1014 to protect.

Capital gains. If a taxpayer sells appreciated property prior to death, he must pay tax on the appreciation. However, if the property is a "capital asset," that accession to wealth may be taxed at favorable capital gains rates. Essentially, the capital gains rate is a special (lower) rate of tax on the sale of investment property as opposed to the common (higher) rate on "ordinary" income. Avoiding technical detail, ordinary income consists of such items as salary, dividends and interest, while capital gains come from the sale or exchange of capital assets such as stocks and real estate.

Owning the right kind of property is crucial to capital gains treatment. First, preferential treatment goes only to property that produces a gain on sale. Depreciated properties, such as cars and real estate in inner city slum neighborhoods, are disfavored if they are capital assets because a taxpayer is often unable to deduct losses resulting from these properties. Further, the capital gains rate only applies when the property is of a type where its appreciation is not immediately realized. Finally, the taxpayer must hold the property for investment rather than for sale to customers. Thus investors are favored over small businessmen. As we will see, all these requirements have adverse effects on blacks because they disfavor the very assets that blacks tend to own.

Gifts. Surely an extra $5,000 received without an obligation to repay is an "accession to wealth." Yet, under § 102 this $5,000 (or $50,000 or $500,000) escapes income taxation if it meets the Code's "gift" definition. Under *Commissioner v. Duberstein*, a transfer with no obligation to repay constitutes a "gift" for tax purposes only if it results from the donor's "detached and disinterested generosity."[3] In combination with other rules, the net result of the "detached and disinterested generosity" requirement is that gifts from strangers (such as prizes and awards) are usually taxed. In contrast, gifts from family members and friends commonly receive the § 102 exclusion. Moreover, wealthy people generally count other wealthy people as their family and friends, while low-asset individuals can only hope to get wealth transfers from strangers and lotteries. The gift exclusion under § 102 thus favors the more fortunate both because wealthy individuals have access to more gifts and because they have access to the "right" gifts.

This emphasis on the right gifts only increases when we consider the rules in § 1015 that govern the donee's basis in gifts. Under § 1015 the donee takes the donor's basis so long as the gift has appreciated in value. This provision allows a

---

[3] 363 U.S. 278, 285 (1960) (quoting Comm'r v. LoBue, 351 U.S. 243, 246 (1956)).

high-bracket donor to arrange for gains to be taxed at the rates applied to a donee, who may be selected for the gift because of his low bracket. But the donee's basis in property that has depreciated in the donor's hands is the fair market value of the property at the time of gift. Thus no one gets the tax benefit of deducting the loss that resulted from the depreciation in value. Therefore, the basis rules mean that only taxpayers who have property with unrealized appreciation can reduce taxes by giving that property to family members.

Wealth and the Social Science Literature

Until the 1970s, studies of race and economics focused on income rather than wealth. Studies of wealth differences by race were few and far between. Once the importance of wealth and race was acknowledged, the reason for the dearth of studies changed from lack of interest to problems with data collection. Income surveys are relatively easy because researchers can obtain income information from pay stubs, tax returns, and bank records. Because value is constantly affected by ever-changing market conditions, information on home and car equity or the value of household goods is harder to obtain. Even today, social scientists point out that wealth data is suspect if for no other reason than that the wealthy are uncooperative subjects with a tendency to substantially underestimate their holdings.

Results of Our Study

Our review of the social science literature confirms a wide gap in black and white wealth, both in gross averages and after controlling for such factors as income, education, region, marriage, and children. The studies also confirm that blacks hold a higher percentage of their wealth in consumption items than whites do, and a lesser percentage in financial and investment assets.

We have conducted our own analysis of available databases for two reasons. First, because we are concerned about tax consequences, we are interested in different categorizations of assets than the social scientists are. Social scientists group houses and cars together as consumption items. Yet we know that the Code strongly favors investment in housing, so much so that we will discuss it separately. Similarly, the social scientists' concept of investment or financial assets fails to distinguish between assets which can benefit from the realization requirement and capital gains rates, such as stocks and bonds, and assets which do not so benefit, such as bank deposits. Our own data analysis takes account of these tax concerns in estimating differences by race in the composition of asset holdings.

Our other addition to the social science literature is to estimate the difference by race in the amounts received by inheritance or gift.

Analysis of race and asset composition. Our analysis of asset composition, which segregates assets into "tax favored" and "tax disfavored" groupings, relies on data that the [*Survey of Income and Program Participation (SIPP)*] surveys gathered. Race is the crucial variable in all of our regression equations. We controlled for various other independent variables to see if race remains a statistically significant predictor of asset holdings in various tax favored categories.

Table 5.1. *Race and wealth composition*

Component of wealth	Black mean $	White mean $	Black % of total	White % of total
Stock/Mutual Funds	207	6,746	0.01	0.04
Real Estate Equity	4,587	11,943	0.05	0.08
Home Equity	21,384	39,711	0.53	0.56
Equity in Vehicles	3,328	5,906	0.41	0.32
Total	29,507	64,306	1	1

n = 32,162
Data Source: 1984 Survey of Income and Program Participation; Wave 4.

We first constructed a dependent variable of total net worth. Using controls for income, education, age, region, and marital status, we ran a regression to determine whether race was a statistically significant predictor of total net worth, as measured in this data set. We found that it was, just as other researchers had previously found using the same and different databases.

In order to separate tax-favored assets from disfavored assets we used the *SIPP* databases to get measures of wealth in equity in one's home, equity in real estate aside from one's own home, stocks and mutual fund shares, and equity in vehicles. The first three of these categories are tax-favored investments. But because vehicles generally decline in value, and the loss is not deductible if the vehicle is held for personal use, vehicles are tax disfavored. Because we have run regressions on each of these new dependent variables, for logistical reasons (division by zero) we had to perform the analysis using only respondents whose wealth was greater than zero. However, that subset of respondents causes us to overlook the fact that more blacks than whites have no wealth at all. As a result, the wealth differences between the two racial groups that we report are most likely smaller than they are in the general population.

Table 5.1 shows the mean amounts owned in each asset category, by black and white respondents separately. The last two columns report the percentage of total holdings in these four asset categories that consist of assets in each individual category, again for black and white respondents separately.

This table indicates that blacks who own assets are less likely to hold assets that are tax favored. Table 5.1 shows that blacks hold a much smaller percentage of their wealth in stock and mutual funds and real estate equity. These are both asset categories where tax-favored appreciation in value is common. In contrast, blacks hold a greater percentage than whites of their wealth in equity in vehicles. Assuming that almost all these vehicles are held for personal use, this is a tax-disfavored investment. We used regression analysis to ensure that the differences displayed in Table 5.1 are not byproducts of socioeconomic and demographic differences between blacks and whites.

Gifts and inheritance. Analysts have sometimes speculated that blacks receive less in gifts and by inheritance than whites, and that this disparity accounts for at least part of the well-documented race and wealth disparity. But little data analysis actually addresses this question. Because of the important tax benefits

Table 5.2. *Gifts and inheritance by race*

	Black (mean per person)	White (mean per person)
Gifts Given	$236	$1,054
Gifts Received	$172	$1,033
Inheritances Received	$1,485	$5,348
Value of Property at Age 65	$15,346	$81,936

associated with gifts and inheritance, we decided to look at this issue in depth. The *SIPP* database did not have enough information on what people receive and what people give, but we were able to get relevant data from the *National Survey of Families and Households (NSFH)*, a database compiled in 1988–89.

Unfortunately, although the *NSFH* supplies data by race on the values of gifts and inheritances, it does not break down the values according to the type of asset that was received or inherited. This information is important because some of the tax benefits associated with gifts and inheritances depend on the donor or decedent transferring property with untaxed appreciation that has resulted from the realization requirement. For example, cash gifts and bequests get none of the benefits of avoiding tax on previously unrealized appreciation, whereas gifts and bequests of appreciated stock commonly capture this tax benefit.

To partially rectify this data deficiency, we constructed a variable from the *NSFH* database that measured the value of assets held by blacks and whites at age sixty-five in four asset categories: home, other real estate, business or farm property, and motor vehicles. Our intent was to get some measure of the value of assets that blacks and whites owned at a time near death, as a way of estimating the differential potential by race of taking advantage of the stepped-up basis for property transferred by bequest. However, our constructed variable is far from perfect because it does not include the value of stocks and bonds, which are most likely to benefit from basis adjustments at the time of gift or death. Furthermore, our variable includes motor vehicles, which rarely benefit from such adjustments.

Table 5.2 reports the differences by race for the value of gifts given and received, inheritances received, and value of assets held at age sixty-five. The data comes from *NSFH*.

The differences by race reported in Table 5.2 are very dramatic and indicate a wide variance in the degree to which blacks and whites enjoy the tax benefits associated with gifts and inheritance. In order to determine whether these differences were simply a product of status differences between blacks and whites, we ran regression equations with respect to the value of gifts received, inheritances received, and property held at age sixty-five. We controlled in each instance for income, education, age, region, and marital status. Race remained a statistically significant predictor with respect to these dependent variables.

Conclusion. It must be emphasized that we have not measured directly the differential impact on blacks and whites of the tax rules we have discussed, because we have been unable to directly examine returns. The evidence that we have gathered cannot account for the fact that not all taxpayers who are eligible for a tax benefit claim it. Nonetheless, we have gathered very strong inferential evidence to support the hypothesis that whites benefit more than blacks from the tax provisions we have studied, each of which deviates from an ideal income tax as set forth in *Glenshaw Glass*.

A BLACK CONGRESS ON WEALTH

As we turn to suggestions about how a Black Congress might amend the Code in light of our findings, two preliminary comments are appropriate. First, if a Black Congress truly existed, we would not expect it to act solely in the interest of blacks, any more than we expect the current Congress, which is mostly white, to act solely in the interest of whites. Our Black Congress, oriented solely to the interest of blacks, is purely a metaphor, useful for analytic purposes.

Second, our Black Congress is not solely motivated by the goal of minimizing black taxes. Blacks are interested in government spending; consequently, some of our recommendations will reflect concerns about the level of government revenues. Moreover, the tax provisions we are considering all have ostensible purposes which may benefit blacks. For example, the realization requirement and the stepped-up basis at death are commonly justified as making the tax system more administrable. The realization requirement permits a sale or exchange to measure the amount of asset appreciation, rather than relying on some alternative valuation method. The stepped-up basis at death avoids the necessity for determining a decedent's basis in property, which can be very difficult when the person has kept inadequate records. Not all of the supposed benefits are administrative. The special tax benefits for home owning, for instance, are justified as explicit incentives for taxpayers to own rather than rent their residences, apparently on the theory that home owners on average are more stable and responsible citizens. We do not agree with all of these justifications, but it is not the point of this article to debate about them. However, a Black Congress would consider these usual justifications for tax benefits.

We next offer some suggested tax reforms that a Black Congress might consider in light of our findings.

Tax Property Appreciation as It Accrues on Investments in Publicly Traded Securities and Nonresidential Real Estate

Except for homes and vehicles, blacks generally do not own property. Instead, blacks earn income in the form of wages that are immediately subject to tax. Depository accounts are probably the most common form of black wealth other than homes and vehicles. Hence repeal of the realization requirement would raise considerable revenue without adversely affecting blacks. We believe that limiting repeal of the realization requirement to publicly traded securities and nonresidential real estate is an eminently practical reform, because it is possible to measure the extent of appreciation on these assets without a sale or exchange. Public listings report the trading value of securities, and property tax assessments provide a usually reliable estimate of the market value of real estate.

Repeal Special Tax Rates for Capital Gains

It is very unlikely that many blacks benefit directly from special rates for capital gains. While some argue that favorable rates for capital gains stimulate economic activity which trickles down to taxpayers who never enjoy a capital gain, we have little faith in trickle-down economics.

Maintain the § 102 Exclusion for Income from Gifts and Inheritances

Although blacks receive few gifts or bequests that benefit from this exclusion, we decline to recommend changing it for two reasons. First, any change in this provision must be coordinated with gift and estate taxes because it may not be appropriate to tax both the grantor and the recipient. But consideration of gift and estate taxes is beyond the scope of this article.

Second, a Black Congress might want to preserve some incentives for savings and intergenerational transfers of wealth. The story of black American life has been one of inability to pass wealth from generation to generation, whether because of slavery, racism, or poverty. The inability to transfer wealth has adversely affected black wealth. We believe that a Black Congress would prefer to encourage, rather than discourage, such transfers.

The Marriage Bonus/Penalty in Black and White

DOROTHY A. BROWN[1]

A marriage penalty occurs whenever a couple pays higher federal income taxes as a result of their marriage than they would pay if they remained single and filed individual returns. A marriage bonus occurs whenever a couple pays lower federal income taxes as a result of marriage than they would pay if they remained single and filed individual returns. Marriage penalties are the greatest where there are two wage earners; marriage bonuses are the greatest where there is only one wage earner. Although numerous articles have been written about the marriage penalty, this essay provides a different perspective.

THE TAX IMPLICATIONS OF THE MARRIAGE DECISION

This section considers the effects of the marriage decision by examining the differences between white and black households. The evidence suggests that there is a difference in the impact of both the marriage bonus and the marriage penalty based upon race. Black families are more likely to pay a marriage penalty; white families are more likely to receive a marriage bonus.

My analysis is limited to an investigation of the differences between black and white households. Without question, a richer, more complete examination ultimately must include Hispanic, Asian, Native American, and other racial or ethnic groups. In that regard, this essay is intended only as a first step in considering the racial and gender implications of the rate structure. This essay also makes the simplifying assumption that there are no racially mixed households. That assumption does not distort the picture much, given that in 1985, 98.9% of black married women and 96.6% of black married men had a black spouse.

The IRS does not keep statistical information according to race, but the Census Bureau and the Bureau of Labor Statistics do. Relying on their data, this section will begin by describing how married black women participate in the workforce at higher rates than married white women. It also will show that married black women contribute a higher percentage of total household income than married white women and that wage discrimination results in white men earning more than white women, black men, or black women. Finally, this section will demonstrate

---

[1] Reprinted by permission from 65 *University of Cincinnati Law Review* 787 (1997).

that because of the marriage rate for black women relative to that for white women, a disproportionate number of black women are single heads of household, which suggests yet another path of inquiry.

Labor Force Participation Rates Based upon Gender and Race

Black women historically have entered the workforce in larger numbers than white women and have stayed there longer. A 1990 study showed that 73% of married black women were in the waged labor force, compared to 64% for married white women. If the marriage penalty exists only in households of two-wage-earner couples, married black couples, with a higher percentage of two wage earners, are more likely to pay a marriage penalty than white couples. Conversely, married white couples are more likely to receive a marriage bonus.

A recent study found that married black women contribute approximately 40% of their household's income. Married white women contribute only 29% of their household's income. These statistics suggest that black couples not only are more likely to suffer a marriage penalty, but also that they will tend to pay more in marriage penalties than their white counterparts with equal household income.

That study is valuable not only for revealing that women's rates of contribution to household income vary across race, but also for highlighting gender essentialism in the tax literature. Married black women contribute a significant portion of total household income. Assuming that 40% is the average household contribution of married black women, it is possible, perhaps even probable, that certain married black women contribute more than 40% of total household income. Accordingly, married black women cannot unequivocally be considered a marginal second wage earner in the way that current tax literature treats all married women. For example, Professor McCaffery recently described working married women as follows: "[H]istorically, of course, wives have usually been the marginal earners.... [M]arried working women earn, on average, forty-six percent of what their husbands do."[2] McCaffery's statistics may be more appropriate when applied to white married women, although he did not so limit his analysis. If a significant portion of married black women earn more than 50% of household income, however, they cannot be considered marginal earners. Given the vast differences between black and white women's working experiences, averages of the sort McCaffery used are wholly inadequate in understanding the operation of the joint tax return and suggest a path for future inquiry.

If any group is likely to view themselves and be viewed as marginal wage earners, it is married white women, who on average contribute 29% of total household income. Although black couples are more likely to suffer a marriage penalty, within the marital unit it is white women as marginal wage earners who are more likely to feel the greater impact of the marriage penalty. This is so because as a marginal earner, the couple may understand the wife's wages as taxed at the highest marginal tax rate. In addition, if the marginal wage earner is a mother of young

---

[2] Edward J. McCaffery, *Taxation and the Family: A Fresh Look at Behavioral Gender Biases in the Code*, 40 UCLA L. Rev. 983, 994 (1993). [This article is excerpted in Chapter 8. – Eds.]

children, the couple also may view the increased child-care costs as an added cost of her working. Of course, this understanding of child-care costs erroneously assumes that they are the costs of the working mother and not of the working father. The Code treats a family member's performance of household services, including child care, as nontaxable imputed income. To the extent that married white couples are more likely to have only one wage earner, with the wife staying home and providing unwaged labor, the Code is more likely to reward them doubly. Not only are white couples more likely to enjoy a marriage bonus because of their household arrangement, they are more likely to enjoy an imputed income bonus from it as well.

Given that black men may contribute less than 50% of household income, any analysis of the marginal wage earner in married black households would seem suspect. However, such an analysis surprisingly might reveal that black men, as secondary wage earners, are more affected by the marriage penalty than black women. This sort of analysis might provide one explanation for the declining labor participation rates of black men in recent years.

Workforce participation for all men, however, has declined over the past two decades, although this decline is more dramatic for black men than for white men. Among younger white men, extended education has been the primary cause for the decline in their labor force participation. That explanation does not hold for black men, however, whose educational enrollments have declined.

The decline in labor participation rates among black men also may affect black women's waged labor participation. Black women, who contribute 40% of their household's income, are less likely than white women to be able to afford to stay at home and raise their children while their husbands provide all of the family's waged income.

The differences in waged labor participation between black and white families just described should not be viewed as static. Recent trends indicate that more married white women are entering the labor force. Those trends are attributable partially to the growing need for both spouses to work in order for the couple to maintain the wage growth previously enjoyed by traditional white, one-wage-earner households. Moreover, as a consequence of continuing efforts toward wage equality in the workforce across gender and race lines, it may be that more white couples in the future will suffer the marriage penalty at rates similar to those historically experienced by married black couples.

Wage Rates Based upon Gender and Race

A more complete picture of the racial implications of the marriage bonus/penalty requires an investigation of the differences in taxable income between black and white households. As noted earlier, black families are more likely to pay a marriage penalty than white families because black women tend to contribute a larger portion of their households' income than white women. One reason behind that phenomenon is employment discrimination.

On average, black women's earnings are closer to black men's earnings than white women's earnings are to white men's earnings. For every dollar earned by a white man, a white woman earned 78¢, a black man earned 74.8¢, and a black woman earned 66¢. Therefore, due to wage discrimination, even if all married women participated in the labor force at the same rates, black families still would be more likely than white families to pay a marriage penalty. Wage discrimination causes black men and women to earn roughly equal amounts, or at least amounts more equal than the amounts earned by white men and women.

Wage discrimination, of course, is not the only factor that tends to equalize earnings between spouses in black families. High labor participation rates by black women also tend to equalize spousal earnings. The combination of wage discrimination and the higher incidence of two-wage-earner households means that black men and women tend to contribute nearly equal amounts to total household income. Within the U.S. tax rate structure, that means that black families are more likely to pay the highest marriage penalty, which occurs when total household income is split equally between the two spouses.

Although wage discrimination penalizes black families, it benefits white families. White men are more likely than black men to earn an income on which their families can live. This allows white women the opportunity to remain at home and gives the opportunity for the couple to enjoy untaxed imputed income. Wage discrimination, then, helps to explain the differing rates of contribution to total household income between black and white married women. It also helps to explain the differing labor participation rates of black and white married women. Given white men's wages, the low wages of white women relative to those of white men, and the tax treatment of imputed income, white married women's decisions to work outside the home are less likely to be related to economic survival than to personal preference. Thus, marriage acts to reduce the labor force participation rates of white women, but not of black women.

Although the impact of the marriage penalty is felt most severely by black families, as more white families have second earners in the labor force, it will become a problem for white families as well. Given the decreased labor participation rates of white men and the fact that white women are being employed in areas that once were the province only of white men, white families are more likely to have two wage earners. That means that in the foreseeable future more white families may suffer the marriage penalty.

Head of Household Rate Differences Based upon Race

Married-couple families are much more economically prosperous than families headed by women. As a result, the increasing number of black single-parent households has caused the black poverty rates to soar. Although one study found that 55% of families headed by white women were either poor or very poor, it also found that 80% of families headed by black women were in poverty. That percentage for black women takes on special significance because only 36% of black women were in married-couple households. Thus, a substantial number of black women are heads of household. These statistics intensify the urgency for scrutinizing federal income tax laws that penalize black women for marrying.

The experience of black women in the labor market has been different from that of white women and must be viewed separately. Black female heads of household experience extreme poverty in part because of the wage discrimination that black women face. Unlike black women, white women have entered middle-income jobs, and during the 1980s, they were more successful than black women in breaking the glass ceiling. Most of black women's gains in the employment sector have come in low-wage jobs, which helps to account for the disproportionate number of black female heads of household in poverty. Black women have been concentrated in a few occupations with a very narrow wage range. Even controlling for the effects of education, black women suffer wage discrimination in areas where white women do not.

ENDING THE MARRIAGE BONUS/PENALTY

Because the marriage penalty occurs whenever there is a progressive tax system that permits joint filing, there are three ways to eliminate the marriage bonus/penalty. The first is by abolishing the progressive tax system and replacing it with a flat tax system. Under a flat tax, neither spouse would be penalized by paying taxes at a higher rate than the other. The second is through abolishing the joint return. If tax returns were calculated for everyone on a single return basis, there would be no marriage bonus/penalty because liability for an individual taxpayer would not change upon her decision to marry.

A third and less drastic alternative would be to target the marriage penalty relief better to those who pay the highest penalty, namely to those couples whose incomes are equal. In addition, some consideration should be given to eliminating the marriage bonus, at least for couples in high-income brackets. By eliminating or reducing the marriage bonus/penalty, the tax law would be acknowledging and counteracting marketplace wage discrimination based on gender and race. In contrast, to leave the marriage bonus/penalty intact serves to exacerbate marketplace wage discrimination. Understood from this perspective, the choice is clear.

Tax and Race: The Impact on Asian Americans

MYLINH UY[1]

The literature on the effect of tax laws on minorities overwhelmingly looks at one minority group: blacks. In this context, "'race' means, quintessentially, African American,"[2] a manifestation of what has been called the "black–white paradigm" or the "black–white binary."[3] Because race is such a complex issue, it is easier to identify the black experience as *the* minority experience. "The risk [of this narrow identification] is that non-black minority groups, not fitting into the dominant society's idea of race in America, become marginalized, invisible, foreign, un-American."[4] In the context of tax law, blacks appear the most negatively affected, especially within the context of their economic reality. In addition, given the de facto segregation of black and white lives, it is understandable that a system developed almost a hundred years ago by wealthy white men would benefit whites more than blacks. When tax and economics are so intermingled, Asian Americans appear too well off to be negatively impacted by the tax laws. Asian American households earn[ed] an average annual salary of $53,635 in 2001, compared to a white household's $46,305. But the empirical data may not always provide a complete picture into the economic situation of Asian Americans. When the data is examined a little closer, the factors that support a disparate impact on blacks could also support a disparate impact on Asian Americans.

In the mid-1800s, Asians began to immigrate in substantial numbers to the United States. Not long after that, taxes were used against them to subordinate and expel them. A study of Asian American history reveals a long legacy of racism from the white mainstream society. The lynching of Chinese in California in the 1800s, the Japanese internment camps, and the murder of Vincent Chin comprise only a small part of the story. In 1988, the Civil Rights Commission reported that Asian Americans still suffer from "a variety of anti-Asian activities" and that the subject of anti-Asian discrimination still merited serious attention.[5] The racism

---

[1] Reprinted by permission of the Regents of the University of California from 11 *Asian Law Journal* 117 (2004). Copyright 2004 by the Regents of the University of California.
[2] RICHARD DELGADO & JEAN STEFANCIC, CRITICAL RACE THEORY: AN INTRODUCTION 67 (2001).
[3] *Id.* at 67–68.
[4] *Id.* at 70.
[5] U.S. COMM'N ON CIVIL RIGHTS, THE ECONOMIC STATUS OF AMERICANS OF ASIAN DESCENT: AN EXPLORATORY INVESTIGATION 15 (1988).

dealt with by Asian Americans, however, cannot be perfectly analogized to the black experience. Unfortunately, the model minority myth obscures the problems Asian Americans face in our society. As a result, Asian Americans' needs and realities are often ignored.

DEBUNKING THE MODEL MINORITY MYTH (AGAIN)

The model minority myth paints a picture of Asian American economic success. The stereotype of the model minority emerged in the 1960s.

The model minority myth is dangerous in a number of ways. First, by assuming group success, the model minority myth masks the great disparity amongst Asian American ethnic groups. The Civil Rights Commission reported in 1990 that Laotians, Hmong, Cambodians, and Vietnamese have poverty rates of 67.2%, 65.5%, 46.9%, and 33.5%, respectively. Only two groups of Asian Americans, Filipinos and Japanese, have poverty rates below the national average, 6.2% and 4.2%, respectively. The needs of recent Southeast Asian refugees are ignored because they are viewed on the same footing as third- or fourth-generation Japanese or Chinese Americans. "Thinking Asian Americans have succeeded, government officials have sometimes denied funding for social service programs designed to help Asian Americans learn English and find employment."[6] Some scholars have even argued that accepting the model minority myth is a form of participation in the oppression of Asian Americans.

The model minority myth also hurts other minorities. This myth's persistence is displayed in the Census's nonreporting of Asian American unemployment rates and median weekly income levels, making it difficult to assess their economic position in relation to other races. This misleadingly creates the belief that since Asian Americans have succeeded on their own, then other minority groups such as blacks and Latinos should be able to do it, too. Such rhetoric condones the subordination of other groups while simultaneously creating racial tensions between Asian Americans and other minorities. The masked success of Asian Americans supposedly serves as proof that the social and economic problems faced by other minority groups have nothing to do with race. But "the reality is that many Asian Americans, particularly recent immigrants, are neither economically well-off nor politically empowered."[7]

When other factors are examined, it is clear that the model minority myth is truly a myth. First, reliance on median family income as evidence that Asian Americans suffer no discrimination in the workforce is misleading. In actuality, because Asian American families have more workers per household than do white families, their median family income is on average higher. The Civil Rights Commission notes that when family income is adjusted for family size, the economic status of foreign-born Japanese and Indian families equals that of native-born whites, but that the economic status of foreign-born Chinese, Filipino, Korean, and Vietnamese

---

[6] Robert S. Chang, *Toward an Asian American Legal Scholarship: Critical Race Theory, Post-Structuralism, and Narrative Space*, 81 CAL. L. REV. 1241, 1261 (1993).

[7] *Id.* at 1308.

families fall[s] behind. Median family income, therefore, is not an accurate measure of how well Asian Americans are doing. Compounding the problem with the empirical data is the fact that Asian families are also more likely to have nonworking relatives living with the nuclear family.

In addition, average income levels of Asian Americans are skewed by the inclusion of the income of Asians who are not Americans. Japanese businessmen, for example, spend several years in the United States doing business, and their upper-management salaries are added to the average Asian American income. This increases Asian Americans' average income and hides the economic reality of most Asian Americans.

The high academic achievement of Asian Americans is another component of the model minority myth. A number of factors, however, explain this "phenomenon" of Asian American academic achievement. University of Hawaii sociology professor Herbert Barringer found that native-born Asian Americans make less than native-born whites, and possibly less than foreign-born whites. The fact that Asian Americans are better educated yet earn less than their white American counterparts undermines the model minority myth. In fact, the studies demonstrate that Asian Americans are forced to overcompensate in their education, because they receive a lower return on their educational investment.

In addition, cultural capital is a big reason for Asian American academic achievement. A study of high-achieving Asian Americans found that 85% had fathers with graduate degrees, 71% with doctorate degrees, and 21% had mothers with doctorate degrees. The idea that overachieving is inherently an Asian trait is a fallacy, because the immigrants from Asia to the United States may not necessarily be representative of all Asians. Immigration by nature is self-selective. Except for the recent refugees from Southeast Asia, the Asian immigrants had to be able to afford to come to the United States, or they came to fill an occupation that American workers could not fill. More than 50% of the professional immigrants to the United States are Asian. Thus, when statistics lump together those who immigrate from a higher economic status with Southeast Asian refugees into a group called "Asian American," the emerging numbers are not representative of either group.

PROBLEMS WITH EMPIRICAL DATA: HOW THE TAX SYSTEM REALLY AFFECTS ASIAN AMERICANS

Asian American Wages and Employment

In 2001, the Census Bureau reported that Asian American families had a median annual income of $53,635 but that Asian American income per household member was $24,933. This falls below the average income for white household members, which is at $25,751. As mentioned earlier, these figures may not take into account that a number of Asian American women work for no pay in a family-owned business, or that Asian Americans often work below their level of educational achievement. In addition, the figure does not reflect the economic reality of many subgroups that fall under "Asian American." A large percentage of Southeast Asian groups and recent immigrants live below the poverty line.

For both native- and foreign-born Asian Americans, the earnings of other relatives make up a larger fraction of Asian American family income than of white family income. In native-born Chinese, Filipino, Japanese, and Korean families, family members other than the husband generate more than 30% of the household income. Compare this to native-born white families, where that number is 25%. In foreign-born Filipino, Vietnamese, and Chinese families, 43%, 37%, and 32% of family income, respectively, come from the combined labor income of wives, children, and other relatives. In foreign-born white families, this number is only 23%. This data indicates that more family members must work to make up Asian American household income.

In addition, Asian Americans tend to live in areas of the country that have higher wages and higher costs of living. The income in these areas would be higher, such that their average family income compared to the national average appears higher. Many scholars argue that when one controls for geographic location, Asian American wages do not look that much better than black or Latino wages. In California, for example, Korean men earn 82% of the income of white men, Chinese men 68%, and Filipino men 62%. According to the Civil Rights Commission, if Asian Americans and whites shared the same regional distribution, the relative average family incomes for most Asian groups would be slightly lower. According to another study, Asian American men make 10[%] to 17% less than white men and Asian American women make as much as 40% less than white women. Therefore, a simple statistical comparison does not reflect the economic reality of Asian Americans.

Asian Americans are also more likely than whites to be self-employed. "Self-employed individuals with the same income as corporate employees tend to put in longer hours, with fewer benefits and increased risks of bankruptcy and other setbacks."[8] Self-employed individuals must pay for their own medical insurance while many employers offer this benefit to their employees. They also must cover the costs of doing business that individuals working for a company do not have to pay, such as other insurance and self-employment taxes. The empirical data may not take into account these expenses that a self-employed individual must account for, since they simply report income.

In addition, the empirical data masks the fact that Asian Americans do face workplace discrimination. In 1992, the United States Civil Rights Commission released a report on the civil rights issues facing Asian Americans. The report found that all Asian Americans suffered some level of employment discrimination such as accent or language discrimination, discrimination caused by immigration control laws, and "artificial barriers" preventing Asian Americans from rising to management positions. Indeed, some believe that "Asian professionals face the worst promotional opportunities of all groups."[9]

Therefore, when Asian American household income is broken down, each family member makes less than what an individual in a white household makes.

---

[8] *See* Frank H. Wu, Yellow: Race in America Beyond Black and White 54 (2002).

[9] *See* U.S. Comm'n on Civil Rights, Civil Rights Issues Facing Asian Americans in the 1990s, at 133 (1992).

In addition, the income of the Asian household members makes up a larger percentage of Asian American household income. Accepting the fact that Asian Americans often make less than whites and that they do face workplace discrimination, they face some of the same hurdles other minorities face in achieving racial equality. These same hurdles may be reflected in the ways Asian Americans are taxed and in the tax benefits they receive.

Home Ownership and Family Structure

Asian American home ownership is not at all near the level of white home ownership. According to a Harvard University study, approximately 53.9% [of] Asian Americans and "others" owned their homes in 2002, compared to 74.7% of whites. The home-ownership rate for blacks was 48.9% and 47.4% for Latinos. Despite the relatively large disparity between whites and the other minority groups, home-ownership rates had increased for all groups, except for Asians in 2002. In fact, the rate for Asians held constant for the last three years while the rate for all other races continued to steadily climb.

That other minority groups increased in their rate of home ownership may be explained by the opportunities they receive in relation to Asian Americans. According to an article on home ownership in Colorado, except for Asian Americans, minority home ownership increased between 1990 and 2000. The article reports that the national mortgage lending company, Fannie Mae, encourages minority home ownership through programs such as continuing education for realtors on how to better serve minority home buyers. The article also reports that the Colorado Housing and Finance Authority, an agency offering down payment and loan assistance, is targeting blacks and Latinos to help increase rates of home ownership in these communities. Given the data on Asian American home ownership, it is surprising that the agency is not targeting Asian Americans as well.

In 2000, Asian Americans' houses had the highest average value, $199,300, more than 50% above the national average. Homes owned by whites had an average value of $123,400, blacks $80,600, and Hispanics $105,600. As mentioned earlier, Asian Americans may own homes with a higher average value because these homes are located in areas of the country where cost of living is higher. For instance, 45% of the Asian households are located in Hawaii or California where average housing prices are the highest in the nation.

Additionally, the higher than average home values for Asian Americans may not be a reflection of their individual ability to buy larger homes but reflective of the fact that they have more family members contributing to the cost of [the] home. At the same time, the inclusion of extended families in an Asian American household may necessitate larger homes. Therefore, factors such as geography and family structure may account for the high average cost of Asian American homes. In turn, these factors demonstrate how numerically, [fewer] Asian Americans benefit from the tax incentives available for home owners.

Family structures informed by cultural differences may account for why Asian Americans are treated differently by the tax system. The tax system benefits nuclear family households where one adult works outside of the home and the other stays at home. This poses problems when extended families live together in one household in Asian American families, for [fewer] Asian Americans are able to take advantage of the tax benefits allowed by the Code. For example, if two sibling families bought a house and lived in one household with their parents, only one of these siblings would take advantage of the home mortgage interest deduction, property tax deduction, or the favorable treatment of gains on that house if they were to sell it.

The Marriage Penalty and Marriage Bonus

Both spouses of the Asian American couple are more likely to work outside of the home, therefore making their economic reality more comparable to black couples. As noted earlier, more Asian American women than white women must work, because the males in their family earn such low wages. Asian American wives are the largest contributor to family incomes next to their husbands, and their earnings make up a larger part of family income than in white families. This suggests that Asian Americans may be in the same position as African Americans in suffering the marriage penalty more often than whites.

In addition, the tax structure does not account for other family members that the working couple may be supporting. Extended family may not always fall into the Code's definition of who a "dependent" could be, further eliminating potential deductions available for Asian American families.

Immigration

An issue affecting a large number of Asian Americans and Latinos is immigration. Under the federal tax system, even if someone does not qualify to be a resident or citizen under immigration laws, [he or she] can be considered a resident for tax purposes. The federal tax law applies the "substantial presence" test, which basically asks whether the taxpayer has been present in the United States for 183 days in the tax year. If the answer is yes, the taxpayer must file a [Form] 1040, just as a citizen or resident immigrant would. This "resident" for tax purposes does not enjoy any of the benefits that may come with full citizenship or resident immigrant status but must pay taxes just the same. Even worse, the person cannot vote, and therefore has no voice in the democratic process.

CONCLUSION

The current scholarship in critical tax theory argues that the tax system disparately affects blacks for several reasons. First, the tax laws were created by a legislature that is generally wealthy, white, and male. Second, due to the wage disparities between blacks and whites, the former are less often able to take advantage of the tax incentives favoring those who make more money and have more savings.

This [article] delineated several reasons for the disparate tax effects on Asian Americans: (1) Very few Asian Americans make up the legislature. Therefore, for the same reason that tax laws benefit underrepresented blacks less than whites, these same tax laws also benefit Asian Americans less. (2) While the empirical data appears to indicate that Asian Americans are economically well off, in reality, there still exists a wage disparity between Asian Americans and whites. Related is the fact that Asian Americans suffer from workplace discrimination. Both factors translate into less favorable tax treatment for Asian Americans. (3) Asian American families form households that differ from their white counterparts, resulting in less available tax benefits for Asian Americans.

Race and Equality Across the Law School Curriculum: The Law of Tax Exemption

DAVID A. BRENNEN[1]

What is the relevance of race to tax law? The race issues are apparent when one studies a subject like constitutional law. The Constitution concerns itself explicitly with such matters as defining rights of citizenship, allocating powers of government, and determining rights with respect to property. Given the history of our country – with slavery followed by periods of de jure and de facto racial discrimination – these constitutional law matters obviously must have racial dimensions.

Tax law, however, does not generally concern itself explicitly with matters of race. Tax law is often thought of as completely race neutral in that its rules do not explicitly hinge tax consequences on matters related to race. In fact, even though the Code refers to discrimination based on nonrace factors twenty-six times, it expressly refers to the concept of racial discrimination only twice, once with regard to racial discrimination by tax-exempt social clubs and once with regard to the foreign tax credit for taxpayers that participate in international boycotts that promote racial discrimination. But despite the paucity of express racial references in the Code itself, there are a myriad of implicit racial issues in tax law that mostly concern the federal tax imposed on individual income or wages. One well-known example is the racial bias inherent in the marriage penalty as a result of a combination of tax law rules and the lingering effects of slavery and postslavery discrimination against blacks. Though teachers of tax law are often quite familiar with this and with similar race issues related to the federal taxes imposed on individual income and wages, few are as familiar with the many ways in which race affects our understanding of tax laws that apply to organizations, particularly tax-exempt nonprofit organizations. This article focuses exclusively on the law of tax exemption (familiarly known as "tax exempt law"), attempting to explain many of the instances in which race is relevant to an understanding of this growing area of legal study.

RACE ISSUES IN TAX EXEMPT LAW

Tax exempt law is a subfield of tax law that focuses on the exemption from the federal income tax for corporations, trusts, and other entities (as opposed to individuals)

[1] Reprinted by permission from 54 *Journal of Legal Education* 336 (2004).

that comply with certain statutory requirements. Tax-exempt organizations typically are charitable organizations, social welfare organizations, labor organizations, business leagues, social clubs, various beneficiary associations, certain insurance companies, cemetery companies, credit unions, employee benefit plans, and many more. The common link is that all of these organizations are not required to pay federal income tax so long as they abide by the relevant tax exemption rules. Tax exempt law consists of laws that enable tax-exempt organizations to maintain their nontaxable (i.e., tax-exempt) status. Instead of focusing so much on the relative fairness (or unfairness) of a particular tax benefit as it affects blacks and whites, the race bias focus in tax exempt law is more on the justness (or unjustness) – with regard to blacks – of the statutory requirements for tax exemption.

This different focus in tax exempt law allows for a rich jurisprudential analysis of tax law. Indeed, one of the primary advantages of conducting an activity through a tax-exempt organization is that such activity automatically receives public and governmental financial support through tax expenditures. Scholars and judges disagree about the constitutional implications of government financial support by means of tax expenditures (tax benefits) as opposed to direct expenditures (direct outlays of cash). But few could deny that many tax-exempt organizations receive a financial benefit from the government as a direct result of their tax-exempt status. The indirect financial support from government means that tax-exempt organizations often avoid many of the political aspects that accompany direct government spending. The uniqueness of tax exempt law issues, as compared to many issues that arise in individual income tax law for example, provides an opportunity to analyze tax exempt law and ask: how should the government allow tax-exempt organizations to use this indirect, but admittedly financial, government/public benefit?

RACIAL DISCRIMINATION BY TAX-EXEMPT CHARITIES

Of the many types of income tax exemptions described in the Code, by far the most cherished is the tax exemption allowed for charitable organizations. A charitable organization must abide by many obligations to secure and maintain its tax-exempt status. The obligations stem directly from the tax law provision that authorizes the tax exemption for organizations performing charitable activities. This statutory requirement imposes several affirmative and negative obligations on tax-exempt charitable organizations. Affirmatively, a tax-exempt charity must show that it is both organized and operated primarily for a proper charitable purpose. Negatively, a tax-exempt charity must avoid private inurement, cannot receive more than an insubstantial amount of private benefit, cannot engage in more than an insubstantial amount of legislative lobbying, and is prohibited from engaging in any political campaign activity.

The charitable purpose requirement is at the heart of the charitable tax exemption, imposing an obligation on the charity to have a special type of mission focus as opposed to a profit focus. The mission is distinctly different from the mutual-benefit mission of the many noncharitable tax-exempt organizations. The mission that constitutes a proper purpose for the charitable tax exemption must be what is collectively referred to as a *charitable* purpose. Some of these purposes are specifically delineated in the statute that authorizes the charitable tax exemption – religious and educational, for example. But many charitable purposes have to be gleaned from the statute by either the IRS or reviewing courts.

A key question for the charitable tax exemption is how to determine whether a particular purpose is "charitable" or not. One instance in which the charitable purpose requirement can become conceptually difficult is when a proposed charitable purpose violates the public policy doctrine – a doctrine adopted by the Supreme Court and now incorporated into tax-exempt-charity law. Pursuant to the public policy doctrine an organization that is otherwise "charitable" will not be treated as such if it engages in acts that contravene "clear" or "established" public policy. The prototypical example of an instance in which the public policy doctrine would defeat charitable status is racial discrimination against blacks. Accordingly, the Supreme Court affirmed the IRS revocation of charitable status for Bob Jones University, a nonprofit religious school that discriminated against blacks in its admission policies.

Administering the public policy doctrine, as applied to racial preferences against blacks, is not problematic. But the doctrine becomes much more difficult to administer in other instances. For example, should the public policy doctrine be applied in such a way as to deny charitable status to organizations that make racial preferences in the context of affirmative action? Though the Supreme Court recently ruled that affirmative action may be constitutional if race is one of many factors considered by a state actor, it also ruled that affirmative action is unconstitutional if race is a deciding factor.

One approach to the issue of racial discrimination by tax-exempt charities might be to say that the public policy doctrine prohibits all racial preferences whether for affirmative action purposes or not. But how would this analysis be altered if the racial preference issue were addressed by a hypothetical black Congress? Asked differently, might a black perspective on this issue yield a different legal result? A black perspective might suggest that, because race-based affirmative action aimed at benefiting society is meaningfully different from invidious racial discrimination against blacks, tax-exempt charities should be permitted to engage in affirmative action even in the face of the public policy doctrine.

Perhaps one reason for this potential issue respecting the legality of affirmative action by tax-exempt charities is the manner in which the tax law rule aimed at combating discrimination – the public policy doctrine – was adopted by the Supreme Court in *Bob Jones University v. United States*.[2] The only tax law issue involved in the case was whether a tax-exempt charity's discrimination against black people necessitated denial of the benefits that flow from the charitable tax exemption. But instead of creating a rule specific to invidious racial discrimination, the Court in *Bob Jones University* adopted a broad neutral-looking rule that, on its face and in a manner consistent with the entire Code, does not even mention "race" or "discrimination." That is, it adopted a facially neutral tax law rule that could conceivably apply to any number of circumstances, some having to do with race

---

[2] [461 U.S. 574 (1983). – Eds.]

and some having nothing at all to do with race. In other words, instead of expressly attempting to include the "black perspective and experiences" of marginalized applicants to Bob Jones University in tax exempt law, the public policy doctrine masks the racial dimensions of this area of law through adoption of an *apparently* neutral tax law rule – the public policy doctrine.

RACIAL DISCRIMINATION BY NONCHARITABLE TAX-EXEMPT ORGANIZATIONS

Another example of an attempted masking of race in tax exempt law is Congress's adoption of a rule prohibiting racial discrimination by tax-exempt social clubs, which do not enjoy many of the "special" privileges bestowed upon tax-exempt charities. Tax-exempt social clubs are not eligible to receive tax-deductible contributions, nor are they entitled to the many state and nontax federal benefits reserved solely for tax-exempt charities. Nevertheless, tax-exempt social clubs are entitled to federal exemption from the income tax – so long as they comply with the statutory requirements contained in the portions of the tax exemption law specifically applicable to them.

A tax-exempt social club is a club "organized for pleasure, recreation, and other nonprofitable purposes, substantially all of the activities of which are for such purposes and no part of the net earnings of which inures to the benefit of any private shareholder."[3] Many private golf and tennis clubs are organized as tax-exempt social clubs so long as they comply with this definition. Many of these clubs have been known to discriminate against women and minorities, including blacks, and such discrimination continues even today. Responding to racial discrimination at social clubs, Congress enacted a tax law provision in 1976 aimed at prohibiting such invidious acts.

Though this nondiscrimination provision is certainly a step in the right direction toward prohibiting discrimination by tax-exempt social clubs, it clearly lacks a black perspective. From a black perspective, one might wonder why this provision applies only to social clubs. Does this mean that racial discrimination by other tax-exempt organizations is permissible for tax law purposes? Although the public policy doctrine announced by the Supreme Court in *Bob Jones University v. United States* clearly prohibits racial discrimination by tax-exempt charities, that doctrine applies *only* to tax-exempt charities. The *Bob Jones University* public policy doctrine does not apply to the many other tax-exempt organizations described in the tax exemption statute.

Aside from the limited applicability of the nondiscrimination rule to tax-exempt organizations other than social clubs, another race issue is why the rule, at least textually, is so restrictive. Indeed, the textual expression of the rule applies only to discrimination contained in a tax-exempt social club's written documents (the charter, bylaws, or other governing instrument, or any written policy statement). Does this mean that official and authorized discrimination by words or actions of key members of a tax-exempt social club cannot cause the organization to

---

[3] I.R.C. § 501(c)(7).

lose its federal tax exemption? This limited applicability to written documents is very different from the much broader public policy rule for tax-exempt charities, which presumably seeks out discrimination wherever it exists. A hypothetical Black Congress today (or even in 1976 for that matter) would most certainly adopt a statute very different from the one actually adopted as a nondiscrimination rule for tax-exempt social clubs. A statute enacted by blacks would likely address discrimination by the many other categories of noncharitable tax-exempt organizations besides social clubs and would likely address discrimination in various forms, whether reflected expressly in written documents or not.

RACIAL DIVERSITY ON TAX-EXEMPT CHARITIES' BOARDS

Another area of tax exempt law that could be influenced by a critical race perspective concerns the composition of the board of directors of a tax-exempt charitable organization. Steven Ramirez's article on federal corporate law reform efforts aimed at lessening the likelihood of corporate scandals like those at the start of the millennium posits that a racially diverse board of directors would make such scandals less frequent. According to Ramirez, cultural and racial diversity on corporate boards "could enhance small group decision-making processes and diminish the inclination of small groups to devolve into a groupthink approach to issues."[4] He explains that groupthink causes small groups, like boards of directors, to mindlessly adhere to group norms and fail to challenge or question group decisions.

Federal tax law does not contain any express provisions concerning laws generally applicable to boards of directors of tax-exempt organizations – a matter left primarily to state law. But tax exempt law does require that the organizational structure of a tax-exempt organization be such that the organization is driven to accomplish its tax-exempt mission. This requirement is most prevalent with respect to tax-exempt charitable organizations. Two major concerns regarding the structure of tax-exempt boards that make tax exempt law open to a racial analysis are the requirement that board members avoid reaping improper financial benefits from the organization and the requirement that the board represent a broad cross-section of the community the organization serves.

Federal tax law prohibits tax-exempt charities' board members from receiving organizational profits except as beneficiaries or as fair compensation for products or services delivered to the charity by, or on behalf of, the particular board member. A board must constantly ensure that all transfers of money or property between the organization and a board member are consistent with this prohibition on improper private benefits. Ramirez's article on racial diversity's tendency to lessen the occurrence of groupthink on corporate boards suggests that a racially diverse tax-exempt charitable board would be less likely to engage in prohibited private benefit transactions. The idea is that a more diverse board creates a culture of scrutiny that encourages board members to speak out whenever improper activities

---

[4] Steven A. Ramirez, *A Flaw in the Sarbanes-Oxley Reform: Can Diversity in the Boardroom Quell Corporate Corruption?*, 77 ST. JOHN'S L. REV. 837, 839 (2003).

occur. Accordingly, while racial diversity does not guarantee that improper private benefits will not pass from the tax-exempt charity to individual board members, it might lessen the likelihood of such improper deals.

Tax exempt law sometimes requires that a tax-exempt charity's board of directors represent a broad cross-section of the community served by the charity. This requirement is most exemplified in the context of the private foundation rules applicable to tax-exempt charitable organizations. Unless a charity serves certain educational, religious, medical, public safety, or governmental purposes, it must demonstrate that it receives substantial financial support from a wide array of public sources to avoid private foundation status. To satisfy the substantial financial support requirement, a tax-exempt charity must show either that it receives more than one-third of its support from a variety of public sources or that it receives more than 10% of its support from these sources and satisfies other factors. Among the other factors is that the board of directors represents a broad cross-section of the community.

Because it does not specifically state that racial diversity is required (or even contemplated) with respect to either the rules that limit private benefits or those that require a charity board to represent a broad [cross-]section of the community, tax exempt law presents an opportunity to consider race. We might ask: To what extent might these two aspects of tax exempt law benefit from a race perspective? Should tax exempt law require, or at least urge, tax-exempt charities to have racially diverse boards in some cases? Further, should tax exempt law apply a racial diversity mandate for all tax-exempt organizations, not just tax-exempt charities?

OTHER AREAS THAT MIGHT BENEFIT FROM A BLACK PERSPECTIVE

There are many other possibilities to consider race in the context of tax exempt law. Broadly speaking, many of these other areas involve looking not so much at explicit notions of racial discrimination or racial diversity, but more generally at how different structures of law affect certain racial populations. For instance, religion is a big part of the black experience and has been since the time of slavery, so laws that affect tax-exempt black churches might have a special impact on the black community. Consider the rule that prohibits tax-exempt charities, including churches, from performing political campaign functions for political candidates. It is not uncommon for black churches to allow political candidates, especially those candidates who advocate the interests of black people in particular, to speak from the pulpit. Even though the no-political-activities prohibition is a neutral-looking provision, a black perspective on this rule might result in a different interpretation of it to reflect the particular interests of black people – or even result in a different rule.

Another example has to do with tax-exempt charities that engage in community development activities. A community development organization is a tax-exempt organization formed to develop areas of a community that are often blighted or otherwise subject to severe deterioration. Charitable tax exemption granted to community development organizations could present an opportunity to explore tax exempt law's ability to recognize the uniqueness of being black in America. For example, the IRS has historically limited the community development tax exemption to organizations that "relieve poverty, eliminate prejudice, reduce neighborhood tensions, *and* combat community deterioration."[5] A race analysis of this aspect of tax exempt law might ask whether the law should permit a community development organization to exist if its only objective is to "eliminate discrimination" in a particular area of a community?

* * *

Issues of race pervade American law – not just constitutional law, but all law. Many injustices – again, racial and nonracial – are explicit and apparent. Many other injustices, though, are hidden from plain view. As Jerome Culp has pointed out, racial injustices are often so well hidden that it takes a special type of "vision," indeed a special type of experience, to discover them. Though many steps toward exposing race bias in tax law have been taken, there is still much work to do. Here, as in other aspects of American life, we still have a long way to go in stamping out the vestiges of slavery. A critical race examination of tax exempt law will get us just that much closer to achieving this laudable social justice goal.

[5] Rev. Rul. 74-587, 1974-2 C.B. 162.

Race and Class Matters in Tax Policy

DOROTHY A. BROWN[1]

As President Bush recently acknowledged, Hurricane Katrina made visible the race and class divide in America. Many questions have been raised in the wake of this tragedy, and hopefully those questions will spark vigorous debates regarding racism and poverty in our country. One question that should be asked, but has rarely been, is what role does tax policy play in creating or exacerbating America's racial and class divide? As President Bush stated earlier this month, albeit in a very different context, "tax policy matters."

Low-income taxpayers are under attack. We recently learned that for the past five years, hundreds of thousands of low-income taxpayers have had their refunds frozen and labeled fraudulent, although almost two-thirds appear to have done nothing wrong. Beginning in 2004, the IRS now requires additional records [to] be submitted in addition to tax returns before 25,000 low-income taxpayers receive their refund. Low-income taxpayers are more likely to be audited than any other taxpayer group. Since 1998, the IRS has spent over $1 billion on audits of low-income taxpayer returns. No other taxpayers are subject to such scrutiny.

Each year 5,000,000 families are lifted out of poverty because they receive the low-income taxpayer credit. More children are lifted out of poverty as a result of the credit than any other governmental program.

Tax scholars who have recently written about low-income taxpayers often either ignore these facts, or assume they are the price to be paid for tax benefits for low-income taxpayers. Politicians routinely demonize low-income taxpayers by decrying all the "fraud" associated with the low-income tax credit.

Politicians are correct to a certain extent. There are errors associated with tax returns of low-income taxpayers. This is true regardless of whether the returns are completed by taxpayers or their paid tax return preparers. In addition, once the tax return is received by the IRS, the staff makes mistakes in processing the claims for a refund. Politicians argue that the error rate is due to fraud, and I argue it is due to complexity.

---

[1] Reprinted by permission from 107 *Columbia Law Review* 790 (2007).

To begin with, the IRS publication associated with the low-income taxpayer credit, Publication 596, is over *fifty* pages long with six separate worksheets. The credit's complexity also results in tax professionals preparing the majority of low-income taxpayer returns at an estimated cost of $1.75 billion annually.

Yet whenever there is an error found in a low-income taxpayer's return, politicians only suspect fraud and not complexity. Why is fraud so much easier for elected officials to believe? The answer lies in the political rhetoric surrounding the low-income tax credit.

THE TARGETING OF LOW-INCOME TAXPAYERS

Low-income taxpayers are eligible for the earned income tax credit (EITC). The EITC is only available for "earned income" such as wages. The EITC rewards work. The expansion of the EITC in the 1980s and 1990s increased employment among single low-income parents, especially single mothers. Numerous studies show that the growth in the EITC increased the labor-force participation of single parents. Expansions of the EITC have also led to large declines in the receipt of cash welfare assistance.

The EITC supplements the minimum wage. It takes a combination of the EITC, minimum wage, and food stamps to allow a family of four with a full-time minimum-wage worker to raise their standard of living to something approaching the poverty level. In order for the minimum wage to support a family of four with a standard of living above the poverty level, the minimum wage would have to be significantly increased from its current level. Given the anticipated outcry by employers at the doubling of the minimum wage, it's easy to understand perhaps why it is in their enlightened self-interest to support the [Food Stamp Program] and the EITC, which they do not directly pay for, as a means of subsidizing their workforce.

EITC taxpayers have been targeted because they are viewed as being the equivalent of welfare recipients. That perception in turn leads to a higher level of scrutiny than that faced by *any* other taxpayer group. First, numerous congressional hearings have been held, and General Accounting Office reports published, studying the high "error rates" associated with the EITC. Second, EITC taxpayers are audited more than *any* other taxpayer group. Third, a certain portion of EITC taxpayers are required to be precertified. In other words, filing their tax return is insufficient. They must file additional paperwork and affidavits to "certify" that their child qualifies them for the EITC months in advance of filing their returns or face delays in getting their refund far exceeding those most taxpayers experience.

WELFARE POLITICS: WHEN RACE AND CLASS COLLIDE

Welfare Is Viewed Through a Race and Class Lens

The American public strongly supports higher government spending levels for "almost every aspect of the welfare state" – except payments to the "undeserving poor."[2] The public generally supports aid to the poor, yet the overwhelming majority opposes welfare.

Welfare, however, is hard to define. It has been defined by identifying those characteristics of welfare that most antagonized its opponents leading to its repeal in 1996. It has also been defined as "cash benefits paid to the working-age, able-bodied poor."[3] Welfare is perceived to be filled with fraud, and any program that wants political support cannot be perceived as welfare. And any program that wants political support *must* emphasize work.

While policy debates about welfare appear to be race neutral, they are anything but. Welfare policy debates strongly cater to and reflect the racial views of the white majority. American opposition to welfare is due to the public perception that the typical welfare recipient is undeserving. They are undeserving because Americans believe that most welfare recipients are black and because Americans believe that blacks are not committed to working. "[R]acial stereotypes play a central role in generating opposition to welfare in America. In particular, the centuries-old stereotype of blacks as lazy remains credible for large numbers of white Americans."[4]

To bolster the claim that welfare is a code word for race, not all welfare is seen as welfare by members of Congress. Government subsidies that flow to predominantly white beneficiaries are not considered to constitute welfare.

Democratic Congress members tried to argue that payments to farmers under the Agricultural Market Transition Act (AMTA) constituted welfare. AMTA was discussed in Congress in 1996, the same year that radical changes in welfare were being enacted, which is why Congress members were making the analogy. Members of Congress who stated that AMTA payments were welfare were roundly criticized.

Low-Income Taxpayers Are Viewed Through a Race and Class Lens

Scholars recognize that welfare is "implicitly a raced issue."[5] Accordingly when politicians refer to anyone as a welfare recipient, they are playing the race card. This is what happened when members of Congress referred to the EITC as welfare.

Republican President Gerald Ford established the EITC in 1975. The legislative history provides that the credit is to "correspond roughly to the added burdens placed on workers by both employee and employer social security contributions."[6] The legislative history continues: "Because it will increase their after-tax earnings, the new credit, in effect, provides an added bonus or incentive for low-income people to work, and therefore, should be of importance in *inducing individuals with families receiving Federal assistance to support themselves.*"[7] In a later section,

---

[2] Martin Gilens, Why Americans Hate Welfare: Race, Media, and the Politics of Anti-poverty Policy 2 (1999).

[3] *Id.* at 1.

[4] *Id.* at 3.

[5] Naomi R. Cahn, *Representing Race Outside of Explicitly Racialized Contexts*, 95 Mich. L. Rev. 965, 966 (1997).

[6] S. Rep. No. 94-36, at 11 (1975).

[7] *Id.* (emphasis added).

the legislative history provides: "The committee believes, however, that the *most significant objective* of the provision should be to assist in encouraging people to obtain employment, reducing the unemployment rate and *reducing the welfare rolls*."[8]

The EITC was made a permanent part of the Code for two primary reasons. First, the EITC was designed to provide an incentive to choose work over welfare and to offset Social Security taxes which were perceived to be a work disincentive. Second, the EITC was designed to financially reward work so that the financial position of those who worked would be better than the financial position of those who remained on welfare.

Because the EITC is only provided for working taxpayers, EITC recipients should be included in the term "deserving poor." Over two-thirds of EITC claimants do not receive a net transfer payment; their EITC is used to offset their income, Social Security, and excise taxes. Accordingly, less than one-third receive their EITC as a transfer payment. Yet congressional statements turned EITC recipients into the "undeserving poor" by referring to them as "welfare recipients." Given the racial nature of welfare discourse, whenever EITC recipients are referred to as welfare recipients, the speaker is inviting opposition by the majority white population – and that is exactly what has occurred.

Thus, EITC recipients who receive payments only if they work receive "welfare," but farmers who receive payments even if they do not work do not receive "welfare." Farmers are insulted if they are referred to as welfare recipients, but hardworking low-income taxpayers are expected to accept the same insult. Farmers who do not have to work to receive government payments are hardworking, proud, and independent, while low-income taxpayers receive "public assistance." Farmers care about their children and their grandchildren, but EITC claimants do not.

INTEREST CONVERGENCE AND THE "SELLING" OF THE EITC

This section seeks to use critical race theory as a framework for ending the attack on low-income taxpayers. The EITC lifts many low-income workers out of poverty. As I have written elsewhere, economic rights should be the civil rights battleground of the twenty-first century. Professor Richard Delgado has also encouraged critical race theorists to spend more time addressing issues of race and class. To the extent that government policies are preventing low-income taxpayers from working their way out of poverty, those policies must be examined and changed.

Tax scholars who have written about the EITC have either ignored the impact the targeting of low-income taxpayers will have on the survival of the credit or have suggested that targeting low-income taxpayers is the price to be paid for the credit's survival. This section will show the harm that has been done to low-income taxpayers when scholars ignore race and class matters in tax policy.

Derrick Bell announced the interest-convergence principle over twenty-five years ago. It states that gains for blacks occur primarily when they coincide with gains for whites. As a result, one would predict that if the primary beneficiaries

---

[8] *Id.* at 33 (emphasis added).

Table 5.3. *EITC-eligible population by race*[9]

Race	Percent of EITC-eligible population
White, Non-Hispanic	54.0%
Black, Non-Hispanic	24.5%
Hispanic	17.9%
Other, Non-Hispanic	3.6%
Total	100.0%

of the EITC are black, white taxpayers and their elected representatives would not be inclined to fight to improve conditions affecting low-income taxpayers. In that instance, low-income taxpayers could only look forward to more targeting, perhaps 100% precertification if they were lucky, and outright repeal if they were not so lucky.

There is reason for optimism, however, because this section shows that the majority of EITC-eligible taxpayers are white and most blacks are not eligible for the credit. Therefore, the targeting of the EITC has missed most blacks and harmed a lot of low-income white taxpayers.

Targeting EITC Taxpayers Means Targeting White Taxpayers

Table 5.3 shows that more than half of EITC-eligible taxpayers are white, while less than one-quarter are black, and less than one-fifth are Latino.

Figure 5.1 shows that slightly more than 35% of blacks with children were ineligible for the EITC because they lacked earned income. Figure 5.1 also shows that a much smaller percentage (between 7% and 9%) of whites with children were ineligible because they too lacked earned income.

Figure 5.2 shows us that the majority of blacks and whites are ineligible for the EITC because they have too much income. Race is similarly a weak proxy for being eligible for the EITC. Figures 5.1 and 5.2 show us that the majority of blacks with children are ineligible for the EITC.

I believe the data just presented hold the key to changing the unfair targeting of EITC claimants. The racial composition of the EITC claimants must be widely disseminated to the public in order to change its perception. EITC claimants are hardworking, barely above the poverty line, and should not have a harder time claiming their tax benefits than their middle-income and wealthier counterparts.

When the white majority – and their elected officials – come to realize that over half of all EITC-eligible taxpayers are white, they will have more empathy for low-income taxpayers. In all likelihood they will find the harsh treatment received at the hands of the IRS and precertification to be unacceptable. Without some

[9] Dorothy A. Brown, *The Tax Treatment of Children: Separate but Unequal*, 54 EMORY L.J. 755, 823 (2005) (citing Jeffrey B. Liebman, *Who Are the Ineligible Earned Income Tax Credit Recipients?*, *in* MAKING WORK PAY: THE EARNED INCOME TAX CREDIT AND ITS IMPACT ON AMERICA'S FAMILIES 274, 286–87 (Bruce D. Meyer & Douglas Holtz-Eakin eds., 2001)).

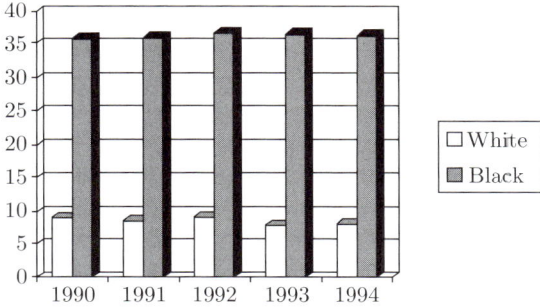

Figure 5.1. Percent ineligible because no earned income.[10]

Herculean effort to protect low-income taxpayers, EITC taxpayers will continue to be targeted. EITC claimants should not be treated differently than all other taxpayers, and I believe that the solution lies in acknowledging the stereotyping that is occurring and working to refute it.

Majority Will Support the EITC, Once It Is "Properly" Raced

This section builds upon the scholarship in the area of school finance reform, which found that white majority taxpayers supported redistributive legislation when they believed that it was primarily going to benefit white children, and welfare literature that shows less opposition to welfare when whites believe that whites are the primary beneficiaries – or put another way, when whites believe that blacks are not the primary beneficiaries.

Two studies provide support for the theory "that race does play a role in popular (and by presumption legislative) opposition to the equalization of resources."[11] The studies indicate that whites perceive school finance reform as primarily benefiting blacks and oppose the efforts, even though *in reality* blacks are not primarily benefiting. Minority school districts therefore do not fare as well as white school districts in school finance litigation. Predominantly white school districts have an easier time gaining legislative reforms than predominantly black school districts.

As a result, we would expect that if the white majority could be convinced of the fact that the primary beneficiaries of the EITC were white, they would support the elimination of the targeting of low-income taxpayers. One issue would be whether or not they could be convinced, since in the education funding context, the voters were ignoring the facts. Nevertheless, in states where whites are the primary beneficiaries of welfare, support for welfare is high. A remaining issue would be whether the white majority could be convinced to put aside long-held beliefs about blacks not being committed to hard work, given that there will still be blacks receiving the EITC.

[10] *Id.* at 825.

[11] James E. Ryan, *The Influence of Race in School Finance Reform*, 98 Mich. L. Rev. 432, 473 (1999).

Dorothy A. Brown

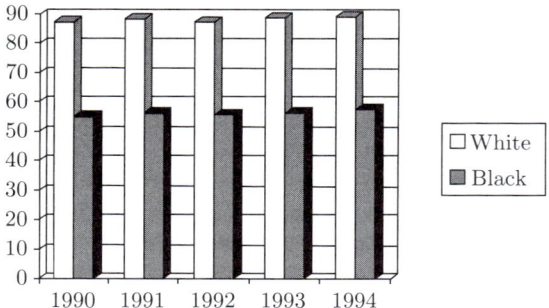

Figure 5.2. Percent ineligible because earned income was too high.[12]

EITC Will Be Reformed to Reduce Its Complexity

Assuming, however, that the hurdles just described can be overcome and the EITC is "raced" white, the stereotypes that apply to low-income taxpayers will dissipate. They will no longer be perceived as untrustworthy and in need of increased government scrutiny. As a result, the discourse surrounding the error rates should change. There should be widespread support to eliminate the complexity currently faced by low-income taxpayers and to worry less about the error rate.

An alternative explanation for the error rate, and one that is more likely to be accepted once the EITC has been properly "raced" in the minds of the public, is complexity. *The majority of EITC taxpayers use paid preparers.*

Low-income taxpayers, who need the EITC to stay out of poverty, have to pay to receive their EITC. One estimate of the costs paid to EITC preparers was $1.75 billion. The EITC is so complicated that mistakes are made regardless of whether the returns are completed by taxpayers, their return preparers, or IRS staff. The EITC's complexity places an undue burden on low-income taxpayers.

Former Treasury Secretary Paul O'Neill also said the IRS has fifty-four pages of instructions for claiming the tax [credit] "for the lowest-income people who struggle to make a living. We've given them an impossible Code to interact with and then we ridicule them" for not following it.[13] If low-income taxpayers were instead raced "white" it is possible that sympathy would take the place of ridicule. They could become "blameless" taxpayers and a move for eliminating the complexity of the EITC could begin.

CONCLUSION

In order for the EITC to remain politically viable, several things must occur. First, the empirical data concerning the racial demographics of who benefits from the EITC must be widely disseminated and "sold" to the American public. As a result,

[12] Brown *supra* note 9, at 826.
[13] *Hearing on the Treasury Before the Subcomm. on Treasury, Postal Serv., and General Government Appropriations of the H. Comm. on Appropriations*, 107th Cong. 672 (2002) (statement of Paul O'Neill, Secretary of the Treasury).

EITC taxpayers will not be viewed as receiving welfare. Second, the EITC must remain within the tax system because it reminds the American public that you have to work to receive it. Third, politicians and academics working to improve the lives of the working poor must stop referring to the EITC as welfare.

Finally, EITC taxpayers should not just accept the cards they're dealt. Low-income taxpayers are being singled out for harsh retaliatory treatment for being poor – and for being perceived to be black. Interest-convergence theory provides hope for improving the future prospects of all low-income workers and their families. Race *and* class matter in tax policy discourse.

The intersection of gender and taxation has been obscured by the operation of "neutral" tax principles. For example, the distinction between deductible "business" expenses and nondeductible "personal" expenses along with the general exemption from tax of so-called imputed income (i.e., income generated by performing labor for oneself or members of one's household) together establish a public/private divide in tax. Activities that take place on the public (i.e., market) side of this divide are acknowledged and valorized for tax purposes, while activities on the private (i.e., domestic) side of this divide are often deemed irrelevant – and, therefore, ignored – for tax purposes. These and other "neutral" principles have led the tax laws to exacerbate discrimination against, and reinforce stereotypes about, women in their roles as workers, caregivers, and wives.

Each of the first three contributions to this chapter brings the intersection of gender and taxation into sharper focus. To begin, in *Not Color- or Gender-Neutral: New Tax Treatment of Employment Discrimination Damages*, Karen Brown discusses the biases that led to the current tax rules that allow employers to deduct employment discrimination awards, but that require women who suffer gender-based employment discrimination to pay tax on those same awards. Turning "neutral" tax principles on their head, Brown makes the argument that employment discrimination awards should be excluded from gross income on the ground that they are merely a reimbursement of the otherwise deductible costs of producing income in a discriminatory workplace. At the same time, Brown demonstrates the interlocking nature of subordination by showing how these rules operate simultaneously along lines of gender, race, and class.

Next, Nancy Staudt argues in *Taxing Housework* that it is important to balance inquiries about how the tax laws deter women from entering the paid labor market with a consideration of how the tax laws can be used to affirm the value of women's labor in the home. Staudt argues that many women do not view labor in the market and labor in the home as mutually exclusive. Notwithstanding the tax incentives that favor women's remaining in the home, many women engage – and find value – in both types of labor. To reflect this reality, she advocates the taxation of women's unpaid labor in the home, both to demonstrate its value to society and to provide women with economic security in retirement – by providing them greater access to

Social Security, disability, and Medicare benefits, which are all tied to the payment of payroll taxes.

In the following selection, Wendy Gerzog explores the estate and gift tax treatment of qualified terminable interest property trusts ("QTIP" trusts, for short). In *The Marital Deduction QTIP Provisions: Illogical and Degrading to Women*, Gerzog explains that Congress's rationale for creating the QTIP trust – and for allowing property in the trust to escape tax – is nominally based on the idea that a married couple is a single economic unit that shares property. In view of this sharing (or so the theory goes), the couple should not be taxed until marital property leaves the marital unit. In practice, however, the QTIP trust is nothing more than a means for men to obtain a tax benefit without having to turn control of marital property over to their wives – out of a fear that the wives will not pass the couple's property to the children from that (or one of the husband's previous) marriage(s). Gerzog maintains that the paternalism of the QTIP provisions is degrading to women and argues that Congress should repeal those provisions and return to the pre-1981 rule that required husbands to give control of property to their wives in order to obtain a tax benefit.

This chapter closes with Marjorie Kornhauser's *A Taxing Woman: The Relationship of Feminist Scholarship to Tax*. In this piece, Kornhauser considers the question of when it is appropriate to apply the label "feminist" to a piece of tax scholarship. Is it only appropriate when the piece consciously applies feminist theory? If not, then is it appropriate when the piece employs a style associated with feminist legal scholars (e.g., narrative)? Or when the piece approaches a topic of concern to women from a viewpoint that is sympathetic to feminist thought? Or when the piece has a feminist outlook? In the end, Kornhauser suggests that this series of questions might be more profitably viewed as sketching a continuum of scholarship that blends tax and gender, with the most conscious uses of feminist legal theory at one end and those that examine gender issues but that do not fit any conceptualization of a feminist viewpoint at the other. Kornhauser further considers the potential positive and negative effects of applying the label "feminist" to tax scholarship as well as the value of engaging in work that adds a feminist viewpoint to tax scholarship and a tax viewpoint to feminist legal scholarship.

Not Color- or Gender-Neutral: New Tax Treatment of Employment Discrimination Damages

KAREN B. BROWN[1]

To support a host of tax giveaways offered as a palliative to small businesses required to pay a higher minimum wage, Congress eliminated a venerated Code provision that supported exclusion from gross income of damages received on account of race- and gender-based employment discrimination. Congress's 1996 amendment of § 104(a) erased seventy years of tax history by limiting tax-free damages awards to only those arising from a physical injury. The amended section reverses case law and administrative rulings of the IRS that interpreted the term "personal injury" broadly to include awards for defamation, alienation of affection, violation of an employee's civil rights, and certain types of employment discrimination claims.

This article explores the ways in which Congress's amendment of § 104(a) exacerbates race-, gender-, and worker-based biases already embedded in the rules regarding taxation of employment discrimination damages. Many tax scholars view the pre-amendment version of the section, which provided a tax exemption for physical and nonphysical personal injuries, as a departure from accepted notions of the ideal income tax base. These scholars find the historical tax exclusion for employment discrimination damages akin to a subsidy or tax expenditure, not justifiable as a structural component of a tax that operates on income net of the costs of earning or producing that income. However, other scholars defend the exclusion because it promotes social justice concerns. I side with the latter group but for somewhat different reasons. Tax-free treatment of employment discrimination damages furthers society's antidiscrimination goals by acknowledging the harm of job bias and reflects true income measurement for workers by acknowledging a setoff for investment in human capital.

NEW TAX TREATMENT OF DISCRIMINATION DAMAGE AWARDS

After the 1996 amendment, § 104(a)(2) provides an exclusion from gross income for "the amount of any damages (other than punitive damages) received (whether by suit or agreement and whether as lump sums or as periodic payments) on account of personal *physical* injuries or *physical* sickness." [Emphasis added.] All recoveries, except punitive damages, that flow from a physical injury or sickness

[1] Reprinted by permission from 7 *Southern California Review of Law & Women's Studies* 223 (1998).

are tax-free. The tax benefit is for a wide range of damages attributable to a physical injury, encompassing recoveries for medical costs, lost wages, emotional distress, and for those attributable to physical injury to another, as in the case of loss of consortium and wrongful death claims.

Amended § 104(a)(2) sets up a dichotomy in which recoveries for "physical" injuries are tax-free and recoveries for "nonphysical" personal injuries are not. While the distinction between "physical" and "nonphysical" has been poorly drawn, the amendment does target recoveries for employment discrimination and defamation. Even though plaintiffs can recover all damages (other than punitive ones) from a physical injury, including those for emotional distress, they cannot recover damages from "nonphysical" injuries without taxation. Apart from a limited exception for emotional distress recoveries, no damages from "nonphysical" injury may be excluded from gross income. Awards arising from the emotional distress caused by employment discrimination or defamation and similar harms deemed nonphysical are only tax-free if substantiated by medical care expenses.

The result is codification of the notion that an injury to the physical part of an individual is real and tangible and, hence, legally perceptible. While the term "physical" remains undefined, for most purposes, emotional injury is considered nonphysical. Harm to an individual in the form of employment discrimination is not cognizable because it is not real (imaginary, not traceable to a cause), and it is intangible (incapable of measurement). The separation of the physical and nonphysical spheres of the individual by establishment of categories of harm that generate tax-free or taxable damages operates to disadvantage the worker injured by on-the-job discrimination. While a worker might recover damages tax-free for the harm caused by a punch or a kick motivated by race- and/or gender-bias (if the worker incurs substantiated medical expenses), damages the worker might recover for equally serious conduct in the form of race- or gender-based discrimination that injures emotional well-being, the ability to perform a job, or one's dignity would be taxable.

Candid appraisal of the rationales underlying the development of § 104(a)(2) case law and Congress's recent amendment reveals the bias in tax law against race- and gender-based discrimination claims. The justification for taxation that states that no personal harm can result from employment discrimination is an illogical one dictated by the Supreme Court's adoption of a requirement that tax-free damages be tort-like. A tort-like standard guaranteed that damages recovered under statutes prohibiting employment discrimination would not qualify because many such statutes were enacted after acknowledgment of the unavailability of tort law remedies to redress these harms. Moreover, Congress did not provide the full complement of damages normally available in a legal action in order to make enactment of antidiscrimination statutes more palatable to protesters. Adoption of a "tort-like" test enabled courts to ignore the injuries caused by employers' actions by resorting to a measure of tax-free damages that could never include those arising from discrimination. That test ignored injury to workers by asking whether the worker could recover prescribed amounts instead of asking whether the worker was harmed.

The revenue maximizing rationale for taxing employment discrimination recoveries is also unconvincing. The law targeted awards to workers independently of revenue concerns. Protection of the fisc did not motivate the amendment of § 104(a)(2) because other revenue losers remained. After the amendment, recoveries for physical injuries to an individual remain tax-free even if the damages are awarded to third parties on a claim for loss of consortium. A recovery of lost wages during a period of incapacity remains tax-free even though some see an attenuated link between a physical injury and foregone wages. The retention of a tax advantage for this latter type of recovery, similar to back pay or front pay recoveries in employment discrimination cases, is a likely revenue loser. Frequently, the loss of future earning capacity is a significant element in the computation of damages awarded in physical injury and wrongful death cases. Another drain on the Treasury, the deduction allowed employers for payments to workers for violations of antidiscrimination statutes, escaped repeal.

RACE- AND GENDER-BASED BIASES IN TAX LAW MARGINALIZE THE HARM OF EMPLOYMENT DISCRIMINATION

Derived from a system built on principles of economic efficiency and horizontal and vertical equity, rules of taxation maintain the appearance of neutrality. Yet the differing impact of tax rules on women and people of color denotes implicit bias that must be dismantled. The bias present in the rules governing taxation of job discrimination damages can be traced to two antecedents.

First, adoption of a tort standard to determine taxability of recoveries led to results that burdened women and people of color compared to others who suffer injury. The incongruity of the use of a tort standard is especially poignant in job discrimination cases. Many scholars have written of the inadequacy of tort law in addressing harms caused by race and gender discrimination. In some cases, tort law fails to appreciate and provide compensation for the emotional harm to workers, because it privileges pecuniary damages. Tort law has failed to view the abusive conduct of employers who discriminate as "sufficiently outrageous to warrant imposition of liability."[2] Moreover, some view tort law's treatment of employment discrimination as isolated interactions between individuals as an inadequate response to what is really a public injury to workers. Yet the public law remedy of back pay to injured workers fails to adequately compensate for emotional, physical, and other harms.

The second cause of bias is marginalization of the harm of job discrimination. The privileging of what are termed "physical" harms, defined to exclude effects of employment discrimination, operates to subordinate the very real injuries experienced by those individuals denied equal opportunity to succeed on their jobs as a result of their gender or race. Amended § 104(a)(2), which limits tax-free recoveries to those arising from physical personal injury or sickness, denies the

---

[2] *See* Lucinda M. Finley, *A Break in the Silence: Including Women's Issues in a Torts Course*, 1 YALE J. L. & FEMINISM 41, 55 (1989).

harm caused by job discrimination by ignoring the physical and emotional effects of race and gender discrimination.

A recent study documented the pervasiveness of what it termed "ethnoviolence" in the workplace. The term "ethnoviolence" is used to describe "prejudiced behavior which causes, or is intended to cause, physical and psychological harm to its victims."[3] In a survey of a corporation in the mid-Atlantic region of the United States, the report noted that one of every five workers "had suffered major forms of discrimination, which included the denial of raises, promotions, or transfers and the differential granting of privileges."[4] Race and gender were the primary bases for the mistreatment.

The data collected in the study revealed the impact of the discrimination on the mental and physical health of the victims. The ethnoviolence not only affected job performance, but it also caused the workers to feel alienated from their jobs and from the people with whom they worked. There was a significant impact on the workers' outside social relationships, which resulted in problems with families and friends.

The report concluded that prejudice-based incidents in the workplace produce a considerable amount of psychological trauma, physical symptoms, and defensive behavioral changes, and notably more harm than to workers who were not victimized or those who were victimized for reasons not related to race or gender. Workers subjected to race- or gender-based prejudice reported depression, nervousness, anger, fear, and feelings of helplessness, as well as physical problems such as headaches, stomachaches, shortness of breath, weight loss or gain, anger, sleep problems, and unexplainable weakness or exhaustion.

When Congress changed the § 104(a)(2) tax benefit in 1996 to one for damages received on account of personal physical injuries or sickness, it targeted job discrimination recoveries for unfavorable treatment. That action reflected Congress's decision to discount the physical and psychological components of on-the-job discrimination. Despite its awareness of the emotional distress component of job discrimination, Congress provided no tax relief. The 1996 provision allowing an exclusion from gross income for reimbursements for medical care attributable to emotional distress arising from job discrimination does not recognize the significant physical and psychological harm of workplace bias. It merely provides a full deduction for medical care expenses.

TAXATION OF EMPLOYMENT DISCRIMINATION RECOVERIES DEVALUES WORKER PRODUCTION COSTS

Missing from jurisprudential developments regarding the tax status of employment discrimination damages and Congress's amendment of § 104(a)(2) to preclude tax-free treatment is an appreciation of the significant costs incurred by workers who

---

[3] *See* Howard J. Erlich et al., *The Traumatic Impact of Ethnoviolence, in* THE PRICE WE PAY: THE CASE AGAINST RACIST SPEECH, HATE PROPAGANDA AND PORNOGRAPHY 62, 62 (Laura Lederer & Richard Delgado eds., 1995).

[4] *Id.* at 71.

face gender and race discrimination on the job. Failure to acknowledge those costs has resulted in a rule that overtaxes job discrimination recoveries. Taxation of those recoveries denies the workers any offset for the costs of working in a discriminatory marketplace. For injured workers it achieves a distortion in an income tax system founded upon the principle that income producers may set off invested expenses against income generated.

Professors Stanley S. Surrey and Paul R. McDaniel have noted that the U.S. "normative concept of income based on the Schanz-Haig-Simons (S-H-S) economic definition of income is an increase in net economic wealth between two points of time plus consumption."[5] Expenditures incurred as a cost of earning or producing income are proper offsets to gross income to arrive at net taxable income because they do not amount to consumption. With certain exceptions, any other exclusions or offsets from income amount to tax expenditures, "special tax benefit[s] [that depart] from the normal structure," which may be lauded or condemned by tax policy analysts.[6]

Early interpretations upheld tax-free treatment of personal injury recoveries, which would include employment discrimination damages under some subsequent lines of authority, as part of the normative structure. Surrey and McDaniel's tax expenditure analysis did not conceive of the § 104(a)(2) exclusion from income as a tax expenditure. Current analysts have adopted that view. I too view the exclusion as consistent with the normative concept of net taxable income because, in the case of job discrimination damages, it respects worker production costs.

Workers may claim a deduction for most costs of engaging in employment. These are allowed as ordinary and necessary expenses of carrying on a trade or business. However, the 1986 Tax Reform Act sharply limited the benefit of this deduction by a provision that limited out-of-pocket expenses of workers to an amount exceeding a percentage of adjusted gross income. For most workers that limitation equals 2% of their salary. Given the limitation, routine expenses like union dues or office supplies obtained by the worker generally are not deductible. It is apparent that the system disadvantages workers because there is no comparable limit on the business expenses of employers.

The bias against workers is further demonstrated by employee tax benefits that depend upon employer control. The 2% floor on expenses described previously does not apply if the employer reimburses the worker. In addition, reimbursed expenses are excluded from the worker's gross income as a working condition fringe, obviating the need for an employee deduction. Connecting the reimbursed expense to performance of the worker's duties is not the measure of a tax-free benefit. Instead a working condition fringe is defined by the relationship of the expense to the employer's business.

The Code's failure to acknowledge the worker's role in employment for non-taxation of fringe benefits sheds some light on current taxation of discrimination recoveries which ignores the costs of working in a discriminatory environment.

---

[5] *See* STANLEY S. SURREY & PAUL R. MCDANIEL, TAX EXPENDITURES 4 (1985).
[6] *Id.*

Amended § 104(a)(2) denies those costs by taxing the worker's recovery. Under present law, taxing the recoveries results in overtaxation of workers because they are denied an offset for inputs into income-productive activity.

By contrast, employers are undertaxed. The cost incurred by the employer in discriminating, measured in part by the recoveries of workers who pursue their claims, are deductible. Given the strong antidiscrimination policies expressed in society and the law, a deduction for expenses connected to discriminatory conduct seems a reward. The Code ignores those policies and sanctions a deduction for any expense, short of a fine or penalty, related to business activity even if it violates strong public policy. The Code thus provides no incentive to treat all workers fairly.

Whether or not the employer's deduction is allowed, taxation of the employment discrimination recoveries marginalizes worker costs. The exclusion from gross income of gender- and race-based job discrimination awards urged here is equivalent to allowing a deduction to workers for the physical, emotional, and other costs of holding down a job in a discriminatory workplace. Treating the worker's recovery as both income and the measure of the expense of sustaining a job in which the worker is a victim of race- or gender-based discrimination would support a gross income exclusion because the otherwise taxable income would be exactly offset by an equivalent deduction.

A current example of this exists in the working condition fringe of § 132(d), which excludes from the worker's gross income a reimbursement of a business expense incurred on behalf of the employer. The worker reports no gross income because there is a "wash" – purported income from the reimbursement offset by a deduction of identical amount for the worker's payment. This logic supports an exclusion from gross income for gender- and race-based employment discrimination awards. For example, an award in the sum of $50,000 would be excluded from the worker's gross income as reimbursement of her costs of working in a discriminatory workplace. The exclusion would encompass all components of a job bias award, including punitive damages.

Two arguments support nontaxation of punitive damages awards that form part of a job bias recovery. First, these damages may be an essential element of compensation for harm to the worker. Discrimination statutes often fail to fully address injuries to workers by limiting the components of recovery. In some cases, even if full injury is redressed by statute, punitives are the most significant form of recompense because mitigating circumstances may reduce compensatory awards. In others, they may provide the only monetary evidence of a legal injury to the worker. For this reason, in employment discrimination matters, a conclusion that punitives are designed to rebuke the wrongdoer and are not linked to harm to the injured party is erroneous.

A belief that punitive damages serve only to punish wrongdoers would not compel taxation of these awards in job bias cases. Job bias recoveries should not be taxed partly because they compensate workers for the physical and emotional harms of holding down a job in a discriminatory workplace. Individualized harm to workers exists and must be acknowledged even in circumstances in which an antidiscrimination statute opts for a public remedy for the harm by imposing a monetary sanction – in the form of punitives – for conduct that injures society's interest in a fair workplace. Taxation of punitive damages in job bias cases would ignore harm to the individual worker, by denying that recompense to the public substitutes for a payment that should have gone to the worker on account of injury. Nontaxation of punitive damages would acknowledge that job bias harms workers as well as the public.

CONCLUSION

Workplace practices that encourage race and gender discrimination are unacceptable. The resulting harm to the physical (including emotional) well-being of workers and to their ability to properly perform duties impedes marketplace efficiency. Accordingly, society has a critical interest in securing a labor market in which all workers are accorded equal opportunity to produce and achieve. The public also has a stake in ensuring a workplace free of the harms that damage the lives of individual workers.

Anti-job bias statutes have acknowledged the harm to the marketplace, but limitations on job bias remedies demonstrate that they have failed to fully appreciate the serious injury to workers. Lawmakers (both legislators and the courts) skirt sensitive but critical issues concerning the validity and measure of damage to workers by emphasizing the public harm of discrimination. Skepticism about job bias allegations has permeated many arenas, including tax law. The 1996 amendment of § 104(a)(2) reinforces the disbelief in the validity of bias claims by removing employment discrimination recoveries from the purview of a statute designed to provide a tax offset for physical and emotional costs of injury. In this article, I expose the race-, gender- and worker-based biases that underpin that amendment and urge tax rules that recognize the considerable costs of workplace discrimination.

Taxing Housework

NANCY C. STAUDT[1]

Congress's failure to tax nonmarket activities has both distributional and behavioral consequences for women. Tax commentators have traditionally focused on the distributional effects of nontaxation. Many have argued that by declining to tax the value of household labor, Congress provides valuable tax benefits to families with stay-at-home spouses. These families obtain the value of household labor tax-free, while the same labor performed in the market is subject to taxation. The tax literature has traditionally viewed this unequal treatment as violating the long-standing and firm principle of tax neutrality. Despite this perceived unfairness, tax analysts have uniformly taken the position that administrative difficulties make taxation of nonmarket household labor impossible.

Recently, feminist tax scholars have begun to examine the behavioral incentive structure of the Code. While these scholars acknowledge the distributional effects of the Code, they focus on how the tax structure discourages women from working in the waged labor force. Feminist scholars argue that by failing to tax the benefits of household labor while at the same time taxing the benefits of market labor, Congress encourages women to undertake a conventional household role that makes them dependent on a traditional wage earner and perpetuates their economic vulnerability.

THE BEHAVIORAL EFFECTS OF EXEMPTING HOUSEHOLD LABOR FROM THE TAX BASE

Although time spent in the household was once viewed primarily as leisure time, there is now little question that the labor performed in the home is productive and valuable. Indeed, economists estimate that the value of household services is equal to at least 25% of the entire gross domestic product or approximately $145.6 billion. Congress's decision to impose a tax only on market activities therefore shelters a significant portion of household income from taxation.

Although the failure to tax nonmarket labor provides a benefit in the form of a lower tax liability, many feminist tax scholars have argued it comes at the cost of

---

[1] Reprinted by permission from 84 *Georgetown Law Journal* 1571 (1996).

encouraging women to undertake a traditional role in the home. Feminist scholars conclude that Congress, in effect, encourages women to undertake a financially insecure and subordinate role in the household by failing to tax these services.

While the Code does theoretically establish a disincentive to work, empirical data is needed to determine whether the Code has actually affected women's labor decisions. Sociological studies indicate that the behavioral effects of taxing only market labor depend on a woman's socioeconomic status. In general, women substitute household labor for market labor when they have access to resources that enable economic survival absent a market wage. Wealthy women or women married to middle- or upper-income men, for example, can substitute unpaid for paid labor without suffering immediate impoverishment.

Many women, however, do not experience market labor and household labor as mutually exclusive. Low-income women, for example, do not have the luxury to leave the market for the home simply because Congress awards tax benefits for such a decision. Indeed, data unambiguously indicate that low-income women and single women have traditionally performed the bulk of the household labor, yet have also had high levels of market participation. Low-income and single women, therefore, usually do not have the option to substitute home labor for market labor and instead must work in both spheres to survive economically.

African-American women of all income levels also have high and steady rates of labor force participation, despite the tax benefits Congress provides to stay-at-home spouses. While middle-income white women often substitute the role of market laborer for the role of mother, black women rarely experience this substitution effect. Rather, black women often add mothering responsibilities to their roles as market workers. Indeed, married black women with children participate in the waged labor force at a higher rate than any other group.

More recently, women of all races and socioeconomic classes have moved into the waged labor force while still maintaining their household responsibilities. Economic downsizing, a desire for greater consumption of goods and services, or simply a general frustration with domestic roles caused nearly 60% of all women to enter the waged labor force in 1990. Thus, while Congress's failure to tax nonmarket activities encourages some women to substitute household labor for market labor, others experience an income effect, which causes high levels of market participation. Consequently, women of most classes and races constitute a significant part of the market workforce, and they continue to be responsible for providing 70% to 80% of the unpaid household services.

THE DISTRIBUTIONAL EFFECTS OF THE EXEMPTION OF HOUSEHOLD LABOR FROM THE TAX BASE

Although the substitution effect is more limited than might be expected, nontaxation of household labor nevertheless provides significant benefits to families in the form of a decreased tax liability. If household labor were included in the tax base, the family's tax burden would increase by the imputed value of the labor. A lower tax burden provides a corresponding higher level of disposable income.

If the additional income is shared by each family member, Congress's failure to tax nonmarket labor would arguably benefit the entire family.

Families, however, do not act as a single economic unit, and individuals within the family do not share benefits and burdens equally. To understand the full extent of the gendered nature of the Code, therefore, we must analyze the economic position of each family member individually. Once the family is disaggregated, it becomes clear that women do not always have access to the family's greater disposable income. Not only are intrafamily resources not shared equally, but failure to tax household labor denies women access to social welfare benefits directly tied to taxation.

The Allocation of Resources Within the Household

Many provisions in the Code indicate that Congress assumes equal sharing of income within the family. Most studies indicate, however, that Congress's assumption that families operate as a single economic unit, sharing income and expenses equally, is flawed. Viviana Zelizer, for example, argues that families historically have operated as hierarchically structured groups in which one person controls the allocation and use of money. Many recent sociological studies indicate that in most cases women do not have meaningful control over family resources. Although access to and control of resources is often tied to the gender hierarchy, the extent of women's power over resources varies between families.

Sociologists have found that women who are married to high-income men are less likely to have meaningful access to disposable income than women living in low-income families. The extent of a married woman's control over disposable income thus appears to correspond to her socioeconomic class.

In high-income families, gender relations shape the circulation and control of money within families, often with the man in control. Studies indicate that often married women working in the home are given only enough resources to pay for the family's necessities such as food, clothing, and utility bills. In this type of allowance system, women rarely have access to personal spending money. Thus, for married women undertaking a conventional caretaking role, a greater level of disposable income resulting from the nontaxation of household labor will not necessarily translate into more resources for the woman.

Married women who earn a wage in the market are more likely to maintain some control over the family's resources. Most studies, however, indicate that the level of economic control corresponds to the level of each family member's market wage. Individuals who bring in a greater portion of income generally have more control over resources. The continuing gendered wage gap almost ensures that women bringing home a wage will have less control over the family's disposable income than men.

Even women who have complete control over the family's resources may have only illusory economic power. In low-income families, for example, the woman is often the manager of the family's finances. Because money is scarce in low-income households, however, this role cannot be seen as a source of power. Indeed, low-income families often perceive economic problems as their greatest worry and responsibility over these matters is often a source of stress.

Social Welfare Benefits Tied to Taxation

Unlike federal income tax revenues, payroll tax revenues are separated from the government's general operating budget and deposited into a trust fund, the proceeds of which are paid to the taxpayers during periods of disability and retirement. These social welfare benefits, the level of which is tied directly to taxation, provide many citizens essential resources, especially in old age. Because household labor is not taxed, women's access to these critical resources is greatly restricted.

Unlike the income tax, which provides for a standard deduction and a personal exemption to all wage earners, the payroll tax applies to the very first dollar earned by a taxpayer. Consequently, the payroll taxes represent a much greater economic burden than the income taxes for low- and middle-income taxpayers. These payroll taxes, however, are returned to the taxpayer in the form of Social Security, disability, and Medicare benefits. By failing to impose a tax on household labor, Congress enables the family unit to avoid paying income and payroll taxes on the housework, but it denies women access to Social Security, disability, and Medicare benefits.

Currently, women must participate in the market to receive independent Social Security benefits. The extent of the benefits that women receive for their market activities is tied to the level of taxes paid. Upon reaching retirement or in cases of disability, market workers are entitled to benefits based on the number of years worked and the average amount earned. High wages and high levels of market participation, therefore, correspond to greater Social Security and disability benefits for the taxpayer. As women begin to spend more time in the waged labor force, the number of women entitled to Social Security benefits based on their own work records increases.

Despite the high numbers of women in the waged labor force, they have not reached benefit parity with men. Because women continue to earn less than men in the market, frequently work part-time, and often leave the workforce completely to care for children and elderly parents, few women earn significant benefits. Although the Social Security laws entitle married women to derivative Social Security benefits based on their husbands' waged labor, women often fail to obtain such benefits due to divorce, death, or because their husbands do not qualify for Social Security. Consequently, women, particularly women of color, suffer high poverty rates in old age.

As Mary Becker has argued, these high levels of poverty partly result from the structure of the Social Security system, which benefits waged laborers and not household workers. By refusing to count unpaid household labor in the calculation of retirement benefits and by tying such benefits only to wages, Congress has almost guaranteed that women will live in poverty at higher rates than men. Thus, although studies indicate that women's combined market and nonmarket labor hours are greater than men's, the Social Security laws treat women as undeserving of equal benefits.

VALUING AND TAXING WOMEN'S HOUSEHOLD LABOR

Past efforts to increase women's economic security through tax reform have had limited success. Women, for a variety of reasons, have not responded to incentives aimed at encouraging their market participation. As a result, feminist scholars must shift their attention to other means for achieving the goal of economic independence.

In particular, scholars must seriously consider the advantages of broadening the tax base to include the benefits of women's unwaged labor. Taxation provides access to substantial, independent social welfare benefits in retirement and disability. Tying the benefits to household labor as well as market labor would ensure greater resources for women and would represent a congressional recognition of caretaking responsibilities as valuable and productive labor.

This tax reform proposal builds on the traditional conception of income, which theoretically includes all increases in the taxpayer's economic wealth. By refusing to make a distinction between labor performed in the private and public spheres, Congress would recognize the value of household labor and the individual laborers regardless of the location of the labor. Rather than viewing women only as nurturing caregivers providing gratuitous services to the home out of love, duty, and custom, women would be treated as autonomous individuals with economic rights. Finally, by taxing household labor, Congress would follow the lead of other areas of law in which the public/private distinction has been seen as both false and problematic.

VALUATION CONCERNS

Taxpayers obtain significant "psychic" income from many nonmarket household activities such as watching the sunset, smoking a cigarette, balancing a checkbook, and recycling paper and cans. By providing self-supplied services, such as mowing a lawn and preparing a meal, the taxpayer also provides valuable economic benefits to the household. Theoretically, because Congress seeks to tax all items that improve the taxpayer's well-being, an ideal Code would include the value of these activities within the tax base. Of course, if Congress attempted to tax all benefits the household received from each family member's labor and leisure, enormous administrative complications would arise.

Rather than attempting to capture the value of all labor and leisure, Congress could focus only on the productive aspects of household activities. Although long viewed as simply an expression of love and commitment, the productive nature of nurturing and caregiving activities has recently gained wide acceptance outside of the law. Sociologists and economists have begun to generate extensive scholarship discussing and analyzing the productive nature of housework, and many scholars have argued that by understanding the nature of women's contribution to the household, we will have a better understanding of the economy outside of the home.

Although economists have not uniformly agreed to a single approach for distinguishing valuable household labor from leisure, and much literature has been devoted to problematic assumptions underlying each approach, they generally agree that separating productive labor from leisure is possible. Thus, although it would certainly not be an easy task, current economic literature indicates that household labor can be distinguished from leisure.

In addition to distinguishing labor from leisure, Henry Simons raised a concern with quantifying women's labor in different households in his classic work, *Personal Income Taxation*. Simons, who was concerned with tax fairness, argued that while imputing an identical value for household chores to each household would not create administrative complications, it would produce unfair results in light of the varying amounts of productive labor each household produces. Simons concluded that it would be impossible to ensure tax fairness between households by independently valuing each household task without suffering enormous administrative difficulties and government intrusion into the private lives of the taxpayers.

Of course, a detailed and thorough measurement of the time each woman spends on productive household labor would be administratively impossible. Productive household labor, however, could be quantified based on the number of children in the household, the presence of a husband, and the women's market participation. Time-use studies providing detailed data about the number of hours each family member spends performing unwaged labor in the household could be used to estimate the amount of labor produced. Thus, there is no need to measure the precise amount of unpaid labor in each household.

Finally, Michael McIntyre and Oliver Oldman have argued that even if Congress could identify and measure productive labor, additional problems still exist with determining and assigning a market value to household labor. First, in contrast to waged work, the actual tasks that women perform vary from household to household. Second, women respond to the demands of spouses and children, as well as other social institutions (such as children's school, the transportation system, and health authorities) when providing labor in the home. Third, standards of performance are obscure and are often set by each woman individually. Consequently, the value of the housework could vary dramatically between households. In light of these complications, many tax theorists have taken the position that income from nonmarket labor cannot be valued by applying a formula based on objectively observable factors. Because the services cannot be valued in market terms, many argue the labor is impossible to value accurately and fairly.

Although Congress has failed to impose a tax on household labor – labor for which a market does exist – economists have devised numerous valuation methods that produce meaningful estimates of the worth of household production. The replacement value method is the most widely accepted method used to value household production. This approach involves equating the value of the household labor with the cost of hiring another person in the market to perform the same work. Determining the replacement value of household labor is easy because the market now provides services formerly available only in the home.

Alternatively, Gary Becker has suggested that household labor could be valued according to the individual's opportunity cost of time. Under Becker's theory, individuals will allocate time to housework until the value of the labor equals the opportunity cost of a market wage. Thus, by determining the amount women could earn in the market, Becker argues that the value of their household labor could also be ascertained.

The third and [simplest] approach would be to estimate the number of hours per week women spend performing household labor and value the labor according to the minimum wage.

LIMITING THE DISTRIBUTIONAL EFFECTS OF TAXATION: A PROPOSED HOUSEHOLD INCOME TAX CREDIT

Although taxation of household labor has the potential to ensure women's access to independent social welfare benefits, it will simultaneously impose an immediate financial burden upon women and their families. This additional burden is particularly problematic for low-income women who often need every available dollar to purchase necessities, such as food and child care. Because this burden might outweigh the value of future benefits, some women will prefer to forgo long-term social welfare benefits to avoid taxation in the short run.

This same tradeoff is present when women are in the waged labor force. Low-income women must pay income and payroll taxes that take resources needed for everyday living expenses. Congress, in response to the problems associated with the burdens of taxation on low-income wage earners, has rejected the conclusion that low-income taxpayers must choose between long-term and short-term financial stability. In 1975, Congress created the earned income tax credit (EITC) program, which aims to offset the tax burden of low-income workers while maintaining access to social welfare benefits.

To ensure low-income women are not harmed by the inclusion of household labor in the tax base, Congress could adopt a household income tax credit (HITC) that parallels, but does not mirror, the EITC. The purpose of the HITC would be to offset only the increased tax imposed on household labor and not to operate as a tax-based social welfare program similar to the EITC. An HITC, therefore, should have a distributional character similar, but not identical, to the EITC. An HITC, like the EITC, should base eligibility on income level and family size. The HITC, however, should be a nonrefundable rather than a refundable tax credit. Thus, while the HITC could decrease or eliminate the tax burden, it would not provide a cash transfer similar to the EITC program.

The structure of the HITC must ensure women at low-income levels and women who depend on social welfare programs have a credit that entirely offsets the increased tax burden imposed on household labor. Like the EITC, the HITC should begin to phase out as income rises. The speed at which the credit phases out will, of course, depend on the value Congress imputes to the household labor and the resultant tax.

The household income tax credit, like the EITC, will ensure that low-income women avoid a tax liability while still gaining access to Social Security benefits. The HITC, however, will offer little or no income assistance to middle- and upper-income women and may potentially decrease middle- and upper-income women's disposable resources. But this would occur only if women had access to such income prior to the imposition of the tax. Households, however, do not equally share income and expenses. Married women tend to use a large portion of their income for family necessities, leaving greater disposable income for their husbands. If the new tax burden is, by necessity, paid out of the disposable income, then the taxation of housework might work more to the detriment of married men than married women.

If the household unit equally shares income and expenses among its members, the burden of the new tax will be shared by the entire household, including the woman. Under these circumstances, this approach will arguably cause less economic hardship on women than the current approach that leaves women without significant economic resources in old age. Women generally live longer than men and often have a low level of Social Security benefits; as a result, women frequently spend the last years of their lives in poverty. By taxing housework, Congress would require the entire family to contribute to women's economic security in retirement.

CONCLUSION

Scholars in many disciplines have recognized that women suffer economic vulnerability due to the division of labor in the home along gender lines. Because many women undertake the time-consuming tasks of bearing and rearing children, they often are unable to participate in the waged labor force at the same level as men. Tax analysts, noting the manner in which the tax structure reinforces this traditional gendered division of labor, have almost uniformly responded by proposing tax reform intended to encourage women to substitute market work for household labor. Many argue that by substituting a traditionally "male" role in the market for the conventional "female" role in the home, women are more likely to reach economic parity with men.

While this market-oriented approach recognizes women's economic vulnerability, it fails to acknowledge that many women who participate fully in the market remain economically vulnerable. This economic vulnerability depends in part on women's continued responsibility for household work even while in the waged labor force. Although some women view this division of labor as oppressive, this view is not universal. Many women welcome household responsibilities and view the labor as an important contribution to the family and to society. Many women, for example, consider nurturing and caring responsibilities in the home as closely tied to the elimination of discrimination and the empowerment of their community.

This article has argued that to improve women's economic security, housework must be recognized as valuable and productive. In particular, I have argued that Congress should value and tax household activities to ensure women have access to social welfare benefits typically tied to waged labor, such as Social Security, disability, and Medicare benefits. Taxation would mark an important step toward the formal recognition of women as important economic and political actors. This reform, together with the market-oriented reform, would go far toward changing society's views of the value of productive activities carried out both in the home and in the market, and more importantly, it would represent a critical step in achieving greater economic security for women.

The Marital Deduction QTIP Provisions: Illogical and Degrading to Women

WENDY C. GERZOG[1]

In 1981, Congress enacted the qualified terminable interest provisions (QTIP) that allow an estate and gift tax marital deduction for the full value of the underlying property where a spouse receives only a qualifying income interest for life and where the executor of the estate or the donor spouse makes a timely election. Generally, however, the availability of the estate and gift tax marital deduction is restricted to the transfer of property ownership itself from one spouse to the other. Congress adopted the QTIP provisions as an extension of its contemporaneous decision to select the marital unit as the unit of taxation for estate and gift taxes. Congress believed that most couples view property acquired during the marriage as "ours." Therefore, Congress reasoned that as long as the property is subject to transfer taxes when it leaves the marital unit it is not necessary that the surviving spouse own, or control the ownership of, the underlying property. However, the reality is that only one spouse (the donor spouse or decedent) controls the transfer of the underlying property. Making a QTIP election, including naming the ultimate beneficiary of the property, does not in fact require both spouses' participation. In the case of a gift, the donor alone makes that election; in the case of a testamentary transfer, the executor of the QTIP trust has that responsibility. In both cases, it is the transferor alone who determines the final recipient of the property, and in both instances it is a transfer to a nonspouse. Thus, it was a rather Herculean leap in logic that led Congress to state that the QTIP provisions reflect the shared decision making of a husband and wife in a marriage.

While the 1981 legislative history of the QTIP provisions is couched in politically correct, gender-neutral terms, the provisions themselves are rooted in the prejudices and stereotypes of the 1960s and can only be explained as a gender-biased, paternalistic, and degrading treatment of women. The QTIP's current income distribution requirement is merely an illusion given to the widow to pretend that an income interest is as valuable as ownership of the underlying property. The QTIP "current beneficial enjoyment"[2] requirement has

---

[1] Reprinted by permission from 5 *UCLA Women's Law Journal* 301 (1995).

[2] FEDERAL ESTATE AND GIFT TAXATION RECOMMENDATIONS ADOPTED BY THE AMERICAN LAW INSTITUTE AND REPORTERS' STUDIES (1968), *reprinted in* HOUSE WAYS AND MEANS COMM., 94TH CONG., BACKGROUND MATERIALS ON FEDERAL ESTATE AND GIFT TAXATION 355 (Comm. Print 1976).

no logical explanation except as a "bone" being tossed to the obsequious surviving spouse.

THE QTIP PROVISIONS: AN EXPLANATION AND ANALYSIS

The QTIP provisions provide an exception to the marital deduction terminable interest rule. The QTIP allows the predeceasing spouse to receive the benefits of a marital deduction without ceding control of the transferred property. Because statistically the majority of predeceasing spouses are men, the QTIP in effect provides a loophole that perpetuates the women-deserve-only-support school of thought by allowing husbands to reap the benefits of the marital deduction without relinquishing control of the ultimate disposition of the underlying property. In so doing, the provisions give an unwarranted tax benefit to married couples based on the fallacy that decisions by the husband are decisions of the marital unit.

The Mechanics of the QTIP

By voice vote the Senate adopted the QTIP provisions, which were not originally in the 1981 tax bill. Senator Symms explained that if Congress enacted an unlimited marital deduction section, it would present the taxpayer with a quandary:

> All estate taxes could be postponed, but only by giving the surviving spouse unrestricted control over the property, which current law requires in order to obtain a deduction. The owner may prefer not to give his or her spouse such control. The point becomes more significant as divorce and remarriage increase, which has occurred. The property owner would like to be sure that upon the death of his spouse his children by a prior marriage or marriages share in his property, including the marital deduction property.[3]

Essentially, the QTIP provisions allow the taxpayer to control the ultimate disposition of the underlying property after the death of, or earlier transfer by, the surviving spouse. They provide that qualified terminable interest property will be treated as if it passed to the surviving spouse and that no part of such property will be deemed to pass to anyone else – although the surviving spouse will receive only a lifetime income interest in the property. A qualifying income interest for life requires that the surviving spouse be entitled to all the income from the property. This income must be payable at least annually, and no person, including the surviving spouse, can have a power over the property to appoint it to anyone other than the surviving spouse during her lifetime.

In order to qualify property as QTIP property, the donor or executor must also make a proper election. However, there is no requirement that the donee spouse participate in any way in this decision. Indeed, Congress added the QTIP provisions precisely to avoid entitling the other spouse to control the ultimate disposition of this property.

---

[3] 127 Cong. Rec. 17,289 (1981) (statement of Sen. Symms).

Congress enacted the terminable interest rule primarily to ensure that property would be included in the surviving spouse's estate. Generally, the transfer of a terminable interest to one's spouse is not eligible for the marital deduction because many terminable interests, such as a life estate, are extinguished at the possessor's death. If such transfers were eligible for the marital deduction, this would provide a chance for tax abuse because the underlying property would never be included in either spouse's estate at its full fair market value. However, the value of the property transferred under a QTIP election by definition is either included in the surviving spouse's estate or treated as a taxable gift. This inclusion ensures that the property will be taxable when it ultimately leaves the "marital unit."

An Analysis of the QTIP

The current distribution requirement of the QTIP provisions is identical to the current distribution requirement of the power of appointment exception to the terminable interest rule. Although the current distribution requirement coupled with a general power of appointment is roughly equivalent to outright ownership, there is no apparent reason to copy this requirement for a QTIP deduction because the QTIP is not intended to convey the parallel control and enjoyment of property inherent in property ownership.

Indeed, estate trusts are allowed a marital deduction because they do not contain a terminable interest; they are trusts where income is accumulated during the surviving spouse's life and where the value of both the accumulated income and underlying property is included in the surviving spouse's estate. Moreover, the surviving spouse, although unable currently to enjoy the property, is allowed to direct, by testamentary transfer, its recipient's identity. Essentially, the power of appointment exception and the estate trust share the element that the surviving spouse controls the final transfer of the underlying property – a basic indicium of property ownership. Partaking of an income interest is neither as valuable nor as reflective of property ownership as controlling the property's ultimate disposition.

If the current distribution requirement is indeed founded on the concept that a married couple considers its property as "theirs," and if the proper time to tax interspousal transfers is when a third party actually comes into possession of its future interest, there is no logical reason for requiring that income be currently paid to the recipient spouse. As long as income is accumulated during her lifetime and then taxed, together with the value of the underlying property, at the time of her death or earlier transfer, that objective will be met.

Thus, a simpler version of the QTIP could be developed as a logical consequence of that rationale. Such a statute would not pretend to give the surviving spouse any equivalence of ownership and would emphasize only the tax deferral consequence of the QTIP. Without the window dressing of the current distribution requirement, Congress would have to find a policy reason for such a tax benefit. With the Emperor's new clothes removed, however, it will be hard to justify retaining the QTIP.

IS THE DECISION TO USE THE MARITAL UNIT AS THE PROPER UNIT OF TAXATION FOR TRANSFER TAX PURPOSES COMPATIBLE WITH THE RATIONALE FOR THE QTIP PROVISIONS?

The decision to use the marital unit as the proper unit of taxation for transfer tax purposes rests on the concept that married persons share and make joint decisions about "their" property. Thus, the best time to tax that property is when it leaves the marital unit, whether at the surviving spouse's death or at earlier transfer. However, the legislative history behind the QTIP provisions reveals a policy rationale incompatible with at least one of these assumptions: that married persons both decide what they will do with "their" property. Rather, the QTIP statute itself does not require any *joint* decision making between husband and wife.

The legislative history of the QTIP provisions is replete with expressions of the decedent/donor spouse's fear of transferring the underlying property to his wife. Basically, the decedent/donor is worried that she will not subsequently transfer the property to his children from either that current marriage or from his prior marriages. Yet the QTIP is based on the theory that a couple shares and makes "joint" decisions about "their" property. If that purported rationale for the QTIP were indeed true, there would be no need for such fear. Underlying the husband's fear is the fact that he does not wish to *share* his decision with his spouse but wants unilaterally to control to whom "his" property is transferred when it leaves the marital unit. In other words, without the QTIP statute the decedent would probably utilize the power of appointment exception to the terminable interest rule. However, the decedent is horrified at this option because he sees the recipient spouse as unilaterally controlling the ultimate disposition of *his* property specifically *not* in accord with *his* wishes. He wants his cake (i.e., the tax benefit of deferral), and he wants to eat it, too (i.e., to control who will finally receive the underlying property). The icing covering this cake is Congress's pretense that the QTIP's preferred tax treatment is based on the decision to use the marital unit as the unit of taxation because married persons *share their* property. Evidently, they do not.

HOW THE QTIP PROVISIONS DEGRADE WOMEN

There are few men in common law states who are willing to grant their widows more than a life estate where there are surviving children. They do not want to grant the widow a life estate plus a general power of appointment as that in effect is to give her the fee simple, and the widow who has unfettered power to dispose of the property may do so and cut off the interest of the children. There are many widows in this country who are experienced and astute in the management of property and business affairs. *But there are many more who have been active only in domestic circles and who lack the experience and judgment to suddenly assume outright ownership and disposal of substantial properties. The tax law should not offer a premium to a husband who ignores his better judgment and grants his widow a general power of appointment leaving his children at the mercy of any charlatan who has his widow's ear.*[4]

---

[4] John W. Beveridge, *The Estate Tax Marital Deduction – Beneficent Intent, Baneful Result*, 44 TAXES 283, 284 (1966) (emphasis added).

It is amidst this climate of paternalism, which is degrading to women, that the American Law Institute (ALI) wrote its proposed changes in Federal Estate and Gift Taxation. While Mr. Beveridge, author of the earlier quotation and a co-author of treatises on Gift Taxation and Estate Taxation, was not on the ALI committees proposing the new exception to the terminable interest rule, his words state the sentiment to which others merely allude.

The QTIP provisions degrade women because they were enacted to enable men to control the ultimate disposition of property but nonetheless the provisions qualify QTIP transfers for a marital deduction. The framers of this new exception to the terminable interest rule further degraded women because they assumed that widows would be content with receiving only one of the indicia of property ownership, for example, current beneficial enjoyment, and would not protest against the enactment of such a provision. Unfortunately, these men were successful. Since the enactment of the QTIP provisions in 1981, no one has called for their repeal.

The source of the QTIP's qualifying income interest for life provision is the current beneficial enjoyment test that was proposed by the ALI Federal Estate and Gift Tax Project in the mid to late 1960s. The current beneficial enjoyment test provides that any transfer that gives the recipient spouse a limited, present enjoyment of the property should qualify the full value of the underlying property for the marital deduction. In 1969, the Treasury Department also recommended such a change.

While the 1981 legislative history is expressed in gender-neutral terms, earlier versions of the QTIP evidence a clear gender bias and stereotyping. All examples in both the ALI Proposal and the Treasury Recommendations envision the surviving spouse as a woman, which is, of course, borne out by the statistical evidence. In fact, in 1969 when it compiled its statistics for recommending the unlimited marital deductions, the Treasury Department only offered statistics relating to the number of years *widows* outlive their *husbands*. If the government had been concerned with both widows and widowers, surely it would have compiled similar data with respect to the men.

While not necessarily indicative of bias, all seventy-five members of the Tax Advisory Group of the ALI, in May 1968, when the recommendations contained in the ALI Report were approved, were men. Likewise, all thirteen members of the Liaison Committee of the Section of Taxation of the American Bar Association (ABA); all three members of the Liaison Committee of Real Property, Probate and Trust Law of the ABA; and all eleven subcommittee chairs of the Committee on Estate and Gift Taxes of the Section of Taxation of the ABA were men. While the all-male composition of the committees creating the QTIP provision is not proof of gender bias, representation by women, and perhaps another perspective, was virtually absent.

When Congress finally adopted these provisions in the 1970s, it merely patched gender-neutral phrases, such as "his or her," into the legislative history without any reexamination of the rationale for the provisions themselves. Essentially, the current income distribution requirement of the QTIP provisions is meant to pacify the surviving spouse. The QTIP's requirement of giving the surviving spouse less than full ownership reveals an intention to delude the surviving spouse into accepting

QTIP treatment as if she truly owned the property. Ironically and interestingly, nowhere else in the transfer tax provisions is a taxpayer deemed to be owner of more property than he or she either controls or once controlled.

CONCLUSION

When a donor or decedent irrevocably relinquishes control over his or her property, that property is subject to a transfer tax. A special deduction, the marital deduction, applies to married persons because Congress believes that husband and wife share decisions about property ownership. Under this rationale, interspousal transfers should not be taxed because the marital unit continues to hold *their* property. Until the enactment of the QTIP provisions in 1981, the marital deduction required that the recipient spouse own, or have the equivalent of ownership of, property transferred to her. In this way, the property would continue to be owned by at least one member of the marital unit and by no one outside that unit.

With the enactment of the QTIP provisions, Congress extended the tax benefit afforded by the marital deduction to transfers of only a life estate to a member of the marital unit and of a vested remainder to third parties outside the marital unit. It did so on the stated rationale that: (1) married couples share decisions about "their" property, and (2) as long as the value of the underlying property would be included in the surviving spouse's estate at her death, the government's right to such transfer tax revenue would not be compromised.

The only legitimate rationale for allowing married persons to receive the tax benefit of deferral is because a spouse must transfer the underlying property itself to the other spouse. At a minimum, Congress should only allow the marital deduction where the transferor's spouse must agree both to the identity of the recipient and to a QTIP election.

Ideally, Congress should repeal the current QTIP provisions because they degrade women; clearly, the motivation for their enactment was gender-biased, and as applied, even today the QTIP disadvantages mostly widows. The QTIP provisions encourage husbands to transfer less than a full property interest to their wives by providing the donors with a marital deduction based on the value of the underlying property although the husbands actually give their surviving spouses only a life interest in that property.

A Taxing Woman: The Relationship of Feminist Scholarship to Tax

MARJORIE E. KORNHAUSER[1]

A recent law review article described me as a "feminist tax scholar." The description made me pause; then my pausing made me wonder: Why was I hesitant about this label? I do, after all, consider myself both a tax scholar and a feminist. What was it, then, about the combination that made me pause?

My hesitancy stems, I believe, from two sources. First, I am not sure what the label "feminist tax scholar" means. Second, whatever the definition is, the mere fact of labeling makes me uneasy. Labels in general worry me because they are rhetorical tools that can, like any rhetorical tool, too easily change from being an aid to communication into a barrier by substituting reaction for thought. At the very least, labels frequently alter the way people perceive the labeled object. What purpose does this particular label serve and does it alter the perception of my work and, by implication, that of other feminist tax scholars?

This article explores my puzzlement and in so doing explores the relationship between feminist scholarship and tax by examining two of my articles that some people have described as feminist. Their themes are most commonly described by others as progressivity of income tax rates and the realities and assumptions underlying joint filing for married couples under the income tax, respectively. Each, however, in fact has other concerns and themes as well. The concept of rhetoric, for example, runs through both. The progressive piece, *The Rhetoric of the Anti-Progressive Income Tax Movement: A Typical Male Reaction* (*Income Tax Rhetoric*) [see Chapter 2], has a section that explicitly applies feminist theory to the issue of progressive income tax. It has been called a feminist article by many people. The joint filing article, *Love, Money, and the IRS: Family, Income Sharing, and the Joint Income Tax Return* (*Income Sharing*) [see Chapter 8], on the other hand, makes no reference at all to feminist theory or feminism in general and does not explicitly deal with a feminist topic.

TOWARD A DEFINITION OF FEMINIST SCHOLARSHIP
AND ITS ROLE IN SCHOLARSHIP

The clearest, narrowest definition of feminist scholarship is an article that consciously applies feminist theory to the analysis of an issue. Under this definition, the

---

[1] Reprinted by permission from 6 *Southern California Review of Law and Women's Studies* 301 (1997).

only one of my articles that is a candidate for the feminist tax scholar label is *Income Tax Rhetoric*. I wrote it in 1987 as a response to the heated debate and politics that accompanied the passage of the Tax Reform Act of 1986, which greatly compressed the progressive income tax rates. My major concerns were the decreased progressivity and the rhetoric that had been used to accomplish that feat. I used the article to explore that rhetoric and the arguments against progressivity, thereby revealing the individualistic rhetoric and philosophy that underlay the nominally scientific and objective economic efficiency arguments favoring a flat tax.

The article began with an examination of the classic arguments against progressivity, especially the economic argument. Next, it explored the philosophy which underlies that argument and suggested that alternative visions of society would support progressivity, using feminism as an example of such an alternative vision. The model of feminism that I used was a Gilliganesque relational "web of care" vision. Finally, the article concluded not only that feminist theory provided a "strong case for progressive taxation" but that the individualistic philosophy undergirding the traditional case against progressivity also did.[2]

Is this "feminist scholarship" under the above definition? The answer is not immediately clear. On the one hand, approximately one-sixth of the pages of the article are explicitly devoted to exploring a connection between progressivity and feminist theory. The mere presence of feminist theory, however, does not make an article feminist. The fact that this discussion is sympathetic to feminist theory perhaps qualifies at least that portion as feminist in the general but vague sense in which a person who writes favorably about a topic is usually described as being a supporter. On the other hand, feminist critique is absent from most of the article and certainly is not its organizing force. Under a narrow definition, then, *Income Tax Rhetoric* may be feminist scholarship only in a general sense of using feminist theory sympathetically, but the major portion of the article, as well as the broader themes, are not.

The article, however, may be feminist scholarship in another sense. Perhaps feminist scholarship is defined as much by form as by content. Traditional scholarship is presented in a third-person, impersonal, and "objective" manner. Feminist scholarship, reflecting a more particularistic and contextual viewpoint, is associated with a more narrative or storytelling style. Many of my articles, including *Income Tax Rhetoric*, are written in a nontraditional style that others have specifically identified as storytelling. Perhaps, then, *Income Tax Rhetoric* and my scholarship in general can be labeled feminist scholarship based on this style. Such a style-based classification of scholarship, however, seems superficial unless it is also a manifestation of something more substantive.

In short, does this narrative style reflect a deeper meaning that may be called feminist scholarship? I think not. It may sometimes be a component of feminist scholarship, but it is not a necessary element, let alone a sufficient one. For example, Nancy Staudt, in *Taxing Housework* [this Chapter], uses feminist theory and literature to enhance her analysis of the tax treatment of women's housework, yet

---

[2] Marjorie E. Kornhauser, *The Rhetoric of the Anti-Progressive Income Tax Movement: A Typical Male Reaction*, 86 MICH. L. REV. 465, 470, 518–23 (1987).

she writes in a traditional, straightforward law review manner. Moreover, some people use the narrative style but are not feminist scholars by any definition. Some critical race theorists, for example, also use this technique.

Perhaps, then, feminist scholarship is defined by something less tangible than an explicit application of feminist theory or of a narrative style. Perhaps feminist articles are those that analyze topics of concern to women from a viewpoint sympathetic to and informed by feminist thought. This definition obviously is broader than my earlier definition but it is also [vaguer] at the boundaries. Much of Professor Edward McCaffery's work, for example, falls in this category [see Chapter 8]. The primary point of view or analytical tool in many of the articles in this category, however, is not feminist. Professor McCaffery's primary analytic tool, for example, is economics, as well as political theory and philosophy. Similarly, Professor Carolyn C. Jones writes sympathetically about women's issues, but does so from an historical standpoint, in articles such as *Dollars and Selves: Women's Tax Criticism and Resistance in the 1870s* [see Chapter 2].

Even more amorphous than the "centrality of women's experience" definition is a definition of feminist scholarship as those articles which have a feminist outlook. Since much feminist theory states that most women view the world differently than most men, perhaps it is merely the presence of this outlook that defines feminist scholarship, even if that outlook is not ever explicitly stated or even consciously recognized by the author. What a person sees; how she interprets what she sees; how she frames the questions and answers them all are affected by her outlook. Her outlook, in turn, can affect how others view her work.

Professor Gwen Thayer Handelman, for example, wrote an article on statutory construction of tax provisions and "was startled by the fervor with which several colleagues disputed" her contentions.[3] Moreover, she noticed that women "were more comfortable" with her proposals than men.[4] She later concluded that although she had written an article on statutory construction of tax laws that never once mentioned feminist scholarship or addressed "women's issues" she had nevertheless "brought [her] womanhood into [her] professional undertakings, that [her] work is that of 'a lawyer and a woman.'"[5] After recognizing this, she then proceeded to write an article that specifically examined the connection between gender and statutory interpretation [see Chapter 4]. This latter article is feminist scholarship under my first definition, whereas the first article meets neither the strict theory definition nor even the "centrality of women's experience" definition. It qualifies as feminist only if we define feminist scholarship to include those articles written simply with a feminist outlook. Should we?

I believe that a female outlook frequently is different than a male one. I also believe this outlook affects what many women see, how we interpret what we see, and how we value it. Although all women do not have the same female-inspired outlook, many have a similar outlook that may be described as feminist.

---

[3] Gwen Thayer Handelman, *Sisters in Law: Gender and the Interpretation of Tax Statutes*, 3 UCLA WOMEN'S L.J. 39, 39–40 (1993).

[4] *Id.*

[5] *Id.* at 41 (discussing her earlier work, Gwen Thayer Handelman, *Zen and the Art of Statutory Construction*, 40 DEPAUL L. REV. 611 (1991)).

Nevertheless, I do not believe that this outlook alone rises to the level of feminist scholarship. In other words, there is a significant difference between Professor Handelman's first and second articles. It is the difference between the unconscious and the conscious; the instinctual and the reasoned argument. Both can bring new insights to an issue, and therefore both are valuable. I would call only the latter, however, feminist scholarship.

Nevertheless, such an outlook can have a powerful effect on scholarship by profoundly affecting what issues an author treats and how she views them. Sometimes the topic or treatment is specifically feminist, but sometimes, I think, the primary effect of the outlook is simply to provide an outsider's perspective. For example, since outsiders have less power than those in the majority, they are more likely to discern power issues in areas where a mainstream observer would see neutrality. My article *Income Sharing* illustrates this. Although the article neither mentions any feminist theory nor draws particularly on feminist literature, the focus on intrahousehold allocations of income may derive from an outsider's sensitivity to power. My relevant outsider perspective is that of a woman; the article might have had some different or additional insights if my class or race also had outsider status.

The preceding discussion suggests that since there is no single definition of feminist scholarship, perhaps the best way to conceptualize feminist scholarship is to see the connection between scholarship and gender issues as a continuum. Feminist legal theory is at one end; it is the most intense and analytically complete method of involvement. Centrality of women's experience comes next, followed more controversially by feminist outlook and style.

At the opposite end of the scholarship–gender continuum are articles that examine gender issues but do not fit within any definition of feminist scholarship because they do not embrace any feminist viewpoint; rather they adopt either a neutral or hostile position. Articles in this category can be difficult to identify since classification may depend on subtle nuances of tone rather than any explicit words. Compare, for example, my article on progressive taxation with a recent one by William Turnier, Pamela Johnston Conover, and David Lowery, entitled *Redistributive Justice and Cultural Feminism* [see Chapter 12]. Mine sympathetically discusses feminist theory and is often associated with feminist scholarship. It is this article, I presume, that causes Turnier et al. to label me a feminist tax scholar. Their article, in turn, also discusses feminist theory; in fact, feminist theory is more central to their article than to mine. Nevertheless, their article is not, in my opinion, feminist scholarship despite its topic and what they call "the feminist orientation of [their] study."[6] Their article uses feminist theory from an external rather than from the internal perspective.

Written in a traditional law review style, the Turnier article begins with an overview of the topic, briefly surveys the fields of feminist theory and jurisprudence, lays out its hypothesis, its methodology, and its findings, and finishes with a conclusion which sets out some implications of the study. None of this makes

---

[6] William Turnier et al., *Redistributive Justice and Cultural Feminism*, 45 Am. U. L. Rev. 1275, 1299 (1996).

it feminist. In fact, despite their study's alleged "feminist orientation" the article's tone is that of nonfeminists examining feminist theory.

CURRENT ROLE OF FEMINIST TAX SCHOLARSHIP AND THE FEMINIST TAX SCHOLAR LABEL

Any discussion about the role of feminist tax scholarship in legal literature is complicated by the difficulty of defining the term. The term's very ambiguity means that the label "feminist tax scholarship" is probably applied to many articles that some would not define as feminist scholarship, such as those with a feminist style or outlook. No matter how the label is defined, it is a double-edged sword, having both positive and negative consequences.

Labels are rhetorical tools that serve as signifiers; their usage communicates a host of unstated ideas and feelings to the reader who filters them through his or her own cognitive and emotional lenses. Labels thus provide the reader with a shorthand method of classifying and evaluating without always doing an analysis on the merits. In other words, the reader's preconceived view of feminist theory (or whatever the label) short-circuits his or her analysis and prejudges the article. Sometimes a label provides positive cues; sometimes negative. The more controversial the theory or the less established it is, the more negative cues it will provide to those who have not yet become comfortable with the theory. They will be more likely to prejudge an article written from this particular viewpoint negatively; similarly, followers of a particular theory in this adverse situation may be more likely to be less critical of a fellow theorist than they otherwise would be. It is this prejudging aspect of any label that bothers me because it makes it easier for readers to accept or dismiss an article without really thinking carefully about it. Even if people don't prejudge, the label can consciously or unconsciously color their reactions.

The less defined the label, as here, the more varied the reaction from reader to reader. Despite the variations in how feminist tax scholarship is defined and how the label is interpreted, commonalities exist. Once again, I will use *Income Tax Rhetoric* to illustrate this.

As I read subsequent tax articles which touched on progressivity, I sometimes thought *Income Tax Rhetoric* was being cited differently than was a contemporaneous article on the same subject by Joseph Bankman and Thomas Griffith, *Social Welfare and the Rate Structure: A New Look at Progressive Taxation*[7] (*Social Welfare*). I used the writing of this article as an opportunity to do a quick search of the citations to check out this impression.

The number of law review cites for both articles [is] similar. Their citation patterns, however, are different. For example, approximately 40% of the articles citing *Income Tax Rhetoric* were nontax articles whereas this was true for only about 10% of the *Social Welfare* cites. In these nontax articles, mostly by women, the citations to my article were generally with regard to its use of feminist theory.

---

[7] Joseph Bankman & Thomas Griffith, *Social Welfare and the Rate Structure: A New Look at Progressive Taxation*, 75 CAL. L. REV. 1905 (1987).

Since both articles had approximately the same number of cites and *Income Tax Rhetoric* had more nontax cites, *Social Welfare* obviously had more tax cites. Some of the cites to *Social Welfare* but not to *Income Tax Rhetoric* were for a point made in both articles. Why does this occur and why, generally, does *Social Welfare* have more tax cites?

One simple explanation would be that their article was more visible than mine, but I do not think that this is the case. We published within months of each other; each article being placed in a top ten law journal. Then, perhaps, the explanation is the most obvious: their article is simply better than mine. I do not think this is the explanation either.

Both articles are good ones; if there is a difference in merit, it is not large enough to explain the difference in citation history. Other differences, however, certainly are significant enough to account for the respective citation patterns. Both articles share a topic – "progressivity" – but little else. *Social Welfare* is an excellent example of a traditional law review article. Both its form and substance are cool, scientific, and impersonal. In particular, it uses economic analysis, which is a well respected mode of analysis in law and tax in particular. My article, on the other hand, is different from most law review articles and, in particular, tax articles. To the extent the content is feminist or perceived as feminist, feminist tax articles at the time of publication were rare and indeed are still rare, though more plentiful than previously. Rhetoric, which was a major theme of the article, also was not (and still is not) a common topic in legal scholarship generally, and tax scholarship in particular. The article's form as well as its content was unusual since it was perceived by some to be written in the nontraditional narrative or storytelling style. Perhaps more startling was the title (and first paragraph) which were designed to be provocative, but not off-putting (as some readers took it).

The citation patterns of the two articles reflect the academy's reactions to all these differences. On the positive side, the perceived feminist aspect of my article made it a much more widely cited article outside the tax area. On the other hand, I believe that this very aspect is the reason it was less likely to be cited within the tax field, and when it was cited it was sometimes cited more for these feminist aspects than for its traditional tax aspects. As discussed before, the style of writing (including the title) could – and did – make some people uncomfortable. Feminist content could also limit citations in several ways. First, the feminist content coupled with the philosophic and rhetorical discussions place *Income Tax Rhetoric* outside the mainstream of most tax articles. Thus, *Income Tax Rhetoric* is less likely to be cited in tax articles than is *Social Welfare* simply because more tax scholars are interested in economics than rhetoric or jurisprudence. When they are interested in jurisprudence, it is more likely to be the jurisprudence of John Rawls or Robert Nozick than feminist jurisprudence.

Second, the feminist aspect, real or perceived, of *Income Tax Rhetoric* was its most unique aspect. It thus tended to overshadow the more traditional tax analysis in the article. As a consequence, even authors who view the article favorably might label it in their minds as that "feminist progressivity" article. As a result, when they are searching for a cite on another tax point (e.g., benefits taxation), *Income Tax Rhetoric* might not immediately come to mind. Third, even a feminist aware of the feminist aspects of *Income Tax Rhetoric* might deliberately choose to cite a nonfeminist article so as not to cloud the point she wishes to make with all the inferences and controversy that accompany the feminist label. Finally, those authors who are uncomfortable with feminism would be less likely to cite the article for its nonfeminist aspects.

In sum, what worries me about the feminist label is that it – like all labels – facilitates prejudging an article without fully considering its merits. Even if it does not lead to prejudgment, a feminist label has a tendency to overshadow other, more traditional, aspects of an article and thus people tend to categorize it as feminist. This skews its use in legal literature. Moreover, as with other new or less accepted theories and disciplines, the label can marginalize the author and her writings.

CONCLUSION

Despite some confusion about the exact meaning of feminist tax scholarship, the field is extremely valuable. The "feminist" portion of feminist tax scholarship (however defined) enriches our understanding of the tax laws by providing an "outsider" perspective on tax which makes us question the heretofore unquestioned or explains the previously unexplainable. The "tax" component deepens other disciplines' comprehension of issues that involve tax and helps build a communications bridge to other disciplines. The term feminist tax scholarship is a double-edged sword, however. Its power to enrich both tax and other disciplines is limited by a potential for marginalization – of being read only for its feminist angle, or worse, being dismissed because of its feminist angle. On the other hand, its interdisciplinary aspect offers the possibility of increased communication among academic fields; such cross-fertilization can only enrich scholarship.

Lesbians and gay men are in the unique position of being the only subordinated group that is the object of both overt *and* covert invidious discrimination in the application of the tax laws. This chapter features the work of three scholars who have criticized the tax laws' biases against lesbian and gay taxpayers.

Reading Patricia Cain's 1991 article *Same-Sex Couples and the Federal Tax Laws* reminds the twenty-first century reader of the old adage that "the more things change, the more they stay the same." In this article, which predates both the federal Defense of Marriage Act and the advent of same-sex marriage, civil unions, and domestic partnerships, Cain uses a hypothetical lesbian couple to illustrate the thorny income and gift tax issues that same-sex couples face when they share income and property. To ameliorate the problem, she suggests an interpretation of the tax laws that would render transfers from one partner to another tax-free under both the income tax and the gift tax. Importantly (and to critical tax scholars, unfortunately), even with all of the recent advances made by same-sex couples in obtaining access to the rights and obligations of marriage, Cain's analysis remains as relevant today as it was the day it was written.

In *The Internal Revenue Code as Sodomy Statute*, Anthony Infanti picks up on Cain's theme. Using personal narrative, he counters the misguided assertion of some mainstream tax scholars that lesbian and gay taxpayers cannot claim to be victims of discrimination until they quantifiably demonstrate that all of the detriments of not having their relationships recognized for tax purposes outweigh any benefits of being treated as strangers for tax purposes. Infanti explains how Congress's and the IRS's silence on the tax treatment of same-sex couples puts those couples in the untenable position of choosing between (1) hiding their relationships or (2) disclosing them and risking the imposition of confiscatory levels of taxation and, possibly, criminal punishment. In that sense, Infanti argues, the Code is a sodomy statute, designed to criminalize (at worst) and silence (at best) taxpayers who fail to conform to heterosexual norms.

In *Heteronormativity and Federal Tax Policy*, Nancy Knauer draws attention to the heteronormativity – that is, "the largely unstated assumption that heterosexuality is the essential and elemental ordering principle of society" – that undergirds both the tax laws and the tax policy literature. She asserts that both traditional and critical tax scholars focus too much (and too unquestioningly) on the couple as the appropriate tax unit. Knauer suggests that infusing queer theory into the study of tax would provide new insights into basic ideas and move scholars to question the seemingly received wisdom of tax law. Among other things, queer theory would push us to question how we define a "family" and what relationships, if any, should be privileged in the application of the tax laws.

Patricia Cain's article, *Death Taxes: A Critique from the Margin*, takes up Knauer's challenge (although not directly). Cain asks how the tax laws should treat families. Cain again adopts the narrative critique made popular by critical race theorists and feminist legal scholars. In telling a series of stories "from the margin," Cain exposes the burdens that the estate tax imposes on nontraditional families. Cain argues that increased sensitivity to the real-life experience of families – whether gay, lesbian, or not – militates in favor of shifting the focus of wealth transfer tax rules away from traditional rules concerning the transfer of property by one individual to another and toward a focus on the economic sharing that occurs in almost all families.

In Homo Sacer, *Homosexual: Some Thoughts on Waging Tax Guerrilla Warfare*, Anthony Infanti makes clear that dignity does not mean complacency and that demands for justice are not only rhetorical. He proposes mass action on the part of gay and lesbian taxpayers to flood the IRS with tax returns claiming recognition for same-sex relationships. Infanti's strategy would bring the IRS to an effective standstill (at least temporarily). It also would make lesbian and gay taxpayers and their advocates the leaders of a movement for social and economic justice in action, as they educate the country about the discrimination that they suffer.

Same-Sex Couples and the Federal Tax Laws

PATRICIA A. CAIN[1]

One of the arguments put forth by advocates of lesbian and gay marriage is that same-sex couples should be entitled to the same tax benefits enjoyed by married couples. Often, however, advocates of this position overlook the fact that the federal tax laws do not always bestow benefits on married couples. In addition to the "marriage penalty," other tax detriments that married couples experience are: (1) joint and several tax liability on a joint return; (2) the inability to recognize losses on sales between spouses; and (3) numerous tax attribution rules that treat spouses as a unitary taxpayer.

Nonetheless, married couples do receive considerable tax benefits. Husband and wife can transfer wealth to each other free of income, estate, and gift taxes. Employers often provide important fringe benefits to the spouses of their employees. The federal tax law exempts the receipt of these benefits from income taxation. When married couples divorce, income tax rules are structured to allow the couple to unwind their property entanglements tax-free. Finally, for some married couples, the availability of the joint return does produce a tax savings.

None of these specially enacted tax benefits is available to lesbian and gay couples.

AGREEMENTS TO SHARE INCOME

Earned income is always taxed to the earner, unless the income is community property income. Despite the absence of satisfactory justifications for these results, the judiciary has held firm to this underlying rule for over sixty years now. Thus, there is no viable argument under current law by which a private agreement to split earned income can serve to split the income tax burden.

Consider a lesbian couple, Anna and Beth. Assume that Anna earns a salary of $60,000, which she has agreed to share with Beth. Anna remains taxable on the $60,000 despite the agreement. But does the agreement affect Beth's tax liability?

Exclusion from Gross Income

Are the transfers from Anna to Beth gifts under § 102 of the Code? The starting point for answering this question is *Commissioner v. Duberstein*. Under *Duberstein*, a

---

[1] Reprinted by permission from 1 *Tulane Journal of Law and Sexuality* 97 (1991).

transfer is a gift if the transferor's motive is "detached and disinterested generosity," stemming from "affection, respect, admiration, charity or like impulses."[2] A difficulty in applying this test to Anna and Beth arises if the transfers occur pursuant to a relationship contract. The mutual promises in a relationship contract suggest a certain quid pro quo that is inconsistent with the notion of "detached and disinterested generosity." Additionally, if Beth has promised more than love, affection, and companionship – for example, if she has also promised services (e.g., housekeeping or cooking) – then the *Duberstein* test is clearly more difficult to meet.

Despite warnings that traditional tax analysis could tax both Anna and Beth, the correct approach is to focus on the primary motivation of Anna in making the transfer. Provided the contract itself is motivated primarily by love and affection, then all transfers pursuant to the contract ought to be viewed as stemming from the same motivation. Under this analysis, the transfers would be excludable gifts under § 102.

Although I believe gift characterization is accurate for the transfer from Anna to Beth, another characterization is possible. The agreement to pool income was entered into for the purpose of supporting Beth. Characterized in this manner, the payments technically would not meet the *Duberstein* test for gift exclusion. Can they be excluded from Beth's income under some theory other than the "gift" exclusion?

One possibility would be to analogize support payments between Anna and Beth to support payments between spouses. Spousal support payments are not income to the recipient. Although there may be a number of policy reasons for excluding support payments from income, one of the most obvious reasons is that they are sufficiently similar to gifts (e.g., the motives behind the transfers are similar in that they both stem from love and affection) that it would be administratively difficult to determine when a payment was a "pure gift" and when it was in fulfillment of a support obligation. Thus both types of payments should be excluded from income.

The Gift Tax

Gift and estate taxes are often described as the concern of the wealthy and not of the general population. [As of the writing of this article in 1991,] every person can make $600,000 worth of cumulative gratuitous transfers before any tax will be triggered.[3] This $600,000 "exemption" amount can be transferred in the form of inter vivos gifts [or] at death, or through some combination of lifetime and death-time transfers. The tax will be triggered on the first $1 that is gratuitously

---

[2] 363 U.S. 278, 285 (1960).

[3] [The Economic Growth and Tax Relief Reconciliation Act of 2001, Pub. L. No. 107-16, 115 Stat. 70 (2001) (EGTRRA), provided for gradual increases to the gift tax "exemption amount" to their present level of $1,000,000 in 2009. Under EGTRRA, the federal estate tax is repealed for 2010 and is scheduled to spring back into effect at pre-EGTRRA rates in 2011. If Congress does not intervene before that time, for years after 2010, the unified credit allowed under § 2010 of the Code will protect $1,000,000 of gratuitous asset transfers during lifetime or at death. – Eds.]

transferred in excess of $600,000. The marginal rate applicable to that first $1 is 37%, increasing to a top bracket of 50%. Conceived as a tax on the wealthy, the tax steps in at a comparably hefty rate. The availability of a $10,000[4] annual exclusion from taxable gifts, calculated on a per donee basis, is also thought to mitigate the effect of the gift tax on the less wealthy.

Although $600,000 may seem a high enough figure to some, there are likely to be regional differences of opinion on the matter. California real estate prices, for example, are steep enough to push some middle-income couples into the 37% tax bracket on the basis of home ownership alone. In addition, vested pension plans, together with employer-provided life insurance, can easily produce taxable estates in excess of $600,000 for persons who spend all their available income on support rather than making investments in estate assets. In such cases, it is unlikely that any tax will be due until death, but the amount of that tax at death will be increased if the decedent has made any taxable gifts during her lifetime.

Spouses can make gift transfers to each other free of the gift tax. For all other taxpayers, including Anna and Beth, gift transfers are taxable to the extent they exceed $10,000 per donee per year. The gift tax is assessed against the transferor when the gift transfer is complete. If Anna keeps her funds in a separate account, no gift transfer is completed until she actually transfers funds to Beth or uses them for Beth's benefit. If Anna deposits funds into a joint account, there is no completed gift for gift tax purposes until [Beth] withdraws the funds.

Technically the definition of "gift" is different for income and gift tax purposes. Thus, it is logically possible for a transfer to be considered a gift under the gift tax definition, but not a gift under the income tax definition. In this case, the transfer would be subject to both the gift tax and the income tax. Similarly, it ought to be logically possible to argue for gift treatment under the income tax, while maintaining that a transfer is not a taxable gift under the gift tax.

Having taken the position for income tax purposes that payments made to Beth pursuant to the relationship contract stem primarily from love and affection, however, consistency would seem to require that any such payments be characterized as taxable gifts. This is because the gift tax provisions define "gift" as any transfer "for less than an adequate and full consideration in money or money's worth."[5] "Love and affection" is not adequate consideration in money or money's worth.

Is there any way that Anna and Beth can achieve the same tax result under their relationship contract as a married couple achieves under a marriage contract? In other words, is there any theory under which we might argue that the transfers from Anna to Beth are neither taxable income nor taxable gifts? While it is clear that Anna cannot utilize the gift tax marital deduction, there are several arguments that can be made against gift taxation.

First, we must consider the purpose of the gift tax: to protect against depletion of the taxable estate. The question becomes whether the wealth transfers from Anna to Beth are the sort of transfers that threaten estate depletion. One accumulates

---

[4] [For 2009, the gift tax annual exclusion is $13,000 per donee. Rev. Proc. 2008-66, § 3.30(1), 2008-45 I.R.B. 1107. – Eds.]
[5] I.R.C. § 2512(b).

wealth out of disposable income. If Anna's taxable income is $60,000 for the year, she will have approximately $41,500 in after-tax income. Assuming no other deductions from her payroll check, this is the amount available for income pooling with Beth. If Anna were to write Beth a year-end check in the amount of $20,000, which Beth could spend as she pleased, the transfer would look like a $20,000 gift, $10,000 of which would be taxable. But does this amount really constitute "disposable income" to either Anna or Beth? The relationship agreement calls for the sharing of expenses as well as income. Even if Anna writes a check to Beth for $20,000, Beth is obligated to use those funds to cover her half of the joint expenses. The joint expenses include payments for housing (either mortgage payments or rent), for repairs, insurance, utilities, and groceries. If their joint expenses exceed $20,000, which is likely, then the amount of the unrestricted transfer to Beth is less than $10,000.

Let us assume for purposes of argument that Anna and Beth live in a three-bedroom home, which they rent for $1,500 a month, and that the cost of repairs, insurance, utilities, and food is on average $500 a month. In this case, their total joint expenses are $24,000 for the year. This means that $12,000 of the $20,000 transfer to Beth is not a transfer for Beth's sole enjoyment, but is a contribution toward their joint living expenses. Is this $12,000 amount the sort of wealth transfer that the gift tax was intended to reach? One might argue that it is not because the $12,000 does not represent truly disposable income. It is not a net wealth transfer from one taxpayer to another that necessarily reduces the transferor's taxable estate. Anna might well live in the same house whether or not she was in a relationship with Beth. The cost of repairs, insurance, and utilities might not vary much between sole occupancy and shared occupancy. The grocery bill might be higher for two than for one, but not necessarily. If Anna and Beth were not living together, Anna might spend more money in restaurants and on entertaining friends.

If Anna pays all living expenses out of her separate account, she will be paying Beth's share of the expenses. Under their agreement to share everything, Beth's share is $12,000. But the situation can also be described as one in which Anna is paying $24,000 for living expenses and allowing Beth to live with her at no cost. Although I believe the gift tax question is the same regardless of the mechanics, this latter approach isolates the issue nicely. The issue is: Does the provision of room and board cost-free constitute a gift to the recipient in the absence of proof that the transferor would not have made these payments for self-consumption anyway? Since payments of this type cannot possibly reduce the transferor's taxable estate (they are consumption expenses), they should not be viewed as taxable gifts.

Support for this position can be found in Revenue Ruling 68-379, which held that transfers from a husband to a wife in satisfaction of his obligation to support her are not taxable gifts, because "the satisfaction of this legal obligation does not have the effect of diminishing the husband's estate any more than the satisfaction of any other legal obligation."

In addition, the ruling raises another possibility: that payments in the nature of support are not taxable gifts. The payments in the ruling were made pursuant to an agreement entered into incident to a legal separation. Nonetheless, it assumes that payments that satisfy a legal obligation of support are not taxable gifts. Anna's payments to Beth are similar to the husband's payments to support his wife and they do not have the effect of diminishing her estate. If the analogy holds, Anna's payment of Beth's support should not constitute a taxable gift.

There are, however, arguments against this "legal obligation to support" analogy. First of all, Anna undertook her support obligation voluntarily. The husband's obligation arose under state law. Also, "legal support" is often limited to payments for bare necessities under state law. Thus, the amount of support exempted from gift tax may not include all of the consumption items purchased by Anna for the benefit of Beth.

In the 1960s, the American Law Institute (ALI) began a study of the federal estate and gift tax system. At its May 1968 annual meeting, the ALI adopted a number of recommendations, including the unification of the gift and estate tax and the 100% marital deduction, which have been adopted by Congress. At this same May 1968 meeting, the ALI addressed the transfer for consumption problem and adopted the following resolution:

> An expenditure should be excluded from transfer taxation as a life-time transfer, under either a dual tax system or a unified tax, if the expenditure is for:
>
> (a) the benefit of any person residing in the transferor's household or the benefit of a child of the transferor under 21 years of age, whether or not he resides in the transferor's household, provided that such expenditure does not result in such person or child acquiring property which will retain significant value after the passage of one year from date of such expenditure; or
> (b) current educational, medical or dental costs of any person; or
> (c) current costs of food, clothing and maintenance of living accommodations of any person in fact dependent on the transferor, in whole or in part, for support, provided such expenditure is reasonable in amount.[6]

Note that this proposal offered tax rules that could be applied consistently to lesbian and gay families as well as to traditional families. No special relationship between the transferor and transferee was required. The purpose of the proposal was to clear up what was perceived as "common misunderstanding about the gift tax consequences of responding to the needs of various persons for help."[7] Furthermore, since the IRS had taken the position that support transfers were taxable gifts unless they were made pursuant to a legally binding support obligation and since the state laws were quite varied in their support requirements, geographical location was often determinative of the gift tax question. The ALI proposal would have eliminated this geographical discrimination. But most important, the proposal would have extended this nongift status to support payments that occurred within lesbian and gay couples.

In 1981, Congress adopted part of the ALI proposal. Payments of medical expenses and tuition are now explicitly excluded from the definition of gift, regardless of whether those payments are made on behalf of traditional family members, nontraditional family members, or even good friends. This provision is a major

---

[6] Am. Law Inst., Federal Estate and Gift Taxation: Recommendations of the American Law Institute and Reporters' Studies 20–21 (1969).

[7] Id. at 19.

benefit for lesbian and gay families, but it is not enough. Under an ideal tax system, no support payments would be subject to the gift tax.

Although the failure of Congress to codify the rule regarding support payments generally is troubling, it is difficult to believe that Congress intended tuition payments to escape gift characterization, but not payments for basics such as food and clothing. It is just as likely that Congress thought no specific laws were required, given the existence of prior authority on the question with respect to intrafamily support transfers. In addition, the annual exclusion was raised from $3,000 to $10,000, which no doubt was viewed as sufficient to cover support payments that might exceed the minimum support required under some state laws.

The difficulty is that [prior to the recognition of same-sex unions in some jurisdictions] no state imposes support obligations in lesbian and gay families. The partners can, of course, take on such obligations voluntarily by contract. Whether the IRS would equate such contract obligations with state-imposed ones is an open question. If it does not, then under existing authority, support payments could be taxed as gifts. Whereas, the $10,000 annual exclusion may be sufficient to cover support payments to children that exceed any legally imposed obligations, it is not sufficient to cover all support payments in lesbian and gay families where no state-imposed support obligations exist.

In sum, support transfers ought not to be treated as taxable gifts, because they are not transfers that serve to deplete the transferor's taxable estate. One argument that such payments are not taxable gifts when they occur within a lesbian or gay household is that the payments are primarily for the consumption of the transferor. When Anna satisfies her own consumption needs, she is not depleting her estate and thus not making a taxable gift to Beth. Another argument is that to the extent the lesbian or gay partners have legally obligated themselves to support each other, their support payments are not gifts. There is adequate authority to support nongift characterization in the case of legally imposed support payments by spouses and by parents. There is no reason not to extend this rule to lesbian and gay couples.

CONCLUSION

Our income tax laws are based on the notion that the individual is the appropriate tax unit. Congress recognized that this notion was unworkable for husbands and wives who shared a household and supported each other. The joint return provides a partial legislative solution to the "individual as tax unit" problem. Congress has made similar adjustments for husbands and wives over the years, which, in effect, allow spouses to share income, and make wealth transfers at no tax cost. These adjustments have established the husband and wife (and in some cases, their dependent children) as the tax unit.

The tax laws ignore other real households in which couples share income and property. In particular, lesbian and gay couples are harmed by tax laws that limit tax benefits to married couples. Full parity between married couples and same-sex couples could be obtained if Congress would recognize some form of "tax marriage." In this article, however, I have made arguments for lesser reforms. The arguments I have made are but part of a larger reform that must occur before full tax parity between same-sex couples and married couples will be attained. In an ideal world the tax law would not discriminate against same-sex couples who are similarly situated to married couples. If joint returns are the appropriate reporting device for husband and wife, then I believe joint returns should be available for same-sex couples who consider themselves just as committed as married couples and whose household is just as much a single economic unit. If husbands and wives can acquire joint wealth without paying gift and estate taxes, then I believe lesbian and gay couples are entitled to that same tax treatment. Full tax equity between married couples and same-sex couples who are similarly situated seems so correct a principle that it hardly needs defending. What I have tried to do in this article is to suggest different ways of looking at one type of transaction, the payment of support to a lover, which is currently subjected to discriminatory treatment under existing tax laws.

The Internal Revenue Code as Sodomy Statute

ANTHONY C. INFANTI[1]

I recently had occasion to read an issue of the *North Carolina Law Review* containing a symposium on critical tax theory. Most of the contributors focused their attention on issues relating to race and gender. Nevertheless, one of the contributors, Steve Johnson, did focus significant attention on issues relating to sexual orientation. Johnson concluded: "I believe that scholars and advocates have not yet convincingly demonstrated that, on net, the failure to recognize same-sex couples as married hurts them by imposing substantially higher federal income tax liabilities on them."[2]

My immediate reaction to Johnson's article can be summarized in one word: astonishment. As a gay man, I was puzzled at how equal treatment could be boiled down to a simple cost-benefit analysis. How could Johnson have ignored the ways in which the Code stigmatizes gays and lesbians and attempts to force them into the closet? Can any net tax benefit really make up for the patently unequal and discriminatory treatment visited by the federal government upon gays and lesbians through the medium of the Code?

THE NARRATIVE

Not many people at [my college] were out of the closet, and the environment wasn't particularly welcoming for the few who were open about their sexual orientation. I learned this for myself within a week of arriving at school. I had been assigned to an all-male dormitory that year. The testosterone level in the dorm ran high, and the antigay remarks and fag jokes were more pervasive and biting than I had ever experienced before. During that first week, when everyone feels vulnerable, nervous, and anxious about being away from home, I had a rather negative encounter with two upper-class students. I had just passed them in the stairwell when they started spitting "queer" and "fag" at me – in a tone that oozed venom and with a physical presence that can only be described as menacing. I couldn't understand why they had targeted me. Was it that obvious? Whether it was or not, they had made it abundantly clear that being open about my sexual orientation at college

---

[1] Reprinted by permission from 44 *Santa Clara Law Review* 763 (2004).
[2] Steve R. Johnson, *Targets Missed and Targets Hit: Critical Tax Studies and Effective Tax Reform*, 76 N.C. L. REV. 1771, 1779 (1998).

would likely culminate in hospitalization. After that episode, I became all the more firmly ensconced in the closet, because I was not about to risk having to come out to my parents from a hospital bed.

In law school, I eventually came to the realization that this was no way to live. By the end of law school, I had reached a point where I was relatively comfortable with myself. I finally started dating. I met Michael, a master's student in chemical engineering. We soon became inseparable. When I met him, I was in my last semester of law school and he had not quite finished his master's degree. I had already accepted a clerkship in San Diego that was to start at the end of the summer, and had accepted a summer associate position with a firm in New York that would occupy my time between graduation and the clerkship. But we had fallen in love, and I knew that I wanted to make a life with Michael. So, I asked him to move with me to San Diego, and he agreed.

While working as a summer associate in New York between law school and my clerkship, I lived with my parents and commuted to the City from their house in New Jersey. Shortly before I was to return to California, my mother, prompted by suggestions from others in my family, asked me straight up (so to speak) if I [was] gay. I honestly answered "yes." She then asked if Michael, whom my parents had met at my law school graduation, was my "special friend" (where she got that term from, I still don't know). Again, I honestly answered "yes." Although a little upset, she generally took it in stride. I was her son, and my being gay was not going to change how much she loved and cared for me.

When my mother asked me if Michael was my "special friend," it was the first time that I had seen someone react to homosexuality with a combination of bewilderment and discomfort (rather than unadulterated hostility). She found herself stumped by how to refer to our relationship. By now, I have experienced this uncomfortable groping for words on countless occasions. When my mother acknowledged our relationship, she, like most straight people, was clearly uncomfortable with admitting to herself that there was a sexual dimension to it. This discomfort, when combined with the lack of a ready label for a relationship between two gay men, has generated any number of desexualized euphemisms such as "friend" or my mother's term "special friend" (both of which have a decidedly platonic overtone), "partner" (which sounds like you're in business together), and "significant other" ("significant" – I would describe my dog as a significant part of my life; "other" – other than what?).

THE CODE: A GAY PERSPECTIVE

By recounting this series of experiences, I have tried to explain why I view society's visceral revulsion to homosexuality as being comprised of a fluid mixture of hostility, bewilderment, and discomfort. In this Part, I explore how society's revulsion manifests itself in the Code's treatment of gay and lesbian couples.

Hostility

For many years, the federal government (with the complicity of the states) quietly banished gay and lesbian couples to the closet by failing to acknowledge the existence of their relationships. Congress was content with this arrangement until gay and lesbian couples began to make some progress in having their relationships legally recognized. In the wake of a Hawaii court decision that for the first time raised the specter of legalized same-sex marriage, Congress decided to step in and ensure that gay and lesbian couples would never be treated as married for federal tax purposes. To this end, Congress enacted (and President Clinton signed) the Defense of Marriage Act (DOMA), which provides that:

> In determining the meaning of any Act of Congress, or of any ruling, regulation, or interpretation of the various administrative bureaus and agencies of the United States, the word "marriage" means only a legal union between one man and one woman as husband and wife, and the word "spouse" refers only to a person of the opposite sex who is a husband or a wife.[3]

Not satisfied that a mere slap in the face would keep gay and lesbian couples in the tax closet, Congress apparently decided to deal them a body blow that would ensure that its hostility is clear and unmistakable.

Yet nothing is new or different about this hostility – it is little more than an extension of the hostility that I have experienced all my life. The hostility in the Code has simply moved from the background to the foreground in the same way that the atmosphere of hostility that I experienced in my childhood and adolescence (i.e., the childhood taunting, fag jokes, derogatory remarks, and whispers) gave way to physical menacing when I went to college.

Mixed with Bewilderment and Discomfort

Mixed in with this now-explicit hostility are the twin elements of bewilderment and discomfort. Because Congress refuses to treat gay and lesbian couples as "married," it becomes difficult to settle on an appropriate tax classification for transactions that occur within the couple. Are they transactions between donor and donee? Creditor and debtor? Employer and employee? Parent and child? Business partners? This is the same difficulty that straight people encounter when, refusing to use the word "husband" or "wife" (or even the gender-neutral "spouse"), they grope to find the right word to describe the relationship between two gay men or two lesbians. As a result of its aversion to gay sex, straight society finds itself struggling once again to shoe-horn gay and lesbian couples into desexualized categories that just don't comport with reality. These categories are simply the tax versions of the desexualized euphemisms (e.g., "friend," "partner," and "significant other") that gay and lesbian couples encounter in daily life.

In the context of taxation, this bewilderment and discomfort have more than just symbolic consequences. During the nine years that Michael and I were together, we pooled our income (which, as might be expected, was never equal) and shared all of our expenses. Whenever, like us, a gay or lesbian couple pools all or a portion of its income and investments and one partner earns more than the other, the couple

---

[3] Defense of Marriage Act, Pub. L. No. 104-199, § 3(a), 110 Stat. 2419 (1996) (codified at 1 U.S.C. § 7 (2000)).

must confront the enigmatic task of characterizing the annual net transfer from the higher-earning partner to the lower-earning partner (the "net interspousal transfer") both for income and for gift tax purposes.

For income tax purposes, the higher-earning partner might be treated as making a gift each time the utility bills are paid, a trip is made to the grocery store, or a withdrawal is made from the ATM. If so, the higher-earning partner would continue to pay tax on her wages, and the lower-earning partner would have no income tax inclusion as a result of receiving those gifts. Alternatively, the pooling might be characterized as a support arrangement. In that case, the higher-earning partner would still be subject to tax on her wages, while the lower-earning partner would again have no income tax inclusion as a result of receiving the support payments. A more frightening alternative would require both partners to pay tax on the portion of the higher-earning partner's income that is transferred to the lower-earning partner – on the ground that it technically constitutes "income" to each of them. Yet another possibility is that the net interspousal transfer could represent some combination of [these alternatives] (e.g., part support, part gift; part support, part income; or part gift, part income).

For gift tax purposes, a net interspousal transfer might be treated as a taxable gift. Or, the transfer might be characterized as a nontaxable payment made in exchange for rendering domestic services or for furnishing some other consideration in money or money's worth. Alternatively, the net interspousal transfer might be characterized as a nontaxable support payment. Yet another possibility is that the transfer could represent some combination of [these alternatives] (e.g., part non-taxable support payment, part taxable gift or part nontaxable payment for services, part taxable gift).

Furthermore, when the income and gift tax consequences of a net interspousal transfer are considered together, the tax cost may be even higher than it initially appears. Because the income tax and the gift tax operate independently, the characterization of a net interspousal transfer need not be consistent across these taxes. In other words, a net interspousal transfer might be characterized as income to both partners for income tax purposes and as a taxable gift from the higher-earning partner to the lower-earning partner for gift tax purposes. Consequently, a portion of the income of the higher-earning partner might be subject to triple taxation.

. . . and Back to Hostility Again

Faced with a veritable constellation of potential tax characterizations, gay and lesbian couples must examine all of the possibilities and settle on an appropriate combination of income and gift tax characterizations for their net interspousal transfers. Their task is not made any easier by Congress or the IRS, both of whom have been conspicuously silent on the question of how the tax laws should be applied to gay and lesbian couples. Although Congress took the time to debate and decide that gay and lesbian couples should never be treated as married for federal tax purposes, it did not spend any time spelling out how to treat couples who do not qualify for the marital provisions in the Code. The IRS has made no attempt to fill this gap in the application of the tax laws either; it has been noticeably remiss in issuing public guidance to help gay and lesbian couples comply with tax laws.

Burden of proof and penalties. Yet, despite this lack of guidance, the tax laws place the burden on gay and lesbian couples to prove that their chosen treatment is correct. The tax laws additionally attach a presumption of correctness to whatever treatment the IRS deems appropriate – after the fact and without any advance public notice. Because of the need to shoe-horn interspousal transfers into categories that don't quite fit, these burdens – the burden of proof and the burden of going forward with evidence – will prove difficult for gay and lesbian couples to bear. If they fail to carry one or both of these burdens, gay and lesbian couples may find that they are liable not only for additional tax, but also for one or more of the civil penalties authorized by the Code.

The potentially applicable penalties include: a penalty for failure timely to file an income or gift tax return[;] a penalty for failure to pay any amount of tax required to be shown on an income or gift tax return, but which has not been shown[;] a penalty for negligence or disregard of rules or regulations[; and] a penalty for substantial understatement of income tax. Other more obscure penalties may also be imposed on gay and lesbian couples in connection with net interspousal transfers.

A taxpayer can avoid these penalties if she can demonstrate that (i) she had reasonable cause for her failure and (ii) depending on the penalty, she either acted in good faith or did not willfully neglect her legal obligations. To establish the existence of reasonable cause, the taxpayer must generally demonstrate that she exercised ordinary care and prudence in ascertaining and complying with her tax obligations. Ignorance of the law, by itself, does not constitute reasonable cause for failure to comply with the tax laws.

When it comes to grappling with the uncertainty surrounding the tax characterization of net interspousal transfers, gay and lesbian couples likely fall into one of three categories: (i) the blissfully ignorant, who are simply unaware of this tax issue; (ii) the informed and well-intentioned, who are aware of this tax issue and make their best effort at compliance; or (iii) the informed but civilly disobedient, who are aware of this tax issue but purposefully refuse to allow themselves to be made a party to their own oppression. Only gay and lesbian couples that fall in the second category will be able to avail themselves of the reasonable cause exception, because they will have made a good faith (albeit erroneous) attempt to comply with an uncertain area of the law. Couples in the other two categories will be faced with penalties either because they were ignorant of the law or because they were aware of the law and ignored it – neither of which constitutes reasonable cause.

If they are liable for additional tax, penalties, or both, then the couple will also be liable for interest on the additional tax due and on any penalties – compounded daily. Taken together, compound interest and penalties can quickly increase the size of a tax bill.

Recordkeeping and reporting requirements. Even if a gay or lesbian couple manages to win the battle with the IRS over an alleged failure appropriately to characterize a net interspousal transfer, the couple may find that the war with the

IRS is far from over. The Code also imposes on gay and lesbian couples several recordkeeping and reporting requirements that are ostensibly designed to help the IRS verify the accuracy of the couple's returns.

For income tax purposes, each taxpayer is required to "keep such permanent books of account or records, including inventories, as are sufficient to establish the amount of gross income, deductions, credits, or other matters required to be shown by such person in any return of such tax or information."[4] Likewise, for gift tax purposes, each taxpayer is required to "keep such permanent books of account or records as are necessary to establish the amount of his total gifts . . . together with the deductions allowable in determining the amount of his taxable gifts, and the other information required to be shown in a gift tax return."[5] Moreover, if a taxpayer makes gifts to a person in excess of the annual exclusion, she is required to list separately on her gift tax return each and every gift made during the calendar year to that person, including gifts that are not taxed because of the annual exclusion.

These requirements impose a Sisyphean compliance burden on any gay or lesbian couple who pools income and shares expenses. The Code essentially requires these couples to keep records documenting every penny that they spend, save, or give away to third parties. Every trip to the grocery store, the clothing store, and the bank must be documented to determine who spent what and on whom. Without these records, the couple will find it difficult, if not impossible, to counter an assertion by the IRS that (i) the net interspousal transfer is larger than claimed by the couple; (ii) for income tax purposes, a larger portion of the transfer should be treated as taxable income (as opposed to a nontaxable gift or support payment); and/or (iii) for gift tax purposes, a larger portion of the transfer should be treated as a taxable gift (as opposed to a nontaxable support payment).

Simply put, these recordkeeping and reporting requirements are demeaning and oppressive. Think for a moment of the mountain of shopping receipts that you collect every month. Then think of having to catalogue each of these receipts contemporaneously according to what was spent and on whom. Then think about having to tally up the total at the end of the year. Then think about having to list every one of these transactions on a tax return, showing the particulars of what was given, by whom, and to whom. Finally, think about having to find a place to store this small mountain of paper for six or more years (depending on the relevant tax statute of limitations) in order to provide support for the claimed amount and tax characterization of any net interspousal transfer.

For gay and lesbian couples, these recordkeeping and reporting requirements represent not only an onerous burden, but also a severe invasion of privacy. After *Lawrence v. Texas*,[6] the government can no longer break into our bedrooms to determine with whom and how we have sex, but it can still use the Code to knock on the front door, come in, and probe our every move (financial and otherwise) with our partners. No straight couple is (or likely ever will be) required to put up with this level of intrusion into its relationship.

---

[4] Treas. Reg. § 1.6001-1(a).
[5] *Id.* § 25.6001-1(a).
[6] Lawrence v. Texas, 539 U.S. 558 (2003).

Such a crushing (not to mention insulting) recordkeeping and reporting burden can only breed noncompliance. Noncompliant gay and lesbian couples will again likely fall into one of three categories: (i) the blissfully ignorant, who simply have no idea that the recordkeeping and reporting requirements exist; (ii) the informed and well-intentioned, who attempt to comply, but (as can only be expected) fail to do so; or (iii) the informed but civilly disobedient, who are aware of the requirements but purposefully refuse to comply because they do not wish to be made a party to their own oppression. Whatever the reason, this noncompliance with the recordkeeping and reporting requirements may give the IRS an opportunity to increase the amount of additional tax owed and to impose penalties.

For those who either throw up their hands at the impossibility of the task or who refuse to acquiesce in the oppression, the specter of criminal liability is added to the array of civil penalties discussed previously. Gay and lesbian couples who are aware of the recordkeeping requirements and decide not to comply with them may be found guilty of the crime of willful failure to keep records. This is a misdemeanor punishable by a fine of up to $100,000, imprisonment of up to one year, or both. These criminal penalties are imposed in addition to, and not in lieu of, the civil penalties discussed earlier.

The Code as Sodomy Statute

Given the array of civil and criminal penalties that the IRS has at its disposal, gay and lesbian couples who pool income and share expenses are nearly assured that they will not escape an IRS assault unscathed. Those who remain blissfully ignorant of these tax issues may not be subject to criminal penalties for failing to keep appropriate records; however, they may be liable for civil penalties because of their inability to rely on the reasonable cause exception. Those who are aware of their legal obligations and make a good faith attempt at compliance may be able to avoid civil penalties by relying on the reasonable cause exception; however, they may have a tougher time avoiding criminal penalties if they are aware of the recordkeeping requirements, but voluntarily and intentionally fail to comply with them because they impose a crushing burden. Those who engage in civil disobedience get the worst treatment, as they face the possibility of both civil and criminal penalties for failing to comply with their tax obligations.

Seen in this light, the Code takes on the aspect of another codification of society's hostility toward homosexuality: the (now outmoded) sodomy statute. Like a sodomy statute, the Code targets and punishes gay sex, albeit indirectly through the proxy of gay coupling. And despite being underenforced (much like a sodomy statute), the Code and its civil and criminal penalties nonetheless "hang as an ominous Sword of Damocles over the heads of lesbians and gay men throughout the country."[7]

Moreover, as is the case with a sodomy statute, the impact of the Code on gays and lesbians is not confined to the civil and criminal penalties that may be imposed

---

[7] Evan Wolfson & Robert S. Mower, *When the Police Are in Our Bedrooms, Shouldn't the Courts Go in After Them?: An Update on the Fight Against "Sodomy" Laws*, 21 FORDHAM URB. L.J. 997 (1994).

on the occurrence of the rare audit or prosecution. The Code can also harm gays and lesbians in other ways. As one of the more prominent applications of DOMA, the Code is overtly hostile to gays and lesbians. This overt hostility toward gay and lesbian couples stigmatizes them by branding their relationships inferior to those of straight couples. In effect, the Code at once embodies and perpetuates societal prejudice, discrimination, and hostility toward gays and lesbians by giving such activity the imprimatur of the federal government.

The bewilderment and discomfort that follow on the heels of this overt hostility further reinforce the stigma. In defining marriage for purposes of federal law, DOMA makes no explicit mention of gay and lesbian couples – even though its purpose is to brand them inferior. Its condemnation comes instead by implication and through explanation in committee reports that few will ever read. This discomfort at officially and prominently acknowledging the existence of gay and lesbian couples can also be detected in the noticeable failure of Congress and the IRS to address the application of the Code to gay and lesbian couples. It can additionally be detected in the need to shoe-horn gay and lesbian couples into desexualized tax categories at odds with the reality of their relationships. Relationships between gay men and lesbians are apparently so repugnant that they cannot be acknowledged as such; instead, they must either be ignored or reshaped into more acceptable, and less loathsome, molds.

This bewilderment and discomfort engender a more insidious form of hostility that attempts to make gay and lesbian couples a party to their own oppression by driving them into the closet (or for those already there, further into the closet). The Code encourages gay and lesbian couples not to file returns or statements with the IRS that connect one partner with the other. If they dare to do otherwise, they expose themselves to a panoply of civil and criminal penalties, and, for those in the closet, to the public outing that tax litigation would necessarily entail (should they choose to fight the IRS's determination in court). The Code thus attempts to banish our relationships from sight, making us invisible once again.

CONCLUSION

So, you see, I am not concerned with whether my tax bill would go up or down were I allowed to check the "married filing jointly" box on my Form 1040. As a gay man, that is the least of my worries. Much more important to me is finding someone with whom I can share my life. About two years ago, I was lucky enough to meet a wonderful man and we're planning on moving in together. What is important to me is that we, as a couple, be treated with dignity and respect. But that is not what we get – either from society or from the Code. Instead, both society and the Code treat us with a combination of hostility, bewilderment, and discomfort that demeans our existence and attempts to control our destiny by essentially making our private sexual conduct a tax crime. If that's not discrimination, what is?

Heteronormativity and Federal Tax Policy

NANCY J. KNAUER[1]

INTRODUCTION

The proponents of same-sex marriage demand equal marriage rights as a matter of fundamental human dignity and as a means to gain certain legal benefits that attach to marital status. When they enumerate the benefits of marriage, the proponents invariably place the ability to file joint federal income tax returns near the top of the list, followed by inheritance rights, pension and survivor benefits, and decision-making authority in the case of disability. However, for anyone familiar with the recent congressional debate over the "marriage tax penalty," characterizing joint filing status as a "benefit" seems to be at best ill-informed and at worst just plain wrong. After all, everyone knows that the Code is anti-marriage.

To the contrary, I believe that this assertion by same-sex couples reveals three points that may not be obvious to tax scholars. First, from their vantage point, same-sex couples can see that the joint filing provisions are just one example of a scheme of taxation where considerations of marital status are pervasive. Accordingly, the risk of a marriage penalty may be overstated because the narrow focus on the marriage penalty ignores the numerous other provisions of the Code which reference a taxpayer's marital status. Second, the provisions governing family taxation are prescriptive in nature. They are designed to recognize and privilege a specific type of relationship. Thus, for some same-sex couples, the risk of a marriage penalty may be offset by the value of official recognition. Finally, the stance of the opponents of same-sex marriage highlights another very important point. Any discussion of sexual orientation and/or marriage implicates difficult and divisive questions of morality.

This article uses these three observations to analyze the marital provisions of the Code, the treatment of these provisions in tax scholarship, and the current legislative proposals for "pro-family" tax reform. Central to my analysis is the contention, informed by queer theory, that the scholarly treatment of the choice of a taxable unit, including much of the new critical tax research, is limited by heteronormativity – the largely unstated assumption that heterosexuality is the essential and elemental ordering principle of society. Queer theory offers a particularly useful

---

[1] Reprinted by permission from 101 *West Virginia Law Review* 129 (1998).

perspective for this analysis because it demands that we question the normal. It reminds us that heterosexuality also is a sexual orientation warranting study. Because queer theory rejects stable gay and lesbian subjects, it does not articulate an ethnic or minority program of inclusion. By moving beyond a rights-centered dialogue it invites us to challenge the construction of the taxpayer as married, widowed, or divorced and to grapple with fundamental normative questions, such as how to define family and which, if any, relationships to privilege.

From this perspective, it is clear that the marital provisions are far from punitive. Not all couples see their federal income tax liability increase upon marriage. In fact, many more see it decrease, experiencing a marriage tax bonus. When viewed in their entirety, the seemingly discordant rules offer a composite picture of marriage. The rules reflect, for better or worse, a view of marriage as an economic unit, a fundamental unit of society, and an intimate association whose members may not deal with each other at arm's length. In stark contrast, same-sex partners always act as strangers under the Code regardless of the economic or contractual realities of their relationship and, since the Defense of Marriage Act (DOMA), regardless of a valid marriage under state law. Whether a same-sex couple will owe more or less federal income tax than a similarly situated married couple depends on the couple's individual circumstances. Generally, a single-earner same-sex couple will pay more income tax than its "traditional" counterpart. A high-income dual-earner same-sex couple will pay less income tax, but in the end may be the hardest hit because of the federal estate and gift tax.

In addition to any economic disadvantage, the exclusion of same-sex couples carries a symbolic cost. No matter how much taxpayers resent paying taxes, the Code continues to send a strong prescriptive message each year when millions of taxpayers check the appropriate box for their filing status. Your filing status, the way you present yourself, and the annual tally of your accomplishments to the state depends, not simply on your marital status, but on the sex of your partner. As a result, I will always be "single" regardless of the length of my relationship or the depth of my commitment. The marital provisions exist very clearly as an expression of the way things should be, not simply of the way things are.

Critical tax scholarship has made great strides in bringing new perspectives to bear on issues of tax policy. Surprisingly absent from this progressive critique has been any extended discussion of the heterosexual bias imbedded in the numerous tax provisions that reference a taxpayer's marital status. This relative silence on matters of sexual orientation reinforces the heteronormative nature of the Code and necessarily limits the depth of any analysis of the marital provisions.

Critical tax scholarship has successfully used critical race and/or feminist theory to reveal racial and gender bias in the Code. It examines the "neutral" principles which purport to undergird tax policy and illustrates how such principles maintain and reinforce existing social and economic structures. This new scholarship also identifies the disparate impact of facially neutral statutory language and examines the behavioral incentives produced by specific provisions with regard to both market- and family-based decision making. Too often, sexual orientation is mentioned only in passing within the larger and primarily gender-based discussion of the joint filing provisions. When sexual orientation is present, the arguments for changing the tax treatment of same-sex couples are grounded safely and securely on neutral principles of tax policy.

The pervasive nature of the marital provisions makes the assumption that every taxpayer, if not married, will marry at least once. One challenge for the new scholarship should be to disrupt the normative image of the taxpayer which underlies our present system of taxation (i.e., the quintessential liberal choosing subject who by default is white, male, and who will marry at least once) and ask what impact race, gender, and sexual orientation have on the tax burden of a particular taxpayer. Looking forward, it is equally important to ask these questions early on when considering any fundamental tax reform in order to begin constructing an (in)essential taxpayer.

As tax scholars labor to make the identities of taxpayers visible, special care is necessary to structure the inquiry in a manner that both acknowledges and avoids the essentializing tendencies that have plagued other areas of legal scholarship. Queer theory cautions that identity is fluid and multivalent. It is not a seriatim experience. We do not have an alternative series of identities but have multiple identities or identifications. At any one moment we are not female or gay or Latina or Jewish, but potentially all of those and more.

The assertion that morality is an integral part of any public policy decision making regarding sexual orientation and/or marriage presents an additional challenge to the new tax scholarship and to gay and lesbian scholarship in general. Sexual orientation is not experienced in the same way as ethnicity and/or race because it is framed by questions of morality. Thus, existing minority identity models are not transferable to individuals in same-sex relationships, whether they identify themselves as gay, lesbian, queer, bisexual, heterosexual, or eschew labels entirely. Further, when discussing the tax treatment of same-sex couples (or any married couple) tax scholarship cannot rely on the comfortable commonplace that taxation is morally neutral.

QUEER THEORY: A PRIMER

Queer theory seeks to destabilize the hetero–homo opposition without offering an alternative fixed identity. Queer theory advocates an alternative positionality or perspective. Instead of seeing from a position of presumed heterosexuality (i.e., that of universal subject) we can begin to approach "heteronormativity" and regard it as the object of critique and a powerful prescriptive force.

The contingent nature of identities helps address the essentializing tendencies of legal scholarship, including the new tax scholarship. Recognizing that identity is multivalent, queer theory challenges us to engage one identification without necessarily silencing or excluding other simultaneous identifications.

The historical explanation of contemporary homosexuality and heterosexuality establishes a relationship of dependence between the two concepts. Heterosexuality does not exist (and indeed would be meaningless) without its evil twin of homosexuality. Thus, the privileged position of heterosexuality depends on the existence of a category which defines that which it is not (i.e., homosexuality). A major project of queer theory is to destabilize the boundary between the natural and the unnatural – between heterosexuality and homosexuality. Ideally, "queer," or at least the positionality advocated by "queer," has the potential to be inclusive of considerations such as of race, class, ethnicity, and disability because it does not attempt to foreground one form of social identification to the necessary exclusion of others. This potential offers legal scholarship the opportunity to develop a "scholarship of articulation" where both differences and commonalities are recognized and spoken.

THE APPROPRIATE TAXABLE UNIT

The current joint filing provisions are considered a compromise between competing neutrality principles: marriage should not impact on a taxpayer's tax liability (i.e., marriage neutrality) and married couples with equal income should bear the same tax, regardless of who earns the income (i.e., couples neutrality). The very question of couples neutrality presupposes that as an elemental unit of society a married couple should also be an elemental unit of taxation. Much of tax policy has grounded its explanation for joint filing on the basis that spouses act as a single economic unit. The intense scholarly interest in the joint filing provisions represents a heteronormative "selection bias" because commentators tend to critique only those marital provisions which are potentially detrimental to married taxpayers.

The recent critique of the joint filing provisions has refuted the economic unit theory by showing that the use of marriage as a proxy for pooling behavior is both overbroad and underinclusive. It has also identified undesirable behavioral incentives produced by joint filing and revealed the disparate impact of the marriage penalty. On the subject of income pooling, Marjorie Kornhauser reports less pooling between married couples than anticipated and introduces the concept of nominal pooling where the spouse who earns the income still retains greater dispositive control over the income [see Chapter 8]. The potential that same-sex (or other unmarried) couples could pool their income is often cited as evidence that the economic unit justification for joint filing is underinclusive.

Tax scholarship written from a gay/lesbian perspective tends to try to expand the definition of couples neutrality and not to question it. Lesbian and gay scholars and activists who have addressed this issue generally have argued that the marital provisions should apply to same-sex couples. To the extent same-sex couples want the Code to recognize their relationships, they are at odds with the emerging consensus that the individual and not the married couple should be the appropriate unit of taxation. Thus, lesbian and gay scholars seem to be asking for inclusion in the very regime that other progressive scholars are trying to dismantle in the name of greater female autonomy.

MARITAL PROVISIONS

Far from being anti-marriage, the Code embraces and recognizes marital status in a wide variety of contexts. Beneficial provisions such as the unlimited transfer tax marital deductions and the exclusion of employer-provided fringe benefits from gross income have gone largely unnoticed and unquestioned.

The marital provisions are based on a series of assumptions concerning the terms, merit, and nature of the taxpayer's relationship with his or her spouse. These provisions use marital status to identify (i) a relationship where income or resource pooling occurs (or should occur), (ii) a relationship that is worthy of societal support in the form of tax deferral or other relief, and (iii) a relationship where the individuals never deal with one another at arm's length. To the contrary, for tax purposes, same-sex partners always deal with each other at arm's length or, at best, with "detached and disinterested generosity."[2]

THE CODE, CONGRESS, AND THE CULTURE WARS

Two cases where Congress debated, articulated, and defined marriage and family [are]: (1) the passage of DOMA and (2) the recent debate regarding "pro-family" tax reform. The floor debate, testimony, and the numerous press releases issued by various interest groups and members of Congress [indicate that] the congressional construction of marriage and family is very far removed from the dispassionate theories of income pooling and the apolitical machinations of competing neutrality principles. It stands instead as a harshly normative view expressed in terms of morality and directly informed by conservative Christian thought. Thus, before tax scholars suggest individual filing or tax marriages, I suggest that they take note of Senator Coats's statement regarding jurisdiction over the term marriage:

> The definition of marriage is not created by politicians and judges, and it cannot be changed by them. It is rooted in our history, in our laws and our deepest moral and religious convictions, and in our nature as human beings. It is the union of one man and one woman. This fact can be respected, or it can be resented, but it cannot be altered.[3]

TOWARD A SCHOLARSHIP OF ARTICULATION

The introduction makes three basic observations regarding same-sex couples and federal tax policy: marital status is a pervasive factor throughout the Code, the marital provisions are prescriptive and have symbolic impact, and questions involving same-sex couples (or even marriage in general) are articulated in terms of morality. These three initial observations offer corresponding recommendations to tax scholarship or political scholarship in general: interrogate assumptions, articulate difference, and evaluate avenues for reform based on strategic assessments. These points should help develop a scholarship that is sensitive to the complexity of identity, the pitfalls of essentialism, and the strategic considerations of "political realism."

Caution What We Too Easily "Mistake for Nature"

Couples neutrality represented a demand by taxpayers/voters that the federal government recognize the fundamental ordering principle of society – the married

---

[2] Comm'r v. Duberstein, 363 U.S. 278, 285 (1960).
[3] 142 CONG. REC. S10,100–02, S10,113 (daily ed. Sept. 10, 1996) (statement of Sen. Coats).

couple – as the relevant taxable unit, regardless of the economic realities of the relationship. This signifies one of the many ways federal law privileges married couples, suggesting a strong, and largely unexplored, preference for marriage. The progressive critique of the marital provisions has focused primarily on the marriage penalty while leaving the marital provisions which do not disadvantage married couples in place and seemingly unremarkable. This targeting of the marriage penalty represents heteronormative "selection bias" and limits our understanding of the current marital regime.

Critical tax scholarship has analyzed the Code through the lens of critical race theory and feminism. These efforts have caused us to view the joint filing provisions, the mortgage interest deduction, and the child-care credit in a different light. However, the relative absence of sexual orientation from these critiques risks revealing a hidden bias while practicing the very type of exclusion that the critique purports to challenge. The effect is to produce a series of static critiques which mask the interconnectedness of identity by an appeal to a false universal. Just as women have had to argue that all taxpayers are not men, lesbians have had to argue that all women are not married to men. Just as critical race scholars argue that all taxpayers are not white, gay men and lesbians of color have had to argue that all taxpayers of color are not heterosexual.

Queer theory offers the opportunity to put it all up for grabs. Queer theory does not construct an alternative identity to gay and lesbian. Instead, it offers a position against the normal or the normative. Queer is simply a vantage point and a [same-sex] libidinal object choice is not a prerequisite. This vantage point equips one to see not simply as a gay or lesbian subject but ideally as any subject that is outside or opposite the normal. Thus, from an oppositional stance against the normal, one can begin to contemplate the impact of race, gender, sexual orientation, disability, class, and other outsider identifications.

Toward a Scholarship of Articulation

The next step is to work toward articulating the endless differences and commonalities revealed by the process of interrogation. Although it is not possible to consider every identity configuration within every proposal or critique, at a minimum a scholarship of articulation requires learning to resist the totalizing impulse that drives us to declare that our scholarship speaks a universal truth just recently discovered. Concerns of intellectual honesty and accuracy dictate that a "scholarship of articulation" make explicit the position of the author.

In order to articulate difference, it is important to understand or be aware of different positional or identity configurations. For example, it is clear from the discussion of DOMA and "pro-family" tax reform that approaching issues of sexual orientation from a minority or ethnic model is insufficient to conceptualize the extent to which morality controls the debate concerning same-sex relationships. Remember, there is nothing unintentional about the exclusion of same-sex couples from the marital provisions. Arguments for the inclusion of same-sex couples that are based on formal equality misapprehend the actual policy issue at hand. It is not simply an abstract question of what is the appropriate taxable unit, rather it is a demand for the validation of same-sex couples and what some would call pejoratively a gay or lesbian lifestyle.

Even if we recognize that a discussion of sexual orientation is primarily a morality discourse, there are wide disparities with respect to the impact of this discourse depending on overlapping identity configurations. The experience of nonnormative sexual orientation differs depending upon class, race, disability, gender, age, marital status, employment, geography, education, and political affiliation. To assert otherwise invites the same form of essentialism that [has] taken lesbians and/or women of color so long to unravel within feminism. Within the category of sexual orientation when gender and race are left unmarked, the default position is white and male. Within feminism, the default setting is white and heterosexual.

A scholarship of articulation requires new and innovative ways to disrupt or reveal those default settings. The easiest way to go about this is to include sexual orientation as an add-on: race, gender, class, ethnicity, or sexual orientation. The shortcoming of this approach is that the reader is left with a sense that there are five different stories being described, not a multitude of stories or a convergence of stories. In this regard, critical tax scholarship can benefit greatly from the work on intersectionality that has stressed the importance of addressing the complexity of identity. Specifically in connection with queer theory, Darren Hutchinson advocates the use of the term "multidimensionality" in place of intersectionality, stating that "it more effectively captures the inherent complexity and irreversibly multilayered nature of everyone's identities and of oppression."[4] The multivalent nature of identity insures that every article will not incorporate every viewpoint. There is no dishonor in writing a proposal or a critique that is less than comprehensive, but there is much to be lost in presenting a partial picture as a false universal.

The practice of articulation can add considerably to any discussion of fundamental tax reform. Critical tax scholarship largely addresses preexisting market distortions or gender role expectations under the current taxing system. In this way, it seeks to deploy the insight of critical study in an instrumental manner to address a present bias. The next step is to begin a foundational discussion regarding the construction of an (in)essential taxpayer.

CONCLUSION

Critical tax scholarship has shown that tax is indeed political. Accordingly, it makes sense that the battle over the changing face of the American family is also taking place within the Code. How tax legislation responds to this change can tell us a good deal about not just how society values families but how it defines them and why. A study of "pro-family" tax reform shows that it is part of a larger political agenda designed to strengthen traditional marriage which includes stopping same-sex marriage and securing tax benefits for all married couples. Taxation is an attempt to resolve the most basic question of how to apportion the burdens of citizenship.

[4] Darren Lenard Hutchinson, *Out Yet Unseen: A Racial Critique of Gay and Lesbian Legal Theory and Political Discourse*, 29 CONN. L. REV. 561, 641 (1997).

The choices that a society makes concerning the definition of its tax base reveal fundamental judgments regarding issues of fairness, autonomy, and equality.

The exclusion of same-sex couples from the marital provisions is intentional. As a result, there is nothing hidden or covert about the heterosexist bias of the Code. There is no neutral principle at work. The rationale for the exclusion is not that same-sex couples do not pool their resources like opposite-sex married couples. Instead, the rationale for the exclusion is based on the beliefs that a same-sex couple is not a family, that no civilized society has ever countenanced such unions, and that our Judeo-Christian heritage forbids them.

Although not hidden, heteronormativity remains difficult to identify because as an elemental ordering feature of society it is so pervasive that it is unremarkable. Perhaps for this reason, the existing progressive critiques of the marital provisions have remained only partial. The feminist view focuses on the unfavorable tax aspects of spousal unity and produces a gender analysis that has little relevance to same-sex couples. Scholars writing from a gay and lesbian perspective argue for equal treatment. Both fail to address the heteronormative starting point for the marital provisions – taxpayers demanded that the state recognize the fundamental unit of society as the fundamental unit of taxation.

Queer theory does not get sidetracked by bare claims of equality or a gender-based analysis that ignores issues of sexual orientation. It offers a perspective from which to consider the marital regime *in toto*. It acknowledges that discussions of sexual orientation are primarily morality discourses and that heterosexual society will vigorously defend its institutions against any perceived encroachment by homosexuals. This explains both the terms of the congressional debate on DOMA and its ferocity. Finally, the insights of queer theory may help forestall the essentializing tendencies of some of the critical tax scholarship.

Although queer theory can help conceptualize the competing characterizations of marriage and family, it offers only a provisional, guerilla-type approach to political change. Strategic institutional choice and a realistic assessment of the demand side of legislation can reduce the level of disconnect between the academy and the political process. Consideration of the demand side of legislation might further induce scholars to stop dismissing the morality discourse of the opponents of same-sex relationships as irrelevant. It may be time, as some scholars suggest, to begin a discussion of the moral good of same-sex relationships.

Death Taxes: A Critique from the Margin

PATRICIA A. CAIN[1]

Feminist theorist bell hooks wrote many years ago that if movements were to succeed in making the world better, they ought to pay attention to the plight of the most marginalized. Thus, in the interest of justice, and in keeping with the advice of bell hooks, my critique of the death tax is from the perspective of the marginalized taxpayer, the taxpayer whose position is almost never considered by Congress in the writing of tax legislation, nor by the IRS in the interpretation of tax legislation. My marginalized taxpayer is a gay or lesbian partner in a long-term committed relationship.

I critique from this perspective not to show that gay and lesbian couples are treated less favorably than married couples by the tax law. I assume that most people will agree with me that whenever a tax rule favors traditional families, it consequentially disfavors nontraditional families, who cannot meet the necessary definitional requirements to have the rule applied to them. For those of us who agree that equality is a good principle and that justice requires treating all families alike, we might critique the estate and gift tax laws against our notion of equality. We might, for example[,] take the position that nontraditional families should be treated the same as traditional families. That is, we might adopt the principle of formal equality.

But achievement of formal equality is not the goal of my critique. In part, formal equality is not my goal because I do not begin with the conclusion that the current treatment of traditional families is necessarily just. Rather, I begin with a normative question: how should the estate tax system treat families generally? Thus, my project is one of substantive justice and not mere formal equality.

THE PERSPECTIVE OF THE MARGINALIZED TAXPAYER

To understand the perspective of the marginalized gay or lesbian taxpayer who is concerned about the estate tax, one must know something of how same-sex couples live their lives. Narrative method, or the sharing of specific stories, is one way to create this knowledge.

---

[1] Reprinted by permission from 48 *Cleveland State Law Review* 677 (2000).

Feminist scholars in many disciplines have embraced consciousness raising and narrative as methods that inform their scholarship. One key feature of feminist thought is that abstract theory ought to be based on concrete experience. Much early feminist scholarship, both in law and in other disciplines, focused on deconstructing abstract rules and revealing their hidden biases by showing that such rules were not crafted with women's experience in mind.

The use of personal narrative, of fictional stories, and of real stories of real lives can help make visible experiences that in the past have been ignored. In addition to feminist legal scholars, critical race theorists have embraced the use of narrative. Telling stories of discrimination in rich and concrete detail helps to teach the listener about different perspectives.

Gay and lesbian scholars have also embraced narrative. Because discrimination against gay men and lesbians has been so dominant throughout our legal history, many gay people have lived closeted lives. Even some of us who have been out for years have felt compelled to be silent at times. Our stories, like other stories "from the bottom," have only recently begun to be told in the legal journals, courtrooms, and legislatures.

STORIES OF DEATH AND TAXES

These stories will deal with situations in which the coupledom is ended through death of a partner. These narratives come from lawyers and accountants who have represented gay and lesbian clients in estate tax audits. Confidentiality is maintained because although the stories are based on real people, I have either elaborated on or amalgamated the specific facts from individual cases.

Alice and Barb are a lesbian couple in Ohio. They had lived together for over forty years when Alice died. The auditing agent took the position that since Alice was the wealthy partner, everything she paid for over the forty years that benefited Barb was an adjust[ed] taxable gift. Thus, Alice's ownership of the couple's residence which was used by Barb created an adjusted taxable gift. Vacation trips for the two of them paid out of Alice's funds created an adjusted taxable gift. Entertainment expenses and meals at fancy restaurants – all items of joint consumption – were proposed as adjusted taxable gifts. Although the case was finally settled, the audit lasted over two years.

Carl and Dan are a gay male couple in California. They owned all their property as joint tenants and considered it "community property."[2] The property included real estate and joint checking accounts and a joint CD. They purchased some of the property twenty years ago. Carl was earning slightly more than Dan at the time of Carl's death. The agent asked for proof of Dan's original contribution to every piece of joint property. Dan had not retained cancelled checks for twenty years, but he did have tax returns. He was able to show that he made enough money to enable him to cover half the down payment for the property purchased twenty

---

[2] Please note that this narrative predates the creation of the California domestic partnership registry. 1999 Cal. Legis. Serv. ch. 588 (West). After the writing of this article, California actually extended its community property laws to cover registered domestic partnerships. CAL. FAM. CODE §§ 297.5(a), (k), 751, 760 (West 2008). – Eds.

years ago. On the more recent purchases, Dan was eventually able to produce cancelled checks to account for 40% of the funds needed for the down payment. Data on the bank accounts varied. The agent asked for proof of equal contribution to the mortgage payments. Dan had no cancelled checks to the mortgage company, but was able to show some cancelled checks to Carl which appeared to be partial reimbursements. They had split the interest deduction and property tax deduction equally on their tax returns over the years. Again the case was ultimately settled, but the taxpayer's representative who shared this story with me says she will never allow a gay or lesbian client to own property jointly. Even if they can substantiate contributions, the emotional toll is not worth the benefit of avoiding probate.

ANOTHER STORY: A PURELY HYPOTHETICAL FACT SITUATION THAT DEMONSTRATES THE BURDEN OF THE DEATH TAX

Consider the situation of Anna and Beth, a hypothetical couple, whose income and wealth mirrors that of many lawyers and similar professionals. Anna earns over $150,000 per year. That salary is not in the realm of the very rich, but it certainly means that Anna is well-off. Beth, by contrast, is a dedicated and talented pianist, who pulls down around $25,000 a year from teaching students and performing. They are committed to each other and support each other's career choices. They jointly own a home purchased fifteen years ago for $200,000, which is now worth $600,000. They took title as joint tenants with right of survivorship and financed the purchase with a fifteen-year mortgage, which has been recently paid off. Anna made the mortgage payments and claimed all the interest deductions and property tax deductions on her income tax return. They agreed that, in return, Beth would pay for the groceries, do the shopping, and prepare the meals.

Some years ago, Anna inherited from her father a cabin in Maine. Anna and Beth have used the cabin over the years as their special retreat. It is located on a forty-acre tract and it is the one place in the world that has brought them peace and spiritual happiness. In the early years of their relationship, when they decided to have a holy union ceremony, celebrating their lifelong commitment to each other, they chose this acreage as the site for the celebration.

The first year they were together, they purchased their first piece of art. Both women had appreciated art, but seemed to differ in their tastes. On a visit to New York, they walked into a gallery and instantly fell in love with a painting by a young French artist they had never heard of before. Anna paid most of the $15,000 purchase price, but Beth contributed $500 from her own savings so that the decision to purchase would feel more truly shared.

For Beth's fortieth birthday, Anna purchased a $40,000 Steinway piano to replace the piano that Beth had been using at home. The piano was intended as a gift to Beth, although Anna secretly felt as though she has gotten the major benefit from the gift because she loves to listen to Beth play.

Both Anna and Beth are now in their late forties. Neither expects death to occur. They have done no estate planning other than to write wills leaving all their property to each other. Consider the possible estate tax cost to Beth should Anna suddenly die in a freak accident.

The home, the cabin in Maine, the piece of art, and the piano are all items of property that Beth identifies as key parts of her life with Anna. These assets alone will trigger an estate tax. The residence is worth $600,000 and the Maine property has appreciated to $600,000 as well. The artist of the $15,000 painting has been "discovered" and the value of his paintings [has] skyrocketed. The painting they own is now worth $100,000. The Steinway has similarly appreciated in value to $60,000. Add to these items Anna's retirement plan assets ($300,000) and the group term life insurance provided by her employer (twice her salary, $300,000), as well as Anna's bank accounts, car, and other personal property (assume a total value of $40,000), and the total estate has reached the value of $2,000,000.

An estate of $2,000,000 may sound like a lot of wealth, but in Anna and Beth's case, it is not enough to continue supporting Beth in her current life style, or in fact, anything close to it. If Anna were to die in 2001, the estate tax payable would be around $560,000. The life insurance and retirement plan assets produce just enough cash to cover this tax. If Anna and Beth had lived in a state like Iowa that has a state inheritance tax, Beth would have to come up with another $200,000 to $300,000 to pay the state tax bill.

Obviously Anna should have done some estate planning to avoid this tax problem. She surely should have taken out more insurance than the amount provided by her employer. She probably should have created an irrevocable life insurance trust. However, I use the example not to prove that couples that resemble Anna and Beth should hire an estate planner. Rather I use the example to question whether it is fair to place such a large tax burden on Beth or other taxpayers like her.

There are some specific facts in their situation that cause the tax problem. First of all, Anna, who is supporting Beth, dies early and thus Beth loses her source of support. The $600,000 in liquid assets is probably enough to support Beth if she can invest all of it rather than pay it to the tax collector. Had Anna done sufficient planning, the problem would not have occurred. This fact demonstrates that often the tax falls more heavily on the unwary, or those who die young before completing their estate plans.

Another fact concerns the type of property in the estate. The personal residence, the cabin in Maine, the painting, and the piano can all be described as constitutive property. If Beth has to pay inheritance taxes on top of the estate taxes, she will surely have to sell some of these items. And yet, all of these items represent important connections to her life with Anna. Do we really want to force living people to give up property of this sort in order to pay death taxes?

The home, because it is owned in joint tenancy, is subject to § 2040. While Beth feels she made valuable contributions to the purchase of the home, she has no records that will prove a financial contribution. In the nine months following Anna's death, as Beth is grieving, she will be asked to go through records to prove what she has paid for and will be made to feel as though her contributions to their joint estate don't really count.

Should Anna and Beth face this tax burden? Is the burden a *just* one? I have used variations of this basic hypothetical in presentations before various audiences. Some people think it is outrageous for Anna and Beth to face this burden because married couples do not face it. Others feel that the burden is of their own making through lack of planning. Still others begin to realize that the estate tax is not a tax on only the very wealthy.

My own normative conclusion is that Anna and Beth should not bear a tax burden on these particular facts. Even though tax law might view Anna as the sole owner of most of their joint assets, Beth's ownership rights ought to be recognized. She should not have her property taken away from her solely because her co-owner has died. The estate tax is conceptualized as a tax on the privilege of transferring property. But, from Beth's perspective, it is a tax on her continued ownership of property.

Early supporters of an inheritance or estate tax argued that the tax was proper because it was a way to raise needed revenue without depriving anyone of property. Numerous scholars have viewed the estate tax as particularly appealing because it is a tax on the dead, who cannot experience the burden of the tax. And yet it is difficult to view the tax on Anna's estate as one on Anna, rather than on her surviving partner, Beth.

PROPOSALS FOR CHANGE

There are, in my view, [many] possible options that could resolve the tax problems faced by couples like Anna and Beth. The ideal resolution would find the right balance between individualism and merger. It would also empower couples to make their joint choices, should they wish to do so, about how their particular situation should be viewed. Further, the ideal resolution would preserve the core purpose of the estate tax by taxing wealth that belongs more to the dead than to the living.

I have complained that tax law has suffered from a fallacy of individualism and that more recently it also suffers from a fallacy of merged identities. In an ideal world, tax law ought to strike the correct balance between individualism and the merged couple. One way to strike this balance would be to recognize each individual and allow the individual partners in a couple to decide how coupled or merged they want to be for tax purposes.

The Code allows individuals to form business partnerships in which they allocate capital ownership, share income and losses, and provide for services. Tax law will recognize the allocations provided they have "substantial economic effect." The partnership is not a separate taxable entity for income tax purposes. The tax burden of the profits and losses and the tax consequences of dispositions of property are allocated out to the individual partners in accord with their agreement. When the partnership is dissolved, there need be no tax triggered provided the partners can receive their shares of property with positive bases for tax purposes.

Suppose Anna and Beth could form a similar partnership. They could decide in advance what property would be jointly shared by the partners. They could decide in advance how net income would be shared. They could decide in advance how the property would be distributed in the event the partnership was terminated, either by mutual agreement or by death of one of the partners. Termination of the partnership should not be a taxable event. Rather, property should be distributed according to the joint agreement of the partners and the recipient of the property should take historical cost basis. Any property at death that passes to someone other than the tax partner would be subject to the estate tax, provided the estate were large enough to trigger a tax.

There are numerous pros and cons to this option. A primary initial issue is how to limit the use of such arrangements. For example, who should be permitted to create such tax partnerships and should they be limited to two persons? Should we, for example, only allow intimate committed partners? Or, should we allow siblings or other family members to form such partnerships? If the driving principle is shared property, why limit the partnership to two persons? My version of this option would permit only two-person partnerships and would limit each taxpayer to one partnership. While the limitation might be hard to justify in terms of the principle that partnerships ought to reflect the real-life agreements of sharing, some limitations are necessary to make the proposal workable.

Some have suggested cohabitation as the limiting principle. But, even with co-habitation as a limiting principle, it might be possible for persons in different generations to form such partnerships. If they could, then the partnership arrangement would serve to exempt the partnership property from estate taxes when it passes to the next generation. If such arrangements were permissible, then why not simply repeal the estate tax? If everyone planned carefully enough, they could form partnerships with beneficiaries in lower generations and avoid the tax completely. In that case, the tax would only fall on those persons who neglected to do the necessary paper work. Imposing a tax on only unplanned estates violates the principle of fairness I meant to suggest in the hypothetical case of Anna and Beth. Thus, some limiting rule would have to be constructed.

One possibility would be to limit the partnerships to two people in the same generation, with generation defined in terms of years rather than family relationships. For couples who are in spousal or similar relationships but who fall outside the generation limits, we might exempt a certain amount of property or reduce the tax rate based on the number of years the couple has been together or shared the property via the partnership agreement. The concept here is that ownership rights do vest over time when people agree to share property ownership. Alternatively, we might simply bar such arrangements between parents and children or other related parties of different generations who are barred from the marriage relationship because of the family relationship.

While my immediate focus is on same-sex couples, my critique of the estate tax has in part been based on the notion that, despite the form in which legal title may be held, property is often owned in other senses by partners or family members who share in the upkeep and the use of the property. Just as Anna and Beth's sharing of life and property supports the notion that they should both be viewed as owners for estate tax purposes, a parent and a child might share a home or a business in much the same way and for just as many years. In such cases, I see no reason to ignore the nonlegal title ownership of the child.

Just as marriage has been an inaccurate bright line for determining who shares what, who owns what, and who ought to be exempt from the estate tax, alternatives to marriage appear to suffer from some of the same problems. Tax partnerships of the sort I have suggested are likely to be either overinclusive (i.e., include tax avoiders who don't really share) or underinclusive (i.e., not include true sharers who simply fail to sign the legal papers). While this option, the personal tax partnership, is in some ways the most attractive because it can accord tax significance to sharers who *ought* to be treated as co-owners of property, it may also be the most difficult option to develop.

Homo Sacer, Homosexual: Some Thoughts on Waging Tax Guerrilla Warfare

ANTHONY C. INFANTI[1]

OF PARABLES AND PROVOCATEURS

Lesbians and gay men should be particularly interested in [Giorgio] Agamben's interpretation of Franz Kafka's parable *Before the Law,* which Kafka later incorporated into chapter nine of his book *The Trial.* It is worth reproducing this short parable in full before considering Agamben's interpretation of it:

> [B]efore the Law stands a doorkeeper. To this doorkeeper there comes a man from the country who begs for admittance to the Law. But the doorkeeper says that he cannot admit the man at the moment. The man, on reflection, asks if he will be allowed, then, to enter later. "It is possible," answers the doorkeeper, "but not at this moment." Since the door leading into the Law stands open as usual and the doorkeeper steps to one side, the man bends down to peer through the entrance. When the doorkeeper sees that, he laughs and says: "If you are so strongly tempted, try to get in without my permission. But note that I am powerful. And I am only the lowest doorkeeper. From hall to hall, keepers stand at every door, one more powerful than the other. And the sight of the third man is already more than even I can stand." These are difficulties which the man from the country has not expected to meet, the Law, he thinks, should be accessible to every man and at all times, but when he looks more closely at the doorkeeper in his furred robe, with his huge, pointed nose and long, thin, Tartar beard, he decides that he had better wait until he gets permission to enter. The doorkeeper gives him a stool and lets him sit down at the side of the door. There he sits waiting for days and years. He makes many attempts to be allowed in and wearies the doorkeeper with his importunity. The doorkeeper often engages him in brief conversation, asking him about his home and about other matters, but the questions are put quite impersonally, as great men put questions, and always conclude with the statement that the man cannot be allowed to enter yet. The man, who has equipped himself with many things for his journey, parts with all he has, however valuable, in the hope of bribing the doorkeeper. The doorkeeper accepts it all, saying, however, as he takes each gift: "I take this only to keep you from feeling that you have left something undone." During all these long years the man watches the doorkeeper almost incessantly. He forgets about the other doorkeepers, and this one seems to him the only barrier between himself and the

[1] Reprinted by permission from 2 *Unbound: Harvard Journal of the Legal Left* 27 (2006).

Law. In the first years he curses his evil fate aloud; later, as he grows old, he only mutters to himself. He grows childish, and since in his prolonged study of the doorkeeper he has learned to know even the fleas in his fur collar, he begs the very fleas to help him and to persuade the doorkeeper to change his mind. Finally his eyes grow dim and he does not know whether the world is really darkening around him or whether his eyes are only deceiving him. But in the darkness he can now perceive a radiance that streams inextinguishably from the door of the Law. Now his life is drawing to a close. Before he dies, all that he has experienced during the whole time of his sojourn condenses in his mind into one question, which he has never yet put to the doorkeeper. He beckons the doorkeeper, since he can no longer raise his stiffening body. The doorkeeper has to bend far down to hear him, for the difference in size between them has increased very much to the man's disadvantage. "What do you want to know now?" asks the doorkeeper, "you are insatiable." "Everyone strives to attain the Law," answers the man, "how does it come about, then, that in all these years no one has come seeking admittance but me?" The doorkeeper perceives that the man is nearing his end and his hearing is failing, so he bellows in his ear: "No one but you could gain admittance through this door, since this door was intended for you. I am now going to shut it."[2]

For Agamben, the man from the country in this parable is living in a virtual state of exception [i.e., he is excluded from the juridical order]: the "law applies to him in no longer applying, and holds him in its ban in abandoning him outside itself. The open door destined only for him includes him in excluding him and excludes him in including him."[3] Agamben describes the real danger that faces each of us in this state of exception that becomes indistinguishable from (consumes?) our life as the possibility that we might find ourselves "condemned to infinite negotiations with the doorkeeper or, even worse, that [we] might end by [ourselves] assuming the role of the doorkeeper who, without really blocking the entry, shelters the Nothing onto which the door opens."[4]

Probably the most striking aspect of Agamben's analysis of Kafka's parable, however, is his treatment of its ending. Agamben does not see in this ending "the irremediable failure or defeat of the man from the country before the impossible task imposed upon him by the Law."[5] When the doorkeeper closes the door that was open only to the man from the country, Agamben "imagine[s] that all the behavior of the man from the country is nothing other than a complicated and patient strategy to have the door closed in order to interrupt the Law's being in force."[6] Thus, instead of failure, Agamben sees success, "even if [the man from the country] may have risked his life in the process (the story does not say that he is actually dead but only that he is 'close to the end')."[7] Recapitulating the end of the parable in messianic terms, Agamben essentially contends that deliverance comes

---

[2] Franz Kafka, The Trial 213–15 (Willa & Edwin Muir trans., Schocken Books 1968) (1925).
[3] Giorgio Agamben, *Homo Sacer*: Sovereign Power and Bare Life 50 (Daniel Heller-Roazen trans., Stanford Univ. Press 1998) (1995).
[4] *Id.* at 54.
[5] *Id.* at 55.
[6] *Id.*
[7] *Id.*

only once the man from the country provokes the closure of the door to the law – when he is no longer a virtual "outlaw" but a very real one.

Finally, in closing his discussion of the parable, Agamben underscores the idea that he is not advocating surrender to the power of the state of exception; instead, following the example set by the man from the country, he urges resistance to it and, ultimately, the subversion of it.

TAX GUERRILLA WARFARE

Too often, we do no more than sit idly outside the already open door to the law. We dare not approach the doorkeeper until we receive word from the legal "experts" that the "right" or "best" case with the most "sympathetic" plaintiff has arrived. These experts actively discourage anyone who does not fit this ambiguous paradigm – which serves as a repository for every (real or imagined) heterosexual expectation of our nonthreatening domestication – from even considering the possibility of approaching the doorkeeper. When an ostensibly "good" case finally does happen by, the experts stand and bicker over whether this is truly the right case and the right time to approach the doorkeeper to plead for entrance through the already open door to the law. In the meantime, we sit by suffering needlessly. And pity the poor troublemaker who, on a rare occasion, challenges the experts' judgment and moves to plead her case directly to the doorkeeper; this rogue soon finds the experts attempting to intercept and block her approach for fear that the doorkeeper will bar the way to all.

Perhaps, true change is possible only when we resist being co-opted into serving as our own doorkeeper, when we cease asking politely for entrance through a door that is already open, and when we instead turn our energies to provoking the closure of that door and the creation of a real state of exception. On more than one occasion, it has been suggested to me that government silence on the tax treatment of same-sex couples is preferable to the message that would be sent should the government choose to speak. But, is it really? Might it not be preferable to force the government to express in words the precise nature and the full extent of its antigay animus rather than allowing that animus to remain the unseen and unacknowledged (only by heterosexuals, of course) subtext of lesbian and gay lives?

In other words, the source of our great sorrow and despair – our oppression – may actually be the source of our greatest strength. By provoking the government to close the door of the law on us, we may be able to draw attention to our plight in a way that serves as a catalyst for change. Provoking the closure of the door to the law should serve as a call to action for all lesbians and gay men as well as for any potentially sympathetic straight men and women (all of whom should be horrified when they finally realize the true extent and nature of our oppression at the hands of those among them who wield power by exploiting fear and division). At the same time, the threat of social unrest should shock the remainder of straight society out of its complacency.

Conversely, from this perspective, the paralyzing fear of defeat – of being turned away by the doorkeeper – has been the source of our greatest weakness. Our fear has debilitated and domesticated us by turning us into our own doorkeeper. In place of our current approach of engaging the law on its own terms, we might consider using the law strategically in an effort to provoke the closure of the door to the law and, concomitantly, to destabilize heterosexual privilege. We could begin by recognizing that, despite the quotation marks that so frequently surround the phrase, the "culture war" is more than just a rhetorical device for the reactionary right. It is a very real war, and lesbians and gay men have too often found themselves the victims of reactionary violence. Clearly outnumbered by our foes, we might take a page from the government's playbook when it litigates against its citizens, and adopt (and adapt) the tactics of guerrilla warfare – using the law to harass the government and provoke it to close the door to the law firmly against us – in an attempt to erode support for the hetero status quo among the "civilian" population. I realize that this probably sounds like quite a radical suggestion; yet, as we will see, it might require only the most ordinary of action to accomplish.

I think that tax would be the perfect area in which to test these guerrilla warfare tactics against the government. Despite being an area of the law that touches the life of nearly every lesbian and gay man, tax is the one door to the law that is generally left unattended by the experts who have been co-opted into serving as doorkeepers. As a result, tax is one area of the law where we will be able to approach the doorkeeper of the law directly, without having to pass through a gauntlet of experts attempting to dissuade us – or, worse, actively prevent us – from making our way to the already open door to the law. Approaching such a relatively unguarded door to the law may provide us the advantage of surprise in our attack (depending, of course, on who reads this essay).

In addition to being an unguarded approach, tax has particular attributes that are well-suited to its use in waging guerrilla warfare. Guerrilla warfare is associated with "small, mobile and flexible combat groups" that engage in "long, low-intensity confrontation" to "destabilize an authority."[8] In contrast to conventional civil rights litigation, which normally involves a single or select group of plaintiffs who file suit on behalf of (even if not in the name of) a larger class or group of individuals, tax lends itself to a more diffuse approach. Although taxpayers have, on occasion, filed class action lawsuits, they normally interact with the IRS and the courts on an individual basis, with arguments tailored to their individual situations.

Imagine what would happen if thousands of domestic partners in California were each to file federal income tax returns splitting their earned income [equally between them] in accordance with the U.S. Supreme Court's decision in *Poe v. Seaborn*[9] and were openly to invite the IRS to audit their returns and to challenge their interpretation of the law. Then consider what would happen if, at the same time, thousands of married same-sex couples in Massachusetts were to file joint federal income tax returns, asserting that DOMA is unconstitutional, and likewise were openly to invite the IRS to audit their returns and to challenge their interpretation of the law.

To be clear, when I speak here of an "open" challenge, I contemplate the filing of returns that on their face challenge the current application of the tax laws to

---

[8] *Guerilla Warfare*, WIKIPEDIA, http://en.wikipedia.org/wiki/Guerrilla_warfare.
[9] 282 U.S. 101 (1930).

same-sex couples. Such a transparent challenge could be accomplished by filing the appropriate disclosure forms issued by the IRS and including a cover letter with the return that explains the precise nature of the challenge. Surreptitious challenges simply would not have the same effect. Although the IRS would likely uncover the income splitting by the California couples relatively quickly and easily (because of the mismatch between the amount of earned income reported on the tax return and the amount of earned income reported to the IRS by the taxpayer's employer), the IRS would be far less likely to detect the filing of joint federal income tax returns by the Massachusetts couples. In either case, open challenges are necessary to bring about the desired adverse impact on the IRS, because achieving that impact depends on the IRS's immediate awareness of the challenges.

In this regard, the IRS should be accustomed to, and adequately equipped for, individual challenges to its interpretation of the tax laws; in fact, it has promulgated specific regulations concerning, along with the necessary forms for reporting, tax return positions that challenge rules or regulations. However, the nearly simultaneous arrival of thousands upon thousands of these challenges would, I imagine, leave the IRS nonplussed (to say the very least). We could expect that this initial strike against the law would cause a disruption similar to that caused by a computer virus that is designed to bombard a single website with information until it becomes so overloaded that it is forced to be shut down temporarily. After this initial disruption, the IRS would be saddled with thousands of individual audits and the resulting court cases, which could drag on for years and significantly drain government resources.

With a bit more effort, we could turn the law even more fully against itself, while at the same time facilitating the participation of as broad a swath of the lesbian and gay community as possible in this opening salvo of the guerrilla war. We could encourage low- and middle-income as well as elderly lesbians and gay men to avail themselves of volunteer income tax return preparers who are trained and supported by the IRS when preparing their returns challenging the IRS's interpretation of the tax laws. The IRS sponsors two volunteer tax return preparation programs: for low- and middle-income taxpayers, the Volunteer Income Tax Assistance program provides help in preparing basic tax returns; for the elderly, the Tax Counseling for the Elderly program provides free tax counseling and help in preparing basic tax returns. The sites where help is available are located throughout the country, and the IRS will provide taxpayers with the location of the closest site when they call its toll-free telephone numbers.

Following the initial disruption, the extended audit and litigation process would likely require the participating lesbian and gay taxpayers to employ accountants and/or attorneys to work on their behalf – all of whom would obviously be instructed to be as unaccommodating to the IRS as possible (e.g., by refusing to extend the statute of limitations to allow more time for audit). For those with means, this would entail a financial sacrifice. Those who would find this sacrifice unduly burdensome could turn for help to attorneys and accountants who are willing to work on a pro bono basis. Again, however, an opportunity arises to turn the law even more fully against itself (and, at the same time, to facilitate the participation of as broad a swath of the lesbian and gay community as possible):

low-income taxpayers could contact one of the many independent legal clinics that provide professional assistance in disputes with the IRS. These clinics receive financial support from the IRS and can be found in every state and the District of Columbia.

If this initial strike were to prove successful, lesbians and gay men could then begin to educate the masses concerning their tax grievances. These educational activities could be followed by the expansion of our guerrilla activities into other areas of the law. Naturally, we would need to adapt our tactics as we branch out to other areas of the law, both because other areas might require different approaches and because the government would probably have adapted to (and, therefore, would likely be anticipating) the tactics that we used in the tax context. In each case, however, the goal would be the same – to provoke the closure of yet another already open door to the law.

In contrast to race, gender, and sexual orientation, the family has been a perennial topic in the mainstream tax literature. For example, the family figures prominently in debates about the appropriate taxable unit, the marriage penalty (and its lesser known flip side, the marriage bonus), allowances for the cost of caring for children and other dependents, whether (and, if so, how) the tax system should accommodate family farms and businesses, and the prevention of tax abuse through artificial shifting of income or property within a family. Critical tax theorists bring a new perspective to these old debates and, at the same time, open new areas of debate about the role of the family in taxation.

Marjorie Kornhauser opens the chapter by taking on the question of the appropriate taxable unit in *Love, Money, and the IRS: Family, Income-Sharing, and the Joint Income Tax Return*. She considers whether the justification for the joint income tax return – namely, that married couples pool their financial resources – is in keeping with the reality of how married couples live their lives. Examining empirical studies (and conducting one of her own), Kornhauser paints a complex picture in which some married couples pool their finances, others do not, and many send signals that contradict the outward appearance of their financial arrangement (e.g., by treating jointly held assets as separate property or separately held assets as joint property). She concludes that the joint return should be abolished and replaced with individual tax filing because (1) the extant joint return system is both overinclusive and underinclusive (i.e., it applies to some married couples who do not pool their resources but excludes nontraditional families who do pool their resources) and (2) it would be too complex and intrusive to implement (not to mention too easy to abuse) a system that only allowed for joint filing when couples actually pool their financial resources.

Next, in *Innocent Spouses: A Critique of the New Tax Laws Governing Joint and Several Tax Liability*, Lily Kahng approaches the question of the taxable unit from the perspective of the joint and several liability imposed on married couples when they file a joint income tax return. Kahng asserts that the idea that married couples pool their financial resources was nothing more than the camouflage that Congress employed to create the joint return, when its true purpose was to extend to husbands across the country the income-splitting (and tax-lowering) privilege that only husbands in community property states enjoyed at that time. Having

revealed the tax rationale for joint filing (and joint and several liability) as a mere
fiction, Kahng then turns to other areas of the law that have experience with joint
and several liability (e.g., torts, agency law, and fraudulent conveyance law) to
assess the propriety – and suggest changes to – the "innocent spouse" exception
that affords relief from the general rule of joint and several liability for married
couples filing joint returns.

Adding a host of other tax provisions (not to mention other taxes) to the mix,
Edward McCaffery explains in *Taxation and the Family: A Fresh Look at Behavioral
Gender Biases in the Code* how the tax laws influence decisions whether to marry,
whether to have a one- or two-earner household, and whether the secondary
earner should work full- or part-time. McCaffery demonstrates how the tax laws
have differing levels of influence on these decisions at different class levels, tend
to foster the creation of certain types of families, and further the marginalization
of women in the workplace. To remedy these problems, McCaffery looks to the
economic literature for support in his interesting and controversial proposal to
alter the basic tax rate structure to tax married men more than married women.

In *The Profits and Penalties of Kinship: Conflicting Meanings of Family in Estate
Tax Law*, Bridget Crawford focuses attention on how the tax laws actually adopt
a number of different meanings of family. Taking several estate tax provisions as
examples, Crawford shows how these definitions create a continuum of definitions
rather than one single definition for all purposes. She views these definitions
from a feminist perspective and assesses the extent to which they succeed and fail
in embracing the diversity of family forms in American society. Crawford also
suggests reforms that would expand the definition of family to more closely match
this diversity and reduce the confusion engendered by the ubiquitous use of the
word "family."

In *The Tax Treatment of Children: Separate but Unequal*, Dorothy Brown
describes the starkly different ways that the tax laws treat lower- and middle-
income children. On the one hand, the earned income tax credit (EITC), which
is a tax benefit targeted at lower-income families, is governed by highly complex
rules, requires the taxpayer to work to obtain the credit, contains a ceiling on
the benefit afforded to EITC recipients, and invites stringent scrutiny from the
government. On the other hand, the child tax credit (CTC), which is targeted at
middle-income families, is easy to apply for, has no work requirements or ceiling
on the tax benefit afforded to CTC recipients, and does not invite government
scrutiny. Further underscoring these differences, the EITC is often referred to as
"welfare" while the CTC is often described as tax "relief" for middle-class families.
Brown considers and rejects several race-neutral explanations for these differences.
She concludes that the EITC and CTC, which both serve the same purpose, receive
different treatment because EITC recipients are perceived to be black while CTC
recipients are perceived to be white. Turning to empirical data, Brown demonstrates that whites are actually more likely to be eligible for the EITC than blacks.
Having thus demonstrated that white lower-income children are being treated less
favorably than white middle-income children and relying on Derrick Bell's interest
convergence theory, Brown calls on academics, politicians, and policy makers to

work to ensure that all children – regardless of economic class (and, implicitly, race) – are treated equally.

Mary Louise Fellows closes the chapter with *Rocking the Tax Code: A Case Study of Employment-Related Child-Care Expenditures*, a detailed history of child-care work in the United States and an analysis of the current tax treatment of child-care expenditures. Fellows explores the failure of traditional tax analysis to address how the current tax treatment of child-care expenditures facilitates subordination along race, gender, and class lines. She also calls attention to child-care workers, who are invisible in these debates. Fellows illustrates how the "neutral" principles of mainstream tax analysis provide an incomplete understanding of the current operation – and any proposed reform – of the tax laws. A full understanding of how a law works (or will work) can only come from a careful study of the social context, too.

Love, Money, and the IRS: Family, Income-Sharing, and the Joint Income Tax Return

MARJORIE E. KORNHAUSER[1]

The songs tell us that when two people are in love, their souls unite; their two hearts beat as one. The Code also tells us that their two tax liabilities can be as one, united in a joint tax return – but only if they are not simply in love, but are also married. While tax theorists have debated the appropriateness of the joint return, they have not examined the premise behind the joint return: that married people – and only married people – share not only their hopes and dreams, but also their money.

EMPIRICAL STUDIES OF ASSET POOLING AND CONTROL SHARING

The theoretical justification for the joint return – the belief that married couples share resources – is largely unsupported by empirical evidence. Recently, however, a number of studies have explored intrafamily allocations because of a growing recognition of this issue's importance to a wide array of social welfare programs. These studies indicate "that individual incomes are not simply pooled and then spent to meet household needs in some unified fashion. Rather, they are spent at least in part according to the earner's own preference."[2] This apportionment phenomenon is true even when the couple states that they pool or share resources.

I examined three studies of intrafamily resource allocation as well as my own. My study was an anonymous ninety-three question survey that was distributed twice. The three prior intrafamily studies I examined were the vast study in the 1983 book *American Couples* by Philip Blumstein and Pepper Schwartz, a small 1986 study of dual-career couples in the greater Chicago area by Rosanna Hertz, and an English study of 102 married couples conducted specifically on the issue of money and marriage by Jan Pahl. Despite the many differences in the studies and their limitations, all the studies produce remarkably similar data. Couples do not universally share or pool finances, let alone universally *believe* in such a system. In fact, a significant percentage (ranging from 30% to approximately 50%) do not share all their income.

---

[1] Reprinted by permission from 45 *Hastings Law Journal* 63 (1993).

[2] Beatrice Lorge Rogers, *The Internal Dynamics of Households: A Critical Factor in Development Policy*, *in* INTRA-HOUSEHOLD RESOURCE ALLOCATION ISSUES AND METHODS FOR DEVELOPMENT POLICY AND PLANNING 1, 1 (Beatrice Lorge Rogers & Nina Schlossman eds., 1990).

My survey also shows that the method for handling finances can vary over the course of a relationship. Some respondents stated that while finances were kept separately in the early years of their relationship, they were held jointly later. Others stated that finances were separate while both worked, joint while one was a student, and would become separate once again when the student returned to work. Change from single to married status could also shift financial patterns from separate to joint. As part of my interviewing while developing the questionnaire, but not in the survey, I learned that the birth of children can also cause a switch from separate to joint finances.

Empirical evidence suggests that even among couples who nominally pool assets, true sharing frequently does not occur because power arising from both cultural sources and earning power is distributed unequally. Eighty-seven percent of Shere Hite's respondents felt uncomfortable being financially dependent on their partner and made such comments as, "I felt guilty asking for any money and I wouldn't ask unless it was for groceries" or "I was financially dependent on a man I was married to. I felt guilty spending his money."[3] Hite states that "[e]ven if a woman is comfortable being financially dependent on a man, still there may be insidious psychological effects" such as feelings of inferiority.[4] If a woman feels inferior, is she going to act as if she shares equally in the financial assets and spend them as freely as the earner spouse? According to Hite's study, 82% of women under twenty-five want to be financially independent.

American Couples found that among married couples, heterosexual unmarried couples, and gay couples, the amount of money one partner earned relative to the other determined relative power and control over resources. Among married couples, the higher the wife's income, the more financial autonomy she had, and the more likely she was to have her own personal savings account. This result was even more pronounced among unmarried couples.

The evidence from empirical studies indicates that neither assertions of pooling nor nominal arrangement of assets in a pooling manner accurately reflect the reality of financial arrangements. Behind the facade of sharing is a deep-seated, though often subtle, control of the income by the earner spouse. This control springs both from the individual's feelings of psychological ownership of earnings and from cultural stereotypes of gender and marital roles. Perhaps in recognition of this reality, as women increase their earnings, women will increasingly keep their money separately. As one woman in my survey stated, separate finances are necessary for the stability and longevity of the relationship. Such a reality contradicts the premise of a joint income tax liability.

A SHORT HISTORY OF THE TAXABLE UNIT THEORY AND PRACTICE

Theorists do not agree as to the appropriate taxable unit and throughout our income tax history the law has taken various positions. There are several possibilities from which to choose. Most broadly, the issue is whether tax liability should be

---

[3] Shere Hite, Women and Love: A Cultural Revolution in Progress 432, 433 (1987).
[4] *Id.* at 435.

determined on the basis of each individual or on the basis of each economic unit. In the context of the personal income tax, the economic unit itself may be variously defined as the marital unit (husband and wife), the nuclear family (husband, wife, and minor children), extended family (certain individuals related by blood, marriage, or adoption), or the household family (all individuals sharing the same living quarters).

Different theories underlie the two basic types of taxable units. If the tax unit is the individual, then tax-paying ability is based solely on each individual's earnings and on income produced by property titled in her name. The contrasting theory holds that the family is the taxable unit since the family, not the individual, is the basic economic unit within which financial resources are shared, regardless of the source of the wage or investment income.

If the family is the relevant taxable unit, horizontal equity occurs when two families with identical total income, regardless of how the income is earned or distributed within the family, are taxed equally. If the individual is the proper tax unit, horizontal equity is achieved when two individuals with equal income are taxed equally regardless of their marital status. A tax system that achieves horizontal equity between families will create inequities between families and individuals with similar incomes if the system is progressive. The nature of the inequities will depend upon the schedule of tax rates for individuals and families. Some schedules will favor married couples, thus imposing a "singles" tax, while other schedules might create a "marriage" penalty, taxing married couples disproportionately.

The justifications for treating the marital unit as the appropriate tax unit are economic unity, marital obligations, and economies of scale.

The first and most important justification is economic unity. Traditionally, society views a marriage as an economic unit in which the members share the economic resources. There are several criticisms of this justification. First, people other than married couples pool income. Second, some critics attack the underlying assumption of pooling that couples always share income. Third, the women's rights movement undermines the pooling justification by emphasizing women's increasing access to economic independence as yet another indication that title is significant. Finally, the pooling rationale is criticized because it focuses on income consumption, which is more appropriate for a consumption-based tax than an income tax that measures accessions to wealth.

Another justification for treating a married couple as a taxable unit is that marriage alters an individual's rights and obligations, thereby justifying treating a married couple as one taxable unit. Critics note, however, that individuals other than spouses have a legal obligation of support, and question why these people are treated differently than spouses.

A final justification for treating the married couple as a taxable unit is that economies of scale that result from living together need to be taken into account. It is not, however, exactly clear how to evaluate the economies of scale in determining ability to pay and, hence, tax liability. Again, the critics reply that people other than two married people live together and share resources.

THE DILEMMA OF THE CURRENT SITUATION

Today a taxpayer's marital status affects her tax liability in a variety of ways; the rate schedule is merely the most noticeable. These various provisions are inconsistent in how they treat a married couple. Sometimes the couple is treated simply as one unit so that it gets the same treatment as an individual. Sometimes the couple is treated as a unit but each member is treated as an individual. In these instances, the couple as a whole gets double the deduction or credit. At other times the unit is totally ignored, as in the imposition of Social Security taxes.

Not only is the marital unit treated inconsistently throughout the Code, but even the conceptual definition of the taxable unit fluctuates. The taxable unit is either the individual, the married couple, or the head of household. The common underlying principle is that each is an economic unit within which income is shared. Yet the tests are not only inconsistent, but also inaccurate measures of whether there is in fact pooling. Unlike marital status, head-of-household status requires that the taxpayer and the other members of the taxable unit live together for more than half of the year, presumably to ensure that the group regards itself as a unit. The members of a married couple, in contrast, can live on opposite coasts, keep two separate abodes, and still file jointly. Married status automatically assumes that each spouse pools income, but the reality might be completely separate finances. In contrast, to qualify as a head of household, a taxpayer must meet specific economic tests by providing more than half the support of the dependent living in her home. While married people qualify simply by meeting the state requirements of marriage, heads of households must live with people who are related by law (stepchildren) or related by certain blood relationships (parent, child, or descendant of child).

Another overriding inconsistency is the treatment of the income of the other individuals within the unit. If the proper taxable entity is the economic unit, the income of all dependents should be aggregated with that of the parents (or head of household). However, under § 1(g), our system currently aggregates only the unearned income of children. All other members of the household, including those [children] who have an earned income, are treated as separate taxable units. This rule is directly contrary to the assumption that households pool their income.

Not only is our present treatment of the taxable unit inconsistent and inaccurate, but it is based on outdated, unexamined premises. In 1948, when the joint return was established, certain assumptions prompted creation of the joint return as a response to perceived inadequacies in the system. First was the assumption that spouses pooled all their resources regardless of who earned or owned them. The second assumption was that sharing of income automatically meant that control of the income was also shared. Finally, the joint return, in order to be helpful to married couples, assumed a "traditional" marriage in which there was only one earner in each family. In today's world, these assumptions are no longer tenable.

Even in 1948 these assumptions were not entirely accurate. If all income were jointly shared, then why had all states not switched to a community property system? Carolyn Jones presents evidence that many states rejected community property laws precisely because they gave rights to spouses who had not earned the income. [See Chapter 2.] Nevertheless, pooling of income, at least at the lower levels of income, was generally assumed despite a general absence of empirical evidence to support it. The second assumption concerning equal control, a prerequisite to taxability under general tax principles, lacked universality. The final assumption of one-earner couples also was not uniformly true: In April 1948, 23.1% of all married women participated in the labor force.

These discrepancies are even greater today than they were in 1948. First, many more nonlegal families exist. To the extent that these families are treated differently from married couples, such treatment is inequitable. Furthermore, while the partnership model of marriage may be more true today from a legal standpoint than it was in 1948, pooling, which is a concomitant of the partnership model, is far from universal. Legally, even the community property system still does not require complete joint management and control.

CONCLUSION

As long-term living arrangements have grown increasingly varied and complex, financial arrangements also have been shaped by cultural, sociological, psychological, and economic factors. Because of the complexity and the prevailing myth of marital pooling, survey data is likely to be biased in favor of pooling: Respondents are more likely to overstate, not understate, the extent of sharing. Nevertheless, my study and the others discussed in this article clearly establish several facts: (1) not all couples pool assets; (2) pooling is not confined to married couples, and separation of assets is not confined to nonmarried couples; (3) financial arrangements sometimes change during the course of the relationship; and (4) even among those couples who say they pool, in reality the nonearner spouse often does not have equal access to assets; instead the earner controls the money. In short, the empirical evidence on pooling refutes the basic assumption underlying the joint return. The evidence highlights the unfairness of the current joint filing system, which is both underinclusive (barring some unmarried poolers from its benefits) and overinclusive (bestowing its benefits on nonpooling married couples).

To make any sense from a tax standpoint, the joint return, if it is justifiable at all, is only justified for those families who in fact pool income. This article has shown that not all couples pool their incomes. Consequently, only those groups, married or unmarried, who actually pool should be allowed to file a joint return.

Such a regime, however, would violate another tax principle – simplicity. Because pooling is so fact-specific, proof of pooling would be very intrusive. Further complications would arise because whether a couple pooled could change from year to year. Moreover, true pooling would be difficult, if not impossible, to discern due to the many psychological and sociological factors implicated in the issue. Detailed inquiry into financial arrangements and interpersonal dynamics by the IRS would be expensive and invasive, but not conclusive, and would inevitably result in a great deal of litigation.

Even if the tax system could overcome these problems, a joint return system would not aid all families. The "family" rhetoric often used in connection with the joint return hides the reality that the joint return is disadvantageous for many families. The joint return places an extra burden on the increasing number of two-earner families. It also discourages some women from working outside the home who might otherwise do so for economic and social reasons. As for the "typical" one-earner family that the joint return was designed to benefit, the joint return places the burden of tax liability on the nonearner by making her jointly liable for the tax, but ignores the reality of economic dominance of the earner. The joint return ignores the issues raised by the empirical studies. Many men and women do not want to pool all their income; indeed, the relationship between the couple will be more stable if each partner retains some independence. This evidence suggests that in some situations the joint return not only does *not* promote traditional family functions, but may in fact be detrimental to them.

The joint return ought to be abolished. A system that treats each person as a separate taxable unit is more equitable, more consistent with basic tax principles, more efficient, and ultimately better able to accomplish social family goals.

Separate taxation is more equitable because it treats similar taxpayers similarly. Our system is an *income* tax; by taxing each individual on her income, the system does not unfairly discriminate based on certain taxpayers' living arrangements. If we wish to use the tax system to assist people who have taken on dependents, then Congress can enact tax provisions giving deductions or credits for dependents, be they adults or children.

Separate taxation also is consistent with our tax system's basic principle that the person who controls the income should be taxed on it even if another benefits. The control principle is particularly apt for earned income since only the earner can produce that income. As the empirical studies show, the earner usually controls the income even if the couple states that they pool.

Separate taxation also would be more efficient than joint taxation. For example, the joint return discourages the second earner from working by placing her in a higher marginal bracket. Studies show that the wages of the second earner, usually the wife, are sensitive to the tax rate, whereas the wages of married men and singles are relatively insensitive. Joint returns thus discourage wives from working by placing them in higher marginal brackets than they would be in as individuals. Thus, it is more economically efficient to treat individuals as separate taxable units so as not to discourage women from working.

Separate taxation would also further certain "family values" better than joint taxation. For example, there has been much debate about the plight of children in general and the rising number of poor children; proposals have been made to enact child tax credits to benefit children. Arguably, there is a better chance that the money would be spent for the children if the woman gets the credit. Studies show that women are more likely than men to allocate more of their earnings to children. Separate taxation can strengthen the family unit by permitting the second partner to work without suffering a tax penalty whenever economic or psychological factors encourage or dictate a two-earner family. Separate taxation may also strengthen families by reinforcing a sense of independence and self-worth in both partners.

Such feelings form the basis of modern, healthy relationships which are built not on paternalism, but on true equality. If marriages are partnerships they are or should be partnerships between equal members.

The individual return is not the perfect solution to the taxable unit issue because no perfect solution can exist when it must inevitably rest on social and political values. Nevertheless, because the individual return is a better solution than the joint return, the joint return ought to be abolished.

Innocent Spouses: A Critique of the New Tax Laws Governing Joint and Several Tax Liability

LILY KAHNG[1]

At the first level, our federal income tax system is one of self-assessment. A taxpayer is required to report items of income, deduction, gain, and loss on a return and compute her taxable income and the tax thereon. The taxpayer must sign and file the return, and pay the amount of tax shown due. The IRS is authorized to review and challenge the self-assessed tax liability, and through administrative and judicial proceedings, the taxpayer may ultimately be found to be liable for a deficiency – the difference between the correct tax due and the amount of tax shown on the return. The deficiency may also include interest charges on taxes paid later than their due date and penalties for failure to self-assess and pay the correct amount of tax due.

A husband and wife who choose to file a joint federal income tax return engage in this self-assessment process jointly. The joint return aggregates items of income, deduction, gain, and loss attributable to either spouse; taxable income is computed in the aggregate, and the tax due is a single amount. If a joint return is made, each spouse undertakes to pay the entire amount of tax shown due. Furthermore, each spouse assumes joint and several liability for the entire amount of any subsequently determined deficiency.

From a collection standpoint, joint and several liability allows the IRS to collect from either spouse the full amount of any deficiency. If the IRS collects the entire amount of a deficiency from one spouse, that spouse has contribution rights against the other spouse for the portion of the deficiency attributable to the other spouse. In situations like this, little is known about the extent to which contribution rights are actually pursued or lead to recovery. Nevertheless, the IRS often pursues one spouse rather than the other because prospects of recovering from the other spouse are poor (e.g., the other spouse is judgment-proof, has no attachable income stream, or the other spouse's whereabouts are unknown). From this, one can surmise that the enforcement of contribution rights against this other spouse occurs relatively rarely.

INNOCENT SPOUSE RELIEF

Under certain circumstances, a spouse may be relieved from liability arising from a joint return she has signed. The first statute providing for this so-called innocent

[1] Reprinted by permission from 49 *Villanova Law Review* 261 (2004).

spouse relief was enacted in 1971. Prior to its repeal in 1998, it authorized the IRS to relieve a spouse from joint and several liability for a deficiency if three conditions were met: (1) there was a "substantial understatement" of tax attributable to "grossly erroneous" items of the other spouse;[2] (2) the spouse requesting relief established that, in signing the return, she did not know, and had no reason to know, of the substantial understatement; and (3) taking into account all the facts and circumstances, it would be inequitable to hold the requesting spouse liable for the deficiency attributable to the understatement.

The Internal Revenue Service Restructuring and Reform Act of 1998 (1998 Act) changed the innocent spouse provisions in several significant respects. The 1998 Act liberalized the prior-law relief provision (traditional relief) by eliminating the requirements that there be a "substantial" understatement of tax attributable to a "grossly" erroneous item of the other spouse. Now all that is required is an understatement of tax attributable to an erroneous item of the other spouse. The other prior-law requirements for traditional relief – in particular, the knowledge and equity requirements – remain unchanged.

The 1998 Act also added two new forms of relief from joint and several liability. The first allows a spouse to elect to limit her liability for a deficiency to her allocable share of the deficiency. The deficiency is allocated in the same proportion that the spouse's erroneous items bear to the total amount of erroneous items giving rise to the deficiency.

This first new form of relief (proportionate relief) is available only to a spouse who – at the time she elects such relief – is divorced or legally separated from the other spouse, or has lived apart from the other spouse during the twelve-month period ending on the date relief is elected. In addition, proportionate relief is unavailable if assets are transferred from one to the other with the principal purpose of tax avoidance or if one or both spouses act fraudulently. Finally, a spouse is not relieved of liability for any portion of the deficiency attributable to an item of the other spouse if the IRS demonstrates that the spouse seeking relief had actual knowledge of the item at the time she signed the return.

The second new form of relief created by the 1998 Act (equitable relief) is a residual provision, authorizing the IRS to provide relief in situations where neither traditional nor proportionate relief is available, but it would be inequitable to hold the spouse liable. The legislative history cites as an example the situation where there is no under*statement* of tax, but there is an under*payment* of tax – that is, the return correctly reports the couple's tax liability, but the liability is not paid. In this situation, neither traditional nor proportionate relief is available because both of these require that there be an understatement of tax. The legislative history envisions the third relief provision possibly applying in the underpayment situation. The legislative history also makes clear that this is not the only instance where residual relief might be available.

---

[2] I.R.C. § 6013(e)(1)(B), (C) (1998).

TAX RATIONALES FOR JOINT AND SEVERAL LIABILITY

The concept of marital unity appeared in 1921, shortly after the inception of the joint return, but it did not begin to evolve into orthodoxy until the tax law changes of 1948. It was at this time that Congress created an income-splitting scheme, which allowed husbands residing in common law states to shift one-half of the income they earned to their wives for tax purposes. Under a progressive tax rates structure, this had the effect of reducing their tax burden. Prior to 1948, only husbands residing in community property states could take advantage of income splitting. The political motivation for the 1948 tax law change was to procure for husbands in common law states the lower tax burden enjoyed by their counterparts in community property states, thus rendering meaningless for tax purposes the stronger property rights of women in community property states and quelling the movement toward adoption of community property laws. The camouflage for the political motivation was the unfounded assertion that a married couple is a single unit and that equal-income marital units should bear the same tax burden no matter what their state of residence.

That marital unity was a convenient fiction, serving as political camouflage, was forgotten over the years. By 1976, marital unity had been elevated to a first principle of taxation, as evidenced by an observation of Professor Boris Bittker, one of the most influential tax scholars of the twentieth century: "[T]he 1948 statutory principle of equal taxes for equal-income married couples has been 'almost universally accepted' by tax theorists. . . ."[3]

EVALUATION OF CURRENT LAW

This part evaluates the current law treatment of married couples filing jointly by reference to [nontax] rationales for joint and several liability.

Traditional Relief

Tort rationales. The tort rationales for joint and several liability posit that there are *multiple wrongdoers* who have contributed to a *single harm* to a *victim*. A threshold problem in applying the tort rationales in the tax context relates to the identity of the wrongdoers. As applied in the tax context, the *harm* is the failure to accurately report and pay a tax liability. The *victim* is either the government, or more generally, all other taxpayers, who will have to pay more in taxes to make up the revenue shortfall. Identifying the *wrongdoer(s)* in the tax context is more difficult. It begs the question to assert that both husband and wife are responsible for the tax, and that, therefore, they are both wrongdoers if the tax is not reported and paid. The underlying question is who should be responsible for the tax?

A basic principle of taxation is that each individual ought to be responsible for the tax relating to his or her income-producing activities or investments. The fiction

---

[3] Boris I. Bittker, *Federal Income Taxation and the Family*, 27 STAN. L. REV. 1389, 1395 (1975) (citation omitted).

of marital unity does not warrant modifying this basic principle. The first element under traditional relief – which essentially imposes liability for any taxes relating to the activities of the spouse seeking relief – is consistent with this approach and splinters the marital unit, underscoring the artificiality of the construct. Each married individual is a "wrongdoer" with respect to tax liabilities relating to her own activities, just as each unmarried individual is.

Even if one views both spouses as wrongdoers contributing to the harm, the tort rationales for joint and several liability are ill-fitted to the tax context. The three [tort] rationales for joint and several liability are (1) fairness to the victim, (2) difficulties in ascertaining each wrongdoer's contribution to the harm, and (3) heightened deterrence.

The fairness rationale assumes blameworthy wrongdoers and a victim who deserves full compensation. In the tax context, the fairness rationale loses force because the failure to report and pay taxes does not inflict significant harm on any particular individual. Moreover, in the tax context, it does not seem particularly unfair that the victim (the government) should bear the burden of collection and the risk of insolvency. The government-as-victim is not lacking in resources to pursue compensation for the harm, nor is it likely to suffer unduly if one or more of the wrongdoers turns out to be insolvent. Indeed, one of the common complaints about imposing joint and several liability in the tax context is that the government has superior collection capabilities and a greater ability to absorb the risk of loss and should not be permitted to shift these burdens to a spouse who is left only with unenforceable contribution rights against the other spouse.

The second tort rationale, that it is difficult to ascertain each individual's contribution to the harm, also applies poorly in the tax context. Under traditional relief, each spouse's contribution to the harm – that is, the failure to report and pay tax – is quite clear. There are two possibilities: (1) the understatement of tax is related to the activities of the spouse seeking relief or (2) the understatement is related to the activities of the other spouse.

In the tax setting, then, it is relatively easy to ascertain each spouse's role in producing the harm. Compare this to the paradigm tort case for joint and several liability: two defendants shoot toward the plaintiff with shotguns; only one pellet hits and injures the plaintiff, but it cannot be ascertained which defendant caused the injury.

Increased deterrence is the third tort rationale for imposing joint and several liability. In general, deterrence is not a principal goal of the tax system; on the contrary, its goal is to raise revenue while affecting behavior as *little* as possible. The tax system does have a deterrent aspect, however. It is designed to deter individuals from failing to report and pay tax on income they produce. Monitoring for compliance is accomplished by audits and other enforcement devices, and the penalties for noncompliance include any tax liability owed along with interest charges and penalties. In this way, taxes act as penalties intended to deter the behavior of noncompliance.

Information reporting obligations are imposed on those who, like the taxpayer himself, have knowledge of the item they are required to report, for example, in the case of a bank that pays interest to the taxpayer or an employer who pays wages to the taxpayer. The penalties for failure to report are relatively low – generally $50 per violation, subject to overall yearly limitations – presumably because the third parties have little disincentive not to comply.

Withholding obligations are imposed on those who are the source of payments made to taxpayers. The payor withholds and remits amounts to [the] government as advance payments of the taxpayer's tax liability. The penalties for noncompliance are high – 100% of the amount required to be withheld and remitted – presumably to deter the payor from diverting the withheld amounts for his own benefit rather than remitting them to the government. Within the deterrence scheme of the tax system, information reporting and wage withholding are instances where compliance is enhanced by imposing obligations to report or pay on parties other than the taxpayer. Spousal liability might be justified as a similar means of enhancing compliance, but upon closer examination, the parallels prove to be superficial.

Like a bank who pays interest to a taxpayer, the spouse of a taxpayer may have information that, if reported, would increase compliance by the taxpayer. One could argue that imposing liability on her for failure to report this information has the effect of imposing on her a duty to report and that the duty is imposed in order to increase the taxpayer's compliance. Nevertheless, a spouse's obligation to report, such as it is, differs in significant ways from the bank's.

First, under traditional relief, she is obligated only to report information of which she has knowledge or reason to know. This suggests a further duty to investigate, which is borne out by the courts' interpretation of the "reason to know" requirement. While the duty to investigate may at first blush seem unobjectionable, when stated in terms of the deterrence framework, it is less innocuous: to increase the taxpayer's compliance, the spouse has a duty to investigate those activities, and to report her findings to the IRS. The spouse is forced to step into the shoes of an auditor, a role that is wildly incongruent with the love, intimacy, and trust usually associated with the marital relationship.

A second problem with analogizing spousal liability to information reporting is the magnitude of the penalty imposed on the spouse. While a bank incurs a $50 penalty for failure to report, the spouse incurs a penalty equal to the tax liability relating to the information she failed to report, along with any interest charges and penalties. The spouse's penalty is seriously disproportionate when compared to the bank's. This becomes even more apparent when one considers the reporting "requirement" most comparable to the spouse's: friends, neighbors, and co-workers of the taxpayer are rewarded if they provide information about the taxpayer to the IRS (the "reward for rats" program); they are not penalized for failing to do so.

With regard to the duty to pay, the analogy between third-party withholding agent and spouse is even more attenuated. Unlike an employer, the spouse does not have control of amounts paid to the taxpayer and, thus, does not have the opportunity to withhold before such control is transferred to the taxpayer. Furthermore, although the spouse may nominally have some control by reason of jointly owned assets, the spouse is not likely to have actual control over amounts earned by the taxpayer. Finally, even if the spouse did have control, it would be incongruous with the marital relationship to impose on her the obligation to set aside funds for the benefit of the government.

Agency rationales. The agency rationales for vicarious liability add little to the analysis of traditional relief thus far. A threshold problem is that spouses do not have a principal/agent relationship with each other, either in the legal sense of one being controlled by the other or in the economic sense of one contracting with the other. In some instances, an agency relationship has been found to exist between married persons. The marital relationship, however, differs from an agency relationship in significant ways. There are complex psychological, emotional, and financial facets of marriage that are not present in an agency relationship.

Even assuming that the spouse does control the taxpayer, the two rationales for imposing vicarious liability (fairness and deterrence) are problematic for the reasons described previously.

Fraudulent conveyance rationales. There are thematic similarities between fraudulent conveyance laws and the traditional relief innocent spouse rules. A classic fraudulent transfer might involve a debtor transferring assets to a family member, either as a gift or without adequate consideration, in order to avoid paying a creditor. Applying this template to spousal tax liability, one could view the taxpayer (debtor) as transferring assets to a family member (the spouse) without adequate consideration (as evidenced by significant benefit to the spouse) in order to avoid paying his creditor (the government).

The parallels exist, but there are differences as well. One important difference is that fraudulent conveyance law focuses on the fraudulent intent of the debtor, while the traditional innocent spouse rules completely disregard the taxpayer's intent. Another is that a fraudulent conveyance can involve a transfer to anyone – a family member, friend, another creditor – not just the debtor's spouse. It is beyond the scope of this article to analyze all of the ways in which fraudulent conveyance law diverges from the traditional innocent spouse rules. Nor would it be productive to do so, for the Code has a separate fraudulent conveyance statute and does not need another one in the guise of innocent spouse relief.

In summary, the tort, agency, and fraudulent conveyance rationales for imposing multiple liability do not satisfactorily explain or justify the traditional innocent spouse rules. Imposing liability on a spouse for an understatement attributable to her erroneous items is consistent with the fundamental principle that each individual is responsible for paying tax on the income arising from her activities. Where the understatement is attributable to the other spouse, however, liability should not be imposed on a spouse merely because she knows, or has reason to know, of the understatement or because she received a significant benefit from the understatement. These liability rules under traditional relief should be repealed.

Proportionate Relief

Proportionate relief allocates a deficiency between two spouses in proportion to their respective shares of erroneous items that gave rise to the deficiency. Much of the analysis of the traditional innocent spouse rules can be applied here. Thus, the first condition of liability under proportionate relief – under which a spouse is liable to the extent the deficiency is attributable to her erroneous items – underscores each spouse's distinct identity as a taxpayer and supports the claim that marital unity is a fiction. In addition, the fairness arguments for imposing liability are not persuasive in the tax setting, where there is no identifiable victim and where, to the extent the government is the victim, its ability to absorb loss and its collection powers vastly outmatch those of the taxpayer's spouse.

Viewed from a deterrence standpoint, the proportionate relief rules differ from the traditional relief rules in that they impose spousal liability only if a spouse had actual knowledge of the other spouse's erroneous items, and not if she had reason to know of those items. In terms of compliance, the proportionate relief rules can be viewed as imposing on the spouse a duty to report what she knows, but arguably they do not impose the further duty to investigate. Imposing a duty to report is problematic: such a duty is inconsistent with the marital relationship and the penalty for failure to do so is disproportionately high.

The third condition for proportionate relief imposes liability if assets were transferred by the other spouse to the spouse seeking relief with the principal purpose of tax avoidance, or if one or both spouses acted fraudulently. Like the significant benefit test under traditional relief, this condition for liability bears a resemblance to fraudulent conveyance law and, like the significant benefit test, it is unnecessary in view of the Code's fraudulent conveyance law.

Equitable Relief

Equitable relief is a residual provision, providing relief in situations where traditional and proportionate relief are not available, but it would be inequitable to hold the spouse liable. There has been relatively little interpretation and application of this provision. In determining the scope of the provision, there is an opportunity to mitigate some of the problems with traditional and proportionate relief. In addition, the equitable relief provision should be interpreted in a manner consistent with a cohesive theory of the tax treatment of married individuals. There follows some suggestions along these lines.

One critical category of relief that remains to be fleshed out is the situation where traditional and proportionate relief are not available because the spouse seeking relief had knowledge (or in the case of traditional relief, reason to know would suffice) of erroneous items of the other spouse. The Treasury Department has indicated an unwillingness to provide relief in this situation. The Tax Court has disagreed in several cases, substituting its judgment that equitable relief was warranted even if the spouse had actual knowledge. This article argues that a spouse's knowledge or reason to know of the other spouse's erroneous items is not a justifiable basis on which to impose liability. Accordingly, the Tax Court's approach is preferable, despite concerns about the Tax Court's disregard of administrative deference.

Another general category of relief that is likely to be controversial is the situation where traditional and proportionate relief are not available because an understatement (or underpayment) is attributable to erroneous items of the spouse seeking relief. Again, the Treasury Department has been reluctant to concede that equitable relief could ever be available, while the Tax Court reveals a more generous attitude toward taxpayers. This article has argued that each individual is responsible for tax liabilities related to the individual's own activities. That an individual is married should not change this result. The equitable innocent spouse provision should be interpreted to preclude relief in this situation.

CONCLUSION

The principal tax rationale for joint and several liability – marital unity – is little more than a fiction adopted by lawmakers and scholars in order to rationalize a political compromise between community property and common law states. Furthermore, the other, secondary justifications for joint and several liability are unsatisfactory at best. Nonetheless, with the fiction of marital unity deeply embedded in our tax system, joint and several liability for married joint filers is likely to remain the law. While it can sometimes promote legitimate goals of fairness and efficiency, as an examination of joint and several liability in tort, agency, and fraudulent conveyance law reveals, it can also produce unjust or irrational results. Where possible, therefore, the new innocent spouse laws should be interpreted and, in some cases, reformed to alleviate these injustices and irrationalities.

Taxation and the Family: A Fresh Look at Behavioral Gender Biases in the Code

EDWARD J. McCAFFERY[1]

Despite increasing levels of participation by women in the workforce, a significant gender gap persists. Married women are working more than ever, but their wages lag far behind those of their husbands. In the newly prototypical two-earner family, each spouse devotes an almost equal amount of time to market work, but the wife typically spends twice as many hours as her husband in home production. Despite the supposed "liberation" of women that has transpired over the last several decades, our social models of the family and workplace remain largely unchanged. For example, part-time labor, which would seem an attractive option in a reconceived work–family dynamic, predominantly remains lower paying, less prestigious, and less desirable than full-time labor. More generally, the "new" two-earner family seems largely to have added extra workplace responsibilities to the wife's burdens, while holding most of the husband's activities and the wife's nonmarket production constant. And, while fewer than 10% of all Americans still live in a version of the "traditional" family of some time ago – the working husband and the stay-at-home wife – society has struggled to develop alternative visions of the family.

Tax laws play a role in all of this. A reformulated tax policy could be more sensitive to the character and aspirations of mundane existence; tax laws are well suited to a system of individualized incentives. Yet traditional tax policy often seems stuck in a rut of static, distributive thinking, typically asking who "wins" and who "loses" – that is, who presently pays more dollars out-of-pocket to the fisc – from a putative tax reform. With respect to families, this focus has produced a battle of the "neutralities." The politically dominant school advocates "couples neutrality," a norm whereby "equal income couples should pay equal tax."[2] An opposing camp, gaining prominence in the literature, argues for "marriage neutrality," under which marriage is irrelevant and individuals pay the same tax whether they are single or married.

This article takes a fresh look at taxation of the family, one that focuses on taxation's impact on the character of everyday life. It examines tax rules in terms

---

[1] Reprinted by permission from 40 *UCLA Law Review* 983 (1993).

[2] Michael J. McIntyre & Oliver Oldman, *Taxation of the Family in a Comprehensive and Simplified Income Tax*, 90 HARV. L. REV. 1573, 1590 (1977).

of the *types* of families they foster and suggest. Specifically, the article explores how the tax laws provide behavioral incentives that affect three types of decisions: whether to marry, whether to form a one- or a two-earner household, and whether to work full- or part-time. The bottom line that emerges is that tax laws contribute to the marginalization of women in the workplace, and impede a more creative formulation of alternative models of work and family. In stark contrast to these effects of existing law, a reformulated tax policy, conceived in terms other than the traditional neutrality norms, would offer hope for overcoming some of the entrenched biases concerning family, work, and gender.

THE CLASS DIMENSIONS

The Lowers

Among the lowest income earners, all three incentive effects are rather severe. Perhaps most striking is the marriage penalty. Among the lower income classes, as elsewhere, the rate structure aggregates husband and wife, so they face the same nominal marginal tax rate at all times. But the presence of the earned income credit seriously alters the usual pattern of rate-based incentives. Consider the Lowers. Mr. Lower presently earns $10,000, and the Lowers have two children, qualifying for the maximum 1991 earned income credit of $1,235. Assume that Ms. Lower was considering a job paying $7,000, before taxes, to help make ends meet. With this job, the Lowers' earned income credit would fall to $521, and some portion of the $7,000 would be taxed in the 15% marginal rate bracket. Adding the 7.65% Social Security tax, and some amount for state taxes, brings the total marginal rate facing Ms. Lower to approximately 40% – and the number would approach 50% with the usual incidence assumption regarding Social Security.

In [this] story, the Lowers ultimately get $116 from the federal government. But if the couple were to divorce, the situation would change. If Mr. Lower were to claim the children as dependents and become a head of household, he would still get the maximum earned income credit of $1,235, and the family's total federal income tax bill would drop to a *negative* $1,017.50. Thus the family loses over $900 by remaining married.

The second incentive is the push toward single-earner households. This is brought about by the potentially high marginal tax rates facing the secondary earner, and a woefully inadequate child-care credit that cannot cover the tax costs of working to pay child care in this income range.

The final incentive effect, the tendency to encourage workers to make all-or-nothing labor decisions, follows naturally from [these] discussions. Unless the secondary worker enters the workforce at a sufficient quantum, she cannot cover the high after-tax costs of working with her sharply reduced wages. For the Lowers, it is probably enough to see that working to cover child-care costs is a losing proposition: the secondary worker must earn much more than the costs of child care just to break even.

When we factor these elements together, an unpleasant picture emerges. Our lowest-income families are certainly under stress. The earned-income and child-care credits seem designed to alleviate some of this stress. But the law ironically discourages marriage in the first instance, and creates a bias against secondary worker participation. The child-care credit clearly has two-earner couples in mind, but in practice it is a highly limited tool that does little to encourage secondary worker participation at lower income levels. Especially because simple survival creates a strong economic incentive to work among lower income classes, the discouragement of two-earner families at this level stimulates marital breakdown. Indeed – contrary to the conservative cultural wisdom on work and family – rules that discourage two-earner families will typically also discourage marriage, especially among the poor, where the need for money income is strong. For our lowest income citizens, we see the worst of two worlds – labor markets featuring low pay, few benefits, and little flexibility, and family structures in disarray. Tax rules may play some role in generating these effects. More to the point, tax policy could be more sensitive and helpful, especially if it freed itself from the seductive allure of naively "neutral" rules.

The Mids

Among the middle income ranges, the incentive effects noted for the lower income classes are not nearly as severe. First, the marriage penalty is comparatively small: a couple earning $40,000 pays a maximum marriage penalty, where each spouse earns $20,000, of $165. Second, the relative push toward single-earner families is also much smaller: the marginal rates facing a secondary earner are lower than they are for either the upper or the lower classes, and the child-care credit is relatively effective in offsetting the tax costs of working to pay for child care. But the third incentive, that toward all-or-nothing labor decisions, is clearly present. The reason lies in the fact that these workers face significantly positive marginal rates in entering the workforce, and generate sizeable work-related expenses with only limited tax relief. The need to cover the high after-tax costs of child care, other lost imputed income, and miscellaneous costs of work with reduced pretax dollars, and to do so out of salaries that often reflect entrenched gender biases, drives toward an equilibrium outcome that requires more than part-time labor. In a possibly complex cycle of cause-and-effect, these incentives play out against a backdrop in which part-time options are not very attractive.

The "all-or-nothing effect" has some unfortunate consequences, especially in conjunction with the other two tax-induced incentives. The effect may make women's presence in the labor force unstable because, as circumstances change – most notably, as children enter the picture – the major option facing the family is for the wife to leave her job; simply cutting back one's hours is not often feasible or desirable. If women remain committed to their jobs, the all-or-nothing effect creates a disincentive against having children in the first place, or forces the couple to juggle two full-time careers and child care. This latter solution puts pressure on marriage itself, since two equal earners with children are the most burdened family. More generally, the all-or-nothing effect forecloses options, and contributes to the stressful sense that society is not fostering creative alternatives to traditional family models. It is not just hard to be a two-full-time-earner family. It is also hard to be a full-time/part-time family, and harder still to be a two-part-time-earner family.

The Uppers

Finally, we look at the highest earning Americans. Two effects are especially strong. First, the marriage penalty on two-earner families once again becomes significant. Second, there is a strong bias in favor of single-earner families. This is due to a confluence of factors: the provisions for relieving the tax costs of working to pay for child care are inadequate; the incentive to cultivate imputed income is aggravated by the relatively high marginal tax rates; and the secondary earners face higher rates than primary earners.

In the real world outside of tax rules, the image of two-earner families is strongest in the upper income levels: such couples are apt to be younger, better educated, and have higher incomes than the more "traditional" single-earner families. But the tax laws by and large do not support this reality; they stick to a single-earner model. The results are tax-related incentives not to have children, not to marry if the spousal incomes are apt to be equal, and to specialize between market and nonmarket production. In various ways, these outcomes all oppose the two-earner family. The fact that many upper-income families have resisted these incentives is testimony to the appeal of different familial models, as well as to the flexibility that money brings to ignore certain economic incentives.

The situation of upper-income families – indeed, the whole range of treatment by class – introduces highly unfortunate discontinuities. Among the lower classes, the tax laws discourage formal family structures. This might retard economic improvement to the middle class. At the middle income levels, the laws encourage women to work full-time or stay at home. Either such women fail to develop valuable job market skills, or they find themselves pushing against the upper income levels. But as soon as they do, they face even greater incentives to stay home. Secondary earners in general, and married mothers in particular, are thus pushed in different directions as they cross income levels. The whole pattern is reflected in a social structure that finds poor women alone, middle-class women in a bind, and upper-class women disempowered. One among many ironies is that the corresponding tax system is defended precisely on the grounds of its alleged neutrality.

BEYOND STATIC NEUTRALITY: ALTERNATIVE APPROACHES TO TAXATION AND THE FAMILY

Optimal Taxation: Looking at Elasticities

The optimal tax literature provides a formidable tool for challenging the traditional, static notion of neutrality. Optimal tax literature teaches that goods should be taxed based on their relative elasticities, to minimize "deadweight" losses.

A deadweight loss, also referred to as the "excess burden" of a tax, comes about because of the lost consumer or supplier surplus when the after-tax world is compared to the before-tax world. It may be easiest to understand the concept in simple, prosaic terms. Imagine that some individuals are willing to work for $5.00 an hour, but no less – this is their "reservation wage." They are currently paid a $6.00 hourly rate. But an income tax goes into effect, at 30%, and the workers' after-tax rate drops to $4.20 an hour. Their response is to quit. No one benefits from the tax in this example – neither workers nor employers, nor the government (which gets nothing from the tax). This is a clear example of a deadweight loss – a burden with no compensating benefit.

The actual amount of the deadweight loss turns on what are called the "compensated elasticity," or "substitution effects," of the tax. Any tax will have two general types of effects: income and substitution. Substitution effects unambiguously lead the individual away from the taxed activity, as other goods or pursuits ("substitutes") become more attractive. Income effects, in contrast, lead the taxed individual to have less money from continuing to engage in the taxed activity. In the case of an income tax, these two effects are believed to work in opposite directions: when the government taxes wages, leisure becomes more attractive, leading taxpayers away from work, but the income effects may push the taxpayer to work more hours to maintain her after-tax cash flow.

The optimal tax literature hinges on the notion of deadweight losses and hence focuses on compensated elasticities. The practical prescriptions of the optimal tax literature are clear: the more responsive the demand for a good is to its price, the less should be the tax, and vice versa. Thus, gasoline, cigarettes, and other inelastic goods should bear high tax rates.

Elasticities are a tricky and treacherous business; they vary among the short and long terms, are difficult to measure, incorporate numerous expectancies regarding the future, and are highly particularistic. But a good deal of evidence supports the proposition that the labor elasticity for secondary earners in general, and married women in particular, is higher than it is for primary earners, or husbands. In other words, husbands tend to work no matter what, but wives do so only if their after-tax wages are attractive. Recent studies are beginning to suggest that the elasticity of working women may be quite close to that of men, but that the elasticity of nonworking women is much higher. Considering the survey of tax laws presented earlier, this should not surprise us. Many women face something of an all-or-nothing decision. The elasticity at the participation-decision stage may thus be high. But once a woman is in the workforce (and she is apt to be working full-time), it is not obvious that she will be significantly less committed than a man.

Economists who have studied optimal income taxation of the family, and who tend to take the elasticities as exogenous givens, have advocated separate rates for husbands and wives, with much higher rates on husbands – even possibly negative tax rates on wives. If the participation decision is the most elastic, the lower rates need be concentrated only on the initial ranges of the secondary worker's income – much like the earned income credit operates. If, as would appear likely, mothers are especially elastic, the secondary worker credit could be further tailored to especially benefit parents. Such a credit would lead to an unambiguous improvement in total welfare under a straight application of optimal tax theory: deadweight losses would be lessened.

Pigouvian Taxation: Looking at Market Failures

A second economic theory of venerable lineage that opposes the traditional neutrality of tax policy is often called Pigouvian taxation. As with optimal tax, Pigouvian tax theories give us both a perspective on what might be wrong with the status quo and some insight into correcting it.

Pigouvian taxation is a direct response to observed market failures. Pigouvian tax holds that when free markets do *not* work, as for example because of the presence of externalities, a legitimate role of taxation is to correct for the failure. Free markets thus provide a normative baseline to which tax policy should attempt to move us. A simple example is that of a tax on pollutants, which would force polluting firms to internalize the costs of their polluting behavior.

Labor decisions are classic market outcomes, where workers sell and employers purchase labor at a price, the wage rate. We might therefore expect, in the first instance, that the results reached by private consumers and firms in these matters are superior to those obtained through public intervention, thereby buttressing our inclination not to intervene. But in fact labor markets might break down in a number of important ways. In such a case, a Pigouvian tax, like an optimal tax, will not meet the traditional static distributive test of neutrality. Instead, Pigouvian techniques call for a delicate correction of market imperfections.

Pigouvian taxation gives a rationale for using the income tax to correct these problems. Just as it can be efficient to tax the polluting firm to drive it to internalize the social costs of its activities, we might tax the labor market to prod it to address its systematic biases against married women. One approach might be to subsidize firms that hire married women. But perhaps more attractive approach, given the uncertain incidence of a firm-side remedy, would be to subsidize the women directly, through income tax credits targeted to secondary earners. Financing such credits out of higher rates for primary earners may actually serve the same normative, market-correcting goal. The resulting taxation system will not appear "neutral," in the usual, naive, and static sense of the term. But this might mean only that it is time to move beyond such neutral notions. The Pigouvian taxes are neutral in the more important sense of justificatory neutrality, because they rest on a market-correction rationale, which takes no position on the relative merits of different familial models, or on different substantive visions of the good life.

CONCLUSION

Traditional tax policy looks at distributive burdens. This focus leads, in the taxation and family area, to norms of "couples" and "marriage neutrality." A different picture emerges if we focus on behavioral incentives. This article draws out some lessons from its study of the interface between tax laws and daily life. The tax law's basic rate structure is nominally indifferent to who earns any given amount of income, but the interface with other aspects of the tax law and real-world conditions pushes toward a traditional, gendered division of labor.

The actual pattern of effects has strong class dimensions. Among our poorest citizens, we have disincentives for marrying, or staying together. For the broad middle class, there is something of an all-or-nothing effect, pushing against part-time labor options for either spouse. The upper classes suffer a distinct bias toward specialized households. When these various effects are put together, there are unnerving discontinuities across the income classes, and potentially profound dynamic effects. Married women become marginal workers. Small initial discriminations, perhaps rationally based, can easily explode into a vicious and self-perpetuating cycle of entrenched gender bias. Everywhere women, especially married women and even more especially married mothers, are hurt. If the tax laws are not a cause of these problems, neither are they much of a cure. With more imagination and resolve, they easily could be.

A strong theoretical case exists for altering the basic rate structure to provide significantly lower, even negative, rates for secondary earners, financed by higher rates on primary earners. The welfare economic theories of optimal and Pigouvian tax both support this proposal, the former as a means of maximizing welfare, the latter as an antidote to sexist discrimination and related other market failures in the labor markets. Such a step, which represents a dramatic break from prior orthodoxy on the subject, may also be justified by appeal to the justificatorily neutral norms of freedom to select family structure and equality of opportunity and respect for women.

The ultimate conclusion is a methodological one. It is time to rethink our first premises of taxation and the family. The family is a complex and central social institution, and we can no longer treat it in a two-dimensional manner. Tax laws are too deeply intertwined with contemporary social reality to allow for simple, distributive norms to guide us. We can no longer afford the intellectual luxury of clinging to handy maxims like "equal taxation for equal-earning couples" as a substitute for the difficult, contestable, but ultimately unavoidable chore of constructing normative principles for regulating the story of taxation and the family.

The Profits and Penalties of Kinship: Conflicting Meanings of Family in Estate Tax Law

BRIDGET J. CRAWFORD[1]

You can choose your friends but the Code chooses your family, at least for estate tax purposes. In broad terms, the estate tax provisions of the Code impose a tax on any gratuitous death-time transfer by an individual. For the most part, precise tax liability will depend on the amount of the transfer. Estate tax liability also may depend on the identity and even the business activities of the transferor, the transferee, and each of their respective "family" members. Depending on the particular Code section involved, however, the term "family" has widely divergent meanings for estate tax purposes.

VARIED DEFINITIONS OF "FAMILY" IN ESTATE TAX LAW

Transfers with a Retained Interest

The basic rule of § 2036(a)(1) is that a decedent may not avoid estate taxation if he or she transfers property to another but retains some benefit from the property. A classic example of a retained interest is a life estate. A similar but less well-known example of a retained right that will cause estate tax inclusion is the right to vote shares of stock in a "controlled corporation."

Section 2036(b)(2) defines a controlled corporation as one in which the decedent "owned (with the application of § 318), or had the right (either alone or in conjunction with any person)" to vote stock carrying at least 20% of the aggregate voting power of all stock classes. Note that § 2036(b)(2)'s definition of a controlled corporation focuses on the ownership of more persons than just the taxpayer-transferor. Under § 318, an individual is deemed to own any stock that is owned (whether directly or indirectly), by or for "(i) his spouse (other than a spouse who is legally separated from the individual under a decree of divorce or separate maintenance), and (ii) his children, grandchildren, and parents." Even if the taxpayer personally owns a very small percentage of the stock (or even none at all), and the corporation initially does not appear to be a "controlled corporation" with respect to the taxpayer, the attribution to the taxpayer of the holdings of his or her family members can have unexpected consequences.

---

[1] Reprinted by permission from 3 *Pittsburgh Tax Review* 1 (2005).

Transfers with a Retained Right to Designate

Section 2036(a)(2) includes in a decedent's gross estate the value of all property to the extent that the decedent retains the right to designate the persons who benefit from the transferred property. There are situations where a transferor-decedent retains rights to remove and replace a person (typically a trustee) who has the authority to make discretionary distributions of assets transferred to a trust. The IRS takes the view that if a transferor-decedent has the power to remove a trustee and replace the removed trustee with a family member who is "related or subordinate" to the transferor within the meaning of § 672(c), the trust assets will be included in the decedent's gross estate.

Under § 672(c) a related or subordinate party is one who is both (a) "nonadverse" and (b) a member of a specific class of individuals. A nonadverse party is a person who does not have any "substantial beneficial interest" in a trust that would be adversely affected by the exercise or nonexercise of a power with respect to that trust. The specific class of individuals includes the taxpayer's spouse, father, mother, issue, brother, or sister.

Special Valuation of Real Property

Section 2032A is an exception to the basic principle that the estate tax value of a decedent's property is its fair market value as of the decedent's date of death. Specifically § 2032A provides that "qualified real property" may be valued for estate tax purposes at its value for use as a farm for farming purposes or its use in a trade or business other than the trade or business of farming. In almost all cases, a property's value for farming or trade or business purposes will be less than the property's fair market value. The estate tax savings resulting from this alternate valuation may be significant.

As a threshold matter, to be eligible for the special valuation rules of § 2032A, property must be acquired from or pass from the decedent to his or her "qualified heir." A qualified heir is defined as a "member of the decedent's family." For purposes of § 2032A, a taxpayer-decedent's "family" consists of any of the taxpayer's ancestors; the taxpayer's spouse; any lineal descendant of the taxpayer; a lineal descendant of the taxpayer's spouse; any descendant of the taxpayer's parents (i.e., a taxpayer's siblings, nieces and nephews, etc.); and the spouse of any lineal descendant of the taxpayer, [of any descendant of] the taxpayer's spouse, or [of] any descendant of the taxpayer's parents.

Extension of Time for Payment of Estate Taxes

The general rule is that the executor must pay estate tax within nine months of the decedent's date of death. In certain limited instances, however, an executor may elect to pay the estate tax liability in as many as ten annual installments. This installment option is available under § 6166 to those estates in which the value of an "interest in a closely held business" that is included in the decedent's gross estate exceeds 35% of the adjusted gross estate. Whether a particular interest is one in a "closely held business" for § 6166 purposes is a complex determination that depends on the definition of family. Perhaps not surprisingly at this point in the analysis, § 6166's definition is different from each of the previous definitions.

A partnership or corporation is "closely held" for purposes of § 6166 if either (a) the decedent's gross estate includes 20% or more of the partnership's total capital interests or the value of the voting stock of the corporation or (b) the partnership or corporation has forty-five or fewer partners or shareholders. Consider a scenario in which individual ownership does not rise to the requisite level. [The] estate nevertheless may be able to qualify for the extension of time to pay estate taxes. A decedent is deemed to own all partnership interests and stock owned by any "member" of his or her "family," as defined in § 267(c)(4). In other words, a decedent is deemed to own all partnership interests and stock owned by his or her siblings, spouse, ancestors, and lineal descendants. As a practical matter, the decedent and members of his or her family are treated as one taxpayer.

A Spectrum of Definitions

Each of the Code sections defines "family" (or "related" persons) differently. The Code sections could be arranged on a definitional spectrum with restrictive and expansive definitions at opposite ends. At the restrictive end of the spectrum would be § 2036's inclusion rule for retained interests in "controlled corporations." Section 2036(b)(2)'s reference to § 318 attributes to a taxpayer the ownership of his or her spouse, children, grandchildren, and parents. At the broad end of the spectrum would be § 2032A and its vision of family as including stepchildren and various relations by marriage. Somewhere in between would be § 6166 and § 2036(a)(2).

FAMILY VALUES: PERSPECTIVES ON THE FAMILY

The great variety in existing estate tax definitions of the family underscores the importance of the family to the overall system of wealth transfer taxation. Indeed estate taxation arose in response to the desire on the part of wealthy individuals to transfer wealth to their children. As people accumulated great fortunes that could not be consumed in a single lifetime, the government sought to tax the transfer of wealth from one generation to the next. In response to early estate tax legislation, taxpayers became creative in minimizing their tax bills, and the law in turn became more complicated.

Apart from taxpayer creativity, one reason for the complexity of current estate tax rules is the complexity of modern family arrangements themselves. Family households constitute the majority of American households. Approximately 60.7% of all family households include children, but very few families resemble the traditional model of a working husband and a stay-at-home wife. According to the most recent census data, most women work. Many children live with one parent or neither parent, although the majority (68.7%) of all children live with two parents. Multigenerational households (e.g., a grandparent, parent, and child all living together) are a significant percentage of all households. Of all persons over the age of fifteen years, a large percentage (18.5%) are divorced and remarried, but only 27.1% have never married. These statistics point to the great variation in family composition. In light of the many ways in which American families differ from the traditional model, complexity in the estate tax law is perhaps not surprising, given that the estate tax arose in response to family wealth transfers.

Apart from its revenue-generation function, viewed in a larger cultural context of family relationships, the estate tax rules perform two distinct functions: first, they acknowledge the personal and economic interconnectedness of individuals within families, and second, to a certain extent, they take into account diversity in family arrangements. From the perspective of certain family law scholarship and gender theory, however, the estate tax rules are flawed in theoretical and practical terms because they fail to recognize the full diversity of American households and they valorize market labor. This part borrows the lens of gender theory to explore how the current tax rules embrace progressive constructions of the family, but do not go far enough in recognizing the complexity of human household relationships.

Tax Rules and Interconnectedness

Typically women's interests have been said to center on "caretaking and relationships, particularly with dependents."[2] Recognition of the multiplicity of human connectedness reinforces values and knowledge that some scholars suggest are unique to women: an understanding that no person is ever wholly independent from others. To the extent they are concerned especially with the identities (and business activities) of a particular transferor, transferee, and his or her respective family members, the estate tax rules of §§ 2036, 2032A, and 6166 are consistent with a jurisprudence of connectedness. That jurisprudence would suggest that no person is a classically individual rational actor, and every transfer must be viewed in its larger human context.

The estate tax law's preferences (and penalties) for families acknowledge the human dimension of wealth transfers, particularly that the economic realities of any one transfer may depend on the identity of either the donee of an inter vivos gift or the legatee of a death-time transfer. Transfers to family members are treated in some instances more favorably than transfers to strangers, but replacement of a removed trustee is fraught with greater potential estate tax penalties when the replacement is a family member instead of a stranger. The estate tax rules' embrace of a jurisprudence of connectedness is not complete, however. The rules do not fully account for the multidimensional aspects of human relations. The existence of family hostility, for example, is irrelevant to the determination of whether a corporation is "controlled" for purposes of § 2036(a)(1)'s estate tax inclusion rule. The definition in § 2036(b)(2) focuses on the holdings of the taxpayer and family members without regard to the qualitative nature of the interpersonal relationships (i.e., whether a person is in fact "controlled" by another). Similarly

---

[2] Mary Becker, *Patriarchy and Inequality: Towards a Substantive Feminism*, 1999 U. Chi. Legal F. 21, 49.

whether a particular family member–trustee is in fact "subordinate" with respect to the taxpayer-transferor is irrelevant for purposes of § 2036(a)(2)'s inclusion rule. The only relevant criterion is whether the trustee is a member of the prohibited class. So the tax laws recognize interconnectedness to a certain extent, but efficient application of the tax rules requires the overlay of bright line rules that may or may not reflect the realities of particular family relationships.

Tax Rules and Diversity in Families

Family law scholarship draws attention to the diversity in American families. That diversity requires the estate tax definitions of "family" or "related" persons to embrace modern family configurations to some extent. For example, perhaps in a nod to the prevalence of divorce, § 2036(b)(2) provides that the holdings of a taxpayer-transferor's spouse will not be aggregated with the taxpayer's if the spouses are separated under a decree of divorce or separate maintenance. In possible acknowledgment of multigenerational families (and the likelihood that an adult may be taking care of elderly parents as well as minor children), a parent is a "related or subordinate" party for purposes of § 2036(a)(2), and therefore cannot be removed or replaced as a trustee of a trust created by the taxpayer. Similarly, siblings are defined as members of the "family" for purposes of §§ 2032A and 6166, recognizing the role of extended family in closely held or family-owned businesses. Given the irregular nature of the American family, these expansive definitions of families are appropriate.

At least in the popular imagination, the term "family" calls up an image of a grouping of persons related by blood or marriage. The stereotypical family is organized around a heterosexual married couple and their descendants. The estate tax rules are oriented toward this vision of the nuclear family, allowing for some variations within a traditional bandwidth. Yet the multiple estate tax definitions of family do not recognize the same variations on the traditional structure. For example, § 2032A is the only one of the four provisions to include within the definition of "family" stepchildren and spouses of lineal descendants of the transferor or the transferor's spouse. Likewise, § 2036(b)(2)'s definition of a controlled corporation is the only one of the four not to include siblings. The inconsistency of the estate tax's definitions of family is matched by their underinclusivity. Existing estate tax definitions recognize traditional families, stepfamilies, and extended families, but they do not recognize nonmarital associational relationships that some people consider to be "family." The estate tax maintains this approach even in the face of state laws that grant some of those "families" limited legal recognition. For example, under New Jersey's Domestic Partnership Act, opposite-sex partners who are both sixty-two years of age or older and same-sex partners (who are not permitted to marry under New Jersey law) may register as domestic partners. Registration of the domestic partnership is meant to afford domestic partners certain legal benefits under state law. Yet for federal estate tax purposes, these persons are not considered members of the same "family" in the several ways that the statutes define that term.

PROPOSALS TO RESOLVE THE ESTATE TAX'S CONFLICTING
DEFINITIONS OF FAMILY

No single definition of family discussed here would effectuate legislative intent, and it is unlikely that any single definition would be appropriate for all estate tax purposes, given the diverse purposes for which the laws were enacted. Eliminating all family-based estate tax rules likely would result in systematic overtaxation or undertaxation, using legislative intent and existing levels of taxation as a reference.

In light of these unsatisfactory options, the best (and perhaps the simplest) solution is revising the statutes to eliminate internal conflict over terms like "family" and "related" persons and to reflect each Code section's unique purposes. Within a body of law, words should be used consistently and, to the extent possible, in ways that comport with lay understanding. Statutory integrity is a fundamental requirement for public confidence in the legal system. If it is not possible to use terms like "family" and "related" persons consistently across Code sections, then it is appropriate to consider using distinct terms for their unique and limited purposes.

Revisions would need [to] be made to the definition of "controlled corporation" of § 2036(b)(2) that is made applicable to § 2036(a)(1). The definition of "controlled corporation" could be revised to use a self-contained attribution rule, instead of incorporating the attribution rule of § 318 by reference. The self-contained attribution rule could refer to members of the "Attribution Group" instead of members of the decedent's "family." That way, it would be plain that the language of § 2036(b)(2) should not be read and was not intended to harmonize with any other Code section.

Similarly, the IRS should withdraw Revenue Ruling 95-58, applicable to the interpretation of § 2036(a)(2), and issue a new ruling that prohibits removal of a trustee and replacement by a person who is a member of the "Prohibited Class," for example, instead of a person who is "related or subordinate."

As part of the statutory change of terms to "Attribution Group" and "Prohibited Class," those terms could be drafted to include any person who is defined for purposes of local law as a registered domestic partner or "spouse" of the taxpayer. This would allow the estate tax inclusion rule to reach transfers in the context of family-like relationships that presently are not recognized as "family" for federal tax purposes. Including domestic partners and state-law spouses within the § 2036 definition would be consistent with the legislature's concern over taxpayer control. Furthermore, insofar as the revised § 2036 would apply only to domestic partnerships and marriages that are recognized by the state, there should be little, if any, evidentiary concern over who is a registered domestic partner or spouse for state-law purposes.

Section 2032A would need more extensive revisions to achieve the desired statutory integrity. Apart from the purely semantic change of replacing "family" with a term such as "Qualified Heir Group," it would be appropriate to consider expanding the definition's substance in light of § 2032A's underlying policy goal of providing tax relief to the family farmer or small business owner. The "Qualified

Heir Group" could be defined as all of the persons who are included under existing law as members of a taxpayer's "family" as well as any other individual whose total real estate and farm holdings are below a certain fair market value. That would allow a decedent to leave real property to a long-time employee who, for example, spends thirty years working on the farm before the decedent's death, without extending the special valuation rule in cases where a decedent's family decides to sell the family farm to a large agribusiness conglomerate. As a matter of practical politics, it is extremely unlikely that Congress would expand the definition of "Qualified Heir Group" to include persons who are registered as domestic partners or recognized as spouses for state-law purposes. From a policy perspective, however, renaming and expanding the definition of a "qualified heir" to include domestic partners (as well as their descendants) is consistent with the statute's desire to foster small farms and business activities.

Section 6166 might be rewritten to attribute to a taxpayer the holdings of his or her "Closely Held Business Associates" instead of his or her "family" as defined in § 267(c)(4). The Closely Held Business Associates could include all persons defined under current § 6166 as a "member" of a decedent's "family." To the extent that Congress is concerned about the longevity of small businesses, it may be theoretically appropriate, if politically unfeasible, to include registered domestic partners and state-law spouses within that group. Ultimately the estate tax law's account of "family" will need to be broadened to include a greater range of the relationships that people call by that name.

CONCLUSION

Family is both a burden and a benefit for estate tax purposes. Family is a burden to the extent that attribution rules trigger estate tax inclusion under § 2036(a)(1), or if the ability to replace a removed trustee with a relative runs afoul of the prohibition on the removal of related or subordinate parties under § 2036(a)(2). Family is a benefit insofar as it may cause special valuation rules to be available under § 2032A or for an estate to have more time to pay taxes under § 6166. Each of these already intricate Code sections is complicated by a unique definition of "family" or "related" persons.

The variety in the estate tax definitions of family reflects, to some extent, the diversity in the composition of contemporary American families. In a society in which two-career couples, divorce, remarriage, and multigenerational families are common, laws that seek to tax the transfer of wealth necessarily will have a certain level of complexity. Recent family law scholarship, with its emphasis on connectedness and interdependency, provides a useful lens for examining the strengths and shortcomings of the existing tax rules. But insofar as family law theorists criticize the relatively low value accorded to women's caretaking activities, those theorists should have little quarrel with the estate tax laws which do not tax the fruits of those caretaking activities.

Unless the statutes are revised to achieve some degree of integrity, they will continue to contribute to the general public's sense that the tax laws are unfair and overly complex. This article proposes using terms like Attribution Group,

Qualified Heir Group, and Closely Held Business Associates instead of terms like "family" and "related" persons. Although the changes are semantic in some sense, they embody the larger belief that statutes ought to use words consistently and in ways that comport with lay understanding. This will also align the definitions more closely with legislative intent. The rigorous demands of statutory integrity require nothing less.

The Tax Treatment of Children: Separate but Unequal

DOROTHY A. BROWN[1]

This article considers the question of why the Code has two separate provisions that affect children, namely the earned income tax credit (EITC) and the child tax credit (CTC). They are separate but serve similar purposes, and they are unequal because CTC families receive far greater tax benefits than EITC families. This article seeks to uncover why there is a need for two tax credits which benefit children differently and concludes that the only plausible explanation is related to race.

EARNED INCOME TAX CREDIT

The primary requirement of the EITC is that it only applies to "earned income." It provides a refundable credit for the working poor, which means low-income taxpayers may receive a refund in excess of their income tax withholding and, in certain instances, in excess of their Social Security withholding. In many instances, EITC-eligible families would live below the poverty line without the EITC refund.

As originally enacted, the EITC did not increase for family size. Subsequent amendments now allow the EITC to increase both for family and low-income wage earners without children. Married couples must file joint returns.

The EITC creates marriage bonuses and marriage penalties in certain households. Marriage bonuses occur when the spouses pay less in taxes (or receive a greater refund) as a result of marriage. Marriage penalties occur when the spouses pay more in taxes (or receive a smaller refund) as a result of marriage. In 2001, the EITC was amended to minimize the marriage penalty paid by EITC-eligible taxpayers. Although the EITC phase-out amounts are currently $1,000 higher if the taxpayer is married, that $1,000 does very little to reduce the marriage penalties associated with the EITC. Married taxpayers in equal wage-earning households are most likely to pay a marriage penalty.

The EITC varies based upon income and the number of children in the taxpayer's household. The EITC is greatest for households with two or more children. It is the least for households with no children. The EITC amount does not increase for households with more than two children. The EITC per child is greatest for

---

[1] Reprinted by permission from 54 *Emory Law Journal* 755 (2005).

households with one child since the EITC calculation for two or more children is not twice the value of the one-child EITC amount.

The credit amount increases as long as income increases, up to a certain level of income. Once income reaches a certain level, the credit remains the same even as income continues to increase. As the taxpayer's income reaches another level, the credit begins to decrease as income increases. This resembles a means test. As income increases, the EITC decreases. Eventually, as income continues to increase, the credit will decrease to zero.

Over the past decade, the EITC has been the subject of scrutiny by members of Congress. The government has focused significant resources and energy on these efforts. Numerous General Accounting Office reports were published and governmental hearings were held addressing the EITC. Most of these reports and hearings, if not all, focused on noncompliance issues.

Audit rates for EITC taxpayers are higher than for other income groups. Beginning in 1962, the IRS started the Taxpayer Compliance Measurement Program (TCMP). The TCMP allowed the IRS to perform line-by-line audits on a random sample of tax returns. TCMP audits covered eleven different types of tax returns and were done every three years until Congress decided to end the program in 1994.

Congress stopped the IRS from conducting TCMP studies generally because "the filers selected for review when past studies of general noncompliance were conducted were subject to excessive burdens and intrusion."[2] As a result, audit rates have generally decreased since fiscal year 1988 for the highest-income taxpayers, while rates have increased for the lowest-income individuals. IRS officials acknowledge this is mainly a result of the recent emphasis on nonfilers and EITC claims.

While the budget for IRS audits has generally decreased because Congress considers them to be "intrusive" to taxpayers, the budget for EITC taxpayer audits has increased. Since 1998, almost $900,000,000 has been appropriated specifically for earned income compliance initiatives. This was the result of new laws enacted by Congress and funding specifically approved by Congress for IRS-directed EITC activities. Significant taxpayer dollars are being spent on EITC audits when compared with the revenue that is being generated. While the assumption has often been made that errors on EITC returns are the result of fraud, given the credit's complexity one could easily imagine alternative explanations for the errors. It is entirely possible that the belief that EITC errors are the result of fraud is a function of racial stereotyping about EITC recipients.

In the summer of 2003, Congress denied tax benefits to 12,000,000 children who lived in low-income taxpayer households, but benefits were granted to children who lived in middle-income households. Beginning in 2004, certain EITC-eligible taxpayers will have to be precertified – namely, they must prove to the IRS prior to receiving the credit, that they are eligible. EITC filers who are not married parents claiming their children or who are single fathers claiming their children are subject

[2] Robert Greenstein, *The New Procedures for the Earned Income Tax Credit*, 99 Tax Notes 1525, 1528 (2003).

to the new precertification procedures. These taxpayers must prove they have the proper relationship to the child for EITC purposes before they will be able to receive their EITC.

CHILD TAX CREDIT

The CTC is commonly referred to as middle-class tax relief. There is no requirement that the taxpayer have only earned income. Therefore a trust fund beneficiary with a child who does not work is eligible for the CTC. The CTC was enacted to support families with children. The legislative history provides that the decision to increase the CTC for each child was necessary because of the reduced ability to pay taxes as family size grows.

A taxpayer is entitled to the CTC for each "qualifying child." Each "qualifying child" must be less than seventeen years of age. In addition, there is a limitation on the CTC if you are eligible for the EITC. Finally, there is a limit on your CTC eligibility if your income is too great.

The interaction between the CTC and the EITC adds a great deal of complexity to the EITC, and is a result of the decision to make the CTC partially refundable while the EITC is fully refundable. The maximum refundable CTC is allowed only to the extent the taxpayer's Social Security taxes and income tax liability exceed the taxpayer's EITC. At lower income levels, the standard deduction and personal exemptions will eliminate the income tax liability of many families, making the CTC only available to the extent that the employee's share of Social Security taxes exceed[s] their EITC amount. However, it is at the lower income levels that the EITC is at its highest. As a result, many low-income parents will not receive the full amount of the CTC. In those households, their Social Security taxes and their income tax liability will not be greater than their EITC, which makes them ineligible for the CTC.

COMPARISON OF THE EITC AND THE CTC

The CTC is rather straightforward and only becomes complex when taxpayers are also eligible for the EITC. The EITC is complex from beginning to end and the subject of serious government scrutiny, while the CTC receives no government scrutiny. The EITC is only available for taxpayers with earned income, while the CTC is available to taxpayers with income from any source. The EITC does not increase after the taxpayer has two children, while the CTC increases with every child. There is a maximum EITC, while there is no maximum CTC. The legislative history of the EITC was concerned with not providing economic incentives to large families, while the legislative history of the CTC was concerned with lessening the economic burdens of large families. The EITC is fully refundable, while the CTC is only partially refundable. The CTC phase-out for married couples, when compared to singles, is far more generous than the phase-outs for the EITC. This results in very high marginal tax rates for EITC recipients. The CTC permits married taxpayers to file separately and receive the credit, but the EITC does not. There is no CTC for taxpayers with no children, while there is an EITC, albeit a small one, for taxpayers with no children. The amount of the EITC and the CTC are a function of [the] taxpayer's income and the number of children present in the household. Qualifying children for EITC purposes must be under nineteen, while for CTC purposes qualifying children must be under seventeen.

Given that the CTC was enacted to take into account the decrease in the ability to pay taxes as family size increases, it is indeed curious that the CTC is not fully refundable to low-income taxpayers. The CTC's legislative history provides that the CTC should be increased for every child because of the "reduced ability to pay taxes as family size increases."[3] The ability to pay is, at worst, no less a concern for low-income taxpayers than it is for middle-income taxpayers, and at best, more of a concern. One can explain the decision on political grounds, but it is more difficult to explain on policy grounds.

SEPARATE BUT UNEQUAL: THE CTC AND THE EITC

This section considers race-neutral explanations for why the provisions of the EITC and the CTC are so different and why EITC recipients are singled out for such harsh treatment. One explanation could be that the tax credits benefit such different groups that the disparity is justified. Both tax credits, however, were enacted to benefit families with children. (Only within the last ten years was the EITC amended to permit a nominal EITC for households with no children.) The tax credits' purposes do not provide an adequate explanation for the disparity in the tax provisions. Nor do their purposes provide adequate explanation for why the EITC originally did not increase for family size because of fear that it would provide an "economic incentive for having additional children," while the CTC originally increased for every child in the household.

Another possible explanation is that it is easier to administer the provisions if they are separate. Yet the interaction between the EITC and the CTC exponentially increases the CTC's complexity. The interaction occurs when a taxpayer is eligible for the EITC and the CTC and when the CTC is only partially refundable. Ease of administration similarly does not explain the disparity.

Another explanation could be that the EITC recipients receive such harsh treatment because they deserve it. The error rate associated with the EITC that results in the $6 billion tax gap attributable to all tax credits, including the EITC, justifies the targeting of EITC recipients. But the $6 billion tax gap is only slightly more than 5% of the total $100 billion tax gap and the IRS is not pursuing any other taxpayer group with such vigor. The IRS is also not pursuing EITC tax preparers to the extent it is pursuing EITC recipients. It cannot be fairly said that EITC recipients deserve harsher treatment than taxpayers who promote and benefit from the corporate tax shelters that cause a greater percentage of the tax gap.

The publicly provided explanation for the disparity, however, is that EITC recipients do not deserve additional benefits because the EITC is welfare. Several members of Congress referred to EITC-eligible taxpayers as welfare recipients. Republican members used the analogy to seek public support for their decision to

[3] S. Rep. No. 105-33, at 3 (1997).

deny 12,000,000 low-income families tax benefits, while at the same time providing those tax benefits to more "deserving" middle-income families. In the debates that considered extending the CTC to EITC-eligible taxpayers several Republican members of Congress also described the EITC as analogous to welfare.

This article argues, however, that the analogy between EITC refunds and welfare payments is a poor one. EITC recipients who work in the paid-labor market pay income, property (even if renters), sales, Social Security, and Medicare taxes and do not fit the traditional definition of welfare recipients. Calling taxpayers welfare recipients and their refund "welfare" is inappropriate. Yet, the analogy is a powerful one, and it worked.

WELFARE, POLITICS, AND THE UNDESERVING POOR

When the term "welfare" is used, it generally refers to Aid to Families with Dependent Children, or its replacement, Temporary Assistance to Needy Families. One consistent theme of U.S. welfare policy has been to differentiate between the "deserving" and the "undeserving" poor. No one readily admits to being part of the "undeserving" poor because they would then be ineligible for governmental benefit. Being viewed as part of the "deserving" poor becomes the goal. Welfare policy is therefore best understood as producing symbols designed to validate societal norms and values – thereby making welfare recipients the "deserving" poor. One of those societal norms and values is encouraging the work ethic.

The presence of a means test in a federally funded program increases the stigma attached to its recipients. The absence of a means test is intended to show that the recipient is legitimate and deserving. For example, Social Security benefits are not means tested. In fact, Jack Welch, the former chairman and chief executive of General Electric Co., reportedly receives $1,000 a month after taxes in Social Security benefits, even though he nets $357,128 a month from his pension and continues to earn income from his consulting business. The decision of whether to have a means test is therefore a reflection of whether the recipients are "deserving."

Professor Martin Gilens explains that American opposition to welfare is a result of public perception that most welfare recipients are undeserving, primarily for two reasons. First, Americans believe that most welfare recipients are black. Second, Americans believe that blacks are not as committed to working as nonblacks. As a result, welfare has become synonymous with African-Americans.

Blacks are not like whites because they have "warped values" and do not want their children to attend good schools, do not want good jobs, and do not wish to live in safe neighborhoods. The centuries-old stereotype of blacks being lazy and not hardworking is still firmly believed by a significant majority of the white population. As a result, the public views them as "undeserving" and properly excluded from receiving benefits until their behavior changes.

Given the lack of public support for welfare, political leaders who describe funding programs as "welfare" are inviting a hostile reception by whites. Whether payments are characterized as welfare will be a strong factor in determining the strength of public support of the program. If a Congress member wants a program to garner widespread support, she will avoid characterizing the program as welfare. If a Congress member wants to garner opposition against the program, all she needs to do is characterize it as welfare. You can see this clearly when you compare statements made about EITC recipients with those made about another group of recipients of government largesse – farmers. EITC recipients receive welfare, but to describe farmers in similar terms is deemed "an insult." Anyone looking for consistency in the definition of welfare is left sorely disappointed.

Government subsidies to farmers [have] a racial component. Professor Jim Chen stated that government subsidies to farm owners are "an almost perfectly race-matched system of affirmative action for whites."[4] Farm owners are 98% white, which is one of the highest percentages of white owners in any segment of American business. Professor Chen further provided that "[l]egislative statements favoring 'family farms,' . . . create in their aggregate a *de facto* preference for white enterprise."[5] In addition, the racially disparate impact of the benefits flowing to black farmers was the subject of a lawsuit against the Department of Agriculture that was recently settled.

EITC recipients who receive payments only if they work receive "welfare," but farmers who receive payments even if they do not work do not receive "welfare." Farmers are insulted if they are referred to as welfare recipients, but hardworking, low-income taxpayers are expected to accept the same insult. Farmers who do not have to work to receive government payments are hardworking, proud, and independent, while low-income taxpayers receive "public assistance." Farmers care about their children and their grandchildren – low-income taxpayers presumably do not.

EMPIRICAL DATA AND THE EITC

The [*Survey of Income and Program Participation (SIPP)*] data [see Chapter 5, Dorothy A. Brown, *Race and Class Matters in Tax Policy,* for a brief exposition of the data] show that most blacks are ineligible for the EITC. For the blacks that are eligible, their average EITC is very similar to the average EITC for whites. The disproportionate analysis starting point should be the EITC-eligible population – not the percentage of blacks in the population. At that point one can contrast EITC differences of similarly situated black and white taxpayers. The fact that blacks are more likely to be poor does not mean that blacks are more likely to be the working poor, making them eligible for the EITC. That disproportionate analysis shows that there is a far greater percentage of the EITC-eligible population that are white than are black.

Most EITC-eligible families are not subject to the marriage penalty. While most blacks are not married, they are more likely to pay a marriage penalty because they are more likely to be found in the phase-out income levels. The fact that blacks are less likely to be married does not mean that whites are paying a disproportionate share of the EITC marriage penalty.

---

[4] Jim Chen, *Of Agriculture's First Disobedience and Its Fruit*, 48 Vand. L. Rev. 1261, 1307 (1995).
[5] *Id.*

Finally, because blacks are more likely to have more children than whites, they are penalized by the EITC. White households are, however, slightly more likely than black households to have two children, which is the category with the greatest EITC.

CONCLUSION

This article shows that whites are more likely than blacks to be eligible for the EITC – in fact, the EITC-eligible pool includes twice the percentage of whites as blacks. By focusing on the racial impact issue, academics and politicians have ignored the larger class issue: Low-income families with children are treated very differently than middle-income families with children under federal tax laws.

Federal tax policy should not favor middle-income children over low-income children. This is especially true if the reason for treating low-income children poorly is because they are perceived to be black. The data presented herein shows the vast majority of EITC-eligible taxpayers are white. Low-income children are in greater need and at the very least should be treated as well as middle-income children. This article seeks to start a dialogue among academics, politicians, and policy makers to ensure that federal tax policy treats all children equally.

There is no reason to assume that what may be good for black taxpayers has to be bad for white taxpayers. Professor Derrick Bell's interest-convergence thesis argues the opposite. It is only when tax provisions hurt whites as well as blacks that real change is possible. By assuming that the EITC disproportionately advantaged blacks, academics never considered the possibility that whites or blacks were being disadvantaged when compared with their CTC counterparts.

The empirical data provided herein can provide the impetus for far-reaching EITC reform that will help whites as well as blacks. To the extent that current law benefits middle-income children to the detriment of low-income children, current law disadvantages low-income whites as well as blacks. Once the empirical data is examined, it is easy to get past race to see the larger class issue. The existing literature has maintained the status quo by focusing on proving that the EITC was a benefit to blacks. This, in turn, has penalized all low-income taxpayers – whites as well as blacks. Consider the following as a possible model for reform.

My prior research, which uncovered the racial bias in the joint return showed that middle-income white married couples were the most likely of white married couples to pay the marriage penalty. Any elimination of the marriage penalty will help both black *and* white taxpayers. Recent legislation has minimized the marriage penalty. That will help all taxpayers. I seek the same goals regarding all EITC-eligible families.

Rocking the Tax Code: A Case Study of Employment-Related Child-Care Expenditures

MARY LOUISE FELLOWS[1]

Through an examination of the tax law's treatment of child-care expenditures, I intend to show both how the current tax law facilitates class, gender, and race subordination and how it could be designed to disrupt it. By looking at the tax law's treatment of employment-related child-care expenditures, I will make the argument that a comprehensive tax analysis requires not only an examination of the well-recognized issues of equity, administrability, and economic rationality, but also consideration of other issues of social justice – specifically, consideration of the implications of economic exploitation, racism, and sexism on economic arrangements.

The conventional tax analysis of child-care provisions focuses exclusively on the effects of the provisions on the parents, usually mothers, to engage in waged work. Little or no consideration is given in traditional tax analysis on the effects of the provisions on the waged child-care worker. This omission is particularly confounding because the economic arrangement that is the very subject of taxation is the purchase of child-care services. The antisubordination principle, which is based on the proposition that economic exploitation, sexism, and racism operate together, holds out the promise of uncovering this type of analytical shortcoming and thereby enhancing our understanding of the economic implications of a tax rule.

CURRENT TAX TREATMENT OF EMPLOYMENT-RELATED CHILD-CARE EXPENDITURES

Section 21 provides a nonrefundable credit equal to between 20% and 30% of the expenditures incurred for child care during the taxable year that enable the taxpayer to be gainfully employed. The percentage of expenditures allowed varies depending on the taxpayer's adjusted gross income. The amount of the employment-related child-care expenditures that may be taken into account to determine the amount of the credit is limited. If a taxpayer has one child in child care, no more than $2,400 can be used to determine the credit, and if the taxpayer has two or more children, no more than $4,800 can be used to compute the amount of the credit. Section 129 authorizes an employer-provided assistance program for child care.

[1] Reprinted by permission from 10 *Yale Journal of Law and Feminism* 307 (1998).

An employee is allowed to exclude from gross income up to $5,000 of child-care expenditures that are either paid, reimbursed, or provided in kind by the employer.

One significant practical limitation of both §§ 21 and 129 is that the child-care expenditures taken into account are less than the costs incurred by the taxpayers. Section 129 is further problematic because it is available only if an employer establishes the program. A significant decrease in the use of the credit occurred in 1989 after the passage of the Family Support Act of 1988, which required that taxpayers claiming the credit include the provider's name, address, and taxpayer identification number. One explanation might be that some taxpayers were claiming expenditures that they were in fact not paying. A more likely explanation is that child-care workers who do not report their income did not give their employers their taxpayer identification numbers.

THE HISTORY OF WAGED CHILD CARE

Child care is part of a whole range of activities, such as housecleaning, food preparation and service, and laundering and repairing of clothing, frequently referred to as *reproductive labor*. A history of waged child care must therefore be placed within the broader history of waged domestic work. A review of waged child care in the United States shows that the wages and working conditions for child-care workers have not been, and are not currently, the product of a free competitive market establishing an equilibrium between supply and demand. The labor history instead shows how social prejudices and government intervention have produced those wages and working conditions. With an understanding of that market, a tax analysis that looks at the purchasing of child-care services as an objective fact unrelated to the political and economic strongholds of power that influence the nature of that transaction becomes inadequate. A comprehensive tax analysis that applies the antisubordination principle would necessarily take into account the economic exploitation, racism, and sexism that occur in the child-care labor market.

A substantial amount of the historical data relates to domestic work in general, rather than child-care work specifically. Although considering child care within the broader context of domestic work is useful, it cannot be done without paying attention to the historical data which indicate that, within domestic work, employers frequently favored white native-born or immigrant women to do child-care work. As child-care workers, the women frequently enjoyed higher status, and concomitantly better working conditions, than many women who were performing other forms of reproductive labor, such as laundry, cooking, or housecleaning. The higher status of the work depended on it being performed by white women, and it was performed by white women because the work did have higher status.

CONTEMPORARY "SOLUTIONS" TO PROVIDING CHILD CARE
FOR MIDDLE-CLASS FAMILIES

Although statistics reveal significant progress in removing discriminatory barriers to employment for women of color, in light of current policymaking, it is not surprising that domestic work largely retains its gendered and racial cast. Class, gender, and racial hierarchies that influence our views of motherhood, child care, and child-care workers explain how it is possible that the need for quality, affordable child care remains high while at the same time many child-care workers work for low pay under bad working conditions. The answer is not that child care is impervious to the rules of supply and demand. It is that the child-care market is largely determined by class, gender, and racial hierarchies, and those hierarchies determine what types of child care are demanded and how it is supplied.

Both the influence of the domesticity ideal of the stay-at-home-mom and its economic viability have predictable race and class implications. One implication is that the father's salary is likely to be affected by the racial stratification of wages in the labor market. Given the higher the salar[y] of the father the more feasible the decision of a mother to stay at home without the benefit of money wages, the racial stratification of the labor market affects which mothers stay home and which must find waged work. Data show that more married African-American women participate in waged labor than married white women. They also show that married African-American women contribute a higher percentage of income to the household than white women do.

Another race and class implication is the role that women who hold professional and managerial positions play in the child-care labor market. Armed with economic wherewithal and the domesticity ideal, a significant number of these mothers hire child-care workers to work in their homes on a full-time or live-in basis. Notwithstanding that live-in care remains atypical among waged working mothers, it has had a significant effect on the child-care labor market. With live-in care viewed as the best form of care because it comes closest to reproducing the ideal of middle-class parenting (mothering), the exploitative working conditions of live-in child-care workers has the further effect of depressing compensation throughout the child-care labor market. The expectations of prospective parent-employers regarding market wages, working conditions, and the general view of the economic worth of the service are greatly influenced by the market reality that undocumented migrant women of color are available to mimic unwaged, home child care for low pay.

Through live-in child care, the ladylike worker has found a way to maintain respectability and thereby mark a boundary between herself and her family and other waged working mothers and their families. She has done it by modifying, while at the same time perpetuating, the historical meanings of domestic work, gender, and race. In the nineteenth century, the lady adopted practices that maintained her hold on respectability by separating herself from the waged worker with whom she shared her home; in the twentieth century, the ladylike worker maintains her respectability in the home and in the marketplace by adopting practices that separate herself from the waged worker she leaves in her home while she enters the marketplace.

TRADITIONAL TAX PRINCIPLES: THE MYTH OF OBJECTIVITY

The Business/Personal Distinction

The business/personal distinction arises out of the widely accepted understanding of what should constitute income under an ideal accretion tax system. The ideal income definition requires that every expenditure be classified as either personal, which means that it should not be taken into account as a reduction of income either now or later, or business, which means that it should be deducted from income either now or later. One difficulty, of course, is that "[a] thoroughly precise and objective distinction [between personal and business] is inconceivable."[2] Child-care expenditures provide an excellent example of how difficult the distinction proves to be. It [is] necessary to determine whether taxpayers go to work for the purpose of earning sufficient funds to purchase child-care services for their children, or whether they purchase child-care services for the purpose of earning income in the waged labor market.

The difficulty of distinguishing business and personal expenditures is far more complex than merely a problem of determining taxpayer intent. The problem with the distinction is that it marks business expenses as productive, and personal expenses as unproductive in a way that misapprehends productivity in the home and nonproductivity in the marketplace. Rather than acknowledging that household cleaning, cooking, and child care, among other reproductive tasks, are socially and economically necessary, the intense monitoring of the business/personal distinction that occurs in the tax law denies the intermediate value of reproductive tasks – a value based on how the results from reproductive labor produce further value. The binary classification system requires a willed ignorance of the unproductive aspects of the public marketplace and the productive aspects of the private home.

The public/private distinction justifies and supports class, gender, and racial hierarchies. The public/private distinction is mirrored in the tax law's business/personal distinction. Within an antisubordination framework, the business/personal distinction is no longer seen as an abstract tax concept disconnected from social and economic relationships. Rather, the distinction takes on a different meaning once it is understood as being the functional equivalent, in tax terms, of the public/private distinction, the production/reproduction distinction, and the cult of respectability. Reconnecting the business/personal distinction to its social roots removes its seeming objectivity and makes the widespread willingness to tolerate its "inescapable" problems seem less benign.

Imputed Income

When taxpayers personally provide services for themselves, they are producing in-kind income that is referred to in conventional tax analysis as imputed income. When taxpayers use their own personal property for their own benefit, their property is producing in-kind income that is also referred to as imputed income. Both types of in-kind income are labeled as income because the services and the property produce an economic benefit to the taxpayer. Both types of in-kind income are labeled imputed because the activities take place outside of the marketplace and because the services and property are used for personal (consumption) purposes by the person producing them.

---

[2] HENRY C. SIMONS, PERSONAL INCOME TAXATION: THE DEFINITION OF INCOME AS A PROBLEM OF FISCAL POLICY 54 (1938).

Frequently, commentators define imputed income in such a way as to include in-kind income produced by one family member for another. For example, when one parent enables the other parent to enter or remain in the waged labor force by providing necessary child-care services in the home, this transaction usually is analyzed under the rubric of imputed income.

Making the antisubordination principle a part of tax analysis leads to the question of why policy makers have relied on imputed income, rather than other tax concepts, to conclude that intrafamily transfers of in-kind income should not be taxed. The effect of treating an intrafamily transfer of in-kind income from services, mostly reproductive labor, as imputed is to make the person who produces the work and the productive value of the work itself invisible under the tax law. Within this family context, submerging the identity of the worker into the identity of the beneficiary of the work means that the tax law is indifferent as to who is actually doing the work. Through that indifference, the tax law devalues the reproductive labor even as it acknowledges the economic value produced by it. The historical role that class, gender, and racial hierarchies have played within reproductive labor makes the tax law's submergence of reproductive labor and the reproductive laborer under the rubric of imputed income particularly pernicious.

APPLYING THE ANTISUBORDINATION PRINCIPLE

Supplementing a discussion of the business/personal distinction and the concept of imputed income with a historical analysis of class, gender, and race in the child-care labor market leads to a reevaluation of current tax law provisions. On the one hand, the tax rules for employment-related child-care expenditures provided under §§ 21 and 129 suggest an acknowledgment of the business nature of these expenditures. On the other hand, the segregation of child-care expenditures from other employee-related or self-employed expenditures suggests their personal nature. Arguably, the conflicting interpretations of the tax provisions appropriately reflect the ambiguity inherent in the business/personal distinction. In the political arena, where ambiguity and compromise are coins of the realm, the idea of an expense having both a business and personal nature appears to have found support.

The historical devaluation of reproductive labor adds another dimension to the business/personal controversy surrounding employment-related child-care expenditures. For expenditures where the distinction between business and personal is otherwise difficult to make, arguably the tax law should err on the side of classifying an expenditure as business related. Treating an expenditure, such as child care, the same as other business deductions would disrupt the hierarchical distinction between productive and reproductive labor. By treating child-care expenditures as personal, the tax law perpetuates the economic exploitation, sexism, and racism that [are] rationalized by distinguishing between public production and private reproduction. Reconnecting the business/personal distinction to its social, cultural, and economic roots makes the limited tax relief provided under §§ 21 and 129 seem inadequate.

Another reason for favoring a deduction that is not limited either by the income level of the taxpayer or the amount spent for employment-related child care concerns the tax inequity created by the exclusion of child-care services, performed in the home by parents, from the tax base, and the class, gender, and race implications of that exclusion. Recent statistics show that the percentage of married couples with children in which both parents work exceeds 70% for couples with children over age six and is nearly 60% for couples with children under age six. Considering the increasing number of single mothers, we can conclude that the great majority of taxpayers do not enjoy the tax benefit of excluding child-care services performed by a parent. Arguably, these statistics suggest that the exclusion creates only minor issues of tax equity because of the ever-increasing rates of two-income couples and single mothers.

The antisubordination principle, however, encourages us to look in more detail at who is most likely to accrue the benefits of tax-free imputed income. Data on earnings suggest that the substantially higher salaries and wages paid to white married men places them in a better financial position to forgo their wives' waged earnings and enjoy the tax-free benefits of her child-care services. These statistics suggest that excluding child-care services from income has significant class and race implications. By allowing a deduction for child-care expenditures, the tax law indirectly taxes the child-care services enjoyed by one-earner couples. An unlimited deduction would indirectly ameliorate some of the effects of wage and salary discrimination experienced by women and men of color in all sectors of the labor market. Yet another consequence of providing an unlimited deduction for child-care expenditures would be the removal of one potential economic barrier for women entering the waged labor market.

The arguments just presented for an unlimited child-care deduction demonstrate how the integration of [the] antisubordination principle into an analysis of the business/personal distinction and conventional notions of imputed income can change the character of those common staples of tax analysis. The antisubordination principle transforms seemingly objective criteria by reconnecting them with various social and economic institutions. The veil of objectivity surrounding traditional tax principles is lifted once the historical context from which they were derived and operate is revealed.

The foregoing analysis remains woefully incomplete because it only indirectly addresses the issue of economic exploitation of child-care workers. One response to this problem might be that an unlimited child-care deduction be accompanied with increased enforcement of federal and state labor laws and federal immigration laws to address directly problems in the child-care labor market through governmental intervention. Linking an expansion of the child-care deduction that is likely to benefit the child-care consumer to other labor and immigration policies, however, without first changing the underlying structures supporting those policies would seem to betray any commitment to take seriously the economic exploitation and racism experienced by migrant household workers.

The question then arises as to what kind of tax reform could avoid the reinforcement of class, gender, and race hierarchies identified with the current approach and simultaneously disrupt the economic exploitation of child-care workers. Two reforms warrant serious consideration in any discussion of the tax treatment of employment-related child-care expenditures. One would entail a direct response to the issue of economic exploitation of child-care workers by abandoning the idea of an unlimited deduction and allowing instead employment-related child-care expenditures to be deducted only for those child-care expenditures that exceed some percentage of the taxpayer's adjusted gross income. The amount the taxpayer spends on child care becomes the tool by which the tax law intervenes into a sector of the labor market that is economically exploitative due to class, gender, and race subordination. Keying the amount deductible to the taxpayer's adjusted gross income ameliorates, to some extent, the problem that an unlimited deduction would disproportionately benefit higher-income taxpayers.

One criticism of denying a deduction for some portion of child-care expenditures incurred is that it undermines the benefits otherwise achieved by having the tax law unambiguously treat employment-related child-care expenditures as a business expense. Although the motivation for the limitations [is] quite different, the limitations for child-care expenditures would resemble the limitations placed on other controversial deductions, such as medical expenses and casualty losses. Perhaps one way to counteract this perception is to allow the deduction to be taken to reach adjusted gross income so as to distinguish it from other deductible expenses viewed as personal in nature.

Another criticism is that consumer expectations and the general view of the economic worth of child-care services will combine to make the availability of the tax deduction irrelevant. Instead of encouraging consumers to increase the wages and improve the working conditions of child-care workers, it may lead to increased reliance on the underground economy. The history of the child-care labor market certainly suggests that consumer resistance will be strong. Whether it is possible to overcome that tradition by setting a standard of fair wages through the tax law is unknown. To design a tax provision that ignores the reality of economic exploitation in this labor market, however, seems wholly unacceptable.

Some of the concern about consumer resistance could be addressed through an additional reform that would work in conjunction with the first. This reform entails two substantial amendments to § 129. The first change would be to eliminate the limitation on the amount of child-care assistance employers are allowed to provide for their employees. The other change would be to allow the employee to exclude the in-kind or reimbursed amounts from income only if the employer assures that the child-care workers' working conditions meet certain criteria, such as a fair salary, reasonable working hours, and provision for family health care. The exclusion provided under § 129, as amended, would be more valuable to an employee than the limited deduction proposed earlier because the amount of the exclusion would not depend on an employee's adjusted gross income. This difference would encourage employers to establish child-care assistance programs. One major advantage of employer-provided child-care assistance is that high standards of care by, and working conditions for, child-care workers are more likely to be achieved. The government can assure proper working conditions for child-care workers far more easily through IRS audits of employers of child-care consumers than it can by trying to regulate the child-care market by investigating individual child-care workers and consumers.

A second major advantage of employer-provided child-care assistance is that it would acknowledge employers' partial responsibility for the well-being of their workers' families. The historical tradition of viewing child care as private has not only supported the production/reproduction hierarchy, but has also obscured the relationship of child care to production itself. Tax incentives for employer-provided child care will encourage the marketplace to recognize its co-responsibility for the care and nurturing of young generations who represent the workers of the future.

The solution I am proposing to the complex set of problems concerning child care is imperfect because it is produced out of a set of constrained circumstances that presents only bad choices. What is more important than the particulars of the proposal is that the discussion helps us to appreciate how the tax law is implicated in the social and economic relationships of the parties to an economic arrangement. What the discussion of current tax law and possible reforms shows is that no tax debate about employment-related child-care expenditures should exclude consideration of how child care has been constructed through our social and economic institutions. What the discussion further accomplishes is the removal of the artificial boundary between tax concepts designed to implement an ideal accretion tax and the social and economic environment in which those concepts operate. The point is not to diminish the importance of the distinction between business and personal or the concept of imputed income. Rather the point is that those concepts can gain more analytical power when they are analyzed within a framework that includes the antisubordination principle.

"As a whole, the tax field tends to emphasize the rich rather than the poor," observes Michael Livingston in *Women, Poverty, and the Tax Code: A Tale of Theory and Practice.* Three of the authors in this chapter – Livingston, Francine Lipman, and Dennis Ventry – invert the traditional emphasis of tax scholars to explore how the Code addresses, or fails to address, poverty. Livingston calls for a dialogue between academics and politicians on the intersection of gender and poverty. In *The Working Poor Are Paying for Government Benefits: Fixing the Hole in the Anti-Poverty Purse,* Lipman exposes professional tax preparers as the disproportionate beneficiaries of the EITC program, which is designed to assist the working poor. She offers solutions that would reduce the significant costs, presently borne by poor taxpayers, for demonstrating eligibility for the EITC. Dennis Ventry, in *Welfare by Any Other Name: Tax Transfers and the EITC,* evaluates the general effectiveness of the EITC program. Despite its efficiencies, Ventry raises concerns about relying on the Code to function as the country's main anti-poverty program.

Wilton B. Hyman's article, *Race, Class, and the Internal Revenue Code: A Class-Based Analysis of* A Black Critique of the Internal Revenue Code, makes the case for taking a more nuanced approach to the categories of "wealth," "poverty," and "race." He praises the critical race theory lens that scholars like Beverly Moran and William Whitford have brought to the Code (in their contribution to Chapter 5 of this book, for example), but suggests that we complicate those critiques by appreciating that the tax laws do not have a uniformly discriminatory impact on African Americans, and that the effectiveness of any particular proposal to remedy the disparate impact of certain tax laws should take into account the social, political, and economic history of African Americans in the United States.

Each contribution to this chapter employs a class-based analysis to better understand the workings of the tax laws.

Women, Poverty, and the Tax Code: A Tale of Theory and Practice

MICHAEL A. LIVINGSTON[1]

Being a tax professor at a conference on women and poverty is a little bit like, well, being an expert on women and poverty at a conference on taxation. For one thing, there is the topic, which suggests a political approach not necessarily consistent with that with which one is familiar. For another thing, there is the sense that other lawyers look at tax experts the way everyone else looks at lawyers: about as interesting as plumbers, but without the self-confident charm. Additionally, there is the tax professor's fear that the more one tries to escape these contradictions the more deeply the contradictions will engulf him: poverty is a serious matter, and the nerdy cleverness of most tax scholarship is hardly likely to satisfy those who live in economic deprivation. Rather than being clever, then, I will simply discuss some current issues in tax policy as they relate to women, poverty, and the relationship between the two.

TAX SCHOLARSHIP AND THE SPACE FOR GENDER AND POVERTY ISSUES

Tax scholars see women and poverty through a very particular lens. On the one hand, the tax field has a long history of concern with distribution and "fairness" issues. The progressivity of the Code – that is, the imposition of higher tax rates on those with higher taxable incomes – is a major theme in tax scholarship and is often justified by reference to political philosophers and other nontax sources. There is also a historic understanding that individual tax provisions are not merely technical in nature, but also reflect society's view of economic and social relationships and are themselves constitutive of those relationships. For example, the deductibility of home mortgage interest reflects the high value placed on private home ownership, while the nondeductibility of child-care expenses, at least arguably, reflects the low value traditionally accorded to such activities.

The issue of women and poverty is clouded by two problems. The first is the tax field's historic myopia concerning the issue of poverty. The income tax originated as a "soak the rich" levy that was paid only by a small number of wealthy people. Even today, most of the very poor pay little or no income tax, and the percentage is

[1] Reprinted by permission from 5 *Journal of Gender, Race, and Justice* 327 (2001–2002).

declining as a result of perfectly reasonable efforts to reduce the tax load on poor working families. That is not to say that individual tax provisions, notably the earned income credit, are not very important to poor people, or that individual tax scholars have not paid a lot of attention to poverty issues. But as a whole, the tax field tends to emphasize the rich rather than the poor. Even progressivity is justified by the superior taxpaying ability of wealthy people, rather than the needs of poor ones; one could attend a stream of tax meetings without hearing much about the problems of low-income families.

The second problem relates directly to gender issues. Tax is historically a male-dominated field, even by law school standards, and is not particularly sensitive to issues affecting women and minorities. One famous case lampooned the request for child-care deductions, fearing it would lead to deductions for food, clothing, and other household expenditures. This historic insensitivity is compounded by the law-and-economics methodology of contemporary tax scholarship, which tends to assume the presence of a rational economic actor, and has little room for consciousness-raising or other noneconomic goals in scholarship and public policy. Thus, child care and other feminist issues tend to be discussed in a dry, gender-neutral manner, as if men and women were equally likely to stay at home with the kids. In reality, men are not, and that is what makes the issue interesting in the first place.

In the past decade both of the previously mentioned limitations have been challenged. To begin with, there has been renewed attention, by a small number of committed and talented individuals, to the poverty question. A "critical tax scholarship" has [also] emerged that in theory challenges the foundations of the entire tax field and in practice means a liberal-left tax scholarship with a special emphasis on women's and minorities' issues. This scholarship has taken two principal tacks. The first is to tackle old, traditional tax issues from the perspective of feminism or critical race studies. A second approach is to renew an interest in tax provisions that specifically affect female and minority taxpayers, or affect them so disproportionately as to constitute, in effect, a form of discrimination by the Code against them.

Not surprisingly, given the conservative nature of the tax field, [these] efforts have provoked a strong counterreaction. One author suggested that, while there exists some good critical tax scholarship, the field as a whole is characterized by sloppy thinking and a failure to understand the varieties of critical, as well as tax, thinking. Although many tax scholars are more sympathetic, the largest numbers have simply ignored the critical tax endeavor, leaving women's and minorities' concerns somewhat peripheral to the broader tax subject.

Even within the critical tax community, a high degree of specialization remains, impeding the development of a broader critique of the existing tax system. This internal division is exacerbated by the isolation of the entire tax field, which by definition emphasizes tax issues and may not always be sensitive to the interplay of government policies that impact the poor, such as tax, welfare, and health care policies. When one discusses an issue like the "feminization of poverty," one faces the problem that many people in the field may be indifferent; even among those who do care, the issues of women and poverty may be so conceptually separate that it is difficult to form a coherent or united theory that can serve as a basis for a particular reform program. These problems are exacerbated by the slow pace of scholarly developments: the feminization of poverty is a relatively new, or at least newly recognized, problem, and it may be decades before it is wholly assimilated into the literature on women, progressivity, or other relevant tax issues.

SYMBOLIC MEASURES AND STUDIED INDIFFERENCE

The feminization of poverty describes an economic or social trend rather than a specific area of public policy. As such it is affected by numerous forms of government activity, ranging from tax, welfare, and health care policies to environmental and labor regulations to international trade and immigration policies, which affect the broader market in which women's issues play out. The relevant tax policies alone would include the underlying tax rates; the issue of filing status, including single, joint, and "head of household" returns and the treatment of gay and lesbian couples; family tax issues, including the deductibility of child-care expenditures, personal exemptions and credits, and the tax treatment of alimony and child support payments; and other, narrower provisions, such as the earned income credit and the taxation of welfare and Social Security payments. State sales, excise, and property taxes, together with federal employment (Social Security and Medicare) and other nonincome taxes, also play a significant role. Government inaction, by allowing "globalization" to proceed without interference or failing adequately to enforce child support and similar protective laws, may also be considered a form of policy decision that contributes to the feminization of poverty and associated phenomena.

It is not possible here to consider all these provisions in detail. Instead, let me talk about a few major themes in tax policy as they relate to women and poor people and how these themes have played out in recent debates. This brief discussion will be sufficient to show the distance between the intellectual and political debates and the problems of addressing the feminization of poverty by means of tax and other public policy measures.

In recent years there have been two principal approaches to women's and family tax issues, albeit with some convergence of the two. The Republican philosophy tends to emphasize tax cuts and encourage private enterprise. Republicans see this as helping both rich and poor Americans and, although it is not typically addressed in these terms, both male and female taxpayers. To the extent that they have addressed the family/child-care issue, Republicans and other conservatives tend to favor an increase in the personal exemption in place of, or in addition to, a deduction for child-care expenditures. The personal exemption would benefit families with one stay-at-home parent as well as families with two working parents. Republican thinking on poverty tends to emphasize the destructive effects of welfare and the importance of traditional, quasi-religious values (education, hard work, etc.) in lifting people out of poverty into the middle class; this approach has been lampooned by liberals as a laissez-faire or "trickle-down" policy. However, the Democrats themselves have adopted the policy in several key instances, notably welfare reform (where the Democrats adopted an essentially conservative philosophy of time limitations and a requirement of job training) and the earned income credit (where both parties supported the earned income credit which was designed to increase the attractiveness of low-wage labor as an alternative to welfare or similar programs).

Democrats, although increasingly less liberal on social policy, emphasize what might be called a scaled-down liberalism, relying heavily on targeted tax credits for items like postsecondary education, health care, and other "pro-family" activities with a large middle-class constituency. Democrats have pursued a largely symbolic redistributive policy by limiting many of the previously mentioned benefits to taxpayers below a specified level of income. They have similarly pursued modest nontax (e.g., increasing the minimum wage) and quasi-tax (e.g., liberalization of the earned income credit) initiatives that at least theoretically advance the interests of low-income people. These measures have often been criticized as half-hearted, especially when combined with the Clinton Administration's macroeconomic and trade policies, which supported globalization and did relatively little to address the concerns of labor and disadvantaged groups. Yet the combined effect of these programs is not insignificant. Together with the 1990s economic boom that pushed many Americans into higher tax brackets, the programs resulted in a tax system that was and is surprisingly progressive for a supposedly conservative era.

Although the political debate is less focused than an intellectual discussion, a few major themes do stand out. The first is the relative weakness of the critical or progressive outlook in the political process. When politicians speak of working families and their tax and economic burden, they tend to mean middle, or at least solidly, working-class families, rather than the genuinely poor. Indeed the focus on traditional families excludes single individuals outright and implicitly reduces one-parent or female-headed households to a sort of second-tier status. While Democratic proposals (e.g., targeted tax cuts and partial rate reduction) tend to be somewhat focused on low-income individuals and Republican proposals (e.g., broader tax cuts together with estate tax and marriage penalty relief) on middle- and upper-income taxpayers, the difference between the approaches is an incremental one. Neither party has placed an emphasis on poor people in their tax and spending proposals.

A second notable feature is the ad hoc, symbolic nature of many policy proposals. Proposals relating to women, minorities, and poor taxpayers, if not exactly afterthoughts, are often highly convenient in nature, designed to serve as wedge issues or to demonstrate the candidate's "compassion" (Bush) or "populism" (Gore), even as the same candidates accept large campaign contributions and make significant commitments to other, more powerful interests. There is, accordingly, relatively little coordination between Democratic and Republican proposals and little sense of how these proposals would interact with one another in the case of specific individuals who might be subject to them. This is especially relevant for issues like the feminization of poverty, that cross traditional lines. Since "women" and "poor people" are two distinct political categories, politicians are likely to make separate appeals to these two groups (especially the poor) without thinking about the intersection of the two groups or the effect that proposals designed for one constituency might have upon the other. For example, the Republican marriage penalty proposal and the Democratic tax incentives appear to target women and families. Yet neither incentive does much for the very poor and in some cases they may actually heighten the disparity between lower- and middle-income families.

[These] assertions may be another way of saying that the mood of the country remains essentially conservative, and that the interests of poor women are correspondingly low on the political, as opposed to intellectual, agenda. But it is also important to note that several conceptual issues are common to the intellectual and political realms. These include a blindness toward poor people and a tendency to categorize issues (women vs. the poor, tax vs. nontax policy) in a manner that inhibits broader interdisciplinary discussions. It is also important to remember that many of today's conservative policies originated in academic discussions and that future choices will likewise be circumscribed by today's theoretical debates. These factors suggest that there is at least something to be gained from an academic reconsideration of women's and poverty issues in the tax arena. Progress in the intellectual area might have real impact on the policy process, if not immediately then several years or decades down the road.

TOWARD A CONSTRUCTIVE DIALOGUE

A dialogue between academics and policy makers on the question of women and poverty seems important and overdue. Indeed, it might be useful for academics to conduct a prior dialogue among themselves to clarify their own views and the ways in which their different intellectual agendas (progressivity, feminism, critical race studies) interact with the feminization of poverty. This discussion would be more profitable if mainstream and critical legal scholars ceased attacking each other and instead sought common ground for the discussion of policy issues. For example, mainstream tax scholars should recognize that under current conditions, the progressivity of the Code is a function, not merely of distributional tables, but of the way that the tax laws affect groups (women, minorities, immigrants, etc.) who are historically disadvantaged in the broader society. For their part, critical scholars should recognize that women's and minorities' tax issues are but one part of a broader fairness critique, in which traditional scholarship may play an important and even a vital part. Both mainstream and critical scholars should devote increased attention to empirical and interdisciplinary work and to work that considers tax and its relation to other subjects (e.g., health care, welfare, and retirement planning) that raise similar distributive issues.

The result of reconceptualizing tax issues would be an integrated, vibrant scholarship that considers taxation as one of a series of government policies that impact poor people and social groups (women, minorities, etc.) that are historically overrepresented as beneficiaries of government programs. Such a scholarship would be particularly useful in addressing issues like the feminization of poverty, which crosses traditional academic lines and has unpredictable, sometimes contradictory effects. An integrated scholarship would be better able to evaluate the causes of this phenomenon, and to propose solutions that complement rather than contradict each other.

Critics may say that the political process is too indifferent to poor women to pay attention to academic proposals. A bit of history may be relevant at this point. Thirty years ago, conservative think tanks began to think about public policy in a detailed but unified way. They began to consider how various aspects of the liberal state, including tax, welfare, and various other policies, interacted to undermine traditional values and replace them with a state-centered, liberal creed. By developing expertise in numerous areas, but with a unifying philosophy, conservative think tanks were able to affect public policy in a more extensive manner than anyone had deemed possible. In procedure, if not substance, there is much to be gleaned from them. Those who wish to reverse the feminization of poverty, together with other relics of the past two generations, would do well to learn from their example.

The Working Poor Are Paying for Government Benefits: Fixing the Hole in the Anti-Poverty Purse

FRANCINE J. LIPMAN[1]

There is universal agreement that the federal income tax laws are too complicated. The complexity of these laws is especially frustrating for the millions of low-income working families who qualified for more than $30 billion of federal earned income tax credit (EITC) in 2002. The EITC is one of the nation's largest and most effective anti-poverty, income transfer programs. Low-income families will receive more federal expenditures from the EITC than from the Food Stamp Program, Supplemental Security Income, or Temporary Assistance to Needy Families. Without the EITC, an average of 4,300,000 working American households, including 2,200,000 children, would live in poverty.

Unfortunately, the complexity of the EITC rules and compliance requirements is notably daunting. Congress has created an extensive anti-poverty program, which is almost impossible for the targeted families to obtain without professional assistance because it is too complicated to comprehend and claim. Academics, practitioners, members of Congress and National Taxpayer Advocates have prepared detailed and broad-ranging recommendations for simplification of the EITC. Despite the numerous and thoughtful recommendations, the current evidence suggests that Congress will not enact comprehensive EITC tax simplification in the near term. Indeed, over the last twenty-plus years Congress has added more complexity to the already cumbersome EITC.

Despite the inconceivable complexity in the EITC, in 2000, 19.3 million taxpayers claimed $31.2 billion in EITC benefits. How did these families get this critical relief? The American marketplace, rather than Congress, has provided a response to the working poor's desperate demand for assistance. Sixty-eight percent of tax filers who received the EITC hired paid tax practitioners to prepare their income tax returns. The American marketplace has responded to the demand and carved out a profitable business niche. Many of these tax services offer not only assistance in preparing and filing returns, but also provide refund anticipation loans, refund transfers, and other products intended to help taxpayers obtain their critical EITC dollars quickly.

Tax practitioners exact significant fees and costs for providing these services. These fees and costs consume a significant portion of available EITC dollars.

---

[1] Reprinted by permission from 2003 *Wisconsin Law Review* 461.

An estimated $1.75 billion of the EITC intended to benefit low-income working families and their neighborhoods has been shifted to profitable paid tax practitioners. As a result, the American marketplace is progressively undermining the anti-poverty effectiveness of the EITC.

IDENTIFYING THE PROBLEM

In an extensive collaborative study released in May 2002, the Brookings Institute (Brookings) and the Progressive Policy Institute (PPI) analyzed the shifting of anti-poverty benefits from low-income working families. Brookings and PPI determined that "roughly $1.75 billion" of the $30 billion of EITC benefits in 1999 went to paid tax preparers and affiliated national banks rather than the working poor.[2] In response to demand for tax preparation services and quick access to refunds, the survey found that tax preparation businesses have concentrated in low-income communities and grown significantly over the last several years. Brookings and PPI discovered that the EITC has become "an important profit center for [this] multi-billion dollar industry."[3] High-cost [refund anticipation loans (RALs)] are a significant "reason for the industry's recent growth, and a large revenue source for the commercial chains."[4]

Why do low-income taxpayers use paid tax preparation services? Complexity in the tax laws, especially low-income taxpayer items such as the ever-changing EITC, child tax credits, and the child and dependent care credit, has created a morass of impenetrable rules. To make matters worse, literacy limitations are sharply higher among low-income adults. Literacy limitations are especially prevalent among the 25,000,000 foreign-born persons who reside in the United States, 4,600,000 of whom live in poverty. Many of these low-income people speak English as a second language or do not speak or read English. If they work in the United States and have any tax liability or claim the EITC, they must file an annual income tax return. Given these factors, low-income workers demand and are willing to pay for professional tax assistance.

Ironically, because tax preparation services are so expensive, the ability to pay for critical tax services with the anticipated refund has itself created a lucrative industry. In the pile of paperwork produced during the tax preparation and refund loan application process, most low-income clients probably do not understand that they are entering into a loan or comprehend the overall cost of their tax services. Moreover, because tax practitioners deduct service fees directly from the refund, the transaction costs and fees are less transparent.

Approximately 22% of the 19,000,000 EITC families do not have bank accounts or access to routine financial services. Working poor desperately in need of cash flow and with no alternatives are faced with high-cost RALs or waiting many weeks for a check from the IRS in addition to the high cost of check cashing fees. Check

---

[2] Alan Berube et al., The Price of Paying Taxes: How Tax Preparation and Refund Loan Fees Erode the Benefits of the EITC 12 (Ctr. on Urban & Metro. Policy, Brookings Inst., Survey Series, May 2002).

[3] Id. at 14–16.

[4] Id. at 4.

cashing outlets charge a premium to cash tax refund checks despite the minimal business risks.

While H&R Block and Jackson Hewitt respectively prepared about 13% and 1.7% of all 2001 individual income tax returns filed with the IRS, the Brookings and PPI survey determined that a "significant number" of tax preparers are one-person storefronts and operate only during the January through April filing season.[5] The seasonality of tax preparation services available to low-income taxpayers creates a greater burden for families claiming the EITC who are significantly more likely to be audited than other taxpayers.

POSSIBLE SOLUTIONS

Ignoring the Obvious? Simplification

The most obvious solution to relieve low-income taxpayers from the costs of professional tax preparation is to eliminate their demand for professional tax assistance. Significant simplification of low-income taxpayer issues would ensure that the working poor receive their intended benefits. If tax compliance for low-income taxpayers were user-friendly for the targeted group, then the demand for and cost of professional tax assistance by these taxpayers would be reduced significantly. Simplification may even eliminate the demand for after-filing correspondence and audit assistance. If the tax preparation and filing process is simple for the targeted taxpayer, then the incidence of tax preparation and filing errors and incomplete and misinformation regarding the tax return should be reduced markedly. Simplification of the EITC may also provide an answer to the problem of lack of fast access to tax refunds. If the EITC is redesigned as a direct offset against Social Security taxes paid, then the working poor would not have to wait until after the close of the tax year to receive their tax refund, but would receive the EITC throughout the year in each paycheck.

There is and has been universal outcry for simplification of low-income taxpayer issues for several decades, and most often for simplification of the EITC. In response to this outcry, Congress has simplified some components of the EITC, but it continues to be too complicated for the targeted taxpayer. Moreover, the complexity inherent in recent tax legislation and the expansion of refundable child tax credits has complicated further low-income taxpayer issues. Given the complexity of our tax and welfare systems, individually and working together, it is not likely that the working poor will experience simplification. Accordingly, this article will focus on alternative solutions.

Tax Credit for Low-Income Tax Preparation Costs

One solution to reduce the significant cost of compliance for low-income taxpayers is to reimburse these taxpayers for some or all of their compliance costs.

[5] *Id.*

The government could provide the reimbursement to qualifying low-income individuals through the federal income tax system as a tax credit. The tax credit would provide a reimbursement of any qualifying low-income taxpayer's costs for qualifying tax return preparation and filing costs. The credit would shift the cost of low-income taxpayer compliance to the government. In effect, the government would be paying for professional tax assistance for the working poor.

The tax credit would only be available for qualifying tax assistance, which would only provide assistance from tax preparers who the IRS deemed "qualified." Through the credit requirements, the IRS could motivate the working poor to use qualified professional tax assistance. With qualified professional tax assistance, the working poor would be more likely to benefit fully from the EITC, and EITC compliance errors and incomplete and inaccurate information should be reduced.

Unfortunately, even if the tax credit were to perfectly offset all of the tax compliance costs, the working poor would still not have fast access to their EITC benefits. In fact, the lack of fast access would be more troublesome because the tax credit would increase the demand for a fast refund. Tax refunds would be larger, because they would include the reimbursement for the tax compliance costs. The taxpayer would be even more anxious for the refund because she may have to pay the tax preparer up front and wait for her refund to receive reimbursement and her EITC benefits. This additional pressure for fast access to tax refunds could add to the demand for and costs of RALs. The additional costs for RALs could diminish significantly any benefits provided by the tax credit.

Access to Free Tax Preparation and Filing Services

Another alternative solution is to provide low-income taxpayers with free tax preparation and filing services, not through a tax credit to offset their tax compliance costs, but through the direct provision of free tax compliance services. On October 30, 2002, the IRS entered into a final agreement with a consortium of companies in the electronic tax preparation and filing industry (the Consortium) to provide free, online tax return preparation and filing services. The IRS and the Consortium structured their agreement to provide free online tax return preparation and filing to at least 60% of all taxpayers through a link from the IRS's website.

The Brookings study estimates that the average tax preparation and electronic fees for federal and state tax returns is approximately $100. Other estimates are that 78,000,000 taxpayers would be eligible to file for free under the Consortium agreement. As a result, businesses in the tax services industry could lose $7.8 billion of tax services revenue. These businesses will have to make up for this lost revenue with alternative revenue streams. Groups and individuals opposing the agreement believe that one alternative revenue stream will be low-income taxpayers who will end up paying for their free tax services through new costs and fees. If so, the cost of the free tax services will not be shifted to the Consortium, but will remain with low-income taxpayers, albeit through alternative cost and fee structures. Low-income taxpayers may be exposed to even more high-priced ancillary products and services and may mistake the IRS's link as evidence that the services or products are required and priced fairly. Opponents to the agreement fear that members of the Consortium will charge low-income taxpayers excessive fees for (1) customer service support and assistance, (2) state income tax preparation and filing fees, (3) enhanced RALs, and (4) other advertised fee-based services and products.

Consortium members will only enter into the agreement if they anticipate some benefit. If the anticipated benefit does not materialize or is less than required for participation, then they will likely try to terminate their membership in the Consortium. If the Consortium dissolves, then the IRS will not likely provide free online tax compliance services. Although taxpayer advocate groups have proposed this alternative, the costs are too great. Congress would be unlikely to provide funding of the potential $100,000,000 cost of a government-created e-filing system. If the IRS's web-based tax preparation and e-filing system was successful, then the IRS would have significant and ongoing site maintenance costs to update the site regularly and provide customer support services.

One problem in the IRS-Consortium's agreement is that low-income taxpayers do not have access to the Internet. The Legal Aid Society of Orange County & Community Legal Services has identified lack of Internet access as a problem for its many low-income clients. In response, this group has designed and installed I-Can! kiosks throughout Orange County, California[,] and an Internet-based module to help a user prepare her tax return claiming the EITC. I-Can! kiosks are located in courthouses, legal aid offices, community centers, women's shelters, and libraries. The Legal Aid Society staff designed I-Can! modules specifically for individuals with little knowledge of computers and many modules are in Spanish and Vietnamese. Users can get instant assistance from a Help Center by touching an icon on the screen. Specifically, the newest I-Can! module allows taxpayers who are eligible for the EITC to prepare their own tax returns online for free. The EITC module assists the taxpayer using text and a video tour guide in English, Spanish, or Vietnamese.

Expanded VITA Clinics

Another alternative solution to the problem is to provide low-income taxpayers with free tax preparation and filing services, through the direct provision of these services through an expanded and funded version of the IRS's formal volunteer program [Volunteer Income Tax Assistance (VITA)]. The IRS established the VITA program in 1970 using trained volunteers to assist low-income taxpayers with free tax preparation services in libraries, community centers, college campuses, and other public facilities. While there is no direct funding from the IRS to support VITA clinics, the IRS does provide on-site training, extensive training materials, free tax preparation software, and temporary use of computer equipment.

An expanded and funded year-round VITA program would shift the cost of taxpayer compliance from taxpayers to the government and other nonprofit organizations and local sponsors. The proposals for expanded and funded VITA clinics mirror the IRS's matching fund grant program for [low-income taxpayer clinics (LITCs)]. LITCs are one of the true successes of the IRS Restructuring and Reform Act of 1998. Currently, there are more than 100 LITCs providing services to thousands of taxpayers. In 2002, Congress appropriated $7,000,000 for LITCs to provide legal assistance to thousands of individuals attempting to resolve tax disputes.

Expansion and funding of the VITA program is a multilayered complement to the success of LITCs. As a result, LITCs will be able to focus more specifically on their mission to assist in legal taxpayer representations. VITA programs will have the resources to hire full-time, permanent professionals and buy computer equipment to support the Consortium's free tax preparation and filing software, I-Can! EITC modules, mobile tax preparation vehicles, and tele-filing. VITA volunteers and employees will be integral in the regulation of RALs by their educational and disclosure efforts for low-income families and their constant monitoring of the Consortium member's websites and services. State and local government and nonprofit groups should support VITA programs with cash and noncash resources to ensure that they achieve their complementary goals of providing user-friendly state tax preparation services to low-income individuals.

CONCLUSION

While all of the foregoing solutions offer some promise and some challenges, there is no one remedy to the problem of expensive and burdensome low-income tax preparation and filing. Unfortunately, complex national problems demand complex national solutions. Simplification of our tax system has been a persistent, unfulfilled dream and may be an unreachable star. The working poor and their children have neither the time nor the patience for Don Quixote and Sancho Panza to right this unrightable wrong. These families have upheld their side of the welfare to work contract; they are out in the workforce scraping out a living. We owe these children and their working parents a fighting chance at survival; that is, the funding necessary to provide adequate shelter, food, clothing, and warmth.

The last two options packaged together may provide the most effective patch for the hole in the anti-poverty purse. The IRS should amend its Consortium agreement as follows: Consortium members must provide effective customer service regarding technical applications of their software at no cost to taxpayers using the free software. State tax returns may be included in the software for free or for a reasonable fee. Consortium members already have facilities to service customers and provide state tax preparation and filing and any increased costs should not be material. RALs and similar fast cash products and services should be government regulated and strictly monitored by the IRS under its existing rules.

The government should save more than $100,000,000 by entering into the agreement with the Consortium. The government should spend some of these savings to fund year-round VITA clinics, I-CAN! kiosks and mobile units, and increased tele-filing capability to support active and ongoing assistance for low-income taxpayers. These programs would provide free tax preparation and e-filing services and assistance using the Consortium's or alternative free tax preparation and filing products. VITA clinics could use the Consortium's free tax preparation and filing products and provide a regular check and balance on Consortium products, services, and each member's compliance with the IRS's requirements. Year-round VITA clinics could assist low-income taxpayers with after-tax season IRS correspondence and audits, and education regarding and monitoring of RALs.

Welfare by Any Other Name: Tax Transfers and the EITC

DENNIS J. VENTRY, JR.[1]

What exactly are we trying to accomplish by delivering social welfare benefits through the tax system? This article will explore this systemic question, and pose two further questions. First, what and who are we targeting when we advocate tax-transfer programs like the [earned income tax credit (EITC)]? And, second, are our current efforts effectively assisting the targeted beneficiaries? In addition, this article will discuss the current political and administrative state of the EITC, and recommend several ways in which the EITC, already the largest anti-poverty program in the United States, can further expand its reach and efficacy.

QUESTION #1: WHAT EXACTLY ARE WE TRYING TO ACCOMPLISH BY DELIVERING SOCIAL WELFARE BENEFITS THROUGH THE TAX SYSTEM?

Historically, advocates of tax-transfer programs have perceived multiple benefits to administering social-welfare programs through the Code. These benefits include obvious, structural advantages such as lower administrative costs. In the case of the EITC, would-be tax-transfer claimants self-declare eligibility simply by filing a tax return. Delivering benefits through the Code can also be more efficient and even operate as a countercyclical device, particularly if transfer payments are reflected in regular paychecks, a feature offered – but severely underutilized – in the current EITC's "advance payment" option. The structural advantages of tax-transfer programs such as the EITC also include a less intrusive administrative presence. Unlike traditional transfer programs administered outside the tax system, tax-transfer programs do not require claimants to interact with social welfare workers to initiate or continue receiving benefits. Generally, a claimant need only prove eligibility by filing an extra form with the IRS, the Schedule EIC.

The sum total of these administrative benefits results in lower costs and higher participation rates relative to direct transfer programs. The IRS administers the EITC at a cost between 1.00% and 1.85% of benefits paid. By comparison, estimated administrative costs for Food Stamps range between 20% and 25% of program benefits, while administrative costs for welfare programs equal 10% of benefits. In addition, considerably higher percentages of EITC eligibles participate compared

[1] Reprinted by permission from 56 *American University Law Review* 1261 (2007).

to other transfer programs. The EITC boasts participation rates as high as 89% while the Food Stamps program achieves a participation rate closer to 70%.

It should already be clear that these benefits – lower administrative costs, greater efficiency, less intrusion and coercion – are all defined vis-à-vis "welfare." In fact, one of the primary explanations for why we deliver transfer payments through the tax system is to position these programs opposite welfare.

The history of the EITC is a case in point. Congress enacted the low-income credit in 1975 because politicians viewed it as a work-oriented alternative to existing welfare programs. It flourished when beneficiaries were perceived as deserving workers. But it faced increasing threats when claimants began to resemble the apocryphal welfare cheat who bilked the government and lived off the dole; that is, when noncompliance rates for the program skyrocketed to 35% and 40% in the 1980s and 1990s. Only after supporters of the EITC mounted a protracted effort demonstrating the program's pro-work, anti-welfare features did the threats subside.

Thus, delivering transfer payments through the tax system requires a precarious balancing act. Tax transfers must navigate not only administrative and economic priorities surrounding social welfare policy. They must also negotiate the treachery of welfare politics, and, in particular, avoid all associations with the moniker "welfare."

While tax transfers can be effective in shielding work support programs from the politics of welfare, we may view the policy trend toward tax transfers and away from direct transfers as an opportunity to jump directly into the lion's den, re-imagining our definition of welfare itself. Indeed, one could argue that the sum of "ending welfare as we know it" plus "making work pay" equals a twenty-first century, work-oriented welfare state. Rather than restrict our notion of welfare, we expand it to include the "deserving poor" in the form of the working poor.

This goal is fraught with difficulties. "Welfare" has fallen almost completely off the public agenda since 1996, the year Congress devolved national welfare policy to the states, and replaced the much-maligned Aid to Families with Dependent Children with Temporary Assistance for Needy Families (TANF). Attempts to reignite public discourse over welfare, and expand rather than contract its constituent parts could prove disastrous. If tax credits like the EITC became linked with welfare, they might cease to exist. Ideally, the poor and disadvantaged would be better off with a system of social provisions that recognized public assistance as a matter of right – as an entitlement – much like the basic income guarantees in many countries throughout the world. In reconceiving longstanding notions of "welfare," and expanding the inventory of "welfare" programs to include tax-transfer programs and their beneficiaries, however, we raise the possibility of losing our most effective anti-poverty programs.

We might have more success in expanding our notion of "work" rather than of "welfare." Recently, Noah Zatz has compared the definition of work in the EITC and TANF, showing that "work" for EITC purposes equates exclusively with earnings from employment or self-employment, while "work" for TANF purposes is substantially more flexible, and includes unsubsidized employment, subsidized private sector employment, work experience, on-the-job training, job search and job readiness assistance, community service programs, vocational educational training, and providing child-care services to persons participating in community service. If TANF claimants perform at least twenty hours of "work" from the previously mentioned activities, moreover, they may also participate in three additional forms of work, all unpaid: job skills training directly related to employment; education directly related to employment for non–high school graduates; and high school or [General Educational Development (GED)] coursework for non–high school graduates. Although the list of what qualifies as work under TANF emphasizes the attainment of paid employment, it is considerably more expansive than the narrow category of work recognized for receipt of EITC benefits. Among the states, there is further variation with respect to permitting TANF recipients to satisfy work requirements from unpaid activities, which includes unpaid community service, care for family members suffering from physical disabilities or severe health problems, and subsistence production to meet basic household needs.

Two points are worth emphasizing in comparing "work supports" in the nation's largest tax-transfer program and its largest direct-transfer program. First, "welfare" in the twenty-first century requires that recipients work, seek work, or develop sufficient skills to attain work. There are no free lunches under the welfare state as we have come to know it. Second, unlike welfare, the EITC "makes work pay" only if the work takes place in the paid labor market. The EITC does not reward unpaid work, efforts to find work, or skills training that facilitates paid employment. "Work" under the EITC remains categorical, strictly limited to current paid employment, and generally less inclusive than "work" for welfare purposes.

[Another] potential benefit of delivering social welfare through the tax system rather than through direct expenditure programs may involve our desire to hide these programs in the tax system. We might seek the cloak of the Code for several reasons, including: (1) the hope that opponents of a generous social welfare state will not find out what we are doing, (2) to destigmatize and legitimize tax-transfer programs by tying them and their beneficiaries to the unassailable virtue of work, and (3) to prevent the programs from having to undergo the annual scrutiny of the general appropriations process. As to the last motivation, the EITC, for one, became a permanent part of the Code in 1978, and if Congress wants to defund it, it must do so explicitly.

QUESTION #2: WHAT AND WHO ARE WE TARGETING WHEN WE ADVOCATE TAX-TRANSFER PROGRAMS LIKE THE EITC?

Are we defending wage subsidies? Income supplements? Negative income taxes? Are we providing a "work bonus"? Are we defending progressivity by adding it to the bottom of the income scale rather than to the top? Are we bolstering a weak and ineffective social safety net? Or are we protecting what the Congressional Research Service recently called, when referring to the EITC, the country's "largest anti-poverty entitlement program?"[2]

---

[2] Cong. Research Serv., The Earned Income Tax Credit (EITC): An Overview 27 app. (2007).

Correspondingly, for whom are we fighting? Low-income workers? Their children? Persons below the poverty line? Persons above the poverty line? The transitionally unemployed? Or are we concerned about secondary earners who face significant disincentives to enter the labor market due to high marginal tax rates? Without yet offering answers to these questions, let us turn to our third thematic question.

QUESTION #3: ARE OUR CURRENT TAX-TRANSFER EFFORTS EFFECTIVELY ASSISTING THE TARGETED BENEFICIARIES?

Transfer programs that run through the Code help persons who pay taxes. If you do not have taxable income, tax-transfer programs do not help you, at least currently. But "work" is broader than paid employment. In very real terms, the EITC, as a "work support" program, discriminates among different kinds of workers, and distributes anti-poverty benefits only to one category of persons living in poverty; it supplements the income of paid workers but neglects unpaid workers. In addition, low-income individuals engaged in unpaid work may be ineligible for EITC benefits but considered "working" for other transfer programs, including TANF. The different treatment of "work" under the two programs raises serious concerns about horizontal equity (i.e., the equal treatment of equals). Two individuals, one "working" in paid employment and the other "working" in unpaid employment (with income from nonemployment sources), and each with identical incomes, are treated differently under the EITC. Yet if both of these workers are equally deserving of assistance – they have equal incomes, after all, and are both engaged in work-oriented activities – then "it is hard to see – from an anti-poverty perspective" why one would be helped while the other would be on the outside looking in.[3] The discrimination is further unjustified after accounting for the observation that the EITC extends benefits to low-wage workers in nonpoor families; that is, workers less "deserving" from an economic perspective than the hypothetical individual described earlier.

If the target beneficiaries of tax transfers include all low-income, working Americans, running social welfare through the tax system excludes many members of that group. Of course, we could adopt a universal tax credit, which would provide benefits as a matter of right and not as a consequence of paid employment. But we tried that already, and it did not work; in fact, it failed miserably.

To the extent we see tax credits as the solution to all of our anti-poverty woes, we are in serious trouble. Tax transfers can be powerful anti-poverty tools. But we can lean on these programs only so much. If we shift our entire system of social provisions to the tax system, all the problems that previously plagued, say, welfare policy or health care policy will likely persist under the stewardship of tax officials. In fact, new problems will likely emerge as the tax system assumes responsibilities it was not designed to shoulder, and as policy makers shift responsibilities – perhaps for political rather than informed reasons – from direct expenditure programs to tax expenditure programs.

---

[3] Noah Zatz, *Welfare to What?*, 57 HASTINGS L.J. 1131, 1183 (2006).

HOW WE CAN "SAVE" THE EITC

By raising so many questions as to the nature and purpose of low-income tax credits, I hope to clarify rather than problematize our reliance on tax-transfer programs. To be frank, however, there is an inherent danger in this clarification project. Tax-transfer programs like the EITC have enjoyed political success largely because of confusion – rather than clarity – over what they are and what they are not. Indeed, the EITC gained bipartisan support over the years because it has meant different things to different people. For Republicans, it is a reward for working, while for Democrats, it is an anti-poverty program. By clarifying with precision what we are trying to accomplish with tax-transfer programs such as the EITC, we run the risk of disturbing the delicate balance of bipartisanship that many of these programs currently enjoy.

In fact, some commentators suggest that the EITC is already in mortal danger. Congress reacted aggressively in 2003 upon learning that as much as 31.7% of total EITC claims for tax year 1999 should not have been paid. Congressional pressure to reduce overpayments prompted the IRS to roll out a pilot "certification" program for a limited number of EITC claimants. The program amounted to a prereturn audit for all EITC eligibles swept up in its net. Compared to audit rates of less than 1% for the general taxpayer population, the scrutiny paid low-income taxpayers appeared draconian. In addition, since 1998, the IRS has allocated over $1 billion of its budget to auditing low-income taxpayers, such that low-income audits comprised 50% of all individual income tax examinations between 2000 and 2003; if you were poor during those years, you were audited more than four times as frequently as any other taxpayer. And just over a year ago, the Taxpayer Advocate Service (TAS) reported that between 2001 and 2005 nearly 1,600,000 low-income taxpayers had their refunds frozen without notice and deemed fraudulent under the IRS's "questionable refund program." In two-thirds of the cases, TAS found no evidence of fraud, and the wrongfully accused taxpayers ultimately received at least 100% of the refunds originally claimed on their returns.

These attacks on low-income taxpayers and their tax-transfer benefits are serious. But doomsayers overstate the threat. To the extent a small number of EITC claimants are required to precertify their eligibility for benefits, or that otherwise EITC eligibles shown to have made erroneous claims in previous years are prevented from claiming the EITC for as many as ten years (for fraud), is, to my mind, a realistic price to pay. Therefore, with respect to "how we can save the EITC," the EITC does not need saving. The war over the future of the program was fought and won by its supporters ten years ago. Recent compliance efforts directed at the EITC do not in any way endanger the program, unless, as others have argued, we overreact to what amounts to reasonable oversight of the nation's largest anti-poverty program.

CHARTING THE EITC'S FUTURE

I do not mean to imply that proponents of low-income tax-transfer programs should rest on their laurels. Rather, as I have argued elsewhere, tax-transfer advocates must be mindful of social and political winds, and shape their advocacy accordingly. They require tax-transfer advocates to acknowledge fairly the shortcomings associated with delivering transfers to low-income individuals through the tax system. They also require advocates and administrators to address directly those shortcomings, to reduce unacceptably high noncompliance rates, research the labor participation effects of tax-transfer programs, model optimal delivery of transfers through the Code, and assist eligible low-income taxpayers in claiming the credit.

Some recent efforts are exemplary. In early 2007, responding not only to excessive noncompliance rates but also to growing nonparticipation rates (which may run as high as 25%), the IRS launched an aggressive educational campaign to help eligible low-income taxpayers claim the EITC for tax year 2006. Treasury Secretary Henry Paulson and IRS Commissioner Mark Everson announced "EITC Awareness Day" as part of a concerted effort to inform taxpayers about the EITC and the availability of free tax filing assistance. More than 150 coalitions and partners across the country marked EITC Awareness Day with news conferences, press releases, and media coverage. The United Way and Bank of America announced a new national initiative, which included a $500,000 grant to help low-income individuals obtain tax preparation assistance and unrealized tax refunds through the EITC.

The most important task for proponents of the EITC will be to continue differentiating it and other tax-transfer programs from welfare. This will be no easy undertaking. Apart from the stubborn error rates, the EITC amounts to a hybrid tax-welfare program whether we want to admit it or not. Welfare politics, somewhat counterintuitively, may provide opportunities for expanding rather than contracting social provision in the United States. Exploiting welfare politics may be a suboptimal way to advocate a more inclusive social welfare state. But the political arena often forces its participants to adopt imperfect solutions, particularly with respect to tax-transfer programs, which have thrived over the last generation because they were characterized as tax programs rather than as welfare programs. Political realities continue to force proponents of these programs to emphasize – even overemphasize – the differences between transfer payments associated with work, and transfer payments received as a matter of right, as an entitlement of citizenship in a rich and democratic state.

CONCLUSION

In the United States, social welfare programs run through the Code have been hugely successful, both from the standpoint of delivering benefits to needy recipients and generating bipartisan political support. Still, the shadow of "welfare" hangs over all forms of social provision, whether run through the tax system or the direct expenditure budget. Policy makers need to remain sensitive to criticisms that tax transfers amount to welfare payments, and that tax-transfer recipients should be subject to the same administrative scrutiny and eligibility requirements as welfare recipients. Such sensitivity, however, also requires policy makers to extol the virtues of tax transfers without undermining the usefulness of direct-transfer programs. Celebrating the work incentive features of the EITC that emphasize paid employment, for instance, should not delegitimize the more expansive – and creative – work incentive features of TANF. Rather, such a comparison should encourage policy makers to consider what counts as "work" worthy of public support in a society where work takes all forms, both market as well as nonmarket and paid as well as unpaid. Broader conceptions of work translate into broader social supports, some of which should be delivered through the tax system – for administrative, political, cultural, or economic reasons – and some of which should be delivered through the direct expenditure budget. Indeed, for the U.S. tax-transfer system to build on its three-decade run of success, policymakers need not only appreciate the history of social welfare and the Code, but also its untapped potential to further alleviate poverty and provide opportunity for low-income Americans.

Race, Class, and the Internal Revenue Code:
A Class-Based Analysis of *A Black Critique of the Internal Revenue Code*

WILTON B. HYMAN[1]

Economic class differences within the black community should be considered, in conjunction with the history of black racial oppression, in developing proposals to reduce economic disparities between whites and blacks. In *A Black Critique*,[2] Professors Beverly Moran and William Whitford documented the white and black tax gap by analyzing the extent to which blacks and whites benefit from certain provisions of the Code. They focused primarily on Code sections related to wealth while controlling for factors such as race, "income, education, region and marital status."[3] They concluded that race was a statistically significant predictor of the benefit that whites and blacks receive from the Code, with whites benefiting disproportionately.

Professors Moran and Whitford did not analyze class differences within the black community; they focused on the tax provisions' impact upon blacks in the aggregate in developing strategies to remedy the tax gap. Their proposals, however, reflect a bias toward lower-income blacks and against the economic interests of middle-income blacks due to their focus on race as the primary determinant of the tax disparities. That analysis leads to overly broad prescriptions. The racial tax disparity is a consequence of the historical effects of racial subordination, reflected in wealth disparities between whites and blacks. As a result, a race-based approach will not adequately address the problem because it may eliminate tax provisions that benefit middle-income blacks in an effort to assist lower-income blacks who are unable, due to their economic condition, to utilize those provisions. This article supports the incorporation of class-based considerations in creating tax legislation to resolve black–white economic disparities because class allows for a more particularized approach, and for specific segments of the black community to be identified and targeted for assistance.

---

[1] Reprinted by permission from 35 *Capital University Law Review* 119 (2006).
[2] Beverly I. Moran & William Whitford, *A Black Critique of the Internal Revenue Code*, 1996 WIS. L. REV. 751 [see Chapter 5 – Eds.].
[3] *Id.* at 769.

THE CLASS-BASED IMPLICATIONS OF *A BLACK CRITIQUE*
OF THE INTERNAL REVENUE CODE

One of the most significant findings by Professors Moran and Whitford was that blacks who have incomes equal to that of whites benefit less from the Code. As they acknowledged, blacks generally earn less than whites, so most would assume that whites benefit more from tax deductions and other preferences. The fact that blacks of the same or similar income level benefit less than comparable whites is not only unexpected, but provides support for the critical race critique since the Code is race-neutral in terms of its application.

The foundation of their argument is horizontal equity, which means that tax-payers earning similar incomes should be subject to similar tax liabilities. However, the wealth disparity between whites and blacks is what accounts for the differential tax treatment documented in *A Black Critique*. As observed by Professors Moran and Whitford, the types of assets owned by whites benefit from tax deferrals, exclusions, and deductions. These benefits are unavailable to blacks of the same income level who do not own tax-favored assets or possess comparable wealth.

A class-based analysis does not allow for the numerical certainty of income, but the development of class differences, particularly among blacks, does provide a basis for understanding the factors that have contributed to the present-day wealth disparities. Without further elaboration or the consideration of other contributing factors, Professors Moran and Whitford's analysis may create the impression that the tax system alone contributes to the tax disparities suffered by blacks.

CLASS DEVELOPMENT AND DIFFERENTIATION WITHIN
THE BLACK COMMUNITY

To appreciate how class differences affect wealth and asset accumulation within the black community, a look at the development of black class differentiation is necessary. The ability of blacks to progress economically and socially was and still is directly tied to the degree of hostility and oppression exhibited toward them by American society.

What has occurred, especially since the Civil Rights Movement, is that race as well as class are the significant determinants of an individual's economic prospects. But neither alone is sufficient to comprehend fully the current circumstances of blacks. As a result, the lesson derived from history is that race and class are intertwined, and analysis of both allows a more complete appreciation of the economic condition of blacks as a group.

The Antebellum Period

Slavery imposed upon all blacks a racial caste order that held them to the lowest status within American society. There were no meaningful distinctions between slaves; house servants participated more in the daily lives of their white owners but were still subject to discipline and complete subordination. Emancipated blacks had some opportunity for social and economic advancement, but "the majority

of the free Negroes in the South did not live much above a subsistence level."[4]
Slavery also marginalized poor and lower-class whites economically as a result of
the slaveholders' reliance upon slave labor. As a result, white laborers sought laws
to restrict employment for slaves outside of the plantation system, but they settled
for laws restricting the employment of free blacks.

When allowed, free blacks worked in many different occupations and served as
important sources of skilled labor. Some freemen owned businesses and acquired
wealth during that time. Northern free blacks, however, were more dependent
upon domestic and laborer work. Further inhibiting the progress of northern
freemen was opposition to black employment, attributable to competition with
European immigrants and other northern whites for jobs.

The Postbellum Period and the Emergence of Jim Crow

After the Civil War, slaveholders' control over the economic and political structure
of the South was maintained through the "Black Codes," which restricted movement, voting, and other freedoms of recently emancipated blacks. The eventual
decline of agriculture as the South's primary economic activity led to the erosion
of the slaveholders' influence, paving the way for poor whites to restrict black
competition for jobs. Poor whites were in competition with blacks for industrial
employment, which grew due to capital investment in the South. Jim Crow eventually replaced the Black Codes, which were abolished in 1886, continuing to restrict
blacks from meaningful participation in southern society.

Black Migration to the North

In 1900, 90% of all blacks lived in the South, with the majority residing in rural
areas, making them dependent upon agricultural employment. Nonagricultural
employment was limited to laborer and domestic work. Those constraints, coupled
with oppressive social conditions under Jim Crow, forced many blacks to leave the
South.

Black migration, which began prior to World War I, greatly increased black
populations in northern areas. Some blacks found better job prospects and living
conditions due to the absence of Jim Crow. They also experienced improved
educational options and growing black political influence. Despite those benefits,
most blacks migrating north were still limited to low-skilled employment.

A small black professional class began to develop during the first quarter of
the twentieth century, though it comprised a very small percentage of all workers.
This group included doctors, lawyers, teachers, and other professionals who relied
upon the segregated black population for their livelihood. Members of this black
elite were descendants of blacks who were emancipated prior to the Civil War and
maintained "close economic and social ties with the white community."[5] They also

---

[4] E. Franklin Frazier, Black Bourgeoisie 14 (1997).
[5] William Julius Wilson, The Declining Significance of Race 125 (2d ed. 1980).

supported integration as the most effective approach to resolving racial divisions within American society.

Another group of black businessmen, intent on developing a self-sustaining, independent black community, supplanted the earlier black middle class. This new black leadership depended upon the segregated black community also, but did not interact with the white community. Their ideology was in reaction to Jim Crow in the South and the racial animosity encountered by blacks in the North. They identified with Booker T. Washington and his message of black self-help and uplift. Their tenure, however, was short-lived, because the Great Depression and financial difficulties led to the collapse of many of their businesses.

In spite of the Great Depression and its impact upon black businesses, black gains in occupational differentiation continued, but at a slower rate. Less than half of all southern blacks were employed in agriculture at that time and many northern blacks retained employment advantages secured prior to the Depression. Occupational differentiation among blacks continued up to and during the 1940s. In addition, a study of cities with black populations of 100,000 or more found that the black middle class represented over 20% of the black population in northern cities and about 17% in southern cities. In spite of the advantages blacks gained in northern cities, residential segregation, coupled with housing shortages and high housing costs, led to the creation and growth of urban ghettos.

The World War II Era

World War II industrial expansion allowed blacks to obtain semiskilled jobs in the industrial sector and some white-collar employment with government agencies. These opportunities led to a large migration of blacks to urban areas, which continued through the 1960s.

From the 1950s to the 1970s, the percentage of black males employed in middle-class jobs more than doubled. This growth in black economic mobility was due to: (1) the post–World War II economy; (2) access to white-collar jobs for educated blacks; (3) greater black membership in labor unions; (4) equal employment legislation, at the local, state, and then federal level; and (5) the migration of blacks from the South to other regions that offered better opportunities.

The postwar period saw industry begin to leave the cities (where the majority of blacks resided) and relocate into outlying areas. Slowdowns in central city manufacturing and industrial job growth led to decreases in blue-collar jobs, while white-collar and entry-level service employment increased. These changes benefited educated white-collar workers and provided job opportunities for low-skilled workers in support-type jobs, which were low paying and did not offer many opportunities for advancement. These changes contributed to the high rates of unemployment that plagued residents of urban areas.

The Civil Rights Movement and Affirmative Action Policies

During the 1940s, black leaders returned to the integrationist goals of the black middle class that existed around the turn of the century. The National Association for the Advancement of Colored People and the Urban League provided leadership in the drive for racial equality. These organizations adopted goals reflecting the aims of middle-class blacks, at least in their initial stages.

Legislation outlawing discrimination in public accommodations and the housing market reflected the concerns of the black middle class, but were of limited benefit to poor blacks. The Civil Rights Movement's incorporation of voting rights and employment discrimination made its aims more relevant to the concerns of the poor.

However, the major contributor to black middle-class expansion during the 1960s was the passage of Title VII of the Civil Rights Act of 1964, prohibiting employment discrimination on the basis of race. That legislation, coupled with the growing economy of the 1960s, led to tremendous gains in the black middle class. In addition to legislation and increased enforcement of antidiscrimination laws, affirmative action policies benefited educated blacks. Generally applying to jobs requiring some level of education and training, affirmative action helped blacks seeking government and private sector employment.

Black class development illustrates that class differentiation did not begin in earnest until around the World War II era, and growth in the black middle class did not take root until the 1960s. As a result, we can look to the 1960s as the period of time to begin tracing the black middle class as we know it today. The black middle class is, however, vulnerable to economic declines and resistance to minority advancement, both of which occurred during the 1970s, leading to declines in black middle-class growth.

The Modern Black Social Class Condition

The power and influence of urban areas has diminished due to middle-class families leaving the cities for the suburbs, the relocation of manufacturing and other industry outside of urban areas, increases in poor and working-class populations, and a decline in tax revenues. This consequence is significant to poor and working-class blacks who lack the resources to reside elsewhere and whose educational background may not qualify them for jobs other than low-skilled service employment. Middle-class blacks, due to their economic resources, have more housing, educational, and employment opportunities.

The Significance of Wealth

Wealth creates opportunities that sustain class status and support upward mobility within families and through generations. Without the transmission of wealth to aid future generations, each one starts from scratch in the climb up the economic ladder, relying on income without the benefits of accumulated wealth to assist them.

Viewing the black economic condition in terms of wealth, as opposed to employment or income, the historical effects of racism and discrimination are much more conspicuous and oppressive. An example of these effects is that middle-class blacks earn approximately 70% of the income of middle-class whites, but blacks only possess 15% of the wealth of similarly situated whites.

A partial explanation for the wealth disparity is that the black middle class has existed for only a short length of time, with most of its growth occurring during the 1960s. This compromises its ability to develop traditions, to pass along class status to future generations, and to accumulate wealth.

DISCUSSION

Professors Moran and Whitford did not find intentional discrimination on the part of Congress, but they found a lack of awareness on Congress's part as the basis for the tax laws being harmful to black interests. They argued that if the Code as a whole is consistent in this manner, it provides support for the critical race critique that racial subordination is reflected in American institutions, even those that are seemingly race-neutral like the Code.

The critical race component is evidenced by the disproportionate tax benefits shown by their study of black and white tax outcomes. Based on that standard, Professors Moran and Whitford succeeded in showing that the tax provisions they studied reflected racial subordination. Acknowledgment of historical racial subordination as a contributor to or cause of tax disparities supports remedying the historical racial disparities as a more direct means of addressing the problem. This argument has validity in that the disparities are not due to the Code applying different rules to blacks as opposed to whites; the disparities result from blacks not qualifying for similar tax treatment due to their economic position.

Yet, Professors Moran and Whitford's recommendations did not address the historical economic disparities that were the foundation for the tax disparities they documented. Their approach focused instead on adjusting tax outcomes as the remedy. Based on their critical race analysis, their approach appears reasonable. Because the racial disparity is reflected through the Code, fixing the Code would remedy the problem.

Professors Moran and Whitford concluded that the Black Congress would: (1) retain the gift and inheritance exclusion; (2) repeal the capital gains preference; (3) tax unrealized appreciation on publicly traded securities and nonresidential real estate; (4) replace the mortgage interest and property tax deductions with a tax credit; (5) retain § 121; (6) possibly repeal § 401(k) while retaining the health benefits exclusion; and (7) adopt a single tax rate or allow optional tax filing statuses to eliminate the marriage penalty.

The retention of § 102 and the exclusion of health benefits would not be particularly harmful to the interests of either poor or middle-class blacks. In fact, it would probably be more beneficial to middle-income blacks because they are more likely to take advantage of those provisions. Professors Moran and Whitford's recommendations regarding the marriage penalty are probably more beneficial to lower-income black couples because their income levels may make them more susceptible to the penalty; however, this recommendation would not harm the interests of middle-income blacks, either.

The recommendation to repeal the capital gains tax preference would harm middle-income blacks who are more likely to take advantage of and benefit from this provision. Looking at the capital gains tax preference and its relevance to blacks as a group, Professors Moran and Whitford had a justifiable argument for repeal: most blacks do not use it; therefore, its elimination will not be significant to their interests. That analysis is particularly persuasive if the focus is on lower-income blacks, who are least likely to own capital assets. Even though census data shows that whites have a higher percentage of their net worth in stocks and mutual funds, black ownership percentages, based on their net worth, are increasing.

Furthermore, blacks with investment assets tend to invest in real estate. Assuming those real estate holdings qualify for capital gains treatment, the owners would benefit from the lower capital gains tax rate. In addition, more so than with stocks and mutual funds, rental and commercial real estate holdings reflect greater parity in terms of black and white ownership rates. Despite the minimal rate of capital asset ownership among blacks, the elimination of the tax preference would harm the interests of those blacks most likely to benefit from this provision.

Likewise, Professors Moran and Whitford's recommendation to eliminate the home mortgage interest and property tax deductions and replace them with a tax credit would harm the interests of middle-income taxpayers. Equity acquired through home ownership is the most significant financial asset owned by blacks. Eliminating the home ownership tax provisions would harm the interests of those blacks most able to utilize them and would impair the ability of many blacks to acquire their most significant asset.

The repeal of § 401(k) would harm middle-income blacks because they are more likely to have sufficient resources to put away for retirement and because their jobs are more likely to make these plans available. With 401(k)s representing a significant portion of the overall net worth of blacks, it provides a strong basis for the continuation of these tax benefits.

In the end, the question is whether the elimination or alteration of these tax provisions will benefit blacks in the aggregate. Some of these recommendations will harm middle-class blacks; however, no clear demonstration has been made that lower-income blacks will benefit, with the possible exceptions of the marriage penalty and the mortgage tax credit provisions.

Middle- and upper-income blacks are more likely to support the capital gains tax preference, the mortgage interest and property tax provisions, and the exclusion of gifts from income tax. In an effort to ensure that the interests of those members of the black community are not negatively harmed, targeted tax incentives would be preferable to the policies supported by Professors Moran and Whitford. Their use of race as the primary basis for measuring tax disparities resulted in an overly broad approach, which, to some extent, explains the nature of their recommendations. Because the Code does not identify taxpayers by race, their approach eliminated provisions that are disproportionately favorable to white taxpayers.

This article approaches the racial tax disparities documented by Professors Moran and Whitford with a class-based approach because it provides more insight into the historical aspects of class mobility and differentiation within the black community, and illustrates that race alone is not sufficient to explain the economic differences between whites and blacks. Race is still significant, but the analysis is much more complicated due to the social advances of the 1960s.

Using the Code to reduce racial disparities in home ownership rates and wealth accumulation is an additional weapon against a continuing and persistent societal problem. It also affirms, however, that conventional methods are ineffective or incapable of resolving these problems. Either of those conclusions provides sufficient justification for *A Black Critique*. Despite its unconventionality in terms of its topic or approach, it should be acknowledged as a serious attempt to address an issue that will persist and continue to impair the black community.

CHAPTER 10. DISABILITY AND TAXATION

The authors in this chapter explore the scattered provisions of the tax laws that impact people with disabilities. Theodore Seto and Sande Buhai, in *Tax and Disability: Ability to Pay and the Taxation of Difference*, illuminate disability theory, traditional tax policy, and the insights that emerge from applying both perspectives to the very structure of the tax system. Seto and Buhai suggest that cultural conceptions of disability as exclusively a medical, charitable, or even a civil rights issue should yield to what they call a "human variation paradigm of disability rights," which would recognize that the removal of formal legal barriers to equality does not necessarily provide disabled individuals with equal opportunities. Seto and Buhai develop a set of proposals for change to the current tax system that would both fit within this paradigm and comport with generally accepted notions of the comprehensive tax base and varying individual tax burdens based on ability to pay.

Francine Lipman, in *Enabling Work for People with Disabilities: A Post-Integrationist Revision of Underutilized Tax Incentives*, reveals the underutilization of available business tax incentives to employ disabled people. Lipman points to lack of awareness and the complexity of applicable Code sections as principal reasons that more businesses do not take advantage of these incentives. As a result, Lipman concludes, people with disabilities remain underemployed and marginalized, and the workforce lacks a real diversity. To remedy this situation, Lipman suggests changes to the existing work incentives in the Code.

In *Disability and the Income Tax*, David Duff provides a Canadian perspective on disability and taxation. Duff draws a helpful distinction between the tax policy concerns and social policy concerns that are relevant to the expenses incurred by disabled taxpayers. Though Duff focuses primarily on the tax policy aspects of these expenses, he does touch on broader social policy issues in his discussion. Like Lipman, he finds his country's tax treatment of disabled taxpayers to be wanting. In an exhaustive analysis that can only be reproduced in small part here, Duff suggests ways to improve the Canadian tax system's treatment of disabled taxpayers.

Taken together, these scholars remind us about the importance of the tax system in creating an integrated and just society that provides all of its citizens the right to work. Without a meaningful right to work, disabled people remain second-class citizens in theory, and impoverished in reality.

Tax and Disability: Ability to Pay and the Taxation of Difference

THEODORE P. SETO AND SANDE L. BUHAI[1]

INTRODUCTION

The Census Bureau estimates that at the end of 1994, approximately 54,000,000 Americans (over 20% of the U.S. population) had some type of disability; 26,000,000, a severe disability. Since that time, the U.S. population has both grown and aged; the number of people with disabilities is therefore probably larger today. The Code contains numerous discrete and largely uncoordinated provisions dealing with or of particular relevance to people with disabilities. Yet so far as we have been able to ascertain, no serious academic analysis of the policy issues underlying the U.S. taxation of people with disabilities or of those who interact most closely with them has ever been published. Disability and tax scholars, each largely ignorant of the others' specialties, appear for the most part to have avoided the subject. This is regrettable. Tax rules of particular relevance to people with disabilities are too important for disability specialists to ignore in assessing federal disability policy. Conversely, the problems of people with disabilities raise issues that go to the heart of income tax theory and policy.

Disability theory has changed markedly over the past century. The early 1900s saw the replacement of an affliction paradigm, in which disability was viewed as a punishment or test imposed by God, with a medical/charity paradigm, in which people with disabilities came to be viewed instead as appropriate objects of pity and philanthropy. The result was the enactment of a wide variety of special programs to help Americans with disabilities. The second half of the twentieth century, in turn, witnessed rejection of this medical/charity paradigm, viewed by the disability rights community as demeaning, in favor of a more militant civil rights model, in which people with disabilities claimed a right to equal treatment. This time, the result was the enactment of extensive disability rights legislation, culminating in the Americans with Disabilities Act of 1990. Disability theorists then began to realize that the equality model they were using was inconsistent with many of the assistance programs they had won on the basis of the older medical/charity paradigm – programs still important to Americans with disabilities. Recent years have therefore seen the development of a new "human variation"

[1] Reprinted by permission from 154 *University of Pennsylvania Law Review* 1053 (2006).

paradigm that attempts to reconcile the two. This new paradigm asserts that society should be structured affirmatively to take differences into account, with the goal of allowing equal participation by all, despite those differences, to the greatest extent possible.

Standard tax theory largely ignores differences – other than differences in "income" – in the ability of taxpayers to pay taxes. This, in turn, seriously limits its capacity to model popular moral intuitions about fair taxation. The mechanical structure of the system, caught between theory and moral intuition, has in turn become profoundly stressed – to the point that today many are ready to scrap the system altogether.

We suggest that ability to pay be revived as an analytic tool. We believe that a nonutilitarian ability-to-pay theory fits and justifies significant portions of existing law, offers a coordinated explanation of both base and rates, and is consistent with popular notions of tax fairness. In particular, such a theory explains existing tax provisions of particular relevance to people with disabilities far better than standard tax theory does. It may also permit significant simplification of the conceptual – and therefore also the mechanical – structure of the individual income tax system as a whole.

AN INTRODUCTION TO DISABILITY LAW AND THEORY: STRUGGLING TO FIND A PARADIGM

Whether existing U.S. income tax provisions of particular relevance to people with disabilities make sense depends on what those provisions are supposed to accomplish. Tax policy regarding people with disabilities should, of course, be consistent with overall federal disability policy. Unfortunately, there is as yet no such coherent policy. A civil rights paradigm has dominated recent congressional action with regard to disability issues. That paradigm, however, does not explain important parts of disability law grounded in an earlier medical/charity view of disability. A new human variation theory, recently proposed by a number of disability scholars, may reconcile the two.

Despite its legislative successes, the civil rights model does not fully explain federal disability policy; indeed, it does not even fully explain those laws that most clearly invoke it. The Social Security Act and other "safety net" programs – essential to many people with disabilities – are difficult to reconcile with a simple call for equal treatment. A deaf individual, if treated exactly the same as hearing individuals in a movie theater, classroom, or court proceeding, would effectively be excluded from participation. Mere equal treatment may not result in the integration of people with disabilities into the societal mainstream.

Is equality enough? Today, many in the disability rights movement are moving toward the conclusion that it is not. Even after the ramps are built, the paraplegic must still buy the wheelchair and the specially modified car. Some people with disabilities will be limited in the work they can do and the income they can earn, no matter how extensive the accommodations. Many will never work. Notwithstanding extensive congressional action, people with disabilities continue to be less well-educated and more likely to be unemployed than those without. The challenge to the disability rights movement is to formulate a theory that retains the dignity of the civil rights model but acknowledges these special problems.

Several scholars have attempted to articulate such a theory, which Richard Scotch and Kay Schriner label the "human variation" model. Under this emerging paradigm, problems faced by people with disabilities are viewed "as the consequence of . . . social institutions . . . having been constructed to deal with a narrower range of variation than is in fact present in any given population."[2] Features of the human-made environment that segregate disabled citizens from the rest of the population have not been decreed by immutable natural laws, nor were they produced by historical happenstance or coincidence. They represent conscious choices that had the effect of including some groups, such as the dominant segments of society, and excluding others who were "different" or disabled. Harlan Hahn advocates a world adapted to the needs of everyone, not just those of the dominant majority.

A human variation paradigm would appear to solve many of the problems of the civil rights approach, while retaining much of its normative power. It justifies both a safety net and accommodation on equality grounds. In effect, it invokes John Rawls's choice from behind the veil of ignorance: if it were possible that you might be paralyzed from the waist down, how would you like society to be structured?

AN INTRODUCTION TO THE FEDERAL INCOME TAXATION OF INDIVIDUALS: FROM THE THEORETICALLY ELEGANT TO THE INCOHERENT

Until we began this article, we had never had occasion to question standard tax theory. Comprehensive tax base theory, commonly used to define the appropriate base for income taxation, has enormous explanatory power. Progressivity we took for granted. As we attempted to apply standard theory to the problems of people with disabilities, however, we discovered that it has almost no capacity to deal with differences – other than differences in income – in taxpayers' abilities to pay taxes. Under comprehensive tax base theory, for example, a quadriplegic taxpayer who earns $50,000 but must spend $20,000 for a full-time assistant to help her go to the bathroom, wash, dress, and eat is treated as having equal ability to pay taxes as a "normal" taxpayer who earns the same amount but can choose to spend that same $20,000 on skydiving, cello lessons, or long-term investments. We found it implausible that the two should be expected to contribute equally to the functions of government, as comprehensive tax base theory implies.

A Comprehensive Tax Base Theory

At the core of the U.S. income tax system is a single elegant premise: income includes any value received unless that value is paid for with dollars that have

---

[2] Richard K. Scotch & Kay Schriner, *Disability as Human Variation: Implications for Policy*, 549 ANNALS AM. ACAD. POL. & SOC. SCI. 148, 155 (1997).

already been taxed. Expenditures to produce future income are not treated as resulting in personal consumption benefits. The tax system should allow you a deduction reflecting the costs of producing income. And in general it does. The tax system should not allow deduction of personal expenses. And in general it does not.

The part of our economy that would ideally be taxed under the foregoing theory is sometimes known as the "comprehensive tax base." Comprehensive tax base theory tells us a lot about what must be includible or deductible if Congress's purpose is to tax "income." Applied in the myriad contexts in which taxpayers make, lose, or recover money or other value, this theory commonly tells us what the rule "must" be, even if no statute or regulation has yet addressed the issue. Many exclusions, credits, and deductions relevant to people with disabilities are treated as deviations from tax theory, justified primarily on the nontax ground that such people are the appropriate objects of solicitude – in other words, by reference to the medical/charity paradigm of disability.

Theories of Progressive Taxation

Comprehensive tax base theory does not itself justify progressive taxation. What does? Here, standard U.S. tax theory and popular sentiment diverge. The most widely accepted popular justification for graduated rates remains differences in ability to pay, focusing on the sacrifice taxpayers make in giving up a portion of their earnings to fund the operations of government. Taxpayers with little income generally need it to pay for essentials, such as food, clothing, and shelter. Giving up a significant part of these essentials would be a major sacrifice. We therefore keep tax rates very low at lower income levels or do not tax such income at all. By contrast, depriving a wealthy taxpayer of a fifth luxury car, third vacation home, or fiftieth pair of shoes imposes a relatively small objective sacrifice on that taxpayer, regardless of how passionately he desires that fiftieth pair of shoes. Assuming that government needs a given amount of funding, taking income the wealthy taxpayer would have used to buy a fifth luxury car is thought to be fairer than taking income that less wealthy taxpayers would have used to buy food, clothing, or shelter.

Contemporary U.S. tax theorists, however, commonly reject ability to pay as a justification for progressive taxation of income in excess of this initial exempt amount. Graduated marginal rates on such additional income are best justified, they argue, as part of a larger governmental project to maximize social welfare by redistributing income from the wealthy to the poor. The result of theoretical developments is that mainstream U.S. tax theorists now justify progressivity with a theory (utilitarian redistribution) that is both (1) distinct from and uncoordinated with the theory they use to define the income tax base (comprehensive tax base theory) and (2) inconsistent with public and congressional intuitions about tax fairness. This means there is no consensus theory of the U.S. income tax as a whole – a rather astonishing fact, given how long the income tax has been around. It also means that mainstream tax theorists are poorly positioned to explain, refine, or guide congressional action.

Reframing the Income Tax, in Part, as a Tax on Ability to Pay

We believe it would be useful for U.S. tax scholars to articulate more formally the moral intuitions that underlie continued popular and congressional adherence to ability to pay. Such an articulation would help Congress systematize its implementation of those intuitions and thereby begin to move the individual income tax system back toward coherence. We do not mean to suggest that ability-to-pay analysis can answer all, or even a preponderance of, interesting individual income tax questions. So long as Congress and the electorate believe ability to pay to be relevant, however, we do not believe tax policy scholarship can properly reject or ignore it. Nor do we mean to suggest that scholars should abandon other projects, including utilitarian projects. We believe it is clear, however, that utilitarian theory often does not accurately model popular moral intuitions. Regardless of whether utilitarianism is correct in any ultimate sense, its failure to fit and justify popular moral intuitions limits its ability to explain, refine, or guide congressional action.

What would a more fully articulated ability-to-pay tax system look like? Although the question raises many complex issues, we expect that it would begin with comprehensive tax base income, accurately measured. All economic income would be includible; all current costs of producing such income would be currently deductible; all capital costs of producing such income would be amortized over realistic periods. Some initial amount of such income would be exempt from taxation – an amount large enough to permit the taxpayer to live a frugal but adequate life. Above this initial exempt amount, we would expect moderately progressive rates, consistent with our sense of the American electorate's values. Perhaps most importantly, such a tax system would allow simple targeted deductions to deal with differences in ability to pay.

TAX PROVISIONS OF PARTICULAR RELEVANCE TO PEOPLE WITH DISABILITIES

It is against this background that we turn to current tax rules of particular relevance to people with disabilities. These rules are scattered throughout the Code and follow no overarching logic.

Provisions Consistent with the Medical/Charitable Model of Disability

Perhaps the single most important tax rule of particular relevance to people with disabilities, a set of rulings known collectively as the "general welfare doctrine," excludes most safety net payments from income. It also appears to justify exclusion of the value of governmental services from income. Unfortunately, the doctrine is of uncertain legal foundation and uncertain scope. It is also inconsistent with both comprehensive tax base theory and modern disability rights paradigms.

Governmental benefits and services are clearly income to taxpayers who receive them. Standard tax theory therefore requires that we look outside the tax system for the doctrine's justification. To the extent that the doctrine exempts benefits to people with disabilities, it appears to do so because they are the natural objects of charity – that is, for reasons founded in the medical/charity paradigm rejected by the disability rights community. This means that the general welfare doctrine – perhaps the single most important tax rule for people with disabilities – is inconsistent with both standard tax theory and modern disability rights paradigms.

Fortunately, the doctrine can be reframed in terms consistent with the human variation paradigm under an ability-to-pay theory of the income tax. For this purpose, we break the doctrine into two parts: a rule excluding benefits in kind and a rule excluding payments of cash.

Benefits in kind should, of course, be includible in income. At the same time, benefits in kind are typically provided because governments believe they are needed – in effect, because governments believe they are nondiscretionary. Although some parents might choose not to educate their children, for example, or although some parents of children with disabilities might choose not to provide their children with the special services they need, the government has decided that such services are essential and for this reason provides them free of charge. In a first-best ability-to-pay system, therefore, the value of such services would be includible, but their cost would be deductible. A simple exclusion produces the same bottom-line result.

The same argument cannot be made with respect to payments of cash. In a first-best ability-to-pay system, however, although such payments would be includible, an adequate initial amount of income would also be exempt. Our current zero-bracket amount is probably not adequate. Assuming an adequate zero-bracket exemption, most recipients of need-based general welfare payments would unlikely rise to taxpaying levels in a first-best ability-to-pay system. In a second-best world, therefore, exclusion of general welfare payments can be justified as well, so long as the exclusion is limited to payments based on individual need.

Provisions Consistent with the Human Variation Model of Disability

Section 67 imposes a 2% floor on "miscellaneous deductions," as a result of which taxpayers can claim such deductions only to the extent they exceed 2% of adjusted gross income. Since the work-related expenses of employees fall into the "miscellaneous deduction" category, this has the effect of mismeasuring the income of employees with work-related expenses. Section 67(b)(6), however, exempts "impairment-related work expenses" from the operation of this floor. For this purpose, "impairment-related work expenses" are defined as "expenses . . . of a handicapped individual . . . for attendant care services at the individual's place of employment and other expenses in connection with such place of employment which are necessary for such individual to be able to work, and with respect to which a deduction is allowable under § 162."

The exemption itself is consistent with comprehensive tax base theory, an ability-to-pay tax system, and the human variation paradigm. It is also consistent with the civil rights paradigm as implemented in the Americans with Disabilities Act. As a result of the exemption, people with disabilities are more likely to be able to deduct the extra costs they incur to earn a living. This more correctly measures their economic income for comprehensive tax base purposes, adjusts for ability to pay, and does so without granting people with disabilities a charitable preference. People with disabilities, like their nondisabled peers, are equally subject to the 2% floor with respect to ordinary employment-related costs like union dues. Finally, the exemption facilitates the reintegration of people with disabilities into the societal mainstream, as envisioned by the Americans with Disabilities Act. In effect, it renders it more likely that such taxpayers will be able to deduct accommodations required to enable them to work when they themselves pay for such accommodations.

The practical effects of § 67(b)(6), however, are modest. The section does not change the Code's characterization of such costs as below-the-line deductions, nor does it make those costs deductible for alternative minimum tax purposes. It is therefore only a beginning; its beneficial effects may easily be thwarted by the incoherence of the mechanical structure of the Code as a whole. In a first-best ability-to-pay system, all costs of producing income would be deductible in addition to, not in place of, the standard deduction for regular tax purposes and would be fully deductible for alternative minimum tax purposes (if any such tax continued to exist).

CONCLUSION

Tax provisions of particular relevance to people with disabilities pose serious challenges to both disability and tax theory. The problem for disability theorists is that many of the most important such provisions were originally justified by reference to the now-rejected medical/charity paradigm and are inconsistent with a strict civil rights approach. As a practical matter, such provisions remain profoundly important to people with disabilities. Fortunately, the most important such provisions can be reframed in a manner consistent with the new human variation paradigm of disability.

The challenge for mainstream tax theory is much more severe. Mainstream tax theory has always assumed that taxpayers are identical except with respect to income and family status. It is precisely this assumption that the human variation paradigm of disability contests. Wholly apart from any such theoretical disagreement, the reality of disability itself strains this assumption to the breaking point. A quadriplegic's decision to hire a personal assistant to help with bathing and personal hygiene cannot credibly be characterized as just another consumption choice, normatively indistinguishable from a decision to throw a big party. Our moral intuitions, reflected in the expansive modern medical expense deduction, tell us that at equivalent income levels the quadriplegic simply cannot afford to contribute as much to the costs of government as a taxpayer who can bathe and care for herself without assistance.

At the core of these intuitions lies a sense that a taxpayer's ability to pay really does matter. It may be that, as tax theorists have asserted repeatedly over the decades, ability to pay lacks the precision we would prefer in a guiding moral principle. Be that as it may, the vast majority of Americans continues to believe it relevant. If tax theory is to be useful, rather than merely "correct" in some academic sense, it has to at least nod in the direction of the electorate's notions of fairness.

We believe it impossible to give a coherent account of tax provisions of particular relevance to people with disabilities without explicitly considering ability to pay. If others disagree, we look forward to reading their competing accounts. More generally, our account of the history of the tension between standard tax theory and popular moral intuitions leads us to conclude that until those tensions are resolved, tax theorists are as likely to contribute to our tax system's incoherence as to resolve it.

Enabling Work for People with Disabilities:
A Post-Integrationist Revision of
Underutilized Tax Incentives

FRANCINE J. LIPMAN[1]

There are 54,000,000 Americans with disabilities, millions of whom long to work. Yet people with disabilities unfailingly have had the highest rate of unemployment among all minority groups in America. For more than a decade, the unemployment rate for people with disabilities has been at staggering levels, ranging from 66% to 75%. Given this high rate of unemployment, it is not surprising that one-third of all people with disabilities have annual household incomes of $15,000 or less and are three times more likely to live in poverty than people without disabilities.

Federal employment initiatives for people with disabilities do not seem to be working. Scholars argue that the [Americans with Disabilities Act (ADA)] and similar legislation that exemplify the disability theory of "integrationism,"[2] with the goal of integrating people with disabilities into mainstream employment, cannot succeed. Barriers to employment for people with disabilities cannot be eradicated simply by the modest integrationist approach of reasonable accommodation. A "post-integrationist" approach[3] may be required to provide legitimate equal employment opportunities for people with disabilities.

POST-INTEGRATIONISM

Post-integrationism evolves from the critical limits of integrationism. Integrationism embodied in antidiscrimination legislation and reasonable accommodation has not resulted in equality for people with disabilities. Post-integrationism proposes more aggressive measures to fulfill the promises of the ADA based on the following principles.

"Strategic Essentialism"[4]

Like many oppressed minorities, people with disabilities should encourage each other to reaffirm, celebrate, and explore their unique identity and culture. People

---

[1] Reprinted by permission from 53 *American University Law Review* 393 (2003).

[2] Jacobus tenBroek & Floyd W. Matson, *The Disabled and the Law of Welfare*, 54 CAL. L. REV. 809, 815 (1966).

[3] Mark C. Weber, *Disability and the Law of Welfare: A Post-Integrationist Examination*, 2000 U. ILL. L. REV. 889, 915–19.

[4] *Id.* at 914.

with disabilities must affirm their equal citizenship and demand equal rights, not because the disabled deserve pity, and not because they have sufficiently blended into mainstream society in order to achieve some level of success, but because the American ideal of equality demands such treatment.

People with disabilities must openly affirm their unique identity as different from the mainstream to facilitate them in organizing politically and demanding specialized treatment based upon this difference. The ADA's treatment of disability as a private matter that confidentiality provisions protect is inconsistent with post-integrationism principles.

Due to the uniqueness of people with disabilities, specialized treatment beyond simple integration and reasonable accommodation is necessary to equalize the rights and well-being of those with and without disabilities. People with disabilities deserve equal benefits, not merely access. Under integrationism, people with disabilities must adapt to the "normal," nondisabled world with only reasonable accommodations. This approach has not resulted in increased mainstream employment for people with disabilities. Specialized treatment is necessary to provide people with disabilities as a group sufficient power to end their disadvantaged status. Under post-integrationism, society would respond to the needs of people with disabilities and redefine the norm to adapt it to each unique and essential person. As a result, a person with a disability would not bear the burden of adapting to an existing nondisabled norm, but would define an individualized, unique norm. The world would be reshaped to ensure that within this norm, a person with a disability would enjoy equal benefits rather than merely an equal opportunity to access the nondisabled norm. This approach focuses on the specialized treatment that each person requires to receive equal benefits rather than adapting all people to a preconceived norm for equal opportunity. Post-integrationists do recognize, however, that specialized treatment for people with disabilities comes at a significant cost.

Costs of Disability Should Be Borne by Society

If society is dedicated to the emancipation of people with disabilities, post-integrationists argue that the financial costs must be shifted from people with disabilities to society as a whole. Society has exacerbated the cost of disabilities by creating inaccessible communities and fostering intolerance and discrimination; now, society must pay the full price of undoing its damage. To achieve legitimate, equal opportunity for people with disabilities, society "must eliminate the cost-based incentives to discriminate by funding reasonable accommodations fully."[5] In addition to the altruistic desire to provide equal rights for citizens, public funding for these costs provides social insurance for anyone who, at any moment, could become disabled.

---

[5] Scott A. Moss & Daniel A. Malin, *Public Funding for Disability Accommodations: A Rational Solution to Rational Discrimination and the Disabilities of the ADA*, 33 Harv. C.R.-C.L. L. Rev. 197, 221–26 (1998).

Move to Interdependence and Balancing Relationships Among All People

Full funding for accommodations and other special treatment for people with disabilities would reduce lawsuits that poison relationships and present other serious deficiencies for enforcing antidiscrimination laws. Integrationism promotes individual enforcement of civil rights, which may not be asserted "because of ignorance, irrational fear, or well-founded reluctance to disrupt existing relationships with those who have power over them."[6] Achieving equality is not simply litigating discrimination claims or promoting integration. It requires "identifying the relationships that affect the well-being of persons with disabilities, examining the justice of the relationships, and modifying them to increase social choices and balance power among the persons involved."[7] Post-integrationists emphasize balancing relationships among all people rather than focusing on the competing rights of people with disabilities and people without disabilities.

TAX INCENTIVES DESIGNED TO MOTIVATE EMPLOYERS TO ACCOMMODATE EMPLOYEES WITH DISABILITIES

Barrier Removal Deduction

Congress enacted the barrier removal deduction in 1976 "to encourage the more rapid modification of business facilities and vehicles to overcome widespread barriers that hampered the involvement of people with disabilities and the elderly in economic, social and cultural activities."[8] This tax provision allows taxpayers to immediately expense and deduct rather than capitalize and depreciate, over an extended time period, qualified architectural and transportation barrier removal expenses. For purposes of this tax provision, the Code defines architectural and transportation barrier removal expenses as expenditures "for the purpose of making any facility or public transportation vehicle owned or leased by the taxpayer for use in connection with his trade or business more accessible to, and usable by, handicapped and elderly individuals."[9] "Qualified" architectural and transportation barrier removal expenses must meet standards promulgated by the Secretary and the Architectural and Transportation Barriers Compliance Board as described in Treasury Regulations. The Treasury Regulations describe in great technical detail twenty-one facility and public transportation conformity requirements. Expenses incurred to remove a barrier so that facilities or public transportation conform to one or more of the enumerated requirements are qualified architectural and transportation barrier removal expenses. Any expenses incurred "in connection with the construction or comprehensive renovation of a facility or public transportation vehicle or the normal replacement of depreciable property"[10] are not allowed as qualifying expenses.

---

[6] Weber, *supra* note 3, at 906.

[7] *Id.* at 918.

[8] U.S. GEN. ACCOUNTING OFFICE, BUSINESS TAX INCENTIVES: INCENTIVES TO EMPLOY WORKERS WITH DISABILITIES RECEIVE LIMITED USE AND HAVE AN UNCERTAIN IMPACT 7 (2002).

[9] Treas. Reg. § 1.190-2(a)(4).

[10] *Id.* § 1.190-2(b)(1).

When the barrier removal deduction was enacted in 1976, it was limited to $25,000 of qualified expenditures per tax year. For tax years beginning after December 31, 1983, the barrier removal deduction limit was increased to $35,000 per tax year. Any qualifying expenditures in excess of the deduction limit must be capitalized and depreciated over the applicable recovery period. On November 5, 1990, three months after Congress enacted the ADA, Congress reduced the maximum amount of the barrier removal deduction to $15,000 and enacted the disabled access credit.

Disabled Access Credit

The disabled access credit provides qualifying small businesses with an election to receive a 50% tax credit for "eligible access expenditures."[11] A tax credit is a dollar for dollar reduction of a taxpayer's tax liability. Accordingly, a tax credit generally provides a greater economic benefit than a tax deduction. The disabled access credit is one of numerous tax credits comprising the general business credit. The general business credit is a nonrefundable tax credit that offsets a taxpayer's regular income tax liability after certain adjustments to, but not below, zero. If a taxpayer does not have any current regular tax liability, she may benefit from her disabled access credit (as included in her general business credit) through a tax credit carry-back to a past tax year or a carry-forward to future tax years.

The disabled access credit is limited to $5,000 or 50% of up to $10,000 of eligible access expenditures in excess of the first $250 of expenses per tax year. Eligible access expenditures include "amounts paid or incurred by an eligible small business for the purpose of enabling such eligible small business to comply with applicable requirements under the ADA."[12] The Code further defines "eligible access expenditures" to include reasonable amounts incurred to (1) provide qualified interpreters, readers, or other effective methods of communicating with visually or hearing impaired individuals; (2) to acquire or modify equipment, devices, materials, or services for individuals with disabilities; or (3) remove "architectural, communication, physical, or transportation barriers which prevent a business from being accessible to, or usable by, individuals with disabilities."[13] In addition, and consistent with the barrier removal deduction, qualifying expenditures must not be in connection with new construction and must meet standards agreed to by the Architectural and Transportation Barriers Compliance Board as set forth in the Treasury Regulations.

Notably, only qualified small businesses are eligible for the credit. The Code provides that qualified small businesses are defined as businesses with gross receipts of $1,000,000 or less for the preceding tax year, or businesses employing thirty or fewer full-time employees during the preceding tax year.

In 1999, an irrelevantly tiny percentage of taxpayers, one out of every 686 corporations and one out of every 1,570 individuals with a business affiliation, reported the disabled access credit on their tax returns. The [General Accounting Office

---

[11] I.R.C. § 44(a).
[12] *Id.* § 44(c)(1).
[13] *Id.* § 44(c)(2).

(GAO)] interviewed representatives from business, government, and disability groups, as well as scholars and tax preparers, on the usage and effectiveness of the accommodation tax provisions. These interviews identified two primary barriers to increasing the use of the accommodation tax credits, including unfamiliarity with these incentives and misconceptions regarding the difficulty involved in qualifying for them. The general lack of familiarity with these incentives was the most frequently cited reason for their infrequent use.

Redesigning the Accommodation Tax Provisions

The most frequently cited reason for underutilization of the accommodation tax provisions was a lack of awareness of their existence. Consistent with the post-integrationist principle that people with disabilities must affirm their equal status, people with disabilities individually and in organized groups must take an active role in generating awareness of these incentives. A number of government guides describing these tax incentives are currently available; disability advocacy groups and their partners should make these guides readily available to people with disabilities so that they may deliver them directly to hiring and other human resource managers during the interviewing process. People with disabilities must proclaim their unique identity and demand specialized treatment.

Complexity and lack of clarity was another criticism noted by the GAO[,] especially regarding the disabled access credit. Simplification of these provisions should increase usage. If these tax provisions are simplified, people with disabilities and their employers can better understand, promote, implement, and enjoy the intended benefits. Moreover, if the tax provisions are simplified, they will be more transparent and misperceptions regarding their burden on businesses should be reduced. To accomplish this goal, the two rather cumbersome accommodation tax provisions will be redesigned as one simplified tax credit, in the form of the new expanded disabled access credit. In addition to combining the two provisions into one streamlined tax credit, the new credit will provide tax benefits using preexisting definitions from the ADA rather than by supplementing and qualifying these existing definitions and adding unnecessary complexity and confusion. Finally, the revised disabled access credit must not be burdensome for employers to claim. Similar to the old disabled access credit and the barrier removal deduction, the revised disabled access credit will require nothing more than claiming the tax credit annually on the IRS tax form. The amount of the credit claimed, however, must be increased.

A primary post-integrationist principle is that society, and not people with disabilities, should bear the costs of providing equal benefits for people with disabilities. Based on this principle, the new access credit will be enhanced to reach all employers covered under the ADA. Moreover, any accommodations that employers must make to reasonably accommodate potential and current employees with disabilities under the ADA will qualify as "eligible access expenditures" without any dollar limit. Finally, the new disabled access credit will not be limited to the amount of a taxpayer's tax liability. The new credit will be a refundable tax credit.

The expansion, enhancement, and simplification of the new disabled access tax credit should reduce ADA accommodation litigation, because employers will know that the government will compensate them for making the necessary accommodations. Reduced litigation should facilitate the building, rather than the destruction, of enabling relationships between employers and employees. In addition, businesses will no longer be motivated to offer inadequate accommodations or pass the cost of accommodations onto employees with disabilities. Most importantly, employers will no longer have a financial incentive not to hire people with disabilities. Consequently, the relationship between employees with disabilities and employers will be more balanced, with power shifting from employers to employees, and affording employees with disabilities more social choices and opportunities in mainstream society.

EXPANSION OF THE EITC – A POST-INTEGRATIONIST APPROACH

Congress enacted the [earned income tax credit (EITC)] in 1975 to ensure that poverty-level individuals who work do not pay any federal income or payroll taxes. While most of these individuals do not pay any federal income tax because of their low income levels, they are subject to regressive Social Security payroll taxes. The EITC reimburses Social Security payroll taxes paid by low-income workers with a refundable tax credit. The EITC generally provides a cash tax refund for working poor families.

Most notably, through the EITC, Congress has created a significant incentive to work. The EITC increases the value of work for low-income individuals, especially for individuals who are unemployed. The EITC is the largest and most successful welfare-work program, enjoying broad bipartisan support. In addition to being cost-effective, such cash transfers promote the dignity and sense of equality of the recipient.

Given the staggering rate of unemployment among people with disabilities, the EITC should provide significant motivation to unemployed people with disabilities to work. However, the current structure of the EITC likely results in *de minimis* work incentives for people with disabilities. Workers with and without disabilities are eligible for the EITC if they satisfy certain earned and other income level requirements. In addition, while the EITC is available to persons with or without a qualifying child, the benefits provided to persons without a qualifying child are extraordinarily less than the benefits provided to persons with one or more qualifying children. Accordingly, low-income workers with and without disabilities without qualifying children receive little or no motivation to work under the EITC. Indeed, many low-income workers with disabilities are motivated not to work.

Persons with disabilities who desire to work face daily barriers including humiliating discrimination in a society designed for and controlled by able-bodied people. Some of these work disincentives are economic, such as heightened work costs; diminished earning capacity; [and] loss of [Supplemental Security Income (SSI)], Medicaid, and other government benefits as earned income levels increase. These significant economic disincentives to work are unique to people with disabilities and rationally discourage any motivation to work. However, work provides the opportunity for self-sufficiency through wages, a productive role in society, enhanced self-esteem and self-worth, order, sources of friendship, and social support. The EITC must be expanded for people with disabilities to offset their significant disincentives to work and open the door to mainstream society.

Because of the uniqueness of people with disabilities, specialized treatment beyond simple integration and reasonable accommodation is required to equalize the rights and well-being of those with and without disabilities. People with disabilities deserve equal benefits, including the benefits of work. The cash EITC work incentives currently available to workers with disabilities must be enhanced to offset the significant disincentive costs of work borne by people with disabilities.

The expanded EITC will provide an enhanced incentive to individuals with "disabilities" as such term is defined under the ADA. This modification, which is consistent with the modifications made to the new disabled access credit[,] provides uniformity and should facilitate promotion and outreach. Most people with disabilities are well aware of the ADA and its definition of disability. The IRS has a significant outreach and education program for the EITC targeting the working poor. These existing programs could incorporate and be used to highlight the expanded EITC for people with disabilities.

The expanded EITC will shift some of the additional costs of work from people with disabilities to society. Society has exacerbated the cost of disabilities by creating inaccessible communities and fostering intolerance and discrimination; now society must pay the full price of undoing its damage. The expanded EITC is intended to reimburse people with disabilities for some or all of their additional costs of working.

EITC benefits will be enhanced for individuals with disabilities by modifying how they are characterized for purposes of qualifying for and determining the amount of their credit. The structure of the EITC will be modified so that for purposes of the EITC an individual with a disability will be deemed to have at least one qualifying child in addition to any actual qualifying children. As a result, more people with disabilities will qualify for the EITC and their EITC benefits will be increased.

In addition to mitigating disincentives for workers with disabilities, the expanded EITC may motivate people with disabilities to move from autonomy to interdependence. People with disabilities will be required to obtain a certificate from a designated local agency evidencing their disability status. While the certificate requirement may seem onerous, it will be structured in such a manner as to ensure that the process is administratively practicable and acceptable for people with disabilities, designated local agencies, and other relevant government agencies. The certification process is intended to emancipate and not compromise people with disabilities. People with disabilities routinely interact with government agencies. For those people with disabilities who are not familiar with these agencies, they should benefit from being motivated to work with government agencies that may provide assistance above and beyond the eligibility certificate. Most importantly, the certificate should deter IRS audits or litigation over perceived EITC fraud.

SOCIETAL BENEFITS VERSUS SOCIETAL COSTS

Society benefits if people with disabilities work. Society spends at least $120 billion in annual costs supporting individuals with disabilities. If people with disabilities work, studies show that taxpayer burdens are decreased and the national economy is enhanced. Increased employment translates into increased consumer spending and tax revenues.

An integrated workplace promotes innovation and efficiency. The accommodation of workers with disabilities benefits all members of society by providing progressive goods for public use and consumption. Efficiency-enhancing technologies developed for people with disabilities can be used by all employees to enhance the workplace experience and bottom line.

Society benefits from the employment of people with disabilities through economic benefits realized by tapping a vast, determined, and dedicated labor pool. Quantitative data, surveys, and anecdotal accounts evidence that workers with disabilities have lower turnover and absenteeism rates, higher productivity, and greater dedication, resulting in economic savings in recruitment, training, and replacement expenses.

Society benefits from valuing the identity achieved from productivity versus one achieved from "being excused from productivity."[14] Enabling work for people with disabilities will bring all members of society rich quantitative and qualitative rewards.

---

[14] Michael Ashley Stein, *Labor Markets, Rationality, and Workers with Disabilities*, 21 BERKELEY J. EMP. & LAB. L. 314, 327 (2000).

Disability and the Income Tax

DAVID G. DUFF[1]

In recent years, federal, provincial, and territorial governments have devoted increasing attention to the status of disabled Canadians, emphasizing the integration of disabled persons as equal citizens within the broader community through policies designed to promote equal access to generic programs and services, while simultaneously recognizing the need for specific measures to address the costs of disabilities, to facilitate participation by disabled persons in the paid labor force, and to provide income support for disabled persons who have difficulty supporting themselves.

With respect to persons with disabilities, the [Canadian] Income Tax Act [(ITA)] recognizes the costs of disabilities through credits for itemized medical expenses ("medical expense tax credit") and for mental or physical impairment ("disability tax credit"). Other provisions recognize additional costs associated with the care of disabled relatives by providing credits for infirm dependents over the age of eighteen ("infirm dependents credit"), and for specified relatives living in an individual's home who are over the age of eighteen and dependent on the individual because of mental or physical infirmity ("caregiver credit"); additional provisions encourage private savings to support disabled persons through special tax rules for inter vivos trusts with disabled beneficiaries. Participation by disabled persons in the paid labor force is facilitated by exempting specified disability-related employment benefits from tax, by allowing individuals eligible for the disability tax credit to deduct the cost of attendant care provided to enable them to participate in the paid labor force, by compensating disabled individuals who participate in the paid labor force for lost subsidies for disability-related supports under provincial social assistance, and by permitting employers to claim an immediate deduction for prescribed disability-related modifications to buildings and prescribed disability-related equipment. Finally, income support for disabled persons is encouraged by nontaxation of employer contributions to group sickness or accident insurance plans, and enhanced by nontaxation of social assistance benefits, workers' compensation, and tort compensation for personal injuries.

Notwithstanding these many provisions, however, the pursuit of disability-related policies through the income tax appears to reflect a series of ad hoc

[1] Reprinted by permission from 45 *McGill Law Journal* 797 (2000).

adjustments rather than a comprehensive approach to the income tax treatment of disabled individuals and families with disabled persons. Nor are these provisions always consistent with their primary rationale to promote horizontal equity between individuals with and without disabilities and between persons who support disabled individuals and persons without such support obligations.

This paper reviews and evaluates current income tax provisions and possible reforms relevant to families with disabled persons, with the goals of better recognizing the impact of disabilities on appropriate tax liabilities and bringing a greater degree of coherence to current income tax provisions bearing on families with disabled persons.

TAX POLICY AND SOCIAL POLICY

As one of the most significant policy instruments available to the federal government, it is not surprising that the ITA might be used to pursue a variety of social policy objectives. Indeed, to the extent that a progressive income tax is designed to collect a larger proportionate share of revenue from high-income taxpayers than lower-income taxpayers and exempt those with very low incomes, the tax itself can be said to serve a broad social policy objective of moderating inequalities in the pre-tax distribution of income.

Nonetheless, in reviewing the characteristics of an optimal tax system, commentators generally distinguish between broad social policy goals regarding the appropriate allocation and distribution of economic resources, and the aims of tax policy more narrowly defined to raise revenue in a manner that is equitable among different taxpayers, that minimizes unintended effects on economic decisions, and that is relatively easy to understand and collect. Among those writing in the area, these [narrower] tax policy goals are referred to as equity, efficiency, and simplicity.

With respect to the income tax, efficiency considerations tend to favor a broad definition of income and relatively low rates to minimize tax-induced distortions in economic behavior, while simplicity concerns favor a relatively straightforward and uniform set of rules to minimize the cost of administering the tax (involving government collection costs and the costs of taxpayer compliance). While some equity objectives are consistent with these efficiency and simplicity goals, others may contradict economic efficiency and administrative simplicity by supporting higher tax rates at higher income levels or special allowances to account for relevant differences in taxpayers' personal circumstances. As a result, like other areas of government policy, tax policy may involve difficult choices among different and conflicting policy goals.

When considering issues of tax equity, commentators generally distinguish between horizontal and vertical equity. According to the former principle, taxpayers with the same ability to pay tax should pay the same amount of tax. According to the latter principle, taxpayers with a greater ability to pay tax should pay an appropriately greater amount of tax. In the context of the income tax, horizontal equity considerations apply to the definition of the tax base, while questions of vertical equity concern the rate structure.

Although the elaboration of these abstract tax policy principles in the actual design of a specific income tax is by no means uncontroversial, horizontal equity is often said to favor a broad or comprehensive definition of income, while vertical equity is said to favor graduated or progressive rates which impose a proportionately higher tax burden at higher income levels. In computing the income that is subject to progressive tax rates, however, commentators generally agree that horizontal equity requires that taxpayers be allowed to deduct all costs that are necessary to obtain this income. Moreover, to the extent that a taxpayer's ability to pay is further diminished by various involuntary expenses (e.g., various disability-related expenses), it is arguable that horizontal equity also requires that taxpayers be permitted to deduct these expenses in computing the income that is properly subject to tax. Where the income tax base is determined in this manner, progressive rates ensure that taxpayers with more discretionary income pay a proportionately larger share of this income in tax.

In contrast to these tax policy goals narrowly defined, social policy addresses broader questions concerning the manner in which goods and services are allocated and economic resources distributed among members of a political community. Taking disability-related expenses as an example, social policy is concerned less with the deductibility of these expenses in computing an individual's taxable income than with the extent to which the additional costs incurred by persons with mental or physical disabilities are properly borne by the disabled person and/or supporting individuals, or by the community as a whole. Likewise, where a disability affects a person's ability to participate in the paid labor force, social policy is concerned less with the tax implications for supporting individuals or the deductibility of additional expenses that the disabled person must incur in order to earn income than with the respective roles of the private or public sectors in providing for the individual's support and with the implementation of effective measures designed to make the workplace more accessible to persons with disabilities.

These social policy goals can be and often are pursued through the ITA. Where a social policy decision is made to insure half of all disability-related expenses, for example, this policy may be effected through a refundable tax credit equal to 50% of all eligible expenses. Likewise, where a social policy decision is made to provide a guaranteed annual income to persons with disabilities, this policy may be implemented through a refundable tax credit the value of which diminishes as the recipient's income increases. Similarly, investments in disability-related equipment or modifications to a workplace may be encouraged by accelerated deductions or tax credits (refundable or nonrefundable) through which these costs are shared by the public sector.

Where social policy goals are pursued through the ITA, however, neither they nor the provisions by which they are implemented should be regarded as alternatives to tax policy goals more narrowly defined. Where a social policy decision is made to reimburse 50% of all privately borne disability-related expenses through a refundable tax credit, for example, a tax policy issue remains as to whether disability-related expenses that are not reimbursed are properly deductible in computing the payor's taxable income. Correspondingly, where a refundable tax credit is paid to low-income persons with disabilities, tax policy considerations continue to apply in comparing the ability to pay of higher income individuals with or without disabilities.

Conversely, while tax policy considerations are central to the equitable distribution of income tax burdens among different taxpayers, neither they nor the basic provisions through which an equitable income tax is applied can substitute for the broader social policy goals that might also be pursued through the ITA. Indeed, where the income tax provides a deduction or nonrefundable credit to recognize privately borne disability-related expenses, this allowance is irrelevant to individuals whose income is too low to pay any tax. As a result, although such a provision may be necessary to achieve horizontal equity among different taxpayers, it is neither an effective nor equitable method of reimbursing a share of privately borne disability-related expenses, nor a coherent way to provide income support to low-income individuals with disabilities or low-income families with disabled persons.

THE COSTS OF DISABILITY

As the Standing Committee on Human Rights and the Status of Disabled Persons has emphasized, "Disability involves costs – to governments and society as a whole, but most importantly, to disabled persons themselves."[2] For families with disabled persons, these costs are also borne by supporting individuals – both directly in the form of out-of-pocket expenses and indirectly in the form of foregone income attributable to time lost from employment or business activities in order to care for the disabled person. While these costs are partly covered through a variety of public and private programs, including social assistance, worker's compensation, public health care, and supplementary health insurance, uncompensated costs are necessarily borne by disabled individuals and their families. It is these privately borne costs that give rise to tax policy issues.

Medical Expenses Tax Credit

The medical expenses tax credit ("METC") provides a credit against basic federal tax otherwise payable equal to 17% of eligible medical expenses paid during any twelve-month period ending in the taxation year exceeding the lesser of 3% of the individual's net income or $1,637.35. Taking provincial income tax into account, the combined value of this credit for taxpayers with tax otherwise payable is roughly 25¢ for each dollar of eligible medical expenses exceeding the applicable threshold.

For the purposes of this provision, eligible medical expenses must be proven by filing receipts, and are limited to expenses in respect of specifically defined goods and services provided to the individual, the individual's spouse, or a related dependent (the "patient"). In applying these provisions, the courts have tended to adopt a more liberal approach than the strict method of interpretation traditionally employed. In one case, for example, the Tax Court of Canada adopted a broad

---

[2] Standing Comm. on Human Rights and the Status of Disabled Persons, As True as Taxes: Disability and the Income Tax System, in House of Commons Debates 3 (March 1993).

interpretation of the word "care" in order to permit the taxpayer to claim as eligible medical expenses tuition and other fees paid by the taxpayer to a private school for the "care and training" of his learning-disabled children. In other cases, courts have allowed taxpayers to claim the cost of a hot tub, whirlpool equipment, and a security alert system as eligible medical expenses on the basis that they constituted reasonable expenses relating to renovations or alterations to a dwelling. Notwithstanding this general tendency toward a more liberal interpretation of the METC, at least some decisions continue to reflect a narrow reading of the statutory provisions.

In evaluating the METC, critics have questioned the name of the credit, the definition of eligible expenses, the structure and existence of the threshold, the 1988 conversion of the previous deduction into a credit, the rate at which the credit is computed, and its nonrefundability. With respect to the name of the credit, critics have suggested that the METC be renamed "to make it clearer that disability-related items are included."[3] Indeed, since many of the items added to the list of eligible expenses over the last fifteen years have included disability-related expenses (e.g., home renovations, van purchases and modifications, sign-language services, and various devices to assist visually or hearing impaired individuals), it is arguable that the primary purpose of the credit has evolved from recognizing extraordinary medical expenses to recognizing both extraordinary and recurring costs associated with physical or mental disabilities. For this reason, as several commentators have suggested, it seems both appropriate and desirable to rename the credit the "medical and disability expenses tax credit."

Regarding the definition of eligible medical expenses, some commentators have questioned the restriction on allowable expenses to those incurred for goods and services provided only to the individual, his or her spouse, and a related dependent. Although it might be argued that tax recognition for such expenses should be limited to goods and services provided only to the individual taxpayer and others whom the taxpayer has a legal obligation to support (e.g., spouses and dependent children) on the basis that only these expenses are truly involuntary, the ITA currently recognizes expenses incurred for goods and services provided to grandchildren, parents, grandparents, siblings, aunts and uncles, and nieces and nephews, provided that the recipient of the good or service is "dependent on the individual for support" at any time in the year. Having thus expanded the scope of allowable expenses, it is difficult to understand why it should not be further extended to include payments for goods and services provided to anyone who is dependent on the individual for support at any time in the year, whether the person is a close or distant relative or simply a friend.

While many additions [to the list of allowable expenses] would improve the METC, the number of items on this list and the regular additions to the list of eligible expenses since the medical expense deduction was first introduced in 1942 suggest a more general concern that changes in technology and prescribed therapies are certain to lead to the emergence of comparable items that are not contemplated within the existing categories. For this reason, it might be appropriate

---

[3] COUNCIL OF CANADIANS WITH DISABILITIES, TAX REFORM POSITIONS 6 (1999).

to supplement the categorical list with a general statement of principle according to which eligible medical expenses would include all reasonable amounts to the extent that they are paid for the purpose of acquiring goods or services certified as medically necessary by a qualified medical practitioner.

In relation to the threshold on eligible expenses in the year (expressed as 3% of the individual's net income or $1,637, whichever is lower), a number of concerns have been raised. First, to the extent that the dollar amount caps the net income threshold for individuals with net incomes exceeding $54,567, the structure of the threshold has been rightly criticized as regressive, allowing a larger share of medical expenses as a percentage of net income to be claimed by high-income taxpayers than by low-income taxpayers. From this perspective, a possible reform might be to eliminate the dollar limit on the net income threshold, using the revenue saved from this amendment to finance other disability-related tax reforms. Moreover, one should not forget that the primary purpose of the original deduction was to recognize catastrophic medical expenses incurred by otherwise relatively healthy individuals, not the ongoing costs associated with a prolonged disability. While an annual threshold is ideally suited for the former purpose, it is entirely inappropriate for the latter. To the extent, therefore, that the primary purpose of the METC has evolved from recognizing a limited number of extraordinary medical expenses to recognizing both extraordinary and recurring costs associated with mental or physical disabilities, it is arguable that the existing threshold should be eliminated altogether.

With respect to the 1988 conversion of the deduction into a credit, commentators have taken different positions. To the extent that the provision is designed to recognize the reduced ability to pay of individuals who must incur extraordinary medical expenses, some have argued that a deduction in computing taxable income is a more appropriate measure than a credit computed at a flat rate of 17%. Others, noting that deductions are worth more to high-income taxpayers than to low-income taxpayers[,] are more favorably inclined to the 1988 reforms but nevertheless criticize the current nonrefundable credit on the grounds that it is of little or no value to low-income taxpayers, among whom disabled individuals are statistically overrepresented. Yet others have criticized the rate of the credit, suggesting that it be increased from its current rate of 17% to 30% or more.

To the extent that medical and disability-related expenses are not fully reimbursed, the tax policy issue more narrowly defined concerns the manner and extent to which these privately borne costs should be taken into account in determining the individual's tax liability. While deductions are often criticized on the basis that they are worth more to high-income taxpayers than they are to low-income taxpayers, this argument assumes that the income tax should apply not to the discretionary income that remains after deducting involuntary expenses (such as medical and disability-related expenses), but to net income from various sources without taking into account the personal circumstances of the individual taxpayer. A deduction for extraordinary medical expenses (and arguably a separate deduction for necessary costs associated with a prolonged mental or physical disability) may be justified as a necessary measure to achieve horizontal equity among taxpayers with different involuntary expenses. Although a nonrefundable credit equal to the lowest marginal rate of tax might be justified on the grounds that medical and disability-related expenses are entirely involuntary for low-income taxpayers and increasingly discretionary for taxpayers subject to tax at higher rates, it is implausible that discretionary and nondiscretionary aspects of these expenses are perfectly correlated with the rate schedule.

Having defined this tax policy objective, it is important to emphasize that it cannot take the place of broader social policy goals that might also be pursued through the ITA. To the extent that that the federal government considers it desirable to assume a larger or more direct role in the reimbursement of medical or disability-related expenses than it currently does through the Canada Health and Social Transfer, a refundable tax credit might be appropriate for this purpose. In addition or as an alternative to such a measure, the federal government might provide direct income support to low-income individuals with disabilities or low-income families with disabled children through a refundable tax credit the value of which diminishes as the income of the individual or family increases. In either case, however, these social policy objectives and the tax measures through which they might be implemented should be distinguished from the more narrow tax policy goals supporting a deduction for extraordinary medical expenses and disability-related expenses.

CHAPTER 11. GLOBAL CRITICAL PERSPECTIVES
ON TAXATION

As previous chapters of this book evidence, critical tax perspectives are not unique to the United States. This chapter adds another dimension to the international application of critical tax perspectives by demonstrating their relevance to cross-border tax issues. The relevance of critical perspectives to cross-border tax issues should come as no surprise, because what is commonly referred to as "international tax" is not really a separate and distinct set of tax rules. Rather, it is more akin to an overlay that must be placed on top of the generally applicable rules in the Code – which have been addressed at length in all of the previous chapters of this book.

In international tax parlance, cross-border issues generally fall into one of two categories: inbound and outbound. "Inbound" refers to situations where non-U.S. persons come to (or engage in transactions in) the United States, and "outbound" refers to situations where U.S. persons go (or engage in transactions) abroad. The contributions to this chapter have been grouped together in keeping with this common division of cross-border tax issues.

The first three contributions to this chapter concern what might be termed "inbound" situations. In *Toward a Global Critical Feminist Vision: Domestic Work and the Nanny Tax Debate*, Taunya Lovell Banks begins with an examination of the "nanny tax" debate that followed Zoe Baird's failed nomination for U.S. Attorney General by President Clinton in 1992. Baird withdrew from consideration after it came to light that she had failed to pay Social Security taxes for her live-in child-care worker, who was an undocumented immigrant. Nonetheless, as Banks demonstrates, the plight of undocumented child-care workers, whose vulnerability is too often exploited by their employers, was nearly invisible in the "nanny tax" debate. Banks argues that feminists missed an important opportunity here to engage in a meaningful dialogue about undervalued and underregulated domestic labor.

In *The Taxation of Undocumented Immigrants: Separate, Unequal, and Without Representation*, Francine Lipman describes another ramification of undocumented workers' invisibility, namely, the separate and unequal tax regime that applies to them. As Lipman indicates, despite lacking a voice in government, undocumented workers are subject to U.S. federal income tax on their worldwide income. They are also required to pay payroll taxes on their wages even though they lack access to Social Security benefits. In addition, in computing their federal income tax liability, those with families are often relegated to "married filing separately" status, which causes them to pay more tax than they would under other filing statuses. Furthermore, notwithstanding the general consensus that low-income working families should not pay income or payroll taxes, undocumented immigrants are generally denied access to the earned income tax credit and are only afforded meaningful payroll tax relief under the child tax credit under narrow circumstances.

Rounding out the "inbound" contributions to this chapter, Anthony Infanti explores the radical potential of international tax in *Prying Open the Closet Door: The Defense of Marriage Act and Tax Treaties*. Infanti argues that the same-sex marriages of couples from Belgium, Canada, the Netherlands, and Spain must all be recognized for U.S. tax purposes. Infanti explains how each of the income tax treaties concluded by the United States with these countries contains a "nondiscrimination" clause that requires same-sex couples' marriages to be recognized for federal – and, in some cases, even state – tax purposes. He also explains why the federal Defense of Marriage Act does not override the treaty nondiscrimination clauses under the later-in-time rule that generally governs conflicts between statutes and treaty provisions.

The first of two "outbound" contributions to this chapter is *Missing Africa: Should U.S. International Tax Rules Accommodate Investment in Developing Countries?* In this piece, Karen Brown proposes that the United States enter into tax treaties with sub-Saharan African nations that would create a narrowly tailored territorial system of taxation. This would entail a shift from the current residence-based system of taxation, under which U.S. residents are taxed on their worldwide income – no matter where it is earned – subject to a foreign tax credit for foreign taxes paid. Under the territorial approach, U.S. persons would not pay any U.S. tax on prescribed income from the African treaty countries, and would only pay the (lower) taxes imposed by the African nations themselves. The treaties would also contain built-in safeguards for the African nations, including provisions regarding required labor practices and environmental protections. Brown argues that her treaty proposal would more effectively draw U.S. investment to Africa and provide more of a benefit to African nations than current aid initiatives.

Finally, in *Global Trajectories of Tax Reform: The Discourse of Tax Reform in Developing and Transition Countries*, Miranda Stewart examines and critiques the role of developed country governments, international institutions (which are often controlled by developed countries), and tax experts (again, from developed countries) in tax reform projects in developing and transition countries. Stewart describes how the international institutions and tax experts have reached what she terms a "remarkable consensus" about the appropriate tax reforms for developing and transition countries. This remarkable consensus has led to cookie-cutter advice and mass-produced tax reform that is not tailored to the needs or culture of these countries. Stewart then dissects the tax reform discourse to show how that discourse (1) posits a linear development that naturally (and only) leads to a tax system patterned after those of developed countries; (2) generally ignores the continuing failure of tax reform projects and elides discussion of how the reformers might be contributing to the propensity of their own projects to fail; and (3) has moved decidedly away from a focus on inequality, poverty, and the possibility of effecting redistribution of wealth through the tax system. Stewart raises the need for developed country tax reformers to take into consideration the social, political, legal, and cultural context of the developing and transition countries that they purport to help.

Toward a Global Critical Feminist Vision: Domestic Work and the Nanny Tax Debate

TAUNYA LOVELL BANKS[1]

In December 1992, Zoe Baird became the first woman nominated as Attorney General of the United States. Baird subsequently withdrew her nomination following the disclosure that she failed to pay Social Security taxes for her undocumented live-in child-care worker. Baird, like a majority of working affluent women, knowingly and unlawfully failed to pay Social Security taxes for her domestic employee.

Initially, most senators and political analysts discounted the effect of this disclosure on Baird's nomination, but by January talk radio was calling the controversy Nannygate. Some news commentators framed the issue solely in class terms. The issues raised by Nannygate, however, are much larger, reflecting how work and workers are constructed and valued in American society. Nannygate also raises hard questions long avoided by American feminists about mothering as women's work.

Influenced by Zoe Baird's plight, Congress enacted the Social Security Domestic Employment Reform Act of 1994, popularly known as the Nanny Tax law. The new law increases the threshold amount of employee wages required to trigger the tax from $50 quarterly to $1,000 annually and requires annual instead of quarterly payments of the tax to ease the reporting burden on employers like Baird. Throughout the legislative debate little attention was paid to the real nanny at the heart of the Nannygate controversy, Lillian Cordero, the undocumented Peruvian woman. This essay explores how gender, race, class, and immigrant status influence legal policies affecting paid household workers.

LEGISLATIVE NARRATIVE: FRAMING THE PUBLIC POLICY DEBATE

The narratives of members of Congress and witnesses who participated in the hearings juvenilized, gendered as female, and raced as black in-home or resident child-care workers. Professional women like Baird called child-care workers nannies, powerful male members of Congress called them babysitters, and black members of Congress called them "Black female domestic workers."[2] Whether nanny, babysitter, or black female domestic worker, resident child-care workers

---

[1] Reprinted by permission from 3 *Journal of Gender, Race, and Justice* 1 (1999).
[2] Sidney Blumenthal, *Adventures in Babysitting*, NEW YORKER, Feb. 15, 1993, at 54.

discussed in the hearings also are presumptively native-born, virtually erasing foreign-born workers like Lillian Cordero from the debates.

The Legislative Debates About Employees

Although Congress, as a whole, agreed that simplification of the taxing scheme was needed for the employer's sake, members disagreed over the amount of annual wages needed to trigger payment of the tax. Those arguing for a higher threshold focused on the needs of employers for a simplified means of reporting that excluded occasional or part-time employees.

Under the new law, workers whose earnings from a single employer fell short of the $1,000 annual threshold had no Social Security coverage. Thus, the law does not cover workers earning less than $4.25 per hour, then the minimum wage, or workers earning as much as $5.00 per hour who only work one day every two weeks, or half-days every week for the same employer. A home care worker employed four hours each [day], for five or six different households every week at $5.00 per hour, could earn a yearly income between $4,000 and $5,000, but still not be covered under the new legislation. Under the old law, this worker's employers would be legally obligated to pay Social Security and Medicare taxes on the worker's wages.

The loss of Social Security coverage for some domestic workers was foreseen by Congress. Black members of Congress, while supportive of any measure to increase employer compliance with the Social Security law, feared that a higher triggering threshold would remove some currently covered workers from the Social Security system. During the legislative debates, black members of Congress argued that under the new law, a worker earning $9,000 annually in aggregated wages might receive no Social Security credit if no single employer paid the worker $1,000 per year.

Representative [Carrie] Meek alluded to her prior support for a simplified reporting system to offset the "detrimental effects on the hiring of domestic workers who work independently of companies that contract for services in the home."[3] The current system, she argued, encourages employers to pay their household workers under the table. It is ironic, Meek said, that the problems of "Zoe Baird and other prominent people," and not the interests of domestic workers, were the impetus for the current bill.[4] Meek understood whose interests were driving the legislation.

According to her legislative aide, John Shelby, Representative Meek, a freshman legislator with little influence, supported the $1,000 annual threshold even though she wanted a lower triggering amount because she believed that the law could be perfected later. She and a few others remained focused on the need to ensure retirement benefits for many household workers. Thus, Representative Meek focused on how to protect the retirement needs of some household workers, constructed by her as native-born minority women. Her pragmatic compromise meant that the poorest paid women either remained uncovered, or lost coverage all together.

[3] 139 Cong. Rec. 2580 (1993) (statement of Rep. Meek).
[4] Id.

A black woman who testified during the legislative hearings also focused on native-born women workers. Diane Williams, the daughter of a household worker, clearly positioned native-born women in opposition to immigrant domestic workers like Lillian Cordero. Ms. Williams testified that too much media attention was focused on undocumented domestic workers and not on "the thousands of black and white Americans who have lived here legally, [and] worked for years as domestics and day workers "[5] Rather than advocate on behalf of all working women who occupy this female-dominated labor category, Williams asserts the citizenship status of native-born black and white Americans as the basis for greater government protection.

The Legislative Debates About Employers

While Representative Meek spoke of native-born minority domestic workers who needed financial security, other legislators spoke of babysitters and nannies who created legal problems for employers. Most members of Congress identified with Zoe Baird and her husband, Paul Gewirtz. Thus, the mainstream legislative and public debate focused on the problems faced by employers – well-to-do women and their husbands – not household workers, and especially not foreign-born resident child-care providers. Either the law or the workers were the cause of the problem, never the employer.

During the legislative debate, one commonly cited excuse for nonpayment of the tax by employers was the "complex" quarterly paperwork required to comply with the law. Therefore, many members of Congress argued that employers should not have to pay Social Security taxes on quarterly employee wages of $50 or more. They reasoned that employer compliance with the Social Security law would increase by requiring annual instead of quarterly payments and a higher triggering wage threshold. Proponents of a higher triggering wage, however, never adequately explained how raising the triggering wage threshold would increase compliance with the Social Security law. In fact, there was evidence to the contrary. A former IRS Commissioner accurately predicted that if the proposed legislation became law, compliance rates "would fall 'straight to zero.'"[6]

Another argument advanced during the hearings was that the current law covered women who were not real workers. For many legislators, child-care labor was not real work, it was child's work. Thus, the Social Security law made otherwise law-abiding households tax cheats because they occasionally hired teenagers to babysit their children, yet were liable, under the law, for the Social Security taxes on their wages. *Remember now, Lillian Cordero was neither a part-time nor an occasional worker.*

Some members of Congress blamed household workers for encouraging their employers to evade minimum wage and Social Security laws by paying wages

---

[5] *Proposals to Simplify and Streamline the Payment of Employment Taxes for Domestic Workers: Hearing Before the Subcomm. on Soc. Sec. and Subcomm. on Human Res. of the House Comm. on Ways and Means*, 103d Cong. 73 (1993) (statement of Diane Williams, daughter of a household worker).
[6] *Raising Wage Threshold Will Not Boost Compliance*, Lab. Rel. Rep., July 26, 1993, at 410–11.

under the table, a point countered by Diane Williams[, the daughter of a household worker,] and Queen E. Sledge, a former household worker. Both women testified that most household workers did not know the law and just assumed that their employers would pay in cash. Ignoring the tremendous power and informational imbalance between employer and worker, legislators persisted in justifying employers' failure to comply with the law by asserting that household workers resent having to pay Social Security taxes and income taxes. According to these legislators the employees, not the employers, were the real tax cheats. Their arguments blindly ignore what drives workers' concerns – low wages for hard labor.

PUBLIC DEBATES: WHAT'S IN A NAME – RACIAL MARKERS

The news media labeled the controversy surrounding Baird's nomination Nannygate because Baird called Lillian Cordero a nanny. Job titles are important because they do invoke certain images in the minds of the public, and these images influence public policy. The term "domestic worker" invokes the historic image of a native-born black woman, the mammy, an "ideological construct of the plantation's faithful household servant and the South's most perfect slave."[7]

Even the names domestic workers call themselves are significant. To European immigrants in the nineteenth century "hard, drudging labor" was synonymous with the kind of labor reserved for black workers – "arduous unskilled jobs or ... subservient positions."[8] In the northern United States the term "servant" became closely associated with black labor, whether slave or free. For this reason, Irish immigrant women, overrepresented as household workers during this period, resisted the "servant" and "domestic" labels in order to distinguish themselves from black women. Thus, white workers who performed domestic work advertised for work describing themselves as "help," "helper," and "hand" rather than "servant" and "domestic" to convey a more equalitarian notion of their labor. These labels also served as a means of separating the labor performed by white workers from that performed by black workers, whether free or slave.

Today the terms "nanny" and "domestic worker" serve similar purposes. The term "nanny" invokes the image of a "foreign" woman, unless you are a Brooklyn-accented television nanny. Literature and mass media construct nannies as cultured, educated, unmarried women – surrogate mothers for upper-class children. Therefore, it is no accident that both the press and Zoe Baird called Lillian Cordero a nanny. The term erases the most negative connotations of in-home child care – low-wage work often performed by nonwhite women in a potentially exploitative environment. The significance of job titles is apparent in the public and congressional debates surrounding the enactment of the Nanny Tax law. Strangely, strong feminist voices were missing from the public debates.

---

[7] Peggie R. Smith, *Regulating Paid Household Work: Class, Gender, Race, and Agendas of Reform*, 48 Am. U. L. Rev. 851, 864 n.75 (1999).

[8] David R. Roediger, The Wages of Whiteness: Race and the Making of the American Working Class 144–45 (1991).

PAID DOMESTIC WORKERS: WORKING-CLASS WOMEN IMMIGRANTS

Largely ignored during the Nannygate controversy was Cordero's status as an undocumented worker. Baird raised the issue of Cordero's immigration status only to justify nonpayment of Social Security taxes. In the end, Baird employed an undocumented foreign-born woman as a child-care provider, driven, she claimed, by the fact that she could not obtain satisfactory services from native-born workers.

Starting in the 1980s, the number of women household workers grew steadily, reaching levels comparable to the early twentieth century, when domestic work was the most common women's occupation. Increasingly, immigrant women in the United States perform this work; thus, domestic labor has a global dimension.

Today, approximately 25% of foreign-born women in the United States are household workers. Like the past, there is a racialized hierarchy among immigrant domestic workers. In New York City, for example, non-English-speaking Haitian women are paid less than women from English-speaking Caribbean countries. Latinas who do not speak English earn more than black women from Haiti or English-speaking Caribbean countries because some employers consider (presumably light-skinned) Latinas white.

Some migrant women work as in-home child-care providers. These foreign-born household workers with limited job options are especially vulnerable to employer abuse. Although protected by labor laws, undocumented (and documented) foreign-born workers rarely report employers because they fear loss of income and possible deportation. Their stories of abuse are common and horrifying.

SEARCHING FOR SOLUTIONS

Complex Problems Suggest Complex Solutions

The absence of any comprehensive regulatory scheme for paid domestic labor helps perpetuate potentially exploitative employment situations, and poor women workers are most likely to be exploited under the current regime. Legal feminists have not focused on the plight of domestic workers.

Given the multiple issues connected to paid domestic work, developing an analytical lens through which to process and address all the issues is difficult. A decade ago critical race feminist Kimberlé Crenshaw advanced her intersectionality theory, the notion that some types of subordinating conduct cannot be analyzed using "a single categorical axis."[9] Professor Crenshaw's theory of intersectionality captures an approach to feminism similar to the unified-systems theory adopted by some socialist feminists. Unlike liberal, radical, or cultural feminism, socialist feminism argues "that because male dominance, capitalism, and racism are

---

[9] Kimberlé Crenshaw, *Demarginalizing the Intersection of Race and Sex: A Black Feminist Critique of Antidiscrimination Doctrine, Feminist Theory and Antiracist Politics*, 1989 U. Chi. Legal. F. 139, 140.

inextricably intertwined, it is necessary to construct a [feminist] theory that takes account of the multiple bases of oppression[, because] a challenge to any one alone is inadequate."[10] As a result, socialist feminists might view the status of women household workers in the context of how the underregulation and gendering of child care and other domestic work as women's work reenforces both the public–private and worker/mother dichotomies, and creates a market for migrant women workers, an approach used in this article. Socialist legal feminists, for example, might argue that women who stay home to care for young children should be paid a salary commensurate with schoolteachers since mothering involves many of the same skills. Mothering must be seen as work that is highly valued in both moral and monetary terms.

Socialist feminism also is a helpful analytical lens because it allows us to consider how globalization contributes to the resurgence of a female, largely nonwhite servant class in the United States. By looking at domestic workers from a global perspective it is easy to understand how the lack of work in poor countries creates a flow of low-paid workers into more developed countries. Adopting a socialist feminist approach to the plight of home care workers, however, might result in a theory without practical application. Socialist feminism requires significant structural changes that are unlikely to occur in a capitalistic country like the United States. Socialist feminism also requires a level of activism and involvement to reach and mobilize working-class women.

Collective action, while useful, will not address the concerns of all household workers. Domestic work in this country has both racial and citizenship components which tend to separate rather than unite working-class women. In addition, household workers often labor in isolation from each other, further hindering mobilization efforts.

Mobilizing Household Workers

Almost a decade ago Suzanne Goldberg wrote about the limitations inherent in relying only on legal regulation to improve the working conditions and wages of household workers. Goldberg advocates developing laws that "enhance 'community' organizing" so that workers might support laws that facilitate a balancing of the often conflicted interests of people who do the same type of work.[11] History suggests, however, that community organizing alone seldom produces significant structural changes. At various points in the twentieth century, household workers organized to improve working conditions. Most of these efforts were either unsuccessful or resulted in small changes.

More recently, social scientist Mary Romero studied Chicana household workers in Denver, documenting the humiliation and degradation of the workers at the

---

[10] Marion Crain, *Between Feminism and Unionism: Working Class Women, Sex Equality, and Labor Speech*, 82 GEO. L.J. 1903, 1931–32 (1994).

[11] Suzanne Goldberg, *In Pursuit of Workplace Rights: Household Workers and a Conflict of Laws*, 3 YALE J.L. & FEMINISM 63, 104 (1990).

hands of their employers. Romero found, however, that the Chicana household workers she studied resisted their subordination, establishing informal strategies to improve their position, negotiating schedule changes, length of workday, and payment by the job rather than the hour. They negotiated with individual employers for their labor.

The women in Romero's study may be exceptional, and if not, then the reasons for their success bear closer scrutiny by feminists as we search for solutions. Nevertheless, the household work most likely to be transformed into a fee-for-service occupation is housecleaning and group child care outside the home, not residential child care. Residential or in-home child care, the preferred model for affluent parents, will remain a potentially exploitative and underregulated employment situation. Feminists, some of whom are employers of domestic workers themselves, may find it difficult to encourage their workers to press for better employment conditions because of conflicting interests.

Ambivalent and Affluent Mothers

The Zoe Baird problem touches very few working women, only those at the very top and bottom of the labor hierarchy, since the vast majority of working families cannot afford in-home or residential child care. Legal feminists should initiate public debates about parenting and the construction of motherhood. In the absence of such debate, the ambivalence and guilt of affluent feminists about mothering remains a barrier to meaningful change.

Affluent feminists who supported the Nanny Tax law constitute a group against patriarchy, yet not for women. The failure of women's groups to strongly support comprehensive government regulation of wage and hour provisions for household workers, which is a rather modest proposal, leaves labor performed in the home undervalued, underpaid, and underregulated. Although black feminists, using race as a starting point, acknowledge that the gender and class of the employer and the worker influence government labor policies, their critique does not go far enough. There is an international market for household workers and few regulations to protect women like Lillian Cordero from exploitation. Thus, a more global analysis is needed.

CONCLUSION

One of the ironies of the Zoe Baird controversy is that her spouse, Paul Gewirtz, not Baird, bore the primary responsibility for securing and paying taxes and other benefits for Lillian Cordero, yet Baird bore the full political flack for failing to comply with the law regulating household workers. So Baird's nomination, which went against tradition because of her gender, failed because of traditional and outdated notions that place responsibility for child care on working mothers, without the benefit of institutional support.

Rather than demonstrate, legislatively, that the work of caring for children is valuable, the Nanny Tax law simply confirms the lack of value society places on the women who perform domestic work, whether paid or unpaid. The failure of all feminists to coalesce around domestic work and press for structural changes, or even effective reforms, leaves labor performed in the home undervalued, underpaid, and underregulated. The narratives surrounding the enactment of the Nanny Tax law illustrate how the venue of work, gender, race, class, and citizenship of employer and worker influenced government labor policies.

The Taxation of Undocumented Immigrants: Separate, Unequal, and Without Representation

FRANCINE J. LIPMAN[1]

Undocumented immigrants, like all citizens and residents of the United States, are required to pay taxes. Despite the historic and strong American opposition to taxation without representation, undocumented immigrants (except in rare cases) have not enjoyed the right to vote on any local, state, or federal tax or other matter for almost eighty years. Nevertheless, each year undocumented immigrants add billions of dollars in sales, excise, property, income, and payroll taxes, including Social Security, Medicare, and unemployment taxes, to federal, state, and local coffers. Hundreds of thousands of undocumented immigrants go out of their way to file annual federal and state income tax returns.

Yet undocumented immigrants are barred from almost all government benefits, including food stamps, Temporary Assistance for Needy Families, Medicaid, federal housing programs, Supplemental Security Income, Unemployment Insurance, Social Security, Medicare, and the earned income tax credit (EITC). Generally, the only benefits federally required for undocumented immigrants are emergency medical care, subject to financial and category eligibility, and elementary and secondary public education. Many undocumented immigrants will not even access these few critical government services because of their ever-present fear of government officials and deportation.

RESIDENT ALIEN VERSUS NONRESIDENT ALIEN CLASSIFICATION

If a non–U.S. citizen is a U.S. resident, under the Code, she will be characterized as a "resident alien" for tax purposes. A resident alien is subject to the same income [tax], employment tax, and tax withholding laws as a U.S. citizen. Accordingly, a resident alien is subject to federal income tax on her worldwide income regardless of its source.

In general, an individual is classified as a "resident alien" for tax purposes if she meets the qualifications under either of two residency tests. The first test classifies any alien that is a "lawful permanent resident" of the United States at any time during the calendar year as a resident alien. Undocumented immigrants do not satisfy the requirements under this test.

---

[1] Reprinted by permission from 9 *Harvard Latino Law Review* 1 (2006).

The second test is the "substantial presence test." Under this test, if an individual is physically present in the United States for at least thirty-one days during the current year, and at least 183 days during the current year and prior two years, she will be classified as a resident alien. While there are several exceptions to this general rule, most undocumented immigrants residing in the United States will be classified as "resident aliens" for tax purposes.

THE IRS INDIVIDUAL TAXPAYER IDENTIFICATION NUMBER

Because the U.S. government classifies undocumented immigrants as resident aliens, they are subject to the same federal income and employment taxes and filing and withholding requirements as U.S. citizens. Under the Code, every taxpayer must have a unique and permanent number. Consequently, undocumented immigrants must obtain [an individual taxpayer identification number (ITIN)]. For most nonbusiness taxpayers, Social Security numbers (SSNs) serve as taxpayer identification numbers [(or TINs)]. However, because undocumented immigrants are not eligible to work in the United States, they cannot obtain valid SSNs.

In response to this void, the IRS introduced a new taxpayer identification number for use by individuals who are not eligible for SSNs. The ITIN is a nine-digit number resembling a SSN, but starting with the number "9" and having the number "7" or "8" as the fourth digit. An ITIN does not authorize work in the United States, and cannot be used for employment tax or [Social Security Administration (SSA)] purposes. Nevertheless, employers are required to pay employment taxes and provide a SSN to the IRS and the SSA for wages paid to each employee. Employers desperate for workers and undocumented immigrants desperate for wages either avoid the system completely through unreported wages, or comply with fraudulently obtained SSNs.

As a result of a convergence of mutually exclusive requirements, undocumented immigrants are in an impossible situation. First, undocumented immigrants are required to use ITINs. The government created ITINs specifically to identify and distinguish unauthorized aliens from other taxpayers. However, ITINs cannot be used for reporting wages or paying payroll taxes to the SSA or IRS. Yet unauthorized workers and their employers are subject to, and must pay, Social Security taxes. Consequently, billions of dollars each year are paid to the SSA with invalid SSNs because properly obtained ITINs cannot be used. Similarly, each year hundreds of thousands of annual income tax returns are filed with valid ITINs and invalid SSNs. The SSA and IRS spend billions of taxpayer dollars each year trying to reconcile earnings and tax payments to wage earners who cannot exist (but do by the tens of millions and growing) because they are unauthorized. Undocumented immigrants will never have their Social Security–covered earnings credited to their ITINs because ITINs cannot be used for this purpose. As a result, unless an unauthorized worker becomes authorized, she will not realize any benefit from these Social Security–covered earnings and tax payments. While confusing and obscure, this treatment is clearly separate and unequal.

APPLICATION OF TAX FORMULA TO A HYPOTHETICAL
UNAUTHORIZED WORKER

A hypothetical unauthorized worker named Abe is an industrious man of twenty-eight years. He came to the United States with his wife, Abigail, by crossing over the border from Mexico. Abe works hard, long hours, and in 2005, earns $15,000. Abigail stays at home with Ariel because Ariel is not yet in school, and the family cannot afford the available day care facilities in their neighborhood.

To compute their taxable income, the family reduces their gross income of $15,000 by the married filing jointly standard deduction of $10,000 and an aggregate personal and dependency exemption deduction for three individuals of $9,600. The federal taxable income is $0. The federal income tax liability is also $0 before consideration of any tax credits.

Abe is subject to Social Security payroll taxes on his wages of $15,000. His share of Social Security payroll taxes is 7.65% of $15,000, or $1,148. His employer's contribution on his behalf is also 7.65% of his wages paid of $15,000, or $1,148. However, because Abe is an unauthorized worker, he does not have a valid SSN, so the SSA posts his Social Security–covered wages of $15,000 to the earnings suspense file. The Social Security trust fund is still increased by an unsuspended amount of $2,296. Abe will not realize any benefit from his Social Security–covered earnings and tax payments because his contribution cannot be credited to his ITIN, even though his contribution increases the Social Security trust fund.

The question of filing status becomes more interesting if we change the hypothetical by assuming that Abigail and Ariel have not yet joined Abe in the United States, but are residing in Mexico. For tax purposes, Abigail and Ariel are classified as nonresident aliens, and Abe will be classified as a resident alien.

Under this fact pattern, Abe and Abigail may file as married filing jointly if they elect to treat Abigail as a resident alien for tax purposes. However, if they make this election, all of Abigail's non–U.S. source income would now be subject to federal income tax and wage withholding unless and until they decide to terminate the election. Moreover, Abigail would have to obtain an ITIN and sign the jointly filed tax return, and would be jointly and severally liable for any resulting tax liability. In many cases where the nonresident spouse has little or no income, this will be the most tax-favorable alternative. However, because of lack of a myriad of resources, including finances, education, language skills, and information, Abigail may not be able to obtain an ITIN or even sign the tax return. Alternatively, Abe could try to file without Abigail under the head of household filing status.

Under the head of household filing status, a taxpayer must maintain as her home a household that is the principal place of residence for a qualified dependent for more than one-half of the taxable year. The taxpayer must also provide more than one-half the cost of maintaining the household during the tax year. Abe more than likely provides most of the cost of maintaining his family's household in Mexico and his own household in the United States. Moreover, because he provides over one-half of Ariel's support, she should qualify as his dependent. Unfortunately, because Ariel does not live in the same household as Abe, he will not qualify for head of household filing status. Therefore, he will have to file as married filing separately. This filing status will cause Abe's federal income tax liability for the current tax year to increase meaningfully from $0, as married filing jointly, to $360.

Abe's gross income of $15,000 will be reduced by the married filing separately standard deduction of $5,000 and his personal and dependency exemptions deduction for himself and Ariel of $6,400. Abe will not enjoy the deduction for personal exemption for Abigail because the couple is not filing jointly. Because Abe does not live with Ariel for more than one-half of the tax year, she will not qualify as a dependent under the new definition of "qualifying child." However, Ariel should qualify as Abe's dependent under the "qualifying relative" definition because Abe provides over one-half of her support.

Abe's federal taxable income will be $3,600 and his income tax liability will be $360. Abe will be subject to Social Security payroll taxes on his wages of $15,000. His share of Social Security payroll taxes will be 7.65% of $15,000, or $1,148. Abe's aggregate tax liability of $1,508 on $15,000 of household gross income will generate an effective tax rate of over 10%.

TAX RELIEF FOR THE "DESERVING POOR" UNDER THE EITC

Low-income undocumented immigrants pay little or no federal income tax because of the offset against gross income of the standard deduction and personal and dependency exemptions. Their dangerous and underground existence, however, has led some undocumented immigrants to file as married filing separately taxpayers and to pay more federal income tax than they would if they were able to enter this country with their families intact. In addition to federal income tax, unauthorized workers pay Social Security taxes on every dollar of reported wages at 7.65%. Therefore, these poverty-level workers are paying federal income and payroll taxes at a minimum rate of 7.65%.

There is a broad-based consensus that low-income, working families should not pay taxes. In early 1972, then-Governor Ronald Reagan, testifying before Congress regarding a workfare approach to government assistance, "suggested that the federal government should exempt low income families from income taxes and give them a rebate for their Social Security taxes."[2] Several years later, in 1975, Senator Russell Long and Congressman Al Ullman were able to package the idea in a refundable tax credit and garner liberal support for the EITC.

Undocumented immigrant families cannot qualify for the EITC. In 1996, Congress enacted sweeping welfare reform, including unprecedented restrictions on federal benefits for many immigrants. Among the long list of benefit restrictions, Congress decided that "individuals who are not authorized to work in the United States" should be denied EITC benefits.[3] In an effort to accomplish this goal, Congress amended the Code to require that any taxpayer include a valid SSN for herself, her spouse if she is married, and each qualified child to receive any EITC

---

[2] Saul D. Hoffman & Laurence S. Seidman, Helping Working Families: The Earned Income Tax Credit 12 (2003).

[3] Staff of Joint Comm. on Taxation, 104th Cong., General Explanation of Tax Legislation Enacted in the 104th Congress 392–95 (Comm. Print 1996).

benefits. While this may seem consistent with the denial of virtually all government assistance for undocumented immigrants, it is not. The SSN requirement is poorly targeted and is both overbroad and underinclusive.

The requirement that every member of the household have a SSN (authorizing work) is ill-conceived because it denies or allows EITC benefits inconsistently with Congress's stated intent. The SSN requirement excludes families in which every member is legally working or present in the United States from EITC benefits. For example, the provision denies EITC benefits to any authorized immigrant worker or U.S. citizen whose spouse or qualifying child does not have a SSN. For example, two U.S. citizen parents with a child without a SSN cannot receive any EITC benefits. The Code precludes any EITC benefits for this legally working and present family including EITC benefits available for eligible individuals without a child. However, if the same family has one child with a SSN and one child without a SSN, but with an ITIN, the family can qualify for EITC benefits for a married couple with one qualifying child.

In addition, a U.S. citizen worker married to a documented immigrant, with a valid ITIN but no SSN, cannot receive any EITC benefits even if the couple has one or more U.S. citizen qualifying children. Even if the family decides to file a married filing separately return so that all individuals on the EITC tax return have SSNs, they will not qualify for any EITC. Married taxpayers cannot qualify for the EITC with a married filing separately tax return. Ironically, only if the couple ends their marriage, or never enters into marriage, will generous EITC benefits be available.

The SSN requirement also permits families who have members that are working in the United States without authorization and without current documents to receive current EITC benefits. For example, a taxpayer, with a SSN that authorized work when it was issued but is no longer valid for employment, will qualify for EITC benefits. The provision requiring a SSN on the tax return does not require that the SSN be currently valid for work or residence in the United States. It only requires that the SSN not be issued to secure federal benefits. Therefore, SSNs issued temporarily for work, that are no longer valid for work, and nonwork SSNs issued to secure state or local benefits are valid for EITC benefits; meanwhile, SSNs initially issued to secure federal benefits, but that are now work-authorized, are not. The SSN requirement as stated and enforced does not assure that only authorized work qualifies an individual for EITC benefits.

Ironically, the government provides EITC benefits to families retroactively for tax years in which they were illegally working and/or present in the United States. If an unauthorized worker, her spouse, or qualifying child obtains a SSN after a tax return is filed, the return can be amended to add the SSN to claim retroactive EITC benefits. The IRS has ruled that EITC benefits are retroactively available as long as the statute of limitations has not lapsed. Therefore, once all members of the family have SSNs, EITC benefits are available, even if no family members were authorized to work or even be in the United States during the tax year at issue.

In an effort to quickly and efficiently deny EITC benefits to the "undeserving poor," Congress and the IRS have devised a mechanical, clerical test. The test categorizes the working poor in America into two separate groups: those that are deserving and holders of SSNs, and those that are undeserving, or holders of ITINs or SSNs issued for federal benefits. The result is separate, unequal, and irrational treatment of certain hard-working poor families under the Code.

TAX RELIEF FOR THE ALWAYS DESERVING
MIDDLE-INCOME UNDER THE CTC

While the EITC was designed to provide tax relief for working poor families, the [child tax credit (CTC)] was designed more than twenty years later to provide tax relief for middle-income families. Ironically, undocumented working poor immigrant families who are barred from current tax relief under the EITC may qualify for relief under the CTC. Because it was designed for middle-income families with children, Congress did not have to include a mechanism for segregating the undeserving from deserving recipients.

The CTC was enacted by Congress and signed into law by President William Clinton in August 1997. The CTC offsets a taxpayer's income tax liability dollar-for-dollar by up to $1,000 per "qualifying child."

The CTC also has an identification requirement. Taxpayers must provide the name and TIN of each qualifying child to receive the benefits of the CTC. Notably, the identification requirement under the CTC is less restrictive than the identification requirement under the EITC. Taxpayers who do not qualify for the EITC solely because they, their spouse, or their children do not have a valid SSN should qualify for the CTC. Holding either a SSN or an ITIN qualifies a taxpayer for the CTC.

The CTC was not designed or enacted to provide tax relief to working poor families who already qualify for meaningful EITC benefits. Seemingly consistent with this goal, the CTC is refundable under limited circumstances. If a working poor family qualifies for the EITC, they generally will not qualify for a meaningful, refundable CTC.

Undocumented immigrant families do not receive any meaningful reimbursement of Social Security taxes because they do not qualify for the EITC. Only if these working poor families have three or more children do they qualify for a refundable CTC that effectively reimburses them for their Social Security tax payments. If the undocumented family has less than three qualifying children, then the refundable CTC will only meaningfully reimburse them for their Social Security taxes paid when their income level significantly exceeds $11,000.

Ironically, some of the poorest undocumented immigrant families pay more in taxes than their richer (either in income level or number of children) low-income neighbors because they do not qualify for either the refundable EITC or the refundable CTC. While these working poor families do not pay income taxes, they do pay regressive Social Security taxes. Notably, workers who are authorized to work in the United States will probably qualify for Social Security retirement benefits, but undocumented workers will never qualify for any benefits with respect to the contributions they make to the Social Security retirement system.

The structure of the refundable portion of the CTC causes the poorest undocumented immigrant families to pay a significantly higher percentage of their income in taxes than higher-income working poor families. If, however, an undocumented immigrant family has three or more qualifying children, it will be reimbursed in full for all taxes paid. Accordingly, the addition of one qualifying child (from two to three qualifying children) causes most of these families' effective tax rate to drop from 7.65% to 0%. This result is inconsistent with fundamental tax policy.

The exclusion of undocumented working poor families from the EITC and the targeting of the CTC for middle-income families have created an abyss in federal relief for hardworking, poor families. Undocumented working poor families have higher effective income tax rates than their neighbors who enjoy higher income levels. Undocumented working families at the lowest income levels, without the ability to pay or the benefit of government services, are subject to regressive Social Security taxes without any reimbursement. Only if these families have three or more children do they receive any relief. The structure of the CTC creates an incentive to increase family size for the poorest of all undocumented immigrant families. Certainly Congress did not intend to create this mess. Fortunately, once the interactions of the EITC, ITINs, and the CTC are understood in the context of the demographics of undocumented immigrants, tax reforms can be designed. Unfortunately, but perhaps not surprisingly, none of the recent proposals for tax or immigration reform include tax relief for undocumented working families.

Prying Open the Closet Door: The Defense of Marriage Act and Tax Treaties

ANTHONY C. INFANTI[1]

Following President Bush's endorsement of a constitutional ban on same-sex marriage, a conservative, "pro-family" organization wrote the IRS Commissioner to alert him about "a potential fraudulent tax scheme."[2] The organization was alarmed by "rebellious state and local officials reportedly permitting persons of the same sex to marry in flagrant disobedience of applicable laws defining marriage as a union between a male and a female," and was further alarmed by the prospect that these "married" same-sex couples (their quotes, not mine) might attempt to file joint federal income tax returns.[3] The organization urged the Commissioner to deter these individuals from attempting to evade income tax by threatening to investigate and prosecute any same-sex couples who attempt to file joint returns.

In [its response], the IRS went beyond the narrow circumstances that alarmed the conservative organization and spoke more generally about the ability of married same-sex couples to file joint federal income tax returns. Citing section three of the Defense of Marriage Act (DOMA), which precludes the recognition of same-sex marriages for purposes of federal law, the IRS reassured the organization that

> [e]ven though a state may recognize a union of two people of the same sex as a legal marriage for the purposes within that state's authority, that recognition has no effect for purposes of federal law. A taxpayer in such a relationship may not claim the status of a married person on the federal income tax return.[4]

Putting aside the questionable constitutionality of DOMA, the IRS was technically correct in making this statement – but only because the statement was confined to the tax treatment of domestic same-sex marriages. Having taken a parochial view of the issue (as only too often proves to be the case), both the conservative organization and the IRS ignored the fact that the United States is not the only place where same-sex couples are seeking (and have been granted) the right

---

[1] Reprinted by permission from 105 *Tax Notes* 563 (2004).

[2] Letter from Eugene A. Delgaudio, President of Public Advocate of the United States Inc., to IRS Commissioner Mark W. Everson (Apr. 13, 2004), *available at* http://www.publicadvocateusa.org/news/article.php?article=115 (last visited July 17, 2008).

[3] *Id.*

[4] Letter from the IRS to Eugene A. Delgaudio, President of Public Advocate of the United States Inc. (June 14, 2004), *available at* http://www.publicadvocateusa.org/news/article.php?article=121 (last visited July 17, 2008).

to marry. Whether the IRS's statement about the inability of married same-sex couples to file joint federal income tax returns will hold true when viewed from a wider, international perspective is an interesting question that has yet to be answered.

DOMA AND TAX TREATIES

On May 17, 2004, Massachusetts became the first U.S. state to allow same-sex couples to marry. Although the legalization of same-sex marriage in Massachusetts has received much attention in the United States, Massachusetts is not the only (nor was it the first) jurisdiction in the world to accord legal recognition to same-sex marriages. In 2001, the Netherlands became the first country to extend the right to marry to same-sex couples. The Netherlands' lead was then followed by Belgium and Canada in 2003 [and Spain in 2005].

In addition to same-sex marriage, those four countries share at least one other trait in common: Each of them has entered into a bilateral income tax treaty with the United States. Each of these treaties contains an aptly titled "nondiscrimination" article, which is a standard provision found in all U.S. income tax treaties.

Although the wording of the nondiscrimination articles in the U.S.–Belgium, U.S.–Canada, U.S.–Netherlands, and U.S.–Spain Treaties is not identical, article 28(1) of the U.S.–Netherlands Treaty provides a general sense of the scope of the relevant nondiscrimination provision:

> Nationals of one of the States shall not be subjected in the other State to any taxation or any requirement connected therewith, which is other or more burdensome than the taxation and connected requirements to which nationals of that other State in the same circumstances are or may be subjected.[5]

The U.S.–Netherlands Treaty defines the term "national" to include "all individuals possessing the nationality or citizenship of one of the States."[6]

THE UNANSWERED QUESTION

A question that is bound to arise is how to square this treaty prohibition against discriminatory treatment of foreign nationals with DOMA's codification of discrimination against same-sex couples. It is easy to imagine the series of events that will draw the relationship between DOMA and tax treaties into question. To continue using the Netherlands as an example, picture a gay or lesbian couple comprised of two Dutch citizens. This couple was married in the Netherlands, and they continued to reside there after their marriage. The couple has now, for whatever reason, come to the United States and remained here long enough for each of them to be classified as a resident alien for U.S. federal income tax purposes. After completing their first full year of U.S. residency, the couple has concluded

---

[5] Convention for the Avoidance of Double Taxation and the Prevention of Fiscal Evasion with Respect to Taxes on Income, Dec. 18, 1992, U.S.-Neth., art. 28, para. 1.
[6] *Id.* art. 3, para. 1(g)(i).

that it would be advantageous to file a joint federal income tax return because they would benefit from a marriage "bonus."

Normally, two married citizens or resident aliens would be entitled to file a joint federal income tax return. But, as mentioned at the beginning of this article, section three of DOMA provides that, when interpreting any federal law, "the word 'marriage' means only a legal union between one man and one woman as husband and wife, and the word 'spouse' refers only to a person of the opposite sex who is a husband or a wife."[7] As a result, when the joint return provisions in the Code are read in conjunction with DOMA, it appears that a married same-sex couple (including a married same-sex couple comprised of two resident aliens) is barred from filing a joint federal income tax return.

For our Dutch couple who would benefit from a marriage bonus, this treatment appears to be both different from and more burdensome than the treatment afforded to most married U.S. citizens. However, the nondiscrimination article in the U.S.–Netherlands Treaty clearly prohibits the United States from taxing Dutch citizens – including a Dutch same-sex couple – in a different or more burdensome fashion than it taxes its own citizens *in the same circumstances*. Whether the treaty nondiscrimination article will actually dictate a different result from that ostensibly dictated by DOMA will turn on the interpretation and application of the italicized qualifier – "in the same circumstances."

As a commentator has noted, this qualifier "does not require a complete identity of circumstances."[8] This view finds implicit support in the legislative histories of the U.S.–Belgium and U.S.–Canada Treaties (the legislative histories of the U.S.–Netherlands and U.S.–Spain Treaties merely repeat, and do not elaborate on, the language of the treaty) as well as in Treasury's Technical Explanation of the U.S. Model Income Tax Convention. Furthermore, explicit support for this view can be found in the commentary to the model tax treaty published by the Organization for Economic Co-operation and Development [(OECD)]. In the OECD commentary, the phrase "in the same circumstances" is liberally interpreted to mean "in substantially similar circumstances both in law and in fact."[9]

With these interpretations in mind, we can now continue with our example and consider which U.S. citizens are "in the same circumstances" as a married same-sex couple comprised of two citizens of the Netherlands. In making the comparison, we have several options to choose from: Is a married Dutch same-sex couple resident in the United States substantially similar to two married opposite-sex U.S. citizens, two married same-sex U.S. citizens domiciled in Massachusetts, or two unmarried same-sex U.S. citizens domiciled in one of the other forty-nine states (because [as of this writing in 2004] same-sex marriage is legal only in Massachusetts)?

As a factual matter, the Dutch couple is substantially similar to each of the U.S. couples mentioned previously. In each case, we are dealing with two individuals

---

[7] Defense of Marriage Act, Pub. L. No. 104-199, § 3(a), 110 Stat. 2419, 2419 (1996) (codified at 1 U.S.C. § 7).

[8] RICHARD E. ANDERSEN, ANALYSIS OF UNITED STATES INCOME TAX TREATIES ¶ 20.02[1][b][i] (2004).

[9] ORG. FOR ECON. CO-OPERATION & DEV., MODEL CONVENTION WITH RESPECT TO TAXES ON INCOME AND ON CAPITAL, commentary on art. 24, at para. 3 (2003).

who have decided to make an emotional and financial commitment to each other. They have decided to make a life together and to support each other. Even in the United States, the equivalence of the commitments is increasingly recognized on a social level. In fact, "an overwhelming majority" of Americans feel that gays and lesbians should be given "equal access to the specific obligations, responsibilities and recognitions of marriage" – even if not to the institution of marriage itself.[10] The difference in the gender composition of these couples is, therefore, simply irrelevant to the assessment of the factual similarity of the couples.

As a legal matter, the Dutch couple is also substantially similar to each of the U.S. couples in terms of taxation. All of these couples are subject to tax in the United States on their worldwide income – the U.S. couples because of their U.S. citizenship and the Dutch couple because of its U.S. residency. Consequently, there can be no doubt that, from a tax perspective, the Dutch couple is also "in the same circumstances" as each of the enumerated U.S. couples for treaty nondiscrimination purposes.

Despite these similarities, the Dutch couple does diverge from two of the three U.S. couples in terms of the legal status accorded by the state to their relationships.

Let us begin by contrasting the legal status of the Dutch couple with that of the U.S. unmarried same-sex couple. In terms of legal status, these couples are in drastically different positions. The members of the Dutch couple have taken on an entire set of legal rights and obligations by seeking state sanction of their relationship. In contrast, the members of the U.S. unmarried same-sex couple have (voluntarily or involuntarily) foregone attaching these same legal rights and obligations to their relationship. From a narrowly legal perspective, the unmarried couple is really not much different from any two strangers who pass each other on the street. As a result, in terms of the legal rights and obligations attached to their relationship, it does not seem any more appropriate to equate a married same-sex couple with an unmarried same-sex couple than it does to equate a married opposite-sex couple with an unmarried opposite-sex couple. The legal rights and obligations that exist between them differ so significantly that it would be difficult to argue that either set is "in the same circumstances."

The same-sex couple from Massachusetts seems to be a closer match because they are also married. Nevertheless, the marriage of the Massachusetts couple is recognized only in Massachusetts. Under section two of DOMA, no other U.S. state is required to recognize their marriage, and under section three of DOMA, the federal government emphatically refuses to recognize their marriage. In contrast, the marriage of the Dutch couple is recognized throughout the Netherlands and at all levels of government. The marriage is also recognized in the same way and, with two small exceptions that need not concern us, to the same extent as an opposite-sex marriage. Again, the legal rights and obligations that exist between the two couples differ so significantly that it would be difficult to argue that they are "in the same circumstances."

That brings us to the final possibility – comparing the Dutch couple with a U.S. married opposite-sex couple. The legal status of these two couples is

[10] NAT'L GAY & LESBIAN TASK FORCE, RECENT NATIONAL POLLS ON SAME-SEX MARRIAGE AND CIVIL UNIONS 1 (2004).

substantially similar. Both of these couples have satisfied their respective countries' requirements for entering into a civil marriage. And both of those couples enjoy the recognition of their marriages throughout their respective countries and at all levels of government in those countries. Thus, the Dutch couple seems to be substantially similar to the U.S. married opposite-sex couple both in law and in fact.

If that line of reasoning is accepted by the IRS or the courts, then the nondiscrimination article in the U.S.–Netherlands Treaty would appear to require the United States to accord the Dutch couple the same treatment as a U.S. married opposite-sex couple. The plain language of the nondiscrimination article, which expressly prohibits imposing on the Dutch couple any taxation or connected requirement that is "other" or "more burdensome" than the taxation or connected requirements imposed on the U.S. married opposite-sex couple, seems to dictate this result. Furthermore, the result is consistent with Treasury's explanation that, in this context, nondiscrimination means "national treatment." In other words, the treaty appears to require the IRS to recognize the Dutch same-sex couple's marriage and to allow them to file a joint federal income tax return.

Interestingly, the treaty also appears to require U.S. states and localities to recognize the couple's marriage for tax purposes. Even though the nondiscrimination article is found in a treaty that, on its face, purports to apply only to federal income taxes, its scope is not so limited. The nondiscrimination article in the U.S.–Netherlands treaty applies to any tax imposed at the national, state, or local level in the United States. The nondiscrimination articles in the U.S.–Belgium and U.S.–Spain Treaties are similarly worded, encompassing not only federal but also state and local taxes. The nondiscrimination article in the U.S.–Canada Treaty, however, extends only to federal taxes (income and otherwise); it does not purport to apply to state and local taxes.

LATER-IN-TIME RULE

In light of the differing results dictated by the treaty nondiscrimination provisions and DOMA, a secondary question remains concerning the priority of the treaty nondiscrimination provisions over DOMA.

Under the later-in-time rule, when a statute and a treaty conflict, "the one last in date will control the other."[11] The aphoristic nature of that statement is somewhat deceiving, because application of the later-in-time rule is not simply a matter of comparing a date of ratification with a date of enactment. As an initial matter, the Supreme Court has held that "an act of Congress ought never to be construed to violate the law of nations if any other possible construction remains."[12] Consequently, there is an initial presumption of harmony between a later statute and an earlier treaty.

A construction of DOMA that would avoid a direct conflict with the treaty nondiscrimination provisions does, in fact, exist. By its own terms, section three of DOMA applies in "determining the meaning of any Act of Congress, or of any

---

[11] Whitney v. Robertson, 124 U.S. 190, 194 (1888).
[12] Murray v. The Schooner Charming Betsy, 6 U.S. (2 Cranch) 64, 118 (1804).

ruling, regulation, or interpretation of the various administrative bureaus and agencies of the United States."[13] Section three of DOMA prescribes a definition of marriage that only purports to apply to congressional enactments and interpretations of congressional enactments. The ambit of this "narrow"[14] rewriting of the definition of marriage could easily be confined by the courts to the domestic statutes and interpretations of those statutes expressly mentioned in the text of DOMA. That interpretation would leave international obligations untouched, and would allow the treaty nondiscrimination provisions to coexist with DOMA.

Because the treaty nondiscrimination provisions and DOMA dictate different results for the Dutch couple, one could plausibly argue that the two actually do conflict. Given DOMA's enactment after the Senate ratified the nondiscrimination articles in each of the U.S.–Belgium, U.S.–Canada, U.S.–Netherlands, and U.S.–Spain Treaties, one might be tempted to conclude that, under this interpretation, DOMA would override the treaty nondiscrimination provisions (at least for the time being). However, the Supreme Court long ago "limited and clarified the later-in-time rule by providing that '[a] treaty will not be deemed to have been abrogated or modified by a later statute unless such purpose on the part of Congress has been clearly expressed.'"[15]

The Court has elaborated on this rule of construction by stating that "[l]egislative silence is not sufficient to abrogate a treaty."[16] For example, in *Trans World Airlines Inc. v. Franklin Mint Corp.*, the Supreme Court refused to find a legislative override of the Warsaw Convention (regarding international air transportation), when Congress had made no mention of the treaty either in the enacted statute or in its legislative history. The Court has reiterated "this 'firm and obviously sound canon of construction against finding implicit repeal of a treaty in ambiguous congressional action' . . . in a number of cases."[17]

Applying this long-standing limitation on the later-in-time rule to this case, DOMA still should not override inconsistent tax treaty obligations – even if DOMA and the treaty nondiscrimination provisions are construed to be in conflict with each other. Although DOMA was enacted after the Senate ratified the relevant nondiscrimination provisions, neither DOMA nor its legislative history makes any mention of tax treaties. Because Congress failed to clearly express an intent to override inconsistent tax treaty obligations when it enacted DOMA (and, for that matter, failed even to indicate that it had tax treaties in mind at all when it enacted DOMA), DOMA should not be given priority over tax treaties under the later-in-time rule. Instead, the nondiscrimination articles of the U.S.–Belgium, U.S.–Canada, U.S.–Netherlands, and U.S.–Spain Treaties should be applied to require U.S. federal (and, where appropriate, state and local) taxing authorities to recognize the marriages of resident alien same-sex couples who are citizens of one of those four countries.

---

[13] 1 U.S.C. § 7.

[14] H.R. Rep. No. 104-664, at 31 (1996), *reprinted in* 1996 U.S.C.C.A.N. 2905, 2935.

[15] Anthony C. Infanti, *Curtailing Tax Treaty Overrides: A Call to Action*, 62 U. Pitt. L. Rev. 677, 685 (2001) (quoting Cook v. United States, 288 U.S. 102, 120 (1933)).

[16] Trans World Airlines v. Franklin Mint Corp., 466 U.S. 243, 252, *reh'g denied*, 467 U.S. 1231 (1984).

[17] Infanti, *supra* note 15, at 685 (quoting *Trans World Airlines*, 466 U.S. at 252).

CONCLUSION

As commentators have noted, "claims of discriminatory taxes prove difficult to evaluate."[18] That difficulty is exacerbated by the fact that "[n]either the Treasury Department nor Congress seems to have a strong commitment to nondiscrimination"[19] – even though the nondiscrimination articles "include rather sweeping terms, they appear to be read narrowly."[20] Nonetheless, a tenable argument can – and should – be made that, notwithstanding DOMA, the nondiscrimination articles of the U.S.–Belgium, U.S.–Canada, U.S.–Netherlands, and U.S.–Spain Treaties require the recognition for tax purposes of same-sex marriages contracted by citizens of those countries. A perceived lack of receptivity to claims of discrimination, particularly claims of sexual orientation discrimination, is no reason to remain silent; indeed, it is a reason to protest the discrimination all the more vocally.

[18] Sanford H. Goldberg & Peter A. Glicklich, *Treaty-Based Nondiscrimination: Now You See It Now You Don't*, 1 FLA. TAX REV. 51, 59 (1992).

[19] *Id.* at 108.

[20] *Id.*

Missing Africa: Should U.S. International Tax Rules Accommodate Investment in Developing Countries?

KAREN B. BROWN[1]

THE CASE FOR AND AGAINST USE OF AN EXEMPTION SYSTEM TO INCREASE INVESTMENT IN AFRICA

Just as the case for invigorating trade and other relations with Africa may not be readily apparent to some, the case for revising those features of the U.S. tax system that disfavor investment in the sub-Saharan world is not intuitive. Although European countries, Mexico, Canada, Japan, and some developing nations, such as China, India, and Venezuela, have commanded partnerships with the United States, African nations have not. A continent of vast natural resources and a considerable labor force, Africa is nonetheless "one of the last regions . . . to enter the global economy."[2]

The African continent contains a total population of about 778,000,000. Sub-Saharan Africa includes two-thirds of that total, or 642,800,000, among forty-four countries. To date, the situation of much of Africa in the new economy has been that of aid recipient, region of civil and inter-nation strife, location of catastrophic natural disasters, scene of devastating illness, and situs of relentless poverty and shortened life expectancy. Implicit in President Clinton's campaign to eliminate debt of some of the poorest African nations was an acknowledgment of the critical needs of a population for which annual per capita gross national product ranges from $110 to $4,120. Although the debt relief initiative seems well-intentioned, it may have minimal positive impact on the lives of residents of sub-Saharan Africa. Actual provision of relief has been tied to enumerated improvements in infrastructure, including education, health care, transportation, and economic reforms, which fewer than a handful of nations may achieve in the foreseeable future.

Despite the recent aid and trade initiatives by the industrialized world in favor of Africa, it is apparent that for various reasons – among them political controversy, perceived incompatibility of interests, and even racism – these hold limited power to produce and sustain real change. This article contends that a

---

[1] Reprinted by permission from 23 *University of Pennsylvania Journal of International Economic Law* 45 (2002).

[2] Robert Mallett, *Keynote Address at Symposium on Sub-Saharan Africa in the Global Economy*, 30 LAW & POL'Y INT'L BUS. 569, 570 (1999).

solution in the form of tax relief for specified investments may afford the greatest promise.

This article proposes what some may view as a radical revision of the U.S. system of taxation of foreign source income. In particular, it advocates a shift to an exemption system in which income derived from investment in sub-Saharan nations is free of U.S. income taxation. This experimental regime would expire at the end of a ten- or fifteen-year period. That period would begin on the effective date of an income tax treaty between the United States and the African nation. If review of progress under the proposed regime confirmed a measure of success toward achieving targets, extension of the legislation would be recommended. The goals of the program are to increase the amount of U.S. investment in sub-Saharan Africa and to hold revenue loss to an acceptable level.

In addition to provisions governing the tax rate to be imposed by the African nation on specified income from U.S. operations in that region, the treaty would contain safeguards designed to deter U.S. taxpayers from abusing the resources of the affected African nations. These would include: (1) specification of the type of foreign source income eligible for U.S. tax relief ([e.g.,] from activities relating to manufacturing, technology, natural resource exploration, or research and development); (2) exchange of information and other information-sharing arrangements permitting all parties to monitor investment activity; and (3) sovereignty-preserving provisions detailing minimum standards relating to investment activity required by the African nation in areas such as natural resource protection, infrastructure development (transportation, public utilities, etc.), and labor practices (including minimum compensation provisions). While a multilateral treaty is preferable, involving a negotiation en bloc between interested African nations and the United States, bilateral treaties between a single nation and the United States would also be encouraged.

Potential challenges to implementation of this proposal are numerous. Adoption of an exemption from tax for income from specified investments would counter the reigning mantra of the U.S. international tax regime, known as "capital export neutrality." In systems based upon the capital export neutrality principle, like that of the United States in large part, preservation of production efficiency is a prominent goal. Production efficiency theoretically results in allocation of capital to activities providing the highest rate of return regardless of tax rate. The U.S. system implements this goal by taxing worldwide income of its multinational businesses (firms incorporated in the United States and doing business in domestic and foreign markets) under one rate structure and providing a credit against U.S. tax liability for foreign taxes paid. It removes a possible incentive to shift capital to lower-taxing jurisdictions where rates of return may be lower. The exemption system proposed in this article directly challenges the capital export neutrality principle because it could provide an incentive to initiate investment in an African country if the tax rate were lower than that prevailing in the United States.

Although the production efficiency paradigm has gained hold in international tax policy discourse, it does not provide a persuasive case for rejecting the exemption system proposed in this article. For good reasons, the U.S. tax system has in targeted areas ceded its claim on worldwide income of its multinational firms.

These provisions purport to promote competitiveness of domestic companies and offer incentives for export businesses. The present regime also features prominent loopholes that permit U.S. companies to fashion foreign operations without regard for production efficiency in a manner resulting in moderation of U.S. tax rates on worldwide income. The current economic and social crises in sub-Saharan Africa, indicating a critical need for commercial partnerships with the industrialized world, suggest that modification of U.S. tax rules is essential to attract investment in that region.

Tax incentives for investments in sub-Saharan Africa would serve a redistributive function that comports with the concept of equity, a fundamental principle in the domestic arena. The sub-Saharan region of Africa seems a worthy target of concern. The globalization of the world economy, in which the United States is a determined player, is only strengthened by strong trade partners, including those in sub-Saharan Africa. Moreover, the pressure to focus on stability in Africa after the events of September 11, 2001[,] furnishes additional impetus to undertake measures that will bolster the economies of those countries.

The proposed exemption system raises four additional concerns. First, U.S. obligations under the General Agreement on Tariffs and Trade (GATT) must be considered. This article concludes that the proposal to exempt specified income from African sources would not cause the United States to violate its international trade obligations under the GATT.

The second concern is that a move toward an exemption system as proposed may cause U.S. firms to move offshore in search of lower-cost production, creating the so-called "runaway plant" problem. Labor proponents point to the potential for loss of jobs by American workers as the result of a shift by U.S. firms to offshore production. They have, therefore, challenged tax proposals favoring income from foreign operations. Given the tremendous importance of the labor sector to the social and economic health of this nation, such critiques must be considered seriously.

This article concludes, however, that the proposal does not subordinate the interests of U.S. labor or create a shift of benefits directly from U.S. to foreign workers. There is substantial evidence that expansion of trade opportunities, under agreements like the North American Free Trade Agreement, has created phenomena like the *maquiladora* industry, in which American companies have closed U.S. plants to move assembly to locations just across the border in Mexico to obtain lower-cost labor. These operations have resulted in devastation of the local environment and atrocious abuses of workers, particularly women, who must toil under inhumane conditions for subsistence pay. In these circumstances, the benefits to U.S. firms in the form of zero tariff rates and a partial tax exemption for income cannot be supported because they result in an unacceptable burden on U.S. and non-U.S. workers.

The proposal in this article to eliminate U.S. tax on Africa-source income is not likely to result in the abuse of workers described earlier because it contains safeguards designed to protect both U.S. and non-U.S. workers. No U.S. firm would benefit from the proposed exemption unless a treaty containing protections for African laborers became effective. The treaty would prescribe appropriate working conditions, rates of pay, and other terms designed to ensure that workers would be treated appropriately.

The conditions set forth in the treaty would, in turn, decrease the likelihood that U.S. multinationals would move operations abroad for low return investments made profitable only by the opportunity to abuse the human, natural, and other resources of the host country. Despite these safeguards, it is possible that an exemption system for income derived from African investments nonetheless would result in a move of some U.S. production facilities abroad. Although the capital export neutrality principle underpinning the U.S. international tax system appears to support a shift of production abroad for greater returns to capital, the toll on U.S. workers should not be ignored. If job losses to U.S. workers occur in enterprises in which returns to capital are greater in sub-Saharan Africa, the plant relocations would serve efficiency goals. Equitable concerns could be served by continued support of tax incentives for education and other training opportunities as well as by appropriations for reeducation of American workers.

The third concern raised by the proposal described in this article is whether it actually benefits sub-Saharan Africa. The intention is to move African nations into positions of partnership with the United States. The greatest benefits will result if African nations are able to set appropriate terms and conditions for investment in their borders. These would include a tax rate that provides revenue necessary to finance public expenditures for infrastructure, administration, and other public needs, or investment allowances and tax credits for given investments. Whether treaty negotiations give rise to a system that provides reduced tax rates or tax incentives (such as allowances or credits against tax liability), this article's proposal advances sub-Saharan nations to positions as actors in the development of a tax system that will encourage and support investment gains.

The final concern is whether the proposed exemption system will cause the United States to violate international taxation "norms." A group of industrialized nations [has] recently advanced a campaign to eliminate what is termed "harmful tax competition." The 1998 Organization [for] Economic Co-operation and Development (OECD) report, *Harmful Tax Competition: An Emerging Global Issue*, advocates elimination of tax regimes which are viewed as unfairly competing for investment dollars of multinational enterprises. The types of practices targeted are those in which preferential tax regimes are established for selected types of income. A list of harmful competition culprits was published in the summer of 2000.

The exemption system proposed in this article, calling for elimination of U.S. tax on income from specified investments in sub-Saharan African nations, may accommodate a regime of the type condemned in the OECD report. Unless an African nation devises a system that meets an exception crafted in the report for OECD-member Ireland, which sanctions adoption of a low taxation rate of general application, a preferential regime would be subject to attack and possible sanctions by the OECD.

This article argues that the harmful tax competition agenda should exclude sub-Saharan nations that employ tax strategies to attract investment from the industrialized world. The OECD report, which currently applies only to financial and passive investment-type income, should not be extended to manufacturing and other active income, which are the types of income most likely to be the subject of treaties with Africa. Considering the significant barriers to investment in Africa, it is difficult to conceive of a case in which a preferential tax regime of an African nation could harm the revenue-raising capacity of an industrialized nation. The industrialized world should resist dictating appropriate tax regimes for Africa, particularly when no African nation constructed or adopted the OECD proposals. Moreover, the change in presidential administration in Washington, D.C. in early 2001 may signal a change in U.S. support of the OECD proposal. Both Secretary of Treasury O'Neill and Assistant Secretary for Tax Policy Olsen have publicly questioned continued U.S. support of these OECD initiatives.

The hegemony of the industrialized nations over establishment of international tax norms should not foreclose a system of compromises implementing strategies for developing nations. For example, from a tax policy standpoint, it is not clear why implementation of a limited preferential rate regime for targeted investments coupled with very sophisticated information reporting and exchange among nations would not be an acceptable alternative for the developing world. An example of such a compromise occurred in the summer of 2000 when the members of the European Union (EU) negotiated a settlement of a dispute among members regarding minimum withholding tax obligations on payments of interest and other investments from savings. Because several members opposed the 25% withholding plan, the EU accepted an alternate plan. Under that plan, those members objecting to the minimum withholding rate were permitted to avoid that obligation by agreeing to comprehensive information exchange. With input by African constituents, international tax norms that accommodate the developing world could be constructed.

CONCLUSION

Much respect is accorded the United States in its position as economic powerhouse and leader of the global economy. To be sure, after the terrorist attacks on the United States in September 2001, its economic position has been challenged. Yet, some of the instability in other parts of the world that has led to terrorism can be attributed to the practice of the United States and the rest of the developed world to underestimate the social and economic crisis facing a large portion of the developing world.

The world faces a critical moment in which the needs of the populations of poorer economies must be acknowledged. Many are seeking solutions. Jubilee 2000, a consortium of religious and public interest groups, has made a commitment to work toward the elimination of poverty in sub-Saharan Africa. The European Union has begun to revisit the so-called "Tobin Tax," a tax on cross-border financial transactions, as a means to achieve a similar end. A group of fourteen industrialized nations has embraced the "Third Way" movement, a coalition of progressive industrialized and developing nations striving to "balance the forces of capitalism with the ideals of social justice."[3] The International Monetary Fund is working

---

[3] William Drozdiak, *Summit Considers "Third Way" to Solve Global Problems*, WASH. POST, June 4, 2000, at A24.

toward a program of debt relief for Africa. Yet, none of these measures alone, or in combination with direct foreign aid, holds the promise to appreciably abate destitution in sub-Saharan Africa.

The current debate concerning the deployment of funds to support antiterrorism efforts or to rejuvenate the faltering U.S. economy must include dedication of funds to alleviate the extremely disadvantaged population of sub-Saharan Africa. If, for example, Somalia or some other African locale is considered a platform for terrorist action, some consideration might be given to alleviating the conditions in those countries that create criminals dedicated to disrupting the status quo in the developed world. A Congress considering allocation of resources for security measures in Africa should consider implementation of the proposal made in this article. A balancing of the interests of the United States in enhanced security measures and a robust economy is short-sighted if it does not include consideration of its long-term interests in development and stability in the developing world.

Global Trajectories of Tax Reform: The Discourse of Tax Reform in Developing and Transition Countries

MIRANDA STEWART[1]

MAPPING AGENCIES AND PROCESSES OF GLOBAL TAX REFORM

The Influence of Developed Country Governments

Historically, developed countries influenced tax systems through imperial relationships. Although it has not been comprehensively surveyed, the importance of colonial influence on the tax systems of developing countries is widely recognized by tax reformers. Even countries that were not colonized modified their legal and economic regimes, including tax laws, by adopting reforms based on those of aggressive countries.

Contemporary tax laws of developed countries have also had a significant influence on the structure of tax regimes in other countries. A well-known example of this phenomenon is the importance of the U.S. foreign tax credit, which allows a credit against U.S. income tax due from American corporations and individuals who invest offshore and are subject to foreign income taxes. The credit only applies to those foreign taxes that have the "predominant character" of an income tax as defined by the United States. Various countries, including Mexico, have considered structuring their taxes to ensure that they will be creditable against the U.S. income tax in order to encourage U.S. investment.

A second means of developed country influence over tax law and policy in developing and transition countries has been through the negotiation of bilateral tax treaties. More powerful countries can typically extract significant concessions in this process. In addition, the form of tax treaties was developed by reference largely to tax laws of developed countries and the shape of international commerce among those countries. The rules apply to particular kinds of income – business profits, rents, royalties, interest, dividends – in a format that is based on dominant developed country norms of taxation, reflecting the tax mix in most developed countries.

The third means by which developed country governments have influenced tax reform projects is through direct foreign aid and technical assistance projects. Foreign aid began as a program to facilitate economic recovery of Western Europe,

[1] Reprinted by permission from 44 *Harvard International Law Journal* 139 (2003). Copyright © 2003 The President and Fellows of Harvard College and the Harvard International Law Journal.

Japan, and the territories occupied by Japan until World War II, with the Cold War political motivations of preventing the spread of communism and establishing stable economies. Tax reform projects formed part of this program from the beginning.

Tax Experts

Since World War II, nongovernment tax experts (usually based in academic institutions) have participated in many, if not most, cross-border tax reform efforts in developing and transition countries. The significant involvement of academic economists and lawyers began when Professor Carl Shoup, an economist based at Columbia University in the United States, led the Tax Mission to Japan of 1949–1950. The hallmarks of this early style of expert engagement in tax reform projects were idealism and experimentation: projects generally involved an eminent tax economist writing a report at the request of a foreign government that put forward "the finest work done up to that time in applied public finance," aimed at prescribing the "best tax system" for the relevant economy.[2]

The most significant single nongovernment source of tax expertise has been Harvard University and the Harvard Institute for International Development (HIID). Since 1952, Harvard Law School has offered an International Program in Taxation focused on developing countries for lawyers and public officials of foreign countries. HIID has been active in tax reform since 1975.

From the 1970s, there was a shift in the style of tax reform projects. The new projects involved longer and more detailed project work with local country officials, incorporated more legal experts engaged in actually drafting laws, and placed a greater focus on administration. In the 1990s, as HIID and the Harvard Program expanded their focus to tax reform in the newly emerged transition countries of Eastern Europe, the style of tax reform projects changed again. A key initiative of the Harvard Program has been the Basic World Tax Code (BWTC), developed as a simple and comprehensive tax law primarily for transition countries. The BWTC epitomizes a new focus on fast implementation of a basic set of tax laws.

The International Institutions

The international institutions that participate in tax reform in developing and transition countries now dominate in the sheer number and scope of tax reform projects worldwide. Not surprisingly, the most important institutions are those that play a key role in economic reform generally: the [International Monetary Fund (IMF)], World Bank, [World Trade Organization], and [Organization for Economic Co-operation and Development (OECD)]. Other regional international organizations, such as the Commission of the European Union, ASEAN, and the inter-American regional organizations also play a role in influencing tax reform projects. Recently, these institutions have attempted to increase coordination among themselves.

---

[2] Glenn P. Jenkins, *Tax Reform: Lessons Learned, in* Reforming Economic Systems in Developing Countries 293, 294 (Dwight H. Perkins & Michael Roemer eds., 1991).

The United Nations is a crucial actor in tax reform because it provides the overall context: a goal of market-driven economic development, including necessary tax reforms. U.N. agencies have participated in tax reform in developing countries since the 1950s. However, the United Nations does not do a great deal of tax technical work itself; instead, it is an active supporter of tax reform projects by the IMF and others. However, one area where the United Nations has played a significant role in tax reform on behalf of developing countries is in the development of a model tax treaty that is an alternative to the model prepared by the OECD for developed countries.

The "Remarkable Consensus" in Tax Reform

While the content of tax reform projects has changed over time, a "remarkable consensus" in tax reform policies and approaches appears to have developed since the 1980s. The policies of this consensus differ from the tax reform policies of prior decades. Dramatic shifts in tax reform discourse have taken place in the context of changes in overall economic development strategies.

The post–World War II economic development strategy of many developing countries included a particular role for tax policy. Dharam Ghai summarizes this strategy as one in which the state largely managed the process of economic growth, giving high priority to the goals of industrialization, diversification, and modernization. For tax policy, this meant tariff protection for domestic industry, input subsidies, and favorable domestic tax regimes (containing tax concessions or incentives) for industry. The agricultural and mineral sectors were highly taxed through mechanisms such as export taxes, heavy taxation of mining surpluses, and low expenditures. Tax policy was a means of intervention in the economy; all taxes, including trade taxes, were legitimate tools of the state in this development process. In the 1950s and 1960s, taxes designed to direct firms and individuals into particular investments and activities were a key part of development policy, and the governments of many developing countries relied heavily on these mechanisms into the 1970s.

Today, tax reform projects aim to undo the tax aspects of the model of development described by Ghai and to establish a "broad based" tax system that will encourage savings and operate in an open market economy. Development policies have shifted away from promoting self-sufficiency and subsidizing domestic industry to encouraging export-led growth. At the same time, driven by a need to fund government activities while reducing debt funding and government deficits, a key goal of most tax reform projects has been to increase tax revenues.

The contemporary tax reform "package" intended to achieve these goals includes a single-rate, broad-based [value added tax (VAT)] to replace older-style sales taxes; a low-rate, broad-based corporate and personal income tax; the goal of tax "neutrality" with respect to different investments and activities; and the gradual reduction and eventual elimination of import and export tariffs. This reform package is now espoused by international institutions and most tax experts.

A final trend in tax reform projects since the 1980s has been a decline in emphasis on progressive and redistributional goals in the tax system. A progressive tax system would place a greater tax burden on high-income earners and a nil or lower tax burden on low-income earners. From World War II to the 1970s, tax reform projects placed significant emphasis on a progressive system aimed at redistributing income and reducing income inequality. Reformers sought to implement this system through steeply rising income tax rates, and through taxation of capital held primarily by the wealthy, via income and wealth or asset taxes. These goals have generally been sidelined in contemporary tax reform discourse. The current consensus is that income taxes with relatively low- and flat-rate scales are more appropriate, and there has been a strong shift toward broad-based consumption taxes such as the VAT. The VAT is regressive in that it imposes a greater proportionate burden on the poor than on the wealthy (at least unless significant exemptions are allowed for foodstuffs and other necessary items such as fuel).

THE DISCOURSE OF TAX REFORM

The history of tax reform in developing and transition countries, which involved many agencies and processes and produced the "remarkable consensus" discussed earlier, is also the history of the development of a new, cross-disciplinary *discourse* of tax reform. A discourse may be thought of as a set of expressed ideas, opinions, ways of thinking, and ways of behaving according to a system of rules, within a social and institutional context. Thus, a discourse has its own epistemology, axioms, experts, and techniques. Discourse is not neutral, but is inherently political or ideological. Above all, discourse is partial although it claims to be universal.

Tax reform projects since World War II have brought together economists, lawyers, statisticians, public finance accountants, and information technology experts to participate in the collection of data, the writing of papers and reports, and the experimentation with new economic and legal forms of taxation in developing and transition states. The cross-fertilization between tax policy experts in the developed world and tax reformers in developing and transition countries – often the same people – has led to the flourishing of tax policy and the development of a set of international norms (the remarkable consensus) that are presented as basic principles for a successful tax system.

Tax reform discourse is primarily an economic discourse, and it claims to be scientific largely through its affiliation with economics and public finance theory. The technical nature of tax reform discourse gives it added authority through a claim to a "superior form" of knowledge. Legal practitioners of tax reform tend to rely uncritically upon the international norms of the tax reform discourse when drafting tax laws for a particular country. In addition, tax lawyers bring into the tax reform discourse a heavy emphasis on rules and drafting as a solution to problems of taxation in developing and transition countries. Both the economic and legal aspects of tax reform discourse depoliticize tax reform, reducing it to a matter of mechanics.

The notion of discourse links regimes of knowledge to power and explains the mechanisms by which such regimes produce "truths" about the world. Tax reform discourse conveys "truths" not only about tax reform, but about developing and transition countries (and their economies), the role of the state and its bureaucracy, poverty and inequality, the populations of taxpayers affected by tax reform.

international investment, and economic growth. Through the assertion of a consensus, tax reform discourse purports to be universal. In fact, it silences alternative "truths" or viewpoints on tax systems, development, progress, and inequality, which might run counter to the policies of economic globalization. For example, the discourse takes certain matters for granted, such as the goal of free trade to reduce tariffs. On the other hand, it ignores such matters as the role that massive debt plays in the perpetuation of fiscal deficits in developing countries – debt that arises not simply on account of countries' internal problems, but of historical international policies and crises. It casts matters that are the product of international and domestic policy, such as the increasing difficulty of taxation of international capital flows, as inevitable. It fails to see or count nonmarket activities, such as women's work in the home or subsistence agriculture. It legitimates inequality as a necessary short- or long-term consequence of the goals of efficiency and growth.

While a large part of tax reform discourse concerns the substance of policy and legal prescriptions for reform, another important element of the discourse establishes the framework, terms, and style of tax reform projects. This element is not simply a matter of method but has implications for the processes and outcomes of tax reform. The remarkable consensus incorporates a particular style of tax reform project. Tax reform projects no longer consist of detailed economic studies focused on one particular country with an "ideal" tax system in mind. Nor is current tax reform conducted as a lengthy policy and reform project. Instead, tax reform projects have been mass-produced and have spread rapidly across the globe through broad, superficial, and generalized tax policy recommendations grounded in the consensus. These recommendations are contained in the IMF Letters of Intent applicable to most developing countries, and the consensus further spreads through the use of legislative models such as the BWTC or the rapid extension of newly drafted tax laws in one country to another country, particularly in transition countries. The contemporary mass production of tax reform militates against any real domestic political participation in the determination of tax policies and laws in the countries undergoing reform.

Tax Reform and Development: "Making the State Safe for the Market"

Tax reform discourse incorporates an explicit vision of the developed, market-oriented state. It participates in the conceptualization of developing and transition countries as "'backward,' 'primitive,' 'feudal,' 'medieval,' 'developing country,' and 'pre-industrial,'" hence representing them as deficient in relation to a "Western" (i.e., "developed," or "international") norm.[3] It overlaps with a discourse of *development* that assumes a linear progress from a state of underdevelopment to a state of development, and positions the developed countries as the (only) models for development. It advances this conceptualization of development partly through two key narratives of the development of tax systems identifiable in the tax reform literature.

---

[3] SARA MILLS, DISCOURSE: THE NEW CRITICAL IDIOM 114, 117 (1997); Jenny Beard, *Representations of the Liberal State in the Art of Development*, 10 GRIFFITH L. REV. 6, 20 (2001).

The first narrative is an account of the *evolution* of tax systems from the primitive and simple to the modern and complex. The evolutionary narrative takes its form from a view of the history of tax systems in developed countries; that is, it relegates the developing country to a past stage of evolutionary development long since superseded by developed countries. The primary language of this narrative is numbers, generated through analysis of the tax structures and tax-related statistics of developing countries by organizations such as the IMF and OECD.

The second tax reform narrative is an account of *transition* or dramatic change from a "bad" to a "good" system – typically, from a socialist state and command economy to a market economy. The transition narrative of tax reform suggests a faster change than the evolutionary narrative. In general, the transition countries were encouraged to convert their institutions and economies as rapidly as possible to a market-friendly system. Tax reformers in these countries debated whether a "big-bang" or an "evolutionary" approach to tax reform should be taken. Many took the big-bang approach, with some external tax reformers suggesting that delays could lead to problems with mobilization of vested interests and a delay in stimulating domestic entrepreneurship and attracting foreign investors. The big-bang approach was facilitated by reformers using a model tax code such as the BWTC and by the apparent existence of a consensus in tax reform policy.

Failure of Tax Reform and the Shift to Governance

Buried in the tax reform narratives of progress and development is the story of the continuing failure of tax reform projects. The failure of reform projects is not unique to taxation – the failure of aid and development projects, in particular when they are based on external conditionality, is acknowledged in the development literature. Such failure has itself become an indicator of a state's less-developed status.

In general, the failures of economic reforms have been explained by international institutions and development experts as the result of weaknesses and mismanagement in target country governments. The failure of tax reform projects is frequently attributed to internal causes and not to the tax reform process itself.

The failure of tax reform projects suggests a number of more significant and interesting conclusions than those discussed in the tax literature. First, failure of tax reform may indicate unwarranted haste in reform or, more seriously, a mismatch or misunderstanding by tax reformers of the fit between particular tax reform proposals and the law, legal culture, and broader social and economic context in which they are applied. In particular, problems in ongoing enforcement may be the result of importation of inappropriate tax laws or mass-produced policy prescriptions.

Second, failure of tax reform may be caused by the lack of ownership of the reform policies or processes by government executives, bureaucracies, and political fora in the object countries. Recently, the issue of government ownership of economic reforms, including tax reforms, that are initiated or influenced externally has been acknowledged by reformers to be central to the success of reforms.

More fundamentally, failure of tax reform may be evidence of serious dissent among the population with respect to the reform. This may be the consequence of reformers, with or without the consent of the government, ignoring the political implications of tax reform. Tax reform projects are frequently constructed in such a way as to remove them from the domain of domestic politics. Tax reform may be required or recommended as a result of international negotiations conducted by the executive of the country, or it may be part of the conditions of a structural adjustment package that are not considered by the political mechanisms in the state. More subtly, but more pervasively, tax reform may be cast by external agencies as an essentially technical project which does not raise issues of politics at all.

Finally, tax reformers must acknowledge that the failure of tax reform may indicate a bind in which developing or transition countries are being asked to reform their systems in unsustainable ways and in an impossible time frame, given the competing economic pressures on the countries concerned.

Inequality and Poverty: What Happened to the Goal of Redistribution?

The goal of redistribution, classically known as the tax policy goal of "equity," has declined in importance over the last two decades. The goal of redistribution was a key element of the tax reform proposals of the 1950s and 1960s. Tax reformers focused not only on economic growth, but also on the role of taxation in development, meaning its role in influencing the sharing of the benefits of growth among the members of society.

Since the 1970s, and the emergence of the trend toward supply-side tax reforms, there has been much less focus on redistribution in tax reform, as goals of economic neutrality and revenue collection have taken precedence. In order to encourage savings and investment, the tax reform consensus emphasizes a shift to consumption taxes (in particular the VAT), which are regressive, and also proposes the imposition of low taxes on capital to encourage capital formation and investment, seen as essential to economic growth. Economic globalization and the ability of capital and highly skilled labor to flow offshore have led to the view that capital cannot be taxed (either at a high rate or at all), and that high marginal tax rates on skilled labor will also drive it offshore to lower-taxing jurisdictions.

I wish to emphasize that I am not arguing that tax theory is wrong in its attempts to model the optimal tax system. However, the marginalization of the goal of redistribution and the legitimization of inequality in tax reform are serious consequences of the wholesale adoption of these theories and should be addressed. Tax reform discourse, in sidelining the goal of progressivity, enables tax reformers to eschew responsibility for continued or increasing inequality and poverty in developing and transition countries. Instead, the task of reducing inequality and poverty has been shifted entirely to those responsible for the spending side of fiscal policy. At the same time, the goal of "fiscal discipline" has been used in developing and transition countries as a reason not only to reform taxes, but also to cut expenditures. In the 1980s and 1990s, this often meant cuts in health, education, safety net protections, and other social expenditures, causing real difficulties for significant parts of the population of adjusting countries. Only very recently has there been an acknowledgment that "public investments in broadly accessible education, health, and nutrition, in other basic social programs, and in the rural sector" are essential.[4]

The reduced attention paid to redistribution in the tax reform literature has occurred in the context of a period of "relative neglect" of issues of inequality and distribution in the broader development discourse, particularly in the 1980s. However, a number of economists and development theorists have recently worked to put inequality and redistribution back on the agenda. The recent concern about poverty is still dressed in the language of "fiscal discipline." Nonetheless, it suggests that there may again be some scope for tax reform discourse (together with the expenditure side of fiscal policy) to address directly issues of inequality, poverty, and redistribution in developing and transition countries, and between those countries and the developed world.

---

[4] U.N. High-Level Panel on Financing for Development, *Report of the High-Level Panel on Financing for Development: Recommendations*, at 5, U.N. Doc. A/55/1000 (2001).

CHAPTER 12. CRITICAL PERSPECTIVES ON CRITICAL TAX THEORY

The authors in this chapter call into question the baseline assumptions, method-ologies, and solutions proposed by critical tax scholars. In *Redistributive Justice and Cultural Feminism*, William J. Turnier, Pamela Johnston Conover, and David Lowery question whether there is any empirical support for a relationship between feminist self-identification and support for particular tax policies. The authors implicitly critique scholars who apply Carol Gilligan's theory of women's different moral reasoning to suggest either that "feminism" – however defined – supports income tax progressivity and the redistribution of wealth, or that a feminist tax system would be different from the current one.

In *Taking Critical Tax Theory Seriously*, Lawrence Zelenak evaluates much crit-ical tax scholarship as biased, lacking practical solutions, and agenda-driven. He exhorts feminist scholars in particular to pay attention to "careful balancing of conflicting feminist goals and careful development of legislative proposals that will actually further those goals." Zelenak scrutinizes the work of a number of critical tax scholars in his article to prove his points; however, space only permits us to reproduce his critiques of a few articles by way of example.

Joseph Dodge extends and complicates Zelenak's critique in A *Feminist Per-spective on the QTIP Trust and the Unlimited Marital Deduction*. Dodge is more inclined than Zelenak to see misogyny in the rule that permits an unlimited estate tax marital deduction for property left in a certain type of trust – a "qualified terminable interest property" trust – which gives a surviving spouse limited rights with respect to the trust property. But Dodge is critical of feminists for accepting the baseline principle of an estate tax marital deduction. Dodge suggests that a more robust feminist analysis might lead to far more sweeping reforms than critical tax scholars have imagined.

In the last article, *Caring Enough: Sex Roles, Work, and Taxing Women*, Amy Wax analyzes the nontax reasons for the different participation by men and women in the paid labor force. She points to social custom as a significant influence on the nature and extent of women's work. The work of Wax – whose primary teaching and scholarly interests are not in the field of taxation – provides an example of how scholars outside the tax academy enrich the academic and political discourse about taxation law and policy.

Redistributive Justice and Cultural Feminism

WILLIAM J. TURNIER, PAMELA JOHNSTON CONOVER,
AND DAVID LOWERY[1]

INTRODUCTION

The year 1982 saw the publication of Carol Gilligan's *In a Different Voice.* In general, Gilligan undertook to establish that differences in the approaches of men and women to moral and social structuring issues are based on a different way of approaching ethical and social issues. She found that males emphasize the autonomy of individuals and an ethos of rights in their approach, whereas females emphasize communitarian values and an ethos of care. Gilligan labeled neither approach as superior. Each provided useful, but different, modes for resolving moral and social issues.

Some legal scholars seized upon Gilligan's work as providing justification for creating new modes for evaluating existing legal rules and creating new rules. These scholars, who are sometimes grouped together under the label of the "cultural feminist school" of jurisprudence, claim that the existing legal construct, which was largely the product of a male-dominated society, is preoccupied with individual autonomy and an ethos of rights. Basing legal rules on communitarian values and an ethos of care would result in the making of dramatically different choices. Unlike Gilligan, cultural feminists often see the ethos of care as superior to the ethos of rights and see the changes that would be wrought in the legal system by application of the ethos of care as improvements on the present state of the law.

The purpose of this article is to test, in the context of redistributive justice, the basic postulate of cultural feminist jurisprudence – that men and women approach major societal issues differently so that were we to listen to [women's] different voice, different choices would be made about legal solutions to social problems. To this end, we employed conventional polling techniques and statistical analysis to determine if there are significant gender-based differences in the degree of support for a number of redistributive justice issues. We chose to test support for redistributive justice because, if the cultural feminists are correct, the combined effect of the female-oriented ethos of care with its emphasis on communitarianism and the male-oriented ethos of rights with its emphasis on individuality should result in women being dramatically more supportive than men of progressive tax

[1] Reprinted by permission from 45 *American University Law Review* 1275 (**1996**).

measures and of social spending measures that benefit the disadvantaged and the effectively disenfranchised.

SCHOOLS OF FEMINIST JURISPRUDENCE

Any attempt to classify the various ways that feminists theorize about legal issues is bound to be subject to criticism. Rather than being monochrome, much feminist scholarship resembles a painting where the artist has made use of a number of the colors on the pallet to provide us with her work of art. Nonetheless, it is useful to identify the four major schools of American feminist jurisprudence.

Although various scholars employ different labels in characterizing the different schools of feminist jurisprudence, we accept the four classifications that Professor Patricia Cain has established: (1) cultural feminism, (2) liberal feminism, (3) radical feminism, and (4) postmodern feminism. Because cultural feminism posits that gender alone can account for the different approaches made by men and women as solutions to social problems, we believed that it was possible to test empirically the cultural feminist postulate by employing conventional polling techniques and statistical analysis.

CULTURAL FEMINISM

The cultural feminist movement is principally based on the work of Professor Carol Gilligan. Professor Lawrence Kohlberg, an educational psychologist, established a theory and scale of cognitive moral development under which men generally outperformed women. Gilligan challenged Kohlberg for positing a moral hierarchy centered on a male-oriented ethos of justice or rights. Gilligan asserted that the female-oriented ethos of care should be accorded equal dignity in creating a moral hierarchy and in making judgments about relative moral maturity.

Gilligan's central exposition of the different approach of females and males in dealing with moral issues involves one of Kohlberg's moral hypotheticals. The hypothetical dilemma involved a situation where Heinz's wife is in desperate need of a drug that can save her life but Heinz cannot afford to purchase the drug from the pharmacist. The responses of Jake, a typical young boy, and Amy, a typical young girl, illustrate the different levels of moral development reached by each gender under Kohlberg's scale of moral development.

Jake quickly sees the moral dilemma as involving a conflict between the right to life and the right to property. He realizes that the former is more important than the latter and concludes that theft of the drug is morally justifiable.

Amy, on the other hand, is torn between stealing the drug and confronting the death of Heinz's beloved wife. She seeks accommodations, such as a loan, whereby Heinz might obtain the drug without stealing it and sees the druggist's failure to provide a mechanism whereby Heinz can obtain the drug as providing the principal moral issue in the scenario.

Gilligan tells us that Kohlberg would have us believe that Amy's reactions were indicative of her inability to view the dilemma as involving a clash between two rights, which occupy different places in a moral hierarchy, and her inability to address the proper choice in this conflict between morally unequal principles. Amy's response is reflective of a level of moral development, which Kohlberg would find inferior to that of Jake. Gilligan sees Amy's response as the result of a moral insight, which does not value abstract moral principles as much as it values sustaining concrete harmonious interpersonal relationships. Amy's approach, which emphasizes accommodating the interconnectedness of all involved in moral conflicts, should be contrasted and compared with, but not subordinated to, Jake's rights-oriented approach to the dilemma.

As support for the proposition that males and females employ different modes of resolving moral conflict, Gilligan notes that studies of children at play demonstrate that groups of young boys and groups of young girls at play manifest different ways of dealing with cheaters. Boys tend to remonstrate with the transgressor and ostracize him from the group. Girls, if they fail in their effort to have all play by the rules, will change the game to maintain cohesion of the group. Each group seeks to carry out worthy goals – strict enforcement of rules and maintenance of group cohesion – and each reflects values that are useful for social organization. Gilligan asserts that the ethos of rights, which characterizes the male approach to moral issues, and the ethos of care, which characterizes the female approach, make equally valuable social and moral contributions and that neither is superior to the other. Contrast this with some later cultural feminists who imply the superiority of the results that follow from application of the ethos of care.

Gilligan also posits that males define themselves by separation from others, whereas females define themselves by identification or connection with others. Gilligan's message that there is both a male-oriented and a female-oriented approach to moral reasoning has spawned a school of feminist jurisprudence that cannot be ignored.

Legal cultural feminists focus on Gilligan's observed differences between men and women and demand that society pay equal, or more, attention to women in creating its legal constructs. They assert that virtually all our existing legal system is the product of the male ethos of rights. They believe that, were society to listen to a woman's different voice, it would construct a somewhat different set of legal rules and mechanisms for resolving legal problems. Some commentators attribute the origin of the different voice to biology (nature); others attribute it to environment (nurture); and still others find it unnecessary to determine its origin.

Cultural feminists see the different voice of women as having two distinct impacts on our legal system. First, as members of the legal profession, women are viewed as having a potential impact on the profession, with female attorneys and judges approaching and resolving legal conflicts in a fashion that differs from the behavior of their male counterparts. Second, if society were to base its substantive rules on an ethos of care, rather than the existing male-oriented ethos of rights or justice, different fundamental choices would be made, choices that reflect care and connectedness rather than individual rights and separation.

Cultural feminists view woman's different voice as having the potential to produce dramatic changes in the legal profession, the judiciary, and in our procedural and substantive laws. While men center their value systems around abstract concepts such as justice and a system of rights based on individual autonomy, women emphasize interconnectedness and center their value systems around preservation of relationships, care, and responsibility. With these two positions as starting points, cultural feminists theorize about the potential impact of women's voice for changing the legal profession and various features of our system of procedural and substantive law.

METHODOLOGY

We decided to measure the validity of some of the claims of the cultural feminists and, to the extent that they are related, of the other schools of feminist jurisprudence by analyzing polling data on two significant redistributive justice issues: (1) support for social spending and (2) support for tax fairness. Given cultural feminist assertions about the potential impact of the ethos of care for changing substantive law and the profession and their emphasis on women's heightened appreciation of our connectedness and responsibility toward one another, we fully anticipated that women would be more supportive than men of redistributive justice in the form of social spending and tax fairness measures.

The data used in our analysis was generated by the Institute for Research in Social Science of the University of North Carolina at Chapel Hill. In the fall of 1992, the Institute conducted an extensive national telephone poll, the 1992 Southern Focus Poll, which employed random digit dialing. The poll in question oversampled in the South. To correct for the oversampling, responses were weighted to reflect a national random sample of persons aged eighteen or older living in households.

To test attitudes regarding redistributive taxation, we chose two issues that have figured prominently during the past few decades in national debates regarding tax issues, the progressive tax system and the preferential treatment of capital gains. Responses from the two items were combined to create a tax fairness index. Responses strongly supportive of redistributive tax policies were assigned a value of four, those that merely supported such measures were assigned a value of three, whereas those who were opposed were assigned a value of two, and those strongly opposed were assigned a value of one. The resulting potential index ranged from two to eight. To test opinions regarding tax progressivity respondents were asked the following:

> The federal income tax is based on the principle that people with higher incomes not only pay more taxes but also a greater percentage of their incomes in taxes. Do you think this is very fair, somewhat fair, somewhat unfair, or very unfair?

A second question focused on the capital gains issue and asked:

> Some say that capital gains – that is the profits people make from the sale of investment property, stocks and so forth – should be taxed at a lower rate than their income from wages and interest. Do you strongly agree, agree, disagree, strongly disagree or have no opinion?

Our central theoretical interests concerned gender and feminism. Our indicator of feminist identification for males and females was constructed using three questions. Respondents were asked whether they thought of themselves as feminists.

Those responding affirmatively were asked if they would describe themselves as strong or not so strong feminists. Those responding negatively were asked if they were strongly opposed, not so strongly opposed, or not at all opposed to feminism. Curiously enough, when responses on these questions were compared with respondents' gender, there was only a weak correlation between gender and feminist identification.

FINDINGS

Our analysis revealed that only two of the control variables strongly related to the tax fairness index. With fairly great confidence, we were able to conclude that lower income and Democratic party identification were strongly associated with greater support for tax fairness. A similar result was obtained when separate analysis was made of each of the two separate components of the tax fairness index, support for progressive taxation, and opposition to capital gains preference. In addition, more highly educated individuals, liberals, and white respondents responded with greater support for progressivity than did their opposites.

The impact of both gender and feminist identification, the main focal points of our study, on tax fairness issues was very weak. Surprisingly, however, the data did indicate that women are slightly less supportive of tax fairness than men when measured by their responses to the capital gains issue and using our two-factor tax fairness index. By a very narrow margin, women indicated greater support for progressive taxation; however, by a slightly wider margin, men indicated greater support for eliminating capital gains preferences. The impact of feminist identification was uniformly positive, as expected, but only the result using the two-factor tax fairness index was even marginally significant.

The picture became no clearer when we examined our two interactive variables, gender-feminist identification and gender-party identification. Although female feminists were more supportive of tax fairness than male feminists as measured on our two-factor tax fairness index and our capital gains index, only the capital gains index produced statistically significant results. Contrary to our expectations, when compared to their male counterparts, female Democratic party identifiers proved to be less supportive of tax fairness on both the progressive tax index and the capital gains index and, consequently, on the combined two-factor tax fairness index. Our analysis indicates that the influences of gender and feminist identification are not simple, uniform, or consistent.

To sort out these conflicting patterns, we employed simulation techniques. When all variables other than gender were held constant at their mean levels, males proved to be more supportive of tax fairness than women. This result, of course, is contrary to the intuitive reaction of cultural feminists. While this indicates that women are less supportive of tax fairness than the general male-female population, the difference is far from profound.

CONCLUSION

The female-oriented ethos of care, with its emphasis on communitarian values, should intuitively result in women being dramatically more supportive of redistributive justice measures than are men. Our data, however, indicate that there is little difference between women and men in their attitudes toward major redistributive justice issues involving tax fairness and social spending. Although women favored social spending to a slightly higher degree than men, they were slightly less favorably disposed toward tax fairness than men. The results are not supportive of the cultural feminist position. Moreover, our data indicated that other variables, such as income, age, party identification, and general support of liberal programs are at least as, and on occasion more, important in predicting support for tax fairness or social spending.

We can offer several possible explanations of the disparity between our results and the observation of cultural feminist psychologists, such as Professor Gilligan, on the differences between male and female behavior in their approaches toward individual personal moral behavior. It is possible that while men and women might speak in different voices on the micro-societal level, they may not do so on the macro level. Thus, while men might emphasize autonomy, individual rights, and justice and women might emphasize care, connectedness, and responsibility when forming opinions on moral issues on the interpersonal level, the two genders may speak in the same voice when addressing issues on the national level. If differences between the sexes in educational levels or other factors such as income, age, party affiliation, or liberalism account for differences in attitudes toward issues, regression analysis will expose that fact. This likely explains the failure of gender to emerge as a significant factor in determining support for redistributive justice. Because women have historically experienced the power of the state as more confining of personal liberties and potential than men have, it is possible that their distrust of government as an arbiter of redistributive justice might mitigate the otherwise likely impact of their ethos of care. This distrust may act to somewhat restrain their natural instincts toward programs that promise care when the government provides that care.

Although our study is helpful in evaluating the legitimacy of cultural feminist jurisprudence in the area of redistributive justice, it provides only modest insight into weighing the claims of competing schools of feminist jurisprudence.

Our analysis indicates that feminism has only a modest impact on the formation of attitudes toward redistributive justice. Moreover, male feminists emerged as more supportive of redistributive justice than female feminists. These facts hardly allow us to conclude that a legal structure that was not dominated by male opinion would be more supportive of redistributive justice than our present system of laws. Radical feminists may criticize the use of a woman's feminist self-identification as a proxy for the undominated woman's position, and we surely must concede that not all female self-identifiers could be classified as not dominated or imprinted by males. Nonetheless, it is in this group of women where one would expect to find such individuals. Given the very modest impact of feminism on shaping women's opinions on redistributive justice, we cannot conclude that women, in a world free of male domination, would significantly provide stronger support for redistributive justice than women provide at present in the existing environment.

We caution that the primary conclusions that we draw about cultural feminism are limited to the subject matters included in our survey. We can offer no comments on the validity of the observations of proponents of these schools of jurisprudence in other areas of the law. Moreover, even in the two subject matter areas of our study, tax fairness and social spending, our data and conclusions are limited in time and to the issues tested. Perhaps, in later generations, gender and feminist identification might prove to be significant in forming opinions on redistributive justice issues that significantly vary from those of the general population. At present, however, that is not the case.

We believe that the methodology and techniques of analysis employed in this study offer significant new opportunities for verifying a variety of theoretical claims. The potential applications of these techniques range far beyond the immediate exercise undertaken in this study. Our society, in general, and the legal profession, specifically, have a keen interest in working to ensure that our social norms reflect the multitude of interests in our increasingly diverse society. Given that goal, we believe that our research demonstrates the need to verify empirically the true opinions of our various national constituencies and to match the resulting data against the claims of theoreticians who seek to speak for various groups. To allow theorists, regardless of their good intentions, to articulate their version of the message of previously excluded voices is merely to substitute a new form of dominance for an old one. It is far more preferable to allow all excluded components to speak for themselves.

Taking Critical Tax Theory Seriously

LAWRENCE ZELENAK[1]

Among the most interesting and important developments in tax scholarship in recent years has been the growth of feminist tax policy analysis. Very recently, several examples of critical race theory tax analysis have also appeared. There also have been several articles proposing reforms in the taxation of same-sex couples. All these approaches can be subsumed under the label of critical tax analysis.

The interest of tax academics in such issues is long overdue. Precisely because of the importance of the endeavor, however, I am troubled that much of the work has not been carefully done. Four problems, in particular, weaken much of the literature.

The first problem is an overeagerness to accuse the tax laws of hostility to women or blacks. In the case of feminist analysis, this often results from failure to acknowledge the fundamental conflict between the feminist goals of changing traditional gender roles and helping those women who are already committed to traditional roles. It is difficult – sometimes impossible – to pursue one goal without interfering with pursuit of the other goal. Yet much feminist tax policy analysis pays scant attention to this dilemma. This is sometimes reflected in a readiness to accuse Congress of sexism (conscious or unconscious) whenever it acts to pursue one feminist goal at the expense of the other.

Closely related to the first problem is a failure to recognize the diversity within feminist thought. This has sometimes led to adoption of difference feminism as a guide to tax policy, without considering the powerful critiques within feminism of difference feminism, and without considering the likelihood that public policy founded on this version of feminism will prove counterproductive for women.

A third problem (also closely related to the first) is selection bias, both in the aspects of the tax laws chosen for study, and in the analysis of those chosen aspects. This is especially true of critical race theorists, who focus on Code provisions arguably disadvantageous to blacks, but pay no attention to Code provisions arguably favorable to blacks. The same problem also appears in the feminist literature, when the possibility that a criticized provision may have pro-feminist effects is disregarded.

[1] Reprinted by permission from 76 *North Carolina Law Review* 1521 (1998).

The most serious problem is the failure to think through proposed solutions with sufficient care. The solutions are often presented as afterthoughts, with minimal consideration of whether the author's goal is best achieved through the tax system rather than through nontax legal reform, and with minimal consideration of whether the proposed tax solution will have the desired effects. It is unfair to criticize current law for its effects on women or blacks without showing a way to do better; more important, mere critique without a workable solution does nothing to better anyone's situation.

These are only tendencies, of course, rather than features of every feminist tax analysis. Still, most feminist and critical race tax analyses feature one or more of these problems. The plan of this article is to discuss a small number of articles in some detail to illustrate the previous points.

Given the sensitivity of the topic, and the critical nature of most of my analysis, the risk of misunderstanding is high. Accordingly, it is important to offer at the outset a brief explanation of where I am coming from. I think the basic project of feminist tax policy analysis is worthwhile and important. (I am less convinced of the merits of the critical race tax project, although it is too early to dismiss the approach.) It may be the most exciting area in legal tax scholarship today. But the few easy battles – against tax provisions clearly sexist in language or intent – already have been fought and won. The problems that remain require careful balancing of conflicting feminist goals and careful development of legislative proposals that will actually further those goals. What I propose is to take feminist and other critical tax policy analysis seriously – more seriously than its proponents have taken it in many cases.

Finally, before beginning to examine the articles in detail, a few words about my own position on feminism. For whatever it may be worth, I have been identified in print as a feminist tax scholar. I earned this designation for arguing that the tax laws should reflect governmental neutrality between one- and two-earner couples, and that the present joint return system inappropriately (albeit unintentionally) favors the one-earner model. I leave it for others to decide whether that is sufficient to make me a liberal feminist, or whether feminism requires calling for more than merely an end to tax distortion of women's choices. In any event, I am comfortable with the feminist perspectives of most of the authors discussed in this article; my criticism is mostly of the underexamined links between means and ends. In the few cases where I disagree on basic premises – most notably with unnuanced versions of difference feminism – I will note my disagreement, but I will also accept those premises for the sake of argument and attempt to engage the authors on their own terms to determine what those premises imply for tax policy.

DIFFERENT VOICES AND PROGRESSIVE TAXATION

In *The Rhetoric of the Anti-Progressive Income Tax Movement: A Typical Male Reaction* [see Chapter 2], Marjorie Kornhauser constructs an argument for a progressive income tax based on Carol Gilligan's book, *In a Different Voice: Psychological Theory and Women's Development*. Gilligan's work describes differences in the developmental psychology of boys (and young men) and girls (and young women). The ethical development of boys centers on a "morality of rights," which emphasizes the separateness and autonomy of individuals. Under this morality, duties to others are only negative – duties of noninterference. By contrast, girls' development is founded on an "ethic of care," which emphasizes interdependence, the web of human connectedness, and responsibility toward others.

Kornhauser characterizes Gilligan's ethic of care as feminist, and describes feminism as "less a theory than a way of knowing and of being, experienced by a large segment [approximately 50%] of the world's population."[2] This is peculiar usage because it seems to reduce feminism to a matter of one's sex. To Kornhauser, all females are necessarily feminist, and all males are necessarily not feminist.

It follows from the ethic of care, according to Kornhauser, that responsibility to others extends beyond friends and relations. What does this entail? "It . . . requires that as my discretionary income grows, I contribute money at a greater rate than previously to help others. . . . Thus, a progressive income tax rate satisfies my obligation to myself and others. It is not a redistribution of wealth, merely a paying of my 'just debts' to others."[3]

Kornhauser's Misreadings of Gilligan

When Kornhauser claims, "We also must maintain a . . . connectedness to the nonproximate stranger,"[4] she moves from the indicative to the imperative. She is no longer in Gilligan's world of describing how girls and women actually are; she is in Kornhauser's world of how "we" ought to be. Her assertion is not supported by any citation to Gilligan – which is not surprising because *In a Different Voice* offers virtually no support for the proposition that the female ethic of care extends to the "nonproximate stranger." The girls and women Gilligan describes see their responsibilities as being toward those closest to them – family, friends, and lovers.

In the final chapter of *In a Different Voice*, Gilligan goes beyond her descriptive approach to a normative vision of fully integrated adults. She explains: "In the transition from adolescence to adulthood, the dilemma itself is the same for both sexes, a conflict between integrity and care. But approached from different perspectives, the dilemma generates the recognition of opposite truths."[5] A young woman, who already has a strong sense of responsibility to others, must temper that ethic of care with a morality of rights. A young man, by contrast, must transform "the ideological morality of adolescence into the adult ethic of taking care."[6] Thus, despite the different routes they take, each finally recognizes "two different moralities whose complementarity is the discovery of maturity."[7] Even after this "convergence in judgment,"[8] differences remain. Men are still founded

---

[2] Marjorie E. Kornhauser, *The Rhetoric of the Anti-Progressive Income Tax Movement: A Typical Male Reaction*, 86 MICH. L. REV. 465, 506–07 (1987).

[3] *Id.* at 511.

[4] *Id.* at 510.

[5] CAROL GILLIGAN, IN A DIFFERENT VOICE: PSYCHOLOGICAL THEORY AND WOMEN'S DEVELOPMENT 164 (1982).

[6] *Id.*

[7] *Id.* at 165.

[8] *Id.* at 167.

in separation, women in attachment. But it is now more a difference of degree or emphasis, rather than a radical difference in kind.

To my mind, this convergence should be good news for anyone trying to find support in Gilligan for progressive taxation. The male capacity for abstraction brings the nonproximate stranger into one's range of vision, and the female capacity for care suggests a responsibility to that stranger. But this is a humanist case for progression, not a feminist one. To Kornhauser, who wants to construct a peculiarly feminist case for progression, the convergence is a problem.

The Implications of Kornhauser's Reading of Gilligan

Suppose that *In a Different Voice* really said what Kornhauser takes it to say – that women, with their ethic of care, feel a sense of responsibility to the nonproximate stranger, and men do not. What guidance, if any, would that information provide in designing a tax system? In particular, what would it tell us about progressive rates? It would not tell me nearly as much as it tells Kornhauser, for several reasons.

Kornhauser believes that everyone is entitled to the financial preconditions for self-fulfillment. Obviously, the money to provide this to those who have less than enough must come from those who have more than enough. But how do we tell whether those with a surplus should contribute in proportion to their surplus, or progressively? Either kind of system could satisfy the societal duty to the needy. According to Kornhauser, the tax should be progressive because "as my income grows, it is easier for me to contribute more without impinging on my ability to reach my own goals."[9] That is her entire argument as to why the feminist ethic of care calls for progressivity rather than proportionality: an appeal to the declining marginal utility of money, with interpersonal comparisons permitted. I have no problem with the argument. At bottom, it is the case for progressivity. What it gains from association with *In a Different Voice*, however, is not apparent.

Kornhauser's feminist case for progression is based on a particular use of tax revenues – providing the financial opportunity for self-fulfillment to the poor. To use an analysis premised on this use of tax revenues as a justification for any particular tax system design is to adopt a rather romantic view of governmental expenditures. At most only about 40% of the expenditures to which income tax revenue is devoted fit Kornhauser's model of the function of government. By contrast, almost half of the expenditures are for national defense and interest on the national debt. What does the ethic of care say about the proper tax system for raising money to pay for a nuclear submarine or to cover the cost of federal borrowing? Probably nothing, since it is doubtful that the ethic of care approves of either nuclear weapons or mortgaging our children's futures, regardless of financing methods. But in that case, the ethic of care has nothing to tell us about how half of general federal tax revenues should be raised.

If Kornhauser is descriptively correct, and men and women really do have fundamentally different beliefs as to the rightness of progressive taxation, what is to be done? Apparently the tax system has to have either a male (flat) or a female

---

[9] Kornhauser, *supra* note 2, at 511.

(progressive) rate structure, and either way half the population will be disenfranchised. Kornhauser does not frame the dilemma so starkly, but her answer appears to be that the feminine approach should prevail because it is objectively right. Its fit is best because there really is altruism in the world, a few examples of which Kornhauser cites. But this appeal to altruism solves nothing, for two reasons. First, she makes no attempt to quantify altruism compared with selfishness; altruism may exist but be uncommon. Second, she does not tell us whether these examples of altruism are disproportionately female, or whether they are equally the work of women and men. If disproportionately female, we are back in the original dilemma. If equally divided between the sexes, then her entire premise – that hers is a feminist case for progression – collapses.

Given the obvious failure of the existence of altruism to prove Kornhauser's case, I suspect she really thinks the ethic of care should govern the choice of tax rate structure because she thinks the feminine ethic of care is morally superior to the masculine ethic of rights. But if that is what all women think, and if all men think the opposite, it is cultural imperialism for either sex to impose its views on the other. How does an ethic of care, however morally commendable it may be, justify coercing the selfish into being altruistic? For that matter, how is coerced altruism altruism at all?

Actually, there are ways out of the dilemma. If the ethics of men call for payment of proportional taxes (at most), while the ethics of women call for progressive taxation, then we could have separate rate schedules – flat for men, progressive for women. Or if for some reason that seems objectionable, we could have a flat tax for all; and if women felt the need to do more to satisfy their responsibility of care to the nonproximate stranger, they could voluntarily give more to their favorite charities or to the government.

This proposal, rather than coercive progressive taxation, is what logically follows from Kornhauser's premises. A system very like this has been championed by a group not normally thought of as feminist – Republicans. Their advocacy of flat taxes, supplemented by "a thousand points of light,"[10] could have been inspired by Kornhauser's analysis.

CRITICAL RACE THEORY AND THE CODE

In *A Black Critique of the Internal Revenue Code* [see Chapter 5], Beverly I. Moran and William Whitford investigate "whether the Internal Revenue Code systematically favors whites over blacks."[11] They consider their study a test of the claim of critical race theory that "racial subordination is everywhere" in American society.[12] To perform the test, they adopt the hypothesis that "deviations from the ideal of a comprehensive income tax systematically favor whites over blacks,"[13] and select

[10] George Bush, *Presidential Nomination Acceptance Speech* (Aug. 18, 1988), *in* N.Y. Times, Aug. 19, 1988, at A14.

[11] Beverly I. Moran & William Whitford, *A Black Critique of the Internal Revenue Code*, 1996 Wis. L Rev. 751, 751.

[12] *Id.* at 751–52.

[13] *Id.* at 753.

four aspects of the Code for analysis. The four aspects are: various benefits granted to owners of wealth, including the exclusion of gifts from income, the failure to tax unrealized appreciation, and the reduced rate for capital gains; the tax benefits for home ownership, including the interest and property tax deductions; tax-favored employee benefits, especially retirement savings; and the marriage penalty imposed by joint returns on many two-earner couples.

According to Moran and Whitford, all four aspects of the Code work to the detriment of blacks. They apply the same basic analysis to each of the first three aspects. The Code provides tax benefits for the ownership of certain kinds of assets, and blacks are less likely than whites to own such assets. This is not merely a matter of the tax benefits being skewed toward higher-income taxpayers. Even controlling for income, blacks own fewer assets in general, and fewer tax-favored assets in particular, than whites. Their analysis of the fourth aspect – the marriage penalty – is different. When persons with roughly equal incomes marry, they suffer a marriage penalty; their tax liability increases. When persons with very unequal incomes marry, they enjoy a marriage bonus; their tax liability goes down. Since black spouses tend to have more equal incomes than white spouses, black married couples are disproportionately victims of the marriage penalty.

An Arbitrary Choice of Baseline

Except for the marriage penalty, all the tax provisions investigated by Moran and Whitford are "tax benefits." They define a tax benefit as "any opportunity for deductions or exclusions from income that deviate from the ideal of a comprehensive income tax base."[14] If a deviation from that ideal disproportionately favors whites, that is evidence in favor of the critical race theory hypothesis. The entire analysis depends on the validity of their assumption that a comprehensive income tax base is the appropriate race-neutral standard. For the Code to be skewed in favor of whites, it must be skewed relative to some standard. That standard, according to Moran and Whitford, is a comprehensive income tax.

Unmentioned by Moran and Whitford, there is an ongoing debate – academic and political – between those who believe income is the appropriate tax base, and those who believe the tax base should be consumption. Most of the deviations from a comprehensive income tax criticized by Moran and Whitford are consistent with the methods of implementing a consumption tax. Tax deferral for unrealized appreciation and retirement savings, for example, is consistent with a cash-flow consumption tax. The reduced rate on capital gains, and the permanent forgiveness of tax on unrealized appreciation held at death, are moves in the direction of the yield-exemption method. Because of these consumption tax features, the current "income tax" is really a hybrid income-consumption tax. By one estimate, actual law is roughly equipoised between a comprehensive income tax and a consumption tax.

Given these different views of the ideal tax system, it is not enough simply to assume an income tax ideal and label as suspect any tax provision which departs

[14] *Id.*

from that ideal. Instead, the first steps in the analysis should be the choice of baseline and a defense of that choice. Consider how Moran and Whitford's analysis would change if the suspect provisions of current law were those that departed from a consumption tax ideal. Tax deferral for retirement savings and unrealized appreciation would not be suspect provisions, but provisions that taxed investment income would be suspect. Key suspect provisions would include the taxation of interest, dividends, rents, and capital gains. If these forms of income are realized disproportionately by whites – as they almost certainly are – then starting from a consumption tax ideal, Moran and Whitford would have to conclude the Code is systematically biased against whites.

My view is that it makes no sense to search the Code for hidden racial bias from either starting point. The arguments between income tax and consumption tax proponents are close to a standoff, both intellectually and politically. Given that standoff, there is no reason to privilege either extreme position as the proper starting point in a search for hidden discrimination. Without a good reason to start from either extreme, there is no reason to accuse the actual hybrid tax of discrimination against any race.

Sampling Bias

Moran and Whitford present their study as a quasi-scientific test of the critical race theory hypothesis of universal racial subordination. Although the test samples only a few Code provisions, they believe the results – of racial subordination in every Code aspect studied – are striking enough to support a tentative conclusion: "The entire Code is likely skewed in the favor of whites."[15] That inference is not justified if the provisions studied were not randomly selected. There is nothing in the article, however, to suggest the selection was random. To the contrary, at two points Moran and Whitford mention tax benefits (the earned income tax credit and head-of-household filing status), which may benefit blacks more than whites, and then announce their study will not consider those provisions. Setting aside provisions likely to work against the hypothesis is not an application of the scientific method.

It is not hard to think of provisions which appear to be pro-black, by the standards of their analysis. The earned income tax credit, which they mention in passing, is one obvious candidate. This is a massive subsidy for the working poor. It seems likely the benefits go disproportionately to blacks.

Other likely candidates for pro-black provisions, which Moran and Whitford do not mention, come readily to mind. The exclusion from income of welfare-type benefits probably disproportionately favors blacks. The very existence of the wealth transfer taxes (estate, gift, and generation-skipping) disproportionately burdens whites, since whites transfer a disproportionate share of total wealth.

In addition to nonrandomly selecting Code sections for study, Moran and Whitford also nonrandomly select from among possible racial analyses of the provisions they do study. They claim that the joint return system disproportionately burdens

[15] *Id.* at 801.

black married couples. The system creates marriage penalties when husband and wife have roughly equal incomes, and marriage bonuses when husband and wife have very unequal incomes. Since the incomes of black spouses tend to be more nearly equal than the incomes of white spouses, Moran and Whitford argue the system discriminates against blacks.

One can argue equally well, however, based on the same law and the same facts, that joint returns are biased against whites. In *Taxing Women*, Edward McCaffery claims that the most significant problem with joint returns is the stacking effect – the fact that joint returns tax the income of a secondary earner in a marriage (traditionally the wife) much more heavily than the income of the primary earner. The stacking effect discourages wives from working outside the home, in the case of wives who view themselves as secondary earners. McCaffery finds marriage penalties less important than the stacking effect. But if, as Moran and Whitford's evidence suggests, black married women are generally not secondary earners, then from the point of view of the stacking effect it is white wives who are disproportionately harmed by joint returns.

The two arguments are not logically inconsistent. It is possible for joint returns to harm blacks in one way and to harm white women in another. The problem, again, is with the selection bias that permeates Moran and Whitford's analysis. Arguments that the tax laws are anti-black are explored in depth; equally plausible arguments pointing the other way are not.

The Problems with the Solutions

Even conceding, for the sake of argument, that Moran and Whitford have identified instances of troubling racial skewing in the Code, some of their solutions are also troubling. For example, they present evidence that black employees participate in 401(k) voluntary retirement savings plans at a rate lower than white employees, even controlling for income. The lesson they draw is that 401(k) should probably be repealed. This is more a surrender than a solution. If the basic problem is that blacks do not save enough, changing the tax laws to make it harder for blacks to save is not a helpful response. A better approach would be to retain tax incentives for savings (especially retirement savings), and to use education and exhortation to increase black response to those incentives. The general question is whether the tax laws should be changed to accommodate black consumption patterns and low savings rates, when those patterns are of doubtful utility. Most of the time, including the example of 401(k), Moran and Whitford favor accommodating current behavior. I disagree.

After explaining how blacks are disproportionately burdened by the marriage penalty of joint returns, Moran and Whitford suggest three possible legislative solutions. The solutions resemble those in much of the feminist tax policy literature, in that they are described only in broad outline, and their implications are not carefully explored. The first solution is mandatory separate filing for spouses. But they go on to propose two alternate solutions, in case a "Black Congress" would want to encourage marriage by eliminating marriage penalties while preserving marriage bonuses.

The first alternate solution would give married taxpayers the choice of filing two returns as if they were single, or of filing a joint return, depending on which choice resulted in a lower tax liability. Solely from a black perspective, would this be desirable? Assuming no change in tax rate schedules, the result of the proposal would be a decrease in taxes paid by married couples as a group. Couples currently suffering a marriage penalty would reduce their taxes by filing separately, and couples currently enjoying a marriage bonus would have no change in their taxes. In addition to a drop in total tax revenues, this would mean single persons would bear a larger portion of the total tax burden. As Moran and Whitford themselves point out, single persons are disproportionately black. The appeal to a Black Congress of increasing the share of the tax burden imposed on a group disproportionately black is not readily apparent.

The second alternate solution would give married couples the same choice as the first, but would extend that choice of filing status to unmarried couples as well. In addition to having marriage bonuses without marriage penalties, the system would have cohabitation bonuses without penalties. This proposal would increase the portion of the total tax burden falling on the "truly single." Although it is impossible to count the truly single without knowing exactly how they would be defined for tax purposes, they are probably disproportionately black (because singles in general are disproportionately black). We do know that a major component of the truly single – and a group in especially difficult circumstances – is single mothers living with children under eighteen. Black women are hugely overrepresented in this category. Would a Black Congress really want to help couples – married and unmarried – at the expense of single parents?

CONCLUSION

Critical tax analysts certainly have no monopoly on one-sided analysis or inadequately considered reform proposals. Is there really anything special about the faults of the critical tax literature? Although I cannot offer definitive proof, I believe there is something special – that problems of one-sidedness and incomplete analysis are more common in the critical tax literature than in the general academic tax policy literature.

If that is true, *why* is it true? One reason may be that participants in the critical tax project do not approach the tax laws in a detached and disinterested frame of mind. In their introduction to *Taxing America*, [Karen] Brown and [Mary Louise] Fellows present "those interested in joining in this project" with "the challenge of . . . uncovering bias and discrimination in the tax law."[16] Within the critical tax movement, there is a reward for examining a tax provision and finding it guilty of hidden discrimination; there is no reward for discovering a provision is innocent. In reading much of the critical tax literature, one comes away with the impression the authors set out on the sort of search for hidden discrimination called for by Brown and Fellows. In the case of Moran and Whitford, they acknowledge as much.

---

[16] Karen B. Brown & Mary Louise Fellows, *Introduction, in* TAXING AMERICA 20–21 (Karen B. Brown & Mary Louise Fellows eds., 1996).

While it is certainly possible that a search will find legitimate grievances, the nature of the project creates a great danger of unfounded complaints and poorly considered reform proposals. This problem is not unique to critical tax theory – other tax academics also have axes to grind – but it seems especially pervasive here.

The biggest problem, however, is that almost no one is engaging critical tax theorists in the scholarly dialogue needed in order to test their arguments and proposals. Those outside the movement have simply ignored it, while those within have mostly chosen support at the expense of discussion and debate. This is understandable, given the small size and outsider status of the movement. What is needed now is vigorous discussion among those both within and outside the critical tax movement. I hope this article – by someone outside the movement but sympathetic to some of its goals – will expand the dialogue.

A Feminist Perspective on the QTIP Trust and the Unlimited Marital Deduction

JOSEPH M. DODGE[1]

Professor Lawrence Zelenak's article, *Taking Critical Tax Theory Seriously* [earlier this Chapter], scores many points, but I am nevertheless moved to critique the part of the article that relates to the [qualified terminable interest property (QTIP)] trust and the marital deduction. I also have some bones to pick with feminist scholarship in this area, namely, its innuendos of a male chauvinist plot, its general inattention to the QTIP trust problem, its acquiescence in the unlimited marital deduction, and its failure to come up with a plausible solution. The foregoing critiques tend to validate Professor Zelenak's thesis that critical tax scholarship betrays a "whiner" mentality: (1) critical tax scholarship obsesses over tax provisions it does not like while ignoring the larger context, and (2) it is weak on plausible solutions.

INTRODUCTION

The full value of the QTIP trust qualifies for the gift or estate tax marital deduction even though the transferee spouse (the "wife" or "widow") has only a right to income for life, with no powers of disposition or control. The "price" to be paid for full qualification for the marital deduction is that the QTIP trust property is included in the wife's unified estate and gift tax base, although the burden of the tax "on" the QTIP trust is usually borne by the trust itself and not the wife's own estate.

Both the QTIP trust device and the unlimited marital deduction entered the estate and gift tax as a "package" in the Economic Recovery Tax Act of 1981 (ERTA). The link between the two was explicit. Previously, to qualify for the marital deduction the husband had to give the wife, at a minimum, not only an income interest for life but also a general power of appointment, that is, an unrestricted power of inter vivos or testamentary disposition. At the same time, under pre-ERTA law (and simplifying matters somewhat) the amount of the marital deduction could not exceed half of the gift, or half of the husband's net estate. The pre-ERTA marital deduction was designed (although poorly) to allow a tax-free splitting of the aggregate marital estate, similar to the result achieved automatically (and without tax) in the case of community property upon divorce.

---

[1] Reprinted by permission from 76 *North Carolina Law Review* 1729 (1998).

With an unlimited marital deduction, the husband can reduce his taxable estate to zero by leaving his entire gross estate in the form of qualifying marital deduction transfers. A more sophisticated alternative is for the husband to make that amount of qualifying marital deduction transfers as will reduce his taxable estate to that amount that will produce a tax which will be reduced to zero after subtracting the unified transfer tax credit available to the husband's estate. Since qualifying transfers will, unless consumed or wasted, appear in the surviving spouse's transfer tax base, the current unlimited marital deduction allows no transfer tax to be paid until the widow dies or disposes of the property.

THE QTIP TRUST AND FEMALE EMPOWERMENT

Feminists attack the QTIP trust arrangement on the ground that it was motivated by male determination to prevent the widow from controlling the devolution of the property. This claim appears to be overstated. The QTIP trust was always viewed as a tradeoff for the unlimited marital deduction. The unlimited marital deduction is assumed naturally (if superficially and indeed wrongly) to be beneficial to wives and widows due to its allowance and its (apparent) encouragement of an increase in qualifying marital deduction bequests.

What caused the appearance of the QTIP provision in the 1981 legislation is hard to determine, but it was clearly an afterthought to the unlimited marital deduction, which was promoted for political reasons. Thus, it is difficult to attribute to the 1981 Congress as a collective body a plot to deprive women of property rights, although it is conceivable that some legislators were aware of the effect of the 1981 package.

There is no doubt that the QTIP device diminishes the autonomy of wives and widows, who statistically are the usual beneficiaries of QTIP trusts. The wife or widow is deprived of any power to control the disposition of the property, and the property is usually in trust, which deprives her of administrative control. QTIP trusts implement the husband's dead-hand control. It should be up to the widow herself to make the decision to self-settle a trust, or perhaps to employ investment advisors. QTIP trusts are by far the most commonly used form of marital deduction for wealthy husbands. The estate planning community (if not Congress) is deeply patriarchal in outlook.

The QTIP trust is a potent, if subtle, technique for the disinheritance of widows. The lure of an income interest for life in a large portion of the husband's estate may seduce the widow into foregoing her inheritance rights. For the deceased husband, the retention of dead-hand control of the property's devolution can be obtained at a minimal price. In short, the QTIP trust offers marginal welfare-type benefits, at best, for widows, but allows husbands to reap supermarginal benefits.

The appropriate baseline for evaluating the QTIP trust is the norm of facilitating (if not mandating) equal estate-splitting, which was the norm that informed the pre-ERTA marital deduction regime and accords with the notion of wealth that is "shared." The pre-ERTA regime did this crudely and in an excessively complex manner, but that need not concern us here. Under pre-ERTA law, in order to obtain the marital deduction, the husband had to leave the widow no less than a power-of-appointment trust.

THE QTIP TRUST CANNOT BE DEFENDED ON THE MERITS

I contend that the QTIP trust cannot be defended on its own, wholly apart from its being a tradeoff for the unlimited marital deduction. The most decisive argument against the QTIP trust is that the widow's income-only interest in trust is not very valuable. First, the concept of "income" under the law of trusts is narrower than economic income: capital gains and appreciation are excluded. Second, the trustee's normal duty is to preserve the corpus against erosion by inflation and to balance fairly the interests of the income beneficiary and the remainder. These conditions produce a situation in which a substantial portion of the economic return is (or can be) devoted to the remainder interest. Third, trustees are subject to the prudent investor rule constraining investments. Fourth, the "income" is net of trustee fees charged against income, an expense that would be eliminated if the widow owned the property outright. The third and fourth points combine to suppress the total economic return. Thus, in the mid-1990s, a QTIP trust beneficiary would be likely to enjoy an income yield of only 3% or 4% of asset value. This income is, of course, subject to income tax in the hands of the widow. Using a 4% discount rate, an income interest in trust for ten years (roughly the median survival period for widows) is worth only about 30% of the corpus. The notion of a 3% or 4% "income" yield is now being touted as a desirable norm in order to "preserve" corpus more effectively against erosion. Such a strategy in the context of an income-only QTIP trust will have the effect of reducing the income to be distributed to the widow and increasing the amount passing to third parties.

Finally, any tax savings attributable to the unlimited marital deduction (which can occur only in large estates due to the generous exemptions) will in most cases inure wholly to the benefit of the non-marital-deduction transfers, since any taxes would otherwise be charged to such transfers. Thus, the widow will rarely benefit from any incremental tax savings attributable to an unlimited marital deduction; any tax savings that do augment the QTIP trust will benefit the widow only in proportion to the value of her income-only interest in such trust.

A deduction that neither provides a tax incentive to benefit widows (beyond about 3% in half of the couple's aggregate wealth) nor gives widows a significant economic stake in any tax savings that result from the system hardly deserves to be called a "marital deduction."

A DEDUCTION FOR THE VALUE OF INTERESTS TRANSFERRED TO SPOUSES?

It has been proposed by Professor Gerzog [see Chapter 6] (among others) that the amount of the marital deduction should equal the value of the interests in property that the wife or widow obtains from the husband. In contrast to the current system, which allows a deduction equal to the full amount of the property in a QTIP trust, the proposal would result, when the husband leaves the wife or widow a life estate, in a deduction limited to the actuarial value of the life estate as of the husband's death. The rationale is that the marital deduction should equal only the value of what the widow or wife gets.

The deduction-equals-value approach has seductive appeal, but it is ultimately a bad idea. From the feminist perspective, it would do little to inhibit a husband from using a spousal income-only trust. Giving wives special powers of appointment or naming them as trustees would be discouraged, since powers would not possess any value. The deductible amount would be a function of the widow's life expectancy, which would create an irrational incentive structure. Most importantly, estate planners would greatly favor income-only trusts because income-only interests are, under the estate and gift tax actuarial tables, greatly overvalued. Thus, the husband's deduction would far exceed (on average) the real value of the widow's benefit in present value terms. Moreover, reliance on actuarial tables allows gaming of the system: the excess of the deductible amount over the present value of what widows actually receive would widen if the widow dies prematurely or the trust can shift economic return from "income" to capital appreciation, which benefits the remainder interest. Finally, the "estate trust" would become the misogynist's dream: a 100% deduction, but no guarantee that the widow will receive any benefits during life.

The only airtight solution that prevents actuarial manipulation would be a quali-fication rule that would require an outright transfer, a power-of-appointment trust, or an annuity for a term of years. The term-annuity option would be unappealing both to the husband, since a widow dying prematurely could control the dispo-sition of the unpaid account balance, and to the widow, who might outlive the annuity period.

CONCLUSION

The analysis of both the post-ERTA system and the deduction-equals-value alter-native leads to the conclusion that the optimal solution is to abolish the QTIP trust (and the estate trust) and to allow qualification only for outright transfers and (perhaps) power-of-appointment trusts. The unlimited marital deduction could be kept for gift tax purposes for reasons of administrative simplicity. For estate tax purposes, the unlimited marital deduction should be replaced by an estate-equalization limitation. This system would create a community-property-like template for interspousal transfers, a template that already is the property regime governing about 30% of the population, and would reasonably accommo-date the interests of both husbands and wives.

The best marital deduction scheme would not be as effective in securing the interests of wives as would the optimal legal regime pertaining to marital property rights and succession. Autonomy feminists should be especially skeptical of the institution of the trust and other forms of long-term, dead-hand control.

Caring Enough: Sex Roles, Work, and Taxing Women

AMY L. WAX[1]

The triumph of the modern feminist movement in Western society over the past thirty-odd years is unprecedented in human history. Although feminism has had many important effects on a range of social practices, the story of its march is, at its core, the story of large numbers of women for the first time being permitted to engage in activities and occupy social roles formerly reserved to men. This change postdates, but itself completely coincides with[,] a development associated with modernity – the creation of modern labor markets. In the wake of feminism, those markets have seen the steady demise of practices that prevented women from offering, or employers from accepting, women's and men's labor on the same terms.

Without giving a full account of how and why these changes occurred, it is sufficient to say that traditional sex role norms have suffered grievously in recent years. Although powerful conventions and expectations still underwrite pronounced occupational segregation in partial disregard of talent or preference, the range of jobs open to women has dramatically expanded. Men and women are now closer to occupying a unitary labor market than ever before, with the consequence that competition for women's labor is keener than in the past. Women's pay is rising and approaching parity with that of similarly qualified men. As a result, the opportunity costs of alternative allocations of time and effort in the unpaid domestic sphere have never been greater. For well-educated women, the payoffs forgone by choosing to work at home are large. Because the returns from a life of domesticity during the same period have, if anything, declined, the relatively greater value of nondomestic uses of women's time has produced the expected result – more women are in the paid workforce than ever before.

There would be little cause for concern if the unpaid, "off-market" domestic sector were competing with the paid sector in an unrigged game. The theory of market failures and externalities suggests, however, that the tug-of-war may well be skewed. Although the domestic sector is off-market and unpriced, it could still presumably equilibrate effectively with the paid sector if domesticity generated accurate returns to women for services rendered. That would occur if women's compensation from domestic labor, including consumption value, share of family

[1] Reprinted by permission from 44 *Villanova Law Review* 495 (1999).

income, and other recompense, reflected the full social value of a full-time wife and mother. Built-in imperfections that undermine the full internalization of investments in children mean that hands-on caring work is underrewarded. If women get fairly accurate returns on investment in the paid labor market, but are undercompensated in the domestic sphere, the domestic sphere will lose. As the paid sector moves ever closer to the ideal of a unitary, free, competitive labor market in which rewards reflect not prejudice or accident of birth, but real economic productivity, the pull of domesticity will weaken by comparison and caring work will suffer more.

In view of these insights, Professor McCaffery's proposals [see Chapter 8] for the reform of the system for taxing dual-earner families can be seen in a new light. Professor McCaffery bemoans a system that taxes secondary earners (usually women) more heavily than primary earners (usually men). Both men's role as primary earner and women's secondary position, however, are a reflection of their respective elasticities on the labor market. Men are relatively inelastic or unresponsive to shifts in the effective level of compensation for labor, including those induced by taxes. In contrast, women are quite responsive, or "elastic," in their supply of labor in response to variations in returns to effort.

The theory of optimal taxation asserts that the goal of a tax system should be to minimize any departure from choices that would otherwise be made on a well-functioning market. Applying the theory of optimal taxation developed for consumer goods to the analysis of labor supply, Professor McCaffery asserts that shifting the burden of tax from elastic to inelastic workers produces fewer "distortions" in the supply of labor because it leaves the patterns of work and effort relatively undisturbed. Assuming a well-functioning market for labor, the untaxed pattern will be an efficient one, because it will result in an equilibrium price for labor that maximizes the social utility generated by the balance of supply and demand.

Professor McCaffery is on firm ground in predicting the likely effects of shifting the burden of tax toward inelastic male workers and away from elastic female workers: women will engage in more paid work and will be (somewhat) better off for it. But McCaffery's account rests on a critical assumption – that the untaxed world of men's and women's labor, as it spontaneously allocates effort as between wage work and unpaid work at home, is one that maximizes social welfare. That is precisely the proposition that this paper seeks to question.

It is critical to the validity of McCaffery's argument that the baseline or untaxed market in labor be unmarred by any serious, systematic deviations from an efficient equilibrium. To be sure, McCaffery does bemoan certain types of market imperfections, which he claims lead to a paucity of attractive part-time jobs. In that respect, he does not posit perfectly functioning markets that always "clear." Apart from those defects, McCaffery appears to assume – and indeed has to assume – that labor markets work fairly well. Only then can he be confident that a tax that depresses the supply of paid female labor moves society away from efficiency. If the paid labor market were the sole focus of attention, the assumption of optimal allocation on an unregulated, untaxed market might be a sound one. The possibility that the off-market caring sector might generate significant and stubborn positive externalities reveals, however, how this bedrock assumption might fail. The existence of such externalities would mean that an untaxed and otherwise unregulated allocation of women's labor might fall short of maximizing social welfare by failing to supply the optimal amount of certain valuable types of services.

One way to attempt to correct for an undersupply in the quantity and quality of care for children is to impede women's entry onto the labor market. The differentially high marginal tax on women's labor that is built into the tax system as we know it can thus be viewed as just one more device in the venerable arsenal of social practices designed to interfere with women's sale of [their] efforts to the highest bidder. In this sense, the observed structure is in keeping with the traditionalist project of the "Contract with America." Although the Contract's authors claim to be freeing families from the burdens that prevent women from "doing what comes naturally" (i.e., staying home), what the Contract actually seeks to do is counter the threat that too many women, if "free to do anything else," will not choose to stay home at all. The Contract's program, by leaving high marginal taxes on women's work intact, might end up advancing the goal of maximizing social utility overall. Paradoxically, getting rid of high taxes on women's paid labor might undermine that goal.

McCaffery proposes taxing women or secondary earners less and men or primary earners more. If elasticities are exogenous in being largely independent of the tax system or of any other easily manipulable parameters, it becomes apparent that McCaffery's proposal does not solve the putative undersupply dilemma. As McCaffery acknowledges, lowering the tax on women's paid labor will generally cause women to engage in more paid work – that is what it means to be elastic. But taxing men more will not cause them to engage in less paid work – that is what it means to be inelastic. The end result will be even less hands-on caring than under the present tax regime.

Perhaps we should not assume that this inelasticity is a fixed feature of the landscape. Even if men's work rigidity loosens in response to higher taxes and changing social conditions, men's reduction in market effort will not likely offset women's increase. In addition, there is no guarantee that men will devote time freed up from working less to caring for children; evidence suggests that they will not. Finally, recent data suggest that at least some women's response to shifts in labor market rewards has begun to converge with men's. The shift toward greater inelasticity for women will, if anything, simply make any undersupply worse by rendering women less responsive to efforts to lower the opportunity costs of domesticity, whether by taxing away the benefits of work or through other normative legal or extralegal devices.

If there is indeed a "market failure" that produces less than optimal allocation of investments in future generations, social customs that restrict women's labor market access, and high taxes on women's labor, represent two possible regulatory "cures" for that disease. But, if it takes a market failure to cure a market failure, eliminating the cure will do nothing to root out the disease. If we assume that children need more care than they would get in an unregulated market, undistorted by cartel-like norms or taxation, then freeing up the market will not bring us to the optimal place we would like to be. McCaffery's proposal will no doubt be more fair to women and will make many women, and also men and children, better off; it will result in women voluntarily entering into more labor market transactions that are utility-maximizing for them and their employers. It does not follow, however, that the overall size of the pie will be larger, or that society will be better off collectively if McCaffery's reforms are adopted. If increasing social investment in children by boosting the supply of domestic labor is our goal, there are more or less efficient (or fair) ways to do this. And some ways may be so inefficient, or so lopsided in their distributive consequences, that the resulting losses may even outweigh the gains from luring women out of the labor force and into the home. But the issue of effects on net social welfare – and on children's well-being – must be squarely faced whenever a change in the status quo is contemplated in this area. Although it may be quite difficult to discern all the ramifications for efficiency and equity of any proposed reform, those effects should not be assessed so narrowly as to leave out consideration of the most vulnerable players.

Index

CW01514003

Show Me
Best Friends

Cowboy Crossing
~ Book 4 ~

By

ALEXA VERDE

Cover Art by Julia Gussman
Edited by Deidre Lockhart.

ISBN: 9798519722902

A "steel cowboy" with a wounded spirit, an ex-cop who's never forgotten him, and a baby in need of love… Can these childhood best friends become more?

Damaged and scarred after an accident that ended his racing career, Maverick Clark returns to his family ranch to find a new purpose. As he starts caring for his buddy's baby, Maverick turns for help to the girl he had a crush on, his childhood friend, Vera. Soon he wants more than friendship. But what does he have to offer her now?

At thirty-seven, jobless, husbandless, and childless, Vera Tsareva feels like she took a wrong turn somewhere. But once the road takes her back to her hometown to help her grandmother, she begins working with the guy she tried to forget. They even go on a trip to the other side of the world together, but he's closed off his heart.

When the investigation about the baby's parents leads her to a shocking discovery, is she close to the destination of love and happiness, or is she at a dead end?

Welcome to Cowboy Crossing, a small town in the Show Me State where swoon-worthy single dad cowboys fall in love with curvy thirtysomething and fortysomething women, though sometimes those rugged handsome men might need a nudge—or a push.

To Sherry!
Thank you for all your support and encouragement.
It means the world to me.

CHAPTER ONE

"WHAT DO YOU THINK you're doing?" Maverick Clark didn't mean to growl, but it sure sounded that way. He shielded his eyes from the bright light coming from the window.

"Good morning to you, too." Vera Tsareva sounded chirpy as she whirled around after opening the curtains.

Argh.

It would be childish to pull the blanket over his face or to throw a pillow at her. Besides, she'd probably throw it right back.

He folded his arms across his chest. "I don't remember inviting you to my room."

Why couldn't people understand he wanted to be left alone? Was it too much to ask? His large family seemed to have finally eased up on trying "to bring him back to life" after insisting he returned to the family mansion in his hometown.

And now this.

His childhood friend/PI/babysitter didn't take no for an answer. Yes, he'd hired her to take care of the baby who'd landed in his lap and to investigate the accident that had left him injured and bitter. But she could take care of that in the afternoon, couldn't she?

"Don't you want to see the baby?" She pulled up a chair to his bed. In a yellow dress and with her blonde hair flowing over her shoulders, she looked like a spot of sunshine herself.

He wanted to squeeze his eyes shut, put the curtain between himself and the sunshine. Vera even smelled like something cheerful and sweet with a touch of spunk, with notes of wild berries and melted caramel. The same perfume she'd used as a teen.

As his heart squeezed at the happy memories, he placed a thick curtain between himself and the memories, too.

"I've seen Izzy yesterday and every day before." He grimaced. "The baby cried as soon as I appeared in the room. I think it's best if I don't visit her."

He'd thought she was the one lifeline he'd gotten after his accident.

So much for that.

At least, his family seemed to be besotted with Izzy, no matter that they weren't blood related. After his buddy, Rance, had left Maverick his daughter to take care of, they'd welcomed her like an addition to the family.

It almost reached a soft spot in Maverick's heart, shattered when he'd had to walk away from his successful car-racing career.

Almost.

"Well, if you scowled at the poor child like that, I wonder why she cried." Vera leaned toward him, giving him another whiff of her intoxicating perfume.

He stared at her. "What part about me wanting to be left alone don't you understand?"

That was ugly of him. He winced. He hadn't always been ugly. They used to be friends, and it wasn't her fault he'd become a grouch. But after all the nightmares last night, his mood had dropped, and his mood wasn't high on a regular day.

She flipped her gorgeous blonde hair over her shoulder as if unaffected by his attitude. "Listen. You hired me to investigate things. I can take care of the baby without your help. Especially considering your family adores her and loves to step in. But I have news about the investigation, and we need to discuss it."

Curiosity piqued, he cocked his head to one side. Which investigation was she pushing to discuss? He didn't have much info to help her find the baby's mother. They'd reported about the child to the authorities, but so far, there was no news yet.

And talking about the accident brought back the scent of burning flesh, the rupture of pain, the grinding of metal.

He'd already spent the night reliving it. He suppressed a shudder. While she'd been away on a trip to Springfield, he'd nearly persuaded himself those failing brakes were part of his imagination.

He needed his soul wounds to heal, not someone poking into them.

Besides, he hated her to see him like this.

Broken.

Vulnerable.

Weak.

For a person used to crowds of adoring fans, to being healthy and capable, to being a leader, this—this *wreck* he'd become—was unacceptable. Even more unacceptable than crashing.

Despite a tight band around his lungs, he feigned nonchalance and appealed to her motherly instincts. "Don't you need to take care of the baby?"

A shake sent those lovely waves flying, giving him another whiff of that sweet scent. Too lovely. Too sweet. Too many memories. "Nope. I already fed and changed her. Now your mother is taking care of her. So it's a good time."

He looked into her eyes, blue like the Missouri sky on a summer day. Not that he cared to notice such things.

3

Well, not any longer. When he had, at fifteen, his teenage hormones had affected him too much. "You're not going to leave the room without me getting up, are you?"

Another headshake.

"I need to dress. So you *do* need to leave for some time." That was a valid request, wasn't it?

Her cheeks pinked. "Oh. Hmm. Okay." Then she wagged a finger. "I'm giving you half an hour. If I don't see you downstairs in the dining room, I'll return. I'll bring the rest of the family with me, too."

She marched to the door.

"You know I'm going to lock up then." He should've already.

"You know I'm going to climb through the window then." She glanced back and had the audacity to wink before closing the door.

A chuckle escaped him against his will.

She hadn't changed.

Not that he'd want her to.

As a child, he used to climb out of his window, thankful for a large oak growing next to it. She'd learned climbing techniques fast, too, so they'd disappear into the fields and meadows together, sometimes—okay, a lot of times—getting into mischief.

Those were good times.

Reluctantly, he dragged himself to the bathroom.

There, he flinched at his reflection.

His brown eyes were hooded, and his stubble unkempt. At least it covered the scars on the lower right side of his face. What a difference from his appearance before his accident!

As a winner of many races, he'd always had to look good in case of paparazzi shots.

Those days were behind him.

Breathing became difficult as if he could still smell burning rubber—or was it his own skin? How could a professional car

racer have an accident off the track, going *just a bit* over the speed limit for crying out loud?

He took a shaky breath and started brushing his teeth, the toothpaste's flavor refreshing.

If he knew Vera—and he did know her—she'd be climbing through that window sometime soon. What a stubborn girl!

Woman.

She was all grown up now, in her what—her late thirties?

Curvaceous and attractive.

Her blonde hair was longer now, and a trace of sadness shaded her blue eyes. But the smirk of her full pink lips hadn't changed. The lips he'd tasted only once and had nearly lost his head.

His pulse spiked at the recollection of the incredible feeling of her lips against his. He'd recovered enough to walk away—or rather run away at eighteen—and they'd never talked about it again.

He brushed his teeth more vigorously as his treacherous heart skipped a few beats.

After a quick shower, he dressed and limped downstairs, each step making his teeth gnash. He'd done months of physical therapy and exercised every day now, pushing himself to the limit in their first-floor gym. His family was fine with him using one of the rooms in the large mansion as a gym and equipping it well.

Still, navigating stairs was… difficult. But no way was he going to move to one of the downstairs bedrooms as everybody suggested—or put in one of those ridiculous single person elevators.

Doing that would show even more weakness.

He hadn't become as successful as he was by being weak.

Used to be successful.

Used to be.

His gut tightened. All his trophies were just living room decorations now.

Hmm. Something smelled good.

He entered the dining room where not much had changed since his childhood. Equestrian paintings and Missouri landscapes decorated latte-colored walls. The same large rosewood antique table that had housed so many family dinners with hand-carved chairs stood in the middle of the room. Polished hardwood floors remained in excellent condition, and the floor-to-ceiling window revealed the same breathtaking rolling emerald hills.

Okay, maybe one significant change. Wedding photos of his siblings lined one of the walls, as well as multiple photos with their children. The smiles and happiness in those photos underscored his loneliness.

The grandfather clock chimed ten thirty. A bit early for lunch, but still good timing because now everyone, except for his mother, was probably at work or out and about. By noon, some people might stop by.

He wasn't in the mood for family meals.

Vera gestured to the opposite chair. A plate with chicken wings, potato salad, and asparagus awaited him.

He lowered himself into a chair. "I can get my own food. Besides, I'm not hungry." His stomach grumbled, contradicting his words.

She rolled her eyes. "Really? Friends don't let friends starve. At least, that's what you told me when I tried to go on a diet when I became too… plump." She reached for one of the biscuits. "If you don't eat, I'm going to feed you." She scooted her chair closer and raised the biscuit toward his mouth as if she were going to make good on her promise.

"I'm not a kid!" Shaming heat scorched him. He was behaving like a spoiled child, wasn't he?

Then a different kind of wave sluiced through him at her hands so close to his face.

Snap out of it.

There could be no possibility of attraction between them again.

He couldn't allow it. Not when he was a shadow of his former self.

Still, he wondered what her story was, what she'd gone through in all the years they'd been apart. "Why don't you get a plate for yourself?"

She leaped to her feet. "Don't mind if I do."

She disappeared into the kitchen, then came back with a plate stacked high. She was always full of energy. Too bad that she couldn't bottle some of it and pass it on to him.

He didn't have a drop of fuel in his tank.

Reluctantly, he took a bite. Even if he didn't have an appetite, she had a point.

"Wait. Aren't you going to say grace?" Her hand flew to him as if to stop him.

They both stared at her fingers on his forearm. She'd done that more than a few times when they'd been children, and then it felt natural.

Now, warmth traveled from her fingers, reaching clear through him, and his heart that had been quiet for a long time picked up speed.

Her cheeks pinking again, she withdrew her hand.

Strangely, he missed her touch as if it were the connection to everything good in her.

Or to whatever good was left in him.

"Well, after my accident, my relationship with God became complicated," he said at last. He couldn't understand how God could give him so much and then, when Maverick was at the pinnacle of his career, break him into pieces.

Literally.

Sadness pooled in the bottomless depths of her eyes. "I'm sorry. Do you mind if I do?"

He shrugged. "Go ahead."

She said grace and included him in her prayers. She prayed for his healing.

Something shifted inside him.

Did God even listen?

His rib cage constricted.

"Okay, which investigation do you want to talk about?" She nibbled a chicken wing.

"Izzy's mother." That should be easier.

"Researching the baby carrier and clothes the baby was dropped off in didn't give any results so far, but I'll keep trying. The same goes for the typed note left with her. No fingerprints anywhere. Standard paper and ink. The text says the baby's name is Izzy and it's Rance's, plus that she was born prematurely. I started doing some research. Looked up articles about Rance on the internet, social media, and tabloids." She gestured while she talked and ate. But then, her arms were always flying during any conversation.

He'd once called her his canary, what with her blonde hair and favorite color—yellow—and how she sang after joining the choir. The memory softened one of the sharp angles inside him. Yet a million of the sharp angles remained.

After a sip of iced tea, she continued, "Yeah, I know the tabloids aren't such a reliable source. But I had to start somewhere."

She ate with gusto. But then, she'd done everything with gusto. She'd always been filled with life, her vibrancy bubbling over the top.

A longing surprised him.

Was he…

Was he attracted to her?

He'd been once, but he'd known he'd wanted to leave this small town, known they were going in different directions. She had her own dreams.

So he'd remained only friends with Vera. Even that kiss… He hadn't initiated it.

During the years away, he'd dated whenever his career had allowed him, which wasn't much. But he'd never been able to find the one…

The one what?

Just the one.

Pain reverberated through him. Spending too much time with Vera wasn't a good idea. She reminded him about everything he'd lost, everything he could never have now.

Way too much.

And the baby…

If Vera found Izzy's mother, he'd lose the baby, too. His family already adored Izzy, and despite their rough beginning, she touched something inside him, too.

His eyes narrowed. "I changed my mind. It's best to leave things as they are. Most likely, Izzy's mother doesn't want to be found. Of course, I'll pay you for the research you've done already."

For a moment, Vera stopped eating. Then she waved the chicken wing she was holding. "But what if the baby was stolen? And it's not fair to Izzy."

Their gazes met, hers unyielding. He should've expected it. "You're not going to give up, are you?"

She resumed eating. "Mm, this is good. How about you give me a week? If we can't find her in a week, I'll leave you alone." She stuck out her clean hand, chicken wing in her right. "If we find her faster, I'll leave you alone."

Oh yes.

The peace and quiet he wanted.

Then why did his heart ache?

"Really?" He took her hand to shake, and something unfamiliar surged through him.

There was that connection again.

She nodded. "Really."

"Okay then." He let her hand go because he didn't want that connection. Couldn't want it. A woman like Vera deserved a great man by her side, not a broken one.

CHAPTER TWO

"YOU DO REALIZE you just signed up for spending every day this week with me, for all the time I'm not watching a baby."

"What?" His jaw slackening, he slumped back against his chair. "I did no such thing."

Vera beamed at him as she polished off her wings, dropping the bones into a little discard pile. "A promise is a promise."

An insufferable woman.

They might as well start now.

He pulled his shoulders back and tasted the wings with rich barbecue sauce, the family recipe. He was a coward, running away from his issues. And he could use some closure, after all. "So tell me the results of your trip to Springfield."

She clapped, smearing barbecue sauce onto both hands now. "Finally! Some interest. I became worried." After bouncing in her seat, she grabbed a napkin and cleaned her hands. "Here it goes. I didn't get much from the police, so I went to the place where you rented your car. I talked to the people on duty that day. Of course, I didn't expect them to admit to any wrongdoing, but I had a feeling none of them were lying."

His heart sank. He didn't expect to get the answer today, but…

Did he really expect closure? Or did he need to blame someone besides himself for his accident? To let out the anger and disappointment like the transmission fluid needing replacement?

"Well, thank you for trying." He kept his voice void of emotion as he sipped sweet tea to chase away the bitterness.

"Hold on. That's just the beginning." She reached for another biscuit, then seemed to think better of it. "Remember, I asked you whether you stopped anywhere before driving to the ranch and you said you stopped at the flower shop?"

"Yes. I always buy my mother flowers when I go to visit her." He could see where this was going.

She took a hurried sip. "So I went to that shop and chatted with the owner." Her smile showed the charming dimples that used to drive him crazy.

Not a thought he should be having! He drummed his fingers on the table. "And?"

"Sadly, they didn't have cameras outside, which I think is a mistake." She drained her tea.

His drumming fingers slowed as his heart sank deeper. "Well, at least, you tried." He cringed. He sounded like a parrot. He sipped the cold sweet liquid again.

"Seriously? Would you give up so easily? I walked around the shop. The attorneys' office opposite the shop *does* have cameras. One can see the flower shop's parking." She plucked the biscuit back from her plate and bit into it, then took a minute to chew and swallow before winking. "It wasn't easy, but I got access to the camera recordings."

He released a breath he didn't realize he was holding. "Did you find anything?"

"Not as much as I wanted to." She licked a crumb from her finger, making his heart do a strange movement in his chest. "But someone dressed in overalls with their cap drawn low *did* slide under your car. That person was wearing a beard and dark glasses,

not much in the sense of facial recognition. I'm sure the beard was fake."

Wow! He touched the stubble on his chin. "So I was right. Most likely, the brakes were damaged."

"Couple that with your affinity for speed." She spread her arms. "Here's the result. Now, who knew you usually stopped by that flower shop?"

He shrugged, digesting this new information. "Pretty much everyone in town. I never made a secret of it."

Her gaze became pensive. "Okay, let's discuss again who'd benefit from your death. I understand some developers were interested in buying part of the ranch for a high-end spa. Your family refused to sell, so there were some... suspicious incidents. Lavigne is behind the corporation intent on building the spa. It's far-fetched, but if something happened to you, it might persuade your family to sell."

He rubbed his throbbing temples. "If Lavigne is connected to it, he hired someone to damage my brakes and also has an inside person at the ranch. We had tractors breaking at a higher rate than usual before we installed cameras and upped the security. My sister stumbled upon a cut tree and also heard something like a shot from a gun with a silencer." A shiver ran down his spine. "Does this mean my family might be in danger?"

"If so, I don't think he'd go after an adult this time. Children are much more vulnerable."

He pushed his plate away, losing whatever appetite he had. "What should we do?" Again, he hated being so weak.

Wait a moment.

We?

Her eyes narrowed. "Can I see camera recordings for the last week?"

"Sure. But my brothers or I go through them on a regular basis. So far, we haven't noticed anything unusual."

His stomach clenched. Shouldn't he be the one protecting her and the children, not the other way around?

No self-pity party, remember?

Head tipped to the left in that endearing way of hers, she studied him beneath her lashes. "How about hiring a bodyguard for the older children? Just to be on the safe side? Preferably one who could also work as a nanny."

A bodyguard?

"Hmm." As an image of a buffed-up man running after little children appeared in his mind, Maverick's lips twitched. "I think they call it 'manny' these days."

"I meant a friend of mine—she's female, by the way." Her chin lifted, and her lips pressed together as if holding something in. It wouldn't last. Vera never kept quiet about her thoughts. "Women work as bodyguards, too, you know."

Right. He'd known she wouldn't stay shushed. He should've known she wouldn't take his perceived slight easily, either.

He coughed a little. "I'm sure they do. Let me run it by the family, and I'll let you know. I like this idea. Even if nothing is going to happen, it'll give us peace of mind that our most vulnerable are going to be all right."

"Okay." She put away her empty plate and glass and returned. "I'm going to check the outside perimeter again, and then we'll revisit this conversation."

Strangely, as much as he'd wanted to be left alone earlier, a part of him didn't want to let her go now. Besides, if there was even a slight chance of danger here, he didn't want her to be by herself. "I'll go with you."

Her gaze moved to his cane, but then jerked to his eyes. Not fast enough to keep from giving him a painful stab, though. "Are you sure?"

"Yes." He resisted the urge to grind his teeth. "If you don't mind walking slower than you're used to."

They put the rest of the food away, and he made sure his hand didn't touch hers as they walked.

The trip upstairs wasn't fun, but he needed to change from a T-shirt into a sweater. By the time he returned, he resolved to keep a part of his wardrobe downstairs. He found her still at the table, studying something on her phone. He doubted she was just idly passing her time. Probably investigating, as always.

As he watched her, he was taken back decades.

As a child, Vera had been sort of a tomboy, just like his younger sister. But by thirteen, Vera wasn't a tomboy any longer. She'd started wearing bright summer dresses that showcased her forming figure and let her gorgeous hair grow. Her body developed curves, and her lips grew fuller, creating in him, a hormone-charged teen, thoughts he shouldn't be having toward a friend.

A rare aura of kindness and spunk about her drew people to her. He'd joked once that she was a brainy cheerleader with a heart. In response, she'd laughed that he'd said it with such surprise—like it was an oxymoron. But it was true. She'd wanted to become a forensic scientist, so she did great in chemistry classes. And, despite being on the plump side, she'd become a cheerleader simply because she was stubborn and goal-oriented.

People noticed the change in her appearance and attitude, especially boys. She'd started dating. Maverick was about to ask her on a date when he caught Rance looking at her and saw the same yearning in his best buddy's eyes that he felt himself.

So he and Rance had an honest conversation and decided not to risk their friendships by pursuing a romance with her. The chances of Vera returning their feelings were slim to none, so preserving their friendship seemed more important.

As time passed, he'd regretted that decision and nearly told Vera how he felt. But something always stopped him. Maybe the fact that, by fifteen, she knew she was going to the University of

Central Missouri to study forensic science, and by then, he'd been crazy about racing.

Watching those "need for speed" Tom Cruise movies—one where the hero had the same nickname as his name and one where he'd been a race car driver—had changed Maverick's destiny. It seemed like a sign. So there was no point in trying to start something with her, only to call it quits in a few years. Rance had seemed to think the same way....

"Sorry to hold you up." Vera rose, interrupting his slow drive down memory lane.

"You're not holding me up." Looking at her, remembering her when he could still have a chance with her tugged at him. It all created a much stronger longing than he'd anticipated.

He retrieved a gun from the safe while she picked up her purse where he had no doubt she stowed a weapon.

When she reached for her wool marmalade-colored jacket on the hall hook, he stopped her with a universal gesture. "I'll help you." He let the cane go to grab the jacket, and the cane rattled onto the floor. He frowned as he picked it up. So much for trying to be strong and gallant.

She didn't notice or pretended not to as she shrugged into the outfit he held out for her. "Thank you. So nice of you."

Her smile reminded him of a ray of sunshine while he resembled a cloud, dressed in charcoal-gray jeans and a mouse-gray sweater, with stubble on his cheeks and a frown on his face. He had difficulty balancing the cane and opening the door, and his frown deepened until his lips pinched tight.

That only highlighted the differences between them.

She seemed to inspect her surroundings before she stepped outside. Then she nodded to him. "All clear."

He breathed fresh air filled with the scents of foliage and hay, so different from the scent of fumes he was used to. As they

walked outside, he wondered how she was going to check a perimeter that stretched for miles and miles.

She answered that question by walking around the house first and looking closely at the windows. "The thing I was working on right now…. I followed up on the background investigation of your ranch hands, especially ones who left recently. Do you know Moulin worked for Lavigne's corporation about ten years ago?"

He winced. "I'm sure if he had that on his resume my family would've noticed."

She inspected the patio door. "He probably didn't. I'm trying to locate him now to talk with him. Now, you might not like what I'm going to say next. As Rance is the next person in line to win the race, I have to put him on the suspect list."

He drew a sharp breath of that hay-scented air as they rounded the mansion. "He's our friend! He's also Izzy's father."

She looked away as if this was unpleasant for her, too. "Yes. And your main competitor. With you out of the picture, he can have what he wants."

Anger boiled his blood, coursing through his veins to his extremities until his hand fisted on his cane. "Okay, Rance isn't always on the straight and narrow. But to cause me an accident?"

Resting a hand on his arm again as she used to, she breathed out a long breath that ruffled the hair by her cheeks. "In my line of work, I learned the people we suspect the least often betray us." Her grip tightened almost fiercely as if she were fighting off anger, and the bitterness in her voice warned she might have personal experience in that. "We can't let emotions affect us."

What had happened to her to cause that bitterness? Something besides her parents creating new families and passing her to each other as if she were a grenade ready to explode. Until one day, she had….

She waved at the large oak close to the house. "As much as I love that tree and, well, it brings good memories… This is a safety

17

issue in several senses. First, someone might climb inside if you forget to close the window. Or the window might be taken out. Second, in case of a tornado."

His heart shifted as he studied the bark, trying to find where he'd once carved three names. His, Vera's and Rance's. He couldn't find them, and disappointment stung.

There *could* be a chance Rance wished him ill, and there was some distance between him and Vera, even if she was walking so close he could touch her. Was their friendship gone like the words carved on the tree?

With an effort, he moved his thoughts to current matters. "You said a window can be taken out. Is it easy to do?"

"It can be." She explained how, and he shivered, wondering how she'd obtained that knowledge.

Then she gestured to the building on the left. "Um, if you don't mind, I want to look at the tractor shed and the cameras. You know, to make sure there are no blind spots."

"Sure." He had an inexplicable urge to wrap his arm around her shoulder as they walked.

Of course, that wouldn't be a good idea. First, he didn't need the unwelcome attraction. Second, she might think he needed to lean on her, and he didn't need that embarrassment. It was bad enough that she was leading the investigation while he was more of a useless listener.

Some bright leaves were already scattered on the ground like abandoned dreams. A few more waltzed in the air in the eternal dance he hadn't noticed since he'd been a teen. A burgundy sugar maple leaf landed on her hair, and he wanted to remove it at first. But it suited her so well, he left it there.

"Now, there could be another motive. Revenge. Um, I looked at social media, and boy, did you leave a string of broken hearts behind." She walked slower than usual, obviously for his benefit, and gratitude mixed with irritation inside him. "Care to elaborate

on the ones who'd go to the length of cutting brakes after you broke up with them?"

Was it jealousy in her voice, or was it his wishful thinking?

"I was married to my career. That didn't leave much time for relationships. Most of the love affairs attributed to me were just gossip. Some of them publicity stunts. Except..." He stopped, then resumed his pace.

"Go on. Except?"

He opened the door for her. The building wasn't really a shed any longer, and its recent coat of green paint gleamed, just like the brown fence stood proudly with not a post or plank missing. This ranch was in way better shape than their far smaller ranch had been he was growing up.

"Except?" she prompted as she entered with cautious steps. Of course, she wasn't going to drop the matter.

"Except Embry. She used to work as a mechanic on Rance's team and then moved to mine. I usually don't mix business with pleasure, but something about her... I don't know. Maybe I was tired of being alone. Maybe we just bonded over our passion for cars. We were together for four months, then went separate ways." His rib cage squeezed.

He'd tried to make it work. He really did. But the spark had been gone fast, and... He'd never felt the same happiness with Embry he'd had with Vera. It didn't help that Embry started dropping hints about marriage.

"Who broke it off?"

"I had to. She wanted more than I could give. She returned to work with Rance, and that was it. I didn't see her afterwards." He didn't want to remember her words, his regret. Or the fact that she was a mechanic, so she knew how to damage a car.

As he breathed in the familiar scents of metal and petroleum, he finally felt at ease. As a child, he'd loved helping repair tractors,

learning how they worked. Even then, the large machine fascinated him.

Certainly, one couldn't race on a tractor, but it had been the first time he'd felt he was good at something, that his father was proud of him. He'd wanted so much to be just like his dad that he'd been torn when his heart started calling him somewhere else. Disappointment in his father's eyes—obviously, his father had thought Maverick would stay on the ranch they all worked so hard for—had cut deep.

Oh, how much he'd loved his dad then, a kindhearted, honest man, highly respected by everyone in town.

Little did he know that his father…

Maverick shook his head as he gave her a quick tour. No need to remember the distant past. No use to regret his angry words.

He ran his fingertips over the metal surface like it was an intimate caress. Or rather a handshake with his past. He couldn't explain it, but vehicles were alive to him and needed to be treated with love and respect like his siblings treated horses. When he started the engine, it was like he could feel their pulse.

No wonder they had called him "steel cowboy." Since he'd been thrown off a horse as a boy, he didn't have his family's passion for horses or this land.

"I remember you used to love this place." Her blue eyes were attentive.

"The moment I discovered I could bring an old tractor to life, the moment I tried a scooter, my heart soared."

Like probably all people, he'd craved admiration and appreciation. And racing had brought it to him, if not from his father, then from millions of fans.

He could leave the cheering crowds behind. Maybe. He'd proved himself.

But as he looked at Vera, he realized there was still one person whose admiration mattered very much to him.

Eyes narrowed, she checked the cameras inside like she'd done in the house when she'd arrived the first day. She'd found several blind spots in the house, places that hadn't been monitored, so more cameras had been installed. Then she did the same with the cameras outside the building that monitored the entrance.

"You all have done a good job on this. I can't find any security breaches." She gave him a satisfied nod.

The growl of a motor made him glance in its direction. A moment later, a skinny person in a purple helmet on a large motorcycle parked near the house and waved frantically at Vera.

Her face lit up. "I've got to go. We can discuss the rest tomorrow, okay?"

He did his best to ignore the inexplicable flare of jealousy. "Okay. Rance promised to send me a list of the women who could be Izzy's mother. I should have it by tomorrow. Considering he likes to party, his memory might be fuzzy sometimes."

Her hand moved toward him as if she wanted to reach out to him, but then she stopped herself. "Great. About the list, not the fuzzy memory. Email me when you have it, okay?" She gave him her email address. "I asked him several times, but so far, he wasn't very forthcoming. I'll see you tomorrow. Please go inside. You've risked enough by being outside already."

He watched her disappear, leaving only the fumes behind. Then he limped inside the house, changed, and visited Izzy who was sleeping enviably.

After the lunch with his family—he didn't have a choice in the matter if he wanted to eat—he punished himself in the gym. With his leg like that, he worked on his upper body strength, and he could barely feel his arms when he finished. He probably wouldn't be able to lift them for a while. He grunted every time as he thought about that mysterious someone on the motorcycle— someone obviously close to Vera, based on the tenderness in her eyes.

So the more his arms ached, the more he pushed himself.

What else could he do? After the accident, he hadn't been behind the steering wheel. Just imagining that burning scent set him hyperventilating. Pain sliced him. From a champion, he'd become a coward.

After a shower, he opened his email on his tablet, then pulled up the list. Then he scanned it for familiar names.

What?

His eyes widened. He couldn't be seeing this. It *had* to be a mistake....

But it wasn't a mistake. He saw the name clearly.

Vera was on that list.

CHAPTER THREE

VERA GASPED as she was having breakfast with Maverick the next day. "What? How? No way!" Good thing she wasn't eating at the time, or she'd have choked. "*I* was on the list?"

"Do I need to know something about you?" Something flashed in his brown eyes.

Jealousy?

Hah! Why would he be jealous?

"You've got to be kidding me." Her throat felt parched.

"I wish."

She looked at her empty glass. "Hold on. I need to drink some water after this news. I'll be right back. Can I get you anything from the kitchen?"

"A little clarity in the situation would be nice, but I don't think you can find it in our kitchen," he said through his teeth.

Really, did the man ever smile anymore?

And he used to have such a nice smile. Especially when he smiled at her instead of smiling into the camera.

Unexpected warmth pulsed through her as she got up. When he smiled for publicity shots, his smile always carried a little more sadness and a little less sincerity—less energy, zeal, and life.

Still, he was so handsome he'd become a media darling fast, and they loved to discuss not only his wins but also his high-profile celebrity romances.

It wasn't that she was jealous. Not at all. She'd had no claim on him. And hadn't all the people she'd loved betrayed her at one time or another? Except for her grandmother, but that was a small consolation.

Right. Exactly what Vera should be worrying about when Rance stated she'd had an affair with him. What had that man been drinking?

She rushed to the kitchen, poured a glass of cold water, and drained it.

Much better.

Then she returned to her seat. "Don't get me wrong. The baby is adorable. But do I look like a woman who abandons her child? I thought you knew me better than that."

He looked away. "People change."

Well, *he* certainly had, and not for the better.

An observation she'd keep to herself.

He was still as handsome as ever, even with that stubble covering most of his face and a scowl snarling up his lips.

Lean in the hips, wide in the shoulders, he was exceptionally well built. And judging by the grunts she'd heard from the gym every day, he'd been adding to building up those muscles nicely. Even if he was wearing jeans and a simple T-shirt that stretched over his muscles instead of his racing uniform or those tuxedos he used to wear to charity galas, her heart fluttered.

Now, *think* instead of salivating.

That was what she'd been hired to do.

Think and search.

Not fall in love with her employer, who also happened to be her childhood friend and her teen crush.

Oh, add the little detail that he thought she might be the mother of that precious baby she'd been babysitting.

She'd returned to her hometown to find herself again, maybe reinvent herself even, besides helping her grandmother. She'd needed some simplicity in life, some anchoring after several heartaches and career disasters.

Instead, her life just became more complicated.

Her grandmother had her mother at nineteen while her mother had Vera at eighteen. At thirty-seven, Vera was way behind on that. Vera hadn't worried about it until recent years when seeing couples with children made her heart squeeze painfully.

She knew a few women who'd made a deliberate choice to put their career first, but Vera had nothing to brag in that department, either.

Where had the years gone?

She slapped herself on the forehead. "Oh, I know why Rance said it."

His gaze was brooding. "Can't wait to hear it."

"Yeah, gotta love your enthusiasm." She couldn't help grinning. He really was obnoxious, but he'd been so much more once. Anyway, that fling Rance claimed. "About a year and a half ago, he was visiting town. And by visiting town, I mean visiting the bar."

Maverick nodded, finally starting to eat his scrambled eggs, but his gaze remained guarded. "That sounds like him."

Lord, please help Maverick.

Her relationship with the Lord was never complicated, even after…

Her gut twisted.

No use thinking about that.

"Well, he called me after he'd gotten wasted. It was either him crawling home or me picking him up…. I chose to pick him up, broke up a bar fight—"

"Excuse me?" His brows shot up. "You did what?"

She shrugged. "He got into a bar fight, and I had to break it up. I'm a former ccp, remember?"

Belatedly, she realized he might not know the details of her life, just as she didn't know the details of his, except for the long-legged gorgeous details showcased in the media. Apparently, despite him stating he was married to his career, he hadn't been always faithful to that spouse.

She waved off her own words. "Okay, never mind. So the bouncer and I loaded Rance in my car, and I drove him home. Then I dragged him inside."

Did his lips kick up just a little? "You did?"

"Hey! I've got muscles. But yeah, that was a feat I never want to repeat. Ever! I dropped him in bed. As he tried to get up and go somewhere, I figured I'd stay put by his side. I didn't want him to end up in a ditch. We used to look out for each other, remember? That's all."

"That's all?" Was it distrust in his eyes?

How dare he?

She lifted her chin. "That. Is. All."

"Are you sure?"

She glared at him. That didn't even deserve an answer.

He coughed a little. "He didn't… make a move on you?"

"Of course, he did." She sighed out her exasperation and finished her scrambled eggs with ham and mushrooms. Yummy. But then, this house always had yummy food and welcoming people. So unlike the house where she'd grown up. Her mother was a busy doctor with no time for cooking—or parenting for that matter—and her father was a traveling salesman, rarely home. "Duh. I said no and kept saying no. He finally figured no actually does mean no."

A muscle moved in his jaw. "What if he didn't figure that out? He was drunk, after all."

She smiled sweetly at him and blinked like some clichéd simpering heroine before drawling in her best Missouri twang. "Then, by the mornin', y'all'd better bet he'd be sportin' a black eye."

"Hmm. I believe you." Now his lips definitely moved up a little.

It wasn't half a smile yet, maybe a quarter. Still, warmth spread inside her as if she'd accomplished something.

She was so tired of seeing sorrow in Maverick's brown eyes that once sparkled with mischief, seeing defeat in his features, in the stance of his body and tone of his voice. She ached to hug him, to tell him things would be better from now on, to run her fingers along that prickly jaw....

Whoa.

Where did that thought come from?

She needed to concentrate on her mission.

So she got up and started pacing. She worked better when she moved. That also kept her from looking at him and her heart from doing all that... fluttering. "This shows me his list might not be great. A lot of women there might, well, not belong there. Still, you should've emailed it to me like I asked."

"I forgot after I saw your name there. I'll email it to you now." He reached into his pocket for the phone and did just that. "So you think it's not much of a help?"

"Call Rance and have it changed to the women with whom he can definitely remember, um..." Heat rose on her neck. "Doing things required to have a baby. I know for a party guy like him, it might not be easy to, well, recall. But otherwise, I might cause issues for people once I start asking uncomfortable questions, especially if they are in a relationship or married."

He pushed his empty plate away, watching her. "Okay. Then what?"

She pulled her phone out of her dress's side pocket. First, she checked for any texts from her grandmother. Then she looked through the names in the email and zoomed in on the familiar ones. "Two people here are worth starting with. One is a friend of a woman who still lives in our small town. Another one is someone one of my colleagues knows. If both women stay on his list after Rance really, *really* thinks about it all and confirms them as possible mothers, I'd like to interview them."

He shrugged. "Worth trying."

Her heart fell at his blank expression. He used to be so energetic when they were growing up, so full of life. Seeing him with such apathy, as if he didn't care any longer what happened to him, made her heart ache.

Lord, please guide me on what to do, how to help him. And please heal his heart.

They cleaned the table, working in tandem easily like they once had.

She carried more cups into the kitchen while he rinsed the dishes. "I checked Rance and Embry's alibis for the time of your accident. Rance said he was at the gym with his personal trainer. The interesting part, the trainer said Rance didn't show up that day. Embry took a day off. She had an appointment with a hairdresser. She canceled, too."

He froze. "Could they have been… together?"

"I'm trying to find out." But not fast enough.

Doubt wormed inside her as her hand was so close to his she nearly touched him. Her pulse went rapid in his presence, and her head spun just from looking into the eyes that could always mesmerize her.

This case was important to her, on many levels. She couldn't afford to fail like she had while she'd been a cop. The memory knifed her. She'd let her personal feelings affect her then, too, and had paid dearly for that.

While they placed the dishes in the dishwasher, he cleared his throat. "So… Did you have a good time with the guy who picked you up yesterday?"

Her hand stilled as her mind went blank. "What guy?"

"On the motorcycle? Not that it's any business of mine."

A laugh escaped her lips. "That was my *grandmother*."

His brows shot up as he leaned against the counter. "You're kidding me."

"I wish. Part of the reason I'm here. Grandma bought a motorcycle and nearly flattened a few neighborhood fences. I guess scuba diving wasn't fun enough. She's also talking a lot about her gun collection. I'm trying to make sure she doesn't drive into someone's window or shoot someone." She suppressed a sigh. Emphasis was on *trying*.

"Seriously?" He fit the last cup in the dishwasher and closed the door.

"Totally. It's payback time after what she went through in my rebellious years. But I don't mind." She made a quick call to her grandmother to check that all the fences were still standing and all instructors at the range where Grandma practiced shooting today were still alive.

"Dear," her grandmother's tone chided, "I've been doing things perfectly usual for women my age today. Getting my hair colored and visiting a jewelry shop."

"You colored your hair blue and got three extra earrings for your left ear, right?"

Her grandma laughed. "Yes. *Now* I'm on the way to the range."

Based on the fact that she could talk, she was driving a car and not a motorcycle. Oh yes, that souped-up truck. Vera shuddered.

"I'm sure you look more beautiful than ever. Try not to knock down the instructor standing behind you this time. Or shoot the ceiling." She'd better explain the benefits of knitting and fishing. Maybe, just maybe…

"Oh dear. How was I supposed to know the rifle has so much recoil?"

"I bought you a small handgun. Use it. Love you, Grandma."

"Love you, too."

After disconnecting, Vera threw her shoulders back as she marched to the door.

We never mind doing things for people whom we love.

Hold on.

She had an idea of how to try to reach him, and the answer had been right in front of her all along. "I need to get back to my babysitting duties. Why don't you come visit Izzy with me?"

Even a person whose heart had hardened as if made of steel would have trouble remaining indifferent to such a precious, precious baby.

Wouldn't he?

Then Vera prayed for Maverick and her grandmother.

Lord, please don't let my grandmother harm anyone on the way to the range. Or at the range. Or on the way back. Amen.

CHAPTER FOUR

THE IMAGE of the little girl with a pink bow in her blonde hair touched something deep inside Maverick. Something he thought had stopped existing since the accident.

But the feeling didn't last long.

The baby, as adorable as she was, wasn't his to keep and to get attached to. And it wasn't about the fact that they weren't blood related. What if Rance came to his senses sooner or later?

When Izzy smiled and giggled once Vera entered the room as if recognizing her, his mother passed the child to her. "I'll leave you two to enjoy the child."

She paused and searched his face as if she wanted to say something else. Then she seemed to decide against it and left the pink room. A myriad of multicolored butterflies spread delicate decal wings across the walls and more toys than three babies could cuddle or slobber on stacked the shelves and huddled in the crib.

His family had treated Izzy as if she were one of their own and lavished her with love and gifts. But then, he didn't expect anything less.

Vera started cooing over the girl, a beautiful smile lighting up Vera's face. Dimples made their appearance.

As he watched the touching scene, his heart shifted, and wistful nostalgia unraveled the walls woven around it. He could easily imagine Vera with their child.

Their family.

The longing became so strong it slammed him like a punch to the gut. He hurried to the large window hugged by salmon-hued curtains so she wouldn't see his expression.

As he stared at the lush emerald-green fields with the distant blue ribbon of a creek, the land his family loved so fiercely, he did his best to school his features to neutral. He, Vera, and Rance used to run in those fields as children, carefree and happy.

A different longing stirred him, for the times far gone and opportunities missed. Why hadn't he noticed then how beautiful and kind Vera was, or when he did notice, why hadn't he tried harder for a chance with her?

Because he didn't want to lose two of his best friends. Because other things had been more important to him.

As she played with Izzy, he stole a glance at her golden hair and bright blue eyes and the generous, sincere smile that had always lit up something inside him. Then he faced the window again.

Maverick raised his hand to touch his scars. The tremendous success he'd been so proud of, all those sparkling trophies, the stars that had shone on his path once, didn't seem to matter anymore.

What could he offer her now? A shell of the man he used to be?

She deserved better.

Much better.

He clenched his jaw. He should've searched her out years ago.

He should have.

Now it was too late.

"Would you like to hold her?" Vera's melodic voice interrupted his musings.

He turned around to see her standing in front of him already and handing him the little girl who eyed him, blue eyes wide.

O–okay.

He'd visited Izzy many times before, yes. But he'd never taken her out of her crib or playpen. She'd seemed so tiny, so fragile, and he still felt shaky on his feet. He shifted back a little. "Um, why?"

She shrugged. "It's about time you learned how to change her diapers."

He must've gawked because she laughed. He'd missed the sound so much and hadn't realized it until now.

"You look like I just asked you to breastfeed her." Vera rolled her eyes as she snuggled the child. "Okay, I'm kidding."

Air whooshed out of his lungs. "You have a strange sense of humor."

"You seemed to like it before."

Oh yes.

But then he liked many things about her, and he still did. It was best not to mention it.

Her eyes narrowed as if she recalled the good old times, too. Then she handed him the baby for the second time. "Come on. Don't you feel tenderness sweeping you up as you look into those baby blues?"

He sure did, for more reasons than one. Another thing he'd better keep to himself. If only he could go back in time... But he couldn't.

She showed him how to carry Izzy so the girl's head rested on his shoulder. A tight band constricted his lungs. Hopefully, those hideous scars wouldn't make the poor baby cry. She'd cried in his presence before.

Izzy blinked a few times, and then she... smiled.

At that moment, something changed inside him. A powerful yearning for things he'd underestimated, like love and his own family, stirred him. Things beyond his reach now.

The corners of Vera's lips kicked up. "I think she likes you. You can kiss her if you'd like to."

He touched the soft skin with his lips. Yearning became stronger, loosening the tight band around his lungs. He breathed in the wonderful scent of baby powder and new hope.

Vera handed him two yellow-red-and-white rattles. "Here. Play with her while I get her bottle ready."

"Wait!" Panic set in, his heart slamming his chest so hard it might scare the baby. "What… what if she starts crying?"

"Start rocking her. Sing her a song." Vera scrunched her nose up the way she did when thinking. "Hold that thought about singing. You might scare her."

Right, that was helping. Not. "You're not very encouraging."

"You'll be fine. And I'll be right back." She flashed a smile, then hurried out of the room.

He and the baby stared at each other.

Hmm…

What kind of things did one discuss with a baby? "Well… The weather seems fine today, isn't it?"

He cringed. He sounded ridiculous. At least, Izzy didn't start crying yet.

Vera was right about tenderness sweeping one up when one looked in the baby's eyes. Izzy's were a lighter shade of blue than Vera's, and both of them had generous eyelashes framing their eyes.

He felt his lips widen. "You're a little beauty, aren't you?"

The girl giggled as if she understood him and was pleased.

True to her word, Vera returned with the bottle soon enough. "Would you like to feed her?"

"Um…"

"Here." She showed him how to hold the bottle and place it in the baby's mouth, how to turn it to make it easier for Izzy to drink.

The smile on Vera's face was so endearing, he didn't know what touched him more—the love in her eyes as she looked at the baby, or the baby's peaceful expression as she enjoyed her meal.

Once that was done and Vera burped the child—he had no idea one was supposed to do that—Izzy seemed to want to get on the floor.

"She wants to crawl. She doesn't walk yet, but imagine how exciting it's going to be when she takes her first step!" Enthusiasm trilled through Vera's words. Was she already getting attached to this baby?

His heart twitched. His lips pressed tight. It might hurt her if Rance took the child away.

Not to mention the little detail that, if Rance had caused his accident, how could he be trusted with a child?

She placed Izzy on the pristine and freshly cleaned beige carpet, and Izzy went exploring, her chubby little limbs pumping. The baby touched toys, walls, and anything on her way, the same happy grin on her adorable face.

Arms hugged around herself, Vera moved to the window. "I saw you admiring the day. It's such beautiful weather. Why don't we all go to the backyard? I mean, if everything looks safe enough."

He shrugged. "Sure."

Didn't make much difference to him.

She pulled a papaya-colored sweater over a lovely pale-pink dress with even more tiny bows onto the little girl, then snugged matching booties decorated with a white kitten over the girl's wiggly toes.

As he stared at this miracle in Vera's hands, his heart squeezed again. It scared him how much he wanted that baby to be his.

Theirs.

It didn't make sense.

Not only because Izzy was Rance's daughter.

Maverick wasn't father material on his best days and especially not now. Growing up, he'd admired the love between his parents so much. His family seemed perfect. He was proud of his father—a pillar of the community, a man with high morals.

But when Maverick had stumbled upon his father's dirty secret, his family turned out anything but perfect. Something had broken inside him that day, together with his trust for his father. Maybe a desire to be a father himself, to be a husband.

As for Vera…

Eventually, she'd go back to her city life. Quite possibly taking her grandmother and his heart with her.

He swept the thoughts into the farthest corner of his mind. "Let me carry Izzy." He surprised himself by volunteering.

Vera's eyes lit up as if he'd just given her a precious gift. "Great. Here we go."

Why did he offer that? Could he possibly balance the baby while walking with a cane? It seemed Vera believed in him more than he believed in himself. Leaving the baby in his arms, she picked up her warm jacket from the dining room while he opted to stay the way he was, in a T-shirt and jeans, reluctant to let Izzy go in order to change.

As his arms tightened around the precious child, they walked to the backyard. Thankfully, the day was exceptionally warm for fall. Everything seemed refreshingly brighter today.

The scent of grass teased his nostrils while birdsongs reminded him of the times the three of them had enjoyed bird watching. After yesterday's rain, grass burst with juice, but the main stage belonged to the leaves, of course. The vibrant golden yellow, just a shade darker than Vera's hair, the auburn, and the wine hues could be breathtaking if one paid attention.

Fall in Missouri was fascinating.

But he didn't care for fascinating things any longer.

Regret sliced him, and the baby whimpered as if feeling the change in his mood.

"Why don't you let me hold her for a while, please?" Vera reached for the child.

"Okay." He let the baby go like he'd had to let go of many things recently.

Vera sat on the swing, and he pushed it to rock her and Izzy. Judging by the excited giggles, the baby enjoyed it. Vera sang some fun children's song he'd never heard before and clapped at the end. Izzy clapped, too, a big, mostly toothless grin on her cute face.

Then for some time, they remained silent, only birds chirruping in the background and occasional giggles from Izzy. It was... nearly peaceful.

Until Vera's phone rang, interrupting that peace. She reached into her pocket and frowned at the screen. "This is my grandmother's neighbor, Mrs. Dorotea. I'd better take this call."

"Of course." He accepted rocking duty with pleasure he didn't expect.

She stepped away but soon returned. "I'm sorry, but I've got to go." Her forehead creased. "Grandma needs me. I can ask someone else to babysit if you'd like."

He got up carefully with Izzy in his hands. "Of course. What happened?"

Her frown deepened as she kissed the baby's head and whispered "Sorry." Then she turned to him. "You're not going to believe it."

"Try me." After the motorcycle, the rifle collection, and the blue hair he was curious about what might happen.

"The neighbors spotted her with her cat on her roof. I think she might've had difficulty coming down."

An unexpected chuckle bubbled inside him, but he managed to keep a straight face. It wasn't right to laugh at something like that. "Who is having difficulty? Your grandmother or the cat?"

Vera sighed as she strode toward the house. "Both."

Then he realized the situation's seriousness, and his heart skipped a beat. What if Vera fell off the roof while bringing her grandmother down? "How about I go with you?"

CHAPTER FIVE

SOME PEOPLE had eccentric grandmothers. And then there was Vera's grandmother.

As much as Vera loved her grandma, she did her best not to cringe as she sped up to the house where she'd spent a significant part of her childhood and teen years. Maverick rode shotgun with her while his mother had gladly resumed babysitting duty.

"What you saw while growing up is nothing compared to what's happening now." She didn't slow down enough to make a turn, and the tires squealed.

"I remember a wonderful woman who loved to bake and to can produce from the garden."

"She still does that sometimes. But she made some changes, too. She decided to follow your sister and color her hair green, only in a salad-green hue instead of emerald. Today, she colored her hair blue. I like both colors, actually. But then she decided to take up scuba diving two months ago."

"Scuba diving? Where did she go?"

"There's the Bonne Terre Mine right here in Missouri that has the largest man-made cavern in the world. And also a man-made lake. She said it's marvelous."

ALEXA VERDE

"Hmm, I traveled the world, but I didn't realize what kind of hidden gems Missouri has. Including you."

Her eyes widened as she passed a car. He thought of her as a hidden gem?

"Oh please." She waved off his praise as she stopped at the red light, though it touched a sensitive spot. "Missouri does have great things, though. Like the only cavern restaurant in the world. Or did you know Kansas City has a large number of fountains, second only to Rome?"

"I didn't. All my life, I searched for fame and adventure elsewhere." Regret tightened his voice. "I wish I could take you to that cavern restaurant. Or to the fountains."

She threw him a surprised glance. He'd never seemed to be a romantic type, at least not with her. In their small company of three, she'd always been one of the guys, even if she'd wanted it to be otherwise sometimes.

Her one pathetic attempt to change it at eighteen, to make Maverick notice her had ended in disaster. Heat crept up her neck.

But they were grown-ups now. What if…

No.

She did a mental headshake as she pushed the gas pedal. No sense entertaining false hope. "Well, she returned from scuba diving. But what worries me more is that she bought a motorcycle."

"There's nothing wrong with that. I own several." His lips curved up just a tad.

Something inside her warmed despite her worry for her grandmother. Why was she so desperate to see him smile? "Well, to be honest, I have a motorcycle, too. But my grandmother is seventy-five! Her eyesight is not the way it used to be. Neither is her memory."

"Has she gotten lost or had an accident?" The genuine concern behind his words reminded her of the boy he'd been—warm,

40

caring, as well as fun and adventurous—not the man he was becoming.

"A few damaged fences. Neighbors were surprisingly understanding. I just… worry about her." Her rib cage constricted as she turned to the quiet street leading to her grandmother's house.

Usually, she loved this drive, especially now in the fall when the trees were decked out in their best wardrobe, pretty and excited like girls going to the prom and wearing bright prom dresses. But today, she couldn't get to her destination fast enough.

"It's understandable. You're being a protective granddaughter." He reached for her hand for a brief moment before moving his away.

Well, this day was filled with surprises.

"That's not all. Grandma says she's tired of being single. She's been a widow for thirty years."

"You can't blame her for wanting to find a new man. You know what they say, age is just a number."

That was what Vera would be saying when she turned forty in three years and was probably still husbandless and childless. She pressed her lips tight, holding in a sigh as she pulled up to the driveway. "Yes, I understand. But she decided she's going to marry a Russian like my great-grandmother!"

He chuckled. "There might be a scarcity of those in this small town."

"You think?" Surely, Grandma had a hard enough time finding her first husband with his Russian-American background! Vera unbuckled and jumped out of the car. Then she had to force herself to slow down because he couldn't move as fast with his banged-up leg. "That didn't faze Grandma. No! She found online pals in Russia she's communicating with and hopes to see soon enough."

"You're kidding me." He kept up with her, his expression strained as they walked to the small crowd on the lawn.

"I wish!" She made sure hers didn't show pity. He wouldn't welcome that. "Imagine what kind of mischief she could get into there?"

Even if only in letters and online conversations, her grandmother had a more interesting love life than Vera. But then, Grandma's cat probably had a more interesting love life than Vera.

"I think I can imagine. But you know, I admire her even more now. Way to live her life to the fullest and on her terms."

Unlike him.

At least, not any longer.

He didn't say those words, but he didn't have to. His bitterness revealed it.

Once upon a time, she'd known him like she'd known her own heart and could often guess how to help him. But not now.

Not that she knew her own heart now, either.

Well, anyway, it was all about her grandma at the moment and not about the things Vera wished she could still do.

"It's not that I judge or criticize her. Or try to confine her into some kind of frame." They reached the small gathering.

Ironic how life came full circle. In her teens, Vera was the one climbing out windows or sitting on the roof. At that time, her grandmother had been worried about Vera getting into mischief, especially after Vera had trashed her father's car.

But that had been different. Vera had been an angry and lonely teenager who'd realized her parents cared about their jobs and new families more than they cared about her. She was obviously a burden to them. A nuisance.

Even after all these years, that betrayal hurt.

"I know," he said. The touch of his hand was fleeting, but it reached all the way to her heart. But then, it always had. "You're just looking out for her."

She steeled herself against her reaction to him, ridiculous after all these years apart, and concentrated on the crisis. She greeted

her neighbors and thanked them for calling her, then shaded her eyes to scan the roof.

Mrs. Dorotea stepped to her, her gray hair tucked into a knot and an apron with a lard stain covering the front of her long-sleeved floral dress.

A nervous smile appeared on Mrs. Dorotea's wrinkled face. "I thought I'd try to climb up the ladder, but then you might have two older ladies to get off the roof."

Sadness settled in her faded eyes after her only daughter's death three months ago, and compassion constricted Vera's rib cage. Mrs. Dorotea had moved to their neighborhood about half a year before Vera had left for college and had become friends with Vera's grandmother fast. Vera had been grateful to her for it.

Vera gave her neighbor a quick hug. "I know. And I appreciate it."

Then Vera looked up.

Her grandmother was sitting on the ledge, dressed in jeans and a maroon T-shirt, and the cat stretched nearby, both of them as comfortable as if this was the most common thing to do.

"Grandma, are you okay? What are you doing there?" Vera shouted.

Maybe that wasn't the most perfect choice of words, but how exactly did you talk to your seventy-five-year-old grandmother perched on the roof like a sparrow?

"I'm perfectly fine, dear. Buddy and I are just enjoying the view."

"Buddy?" Maverick touched her hand again.

"That's the cat." She braced herself for an unwelcome flutter of her heart.

He really should stop doing that. It was too distracting. But she couldn't tell him how he was affecting her. Thankfully, men could be clueless about things like that, and she was eager to keep it that way.

"Mind if I join you?" She strode to the ladder still leaning against the wall.

"What are you doing?" This time, he didn't just touch her hand—he snatched it.

Her heartbeat increased. "Don't you see? I don't think she can come down on her own, so I need to help her. But I can't embarrass her."

Something flashed in his eyes, and he let her hand go. "I can try to climb up there."

His hurting gaze sliced through her. They both realized that, with the way his leg was, it would be difficult for him to climb a ladder.

No pity, she reminded herself. "I think I'm better suited to talk her into climbing down. How about you hold the ladder so it doesn't shift?"

His expression softened. "And that way, if you fall down, I can catch you."

As she stared into his brown eyes a moment longer than necessary, her pulse kicked up even more.

She could be falling already.

Falling for him.

No thinking like that!

She gave him a grateful smile. "Yes. I'd feel safer that way."

Then she had a thought. The last thing she needed to do was chase the cat around the roof once she got there. So she hurried inside the house, opened a can with Buddy's favorite salmon, placed the contents in a Ziploc bag, which went into her pocket, and headed back outside.

She reached the ladder and started climbing. *Would* he catch her when she fell now? He'd done it once when she'd been sneaking out of the window to see him. Then he'd joined the cheerleading squad as a male cheerleader when some guys had

complained she was too heavy for the pyramid. Rance had mocked him, then had surprised everyone by joining, too.

But considering how Maverick had been hurt after the accident…

It was best to make sure she didn't fall.

Didn't fall to the ground.

Didn't fall for him again.

She approached the ledge and squeezed into a little spot between the ladder and her grandmother. Buddy opened his eyes, studied her, then went back to sleep. Getting Buddy could wait then.

She took in the magnificent fields with their rolling hills and breathtakingly beautiful fall foliage as if she'd tried to see further than she'd done before. "I don't blame you for getting up here. It's really beautiful."

Being up here, helping her grandmother felt good. Once Vera had changed her major to criminal science because she'd decided she wanted to bring justice to the wronged, help the ones in need, she'd thought she found her sense of purpose in life.

She'd thought she'd continued in the family legacy of extraordinary women. Her great-grandmother had once flown in the skies as a war pilot. Her grandmother had run a successful restaurant before she retired. Her mother was a well-respected doctor who'd been saving lives as part of her daily routine.

Becoming a cop had felt so right then that Vera couldn't believe it when, years later, the dream had faded. It was as if she'd discovered that what she'd considered a sun turned out to be just a lantern, broken by someone's hand. Maybe because she'd seen too much cruelty and the unspeakable sides of human nature… Maybe that doused the former spark.

She'd persevered out of sheer determination until…

She made a mental headshake.

Best not to think about that.

She had to learn the hard way that her judgment about people couldn't be trusted.

Her grandmother snorted. "Okay, we both know I'm here because I climbed to get Buddy down. And then I got vertigo and was too chicken to climb down."

Vera chuckled. "But you can't argue that it is a beautiful view."

So different from what she'd seen in the city. Maybe because for a long time she'd seen more grime than bright colors, no longer romanticizing her job through rose-colored lenses.

But as she stared at the treetops who'd learned easily how to let go every fall, she didn't know if she could do the same. And she still didn't know what direction her life should take. She'd become a disappointment to her mother who'd wanted her to become a doctor, to her father, who'd yelled that he'd lost his son because of her.

She was probably a disappointment to her heroic great-grandmother as Vera had done nothing heroic while being a cop and then had quit altogether. Vera leaned toward the one person who'd never been disappointed in her.

Her grandmother gave her a shove, a tiny and a careful one— they were on the roof, after all. "Beautiful view indeed. How is working with Maverick?"

"Fine." She did her best to sound nonchalant as she averted her gaze, studiously focusing on the treetops again.

"Just *fine*? Why haven't you ever told him how you felt about him?"

Pin prickles danced over Vera's skin. She'd hidden her feelings from the entire town, including the object of her affection, but not from her grandmother. "What was the point? I didn't want to stop him from following his dream. I didn't want to give up on mine. We were going in different directions."

"But you're both here now." Grandma lifted Buddy onto her lap, and then stroked his fur.

Vera drew in a deep breath of air scented with hay, foliage, and a hint of the sweet scent of apple preserves that clung to her grandmother. Then she let it out with a sound more a sigh than a breath. Not that she was the sighing type. No way. "It's too late."

"It's too late for me and your grandfather. It's not too late for you and Maverick."

Vera opened her mouth to argue, then glanced down to see him trying to climb the ladder. "Um, as much as I enjoy the fresh air and view, how about we continue this conversation in the kitchen instead?"

"Okay. But get Buddy down first." Grandma handed her the cat, who meowed as if displeased to be passed down like a trophy.

Huh.

So she didn't need that salmon after all.

"Maverick, please wait for me. I'm bringing Buddy." When he stepped onto the ground again, she exhaled the breath she'd held.

"It must be difficult for a man like him, all strong, masculine, and successful, to feel like a cripple," Grandma whispered. "Be gentle with him."

"Grandma…" Her heart making a sudden shift, Vera looked at the face she'd loved so much and for so long, her anchor in life when she'd needed it the most. "That's just the thing. To me, he's still strong, muscular, and successful."

"I raised you right." The older woman nodded, then chuckled. "I did say masculine, not muscular, though I admit those biceps don't hurt."

Warmth crept up Vera's neck. "No, they don't."

Climbing the ladder empty-handed was much easier than climbing down with a complaining and squirming cat. Just how was she going to do it with her grandmother?

Then Buddy let out a loud meow and released his nails into her flesh.

Vera yelped and let him go. "Maverick, please catch Buddy!"

CHAPTER SIX

YES, VERA heard that cats landed on their feet—or paws in this case—but she wouldn't want to risk it.

Air whooshed out of her lungs as Maverick caught Buddy. Then he let out a yelp similar to her own, though not as high-pitched, of course. Buddy must've used his claws again.

"Sorry!" She hurried to climb down and frowned at the fresh scratches on his arms.

"I've had worse." He shrugged as if it were no big deal. "Though when I said I was going to catch you, this wasn't what I had in mind."

The cat meowed as if confirming that neither had he.

"Hold on, Buddy." She snatched the cat and wiggled the bag with salmon in front of the little pink nose. The cat seemed to decide it was the time to dig its claws in. "You like it, right?"

"I can get Buddy inside and give him the treat," Mrs. Dorotea volunteered kindly.

"Thank you. Watch out for those claws, please." Vera's heart warmed as she passed the cat and the salmon, grateful for small towns and good neighbors. And to think she'd had difficulty finding someone to water her plants in the city.

Then she and Maverick returned to the ladder.

"I won't have to catch your grandma this time, will I?" He smirked.

Aha! There was the first boy who'd made her heart patter. She smirked back. "I sure hope not."

The mischievous expression vanished, and the intensity of her longing to bring it back startled her. Shaking her head, she started climbing. She realized, of course, that he was never going to be the man he'd been before, that something was broken inside him. But neither was she the same rebellious and naïve girl.

Maybe she didn't even want him to be the guy he used to be, the one who'd placed fame and everything that came with it above all else, who'd wanted to be the first, better than others so badly. She wanted him to be a better man than that.

Was it even possible?

Her grandmother's words rang in her ears as she reached for the edge of the roof, but kept her feet on the ladder. *With God, everything is possible.*

But after seeing what Vera had seen for years, believing in God had become…difficult.

Maybe her relationship with God wasn't so simple, after all.

Her grandmother stared at her. "What are you going to do? *Carry* me down like you did with Buddy? Though I promise I wouldn't release my claws into you."

"I appreciate that." Vera chuckled. "What I can do is guide your feet onto the ladder rungs."

The older woman's forehead wrinkled. "O–okay. Let's try that. Let me pray first because I don't want to take us both down to the ground. And I think Maverick suffered too much already to get flattened by two women."

"I don't think he would…" Vera started saying but saw her grandmother's lips moving and shut up.

Then her grandmother turned around, and from her perch, Vera guided her grandmother's left leg onto the top rung, gently tugging on the jeans and then placing the purple sneaker onto the rung. Then she repeated the process with Grandma's right leg.

"You're doing good, Gran. You're doing good." Vera did her best to sound encouraging even as sweat started beading on her forehead and her heart pounded. She'd been in dangerous situations before, but they hadn't involved people she loved.

Except for once…

Her gut twisted as they made slow progress while people on the lawn cheered Grandma on.

No reason to travel down *that* memory lane. It would only take her to the land of Regret with the first stop in Guiltsville.

"I saw the way Maverick looks at you." The fresh breeze brought Grandma's words to Vera. "Don't make my mistake. Don't wait decades to give yourself a new chance. Sometimes we get to return to the roads once traveled. And sometimes we're given only one opportunity to get it right."

Was she really going to have this conversation with her grandmother's purple sneakers? Suppressing a groan, Vera moved them to the lower and lower rungs.

"How do you know which one it is?" she asked the white rubber soles while her longing intensified.

"You don't." The voice was so low Vera barely heard it.

Finally, they made it to the ground. Stepping aside to let her grandmother pass, Vera pressed a hand to her temple, light-headed with relief. At the same time, her grandmother's words took root in her heart. She pressed her hand to her other temple, both now throbbing, a single question rising above the pulsing—Did she want to water those fragile roots or not?

The little crowd cheered for them. "You made it!"

"Thanks, everyone." The older woman smiled. "Now, how about a slice of pumpkin pie with iced tea?"

51

Unlike the words still ringing in Vera's head, those ones were met with enthusiasm. Her grandmother sauntered to her little red brick home like nothing had happened. "And thank you for not calling the fire truck to get me."

A siren whined in the distance.

Grandma glanced back, her forehead puckering. "I spoke too soon."

"Sorry," Mrs. Dorotea muttered.

Waving a dismissive hand, Vera's grandmother opened the door. "Oh, by the way, Maverick and Vera, did I mention I volunteered you for a booth at the Harvest Festival?"

Maverick's eyes widened. "What?"

Vera groaned. This obvious attempt at matchmaking wouldn't work.

Would it?

"I sure hope it's not for a pie or dessert booth." Despite her grandmother's many lessons, Vera had never mastered the fine art of pie making.

Besides, she wasn't sure manning a booth would be safe. The pressure to solve the case intensified. But would someone assault Maverick in the crowd?

"Nah. It's for the children's slide booth." Grandma led everyone to the kitchen that always smelled like freshly baked pies and applesauce.

While helping Vera spread the plates on the table, Maverick started, "I know it's for a great cause, but—"

"Young man, you can either argue with me until the festival or agree now." The older woman cut the pie.

"I guess I'll just agree now." The corners of his mouth moved up a little, giving another glimpse of his former self, and a new nudge of gratitude spurred Vera to smile at her grandmother.

Then the blaring siren neared, and she suppressed another groan. And she'd thought she might get bored back in a small town.

She'd take a slice of boredom together with a slice of pumpkin pie anytime now. She grabbed two plates and headed outside. "Let's hope the fire chief likes pumpkin pie."

Maverick groaned as Vera opened his bedroom curtains again the next morning. "Is this going to happen every day now?"

"Every day until you start doing it on your own." She beamed at him, brighter than the sun.

Was she taking pleasure in this or what?

But a tiny part of him warmed up at the thought that she cared. "How did you even get here? I locked the door. Don't tell me you climbed through the window. I made sure it was locked, too. And the branches were trimmed like you told us to."

"I know how to pick a lock. I took lessons from your brother. Just kidding. It's one of the things I learned when I… needed to." A shadow passed over her face.

Why would she need to learn to pick a lock? Didn't the police usually just break down doors? He'd seen a few cop shows where the detective picked a lock, but wasn't that usually violating the law, not when assisting it such as with search warrants?

Huh. Maybe it had been while she'd stayed with his father in Springfield who'd moved there after his wife had found out about his affair. Poor girl.

Then he winced.

What had happened to him? Not so long ago, he'd been energetic, had trained for hours, fueled by adrenaline and the desire to succeed, to set a new speed record, not for others, but for himself.

And now he needed to be dragged out of bed by his childhood friend.

Maybe because he hadn't just found himself on the side of the road of life but had crashed and burned.

Literally.

Well, enough self-pity.

Vera propped her hip against the windowsill. "Besides, I have a big announcement to make."

Curiosity got the best of him. "What is that?"

Did she get a break in the case?

Hopefully not. He didn't want to let her go yet.

What?

"Izzy got a new tooth!" She stood there still beaming so brightly she could have just won a world racing championship.

Against his best intentions, the corners of his mouth lifted as a pleasant feeling soothed him. "You say it like it's a big deal."

"It is. She's got only five teeth, and every one of them is special. And guess what? We're going to help her learn to walk today. Isn't that exciting?"

Yup.

That was what his world was going to be. Instead of dizzying speed, thousands of fans, and ovations, he was going to be excited about the first step of a child who wasn't even his.

His heart made a weird movement.

Actually, it *would* be exciting to see Izzy's first step. Longing ignited, too, as if someone turned the key in the ignition. He'd worked so hard not to let this baby into his heart, but it looked like Izzy had crawled inside it already, with just a few giggles and innocent baby blues.

A different blue-eyed beauty stared at him. Her blonde hair was flowing over her shoulders, and he wondered how it would be to run his fingers through it, feel its softness.

A lump formed in his throat, and he hated himself for the sign of weakness.

Why hadn't he returned here earlier? Why hadn't he searched her out when he'd still been handsome, successful, and... healthy?

"Um, my grandmother had an idea for the Harvest Festival, and it involves you. I don't know whether you're going to like it." She studied the ceiling, then rolled her eyes and looked him in the eye. "Okay, wrong. I know you're not going to like it."

Uh-oh. That woman was a torpedo. Wasn't it enough for her that he'd agreed to man the slide-booth thing? "What is that?"

"I have cinnamon buns and coffee downstairs. I'll see you there." She marched to the door.

"I'll be there when I'm good and ready," he called after her.

Well, it just happened that he was ready now.

He got out of bed and got dressed. Then he found his cane and limped to the bathroom. As he shaved, he could practically smell cinnamon rolls, and just like in childhood, it lifted his mood. Mrs. Tsareva made amazing pastries. Honestly, the world over, he'd never tasted anything like her baking.

Once he entered the dining room, a large plate with the rolls was already steaming on the table, as well as an inviting cup of coffee for him. "You knew I'd be here fast, didn't you?"

"Yup. Right, Izzy?" She winked at the baby sitting on her lap. "You're such a pretty baby, aren't you?" Based on the stains of puree, Izzy and her pink bib were having a fun breakfast.

He sipped his flavorful coffee, exhaling as it hit the spot. "You make excellent coffee."

She aimed at the child's mouth with a spoon. But Izzy turned, and Vera fed the girl's ear instead. "Lots of practice due to many night shifts. Coffee is one of the few things I know how to make in the kitchen. Which brings me to my grandmother's idea." Then she waved the spoon, what was left on it threatening to glop off. "Before you say it, I think it's ridiculous."

55

That was *not* a good start. His gut tightened. "What is it?"

She wiped the baby's face and ear gently. "You see, a few years ago, someone came up with the idea of 'Sweethearts Pie.' It's a pie cooked by a couple. Grandma has a recipe she thinks would be perfect for it, but she's lacking a boyfriend...."

A groan tore from his gut, loosening the knots somewhat. "Don't tell me. She entered us in the competition."

This time, she was more successful in making the spoon and the baby's mouth connect. "Okay, then I'm not going to tell you. You figured it out yourself. Great deduction skills, by the way."

Sarcasm didn't look good on her. He rolled his eyes right back at her.

"But... we are not sweethearts." His insides warmed as she jostled the squirmy baby. Why had the idea of having her as his sweetheart seemed so appealing? Well, he'd had his chance and crashed and burned it.

But now she was shaking her head. "Not to mention neither one of us can make toast without burning it, no use even talking about a pie." Her head tipped up. She waggled her eyebrows hopefully. "Unless things changed since high school?"

"I lived on restaurant meals and takeout and then hired a personal chef." That didn't sound like bragging, did it? He helped himself to the rolls, cut into one, and brought the gooey, sugary concoction to his mouth, closing his eyes while it dissolved on his tongue. Man, just as delicious as he'd remembered.

He'd given a lot of his earnings to charities and had done his best to make the ranch prosper, even if he wasn't here in person. His family loved this place, and he loved his family. Would've trusted them with his life.

Well, not all of them.

The sense of betrayal burned in his gut. Should he have told his siblings then that...

No, it would've only hurt them.

The past was in the past.

"What happened? Was there a stone in the roll?" Despite the teasing, which sounded so like they used to sound with each other, concern underlined her voice, drawing him to the present.

"What?"

"You had a strange expression on your face. Okay, never mind." She held the squirming baby tight and continued feeding her. "It's none of my business."

That burning feeling intensified, traveled higher as if wanting out. He ached to tell her, just like he'd told her so many of his childhood secrets. She'd understand.

She'd always understood him so easily.

Until he'd all but left her behind after the most amazing kiss of his life.

Still, she'd come to help him without a second thought because that was the kind of person she was.

He owed her.

Learning to bake a pie was a small price to pay for that. And yes, he wanted to spend more time with her. It sent a long-forgotten delight through him.

He swirled his coffee cup, mixing the sugar into it with a practiced motion, then leaned forward. "I'll do it. I mean, I'll bake the pie with you."

Her eyebrows shot up. "Really?"

"Really."

The baby giggled and clapped, obviously excited, too, even if she didn't know what they were excited about.

"I have to warn you. It's not going to be easy. Grandma says it's easier to make an elephant dance on a rope than to teach me baking."

He'd always loved her grandma and her sense of humor. "It can't be that bad."

"Yeah. It can be done." Vera grinned at him. "Some circuses have elephants that do that, right?"

His heart skipped a beat, and once again, as her luminous smile lit him up, he wished he could turn back time. He coughed to hide the feeling, hoping it wouldn't reflect in his eyes. His voice emerged gruffer than he'd intended. "But aren't you forgetting the investigation?"

"No. I got the new list from Rance. And I cross-referenced birth records at a large number of hospitals. Some of the names are famous people, so I could stalk their social media accounts. Even if pregnancy doesn't show for the first several months, it would be difficult to hide it for the rest of the term."

He nodded. "True that."

"I managed to eliminate a large number of names by doing that. I have several names I'm researching." Her eyes dimmed, and he scolded himself for that. "I talked to the two women in this town I told you about. I called ten others from Rance's new and shortened list. I don't think they are the ones, and I'll keep looking. I called the police, and they didn't have new leads, either."

Izzy gave him a bright smile that now showcased her five teeth.

Vera hugged the baby. "I also had a serious talk with Rance. He didn't want to listen at first, but when I explained to him that he could be spending nearly all he earned on child support, he finally listened. And considering his profession, he can't afford a hangover. I described to him some accidents in detail that resulted from drunken driving. He said he'd never driven drunk, but it might happen one day. I told him I'd drag him to AA kicking and screaming if he wouldn't do it voluntarily."

His lips curved up a little. "I'll help you." He should've intervened himself a long time ago. He was a rotten friend. Unlike Vera.

"Thanks. He said he'd *try* to do it. We'll see. You know I'll do my best to find Izzy's mother." But there was some sadness in her voice.

His heart dropped a little. Vera was obviously getting attached to the baby.

Who was he kidding? So was he.

In the beginning, Izzy had been a bit of an unexpected burden, then an irritation and worry when she'd cried in his presence. But now…

Now she was more of a miracle that just might heal some broken parts of him. He couldn't risk losing that hope, that miracle, if Vera found Izzy's mother and that woman had become remorseful and wanted her baby back.

Sulking and bitter, he wasn't a great model for the child.

But…

Did he want to be?

Could there be more than one miracle in his life?

CHAPTER SEVEN

"MAY I feed her?" Maverick surprised himself by asking.

He'd probably feed the baby's ears and bib more than the girl herself, but for some reason, trying felt important.

"Sure." Vera plopped Izzy on his lap. "She can also eat some finger food now, so we can try it later. Might be easier."

Just like yesterday, Izzy didn't cry, and he considered his attempts a success already. A new wave of tenderness swept over him as he breathed in the baby-powder scent and spooned some puree. The baby squirmed a little, but he managed to feed her.

"You're doing great." Vera high-fived him.

The familiar gesture brought too many memories of happy times in their childhoods. But he needed to live in the present. "Thanks."

Her face took on a serious expression instead of the goofy smile he'd grown to adore. "I check the camera recordings regularly. I also do an outer and a perimeter check several times a day when someone else can stay with the baby. So far, I haven't noticed anything unusual. But I'm glad your family agreed to hire my friend as a bodyguard for the children. And good news, she agreed, too. She should be here soon."

"Thank you." His arm moved when he wanted to reach out for her hand, but he managed to stop himself in time.

Something strange entered her eyes, and if he didn't know better, he'd interpret as wistfulness. Could she have started feeling something for him, too, or was it his wishful thinking?

Izzy whimpered, demanding attention, and he rocked her back and forth.

The expression in Vera's eyes disappeared. "Some more news. The guy who used to work for Lavigne took a day off the day of your accident, too. And he's got a new job in Springfield now."

"Let me take a guess. At Lavigne's company?"

"Close enough. Lavigne's brother's. I'm going to make a trip to Springfield tomorrow morning."

"Want me to go with you?"

She seemed to consider it. "Best not to. If he's guilty, he might get suspicious."

He pressed his lips tight, holding in an odd disappointment.

Vera got up. "Would you mind letting me carry her, please? I want to go back to the nursery."

"Sure." Though he wanted to carry Izzy, doing that and walking with his cane had already proved challenging. He resisted the urge to grind his teeth. He'd need to up his regimen with his physical therapist, and that regimen was grueling to start with. He hated being weak.

When they returned to the nursery with its soft carpet from the dining room, she stood Izzy on the floor. "You're such a pretty baby, aren't you?" Then she wrapped her fingers around Izzy's tiny fingers and tugged her forward. "How about making that step?"

He wanted so badly to be a part of this family that it hurt inside.

When he'd raced, the possibility of an accident filled his veins with an adrenaline rush instead of dread. He'd even been in a few

accidents but always escaped unscathed. But in the end, something he'd loved so much had made him the bitter person he was now.

Could the baby's sweet smile as she stumbled forward sweeten that bitterness? Or maybe the sweetness of Vera?

That reminded him of "Sweethearts Pie," and for some reason, baking a pie didn't sound trivial or discouraging.

And just as the baby moved forward with Vera's help, he made a step forward, too.

A wobbly one, but a step nonetheless.

Without a cane.

Some people knew exactly what they wanted to be, even at an early age.

Vera wasn't one of those people. She'd alternated between a pilot, a doctor, a geologist, a scientist, and many other professions. Then she'd stopped at forensic scientist in high school and changed to criminal justice while in college.

But as she dumped another ruined pie in the trash late the next afternoon, she knew one thing with certainty. Unlike her grandmother, she was *not* born to be a baker.

Maybe she wasn't born to be a PI, either, since the conversation in Springfield didn't yield desirable results. First, the guy stated it was none of her business where he'd spent the day—which was true. Then he'd admitted he'd spent it playing pool and drinking with his buddies. His buddies had confirmed it.

She'd studied a copy of the surveillance for the flower shop parking lot until her vision was blurry and decided the cowhand was way too bulky to match the person in the recording.

He was more Embry's size.

Which brought back the idea that revenge might've been the motive. She'd spent the evening yesterday following up on

Maverick's conquests. Some of them were happily married or in a happy relationship now, so she moved them lower on the list of suspects. The quantity of the rest was still mind-blowing, and she'd been going through them slowly.

Working on the list Rance had given her for the baby's potential mother hadn't yielded great results, either.

She suppressed a sigh as she glanced at Maverick. "I've tracked down about eighty percent of the list Rance gave us. By the looks of it, none of those women were pregnant in the months before Izzy was born. I contacted the police. They didn't have any leads, either. The baby carrier and the baby clothes in which Izzy arrived on Rance's porch were brand-new, bought at a major chain. There is a store where they *could've* been bought located relatively close to Rance's residence. While I'm trying to track down receipts, I have a feeling they were paid for with cash."

A band tightened around her lungs.

Was Maverick as disappointed in her as she was?

She'd been a failure to her parents, never reaching their high expectations. Was she a failure to him, too?

Until she'd realized that her mother had cared about her new family way more than about her, she'd tried hard to please her, had studied chemistry with a passion and anatomy with much less passion so she could become a doctor, too. Then Vera had realized that, even if she found a cure for an incurable disease, it wouldn't buy her mother's love.

She'd wanted her grandmother to be proud of her, but Vera had turned out to be a disaster in the kitchen.

Really, how hard could it be to bake a pie?

Frustration tightened her chest.

"Well, there was a slight improvement from the previous pie." Maverick gave her an encouraging smile after being delegated the courageous role of a taster.

She did her best to ignore the fluttering of her tummy, the effect his smile had on her, and held in a groan. "With this much progress, it'll take us a couple of years to bake a passable pie. And we can't have just a passable pie. We need a great one for my grandmother."

"No offense, but I think we've got a better chance of joining a circus and training elephants." He winked at her.

Despite her failed efforts, she did a mental fist pump. *Finally!* For the first time since his return, he'd winked at her. He'd made a few steps without a cane today, too, and as much as she'd been eager to rush to support him, she'd let him do them on his own.

Baby steps.

In more senses than one.

She looked around the kitchen, the warm feeling inside her returning. This place had been her safe haven while she'd been growing up, and a yearning reminded her how much she'd missed it.

Everything about it was so dear and familiar.

Canned preserves her grandmother had made with gooseberries, apricots, currants, all labeled in her grandmother's neat writing.

A glass cabinet displaying the delicate porcelain tea set with pink flowers that was passed down from her grandmother's mother and would eventually be passed to Vera. Vera's mother had no interest in hot tea in the mornings, preferring lattes from a fancy bistro. Hand towels displayed the teacups' pattern, too.

Hand-painted lacquered wooden dishes and spoons—treasures her grandmother's mother brought with her from her country as a WWII war bride—were decorated with one of the traditional Russian ornaments, red berries and golden leaves.

Mixed in with those were the appliances Vera had given her grandmother, giving the kitchen an eclectic air of classic and modern, beautiful tradition mixed with efficient practicality. This

was a kitchen so different from her parents' kitchens or her own, with their stainless steel appliances and fashionable backsplashes.

She closed her eyes, trying to breathe around the band on her chest. The truth was she'd never felt the joy in those kitchens that she'd felt here. It was like this place had always welcomed her with a wink and a smile, even if it knew Vera's culinary skills left a lot to be desired and could burn it down.

Just like her grandmother, this kitchen accepted Vera just the way she was.

And just like her grandmother and unlike her parents, this place had never judged her when she came short of expectations. Had never betrayed her.

The band around her lungs squeezed tighter.

"How about *I* try to bake a pie?" Maverick said softly.

Crossing her arms over her chest, she eyed him. "You said you can't bake."

"I said I usually didn't do it." He shrugged. "I concentrated on my career."

The career he'd dedicated his entire life to and now thought he'd lost. Her rib cage constricted, and she nearly reached out to him.

Then she forced herself to stay back. "Then why did you choose the role of a taster?"

"Because it was an important and, well, dangerous one." His expression went from sulky to a bit playful, and she welcomed it.

She helped by giving him the ingredients while he did everything else.

"Look at cooking and baking like chemistry." He touched her hand. "We mix different ingredients, and they form a new substance. So there's chemistry in this kitchen."

Delightful tingles traveled over her skin from his touch.

Oh yes.

There definitely was chemistry here.

Buddy walked into the kitchen, sniffed the air still carrying a slight trace of burned pie, sneezed unhappily, and seemed to consider leaving. Poor fella. More than likely, he'd never smelled anything singed in Grandma's kitchen.

"You'll live, Buddy." Smirking at him, Vera reached for his favorite salmon, and he generously allowed her to feed him.

Then he marched out of the kitchen, probably thinking he could make a better pie than she could. The sad part was he could be right.

Hmm, once she looked at what they were doing as combining different substances, their property, and them forming new ones, things clicked. Excitement even zinged through her, maybe because things started making sense. Maybe because she was with Maverick.

Most likely, both.

When Maverick placed the pie in the oven, she picked up her jaw from the tiled floor and turned to him. "I think you did it."

"No, *we* did it." He smiled at her.

She melted as if she were ice cream scooped atop warm pie. She moved a little closer to him, then closer still. "Obviously, baking is not my strong suit."

"It can become one. You did great now. Besides, you have other great qualities."

Her mouth went dry, and her temperature increased. "Like what?"

"You're compassionate, intelligent, witty.…" He paused to tuck away a stray strand of hair that escaped her bun.

Her heartbeat went into overdrive at his touch. It took a moment to find her voice. "Oh, stop it! Hmm. On the other hand, go on."

"And absolutely gorgeous. Your luscious hair smells of wild berries and melted caramel. I can drown in your kind blue eyes willingly. Your… lips…"

She was afraid to take her next breath as his gaze slipped to her lips.

"That guy is too old for me." Grandma barged into the kitchen, Buddy prancing at her heels.

Vera and Maverick jerked back as if they were teenagers nearly caught kissing.

"He's fifteen years younger than you are!" Vera's voice sounded strange to her own ears.

Grandma waved in dismissal. "Well, when I offered him a ride on the motorcycle, he paled. And when I suggested we'd go dancing, he said something about his hip."

Stifling the laughter rising in her chest, Vera gave her grandmother a quick hug. "Sorry, Grandma."

"At least, he lasted through dinner. My previous date glanced at my hair, mumbled something about an emergency, and was out of there."

Vera smiled. She also loved her grandma just the way she was, despite the worry she caused her. "I don't think it was about your hair, but maybe about the holstered gun on your hip."

"Hey, I always say a gun is a girl's best accessory." The older woman sniffed the air. "Something smells good."

Vera opened the oven and gestured at the pie. "Maverick made it."

"Vera and I did."

"Okay, I helped. Mostly, by staying out of his way." She bumped his side like in childhood.

Only they weren't childhood friends any longer, and the gesture felt overly suggestive. Awareness rushed through her.

Could she hope there could be more than friendship between them one day, or was she just kidding herself, like she'd done at eighteen?

Chapter Eight

MAVERICK FELT like his eardrums were about to explode. Baking yesterday had been—dare he say it?—a "piece of cake" compared to this. Izzy had been crying and refusing to fall asleep, despite Vera carrying her around the nursery and cooing for what seemed to be hours.

Izzy's diaper was clean. She'd been fed, and based on the pediatrician's assessment, she was healthy. But, man, was she fussy today! Maybe those new teeth. Hadn't he heard teething was a nightmare? Vera's patience was admirable as she still smiled.

However, he was considering escaping into the garden right through the window and wasn't proud of it.

"You know, I was told when I was a child and was fussy, they'd take me for a drive," he blurted out. "I'd fall asleep from the car movement and motor hum."

Then he stilled, regretting his words already. He hadn't been behind the steering wheel since his accident. Any time he'd wanted to do it, the scent of burning rubber and his own flesh appeared in his nostrils, and pain exploded inside. For a few moments, he couldn't breathe, much less move.

"You loved cars even then, didn't you?" Laughing, she looked up at him, a grateful gleam in her eyes. "But it's a good idea. Let's try it. I'll drive, okay?"

"Okay." He did his best not to sound too relieved, shame consuming him.

How embarrassing that a race car driver couldn't even go for a short drive in the neighborhood! His family thought he'd given up on his career because of his injuries, and he didn't dissuade them, too disgusted with himself.

How could he explain that the reason he had to leave what he'd dedicated his life to wasn't the physical injuries, which he believed would heal in time? But him being a coward?

She dressed the baby while, under her guidance, he gathered supplies, like a diaper bag, sippy cup, a bottle, snacks, and far too many other things apparently needed even for a short time away.

Izzy had outgrown the infant seat, so Vera secured her in a rear-facing convertible seat with plush pink padding that matched Izzy's cute outfit.

He opened the driver's door for Vera, then climbed into the passenger seat, feeling only half the man he'd once been.

She turned on the engine and drove off. "Don't be so sad. You're alive. It's a sunny day. And I'm about to buy you a treat."

He stilled. "Are you talking to me or the baby?"

Vera laughed. "To both of you, I guess. Well, mostly to you, because I had ice cream in mind. It's best to wait until Izzy is a year old before introducing her to ice cream. Remember, we used to beg your parents to take us to the ice cream parlor?"

The sweet memories rushed in, but he sat up straighter. "I don't remember doing any begging."

She returned her attention to the road, the muscles tensing on her face. "Right. You didn't have to. All you had to do was ask."

While she'd had to beg her mother with no results. Her father had taken her to the ice cream parlor or for a walk in the park when he'd been home, but he'd seemed to be on the road all the time.

Compassion squeezed Maverick's heart. The sad story of her childhood and especially her adolescence still pained him. For a moment, he looked at the outskirts of town, the trees dressed up in scarlet red, golden yellow, and burgundy as if trying to outdo each other on the red carpet.

He'd nearly forgotten how beautiful the fall colors were in his hometown.

Hmm, something was different.

Silence!

Well, besides the growl of the motor. He glanced back. Izzy had her eyes closed, her long lashes still, and her breath coming evenly.

He kept his voice low as he turned back. "It worked. She's asleep now."

Vera's lips curled up. "Awesome. You knew what to do to calm her down. You'd make a great father."

Something shifted inside him, and breathing became difficult. While he didn't deserve the praise, his chest warmed, his taut muscles loosening. "Thank you. And you'd make a great mother."

Instead of pleasing her, his words removed her smile. "I messed up too many things in life. I probably would've messed up that, too."

And just like that, compassion tightened around his heart further. She used to be cheerful, spunky, and confident. What had happened to her to make her say things like that? Well, besides what he already knew about her parents. "I don't agree. I'm sure you were a great cop. You did an awesome job for my family as a PI."

"I still haven't found Izzy's mother or the culprit in your accident. I did find two women who'd been pregnant before Izzy

was born, and both children are present and accounted for. I checked hospital records to make sure there were no twins. Nope."

He hated seeing disappointment on her lovely face. "We both know Rance's memory could be, well, sporadic. He could've forgotten to mention someone. And take it from your employer in this case, he thinks you're doing great." He winked at her. "And it was admirable of you to drop everything and come here to help your grandmother."

She grimaced as they passed a small bridge over a sparkling creek. "No. Not really admirable. I did it as much for myself as for my grandma."

He studied the face he thought he knew like he knew his own palm—such sadness and even resignation now lined those familiar features. "You don't have to tell me if you don't want to."

Never mind the fact that he wanted to know everything about her.

She made a turn. "Actually, it might make me feel better to tell you. Remember, we used to tell everything to each other? Well, almost everything."

Yeah, he'd never told her the way he'd started feeling about her. He glanced back, to make sure Izzy was still sleeping.

"I wasn't a great cop. Far from it. And not because the physical training was difficult for a plump girl like me. I just had to work more than others, and that was fine by me. Or because of the long, grueling hours. Or because of the nature of our job when sometimes it's difficult not to become disillusioned. I worked hard, slept little, and believed in myself and what I was doing. I believed I was making a difference." She made a pause, glanced back, then returned her attention to the road.

He didn't say a word, preparing himself for what was going to be next.

"I was so busy at my job I had little in the sense of a social life. Until several years later when I met Todd. He helped me out in the

grocery store when I dropped peaches on the floor. Then he put my groceries into my car in the pouring rain while I held an umbrella. He was handsome and seemingly kind, and I gave him my phone number when he asked for it."

Jealousy needled him, and he turned away to stare at the bright foliage. It didn't look so beautiful anymore. Maybe he was wrong. Maybe he didn't need to hear about her love life, to envy some guy she'd fallen for.

She continued as she made a turn, "We talked on the phone for a couple of weeks until he asked me out. He took me to the best restaurants in the city, brought me large bouquets of red roses every time we met, as well as chocolates and expensive perfume. He was charming, very much so, and my head was spinning."

"You fell in love." He felt deflated.

Empty again.

"I thought I did. I was fully aware of what kind of job I did. So I never shared anything I learned at work with him. But a few times he asked questions that should've put me on guard." Her shoulders drooping, she slowed around a curve.

Oh no.

He could guess where this was going, and his heart started aching. Guilt jabbed him, too. He had no right to be jealous. He should've wished her happiness, even if it was with some other guy.

"But I was too infatuated with Todd to notice. He turned out to be a suspect in one of our cases. By the time I had the chance to report it, a *good friend* of mine already had. Apparently, he was eyeing the same promotion I was. It became known to my higher-ups. All my hard work was erased in one sweep." Her voice bitter, she clenched her left hand on the steering wheel.

His heart sank. Two betrayals at the same time, from a man she'd been falling for and her friend and colleague. Add to this

how her parents had treated her, first her mother, then her father when she'd been a teen, and it must've been devastating.

"Don't blame yourself." He did his best to stop himself from reaching out to her in a supportive gesture. Then he gave up and placed his hand on hers on the armrest between them.

She seemed to hesitate for a few moments. Then her fingers laced through his, making the blood rush faster in his veins. "I was punished. Two years later, when things started getting better, another thing happened."

He squeezed her fingers to encourage her. But the pleasant tingles traveling along his skin told him he enjoyed having her hand in his again. And he had a nearly irresistible urge to ask her to pull to the shoulder so he could take her into his arms.

She sent him a glance. "I had to arrest someone for a GTA—grand theft auto. It turned out to be my baby half brother who was fifteen by then. My relationship with my father was estranged already, given how I broke his new wife's car window after he left us. After the arrest of his beloved son, he stopped talking to me altogether."

"It wasn't your fault. If anything, it could be partly his fault for not raising his son right."

"I should've steered my brother in the right direction, too. But they spoiled that boy so much that, if I suggested anything to discipline him, I immediately was a cruel person." She shrugged as if she didn't care while he knew she cared too much.

"That was wrong." Not that he should be judging. Parenthood was difficult, and he was learning it firsthand. But how could that man blame his daughter? Anger pulsed through Maverick's veins.

"And then... A teen I'd been trying to help—one I did my best to get off the streets—was shot. I didn't feel a passion for my job any longer. It seemed, no matter what I did, the result was... something wrong. I didn't think I was making a difference any

longer. It was better to leave, so I did. I got my private investigator's license."

"How did that go?" He glanced at the fields they were passing, then studied her beautiful profile again. He wanted so badly to make things easier for her. To see the shine in her eyes he'd once seen.

"I was eager to help people and enjoyed it at first. But most of the assignments became following cheating spouses. It reminded me too much of why my childhood became broken." Her voice broke, too.

He squeezed her fingers again, trying to move some warmth and strength into her. Though his father had turned out to be an adulterer, he'd never left them like hers had. "I'm sorry."

She shrugged again as she approached a four-way stop. "Still, I persevered. I should be grateful I had a job. But a part of me was glad to return to my hometown and regroup now. I did want to help Grandma, and I still do. But at this point, I am not sure who is helping whom."

"One thing I am sure about is that you're helping me." He brought her fingers to his lips and kissed them. His pulse went into overdrive from the simple gesture.

"Thank you. I should be glad she's filled with a zest for life. I should support it, not try to squelch it. And if my grandmother wants to find love in Russia..." Vera took a deep breath. "I need to find a way to go with her. And to be her biggest cheerleader. I have a lot of experience in cheerleading."

"For others, but not for yourself."

"Probably." A half-smile twisted her lovely face. "Where do you want to go? Left? Right? Forward?"

"Forward." He answered without hesitation.

For too long, he'd been driving in circles.

In many senses.

She nodded and moved forward after letting another car go first.

He needed to get something off his chest, too. Something he'd carried for too long. He knew she'd understand. He told her how he'd found his father with another woman the day before prom night, all the angry words Maverick had shouted at him.

"I'm so sorry that happened to you," she said as she seemed to slow down. "Have you… ever forgiven him?"

"I did. At his funeral. Too late to apologize, huh?" A lump formed in his throat.

"I believe he knew it. And he still loved you."

For a few moments, only the growl of the motor sounded in the car. But he already felt lighter somehow.

"How about we stop for a bit?" She waved at the country road ahead. "Izzy shouldn't be in the car for long, and a breath of fresh air wouldn't hurt either one of us. Then we can return to town and maybe stop for an ice cream."

A breath of fresh air.

That was what she was for him. What she'd always been. He just hadn't realized it. Or rather had forced himself to forget it while he'd traded the fresh air for gasoline fumes.

"Okay," he said, though he had a small stab of reluctance at letting her hand go.

She turned to the country road.

For the time, it was good to drive without having a destination in mind and end up somewhere beautiful with the people he cared about.

"It's better to be a turtle going in the right direction than a hare going in the wrong one," his father used to say.

The thought of his father brought Maverick a taste of bitterness, and he shook his head as if he could erase unpleasant memories. Like the rest of the family, he used to look up to his father so much. Had put him on a pedestal once upon a time,

really. When that pedestal had crashed, it had buried Maverick's love underneath it.

Jenna's love, too. In one of the phone conversations with his sister, he'd found out she'd left for Europe to run away from disappointment. Also, to make sure she wouldn't blurt out the secret to the rest of the family, so she wouldn't hurt them.

And then something had happened to Jenna.

Vera brought the car to a stop. "I think this is a good spot."

"I'll get Izzy." He clicked his seat belt open and limped around the car as soon as he could, eager to open the door for her.

Not fast enough.

By then, Vera had already slipped out of the car and opened the door to Izzy. Another result of his injury. Disappointment stung.

He reminded himself he was blessed he could walk at all as he unbuckled the belt on Izzy's convertible car seat and retrieved sleepy Izzy. As tenderness filled him again, he stilled, afraid she'd start fussing at being woken up. But she just opened her blue eyes and yawned.

And just like that, he was a goner.

Vera stood near him as he took in the vast fields with occasional oaks and the bright blue sky without a single cloud, the weather unusually warm and sunny for November in Missouri.

"Look at this beauty," he whispered to the child as he lifted her. "When we're back, I'm going to show you the ranch that one day might be yours."

Vera laid a hand on his forearm, sending delicious waves through him. "You love her already, don't you?" She was always perceptive.

"I do. I mean, how can you not fall in love with this precious baby?" He kissed the baby's soft cheek, soliciting more giggles, and stole a glance at a different beauty by his side.

The breeze played with Vera's long blonde hair, and some of the familiar shine appeared in those eyes the color of the Missouri

sky today. Longing for things that couldn't be constricted his lungs.

To hide it, he lifted Izzy. "Look how amazing this land is."

In response, Izzy giggled again, her incredibly long eyelashes casting shadows on pink cheeks. The image of her wide-open, trusting baby-blues and tiny rosebud mouth reached something so deep inside him he didn't even know it existed.

He'd never truly understood the concept of the call of the land, the conception of legacy the rest of his family—except for his older sister—was so crazy about. But as he breathed in the fresh air filled with the scent of grass and wildflowers and looked at the endless fields, something deep inside him started changing.

Maybe because he was holding a child who'd clutched his heart the way she'd clutched his sweater in her tiny fist now. A child who needed him, Maverick, as broken as he was. Or maybe because there was a woman by his side he could trust with his life, one who made him get up in the morning and was becoming the reason he wanted to wake up.

Different images appeared in front of his eyes. He wanted to see Izzy grow up.

To hear her say her first word.

To see her making her first friends.

To wipe her tears and hug her and do his best to make things better when she suffered.

He could see her being a cheerleader or maybe presenting her project at a science fair or lip-synching to her favorite boy bands. Maybe even giving her away at her wedding—that was going to be difficult. Babysitting her children.

He wanted the most wonderful things for her.

Most importantly, he wanted her to be loved.

That was the amazing thing about Izzy. She'd never cared how many races he'd won. She just wanted food, warmth, and love.

Was he going in the right direction now? He wanted to become a part of something bigger than he was, to pass it to future generations like the precious child he'd been holding.

All his life, he'd been so occupied with being the first, with being the winner. But while winning world races, had he lost something more precious in the process?

Like the chance to reconcile with his father.

Or the love of the woman who might be able to heal his heart and break it at the same time.

CHAPTER NINE

TWO DAYS LATER, Maverick's heart expanded as he leaned down and held up two tiny hands in his large ones. He shifted forward, afraid to breathe.

He'd been feeding Izzy every day now and playing with her and even changed diapers twice—with a mask on. He'd attempted a lullaby but switched to one on the phone when the baby started crying. He'd even loved watching her sleep and, for the first time since the accident, felt a trace of peace.

But this... this was new for both of them.

Vera smiled encouragingly as she leaned forward, holding one of Izzy's favorite toys, a teddy bear. "You're doing great, Izzy. Come here. Come closer." She waved her hands in the universal sign to approach her.

Izzy made several steps forward with his support while his heart stuttered.

"Now, let her go," Vera mouthed to him.

He stilled as his lungs constricted.

What if the child fell?

What if she were not ready?

What if she hurt herself?

Only now he understood what his parents had gone through with not one but five children. How difficult it must've been to let them take those first steps on their own and then many steps afterward. What must they have experienced when he'd left his home state for a rather dangerous career?

He'd considered himself a good son. After all, he'd funneled a lot of funds into the ranch. But had he given them his *time*? Had he supported his mother and siblings in their grief?

No, he hadn't. He'd poured himself into his career to numb the pain. He'd chosen a path far from home, and he'd had his reasons to do so. But maybe it was time to reevaluate what truly mattered in life.

Did God give him another chance when He'd spared his life in that accident?

To correct the things Maverick could still correct. But then some things were impossible to correct. Like telling his father he'd forgiven him, mostly. Taking back all the hurtful words Maverick had said when he'd found out his father had been cheating on his mother.

Was it too late to let go of all his well-hoarded bitterness, the stuff corroding him much worse than rust could corrode a car?

"Let go," Vera whispered to him again.

Could he?

He could work on letting the bitterness go. But he didn't want to let Vera go again.

Not this time.

But it wasn't about what he wanted. It was about what was best for Vera. And for this little girl. So, his heart palpitating worse than in a race, he released tiny hands.

Please don't fall.

Please don't fall.

Please don't fall.

Izzy stood motionless for some time while Vera cajoled her closer with the same encouraging sweet smile.

Then the child made a wobbly step.

His heart seemed to want to leap out of his chest.

He'd never expected that a little girl making her first step would have this effect on him. He'd won world championships, but he'd never felt this level of exhilaration.

That step, that giggle from the small child suddenly meant more than all the trophies he'd once been so proud of.

Vera put the toy on the floor and clapped. "Yay! You're doing wonderfully well. How about another step?"

Izzy made another wobbly step, then landed on her bottom.

Oh no!

His heart sank.

Did she hurt herself?

Was she going to cry?

Air whooshed out of his lungs when she didn't.

Vera rushed to Izzy, pulled her up, and hugged her, then gave her the toy. "You did awesome!" Then she looked up at him. "Didn't she?"

Her excitement was contagious.

Before he knew what he was doing, he picked up Izzy and then hugged two of his favorite girls in the world. "Oh yes. Absolutely." Then he whispered to Vera. "You did great, too."

She'd make a great mom, and it was a shame she still didn't have a child of her own. His lips were so close to her that a few inches, just like two days ago, and he could kiss her cheek, claim her lips with his.

Her eyes widened, awareness swimming in them, as if she had the same thoughts.

Did she…

Did she want him to kiss her?

Blood surged faster in his veins.

Only by gathering all his willpower did he manage to pull away. He placed the child on the carpet.

Vera's eyes dimmed with what could be disappointment, but then she shifted away, too, and returned her attention to Izzy. "How about we do this again?"

Izzy thought about it for a moment, then made a step.

"Wow! When did she start walking?" Rance's voice boomed in the doorway.

Maverick tensed at the sight of the guy who used to be his best buddy. Vera's words had taken root. But he'd learned how to smile for the camera without showing his emotions a long time ago, and those skills could be used in real life, too.

The resentment wasn't only because he suspected Rance of causing his accident.

Was Rance here just to visit?

Or?

Maverick's gut twisted as he exchanged glances with Vera whose smile became as wobbly as Izzy's steps. Vera was probably thinking the same thing he was.

They didn't want to lose this precious little girl who'd claimed both of their hearts.

"Izzy started walking just a few minutes ago." Maverick shook hands with Rance.

So did Vera, but she had difficulty showing much enthusiasm. "How have you been?"

"Great. Training. Dating." Rance grinned.

"Partying." Maverick failed to keep the sarcasm out of his voice.

"Nope. None of that lately." Appreciation appeared in Rance's eyes as he took in Vera. "You look gorgeous, as always."

"Oh please." She rolled her eyes while an unwelcome stab of jealousy jabbed at Maverick. "How long are you going to stay?"

"Probably for the Harvest Festival. And when I leave, I hope I won't leave alone." Rance's eyes stayed on Vera.

Maverick's blood boiled. Did Rance insinuate he wanted Vera to go with him?

He bottled up his anger, familiar resentment poisoning him instead. He didn't have a say in the matter. Not when he was a scarred cripple. Besides, he'd been the one to break their friendship pact with Rance in the first place by kissing Vera on prom night.

The memory still filled him with exhilaration and guilt.

The next moment, Rance scooped up Izzy, clearing up the matter. "I thought about it for a long time. It's about time I step up and be a responsible parent."

"No!" Vera gasped.

Maverick felt empty inside as if his heart was ripped out of his chest.

How was it possible to get this attached, this fast, to a child that wasn't even his? Judging by the pain in Vera's eyes, she was asking the same question.

"I appreciate what you did by taking my daughter in." Rance wagged his head, his eyes hooded, then pressed his cheek to the top of Izzy's head. "But I don't think I could live with myself if I left her behind."

Eyes wide, Izzy looked from Maverick and Vera to Rance, then let out a loud wail.

Rance winced, then hugged her, his hold awkward. "Baby, don't cry. Daddy's here. Daddy'll take care of you."

The wailing increased and tore at Maverick's heart. He couldn't bear it. "Let me hold her. At least, let her stay with us and get used to you while you're in town."

Rance hesitated. "I'll pick her up tomorrow."

One day. Just. One. Day. It was something at least.

"Thank you," Vera whispered.

Maverick's heart ached. He didn't want to give up Izzy, especially to a man like Rance. His mind whirled, trying to find a way to keep her.

But surely, Rance wouldn't harm his own daughter? Maybe Rance needed Izzy more than she needed him, to change him like she'd done already with Maverick without even trying or knowing it.

As Maverick held Izzy gently, she hiccupped, then smiled up at him, droplets of tears on her eyelashes.

Something changed inside him forever.

He'd thought he'd learned to let go when he'd left home. But as he held the sweet child in his arms and saw the longing on Vera's beautiful face mirror his own longing, he realized he never had.

And he never would.

Chapter Ten

THE NEXT WEEKEND, Maverick did his best to keep a smile in place as he manned the slide booth at the Harvest Festival. It was pretty simple: accept payment, give out tickets, make sure the children didn't get hurt while hurtling down a rubber slide if their parents were looking elsewhere.

The festival was in full swing with many booths offering a variety of food and refreshments and more offering different souvenirs, from handmade jewelry to cowboy buckles and straw hats. There was a Wild West reenactment, a live band, dance performances, livestock shows, and so much more that made the place humming.

While the slide was relatively popular, it wasn't nearly as much in demand as Mrs. Tsareva's *pierogi* and *pirozhki* booth, or whatever those things were called. So he'd suggested Vera go help her grandmother.

A bad idea.

Apparently, a lot of male customers developed a taste for Russian desserts. It wasn't that Vera was flirting, and Maverick understood she needed to be friendly with the customers and smile

at them. But a knife turned inside him every time she paid attention to someone else.

Ridiculous, of course.

Maybe he'd just been raw since Rance had picked up Izzy, and Maverick already missed that child with his entire being. Yummy aromas of corn on the cob and baked turkey legs reached him, but he didn't feel hungry.

"You really like her, don't you?" His younger brother's familiar voice made him wince.

Kade was with his wife and his adorable son. The nephew whom Maverick hadn't gotten to know at all. He needed to correct that, as well as do better with Kade's future child.

While he was thrilled for his brother and couldn't wait to get to know his nephew, it only underscored his pain from losing Izzy.

"What do you mean?" Maverick feigned nonchalance as he gave a quick hug first to his brother, then his wife, and then the son.

Kade shook his head as he paid for a ticket for his boy. "You've always had a thing for Vera. Even when we were in high school. Why don't you finally ask her out?"

Surely, Kade had never had an issue asking a beautiful girl out, and a large part of the town's female population could confirm it. The fact that his brother could commit to one woman still puzzled Maverick, as well as filled him with gratitude.

"I don't know what you're talking about." Maverick handed him the ticket, though pretending was useless with Kade.

"What's the deal with you? Are you like me and can't see the treasure right in front of you?" Kade sent a loving glance toward his wife who had that surprising pregnancy glow and a baby bump showing now.

Maverick suppressed a bite of envy. After a disastrous first marriage, Kade more than deserved his marital bliss. Maverick loved his siblings. He really did. But as Kade hugged his wife and

lifted his grinning son to go on the slide steps, Maverick had a burning desire to know the same joy with Vera.

"I'm well aware of how amazing Vera is. But seriously, look at me." Grinding his teeth, he swept a hand from his deformed face to his crippled leg.

His sister-in-law touched his arm. "Don't let your self-image define you and keep you away from the people you love. Believe me, I know what I'm talking about."

Kade nodded his support. "Listen to my wife. And make your move already. Don't wait for Vera to propose to you like my wife had to. Though I'm so grateful she did." He placed a kiss on her cheek, and she giggled like a schoolgirl. "Some man might make his move first."

As if to confirm his words, Rance walked to Mrs. Tsareva's stand with his usual swagger.

What in the world?

That set Maverick's teeth on edge. Rance had claimed to want to spend more time with his daughter, but Izzy was nowhere in sight. And as he chatted up Vera, Maverick could understand why.

"If you clench your teeth any firmer, you might break a few." Kade nudged him with an elbow.

"Daddy, Mommy, look at me!" Maverick's nephew yelled from the top of the slide before whizzing it down.

Kade clapped, then helped his son to his feet. "That looked fun!"

Maverick shifted away from the happy family, his focus narrowing on Vera. She shook her head at something Rance said, but her grandmother shooed her away.

Vera looked his way, then hurried to him. "They're having live music, a band and all." She bit her bottom lip. "Would you like to go see it?"

With all his being, he wanted to say yes. But he could barely walk without a cane. He couldn't dance, and she loved to dance. It wouldn't be fair to limit her.

He schooled his features to look indifferent. "No thanks." As much as it pained him to say those words, he had to. "But you can go with Rance. I'm sure he asked you."

It wasn't just about the dance. Rance had been attracted to Vera since they'd been teens. If they hit it off, she could become Izzy's mother, something Maverick guessed she'd craved.

Even if it made a razor shred his insides, Maverick couldn't stand in the way of her happiness—or Izzy's.

"Are you sure?" her eyebrows pinched together the way they used to when her parents hurt her, but then they smoothed out, the expression so fleeting he wasn't positive he saw it.

But…

What if Rance was behind his accident?

No. More likely Maverick'd let his jealousy cloud his judgment. "I can take care of things here. Go. Enjoy yourself."

"O–okay." Her shoulders drooping, she walked away.

His disapproving brother shook his head while Maverick's own heart tumbled onto the ground.

Vera's heart ached while her feet moved according to the music. Maverick's rejection hurt more than it should have. Maybe because, against her better judgment, she'd let herself hope they could have something between them. She'd made the same mistake at eighteen when she'd kissed him at the prom.

But she couldn't be mistaken about the attraction and longing in his eyes, could she?

She thought she knew him well.

It turned out she didn't know him at all.

"Earth to Vera." Rance's teasing voice pulled her out of her sad thoughts.

She stumbled. "Did I step on your feet?"

He grinned at her. "A couple of times."

"Sorry." How had she let herself zone out like this? Some PI she was!

She did her best to pay attention to her surroundings and avoid stomping on Rance's feet. Rance used to be her friend, but he was also one of her suspects—and she'd let suspects close to her go unnoticed too long before.

So the main reason she'd agreed to this dance was to conduct an interview. She'd done her research online and over the phone, but she needed to ask him some questions and gauge his reaction. After all, nonverbal cues often meant much more than verbal ones.

"It's okay. I have reliable boots. It's good to see you again, you know. Without all the drama." His expression turned serious as he whirled her around.

Something in his eyes she didn't recognize, wasn't used to, prompted her to clear the air. "About that kiss at prom… I never meant to hurt you. You never told me…"

Okay, maybe she'd guessed he'd liked her in high school. But despite his good looks and the swagger that had made him irresistible to many girls at the time, she'd never been attracted to him. No wonder, as she'd been pining for Maverick.

Avoiding the topic altogether had been easier then. But she was a grown-up now.

He shook his head, then dipped her. When he brought her back up, he said, "It's in the past. Besides, I think I'm in love."

"Really?" She let out a whoosh of relief.

"Really."

The expression in Rance's eyes was sincere. "She might be the one."

For the first time since the dance began, Vera let herself relax. "Then I'm happy for you."

The music stopped, but he didn't release her. "Care for another dance?"

She nodded, feeling like a hypocrite because she mainly agreed since she hadn't started that interview yet. "Is she okay with you being an instant dad?"

"She supported me fully. It was her idea when I told her what happened. I didn't want to tell Maverick, but she's here with me. She's helping me take care of Izzy right now." A wistful seriousness unusual for him darkened his eyes. "I want to change. To become a better person. For her. And for my daughter."

Vera studied him, discovering a man she didn't know before. Had she misjudged him?

No. She wouldn't be sidetracked from a suspect just because she liked him personally. She did her best to slip into professional mode. She needed to verify his alibi for the time of Maverick's accident.

While she'd searched the internet and especially social media about Maverick's conquests, seeking a past flame capable of revenge, she'd done her best not to cringe from jealousy. She'd managed to talk to a few of them. One of them, some leggy blonde named Carmen, had confessed she'd dated someone famous from the racing circuit. When Vera had pressured for more, it turned out it wasn't Maverick, and she had a hunch.

"Did you happen to be with Carmen that day?" She looked him straight in the eye as she named the day.

He grimaced. "How did you know?"

"Professional secret. Why did you tell me you spent it alone?"

Hmm. He couldn't be in two different states at the same time. She'd checked airline tickets for his name, and unless he used a fake ID, he wasn't on any flights to Springfield.

"We tried to keep it under wraps because she had a boyfriend at the time. Besides, I was a bit hurt you'd suspect me in my best friend's accident." That hurt lingered in his eyes indeed.

"Sorry. Comes with the territory." After a pang of guilt, she figured she'd best change the subject and talk about something Rance loved. "How is it going in your career? Ready to win the championship?"

"You're going to be shocked. I'm thinking about retiring to raise the baby. After I've seen what happened to Maverick…" After lifting his hand from the small of her back, he scrubbed his chin, looking somewhere much further away than she was. Into his future? "I mean, what do all those trophies mean then?"

Her jaw dropped, and she stopped. Then, as another couple bumped into them, she started moving again. "You can't be serious."

"I am. I've been thinking a lot about all this. I want to spend more time with the woman I love. I want to see Izzy grow up."

"Wow." She did her best to follow his lead as she recovered. "You were right. I'm… beyond surprised." There went the motive. "Shouldn't you be with them instead of dancing with me?"

"I needed to talk to you. And she understands we're just friends now." A familiar mischievous grin crinkled his eyes. "If things are going to work out between me and her, do you think it's going to be awkward if I ask Maverick to be the best man at my wedding?"

She lifted her chin, then glanced around. She'd been tired of constantly watching her back. Like the women in her family, she still wanted to make a difference, to live an exciting life. But a boring nine-to-five job appealed more and more now. "Well, if he refuses, I'll be your best man."

It looked like she got it all wrong, and she'd have to return to square one in the investigation. Or was she allowing her feelings to affect her judgment again? Could Rance be playing her? She really needed to change her profession.

His grin widened as he whirled her again. "Thank you. I didn't expect anything less from you. I tell you what. When you and Maverick get married, I'd be honored to be your best man."

She chuckled without mirth. "I don't think there's much chance of me and Maverick getting married."

"I saw the way he looks at you. I saw the way you look at him. It puzzles me why you're not together yet."

"I asked him to dance today, but he refused," she blurted out, her heart twisting.

"Hmm. So he cares about you that much."

Huh? "What's that supposed to mean?"

Hold on.

Something Rance had told her didn't sit well. He wasn't the one who'd initiated bringing back the baby. His new love had.

What if…

No.

It couldn't be.

But then, the words on the note left with Izzy rubbed her the wrong way now. According to the pediatrician, Izzy was a normal, healthy baby. What if she wasn't a preemie?

Vera pulled her shoulders back. She knew what she was going to do. No matter how crazy the idea sounded, she needed to check it. It wouldn't be difficult to purchase a DNA kit. She could get a hair with a follicle from a brush.

Of course, she also needed to swipe Izzy's cheek…. "Could you please stop by Grandma's place with Izzy before you leave? I–I need a chance to say goodbye." Her throat clogged up. She really did, even though she did have ulterior motives. How was she going to give up that sweet girl? "Maverick might want the same, too."

She stopped again, but so did the music.

Before Rance had a chance to reply, she spotted Kade racing to her. He was without his wife and son, his face contorted. "Did you see Maverick?"

Alarm shot through her as they stepped aside when the new dance started. "N–no."

Kade glanced Rance's way, and Rance seemed to understand they needed privacy. "I'll let you two talk. Vera, if you don't mind, I think I'll return to Izzy. Thank you for the dance, and don't be a stranger."

"Likewise." She waved Rance farewell, and her stomach clenched as she and Kade moved away from the crowd. "What happened?"

"My brother refused another offer to sell the ranch. He just received a text that he might regret it if one of his brothers dies."

Oh no!

She flinched but did her best to act professionally. "Did he go to the police?"

"Yes. They are investigating, but the text seems to be from a disposable phone."

She expected that much. "Did you warn Maverick?"

"I tried, but we can't find him. He's not answering his phone. He's not in the mansion. He already closed out the slide stand. We've been searching everywhere at the festival, but… he's not here."

Shivers traveled down her spine. "Maybe he took a drive somewhere."

He used to do that to clear his mind. But not any longer.

Kade's words echoed her thoughts. "He hasn't driven once after his accident."

Her heart racing, she rubbed her temples. "I take it you had a prayer chain started?"

"Of course."

"Notified everyone you knew?"

He nodded again.

"Okay. Okay." She took a deep breath to calm her rapid pulse. "I'm going to check a few places we used to frequent when we

were teens. Maybe he took a taxi or someone gave him a lift. I'll keep in touch."

"Thank you." Kade's face relaxed somewhat, though the apprehension stayed. "I'll keep you posted, too."

She sprinted to her motorcycle and drove to the pond, a fist tightening around her rib cage, making it difficult to breathe.

Lord, I'm sorry I usually remember about You when I'm in dire need. But please, please, please keep Maverick safe in Your care. Please? Amen.

CHAPTER ELEVEN

VERA SAID the prayer over and over in her mind.

What was she thinking going off to dance with Rance? She shouldn't have let Maverick out of her sight. She failed to help a person dear to her.

Again.

Maybe she wasn't cut out to be a cop or a PI.

She gritted her teeth as she made the familiar turn and glided toward the pond's mirror surface. It wasn't about her right now. Or about her failures and mistakes.

It was about Maverick.

Her heart sank when she found the pond to be deserted.

She didn't linger.

The next stop was the ice cream parlor they both had loved to visit. Okay, maybe she'd loved to visit it, and he'd humored her. She brought the motorcycle to a stop near the parlor and rushed inside. The last customers were leaving, and the parlor was closing.

Disappointment sliced her, and her heart dropped onto the asphalt.

It took her a moment to recollect herself. Then she dashed outside.

Soon the motor growled, and she was on the road again. With more visitors for the festival, the traffic was higher than usual in town, and she weaved between cars. The loud growl of the motor, the flapping of her shirt in the wind, the wild feeling brought back memories of motorcycle trips with Maverick.

Only now, she was alone.

Desperate to find him.

She drove by their favorite restaurant, but the windows were dark already. Every time she stopped, she called him on the phone, but he didn't pick up.

Lord, please?

Then she snapped her fingers.

How could she forget?

The motor revved to life again as she steered toward an old oak among a cluster of trees behind the creek. They used to hide notes for each other underneath its gnarled roots.

The terrain was rough, and she was grateful she'd chosen to drive her grandmother's motorcycle instead of her car this evening. As the song of the wind joined the growl of the motor, her heart pounded. But unlike her previous motorcycle travels, there was no sense of freedom, only a sense of urgency.

Please be there!

She rather sensed than saw a lonely figure against the backdrop of a sprawling oak. She nearly cried as she jumped from the motorcycle the moment she brought it to a stop and released the kickstand.

She dashed to him and threw her arms around him. "You're okay. You're okay. You're okay."

Fine, maybe a tear did slide down her cheek. But he probably didn't notice it as she tucked her face in his black sweater and

breathed in the familiar and so comforting scent of his spicy cologne.

He seemed to hesitate, then wrapped his arms around her. "Um, why wouldn't I be okay?"

As much as she wanted to stay in his embrace—craved it even—she made herself look up at him and then told him what his brother had relayed.

Her senses remained on high alert as she watched her surroundings, but she'd feel better once they were inside a house.

He visibly tensed. "You think they meant business?"

"I don't know. The text might be an empty threat, but I don't want to risk it. I–I have a gut feeling something might happen." Just like before. Her heart squeezed painfully. "We need to get out of here."

She made several steps and caught a glimpse of something in a cluster of trees nearby.

Oh no!

She whirled around and tackled him to the ground, then rolled as shots thundered in the air.

Everything happened so quickly Maverick barely had time to react.

One moment, he was standing. The next moment, he was on the ground and rolling with Vera, her body against his as the scent of damp earth filled his nostrils.

Once they were behind the oak and out of the shots' path, Vera scrambled away from him and fired several shots. Then she groaned.

Tremors went through him. "Were you wounded?"

"No. Are you…" Her voice trembled. "Are you okay?"

"Yes." He pulled up on his elbows, retrieved his gun from his holster, and fired in the direction of where the shots came from.

A few shots fired back, then silence.

He heard her calling the police.

"I sent texts to your family, too," she whispered a few moments later.

Still shaken but doing his best not to show it, he nodded. "Thanks. Probably soon half the town will be here."

"I think you're wrong."

Despite the dire circumstances, he chuckled. "You don't know my family or the speed with which the grapevine works in our town."

"I do. That's why I think soon the entire town will be here."

They stilled as he listened intently. Did the shooter try to get nearer?

Then it hit him how close he'd come to losing her, and this time, he couldn't stop shaking inside.

She'd put herself in danger by coming to warn him.

After he'd pretty much rejected her.

That was the exact moment he knew he was falling for her and there was no way back from it.

He sidled closer to her, ready to give up his life for her. He took in her hair covered in dirt and the grimy streaks on her dear face. Something inside him shifted just as the siren shrilled.

She might not be meant for him, but his heart didn't want to listen to reason.

There was no one like Vera.

There would never be.

Not for him.

Vera nursed the cup of hot tea in her hands and stared out her grandmother's kitchen window, her heart heavy.

She'd been shot at like yesterday before.

She'd lost people important to her before, too.

But giving back Izzy left her with an emptiness she didn't know how to fill. Rance had stopped by with Izzy in the morning, and Vera had managed to get a swab when she'd had a few minutes alone with the baby. Then she'd had a long cry.

She sniffled a little right now, too, as she traced her finger along the smooth surface of the round oak table.

Things with Maverick were more complicated than ever, and that was saying something. Since the early morning, he'd been in an emergency meeting with his family that seemed to last for hours. He was supposed to call her when the meeting was over, and she checked her phone for the hundredth time. No missed calls from him.

Her grip tightened on the warm cup. She took another sip of hot minty liquid. She told herself she was disappointed because she couldn't protect him while being away from him, not because she was eager to see him.

He'd invited her to the meeting. But she wasn't part of his family and didn't feel it was her place to be there. Instead, she'd spent the morning researching and calling her connections in the police force. Rance had an alibi as he was still at the fair at the time, and several people saw him. But a few of the cowhands at the ranch didn't have alibis, and from her experience, she knew people could be bought.

After giving her statement to the police and surrendering her gun to them yesterday, she'd followed up with them today, thankful she had a good rapport with them. They found shells that didn't belong to hers or Maverick's weapons and identified the gun they had belonged to.

Sadly, it didn't help much as one of the townsfolks had reported it stolen a year ago.

Grandma entered the kitchen, a faint scent of apple preserves moving with her. Today, she was wearing a jean shirt and khaki

pants that looked… interesting combined with her fluffy pale pink slippers.

Vera rose. "Would you like me to make you a cup of tea?"

"I'll get it myself, dear. Do you mind if I join you?" Grandma poured tea from a small teapot with tiny pink flowers, then added steaming water into the cup.

"Are you kidding me? I'd love you to." Vera brought the pirozhki to the table. Conversations with her grandmother often helped Vera figure things out. "Grandma, I've got to tell you something. I think I'm falling in love."

A knowing smile creased her grandmother's wrinkled face as she took a sip. "I don't think so."

Vera's brows shot up. "Excuse me?"

"I don't think you've ever fallen out of love with him in the first place."

"Oh, Grandma, what am I going to do? And it's not about my feelings." Vera scowled at her reflection in her tea. "I'm so worried about him. You know, after what happened yesterday."

Grandma helped herself to an apple-filled pirozhok she'd baked yesterday. "Some distance could help put things into perspective. And help you figure out what's going on and who is behind the assaults and why."

Vera's heart dropped a little. "Put some distance between us?"

They'd spent decades apart, and she was fine. But now she couldn't imagine a day apart. This half a day apart seemed to drag on forever.

"How do you feel about going to Russia with me?" Grandma studied her over the rim of her dainty pink-flowered cup.

Vera stilled, torn between duty and love, and not for the first time. What had happened when she'd chosen duty the previous time froze her. Her father had stopped talking to her. "I'd love to. I want to go with you."

She'd go crazy thinking something could happen to her grandmother. Or, okay, what kind of mischief she could get herself in there. And Izzy was gone. Besides, maybe it was time to learn more about her roots. Could it even help her understand why her mother was so cold toward her?

But…

What about Maverick?

Or her investigation?

Grandma studied her, her gray eyes seeming to look into Vera's very soul. "But you can't because you want to help Maverick."

"He's in danger. How can I leave him now?"

"Well, with all the technology these days, you can continue your investigation long-distance. And you can ask him to go with us. That might help put him out of harm's way, too."

"Gran, really?" Hope fluttered inside Vera's chest, and her mind started working fast. She didn't want to make her grandmother and Maverick travel under false documents, as airline tickets could be tracked down.

But…

They could use a disguise maybe? Travel to different towns? It should be a nice distraction from missing Izzy, too.

Buddy walked in and demanded food, so naturally, Vera dropped everything and fed him, then refreshed the water in his bowl. She glanced up at her grandmother. "But what about Buddy?"

"Dorotea already volunteered to take care of him while we're gone." The older woman's eyes glowed with such energy. "So what do you think? Russia is a very large country. Very. Do you think it's going to be difficult to get lost? Besides, we could do double dates." She patted Vera's knee, then winked. "That way you could spy on me without being too obvious."

Her heart swelling with careful joy, Vera leaped to her feet and hugged her grandmother in earnest. "I love you, Grandma."

"Love you, too. With all my heart."

When Vera shifted back, she blurted out, "I can't believe how different you are from my mother. Why... Why did she never love me? Was it because I failed to meet her expectations? Didn't become a doctor? Didn't hold down my first job?"

"You never failed anyone's expectations. You've worked hard, and you helped many people. We're all very proud of you."

"But not my half brother."

"He had to take responsibility for his actions. You did what you had to do." Those glowing eyes dimmed. "And it's not that your mother didn't love you. It was... just difficult for her."

"Why?"

"It's not my story to tell. At least, not yet."

Anger exploded inside her. Her father's secret had broken the bubble of her happiness once. So now, her mother had an important secret she'd never told her? "Then when?"

Grandma plopped her chin in one hand and drew circles with her finger on the tablecloth. It was unlike the spontaneous woman to be hesitant. Her blue strands fell on her face, concealing her expression. "Soon. Very soon."

Deflated, Vera leaned against the wooden chair her grandmother reupholstered herself with a pattern matching the teacups.

Her parents had been busy when she'd been a child. But her father, a traveling salesman, had always made up for it when he'd been home. He'd showered her with love and gifts, taken her to the zoo, aquariums, and ice cream parlors. He'd been the one to tell her fairy tales and call her his princess and cover her with a blanket, warm and soft like his affection.

He'd had an amazing laugh, throaty and real. And he'd supported her in everything and held her when she'd been upset.

He'd been her hero, her confidante, her friend, her supporter. He'd been her amazing father.

Then one day, it all had stopped. The trips had become much longer, and he became distant like her mother as if a cold heart could be just as contagious as a head cold.

For a long time, she'd blamed herself, tried to be the perfect daughter. Until he'd left them for another woman in Springfield, crushing Vera's heart. She'd run after his car until she could barely breathe, but he'd never stopped. He probably hadn't even looked in the rearview mirror.

Shockingly, her mother hadn't been devastated, not even surprised, really, and less than a year later moved to Springfield, too, to marry a doctor. They'd started a family right away. Then Vera discovered what she'd yearned for all her childhood.

A doting mother.

Only Vera hadn't been the one her mother had been doting on. The new baby had become her mother's world, and she'd even taken maternity leave.

Vera felt covered in layers of suffocating, heavy blankets, only none of them were warm or comforting.

Guilt.

Anger.

Despair.

Disappointment.

That was when Vera had started acting out and broke the window on her father's wife's car with a baseball bat. Needless to say, the woman wasn't pleased, and weekends at her father's new place had become even rarer. Her mother's new husband wasn't too thrilled with a sulky, rebellious teen who wasn't even his, either. She'd felt the only reason she'd been tolerated was because she was a free babysitter. And while she'd loved her new half sister, Vera had yearned to be loved by her mother, to have even crumbs of the attention her mother had given the new daughter.

Was it too much to ask?

Vera had started hanging out with the wrong crowd and sinking deeper and deeper until her grandmother arrived and took her back to her hometown. Her mother had protested at first, probably because she was losing that free babysitter, but Grandma insisted.

A suspicion formed in Vera's mind as she put the cup in the sink. Something she'd felt in her gut more than once before but had been reluctant to believe.

She took a sip of the drink that was getting cold and decided to look forward to the trip. Excitement surged through her as she remembered all the fun she'd had with her grandmother the previous time they'd ventured to the mysterious land of her ancestors.

Now, how would she talk Maverick into it? She tightened her grip on the cool porcelain cup.

Would he reject her offer like he'd rejected her yesterday?

Like her mother had rejected her when Vera had tried to snuggle up to her as a child?

Her fingers tightened around the cup's handle.

When she'd been growing up, neighborhood children told her all the time how wonderful her mother was. She was the best-dressed girl around, every outfit in the latest fashion. Everyone had loved to invite Vera for sleepovers and birthday parties because she'd brought the latest and most popular toys.

Everyone had wanted to be invited to Vera's birthday parties because there would be lots of great food, entertainment, and expensive party favors. Most of the time, her mother had those parties at expensive restaurants and paid for unlimited tokens for all the kids, besides scrumptious pizzas. Later, she'd paid for short trips to Disneyland for *all* the children several years in a row.

She was an exemplary mother. So what if there was no warmth in her hugs or her eyes when she looked at Vera?

At eight, Vera had donated all the toys and electronics and most of the clothes and shoes her mother had given her to the poor families in town. It had become known, and people praised her kindness. But Vera's ears had been burning up in shame for the real reason. She'd kept the toys her grandmother had given her, including the teddy bear she'd made for her, and the clothes she'd sewn for her.

The next day, her mother had replaced all the clothes, and Vera realized she had to be an ideal daughter, too. So she'd dressed like one and told everyone she was going to be a doctor just like her mother. One day, she'd be saving lives, too. People loved it.

Crying herself to sleep alone at night was going to stay her secret. She couldn't tell her mother. After all, like her mother had said, women in their family had to be strong.

"You're going to break that cup," Grandma said quietly.

Vera released her grip.

Then Vera thought again about the part about the baby being a preemie in the note left with Izzy, and it needled at her. There was a reason why people said it when it wasn't the truth.

Despite drinking hot tea, her insides went cold.

She leaned forward. "Grandma, I wasn't born premature, was I?"

Her grandmother winced. Then she got up, gave her a hug, and left, for the first time leaving Vera without an answer.

And that was an answer in itself.

Going over the list of suspects in her head the next day, Vera walked down to the cellar to get a few jars of her grandmother's canning. For a person dedicated to his career, Maverick still managed to leave many broken hearts behind.

Or maybe she was looking at this wrong?

She'd looked into the ranch employees' financial records—with reluctant help from Kade's wife—and found one of the cowhands/mechanics, Claudia Allende, had received a significant amount twice from a company neither one of them could track down. The first time was when the tractors had started breaking down more often. The second time was two days before Maverick's accident.

Upon further research, it turned Ms. Allende had an aunt in Springfield. She'd taken two days off, claiming the aunt had been sick and she needed to visit her relative. The curious part was that said aunt had been on a cruise at the time.

But wouldn't this be too simple and too obvious?

Something niggled at Vera as she stepped into the cool room and pressed the light switch. What had she missed? Maybe if she let it go, for the time being, it would appear in her mind unexpectedly.

Either way, she'd started watching Ms. Allende closely and made a mental note to talk to her. And maybe it wouldn't hurt to get recordings from the airport cameras.

The visitors' section.

It could be that someone knew Maverick was going to get flowers. Or they might've known about his flights and followed him.

As Vera studied jars with raspberry jams bright as rubies, her thoughts switched to Maverick, and just like that, her pulse picked up speed. She'd vowed to keep her feelings for him at bay, but that was a hard vow to fulfill, considering they had to spend so much time together.

Somehow, it was even more difficult when he wasn't the golden boy of their hometown any longer, destined for world fame. He needed her, and she…

She desperately needed to be needed.

After some deliberation, she settled on two jars of peaches, the color vivid as amber, and turned to go back to the kitchen.

Uh-oh.

What was that?

Some noise upstairs?

She tensed.

With her grandmother gone on one of her dates, this time several hours away, there shouldn't be anyone in the house. Grandma said she'd return in the evening, and it was only midday.

Vera drew a deep breath of slightly damp air.

Buddy meowed somewhere, then something fell.

Okay, he'd knocked down a plant from the windowsill again.

She nearly laughed. She was getting paranoid. Or simply following her training to be always alert and suspicious.

She stilled and listened intently again, to be on the safe side. Everything was quiet, and the tight knot in her stomach relaxed somewhat.

Then, the basement lights went out, and a gasp escaped her lips.

Okay.

Okay.

No need to scream.

Maybe something went wrong with the breaker. After all, the house was older than her grandmother, and that was saying something. Vera had replaced many appliances a few times.

Her heart beating fast, she held onto the jars and made a few careful steps. Then she clutched them to her chest with her left hand while feeling the cold wall with her right hand.

Nothing happened yet.

But the urgency to leave the basement was throbbing in her temples. Not that she was claustrophobic. But the underground cement basement had no windows, and she had a gut feeling she needed to get out as soon as possible.

She walked several steps, wishing she'd taken her cell phone with her. She'd have a flashlight then and a way to contact someone in case…

Premonition squeezed her heart, and she hastened her pace.

A strange click made her wince.

CHAPTER TWELVE

THE JARS slipped from her clasp and shattered on the cement steps.

She knew what the click meant. Someone locked the door. The previous owners used to lock their children in the basement as punishment. Both Vera and her grandmother were going to remove the lock. But somehow, they didn't get to it.

Her pulse thundered in her ears.

No, this was ridiculous.

Why would anyone lock her in the basement?

Breathe.

Breathe.

Breathe.

Even without seeing anything, she made it to the door fast and turned the handle.

Locked.

Her heart dropped to the cement steps to join broken jars. She hit on the door. "Someone! Anyone!"

Now she couldn't be mistaken about the footfalls disappearing in the distance. She drew several shaky breaths to calm her frayed nerves.

Fine, she'd have to spend the day in the basement. She'd been in much worse situations. Even if she got a visit from a mouse, it wasn't that bad. If she got hungry, she could eat some of the jam. As long as she didn't slip on the steps and cut herself on the broken glass, it wasn't that bad.

It was just until her grandmother was back. Or maybe Maverick would come looking for her.

She nearly snorted.

Right.

That was wishful thinking. Despite the interest in his eyes, he'd made it clear he only wanted a professional relationship with her, and that disappointment still hurt. Otherwise, he wouldn't refuse her invitation to dance. Besides, he was so wrapped up in his despair he didn't see anything else. He'd even given her a day off today as if seeing her was a nuisance. And he didn't need her help as a babysitter any longer.

Okay, think about the present matters.

Why would anyone lock her in the basement?

If someone wanted to harm her, that meant something else was going to happen.

But what?

Her mind whirled as she leaned against the wall because her knees buckled. She wasn't on any kind of medication she needed to take regularly to survive.

That left a few other options.

She sniffed the air, and a shiver ran down her spine as a faint scent of rotten eggs reached her nostrils. Her grandmother had kept the old gas stove, despite Vera's many offers to buy her a new electric one.

The plan was simple but at the same time nearly brilliant.

A gas leak.

She shuddered as she slid down the wall, her mind searching for a way out.

"Buddy! No!" The cat was inside somewhere.

No.

No.

No.

If she didn't come up with something fast, she and Buddy were going to die from seemingly natural causes.

Lord, please help us!

Maverick frowned at his cell phone as the third call to Vera went to voice mail. He'd called her after painful physical therapy, then as he collapsed on the leather sofa in the empty living room after a shower. She'd never returned his calls. He left another message.

Obviously, she didn't want to talk to him, and his heart sank a little as a void formed inside him.

Was she still upset that he didn't dance with her?

Okay, he'd given her a day off because she deserved it and because the baby wasn't here any longer.

He hadn't expected a void to grow this fast and this big.

His tired muscles protesting, he sat up on the smooth sofa and stared at the fireplace where photos of their large—and growing—happy family filled the mantel. He was one of the two remaining siblings who was still single with no children. For some reason, that bothered him now, as if everyone had been having steak and potatoes and he was on a celery-and-carrots diet.

He cringed as he rubbed his temples.

Not a great comparison.

The pull to see Vera surprised him.

Granted, he'd thought of her often—fine, every day—while on the racing circuit. But it had never been this overwhelming. In a matter of days, he'd grown deeply attached to her, just like to that sweet baby.

Did he need to lean on her support now just like he had to lean on the cane? Like he couldn't even walk on his own? He pulled his shoulders back. That couldn't be the reason.

His heart shifted, and so did the sofa as he brought himself to an upright position. His muscles screamed in protest, but he'd already accepted pain as part of his life now.

He changed fast into a light sweater and jeans. He just needed to make sure she was okay. Besides, he had a perfect excuse. He had to know how the case was progressing, didn't he?

Then there was the matter of driving.

Embarrassed heat flushed through him. Of all the humiliating things, even the thought of driving a short distance sent him—*him*, Maverick Clark—into a shudder.

Calling a taxi… No.

He called Kade, and credit it to Kade, he dropped his ranch work and arrived minutes later with no questions asked. Then he let Maverick out near Mrs. Tsareva's house. Vera's car was in the driveway, so she must be home.

"Call me later when you need a ride back. I hope all goes well. I'll pray for you." Kade waved at him when he drove off.

Maverick's pulse picked up speed as he rang the doorbell.

No answer.

His heart sank to the welcome doormat. She was obviously home, and he doubted she'd be asleep at this time. Was she *ignoring* him?

He rang the doorbell a second, then a third time.

Still no answer.

His gut twisted as he tried the locked door handle. Should he call the police? Right. He snorted. They'd laugh at him. Still, his gut twisted tighter as he limped around the house and looked into the windows.

If the neighbors saw him, *they'd* call the police.

Thankfully, the curtains were open, which allowed him to look inside the rooms. Hmm, neither Vera nor her grandmother were in any of them. Of course, they could've gone somewhere together, right? Mrs. Tsareva's truck wasn't here, but when he'd called her, she'd said her granddaughter was at home.

He should let her be.

But concern rooted him to one place. He tried to call Vera again and winced when her favorite pop song, her ringtone, played inside the house. A shiver traveled down his spine. Something wasn't right.

Sure, there was a chance she'd forgotten her phone. Still, it didn't fit with what he knew about her. He tried the patio door close to the kitchen. Locked, too. He clenched his teeth.

"Meow!"

The sound made him look to the side.

Buddy strolled to him.

Maverick eyed him, remembering the scratches. "What are you doing here? Did you escape again?"

After all, Buddy was a house cat, but he did manage to escape from time to time.

Buddy sniffed the air, then sneezed, then meowed again.

"You don't like something, do you? What are you trying to tell me?" A moment later, Maverick realized what was wrong.

Mingling with the scent of grass was another faint scent. The scent of rotten eggs. When he'd been a child and they'd had a gas furnace, there'd been a tiny leak once. They'd spotted it soon, and no damage had been done.

But his mother had taught him how to distinguish the scent and what to do when he smelled it. He shuddered as he limped away from the house, punched in 9-1-1, and reported a gas leak. Using a cell phone too close to a gas leak could create an explosion.

Then he made it to the tool shed as fast as his hurting leg allowed him. Thankfully, he knew where different tools were

thanks to helping Mrs. Tsareva in the garden all those years ago. He located the wrench and hurried to the gas meter, despite the pain.

He turned off the gas and wiped the sweat forming on his forehead.

Another thought spurred him on as he located a flathead screwdriver and limped back to the window, grimacing at his crippled gait.

What if Vera or her grandmother were inside? The thought sent another shudder through him. They would've reported the gas leak, wouldn't they?

Unless...

Unless something happened to one of them—or both of them. Even if he couldn't see either of them in the rooms, they could've fainted in the bathroom or the basement, especially considering that Vera's phone was there.

No.

He was imagining things.

But even as he tried to talk himself out of it, he knew what he was going to do. He couldn't imagine anything happening to Vera or the person she loved so much. Neither could he risk waiting for help.

Grateful she'd explained to him how to take out windows when she'd inspected the mansion, he inserted the screwdriver into the channel of the metal strip around the window and pried it out as fast as he could by loosening it, then pulling out.

More cold sweat formed on his forehead while his heart pounded. He needed to hurry up. He should just break the window and pay for its replacement later.

Okay, if this didn't work, he would. He inserted the screwdriver between the glass and the pane and pried it open fast. Soon the glass was in his hands, and he laid it aside.

He climbed inside, his leg crying from pain by now.

Without turning on the light switch as that could trigger an explosion, too, he checked the bathrooms—empty. He didn't know whether to be relieved or to worry. He breathed into the sleeve of his sweater, but it wasn't much help. The rotten-egg smell was much stronger inside. So he needed to get out before he passed out.

Instead, he yelled, "Vera! Are you here?"

Pounding on the basement door answered him. He felt dizzy by now, but he lurched to the basement door. His jaw slackened as he found it locked.

Getting weaker by the moment, he opened the lock, and Vera nearly fell onto him.

Her eyes wide and face pale, she managed to get herself out of the basement and into the room. "We have to get out of here."

He hugged her to support her, but she stumbled as she moved forward.

Without thinking, purely on an adrenaline rush, he scooped her up in his arms.

"What are you doing?" Her eyes grew even bigger. "Put me down. Now!"

Yes, he knew. He could barely move himself, much less carry her.

"Don't talk, please." Somehow, he found the strength to make it to the door, adrenaline working miracles.

Once they were outside, he gasped for fresh air, letting oxygen into his starved lungs. He'd never take oxygen for granted again.

Never.

Shrill sirens resounded in the distance, and a few people clustered on the lawn already. Murmurs of "What happened?" were spreading like waves.

He didn't pay attention to the small crowd as he placed Vera on the grass and collapsed nearby.

Mrs. Dorotea rushed to them. "Are you okay?"

"I hope so." He looked at Vera's beautiful eyes, her too-pale skin, terrified she'd inhaled harmful chemicals for too long.

Buddy scurried to them and nudged Vera's hand with his pink nose, meowing.

Mrs. Dorotea scooped up the cat and stroked him. "I'll take care of Buddy."

"Thank you, Mrs. Dorotea. I... I'm fine," Vera whispered. "Thanks to you, Maverick. Praise God."

Only then did he allow himself to relax. Something snapped inside him.

The world disappeared.

CHAPTER THIRTEEN

VERA WAS still shaking as the nurse in purple scrubs wheeled her out of the hospital emergency room where the ambulance had taken her and Maverick.

She'd refused to stay overnight for observation because she needed to make sure Maverick was all right. His fainting had shattered her.

Besides, they'd already given her plenty of oxygen, and her oxygen level wasn't bad at all, all things considering. She'd also refused to call her grandmother or her parents. She didn't want to worry her grandma, and her parents wouldn't care much, anyway. They had busy lives and other children to worry about far away from her hometown. They'd been concerned about their careers or new spouses way more than they'd been concerned about her.

So much unlike Maverick's family.

Longing unraveled her remaining strength as the nurse wheeled her to the *waiting* room where nobody was *waiting* for her.

What an irony.

On the contrary, Maverick's large family filled the entire space, surrounding him in a loving cocoon. A weak smile appeared

117

on his handsome face as everyone took turns hugging him and he kept reassuring them he was fine.

Longing intensified.

Just like in childhood, she didn't belong with his family.

She was an outsider, looking in.

Even in her own family.

Except with her grandmother, of course.

Vera pulled her spine to its full capacity and got up from the wheelchair, ready to retreat. She needed to get home before her grandmother so she wouldn't worry. Caring neighbors would no doubt enlighten Grandma soon enough about what had happened. Besides, his family might resent her for putting their beloved Maverick in danger, even if she didn't do it on purpose.

After all, her own family resented her for much smaller things.

Okay, no pity party.

She should remember the things she was grateful for. Maverick seemed to be okay, Buddy was okay, and she was okay, too.

Thank You, Lord.

"Vera! Praise God, you're okay!" Kade's voice stopped her departure.

Uh-oh. Too late to escape now.

He ran to her and hugged her. Soon the entire family enveloped her, including Maverick.

He embraced her and for a few amazing moments didn't let go. "I worried so much about you. Don't ever scare me like that again."

"True."

"He was asking about you."

"Sounded so worried."

"We didn't know how to hold him back."

As the chorus of voices resounded around her, something warmed her, but she forced herself to ease out of his embrace. "I'm sorry all this happened."

"It wasn't your fault." He placed his hands on her shoulders as if still reluctant to let her go. "It was probably mine. The only reason I can think of why someone locked you in the basement and turned the gas on was because someone doesn't like that you're investigating for me."

She shuddered inside but did her best not to show it. "Well, it's part of the job. I should've been more careful."

But that meant she might be putting her grandmother in danger. No!

"We'll wait for you outside." His family filed out of the room one by one as if to give them privacy before other patients arrived.

Kade stayed a moment longer. "I'll be glad to give you both a ride when you're ready."

"Thanks, bro." Maverick's gaze never left her face. He ran his finger along her jaw, making her dizzy. Or maybe the dizziness was the aftereffects of gas poisoning.

"Do you have any idea how much I'm afraid to lose you?" His voice croaked, barely audible, and she wasn't sure she heard him right. Then he sucked in a quick breath, and his eyes widened as if he couldn't believe he'd spoken aloud.

A family with children rushed in, stealing their privacy.

"Ditto," she whispered as she slid away.

As they walked outside together, she filled her hungry lungs with fresh air instead of the scent of medicines, antiseptics, and worry. She studied the cars in the parking lot for anything suspicious, then nodded for him to proceed.

In the car, they all kept quiet, and she called Rance as she missed Izzy more with every moment. Hearing the baby's giggles on the phone soothed something raw inside her, and she passed the phone to Maverick so the same could happen to him.

Her feelings for him were growing, but so were her dilemmas. Until he could heal inside from past hurts—and so could she— until he'd stopped trying to always be the strong one, the leader,

and accepted his current weakness as a possibility for growth, there was no chance of them being together.

Ever being anything more than friends.

If that even happened.

Her heart constricted.

Meanwhile, she could be putting in danger the life of the person she loved with all her heart and who'd always been there for her.

Her grandma.

"I'd like to go to Russia with you and your grandmother," Maverick said as the two of them had tea in her grandmother's cozy kitchen. Buddy was a welcome guest, stretching on the rug, and her grandmother was on the way back from her date in Springfield. "Hopefully, right after Thanksgiving. If that's okay with you."

Vera spat out her tea and coughed profusely.

His heart sank.

Was he too forward?

Was that asking too much?

Or maybe she didn't want to spend time with him as much as he wanted to spend time with her.

"I–I didn't mean to make you choke. If you think that's a horrible idea…"

She wiped tea on the table with a napkin, then grinned up at him, her lovely face aglow. "I think it's a great idea. For hours, I've been thinking, trying to figure out how to talk you into it."

Warmth flooded him, and he wanted to hug her so badly it took all his willpower to stay in his chair. And to think *he'd* spent hours trying to figure out how to talk *her* into it. "Is your grandma going to be okay with it?"

She laughed, bright and merry, lighthearted and girlish. "Grandma *suggested* it."

His lips spread in a smile. "I knew there was a reason I love your grandmother. Besides the fact that she's so good to you."

He wondered sometimes what would've happened to Vera if her grandmother hadn't insisted on taking her in all those years ago. As his chest constricted, he didn't want to know the answer. She'd probably end up like her half brother.

Maybe he was a fool for suggesting the trip together. Being near her for several weeks and not touching her, not hugging her, not kissing her...

How was he going to survive that?

The longing left by Izzy's absence intensified. Neither he nor Vera had talked about it as if the wound was still too raw to open. It might be stupid to subject himself to being in Vera's company all the time and not allowing himself to show his feelings.

But then, at the hospital, his family had suggested he needed to vanish somewhere far way because he seemed to be the one targeted. So he'd blurted out how he'd like to go to Russia with Vera and her grandmother. The family had voted it in, as well as asked him to invite Vera and her grandmother to Thanksgiving.

A pleasant feeling spread inside him. His family was such a blessing. Something he'd once taken for granted.

"Of course, we all would love it if you joined us for Thanksgiving. You and your grandmother."

Buddy looked up and meowed.

He smiled. "Sorry, no cats allowed at the table."

Buddy meowed again, this time louder in voicing his disagreement. Maverick got up and rubbed behind the cat's ears, evoking a soft purr. "We're going to miss you."

Hmm, maybe he should get a pet. He smiled at the cat. "Thank you for helping me today." Then he winced at the memory of the

gas leak incident. His head jerking up, he faced Vera again. "But I don't want to put you and your grandmother in danger."

She tapped her fingers against the oak table. "I believe the main thing is for you to make it there unrecognized. How do you feel about wearing a disguise?"

Days later, Maverick looked at the Thanksgiving table, breathing in the scrumptious aromas of turkey, ham, and more trimmings than he could count at once. And that was before the pies were brought out.

While he'd done his best to be home for Christmas every year, Thanksgiving was a different matter. With all the rigorous training, he couldn't afford to take a break and risk someone else gaining an upper hand in a race. Having just come off the Bathurst 1000 in October, he'd kept driving with his focus on the Monte Carlo Rally in January. So he'd skipped a lot of Thanksgivings at home, especially during the beginning of his career while he was competing in the smaller races as well, back when his father was still alive.

A stab of regret made him flinch.

For some things, there could be second chances.

For others, no.

He poured apple cider into Vera's glass and wished Izzy was here, too.

As his pulse increased just from looking at Vera, being around her and being unable to touch her, kiss her, run his fingers through her luscious long hair… well, it was getting more and more difficult.

"Thank you." She smiled at him.

Just that smile could melt his heart.

Oh, what was a guy to do?

It didn't help that almost all his siblings had already arrived in Marriageville while he couldn't even locate Loveville on the map. The way their faces lit up when they as much as looked at their spouses was priceless.

He was happy for them—he really was. But what he resented was the envy twisting his gut.

He needed to talk to the one sibling who'd understand him. The one who was just as lost as he was. His kindred spirit.

"I'm going to be right back," he whispered to Vera and excused himself from the table.

He limped from the mansion's spacious dining room to his room upstairs. His childhood room where he'd never before expected to find himself on a semipermanent basis. Funny how life could make a full circle sometimes—and not in a good way.

How do we know which roads to choose, especially when we try to find the road to ourselves? How do we reverse our course when we find ourselves at a dead end?

He chastised himself as he closed the door behind himself for privacy. He could do way worse than having a loving family accept him with open arms and take care of him when he needed it the most.

Despite the vast difference in the hours, Jenna picked up on the second ring. But then, she worked at night often. Her image stood in front of his eyes, though he could barely remember when he'd last seen her without a disguise. Oh, in one of his visits to Europe for a championship. She'd come to cheer for him in sunglasses with a cap drawn low, and he'd met her afterward for dinner in his room.

He would've taken her to the most expensive restaurant in the city, but she'd insisted on privacy. Her long bangs fell on her hazel eyes, and a leather jacket seemed loose on her frame as if she'd lost weight. Her raven hair was cut short, and a healing scar discolored her neck. But he knew she'd never explain, so he didn't

ask. She'd graduated from the Sorbonne that year with majors in French and German but talked about it with indifference.

His family had secrets, and so had Jenna. The more years passed, the more difficult those would be to tell, and the more damage could be done. Over the years as their relationship got closer, he'd tried to figure out the puzzle that was his older sister. But he couldn't because too many pieces were lacking as she'd kept them to herself.

Sometimes he wondered if she'd withheld them because they were as sharp as shards of glass and she didn't want him to hurt himself, and the same went for his family. But it hurt much more to know she wasn't truly happy and he couldn't do anything about it.

"Happy Thanksgiving, sis." He kept his voice as cheerful as he could.

"Happy Thanksgiving, my favorite brother." She kept her warm voice relatively low, making him wonder if she was on a stakeout again.

"Wish I could send you all the yummy things we're having today." He patted his stomach. "I'll have to spend an extra day in the gym."

She chuckled. "I have a turkey sandwich with me in honor of the day."

He shouldn't ask in case it was still painful for her, and still, he blurted out, "Come home for Christmas."

They'd shared the same secret about their father, though they'd found out about his infidelities at different times. Now when the secret was out anyway, maybe she'd stop her wanderings and return.

He'd love that.

Maybe he should've taken her up on her offer when she'd wanted to come home to help take care of him. But he'd been so

bitter he'd refused, saying enough people were fussing over him already.

Regret stung. He had a chance to bring her back, and he'd failed.

His eyes widened when she said, her voice even lower than usual, "I just might. Especially if you get married around that time."

The image of Vera walking to him while he stood near the altar flashed in his mind. It disappeared just as quickly.

"Me? Married?" He strived for a light tone as he plunked on the bed. "Honestly, I'd do it just to bring you here, but I'm a confirmed bachelor."

He hadn't recognized her at their sister's wedding at first, but then he'd seen past her disguise. Of course, he kept her secret. If she wanted to attend family events incognito, that was her choice—no matter how much he wished she'd return as herself and reconcile with the entire family.

"Oh please." She chuckled. "We're all confirmed bachelors and bachelorettes until we meet the right person. I noticed the way you talk about Vera. I remember the way your face lit up when she stopped by the house when we were teens. Why don't you give yourself a chance with her?"

Warmth rose inside him. That was what he got for telling too much to his sister. "You know the way I am now. She deserves better."

"She can't find a better man than you are." Jenna's voice softened.

"You're just saying it because you're my sister."

"I'm saying it because I love you and because you deserve it. This Thanksgiving and always, I'm grateful for having you in my life. Oh, sorry, I've got to go." Her voice became rushed. "Love you, my darling brother."

It looked like the person she'd been tracking had arrived.

"Ditto. I mean, I'm grateful for you, too. Love you very much." Even after she disconnected, he stared at the phone, reluctant to accept that she continued being on the other side of the world.

But at least, now there was hope. His spirits up, he looked forward to returning to his large family where Vera and her grandmother fit as if they were part of it already.

Invigorated, he pushed himself up and walked to the door. As he opened it, he bumped into Vera. Good thing she jumped back, or he could've knocked her down.

"Oh. Oops." He closed the door behind himself.

A strange look settled in her eyes. Sadness? Disappointment? But why? "Kade sent me to look for you. He didn't want you to miss the pies."

His family must've thought he retired for the evening. Or was Kade matchmaking to give Maverick and Vera a few minutes alone?

What if Jenna was right and he should give himself a chance with Vera?

"Sure." He stepped to her and tucked a strand of her luscious blonde hair behind her ear, making his pulse skyrocket. Unable to resist the pull toward her any longer, he wanted to cup her face.

Disappointment knifed him when she jerked back. "We need to return to the table." Her voice, so void of emotion, stopped him more than her words.

"Right." He did his best not to show how his heart shattered as he limped toward the dining room.

Vera obviously didn't want a chance with him, and it hurt more than it should have.

CHAPTER FOURTEEN

TWO DAYS LATER, Vera could barely contain her laughter as she buckled in on the plane.

But contain it, she had.

Maverick already didn't look too comfortable in his disguise. She didn't need to add to it. At least, they'd cleared the air yesterday. When she'd overheard him on the phone saying "Love you very much," it was to his sister.

Phew!

Not that Vera should've been jealous to start with.

"Don't say a word," he muttered through his teeth as he placed their luggage into the overhead compartment, then slid to the seat near her and buckled up, too.

She didn't, but her grandmother didn't have her restraint.

She reached across Vera and patted Maverick on the arm. "If it's any help, dear, you look beautiful. Why, no wonder a guy in the airport even hit on you."

Vera couldn't help herself as a few giggles escaped.

Based on Maverick's expression, he barely held in a groan. Thankfully, even irritated, he still managed to have his voice high-pitched, playing his role well.

"Seriously?" He tugged at the curls of the auburn wig cascading down his shoulders. Then he leaned to Vera, probably to make sure nobody overhead them. "I thought the point was to stay unnoticed. How is this supposed to accomplish that?" He gestured to his leopard-print coat and matching boots.

The whiff of flowery perfume was unfamiliar, but she couldn't complain since she'd chosen it. She missed his spicy cologne, though.

She whispered into his ear. "When people recall you, red hair and leopard-print clothes are what they're going to remember." Out loud, she said, "Would you pass me the headphones, Mom?"

They were supposed to portray a family. Grandmother, mother, and daughter going on a vacation. Vera had put her hair in two braids to appear younger. While Vera wore a casual outfit of a navy-blue blazer, faded jeans, a white knit hat, and low heeled boots and her grandmother selected clothes of the same modest palette, Maverick made up for it.

It had taken Vera hours to do his makeup while it took only a few seconds for her to swipe lipstick on her own lips.

He threw her a look when she called him her mother, but he passed the headphones nonetheless.

An eccentric outfit or not, there was something comfortable about having him nearby. She could easily imagine them taking trips in the future.

As a real family.

With Izzy when she was more grown-up and could travel. Oh, how she missed that baby girl!

A lump formed in her throat, and she suppressed a sigh. Sadly, it was only a dream.

When the plane gained speed on the ground, ready to take off, her nerves stretched taut, and her fingers tightened on the handle.

"Don't tell me you're scared of flights?" Teasing notes laced his voice, but some concern knit his brow line.

She raised her chin. "It's not that I'm scared of flying. I just don't particularly enjoy the takeoff. Okay, I don't particularly enjoy when the turbulence hits, either." She turned to her grandmother. "Grandma, how about next time we travel we go somewhere where we can get by car?"

"You'll be fine, dear. And you know they say flying is safer than driving."

Maverick leaned to her again. "Would it help if I held your hand?"

Vera's pulse increased for a different reason other than being suspended in the air soon. Red wig and bright makeup or not, he still had that certain effect on her. "Yes, it would."

His hand covered hers. Then he laced his fingers through hers.

Indeed, it calmed her.

That, and the fact that she started praying.

Here I am, Lord, coming for help to You again. I'm sorry I forgot to thank You when You saved Maverick's life or when You had him rescue me from the cellar. I–I will try to do better in the future. Please, please give us a safe trip. Amen.

Soon they were in the air, and she stopped clutching Maverick's hand as if it were a lifeline.

Or was it?

Her grandmother often said everything happened for a reason. Maybe her working with Maverick and going on this trip happened for a reason, too. Maybe God was trying to tell her something.

She stole a glance at Maverick who'd seemed to do the same with her heart years ago. Was God telling Maverick something, too? And was Maverick listening?

Lord, please guide me. I know I can be stubborn sometimes, so please shake me if I don't get it. Well, not too much—and no turbulence, please! But, please, help me see the path You have for me.

In a quiet voice and leaning close, she relayed to Maverick some other details of the investigation. She'd talked to Claudia Allende, the ranch cowgirl/mechanic who'd received significant sums of money at suspicious times, as well as lied about her whereabouts at the time of Maverick's accident.

After some digging and a long talk to Ms. Allende, Vera had found out the woman was having an affair with a rich married man in Springfield which she'd wanted to keep a secret for obvious reasons. When Vera had talked to the man's neighbors, they'd confirmed it. Apparently, it wasn't as well-kept secret as Ms. Allende had thought.

"So, this didn't give any results." Vera sighed. "Checking the airport recordings at the time of your arrival didn't help, either. I'm sorry."

He brushed a strand of hair that had fallen on her face, eliciting a tiny gasp. "You're doing what you can. I'm grateful. And I'm grateful that for some time we can relax and forget about the investigation. Enjoy the trip and each other. Um, I didn't mean that…"

Warmth rose inside her. "Yeah, I know."

As she rested her head on Maverick's shoulder and drifted to sleep, she hoped with all her heart the path God had chosen for her intertwined with his.

CHAPTER FIFTEEN

JET LAG WAS MURDER.

Maverick winced from his choice of words as he fit their luggage in the taxi's trunk after they'd landed in Sheremetyevo International Airport. Despite her initial fright, Vera had slept most of the trip while he'd spent the time either watching movies or watching her sleep.

Walking in these boots was even worse than jet lag. How did women do it regularly? He'd half-limped, half-wobbled most of the way and had to lean on Vera, to his embarrassment. In the end, he'd used his cane again, even if it spoiled the look.

He opened the door for Vera, then for her grandmother.

"I'd love to stay and explore this amazing city, but I think all of us should take the train to…" Mrs. Tsareva named a place he didn't recognize as she slipped inside the yellow car.

But then he didn't know much of Russian topography. He slumped onto the leather seat, promising himself he'd never take sneakers and men's boots for granted again.

As the motor growled and the yellow car took off, Vera leaned to him. "It can take forty minutes or over an hour to get to Moscow, depending on the traffic, which road the driver takes, and

the speed with which the vehicle travels. With a taxi, it'll take us more than an hour, most likely."

He glanced at her lovely face. "Is it because they drive slow?"

She chuckled. "No. It's because they choose the longest route."

"Aaaah." Of course, since the payment depended on the mileage.

At first, he watched as fields, then modern buildings, gold-domed cathedrals, billboards, and different vehicles passed in a blur. A certain beauty impressed him in the combination of past, present, and some futuristic constructions, but his eyelids grew heavy.

The next moment he knew, Vera tapped his shoulder. "We've arrived."

After they boarded the train and found their places, he took in the metal table in the middle, white curtains on the windows, and the long seats wrapped into something he figured was blue faux leather.

A door with a mirror closed off the compartment, and he was glad to see it had a lock.

Hmm, interesting.

"Don't tell me it's your first time on a train?" Vera smiled at him, then lifted the lid of the seat. "You can put our bags here."

Oh how much he loved that smile.

Uh-oh.

No thinking like that.

He shrugged as he slid their luggage under the seat and closed the lid. "I know we have trains in the US, but somehow, I never needed to take one." He helped her take off her blazer and hung it on the hook, then did the same for her grandma.

"It's a little different here." Vera plopped on the seat in her adorable beige sweater, and her grandmother joined her.

"I can see that." He dropped himself on the bench seat opposite her and stretched his long-suffering legs. He was going to throw

these boots out the window as soon as possible. Well, after the train started moving. He didn't want to hit someone on the head.

His scalp itched. The wig might follow the boots.

"There will be a *provodnitsa*, I mean a conductor, coming to check the tickets soon. Every railway carriage here has its own provodnitsa. She's going to ask if you want to take a bed."

His eyes widened. "A bed?"

Both Vera and her grandmother chuckled as if they realized how it sounded, then Vera said, "Well, we're going to be at our destination in the morning. So we'll need to sleep, right?"

"Right. But how are the beds going to fit in here?" He frowned, glad he was on this trip with these two women. He didn't like the idea of her being alone with strangers. At least, it was good the fourth passenger never showed up.

A loud voice announced something via overhead speakers, and soon the train started moving, the rattle of wheels loud.

Vera laughed, and the sound sent a pleasant wave through him, even if his cluelessness was the reason for her merriment. "In this case, *postel'*, or the bed, means fresh sheets and a pillowcase. There are already mattresses, pillows, and blankets here." She pointed to the top shelf.

"Aaaah." He followed her gesture. "What else is the provodni—pravad—the conductor going to ask?"

He might as well be prepared.

"If you'd like some tea." Mrs. Tsareva gestured to the table where she unpacked her homemade cookies.

His stomach perked up. "And tea actually means tea?"

Vera nodded. "It's going to be hot tea, and it'll be served in glasses. Because the glasses will be hot, obviously, and difficult to carry, they are placed in metal containers. That container is called *podstakannik*. It literally means 'under the glass'."

"Pod-sta-kan-nik," he said slowly.

"Close enough." She smiled again.

That seemed like a difficult language, yet she spoke it so easily. One had to respect that.

He glanced at his disguise, eager to look his usual self again. Okay, maybe he'd never be able to return to his former self, the way he'd been before the accident. But the leopard-print clothes made his skin crawl.

Vera seemed to read his mind. "Grandma, how about we wait in the corridor while Maverick changes?"

"Sure thing." The woman opened the compartment door and left first, and Vera followed her.

As he pulled off the wig and changed into black jeans and a sweater, his thoughts shifted to the latest events.

Maybe he didn't need to return to his former self. He'd been successful beyond his wildest dreams, yes, but he'd started valuing trophies more than people.

As he pulled men's boots on—yes!—he thought about Izzy's giggles and her first steps, about the bond Vera shared with her grandmother, about the way his family rallied around him after the accident, even if he'd done his best to push them away.

All his life, he'd been driving at high speed, pushing himself and the motor beyond any limits, and proud of it. But maybe he'd been driving in the wrong direction, away from the people he loved, the people who loved him.

Okay, not that he could hope Vera would fall in love with him.

He pulled down the window, breathed in the cold fresh air with a bit of bite, and enjoyed throwing the boots out. He decided to keep the wig in case he needed to use the disguise again. He closed the window fast so the place wouldn't get cold.

How sad that it took something as tragic as nearly dying for him to realize how much he'd left behind and how far he'd gone. Now, he had ugly scars inside and outside, but maybe what happened could help him become a better person. A person worthy of the love of an incredible woman like Vera.

At eighteen, he'd chosen his dream of becoming a famous racer over what could happen with Vera. The world had been wide open, filled with exciting possibilities.

He hadn't been ready for a family then, didn't want to settle down, only to become someone like his father, an exemplary citizen on the outside with a philandering secret. Maverick had thought then he wouldn't be a good husband to Vera, a good father to their children.

He hadn't been ready then.

But when he'd nearly kissed Vera, old feelings coming with new force, when he'd held Izzy and looked into those baby blues, he'd been surprised by the strength of his longing for the things he'd once dismissed.

Was it too late for him?

Or was God giving him another chance?

Could he, Maverick, come back to God like the prodigal son?

Lord, please help me.

The prayer appeared unexpectedly.

He didn't ponder it as he opened the door and gestured for Vera and her grandmother to come in.

The older woman gave them a wry look. "I think I'll stay here a little bit and watch the landscape roll by in the window."

He didn't ask why she couldn't do the same inside but sent her a grateful smile for giving him some privacy with Vera. Once Vera was inside, he closed the door, caught his reflection in the mirror, and cringed.

She seemed to read his mind as if she were as tuned in to him as ever, like they hadn't spent years apart. "Need some help taking off that makeup?"

He nodded and sat down on the long shelf/bench, to make it easier for her. "I'd appreciate it."

She took out a bottle with what he assumed was a makeup remover and a packet with wipes from her purse. Then she started

swabbing one of the cotton circles along his face. The touch of her fingers was light, but it seemed to leave a trail of fire on his heated skin.

"Close your eyes so I can remove your eyeshadow and mascara, too." Emotion filled her eyes as if she were affected by this simple task, too.

Wasn't she?

He did as she asked.

The intensity of his reaction to her touch increased without the distraction of vision, creating images of claiming her lips with his.

Images he shouldn't be having.

As his heart started beating wildly, he wasn't sure her assisting him with this was such a hot idea—or rather, maybe it was too hot an idea. As her sweet perfume, those scents of wild berries and melted caramel, drifted to his nostrils, they evoked memories of their first and only kiss. He nearly had to fist his hands to stop from reaching out to her.

The pleasant wave caused by her touch mixed with the desire to feel her in his arms again and to kiss her. How was he going to survive several weeks of this? He'd thought once he'd had a lot of willpower. He didn't think he had enough willpower for this.

"All done." Her quiet voice made him open his eyes.

He glanced in the mirror. He'd had to shave off the beard that had partially hidden the scars on the right side of his face. With makeup gone, he frowned at the glaring scars. At the same time, he felt lighter at having himself back.

Now, if only he could bring back that missed opportunity with Vera.

Or maybe God was giving him a new one?

Maverick couldn't resist it any longer.

His arms circled her waist, and he brought her closer. His breathing went shallow, and by the looks of it, so did hers. Anticipation surged through him, but he couldn't rush it.

Wouldn't rush her.

More emotion filled her beautiful eyes as she stroked his face with her fingertips.

When she touched his scars, he tensed for a moment, and a lump formed in his throat. "I know they are ugly."

"They are not." As if to prove her words, she leaned toward him and kissed them softly.

His pulse went into overdrive.

"There's a Russian saying that scars make a man more handsome." She smiled as she looked up at him again. Then she chuckled. "Okay, there's also a Russian saying that a man should be a little more handsome than a monkey."

His lips tugged up. "That doesn't set a bar too high."

"To me, it means it's not about outside beauty—though you still have your handsome looks. But it wasn't what attracted me to you. It's about your passion for your dream, your willingness to take risks, your loyalty to the people you love."

What attracted me to you… what attracted me to you … what attracted me to you …

Was she *still* attracted to him?

Her praise touched something deep inside him, even deeper than the road her kiss had blazed. But he wasn't so sure he had that loyalty. As for his willingness to take risks, he was still afraid to risk his heart.

His arms tightened around her as she dipped her face again. This time, he was going to meet her halfway, and his pulse skyrocketed.

As his lips brushed against hers, a delightful wave claimed him, sending him into the times when happiness was not just possible but also near, so near. Every cell in his body filled with euphoria, and her lips were the healing balm he'd needed so badly.

A knock on the door made her jump back, ending the kiss way too soon, and disappointment sliced through him.

"Must be the conductor." Her voice sounded a little raspy as she opened the door.

Her grandmother walked inside with an apologizing look, followed by a middle-aged woman in a uniform and brown boots.

When the woman said something in Russian, Vera handed her the tickets. Her gaze lingered on him, and he tensed, wondering whether she could already guess he was a foreigner. Then she said something.

"She is asking whether you are going to take the bed and tea." Vera glanced at him.

"Yes to both questions." He was glad to be prepared, or he'd look like a fool asking how three beds would fit in this small space.

After the conductor left, he asked what things one wasn't supposed to do in Russia.

Vera removed the bottle of lemonade he'd just emptied from the table and placed it on the floor. "No empty bottles on the table. Besides, you're not supposed to whistle here."

Hmm. Good to know. "What else am I not supposed to do?"

Vera rubbed her forehead. "Oh, there are plenty of Russian superstitions. Returning for something might lead to something bad. But I think if you look in the mirror, it might mitigate it."

"Or when you go somewhere when a woman with empty pails crosses your path, it's a bad sign," Mrs. Tsareva chimed in as she helped herself to the cookies. "Not that women carry water in pails these days, really."

He did his best to follow her logic while he snatched a cookie for himself. Yummy! "But if the pails are full of water, it's a good sign, right?"

Vera smiled. "You're catching on quick. Hmm, let's see. If a pregnant woman asks you something, you shouldn't refuse her. Um, you might move a little to the left. They say a person who sits at the angle of the table won't get married."

Before, he'd laugh it off. Now he moved in a hurry.

"I consider superstitions part of Russian folklore." Vera moved away from the angle of the table, too.

"Speaking of Russian folklore." He leaned back against the wall. "I'd like to learn more about those matryoshkas."

"They are a symbol of fertility. People have been carving them for centuries. Some are considered masterpieces worthy of museums—"

A knock on the door interrupted her explanation.

The conductor brought in the *beds* and, a few minutes later, glasses with tea.

Vera said, "Spasibo," and he figured it meant "Thank you."

As the tea aroma spread in the empty space, adding to the enticing cookie scent, Mrs. Tsareva gestured for everyone to join her. She said grace, thankfully in English.

He added an amen, surprising himself. While someone had always said grace at family meals, he'd been too upset with God to say amen after his accident.

"We'll be at our destination in the morning." Vera added a generous portion of sugar to her glass, a wistful expression appearing in her eyes. "I can't wait. I loved our trip to Russia when I was a teen, Grandma. Thank you for taking me."

"You're welcome, dear." The older lady patted Vera's hand.

His heart squeezed as he helped himself to the vanilla cookies.

Morning was around the corner, but it would take much longer than that for him to return to God. At least, he'd started that journey and reached the first milestones, and gratitude warmed him.

However, traveling to reach Vera's heart would take forever.

Because first, his own heart, his soul, had to change.

A trip around the world sounded easier.

CHAPTER SIXTEEN

AFTER A NICE night's sleep on the train—even though she'd slept for most of the flight over, too—Vera eagerly looked out the window as the taxi sped them up from the railway station to the building where they'd rented a three-bedroom apartment.

This was the city where her great-grandmother was born, where she'd lived before WWII, and it mattered to Vera. Thankfully, she hadn't shared this part of her family history, the city's name, with anyone, or she wouldn't have brought him here.

She'd love to visit the apartment where her great-grandmother had grown up, but sadly, it was impossible. It had been destroyed during the WWII bombings. Thankfully, her great-grandmother's parents had already evacuated by that time. She'd love to meet her Russian relatives, her grandfather's family having left Russia so many generations ago and her great-grandmother's brothers and cousins dying in the war, Vera hadn't tracked down anyone who was alive now—no matter how much she'd tried.

A band tightened her chest for a moment. This part of her heritage meant so much to her. Feeling rejected by her parents in her teens, when she came of age, she'd been happy to legally

change her last name to her grandparents' name and try to live up to the beauty of its meaning, to believe it applied to her.

Well, she needed to be grateful she could visit this place at all, and even share this experience with the people dear to her.

With such heavy snowfall, it was difficult to see much, so she sighed and leaned back against the seat. She glanced at Maverick since her grandmother had insisted on riding shotgun.

His eyes were wide, and he seemed deep in thought.

Just like in Rance, she'd noticed subtle changes in Maverick, too. As if he'd made an important decision. And when he looked at her now, it was as if he'd finally started seeing her in a new light.

More than a friend, hopefully?

Her heart fluttered when his fingertips touched hers.

Or was it her wishful thinking?

But he'd kissed her on the train, and heat spread inside her at the memory. That kiss should mean something, right?

For an ex-cop and now PI, she wasn't doing too great trying to gauge his emotions. For a moment, their gazes held, and her pulse increased. Then his hand flew to his face and touched his scars, and he looked away.

Her gut twisted.

It wasn't difficult to gauge his emotions now.

It was as if, after the accident, after being on the pinnacle of success, he slid into the abyss of thinking he wasn't good enough.

Less than.

She'd told him his scars didn't define him, and pretty much said she was attracted to him regardless. But he didn't seem to believe her.

She tried to find some neutral topic for conversation. "I wish it were closer to Christmas. We could see some wonderful celebrations."

He turned to her, curiosity in his eyes. Well, that was something. "What are some of the traditions?"

"Hmm, I know more about New Year traditions than Christmas, maybe because New Year used to be the main holiday of the year here, I think." Vera wrinkled her forehead. "It's customary to make a wish when the clock strikes twelve. They say the way you spend the New Year night is the way you're going to spend the year. So there's usually a big celebration with a lot of food and drinks. Oh, and fireworks. There was often a masquerade for children, right, Grandma?"

The older woman glanced back. "Yes, remember the costume I made for you as a Snowmaiden?"

"Yup, and no one recognized who I was. Snowmaiden is a popular Russian fairy tale about a girl made from snow. One of the versions has a tragic ending. She joined children jumping above the fire and melted."

"I wouldn't want you to melt." His hand touched hers again.

That fleeting touch made blood surge through her veins. "I wouldn't want that, either."

But she was melting beneath his touch, even though what she wanted was to thaw his frozen heart.

The taxi driver pulled up to a nine-story building and parked at the curb. He said they'd arrived.

Maverick insisted on paying after Grandma explained how much it was going to be. Meanwhile, Vera observed her surroundings for anything suspicious. Everything seemed quiet, with the trees, ground, and cars covered in snow like something from a Christmas card.

At this early hour, not many people were outside, and pink and yellow lantern lights created a myriad of sparkles in the fresh snow. Just like tiny diamonds. A snowman greeted them from a playground, as well as an empty swing that reminded her of Izzy, making her heart skip a beat.

He limped outside and opened the door for her and did the same for her grandmother.

Vera stepped outside and breathed in the frosty air. She took off a white knit glove and let a snowflake melt on her palm, then another one. The taxi drove away after Maverick retrieved their luggage, and she caught his gaze on her.

She crossed to him. "You see these snowflakes? Each one is beautiful. Each one is unique. If God put so much beauty and care into something that's just going to melt away, how much more do you think He put into you, scars and all?"

Grandma nodded. "Well said, dear."

Something she couldn't identify flashed in his eyes, and he held out his hand to her. "I know it might sound ridiculous right here and right now. And I'm going to be a horrible dancer, but… Would you care to dance?"

Was he trying to make it up to her for the dance he'd refused?

While a pleasant wave spread through her, she wanted to tell him he didn't owe her anything. And she'd been wrong to ask him in the first place, knowing about his injury. He'd barely— barely!—started walking without a cane.

There was no music, and it might be dangerous for them to be outside in the open.

"I mean, once we get inside the apartment," he said quietly.

Then she realized what expression had flashed in his eyes minutes ago.

Vulnerability.

She slid her hand in his. "I'd love to."

Awakening as daylight seeped through the silver-colored curtains, Vera opened her eyes and blinked at the unfamiliar surroundings. The wallpaper with pale roses didn't look familiar, and neither did the room much smaller than she was used to, or the gray carpet. Hmm, a desk with a chair in the bedroom?

Oh, right.

This was the three-room apartment they'd rented yesterday. Each room had a lock, which was an advantage. But there was only one bathroom, actually tiny separate rooms where one had a bathtub and a sink with a shelf and a mirror above it and another one a toilet. Having one toilet was a disadvantage. She'd found that out when she'd bumped into Maverick in the middle of the night.

She suppressed a groan as she leaped out of bed. While he was a perfect gentleman and had let her go first, she didn't want him to see her disheveled and with her hair like a bird's nest.

Oh well.

She opened the silvery curtains, casting daylight on the framed watercolors with bright landscapes that gave the place a cozy feeling.

Snow covered the trees as if poured from a giant feather pillow, and she smiled as the pristine beauty of Winterland sparkled with magical promise. Children were making a snowman, and her heart constricted at the memory of Izzy.

Hmm, something was unusual. She drew a deep breath of air filled with coffee aroma. Her grandmother was a tea person, and it took a lot to get Maverick out of bed lately.

She checked on her grandmother in a different room. She'd forgotten to lock the door and was still asleep. Then Vera schlepped to the kitchen.

Huh. Her brows rose at the sight of Maverick near the stove—a gas one, sigh. For a moment, she shivered at the horror of being locked in the basement with gas spreading. But her grandma had already explained that electric stoves were still a rarity here.

Vera pulled her shoulders back and smiled at Maverick. Well, that explained the coffee aroma.

He smiled back at her, such a welcome change from his brooding morning looks lately. "I wanted to get croissants for

breakfast, but I didn't know where. And from yesterday, I remembered not all taxi drivers speak English."

In childhood, more than once, he'd brought her croissants, and her heart warmed.

"Imagine that. Hmm. Thank you for the coffee. That's more than enough. I see you're up early. The change of scenery must be doing you good." She nudged him playfully as she passed him, ignoring her increased pulse.

They'd gotten a few necessities from the grocery store yesterday, but somehow, croissants didn't seem to be a necessity.

"I think it's more than the change of scenery." He poured her a cup and opened a can with sweet condensed milk. "Care to try this?"

"Sure." She'd given up diets after leaving the police. Life was too short, and she'd seen it at her job firsthand. She added a generous dollop of milk and took a sip. Its warmth and sweetness soothed her, her muscles relaxing as she savored the treat. "Thank you."

Besides the smile and the sudden urge to make coffee for her instead of hiding away from the world, there were other changes in him. His eyes were wider as if he looked at the world more openly, and he stood taller.

Seeing those changes warmed her more than the coffee sliding down her throat.

"Now, you just sit and enjoy your drink. I'll make breakfast." He took out a few eggs from the fridge. "Hmm, I can't add your favorite mushrooms, but I hope with ham it's enough."

She sank onto the chair but got up immediately. "Um, I do remember your success with the pie. But I also remember how your brother, Kade, nearly burned down the house."

He shook his head. "That was a minor incident. Minor! And believe me, I don't want to burn down the apartment we just rented."

145

"O–okay." She sat again and took another sip of the flavorful coffee, pleased he wanted to make her breakfast.

Still, to be on the safe side, she searched the internet for how to call for help in case of fire in Russia. There were different phone numbers depending on whether one needed to call the police, the fire rescue, or the ambulance. Thankfully, all of them were easy to remember.

Oh, oops. She must have morning breath!

She slipped into the bathroom. Not because she'd expected him to kiss her again, though the thought sent butterflies fluttering tender wings in her stomach. But because dental hygiene was important, right?

Seeing his shaving cream on the glass shelf felt strangely intimate and as if she were intruding at the same time. She looked away and enjoyed the toothpaste's fresh peppermint flavor in her mouth. Considering the room also had a washer in the small space and a large medicine cabinet above it, she doubted two well-fed people could fit in there.

Well, unless one stood in the bathtub, of course.

There was no dryer in sight, but probably the clotheslines above the bathtub were well used.

By the time she was done and hurried into the kitchen, her grandmother was already there, enjoying a cup of tea.

A sting of disappointment that she wouldn't be alone with Maverick jabbed at Vera, followed by a stab of guilt. She loved her grandmother and treasured her company always.

"Breakfast is ready." He winked at Vera. "And the apartment is still intact."

"Good morning, dear. It's going to be a beautiful day. Frost and sunshine, like a Russian poet once said," her grandmother muttered.

Vera had to tear her gaze from Maverick.

146

Apparently, he had the same difficulty looking away from her. "Beautiful indeed."

Finally, Vera managed to make herself move. "Let me serve you, Grandma. Thank you for cooking, Maverick."

When she brought a plate to her grandmother, the older lady whispered to her, "He's a keeper, dear."

Maybe, but Vera wasn't the one to keep him.

Vera didn't say it out loud, of course. Maverick piled her plate high, then did the same for himself.

"I'll say grace." Grandma took their hands while Maverick's fingers tightened around Vera's. "Thank You, Lord, for these wonderful people beside me, a beautiful day, this food, and the chance to visit Russia. Please bless this food and the hands that prepared it. And please guide Maverick and Vera in their paths and help them see themselves the way You see them. Amen."

"Amen," Maverick and Vera echoed.

As Vera dug into her food with gusto, she wondered how God saw her. She still saw herself as lost and confused, and that needed to change.

After breakfast, her grandmother called the first man on her list, one of her pen pals. According to Grandma, he already knew about them arriving, so it was no surprise when, about an hour later, the doorbell rang and the double date began.

Yuri Yuryevich, dressed in a dark coat he paired with a white scarf, turned out to be a stately man with gray hair and a mustache. He'd retired from being a pediatrician a few years ago and now dedicated his life to fishing, growing a few vegetables on a small plot he called a "dacha," and babysitting his rambunctious grandchildren.

Vera liked that he cared enough to bring her grandmother a box of chocolates.

As Yuri took them around the city in an older—but not yet a classic—beige car, he showed them the magnificent churches with

golden domes she fell in love with during her first time in Russia. Most of them had white walls, so the stunning teal walls of one of the cathedrals stood out.

"The city was built in 883," Yuri said as he slowed near another white-walled cathedral with golden domes sparkling in the sunlight.

"You mean, 1883?" Maverick's fingers hovered close without touching hers as they sat in the back seats.

Yuri chuckled as he glanced back. "No, I meant what I said."

Vera's fingers moved just a tad toward Maverick's hand, and she tried to recall the mini-history lesson her grandmother had given her the previous time they were here. "Many places in Russia have quite a history. This one is one of the oldest Russian cities. It was the center of the princedom, and by the end of the twelfth century, it was one of the biggest in Eastern Europe. It was also a part of Kievan Rus', a medieval country from the late ninth to mid-thirteenth century."

"What happened in the thirteenth century?" Maverick looked at her, then laced his fingers through hers.

"The Mongol invasion." Warm tingles ran from his hand to hers, and she enjoyed this physical symbol of their connection.

Grandma, riding shotgun, turned back as much as her seat belt allowed. Her lips lifted at their entwined hands. "Different invasions destroyed many parts of this city several times."

"But they were always rebuilt." Pride laced Yuri's voice as he made a turn. "I'm going to take you to the local historical fortress, okay?"

"Sure," the three of them said in unison.

Something inside Vera shifted as she looked out the window at breathtaking architecture. If the entire city could be rebuilt several times and preserve such beauty, maybe she could rebuild her career, too. Rebuild herself.

Maverick's eyes were pensive as if similar thoughts passed through his mind.

Yuri parked not far from the snow-covered walls. "It was built at the end of the sixteenth century. Less than half of it was preserved. First, it was built from wood. But later, they determined that wood wasn't suitable, so they rebuilt it from stone. The walls were about four miles in length."

Russians usually measured distance in kilometers, but he probably mentioned miles for their convenience.

As he talked, Vera went on high alert as she studied their surroundings. Nothing suspicious in this city so far, but still she missed having her gun with her and didn't like being out in the open.

Yuri walked around the car and opened the door for her grandmother, then gave her his hand and helped her climb out of the car.

Vera mentally applauded him for being a gentleman and tried to read her grandmother's eyes. Were there some sparks? Or was it too early to tell?

"Let's give them some privacy," Vera whispered to Maverick when he did the same chivalrous gesture for her. Out loud, she said, "How about we take a walk and then meet up with you inside the museum?"

"Sounds good to me." Grandma linked her hand with Yuri's elbow when he offered it.

Maverick did the same for Vera. "It might be icy in some places."

She gladly accepted it, not just because of the ice but also because she wanted to use this chance to be close to him. Even through the layers of fabric, she felt warmth coming from his skin.

As they strolled near the ancient snow-plastered rusty-colored walls and more towers than she'd expected, she wondered about the people who'd walked the earth in the spot many centuries ago.

What they thought.

How they survived.

Who they fell in love with.

"How could they construct their lives and their homes, knowing it could be taken away any day in an invasion?" she whispered.

A mysterious expression lit in his eyes, a mixture of surprise and curiosity as if he didn't just discover a new country but something new about himself, as well. "I guess it's called faith."

Faith... She thought she'd had faith—her name meant "faith" after all. But had she really had it? Had she relied on God to show her the right path? Or had she tried to run away as far from the pain of her childhood as possible?

Her father hadn't forgiven her for arresting his son, but had she forgiven her father for leaving them, even worse, for stopping loving her? She hadn't entirely forgiven her mother, either, first because she'd thought her mother had driven her father away with her coldness, then for choosing her new family over her teenage daughter.

And she hadn't entirely forgiven Maverick for choosing his career and friendship with Rance over her, for walking away from her kiss and their possible future together at eighteen. She'd thought she had, but her gut twisting at the memory told her no.

Not completely.

Because too many had betrayed her in the past, she'd nearly expected him to betray her, too, sooner or later.

How could she move forward in her journey if she was still stuck in her past?

Her heart twisted, but she squared her shoulders, determined to enjoy the moment. "Do you... like it here?"

"Yes. It's almost... magical." He smiled at her.

Her heart fluttered, and it dawned on her. She didn't just want him to come here for the safety of all of them, though there was that.

Did she believe that, if she took Maverick out of their familiar surroundings to a place where nothing reminded him of all he'd lost, it might heal him? Or more selfishly, did she hope he might fall in love with her here?

They stopped to admire one of the astonishing towers, and he brushed snowflakes from her hair, his touch warm, his misty breath fogging around her in the cold air.

She found herself praying for him.

Then she broke eye contact because the pull toward him was too strong. Besides, she wouldn't be doing her job if she wasn't alert to their surroundings. Her gaze swept over the area, taking in every person, and she listened to her gut.

No internal alarm so far.

As she stared at the historic tower, snippets from her conversations with Maverick appeared in her memory, mixing with the recent conversation. She placed them together with what she'd learned in her investigations, glued it all with the shudder from the day she was locked in the basement.

Uh-oh.

Maybe the clue was in a much more distant past than she'd realized.

A missing piece appeared, like the last brick to finish the wall. The fortress's wall that hid a secret.

Of course, she'd have to wait for their return to her hometown to get proof.

Or she might be wrong altogether. But her gut told her she was finally going in the right direction.

She glanced around, then fished out her cell phone from her purse. "Let's take some photos."

He took a few photos of her, then her and her grandmother as they caught up to them, and Yuri took photos of them together. Vera did the same for Yuri and Grandma, and the older couple left.

Vera looked at the reel, and some things were clear to her. While Yuri looked at Grandma adoringly, she didn't do the same.

Maverick brushed the back of his gloved hand against her face. "Have I told you how amazing you are?"

Even through the fabric, his touch affected her. "Yes, but I don't mind you repeating it."

"You are amazing." He chuckled.

The sound echoed inside her, and paying attention to her surroundings became more and more difficult.

He took a branch and wrote their names in the snow. The inscription would be gone tomorrow—or as soon as the floating flakes covered it—and their time together was going to be over eventually. But for now, she welcomed the pleasant feeling as she looked at the shine in his eyes and the sparkling snow.

She glanced around again. "Let's go inside the museum." Besides the fact that it would be warmer, they'd be less visible there.

"Sure." He seemed to understand her without the explanation.

Grandma and Yuri joined them, and soon they were browsing things that had once belonged to princes.

She gave him a glance, trying to find the right words. "Kievskaya Rus' was divided into princedoms. For a long time, each princedom was independent and defended itself. It's great to be independent. But it also made them vulnerable. I mean, it's okay to accept help. It's okay to ask for it."

Their gazes held. "Why do I feel you're not talking about Russian history any longer?"

She only shrugged and looked at the gorgeous things the princes once had, but her thoughts drifted to Maverick.

From what she knew, his external wounds would heal. But a mental block prevented him from becoming himself again, from returning to his life. Kade had let it slip that Maverick hadn't driven since the accident.

Not once.

At that moment, she knew.

She'd do everything to help him recover emotionally, to be able to drive again, to return to his passion.

"I believe in you." She leaned into him slightly.

"You do?" His gaze was quizzical.

"Yes. And one day you'll believe in yourself just as much."

It would crush her heart, of course, but that was a small price to pay for his happiness. Maybe her reward would be a final glance at her in his rearview mirror when he drove away.

The gentle kiss brushed against her cheek turned her insides to mush. Then, as he kissed her again, just a quick whisper against her lips, she committed it to her memory to cherish forever.

Some couples would always have Paris.

They would always have….

This city Maverick still couldn't pronounce.

CHAPTER SEVENTEEN

THE NEXT DAY, Vera's heart lodged in her throat as she and Maverick stepped inside a small WWII museum. A woman working there asked them if they needed any help, but Vera shook her head and thanked her.

Since discovering her Russian great-grandmother was a pilot during that era, Vera had watched many movies set then. Sometimes feeling pride for the heroism of a woman blood related to her, sometimes a sadness lingering for all the women had endured.

Seeing these artifacts—from rifles to uniforms to black-and-white photos—made the connection more tangible. She touched the showcase's smooth glass surface as if she could touch her great-grandmother's hand.

When she met Maverick's gaze, he stepped closer. "Tell me more about your great-grandmother."

"She was very young when the war started. She joined the army like her brothers. She became part of a regiment of female volunteers who became pilots. The regiment was barred from combat at first. Then they became the Night Bomber. To get close

to the target, they'd idle the engine and glide in. The regiment didn't carry parachutes until 1944."

His eyes widened. "Then what if…?"

"No one thought about self-preservation then. Motherland meant much more. By the end of the war, she'd flown over eight hundred missions."

"That many?" His hand moved to her, admiration lacing his voice.

Somehow, sharing this moment with him felt important. Her throat clogged. She admired this incredible woman, too. But what could she do to honor such heroism? "The airplane could carry only two bombs. Therefore, eight missions per night. Sometimes more. The regiment dropped more than three thousand tons of bombs. There is a Russian movie based on their story."

When she'd watched it, she imagined her great-grandmother as one of the heroines. Only her grandmother survived, and the main heroines died at the end, sacrificing themselves.

The lump in her throat grew bigger. Her issues seemed so small compared with a time when food rations were scarce and people didn't know whether they were going to survive the day—or in her great-grandmother's case—the night.

While he paid attention to different weapons, she studied photos and miniature planes made from wood and paper that imitated the real ones. Compared to modern planes, the wartime constructions seemed so… primitive and small. No wonder they could only carry two people and two bombs.

Then her gaze moved to the people in the photos, some of them smiling. Many of them didn't survive the war.

"My great-grandfather was part of the Allies. She saved his life, actually. Interesting, isn't it, how love can blossom even amid such dire circumstances?"

His gaze was pensive. "She risked her life for him. Just like you did for me. That might be the greatest love of all." He sucked in a sharp breath. "Not that I am saying…"

That she loved him.

Well, she was more than halfway there already. Heat simmered through her, and she hurried to redirect the topic. "He brought her to America and married her, and they had a little girl. All her brothers died in the war, and she felt guilty leaving her family. Then…" She drew a deep breath of slightly damp air.

"Then?" Arms crossed, eyes intent on her, he leaned against the wall.

"She became Russian-American, living on a hyphen, between two worlds. I want to believe she was happy with my great-grandfather, and I'm grateful for the opportunities I have now. But once the political situation started getting more tense, it became more difficult for her. She was an outsider. Different. And people don't like the ones who are different from them."

"What happened to her?"

She looked at the black-and-white photos again as if they could transfer her to the past. "She made friends eventually, and she adored her husband and little daughter. But when they were visiting friends, there was an earthquake. She died trying to help someone get out. She died the way she lived. A hero."

He drew her into an embrace, and for a few moments, she sobbed into his sweater, grateful there were no other visitors at the time.

Once she was spent, she looked up, and he thumbed the rest of her tears away. He didn't say a word, and he didn't need to. They gave silent tribute to the heroes and walked to the taxi without a word.

When they drove off, she strove for a lighter tone. "Probably it was more fun yesterday at the museum with princes' treasures."

156

"I like knowing more about you and your ancestors." The sincerity in his voice warmed her. "Can you trace them to prior centuries?"

"Yes, but if you expect some royalty and nobility, you'll be disappointed." She spotted a couple going to the gold-domed cathedral, the bride wearing a short fur coat over a long wedding dress. A beginning of a new union. Something shifted inside her. "They were *krepostniye*."

"What's that?" He followed her gaze.

"People who belonged to the nobles and could be sold or gifted." She swallowed bitterness. "One of my ancestors was very talented and beautiful. She played in a theater belonging to the count. She fell in love with a guy who was a krepostnoy, too. Once she found out she was about to be sold, they ran away. They were captured and punished. Severely. Needless to say, she couldn't be an actress any longer."

Compassion constricted her lungs, and she turned away from the window.

To think about it. Those women defied the rules, and she was a rebel without a cause. One of the reasons she'd chosen to go to the Police Academy, besides wanting to make a difference, was because both her parents had been against it. Wanting to hurt them the little she could, she'd only hurt herself.

"How sad." He tapped the fingers of his right hand against his thigh. "People with no right or choice. We take our freedom for granted sometimes. I know I have. My father didn't approve of my career choice, but other than that, I had an open road in front of me."

"Choices..." Her hand itched to touch his, but the car was already gliding toward the nine-story building where they'd rented an apartment. She did her best to gauge the area for anything suspicious. "I'm grateful America is a land of opportunities. I really am. But it seems to me there might be a certain destination

for us all. And we can get there sooner or go wrong directions and have accidents on the way."

He winced.

"Sorry. Didn't mean that…" She cringed. Way to go to remind him!

She paid the driver and waited for Maverick to limp around and open the door for her, using the time to observe her surroundings. For some reason, these gestures mattered to him.

"I know." He gave her his hand. Her skin tingled as he touched her, and they walked together inside the building.

Each floor seemed to have four apartments, and somebody in one of the apartments on the first floor must be cooking because it smelled like fried chicken. The scent reminded her of the scents of her childhood while she'd stayed with her grandmother.

When any of her neighbors had been ill, or just had a bad day, Grandma had cooked or baked something and taken it there. Neighborhood children had loved visiting her, especially Rance who'd come from the wrong side of the tracks and whose mother rarely cooked.

At the time, Vera had thought her grandmother did it to please others, trying to fit in, considering that having Russian blood made her an outsider of sorts, too. Now she knew it was just who her grandmother was.

Maverick and Vera reached to press the elevator button together, and she withdrew her hand. The women before her had sacrificed so much for love, and here she was, afraid even to touch his hand.

They stepped inside the tiny elevator, and she looked him in the eye. "God is in control, not us. Our losses can turn to wins and vice versa. The power we have is only an illusion." She paused. "We have great-grandmother and great-grandfather's letters that I'll treasure forever. She said something that it took me a while to understand."

He held her gaze even as the elevator doors opened. "What was that?"

"'Life is made of choices that bring consequences. But maybe the biggest choice we really have is the choice whether to be kind.'"

In the afternoon, Maverick pulled the chair out for Vera while Yuri did the same for her grandmother. The quaint café where they stopped for lunch looked cozy with birch furniture and floors, winter forest landscapes, and latte-hued curtains hugging the windows where frost had drawn exquisite ornaments. The scents of fried potatoes and meat greeted him, mingling with the aroma of rye bread and an additional something he didn't recognize. Cabbage, maybe?

His stomach perked up. Yet a tiny twang twinged his chest as if he expected a samovar with hand-painted lacquer dishes like the ones in Mrs. Tsareva's kitchen. Or maybe, as much as he loved her grandmother, he wanted to spend some time alone with Vera.

Maybe even repeat the kiss shared on the train…

Blood rushed faster in his veins as he did his best to dismiss the thought. Until he became a man worthy of Vera, worthy of their future together, he had to keep his impulses in check, and he'd already succumbed to one of them at the historical museum.

Keeping those impulses in check was going to be a tall order.

A slim blonde waitress took their orders as he studied the menu. Well, he might as well be looking at Chinese hieroglyphs.

Smiling at his dilemma, Vera hurried to translate the dishes' names. All the while, her gaze still moved over the small room. Her back appeared to be stiff, her shoulders tense. He knew her well enough to recognize she was on high alert. She'd also chosen

the table at the end of the room and sat with her back to the wall as if she needed to see the room and exits.

Great. Here he was enjoying himself, and she had to work. His protective instincts woke up. He wanted to be the one taking care of her, helping her, shielding her.

Not the other way around.

What kind of man did this make him?

He nearly gritted his teeth at his helplessness, his earlier appetite gone.

"Are you okay?" Concern settled in her blue eyes as she seemingly sensed his mood change.

He plastered on the smile he usually reserved for publicity. "Sure. I'll have what you're having."

Her eyebrows went up. "For *both* courses?"

He should've been more attentive when she'd translated the menu.

Hmm. He studied the menu again as if he could understand a single letter. "Um, what do you mean?"

Her grandmother patted his hand. "Soup is usually customary for the first course here. We eat it with a slice of rye bread and often a dollop of sour cream. If you're okay with beets, I'd suggest *borscht*."

"That's... fine." Even though he couldn't remember the last time he ate beets.

Vera probably caught his unsure expression. "Maybe *ukha* would work better."

"Ugh what?" He should've looked up Russian food on the internet.

"*Uk-ha*. It's a fish soup. Oh, I know!" Vera snapped her fingers. "*Pelmeni*. It can be eaten as a soup or as a main dish. It's minced meat wrapped in thin dough. They are boiled in water until they float."

160

"Served with sour cream or butter. I'll take mine with sour cream." Grandma gave a firm nod as she made up her mind. "I believe they mean 'ear-shaped bread'."

He'd learned something new today. "Okay."

"I'll take stuffed pike for the main course. And *vinegret*. It's a salad from boiled beets, potatoes, carrots, pickles, onions, sauerkraut, and beans," Vera said. "Huh. Ukha and stuffed pike. It's going to be a fish day for me."

No vinegret for him. She lost him on "beets," though he might need to develop a love for them since eventually he needed to try borscht.

The older woman glanced over the menu. "I'm going to get *blinchiki*. It's like cream-filled crêpes. But I guess you guys need meat. So how about beef stroganoff?"

He and Yuri nodded. At least that was a word he recognized.

Soon lunch was served, and Mrs. Tsareva said grace.

They all said amen.

He wondered whether Yuri was a man of few words, or if he'd already learned the lesson in his long life that it was best to let women talk first.

As they dug in, Yuri apparently decided it was time to speak up. "What would you like to do in the evening?"

Maverick took a bite of his pelmeni, then of beef stroganoff, which was juicy and tender and covered in a sauce he hadn't tried before. "What can one do here in winter?" Most of his outside physical activities he'd done in summer.

Used to do.

For a moment, the food turned bitter.

The man brightened and gestured with his empty fork, seeming to forget about his food. "Oh, there are plenty of things. Skiing, skating, ice fishing, going to a hockey match..."

Vera sent him a worried glance as she tasted fish soup as if realizing those activities were outside and most of them required

some endurance. Something that might not be recommended after all his injuries.

He nearly grunted as her concern both touched and irritated him. He wasn't some weakling who needed looking after!

"How about going to a hockey match?" Vera suggested. Then her shoulders sloped as if she'd thought being in the large crowd might put them, and especially him, at risk. "Or maybe we can watch one in front of the TV, right?"

This time, Maverick clenched his teeth before forcing himself to unclench them and continue his lunch. While he'd stayed indoors after the accident, now the need to be hiding, to be protected grated on his nerves.

"Oh, that's great!" Mrs. Tsareva polished off her pelmeni. "I love hockey."

If it were someone else's grandma, he'd be surprised. But nothing about Vera's grandmother surprised him anymore. At this point, he almost expected her to form a hockey team or two from elderly citizens of his hometown when they got back.

So he just nodded. "Sounds good to me. Thank you for the suggestion, Yuri."

Yuri beamed, obviously enjoying the attention now. "If you're into extreme sports, there are tons of other things to do. One can ski the volcanoes in Kamchatka, but the only way to get there is to be dropped off by a helicopter. Oh, or go on an Amur tiger photo safari in the Russian Far East. Because their golden and white stripes are most noticeable on the snow-white background, it's best to do it in winter. Imagine, Amur tigers used to be almost extinct, but now their population is enough there are guided tours!"

Chapter Eighteen

A SPIKE of adrenaline energized Maverick.

Both activities sounded fascinating.

He winced.

Not with his leg!

Vera coughed a little and hurried to drink some tea. "Please don't give my grandmother such ideas."

Uh-huh. So she worried about her grandma and not him?

Mrs. Tsareva was the first one to finish her first course, never mind that she was the smallest of them. "Hmm. I might need a hip replacement after skiing a volcano. Besides, if I want to witness a volcano erupt, I can just visit one of my friends when she argues with her husband."

"How about the tiger thing?" The man didn't seem to let it go.

The blinchiki were disappearing fast from Mrs. Tsareva's plate. "Well, I do love cats. And I miss Buddy."

Vera coughed again.

Maybe it was time to help her out. "Well, the Amur tiger is the biggest cat on the planet. But I want to bring you both back safe and sound and not become"—Maverick gestured to the plates—"a large cat's lunch."

"I'm sure safaris are perfectly safe," Yuri muttered under his breath.

But air whooshed out of Vera's lungs, and her leg touched Maverick's under the table as she put a dent in her stuffed pike.

He stilled.

Was it an accident?

Or was she playing footsie?

Or even worse, maybe it was her grandmother playing footsie with her new suitor?

"Thanks," Vera mouthed to him.

His chest swelled from her gratitude as if he'd just taken an award-winning tiger photo. Immediately, his beef stroganoff tasted much better.

He touched her leg with his foot, hoping he reached the right leg. Based on her cheeks pinking, he did.

Vera gave due to her burgundy-colored salad—vinaigrette, no, vinegret, right? "I could use some wisdom, Grandma and Yuri. How do you know what road in life to take? What are you meant to do? Who do you want to spend your life with?"

Her grandmother took a sip of tea, paused, staring at the raised cup, obviously considering her question. "I don't want to sound morbid, but at my age, one thinks a lot about the last days."

"Grandma! You're going to live to a hundred! You have to!"

She lifted her other hand in a universal stop signal. "When you close your eyes and imagine you only have one day to live, what are you going to do that day? Who are you with? Remember, in her letter to your great-grandfather your great-grandmother said that, if she only had one day to live, she'd want to spend it with him. Sometimes you haven't met that person yet. But if you did, you shouldn't wait until the last day."

Maverick forgot to eat or even to breathe. He didn't need to close his eyes. There was only one image in front of them.

There'd been only one since he'd been a child.

"They say we need to know history not to repeat past mistakes." He studied Vera as she finished her stuffed pike. "This is important to you, isn't it?"

"Grandma felt I needed to know where I came from. She taught me Russian. She read Russian fairy tales to me. We watched a lot of WWII movies together." Vera sent her grandmother a loving gaze. "We read great-grandmother's letters together. That's my legacy. That's part of who I am. Or maybe rather who I want to be."

"I think I'm finally starting to understand why my family is so big on legacy." Why had it taken him this long and traveling this far to understand?

He'd always thought legacy meant something materialistic. He'd earned a lot to pass to others. Or the legacy was the land and the ranch so important to his siblings.

But as he thought about all the things he'd wanted to teach Izzy and would never have a chance to, as he took in everything he'd learned about five generations of women in Vera's family, he realized something simple.

Legacy was about values and kindness we passed to others.

"I wanted you to pass it all to the future generations." Mrs. Tsareva sipped her tea from the dainty cup.

The café also offered an assortment of desserts, but he couldn't see how he could eat even a crumb.

Vera smiled sadly as she pushed her empty plate away. "So much for that so far."

"It's not too late. And it's never too late to discover who you are." He meant every word.

"Do you think so?" Blue eyes blinked up at him, steadied on him.

Her attentive gaze unnerved him, made him want things that could never be. "I know so."

As he looked at the abundant food on the table, he recalled tiny pieces of bread and daily rations during WWII. He thought about Vera's ancestors from the tsars' times, *krepostniye* who were basically the property of other people.

He'd been born into a wealthy, well-respected family with loving parents and great siblings. He'd been popular at school. Though his father hadn't approved of his career choice, Maverick still had all roads open to him. And then on those roads, he'd driven to success beyond his dreams.

God had given him many blessings Maverick had taken for granted. He'd credited himself and his tenacity for his accomplishments. He'd rarely thanked God for it.

But when he'd discovered his father's infidelity, he'd blamed God for it. Maverick had blamed God for the accident.

In the good times, he didn't remember God. In not so good times, he'd resented God.

Taking a sip of his lemonade, he sat in thought.

His mother had never played the lottery. When he'd asked her about it, she'd said she hadn't played because she was afraid to win. She'd already been blessed so much.

He couldn't understand it then, but he did now. With a big blessing came a big responsibility.

So far, he hadn't handled his responsibility too great.

Lord, please help me help myself. Guide me, please.

Maverick stretched after waking up the next day. This time, different scents mingling with a coffee aroma reached his nostrils.

Meat and cabbage?

Vera was cooking something, and regret spurred him on to get out of bed and dress fast. He'd wanted to surprise her with cooking breakfast today, too.

The way her face had lit up when she'd walked into the kitchen yesterday had warmed something deep inside him.

He opened the curtain and looked out the window. They'd rented an apartment on the seventh floor, but another nine-story building blocked most of the view. From what he'd seen, the locals lived in apartments they owned in one of the many five- or nine-story buildings comprising the city. He was yet to see individual buildings in cities, except for the ones in commercial use.

Tall poplars, their naked branches covered in snow, nearly reached the top floor, and pigeons gathered on the roof. A snow carpet made everything look pristine and fresh, like a new beginning.

He welcomed the sunshine and white beauty behind the window. For a moment, he admired the exquisite frost ornaments on the glass again.

Vera was right.

God created such beauty even when it would disappear soon.

Wait a minute.

He stilled.

These mornings were so different from his grouchy mood, as if indeed he could rewrite some things in his life, as if he'd been given a blank slate as clear and clean as the snow carpet outside.

Or would all his attempts be erased by a new snowfall?

He limped outside his room, eager to see Vera.

She was standing in the kitchen and cutting vegetables with her grandmother, both of them singing in a low tone, probably not to wake him up. He smiled and could easily imagine a third-generation female, maybe even Izzy, joining the cooking and singing one day.

Another bit of wishful thinking.

A kitchen here was a separate room and led to a balcony he'd learned was used as an extension of a refrigerator of sorts, due to the cold temperatures. No stainless steel appliances or dishwasher,

but the cozy kitchen felt fun with its salad-colored cabinets, matching soft curtains, and still lifes featuring different breads and pastries. A large tray, painted with flowery motifs similar to the ones on the cutting board, and a small TV perched on the counter next to an assortment of coffee cans.

Vera's eyes lit up again as she saw him. "Good morning!"

He ached to give her a kiss, a hug, but he made himself only give a wave. "Good morning, ladies. What can I do to help?"

"Set the table for breakfast, please, dear." Mrs. Tsareva scooped the vegetables into a large pot. "We're almost done making *shchi*."

One day, he'd learn more than a few Russian words. Today wasn't that day yet. He reached for the plates in the kitchen cabinets. "*Sh* what?"

"Shchi. It's a two-letter word in Russian. It's a cabbage soup. Plus beef or chicken, potatoes, carrots, onions, spices." Vera opened a large bowl, revealing something similar to those crêpes yesterday. "I hope you don't mind *blini*, or blinchiki for breakfast."

"I'd love it." From her hands, he'd probably accept arsenic gladly.

Arsenic? Ugh. What was he thinking?

He was losing his mind.

He placed plates on the table, wondering what was happening to him.

Vera.

That was the answer.

He'd spent a long time teleconferencing with his family yesterday. For the first time, he was interested in the things at the ranch instead of only financing it. He caught himself on the thought that he might like repairing tractors and other farm equipment again.

His lungs expanded with food-scented air as he set delicate cups on the table. He pulled the chair out for Vera, then for her

grandmother. He might not be as passionate about the ranch as his siblings yet, but he wanted to be useful again. And that would be a good start.

Tractors wouldn't care if he limped or had a few scars on his face. Maybe by repairing them, he could repair something inside himself, too.

Vera's grandmother said grace, as always. As he listened to her giving thanks to the Lord, he gave his own in his mind, adding his prayer.

Breakfast was delicious, and crêpes tender with just the right amount of sweetness. Kind of like his growing feelings for Vera.

For some time, they discussed yesterday's hockey match. For a moment, he longed for his former life, when he was the center of attention like the teams were yesterday. When so many admiring eyes had been on him…

Then he glanced at Vera as she sipped her tea, and their gazes met and held. She put the cup down, and longing for something reflected in her blue eyes, too.

Maybe he was reaching the point when only one pair of admiring eyes mattered.

Hers.

CHAPTER NINETEEN

IN THE AFTERNOON, a train sped them up to a different town Maverick equally couldn't pronounce.

There lived another of Mrs. Tsareva's pen pals, Mikhail Sergeyevich.

"I'm sorry there were no sparks between you and Yuri." Vera sipped hot tea from a glass.

Grandma sighed. "It's okay. When it's meant to be, I'll know it."

Mikhail, with a well-kept salt-and-pepper beard and kind gray eyes, met them at their destination, and Maverick gave him props for that, as well as for bringing flowers and a box of chocolate. The guy was wearing a windbreaker and a fur hat with floppy ears tied on the top that Maverick now knew was called *ushanka* from the word *ushi* that meant "ears."

Mikhail blinked when his pen pal introduced her granddaughter and Maverick. Mikhail gave flowers to Mrs. Tsareva and chocolate to Vera, then switched, then switched again in a show of nerves.

When the older lady thanked him with a smile, he beamed and picked up her luggage while Maverick took the rest.

His leg wasn't doing too great this morning, but he wasn't going to show it, of course. At least, he hadn't reinjured it yesterday.

Mikhail took them to a car covered in a thin layer of snow. He must've been waiting for a while. When Mikhail drove them to the apartment they'd rented, Maverick found himself hoping Mikhail would be rewarded for his efforts, though he'd never been a matchmaker.

"There's a great skating rink nearby that we could visit." Mikhail took a sip of his tea inside the cozy kitchen later.

Vera visibly stiffened, but Maverick sat straighter. Maybe he couldn't ski from the volcanoes yet, but at the very least, he should be able to skate. And if they went for a short period of time and were careful, it couldn't be that dangerous, could it?

Grandma's face brightened, too.

Vera seemed to understand the change in his mood without words because both she and her grandmother said in unison, "Okay."

Then Vera looked at him. "If you're fine with that."

"I'd love it."

In the evening, they approached the skating rink.

Vera sent a worried glance toward her grandmother and Mikhail as they took off together. Maverick understood Vera's worry. A broken hip could happen not only on a mountain slope. But her grandmother and her partner held up well and skated gracefully as if this was something they were doing every day.

Maverick helped Vera tie on her rented skates while she looked around nervously.

"All clear?" he whispered to her when he was done.

"I hope so." She rolled her eyes, then let her shoulders loosen and flicked a gloved hand at a wisp of hair escaping her cozy knit hat that matched her eyes. "Um, okay. I'm also nervous because I

don't know how to skate. I mean, I barely know how to skate at all."

He gave her his hand, standing a little taller. "Why don't you lean on me then? I'm not going to let you fall."

A faint smile curled her lips. "Thank you."

He placed his arm around her waist, enjoying the feeling of having her close and mentally thanked Mikhail for his suggestion. Her gaze moved over the skating rink again. Thankfully, it was filled with children and only one adult couple, besides them and Mrs. Tsareva with her friend.

Vera relaxed against him, and her trust warmed him.

"Place your feet at your shoulder width, bend your knees, and squat a little." He leaned to her, enjoying the frosty air and her faint scent of berries and caramel.

She did as he'd said and staggered, but he held her up. "You're doing good. Now, try to walk like a duck."

She blinked up at him. "Excuse me? Should I quack, too?"

He laughed. "No quacking required. Though I don't mind if it'll help you. Place your heels together and your toes outward and make a few steps."

One of the girls, dressed in a pink jacket and a matching knit hat with blonde braids peeking up from it, made an elaborate pirouette in front of them. Vera released a wistful sigh. But Maverick was proud of Vera for getting out of her comfort zone.

While he still couldn't get out of his comfort zone and even think of driving.

The thought bit more than the frost.

Once Vera was more confident, he asked her to take longer strides and roll further with every one. "I think you're ready to glide. Push with one foot and glide with the other until you feel like you're going to fall."

"Like that?" She glanced in her grandmother's direction, then followed his instructions.

At some point, she'd ask him to let her go, and he wasn't ready for it yet. She was gaining momentum fast, and he taught her how to stop, then how to skate backward. All the while, he loved the shine in her eyes, the pink on her cheeks, and the smile now in her eyes, as well. The smile that showed she started to enjoy it.

Stars twinkled in the sky. Lanterns sparkled off the snow, and the children's laughter added to the magical merriment.

To be helpful, to be capable again, to bring joy to someone he cared about felt so good. His heart swelled inside his chest as he filled his lungs with fresh, frosty air.

So what if his leg muscles started to hurt?

He knew how to work through pain.

She slipped as she tried to skate backward, and he held her up. "I've got you. You're okay."

The feel of her in his arms was priceless, though his injured leg was throbbing.

She stilled in his arms, then said, "Thanks. Let's go forward."

"Good idea."

They glided forward.

She traced her grandmother with a pensive gaze. "Grandma told me how much she loved to skate when she was a little girl. Such wonderful memories. I'm glad she gets to relive them."

"I can't help feeling you're grateful she won't have memories of a tiger safari." He chuckled, despite the pain increasing by the moment.

No way he was going to admit his weakness, to feel helpless again.

She looked up into his eyes, and something he couldn't quite read flashed in hers. "You know, as much fun as this is, I'm getting tired. And cold. And I'm still afraid Grandma might fall. How about calling them and going home? We could have a cup of hot cocoa and maybe some pirozhki?"

He did his best not to show his relief. "Sounds great to me."

At that moment, somebody screamed.

Maverick flinched and skated toward the cry.

The blonde girl with two braids who'd been doing amazing pirouettes was lying on the ice, clutching her right leg. Her freckles and blue eyes stood out on her pale round face, and she kept repeating, *"Moya noga bolit! Moya noga bolit!"*

An image of Izzy at this age, suffering and in pain, flashed in his mind, and a shiver having nothing to do with the cold ran down his spine.

Vera made it to the girl soon after he did. Her eyes narrowed. "She is saying her leg is hurting. She might have a fractured or broken bone."

He met her gaze as he crouched by the girl and knew Vera understood him without words as she often had. Due to their professions, they were both trained in CPR. Besides, sadly, he'd had way too much experience with broken bones. He wondered where the girl's parents were, but there was no time to find out.

He slipped his windbreaker off his shoulders and covered the girl with it. It would be better to carry her away from the ice, but moving her might cause her damage.

"I'll calm her down and do my best to keep her from going into shock while you check her bone. I'll explain what you're doing." Vera shrugged out of her coat and tucked it under the girl's head, talking in a soft, soothing voice.

Then she looked up at the small crowd of the children and said something. In response, a champagne-haired girl in a white sweater pulled out her phone and started calling someone.

That division of duties with Vera made sense since he didn't speak Russian.

Keeping a smile on his face, he knelt near the girl, holding in a groan when his leg protested. Then he removed his gloves and started probing her leg gently. He found it swelling already. His

stomach clenched, and adrenaline pumped in his veins mixed with worry.

Mrs. Tsareva and Mikhail joined them. "What happened?"

"Grandma," Vera spoke without looking up, "please call the ambulance, to be on the safe side."

"Yes, dear." Fabric rustled as she retrieved her phone. Then the unmistakable sound of the numbers being tapped rang out.

The girl flinched when he touched a tender spot. "*Bol'no!*"

Compassion tightened his rib cage. "Sorry," he said as if she could understand him.

"She says it hurts." Vera kept a soft smile on her face for the girl's benefit. "This girl's name is Natasha. The girl in the white sweater is her friend and called Natasha's parents. What's your assessment?"

"The good news—there's no bleeding and no protruding bones. The bad news—there might be a fractured or broken bone. I'll try to make a splint to immobilize Natasha's leg. We don't know how long it'll take the ambulance to get here." He glanced around for a board or any other materials to make the splint as he sent up a silent prayer.

Based on the way her grandma's lips were moving, she was praying, too.

Vera said something in Russian again to the children hovering around them.

"I asked the children to bring several branches," she said in a low tone, then continued calming Natasha down.

"Good idea." He removed his scarf to use it to tie the branches around the injured area while his leg wailed in pain.

Making sure to keep a smile on his face, he studied Natasha for the signs of shock. Going into shock could be dangerous because it would prevent blood from moving to vital organs.

Chapter Twenty

MAVERICK NODDED to himself. While the girl was still pale, there was no cold sweat, and her breathing evened out somewhat. So, hopefully, no shock.

Vera placed her fingers on Natasha's wrist, counted under her breath, then let the wrist go. "Pulse is okay."

Two boys came running with small branches, and Maverick positioned the twigs beside the girl's ankle, then tied them with his scarf. A pack of ice would help, and he considered making a makeshift pack from snow wrapped into some clothes.

Vera asked Natasha a few questions and nodded, a satisfied gleam in her eyes. "Natasha doesn't sound confused, and she says she doesn't feel dizzy. I think she's not in shock."

As a siren shrilled in the distance, he released a breath he didn't realize he'd been holding. The paramedics would take it from here.

A bareheaded blonde woman in an unbuttoned faux fur coat ran inside the skating rink, her eyes frantic. From the similarities of features, one could easily see she was related to the girl. She nearly slipped on the ice as her arms flailed. He staggered and cringed from pain as he got up, his leg now protesting every movement.

Then he hurried to the woman and supported her while leading her to her daughter.

Mrs. Tsareva and Mikhail stepped to her and probably started explaining the situation in Russian. Then the woman dropped on her knees and stroked the girl's hair, saying something fast.

The siren neared, and breathing became easier. Maverick said a prayer of gratitude while his pulse still pounded in his temples.

Once paramedics arrived, he helped Vera up, and Vera explained what happened in Russian.

Then he and Vera glided away to let paramedics do their jobs, and she gestured for the children to do the same. While two guys loaded Natasha into the ambulance, the woman rushed to him and Vera.

She shook Vera's hands, then his. "*Spasibo. Spasibo. Spasibo.*" Then she darted back to the ambulance.

"That means thank you," Vera said, but he didn't need the translation.

While cold seeped through his bones, he picked up her jacket from the ice and snugged it over her shoulders—though it would take a while for the frozen coat to offer her any warmth. Then he took her cold hands and brought them to his lips, doing his best to warm her trembling fingers with his breath. "You did a great job."

"*We* did. I hope Natasha will be okay. We make a good team, don't we?"

"*Da.*" That was one of the few words he knew in Russian.

Yes.

And that was what he wanted to be with her.

A team.

A union.

A couple.

But the throbbing pain in his leg reminded him about his weakness and all the missed chances when he'd been whole

instead of broken. A bag of ice and a whole lot of regrets would keep him company tonight.

The topic of ice fishing came up at a scrumptious dinner the same day, and the women decided to give it a try.

Maybe Mrs. Tsareva indeed wanted to spend a lot of time in Mikhail's company, or maybe it was him saying women usually didn't go ice fishing. Or maybe both.

Maverick agreed to the future endeavor easily. He wanted to support them. Besides, his leg would thank him if he just sat and stared at the fishing pole for hours.

Early next morning—way too early morning!—Mrs. Tsareva decided to spend the day baking instead. But partly out of curiosity, partly out of stubbornness, Vera and Maverick trudged after Mikhail on the fresh crisp snow, frost nipping on his cheeks.

Possibly, Maverick also had a primal urge to bring home the bacon, or fish in this case. So he suppressed a yawn and ignored his leg's complaints as he shuffled beneath more layers of thermal clothes than he'd ever worn in his life, not that Missouri in winter was the tropics. Topping off the bundle was an ushanka, the hat a gift from Mikhail that Maverick appreciated very much this morning.

Mikhail tapped an ice spud on the ice as he walked and listened intently.

"Usually, we don't start ice fishing until mid-December, but this year it's been so cold the ice should be thick enough already," Mikhail said over his shoulder.

Maverick swallowed hard while he exchanged worried glances with Vera. He took in the large lake, doing his best to assess whether the ice was cracked anywhere.

"That information would've been useful earlier," she whispered to him.

No kidding.

She looked funny bundled in so many layers of clothes underneath a waterproof jacket. But he was glad she was wearing all that, as well as waterproof boots with metal cleats that made walking on the ice easier.

Despite the early hour and cold, fishermen already claimed spots on the lake, hunching over the poles. Dark circles spotted the ice, and the lake seemed to stretch as far as the eye could see.

Mikhail found the place he liked and drilled a hole with an auger, then measured the ice. "Six inches. Good enough." He nodded to himself, a satisfied smile on his lips. Then he drilled another hole, then another one.

Maverick set down folding chairs and fishing gear he'd borrowed from Mikhail and carried for himself and Vera. Then he scooped the ice from the holes with a metal ice scoop, making for a nice and clean circle.

She put the bait on the lure and arranged the first fishing pole. "This is still pretty safe, right? I mean, nobody you know ever drowned, right?"

Mikhail rubbed his salt-and-pepper beard. "Well, a few guys I know fell underwater, but they were rescued."

Yeah.

That was promising.

Just the thought of Vera going underwater made Maverick's stomach clench. So he made a mental note to sit as close to her as possible as he arranged his fishing poles. "I imagine they never ice fished again."

"Nah. They were back the very next day." Mikhail rubbed his hands together gleefully, then fit a sinker on the hook and dropped it into the ice hole, probably to figure out the water's depth. "Fishing helps with stress."

"I guess, if you die, there's no stress anymore," Vera whispered to Maverick low enough so Mikhail wouldn't overhear. "You know, like the French say, the best remedy for a headache is a guillotine."

Maverick nearly rolled his eyes, though he didn't have such a habit. While indeed that meant there'd be no more stress, he wouldn't want to resolve the issues that way. Granted, he'd brought a first aid kit, a flotation device, and a rope, but he hoped he wouldn't have to use them.

An image of Vera going under the ice, into freezing waters that could cause pneumonia, at the very least, made him shudder.

Vera leaned to him. "That tiger safari in Siberia doesn't look too bad right now, does it?"

His lips tugged up. He always liked her sense of humor. On the other hand, he did forget about his accident, being shot at, and even the scary possibility of Vera's being poisoned by gas. While he was on the other side of the world, those things seemed so far away as if they had never existed.

He turned to Mikhail. "How long have you been ice fishing?"

"Since I was fourteen."

Well, if the man had been doing it for many decades and was still alive, that should be a good sign.

"Okay, I'm going to make a few holes on the other side of the lake and will be right back," Mikhail said when everyone was settled.

"Um, why?" Maverick took Vera's gloved hands and rubbed them. To ensure she had enough blood flow, of course.

No other reason at all.

Mikhail looked at him as if Maverick didn't understand simple matters. "The fish might bite better on the other side. I wouldn't want to miss it."

So he'd be running back and forth on the slippery lake to check on the fishing poles while there was no guarantee the ice was thick

enough. All the layers of thermal clothing and the large boots he wore weren't exactly inductive to running, either.

It seemed to be worth it. Mikhail came back with a large grin and the first catch of the day, a perch. Adrenaline filled Maverick's veins when his pole dipped, and soon he reeled in a pike. Excitement rushed through him when he helped Vera reel in a large perch, then unhooked it from the line and dropped it into a bucket with water.

She clapped. "Yay!"

Her joy rippled through him. Okay, maybe he could see the attraction of ice fishing. Somewhat.

Mikhail nodded. "We're going to have a great ukha."

Right. Fish soup. Maybe Mikhail had felt that primal need to bring home the bacon—ahem, fish—too.

After some time, Maverick decided he needed to share the duty of checking poles on the other side of the lake. His leg didn't thank him for that when he came back with two pikes. Vera, however, did, and that was enough.

Then Vera shared a Thermos with hot mint tea—grandmother had made sandwiches for later, too. Sips of hot tea warmed up his cooling insides.

"You know, in Yakutia, they had the lowest temperatures on earth recorded to date," Mikhail said proudly.

Vera took another sip, a half-smile playing on her lips. "I guess this place is the Sahara compared to Yakutia."

With a suspicious longing, Mikhail eyed a few other fishermen sharing shots of vodka. He'd offered to bring a bottle of the famous local drink "to keep them warm." However, Maverick's partying days were behind him, and Vera had never had any affinity for alcohol in the first place.

Maverick hugged Vera and rubbed his hand over her shoulder. "Are you okay? You're not cold, are you?"

She stared into his eyes, making time stand still. "I... I'm fine."

A few seconds passed, and he was unable to look away.

Mikhail cleared his throat. "Um, Vera, I think the fish bites. If you'd like, I can reel it in."

Vera broke the eye contact, her cheeks flaming up. "No, thank you. I can do it."

Soon another pike joined the ones in the bucket.

Mikhail asked Vera to share more about herself and her life in America and then listened with an intensity Maverick didn't expect.

"Are you happy there?"

Vera's lips curved up a little. "I didn't realize how blessed and how happy I am until now. It's like I am learning more about myself while learning about my great-grandmother."

Maverick felt the same way. He'd never expected his road to himself would lead him through Russia, though. Go figure. "Tell me more about her." Someone that important to Vera was important to him, too.

"She loved to read and design. She came up with some additions to their plane construction that sadly never came to fruition." Vera paused as she peered at the gray sky, lost in thought. "She said things in her letters that stuck with me. 'The true measure of one's life is how much mercy we give.'"

He chuckled without mirth. "She knew that at eighteen, and I'm only now starting to comprehend this."

"She also had to deal with a lot of adversity while being a pilot. Men didn't treat them as equals, and their regiment often received worse equipment, clothes, footwear, and so on, than the men's regiments did." Vera sighed, shaking her head at the horizon. "She never complained but persevered…. Every night, making eight or more missions. Even when they'd been encouraged to take parachutes, they'd rather take more bombs. She was that patriotic…. I have big shoes to fill."

Something dawned on him, and he reached for her gloved hand, feeling her warmth even through the fabric. "Maybe you don't need to try so much. Did you go into the Police Academy because you wanted to be like your great-grandmother?"

Vera nodded. "One of the reasons. It was the closest I could come to being a hero in a peaceful time. I wanted to make a difference like she did, to measure up."

"You don't need to measure up. God created you the way you are for a reason. You don't need to follow someone else's path, even if it's an admirable one. You're your own person." He squeezed her hand while her beautiful blue eyes reminded him of the Missouri sky, his motherland that he'd never appreciated more than now. "What would bring you joy?"

She shrugged. "I don't know. Bringing joy to others?"

"You seemed to like cooking and baking with your grandmother the day before yesterday."

She chuckled as she leaped to her feet and reeled in another fish, a perch this time. "That's a shocker. But after you explained that cooking is like chemistry when we baked the Sweethearts Pie, something just clicked. I found out I can be good at it. Even enjoy it. Thank you."

His insides warmed more than from that mint-flavored tea before. "I'm glad if I could help."

"But… cooking is not heroic."

Mikhail coughed. "It's a much-needed profession. I'm sure your great-grandmother would be proud of you no matter what you did for a living. As long as you did it with love."

Adding bait to her line, Vera smiled at the gentleman. "I think one of the reasons she fell in love with my great-grandfather was because he treated her as an equal. He admired her plane designs, her courage. While he must've worried sick about her risking her life eight times every night, he never tried to stop her." Her

expression turned pensive as she took out salami sandwiches from the bag.

That was admirable indeed. Maverick had never considered himself sexist, but he didn't know whether he'd be able to do the same with Vera. He'd go crazy with worry.

"There's a Russian saying that men love with their eyes and women with their ears." Mikhail took out a sandwich, too.

"That means the men are visual, attracted to beauty, while women often just need someone to listen to them," Vera hurried to explain. "My great-grandmother called my great-grandfather her best friend and her biggest supporter in her letters. She said some things are so rare that we value them more. Diamonds. Gold. Being understood."

He couldn't agree more.

Being understood and, okay, being admired was what he'd always wanted, too. Vera had also been his best friend, his biggest supporter for him to follow his dream. He'd been too selfish to appreciate it at the time.

They took another break for snacks.

"It would be good to go to *banya* tomorrow," Mikhail said as he munched on a ham sandwich.

Maverick tried to place the word. "Banya?"

"It's like a sauna." An adorable blush covered her cheeks again. "Of course, men and women go separately."

"Of course." Maverick never understood the point of sitting for a long time and perspiring. But it might be part of the culture, so he didn't want to offend.

"If you're up for it, I have plenty of birch *veniks* ready," Mikhail offered as he got up and stretched.

"Veniks?" Maverick looked at Vera for an explanation.

She wrinkled her forehead. "Hmm. How to explain? Well, it's birch twigs tied together. In summer, people use fresh ones, in winter dry ones."

"Why do you need them in a sauna? To sweep floors?"

She laughed as she handed him the Thermos again. "No. One sort of hits themselves with it, or other people do it."

His brows shot up. Thankfully, he wasn't drinking tea at the time, or he could've sputtered. "Why would anyone do that?"

"It's like a massage, I guess." She shrugged.

He did his best to wrap his mind around it and failed, so he just took a sip of mint-flavored hot liquid.

By dusk, Maverick knew more details about Mikhail than he'd ever wanted to, including his career, illnesses, and all the vegetables he was growing on his dacha. However, the man had a sense of humor, too, and Maverick and Vera laughed at more than a few of his jokes.

Mikhail started gathering supplies. "Time to go. Days in winter are short, and we want to make it to the car while there's still daylight. I'll put the auger in the car and will be back."

Maverick was gathering the fishing rods together when a shout chilled his blood.

"*On tonet!*"

Vera's eyes went huge. "Someone is drowning. We've got to help!" She jerked in the direction of the voice.

Maverick's heart dropped to the ice.

She could go under freezing water herself!

CHAPTER TWENTY-ONE

MAVERICK SNATCHED Vera's hand. "Wait. He might've gone underwater because the ice at that part of the lake was too thin, after all. Let me go first." He picked up the flotation device.

She glared at him as she jerked her hand free and grabbed the rope. "Right. I weigh much less than you do. It's safer for me to go."

She raced toward the cries.

"No! You shouldn't risk your life." Everything inside screamed in protest as he sprinted as fast as his leg would allow. He saw more ice packs in his near future.

The need to keep her safe was multiplied by the craving to be the one to save the day.

"I can say the same about you. Let's pray to God and work together." She pulled a phone from her pocket but put it back as a bearded guy close by was already calling for help.

Other men were rushing to the large hole in the ice that had somehow swallowed the fisherman, but Maverick and Vera were the closest.

"We should crawl." She dropped onto the ice. "To be on the safe side."

She had a point.

He followed suit, grimacing as pain shot through his leg. Adrenaline pumped in his veins. Air whooshed out of his lungs when a man's head appeared in the water. Thankfully, the guy didn't sink and stop breathing, though being in the icy water was dangerous by itself.

"I'm worried about him having hypothermia," Vera whispered nearby.

She started saying something in Russian to the guy, and as Maverick moved forward, he had to admit he did need her to complete this rescue. Once they were close enough, she tied a knot on the rope and threw it to the drowning man while Maverick threw the flotation device.

In desperation, Maverick watched as the guy tried to grasp the knot, but his hands were obviously too cold and didn't want to move. No wonder, as in cold water a human body was losing heat thirty-two times faster than in the cold air.

He glanced back. Three more men crawled behind him. One of them was shouting something.

"He's suggesting forming a human chain," Vera interpreted. "One person will hold onto the ankles of the person in front of him. And so on."

"Sounds good to me. They aren't going to let go of you, are they?" He looked into the beautiful face of the person whom he could trust with his life.

"No. And I'm not letting go of you, either." The promise seemed to come from her heart.

He was close to the large dark circle of water now.

So close.

Just as her fingers wrapped around his ankles, he slipped the knot over the guy's head and then down his arms, his own fingers going nearly numb from freezing water.

This was going to be one hard-earned dinner.

Maverick shook off the strange thought as he pulled on the rope. As the rope tightened, she kept her promise. Grateful for all the weight training he'd done, he pulled again, his muscles straining.

One more time!

The guy was out of the water!

Beads of cold sweat formed on Maverick's forehead as he dragged the man along the ice, then got up and helped him do the same. Other fishermen, including Mikhail, wrapped the shivering guy in blankets, saying something in loud voices. His teeth were chattering so badly they gave out a staccato.

"They say they are going to take him someplace warm," Vera said. "And he didn't go underwater because the ice was thin but because he slipped and fell inside. Still, I'm glad we took precautions."

As adrenaline ebbed away and exhaustion started taking its place, Maverick realized three things.

First, he could finally understand the attraction of banya/sauna, though without the birch-twig massage.

Second, who needed extreme sports when one could risk their life just going fishing?

And third—the most important one. He might be walking on thin ice in his relationship with Vera, but he never wanted to let go of her, either.

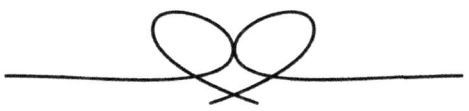

Everyone unanimously decided to stay indoors the next day. Maybe because Mikhail had received a talk down from Vera's

grandmother who'd been none too pleased with her granddaughter taking such risks.

The good part was the fishermen knew each other, and Mikhail reported the guy who'd nearly drowned was fine. Not only hadn't he gotten pneumonia but also he didn't even catch a cold. He'd attributed it to a certain amount of vodka in his system at the time, though Vera disagreed. The guy was fishing again, and Vera said a fervent prayer for him to be more careful this time.

Vera and the rest sat down to the scrumptious dinner of ukha and fried fish with potatoes and pickles and sauerkraut at Mikhail's apartment. She gave sincere thanks for being alive and for the people she cared about being alive, too.

Mikhail mumbled something about going on sleighs. As much fun as that sounded, with the way things were going lately, their horses would get spooked or the sleigh would get disconnected somehow.

Her grandmother said grace, as usual, and all of them echoed her amen.

Vera's heart swelled when Mikhail served her grandmother fish and seemed to catch her every word. When they'd cooked earlier, Vera had been impressed that he hadn't shied away from the kitchen but fried fish like a pro.

And now, a certain warmth in the kitchen didn't come from the stove, and Vera smiled at a gleam she hadn't seen in her grandmother's eyes before. Did Grandma find a man she was truly fond of?

She caught Maverick looking at the elderly couple with a smile as if he thought the same thing before his gaze shifted to her. Just the soft, admiring look in his eyes turned her insides to mush, and she busied herself with the delicious fish soup. Then pleasant tingles traveled over her skin when the rye bread was passed and Maverick's fingertips touched hers.

Maybe away from his familiar surroundings, in a foreign land, he was learning to accept help. He was learning he didn't have to be the leader of the pack. He couldn't do everything on his own.

If he'd tried to rescue the man yesterday on his own, he could've drowned, and she shivered at the thought. Similarly, for some time he'd been drowning in bitter disappointment after his accident.

She helped herself to fried fish after the first course while the guys took away the empty plates. Maverick announced he was going to take dishwashing duty tonight since he hadn't cooked.

She sat up straighter as something occurred to her.

Was she drowning in distrust, too, since she'd avoided getting close to anyone after people she'd loved had betrayed her? Freezing her heart seemed easier than risking suffering again.

"How about going to the theater tonight?" Mikhail helped Vera serve tea.

"Oh yes." Grandma beamed, giving an eager girlish clap of her hands. "I'd love that."

A longing unraveled in Vera's heart as if she were finding more pieces of herself.

The theater had always held a soft spot in her heart because it was a connection to one of her ancestors. She'd even tried to sign up for the acting club in school, but she wasn't good at acting. At all.

She rubbed her forehead.

Maverick was right. She didn't need to live the life of her ancestors to claim her legacy. She could create her own while still enjoying parts of theirs.

Though she missed having a gun with her, she nodded to the theater suggestion. Maverick nodded, too, probably for her sake.

So in the evening, Vera found herself quietly translating a play into English when the lights were out until people around her started telling her to stop.

"It's okay," Maverick whispered to her, his breath hot on her skin. His fingers laced through hers, making her pulse accelerate.

There was something different about seeing a live performance on stage instead of seeing it recorded in the movies, and she shifted closer to him, glad they could share this experience, though the scent of his spicy cologne affected her too much. She tucked the memory inside her, in case they went their separate ways back in Missouri.

The thought stung, but she resolved to enjoy what she had now. Her grandmother sat to her right, mesmerized by the show, and Mikhail seemed mesmerized by her.

If her great-grandmother could risk a romance across the ocean—could try to build in her heart a bridge half the earth long—maybe there was hope for Vera and Maverick, after all.

When the couple kissed on the stage, she didn't need to translate.

It was an international language of love.

The language her heart was speaking now.

The next morning, they all arrived in Moscow.

The capital had a lot to offer, and Maverick hoped it was safe enough for them to be there by now.

Besides, his sister had called him and said she'd love to meet him there in a few days.

The third reason, that Mrs. Tsareva had not just one but five pen pals here, became unexpectedly irrelevant. She'd invited Mikhail on the trip, and he'd declared he'd wanted to visit the capital for years.

Maverick smiled as they walked to the railway station exit and Mrs. Tsareva had her hand in the crook of Mikhail's elbow while he carried her luggage. Snowflakes danced in the air, decorating

people's clothes and hair with a fragile dust. A few snowflakes landed on Vera's eyelashes, framing her beautiful eyes in a delicate lace.

"I'm hoping for the sound of wedding bells," she whispered as she leaned to him. Her gaze darted around, then returned to her grandmother, and then to him.

A pleasant wave went through him as her gloved fingers settled in the crook of his arm, too. Even through the fabric, he could feel her warmth.

"Me, too." He meant it for more reasons than one.

Soon the taxi took them to the hotel he'd insisted on paying for. Well, technically he'd given money for his and Vera's rooms to Mikhail so there wouldn't be a paper trail for either of them. Mikhail had insisted on paying for Vera's grandmother's room. Avoiding the paper trail by paying in cash had been one of the reasons they'd rented apartments previously while booking hotel rooms would've been more convenient. That, and Mrs. Tsareva's affinity for cooking.

Bright and noisy, the city presented a fascinating mix of astonishing classic elegance and modern buildings. The next days passed in a whirlwind, leaving him feeling something akin to a male and older equivalent of Alice in (Winter) Wonderland. It was a different world here.

After a few museums, Mrs. Tsareva suggested for the night out they could enjoy one of Moscow's most famous cultural treasures—the ballet.

So they did.

Illuminated in the dark, the Bolshoi Theater sparkled like a precious jewel in the city's crown. Behind a frozen fountain, its façade offered striking white columns, statues, and elaborate ornaments. Thanks to his cowboy origins, he especially liked the *quadriga*, or a chariot, drawn by four horses on the rooftop.

Inside, the opulent interior nearly blinded him. From luxurious balconies to the gigantic chandelier and ornaments on the ceiling, no expense had been spared.

While he'd never understood ballet—frankly, hadn't tried to—he realized it could be a big deal. Besides, seeing the fascination on Vera's face as she watched the *Swan Lake* performance was priceless.

As he looked around, his eyes widened at how mesmerized the audience seemed to be with ballerinas fluttering on the stage like butterflies, or in this case, swans. He squirmed in his seat and watched that fluttering for some time. When he slid his arm around Vera's shoulders and she leaned into him, it made everything much better.

There was also a big advantage that dancing didn't require translation.

How different Vera's talented ancestor's life could've been if she'd been born free. Maybe she could've even performed in the renowned theater in front of tsars. Instead, she'd suffered for wanting to marry the man she'd loved.

His life was indeed filled with privilege. But, as his mother'd said, privilege came with responsibility. How could he use his privilege—whatever was left from his fame—for something good?

His siblings' idea about the camp for foster children appeared in his mind. A lot of his fans had been teenage boys. His thoughts moved to his brother, Kade, who'd nearly ended up on the wrong side of the law before Maverick's family had adopted him. Then to Vera's half brother whom she'd had to arrest for the auto theft. Then to the teenager whom she'd tried to help and who'd been shot.

Now he could understand why Kade had been so passionate to have the camp for foster teens at the ranch.

Maybe Maverick could use his authority to influence their lives for the better? He could also organize Christmas-gift drives for

older people in town, and he was sure Vera and her grandmother would be happy to join and do some pastry baskets.

The ideas could be endless. He just needed the will to do it.

As his mind wandered and his eyelids grew heavy, he was proud of himself that by the *antract*—a very welcome break in the middle of the performance—he was still awake. He exchanged glances with Mikhail as the lights turned on and everyone got up from their seats. They understood each other without words.

"Wasn't it great?" Vera's eyes were sparkling as their group descended the marble staircase.

"Oh yes." Looking into those eyes, he made a mental note to take her to the New York City ballet the first chance he got.

"It's the world's biggest ballet company. Over two hundred dancers!" she simply gushed. "It's one of the most renowned ballet companies in the world."

Mikhail nodded, obviously taking pride. "The company was founded in 1776. The performances were held in a private home at first. Then the company acquired the Petrovka Theater. It was destroyed by the fire, then replaced by the New Arbat Theatre."

"Wasn't it burned in the Napoleon invasion and then built again?" Mrs. Tsareva touched the banisters in thought.

"Yes, indeed. It went through many rebuildings and renovations." Mikhail beamed with knowledge.

Maverick's hand wrapped around the banister's smooth surface as if having a handshake with renewed hope. Then he touched his scars.

If this amazing beauty could be destroyed in the fire several times and rebuilt again and again to the level of something astonishing, maybe he could do the same.

Was this a sign from God?

Maybe there were other signs from God before, but now, Maverick was ready to listen.

To listen without the growl of motors and the luring song of fame being louder in his mind than the voice of God.

CHAPTER TWENTY-TWO

THEN THERE WAS OPERA.

The singing was in Italian, and Maverick's knowledge of Italian was limited by *buenosera, senora*, and *amore mio*. However, that meant they were on equal footing because Vera didn't speak Italian, either.

Vera explained to him the plot based on the booklet description they'd received, but he felt his eyelids getting heavier by the moment. He did his best to keep them open.

Oh man.

At the end, as he helped her put on her coat he asked how she liked it.

Her smile looked a bit forced this time. "It was, um, great."

It dawned on him. "You're not into opera, are you?"

"No, but they have such wonderful voices here, and…" She blinked. "I thought you were."

He chuckled. So they did this for each other, thinking the other one loved it.

Nearby, Mrs. Tsareva and Mikhail seemed to be having the same conversation as she shrugged into the coat he held for her.

"There was something I loved, though." Vera smiled as they walked to the exit. "That beautiful, romantic scene when the hero serenaded the heroine while she stood at the balcony."

The next morning, they visited the Kremlin and toured the churches behind its walls. As he studied historical frescoes and listened to the history of the golden-domed churches, he stood in awe of how much more was beyond the Red Square he was used to seeing on TV.

Hmm. How often in his life had he failed to look behind someone's walls to discover sometimes beauty, sometimes tragedy?

His leg was thankfully doing better, so all of them bundled up in layers of clothing to explore the city on foot and admire the numerous cathedrals. The city held an amazing quantity of restaurants, too, and one could have a culinary trip around the world easily. He tried *shashlik, kulichi*, and enjoyed pizza again.

They stopped in a Georgian café that smelled of spices and cooked meat and ordered *kharcho*—beef soup—and *khachapuri*— a cheese-filled bread. Now he knew Georgia wasn't just a state in the US.

In the evening, as they drank tea with *vareniki*—boiled dumplings stuffed with cheese, fruits, or other fillings—in the cozy hotel restaurant, they discussed which one of many museums to visit tomorrow. Apparently, one could find hundreds, if not a thousand years of masterpieces on display in this city.

But as he looked into Vera's eyes, he knew he'd already found the most precious masterpiece he'd ever encounter.

In the afternoon, Maverick's heart ached when he met his sister at the airport. He missed Jenna so much, and not only because they'd been bonded by the same secret once. They shared the same

qualities of wanderers who didn't want to admit they'd wandered too. They were the only siblings who were still searching for something—or someone.

The image of Vera appeared in front of his eyes. Or maybe he was just a fool who didn't realize what he'd wanted was right in front of him until it was too late.

Jenna's face lit up when she saw him. In the few times they'd met after the European races or when she'd sneaked into the family weddings, she'd worn a disguise, including a couple of times being dressed as a man.

So his eyes widened at her short-cropped raven-black hair with bangs falling onto her hazel eyes. Maybe she'd decided to be herself because a white scarf hid the bottom half of her face, and the hood of her oatmeal-hued coat hid most of the rest.

The heels of her matching boots that reached her knees clicked against the tile as she hurried to him. She only had one purse and a carry-on. She'd always traveled light.

Jenna hugged him, and they hurried to the exit, not wasting time on small talk out in the open but settling into a familiar routine.

Growing up, he'd looked up to her. They all did. She'd been such a bright student there'd been no doubt she'd become a valedictorian, and so she had. He'd imagined her becoming a professor at some prestigious university, winning awards.

She'd chosen a path none of their family had expected.

Vera glided to them in a rental car nearly as soon as they exited. While Jenna's eyes darted around, he put her carry-on in the trunk fast. They slipped inside the vehicle in silence.

As the car took off, Jenna smiled at Vera. "It's good to see you again after so many years."

"What about me?" He feigned offense.

"Well, I just saw you half a year ago. I haven't recovered yet." Jenna nudged him with her elbow.

Slipping into the familiar camaraderie they'd had as children felt good. "I missed you, sis," he whispered.

Her eyes turned sad. "I missed you, too. More than you can imagine."

The way from the Sheremetyevo airport to Moscow took much less than the previous time by taxi, and then they stopped at the restaurant Jenna suggested.

Once they were seated, he understood why. The small, dimly lit restaurant was away from the popular and overcrowded area. Exactly the place where his sister preferred to meet. Though she'd never been to Moscow, she'd obviously done her research online.

As usual, she chose a booth from which she could see both exits and sit with her back to the wall. Vera seemed to agree with her choice.

He helped the women shrug out of their coats, and they ordered drinks.

"To clear the air, my profession is a tracker. I track down people and/or valuables. I'm the human equivalent of a German shepherd," Jenna said without much emotion.

Vera blinked. "Oh. I didn't ask."

Well, straightforwardness ran in their family. At least, when it came to females.

Jenna's lips curled up. "I don't usually disclose that information. But if my brother trusts you, I trust you, too."

Vera squirmed in her seat a little. "I'm honored."

He wondered what his sister thought of Vera. Her approval had long been important to him. So, when Jenna caught his gaze, then flicked her eyes at Vera and gave a tiny nod, he leaned against the back of his chair and could breathe easier.

Jenna skimmed the menu. "It's all Greek to me. Or, okay, Russian in this case. Any recommendations?"

"Ukha sounds good to me," Vera started, looking more relaxed now as if knowing she'd passed the test. "Blinchiki with caviar,

too. *Zharkoye*, which is fried beef with potatoes. Beef stroganoff…"

"Oh, let me explain." He was eager to show off his newfound language, so he explained what ukha, blinchiki, and beef stroganoff were. "I'll take ukha and baked salmon with caviar. Sounds especially good considering we didn't have to risk going into icy water for it."

Vera's ears pinked. "Ice fishing is rather safe, for the most part. I, um, don't want your sister to think I made you risk your life for fish."

Jenna's eyes sparkled. "I want to hear all about it."

The waitress appeared with their drinks, and they placed orders. For some time, he talked about his visit to Russia, all the things experienced and lessons learned.

Then their food arrived, and the ukha's aroma was indescribable. He savored every spoonful of it, though he still preferred the one Mrs. Tsareva had cooked. Jenna talked about some of her travels and adventures that were safe to share. Vera discussed her ancestors, and Jenna seemed fascinated.

Relaxing into the warm atmosphere, Maverick simply enjoyed being with the two women so important to him, savored seeing them comfortable with each other. They remained for some time after the plates were cleared because none of them wanted to leave.

He knew Jenna was only going to stay for one day, and regret tugged at him. She'd never stayed in one place for long, and he wanted her to. He could show her so much in Moscow. He still needed to tell her so much, too.

Finally, they filed from the warm restaurant into the cold air. "You're going to stay at the hotel with us, right?" he asked his sister as he opened the rental car's door for her.

She hesitated. Then she nodded and hurried into the rear passenger seat. He took the one in the front, in case Vera needed

him to guide her. Though the traffic was busy, Vera drove with enviable ease.

While he couldn't even drive on the country roads.

Pain knifed him.

After some time, he noticed both Vera and Jenna had tensed. "What's going on?"

"I believe we have a tail." Vera frowned as she slipped into a small spot in the left lane.

He glanced back at his sister, who nodded. "A dark sedan with tinted windows."

Premonition tightened his gut as he looked at Vera again. "Can you... can you lose them?"

"I'm trying to! There's too much traffic. We can't go to the hotel before we lose the tail."

Eyes narrowed, he pulled up the city map on his phone. "We need to get into a less congested area." GPS probably wouldn't be much help now, so he found their location on the map.

She exited the road without putting the blinker on while cars around her honked.

"It's probably because of the case I just wrapped up. I shouldn't have come here." Jenna groaned. "Some people weren't... happy."

"Don't worry about it, sis. We had some issues back in the States, too." He sent his sister an encouraging smile, then guided Vera the best he could.

"I think we lost them," Jenna said carefully.

"I don't know for how long. Maverick, we need to trade places." Vera breathed out, her tense shoulders still hunched up to her ears.

"What? No!" Getting air into his lungs became difficult.

"Please?" Vera's pleading eyes skewered him. "I can't do this anymore. I need your help."

He had to come through for her. "Okay." His pulse went into overdrive. He'd never had to trade places with the driver while being on the road, and he hoped he'd never have to do it again.

"There they are again!" Jenna screamed.

The motor growled, pumping fuel into his veins as he floored the gas pedal. He had to do this.

"Please!" he sent up a prayer.

Then he concentrated on being one with the car, on the energy and exhilaration he received from high speed. Adrenaline surged through his veins, bringing memories different from his accident.

When he was capable.

CHAPTER TWENTY-THREE

THE STEERING WHEEL seemed to be the extension of Maverick.

Vera guided him, and they entered a long tunnel. He was pushing the car to its limit as he weaved between cars, then used the open space to speed up even more. Just how he'd explain it to the police if stopped, he didn't know. When he left the tunnel, he took turns at high speed. Several times, the car nearly skidded, but he managed to keep it on the slick winter roads.

He turned so many times he lost count while his heart thudded in his ears.

Risky, so risky.

Worry for Vera and Jenna made him tighten his fingers on the smooth steering wheel. But this was what he knew, what he'd once been so great at. Excitement pumped fuel in his blood. And he felt liquid like gasoline and so light that it seemed one moment more and he'd take off and fly. Another spike of adrenaline took him to the familiar high, and he felt alive—really alive—again.

This time, it wasn't about winning or losing but saving the lives of two people dear to him.

Doing what mattered.

And okay, being himself again. He wasn't beyond repair, after all, didn't have to be discarded like the cars after an accident smashed so badly they had to be totaled.

When it started getting dark, Vera touched his hand. "I think we're fine now."

"Yes!" He did a mental fist pump.

He looked back at Jenna, who seemed to shrink inside herself, and his heart sank as exhilaration leaked out from him like gasoline from a broken tank. Adrenaline ebbed away, too, leaving worry to take the driver seat.

"Please let me take you to the hotel." He tried, though he knew what her answer was going to be.

She shook her head. "I might've brought danger to you. Take me to the airport. Please."

Of course, his sister was leaving because she loved him, but it didn't make it any easier.

Hours later, Vera woke up and blinked a few times. It was still dark, and the room was quiet.

She stretched, snuggled under the warm bedspread, and considered going back to sleep when yesterday's chase made her shiver.

No, she wouldn't be able to go back to sleep now. Yet her limbs asked her to stay in bed a while longer. So she turned on the nearby lamp to cast a soft glow, then reached for her cell phone on the nightstand. She checked her email until she found the email from her friend, Gwendolyn.

Smiling, Vera opened it and glanced through. Gwendolyn had started working for Maverick's family officially as a nanny and unofficially as the children's bodyguard. So far, everything seemed to be peaceful except for the children's mischief.

They'd even tried to set her up with a few cowboys at the ranch, but so far, Gwendolyn had remained a confirmed bachelorette. Well, if Vera knew anything about those children, if Gwendolyn continued taking care of them for a significant amount of time, she wouldn't stay single long.

When Vera made it to the last part of the email, her jaw dropped. She'd arranged for the DNA test results to be mailed to the ranch, care of her friend as Vera couldn't wait to learn the result.

Now she felt like she assumed the man felt when he'd been submerged into icy water. Plunging into that cold, she couldn't breathe.

Slowly, she sat up on the bed, took a deep breath, and read the words again. It shouldn't have been such a shocker. She'd suspected it, hadn't she?

That was why she'd done the DNA test in the first place.

She rubbed her temples, headache brewing.

Now what? She needed to tell Maverick, and he wouldn't be happy she'd done this behind his back.

But when he heard the results…

Would he be glad?

Frustrated?

Angry?

Happy?

Only one way to find out.

First, she needed to do some research and make international calls. She slipped out of bed and changed her pajamas for jeans and a light sweater, then pulled out the chair near the desk. She considered ordering breakfast from room service, but her stomach seemed too queasy to accept food.

Sometime later, she rubbed her throbbing temples and leaned against the back of her chair.

Embry had a leave of absence for five months, she'd said, to take care of her sister in Maryland. After checking tickets to Maryland, Vera confirmed Embry had indeed gone there and stayed with her sister for five months. But the neighbors revealed it was the other way around, her sister had taken care of Embry while she'd been pregnant. She'd given birth to a baby girl and told her sister she'd put her baby up for adoption.

It had taken a lot of digging, but finally Vera found out Embry had a health scare around the same time Izzy had been abandoned. Thankfully, the scary diagnosis had turned out to be wrong.

By the time Vera applied makeup, footfalls in the neighboring room told her Maverick might be up. As she brushed her hair, she heard the water running next door.

Then the knock on his door and the female voice saying, "Room service" made Vera wince.

Her heartbeat picked up for several reasons as she waited for the footfalls to silence in the distance. An incoming text bleeped, and her pulse increased at Maverick's name on the screen. "If you're up, I'd love to have your company for breakfast."

"Thank you," she typed in.

She considered calling her grandmother, but this news was better told alone. She checked the hall for anything suspicious and dragged herself to his door. There she drew in a deep breath of air filled with a mixture of coffee aroma and faint fragrances of colognes and perfumes, then knocked on the door. "It's me."

He opened the door, smiled at her, and waved for her to enter. "Good morning. Come on in."

"Good morning." As she stepped inside, the coffee aroma intensified, mingling with the fresh croissant scent.

Just like hers, the room was done tastefully in earthy shades. Tawny-hued carpet matched the bedspread, and tortilla-colored curtains hugged the floor-to-ceiling window. With the sun up now, the view of Moscow was spectacular. A large rectangular mirror

made the room look bigger, as well, and a long wooden desk housed a flat-screen TV, a lamp, and a phone book.

A welcome addition was a coffee table with two chairs near the window. A tray was already on the coffee table.

He lifted the lid from one of the dishes. "Scrambled eggs with ham and mushrooms. I hope you'll like it. Thank you for having breakfast with me."

Something changed inside her. The domesticity, the normalcy of the scene felt surreal after yesterday's chase. After the news she needed to tell him.

She'd come close to losing him several times already. She'd come close to losing her own life several times, too.

He strode to her and kissed her cheek, making her heart flutter. The scent of his spicy cologne felt as familiar as her favorite perfume. And when he opened his arms and she walked into them, she knew she was home.

Despite being in a foreign country.

And that was how she knew.

She loved him.

Plain and simple.

The infatuation she'd had as a teen had grown into an overwhelming love.

But even as the exhilarating wave washed over her, her throat clogged up. Any time she'd loved someone, her trust had been betrayed. While Maverick wouldn't betray her, he'd leave her just like the others.

She'd seen the confidence with which he'd driven yesterday. He could return to the circuit now. Live his dream life again. And after the news she was going to tell him, he might be sharing that dream with a woman other than her. Just like before, there would be no place for Vera in his life.

She eased out of his embrace, and they sat down. While she had no appetite, it was unfair to snub his kind gesture.

So after saying grace, she poked at what usually was her favorite breakfast and made herself move a croissant past the lump in her throat. She chased it down with coffee and barely sensed the taste.

His eyes dimmed a little at her lack of appetite.

When he was done, she pushed her half-empty plate away.

"We need to talk."

A frown creased his forehead as he put the tray away on the table. "What happened? Are you okay?"

She searched for the right words. "Yes. It's about Izzy."

He leaped to his feet. "Something happened to her?" He lowered his voice as he glanced at the door.

She shook her head, reminding herself to keep her voice low, too. She didn't want to wake up her grandma and Mikhail—or any other hotel guests, for that matter.

What was the best way to break the news? Well, honesty should be the best policy.

She took a deep breath, the intoxicating scent of his cologne affecting her too much. "I–I did something without your permission. I used one of your hairs with a follicle and a swab from Izzy's cheek to send samples for DNA."

He stared at her as he sat down again. "I don't understand. Why would you do that?"

"Because I suspected Izzy might be your daughter."

His jaw slackened. "What? That... can't be."

"Remember, Rance never did a DNA test, which frankly was an oversight on his part. He just believed the note left with the baby."

"But she was left on Rance's doorstep!" Maverick stuttered and leaned against the counter.

"The rumor was that you weren't yourself after the accident. Besides, it was much easier to leave the baby with someone in the same city than fly to Missouri and get to the ranch. And based on

her social media, Embry did have an on-again, off-again relationship with Rance. Frankly, I don't think she was thinking straight at the time. She had a health scare and needed to find someone to take care of the child. Maybe something went wrong with her sister, and Embry couldn't ask her to do it."

He rubbed his forehead. "Hold on. Hold on. The time doesn't line up. I was with Embry a year and a half ago. Izzy was born nine months after I broke up with Embry. The note said Izzy was born premature."

Vera resisted the urge to roll her eyes at the same story her mother had used. "I talked to the pediatrician. Izzy doesn't look like a premature child."

He got up and started pacing the small room. "Do you… do you have the DNA test results?"

She rose to her feet and leaned against the desk. "I do. She *is* your daughter."

His face lit up. Then he froze. "I want to believe this. But I'm afraid to. Why didn't Embry tell me about Izzy's birth?"

"I don't know." Shivers prickled her arms. She chased them down with her hands. "That's a question you need to ask her. Maybe she was afraid you'd try to take Izzy away from her."

For a few moments, he stayed motionless. Then he rushed to her and lifted her up, stealing her breath away. "Do you understand what this means?"

Her head started spinning, and she couldn't say a word.

"I have a chance to bring her back! Or at least see her regularly. I talked to Rance yesterday, and he said how difficult parenting was for him…." He set her down and looked into her eyes. "And you helped this happen. How can I ever thank you?"

"You don't need to thank me." Her heart warmed for his joy, then shattered into a million pieces. This was probably what an emotional roller coaster felt like.

He was going to leave her, and she'd helped it happen. Acid seemed to rise from her stomach, and she started feeling nauseous. Still, she had no regrets.

She wanted him to be happy, and the light in his eyes indicated she'd done the right thing.

"I mean, I can see her grow up. I can be a real dad."

She needed to do something, to distract herself. So she turned away from him and picked up a glass with orange juice from the tray.

But her hand shook so badly she had to put it down. She turned around and touched the stubble on his face. "You *are* a real dad."

He studied her. "Yesterday, you didn't need me to drive, did you? You just... needed me to be able to do it again?"

She looked away, then met his gaze. "I knew you had it in you."

He was finding the road to himself; that much was clear. She should be thankful to God for it.

So what did it matter if that road didn't match with hers?

"Then you know me better than I know myself."

She committed his image to memory, never mind that it was already engraved on her heart. "I just believe in you. Always have. Always will."

And now she'd have to learn to live without him again.

But love had to be selfless, didn't it?

He rubbed his temples. "I have to go back to the US. For Izzy. I mean... You understand, right?"

"I do." Her heart squeezed.

She understood more than he'd ever know.

Despite the nausea, she was glad she didn't tell him about her feelings. That left him an open road.

He paced the room again, his limp much less evident now. "Rance is going to be devastated. Or maybe relieved? I have to

make this work. I might have to move to be closer to Embry and the baby."

Yep.

Vera was still in the room, but he was forgetting her already. She blinked fast to stop the tears. She should be glad for him. She'd sensed how much he'd wanted to be a father. How much he'd needed to.

It was one of the things that had helped him heal.

Her smile was wobbly as she worked up as much gratitude as she could. "I'll book us the tickets."

He stopped pacing. "Us?"

A lump formed in her throat. Even if he didn't care for her any longer, she had to go with him. She'd had her guesses about who'd caused his accident, but she needed proof. When he returned to the ranch, his life was going to be in danger again.

"Well, I was thinking of returning with you. I mean, Grandma hasn't done anything crazy so far, and Mikhail seems to be taken with her."

He rushed to her and hugged her in earnest. "I'm glad. I'd love to have you return with me."

A knock made them look toward the door. She gestured for him to wait, approached the door stealthily, and glanced in the peephole. She felt a little lighter when she saw it was her grandmother, and Vera flung the door open.

Vera's grandmother cleared her throat. "Um, am I interrupting something?"

Warmth rose inside Vera. She tucked her thick hair behind her ears and tipped up her chin to keep from going wobbly. "No, Grandma. We, um, just had breakfast. And we have some news."

As Maverick hurried to explain what had happened, one thought kept appearing in Vera's mind. She needed to wrap up the case. After that, she had to let Maverick go, to live the life he'd always wanted.

Even if it broke her heart for the second time.

After returning to Cowboy Crossing the next day, Vera squared her shoulders as she marched to Mrs. Dorotea's house. Even as her heart was aching from having to say goodbye to Maverick soon, even as her head was throbbing from jet lag, some things needed to be taken care of.

The sooner the better.

After she rang the doorbell, Mrs. Dorotea opened the door and waved her inside. She was wearing an apron, and flour smudged her wrinkled hands. "Oh, hon, great to have you back. Are you here to pick up Buddy? Tell your grandma I'll stop by soon."

Vera stepped inside, easing the door shut behind her. "Thank you for taking care of our cat. Oh, Grandma stayed in Russia for now."

"Such a pity. I was looking forward to talking to her." Mrs. Dorotea handed her the meowing feline. "And I didn't mind Buddy, hon. We became friends." She chuckled. "Buddies, really."

"You do love cats." Vera studied the older woman she thought she knew well. "That's why you let Buddy out before locking me in the basement and turning the gas on."

Mrs. Dorotea gasped. "What *are* you talking about?"

"I didn't think much of it at first. Buddy had escaped before when someone opened the door and we didn't notice. But then I remembered I heard him meowing when I was in the basement. No one left the house after that. He shouldn't have escaped." She pinned her neighbor with a stare.

"You're out of your mind." Grimacing, Mrs. Dorotea waved a hand. "Even if someone let Buddy out, why do you think it was me?"

"The lock wasn't tampered with. You've visited Grandma many times, stayed for hours. You could've gotten grandmother's keys when she was stuck with Buddy on the roof and made a duplicate. You know how to shoot a gun, so you could've been the one to shoot at Maverick. You were friends with the person who had the gun stolen. The one that was used to shoot at him."

"Seriously? Most of the population in the country knows how to use a gun. A lot of people in Cowboy Crossing are friends with that person. It's a small town, after all." Mrs. Dorotea shook her head vigorously, strands of thin hair getting out from her white bun. "Besides, why on earth would I harm Maverick? The only person who'd want to shoot at him is someone from the developers to get the land, to scare the family into signing the deal."

"That's what you wanted us to think. I forgot you used to work as a mechanic. You still stopped by sometimes when the tractors started breaking down. No one realized you were the one to cause the mechanical problems too. You were just an old lady, feeling lonely and trying to bide her time."

"Ridiculous." Mrs. Dorotea ducked her head, her fingers twitching toward the side table.

"I have you recorded near Maverick's car right before his accident." Vera bluffed while Buddy squirmed in her hands as if uncomfortable with the conversation.

"You won't be able to prove anything. I wore a good disguise." Then Mrs. Dorotea's hand flew to her mouth.

Vera did a mental fist pump. "It was because of your daughter, wasn't it? I'm sorry for your loss, but why go to such lengths as trying to kill Maverick? Because he discovered the affair and Maverick's father stopped funding you and your daughter's lifestyle? I researched the house you used to have before moving to a modest home in our neighborhood. It was opulent."

213

Mrs. Dorotea rubbed her eyes and whispered, "We had to sell it. Couldn't pay the mortgage any longer. She had to give up an expensive car. Maverick ruined everything."

Vera stepped closer, pity twisting her gut. "But why wait until now? Did you need to take your anger out on someone after Lenora's death?"

Mrs. Dorotea's eyes narrowed. "You don't know how that feels! How much it hurts! All I have left of her are the photos I keep in this box." She reached to the wooden box on the side table.

A moment later, a small gun appeared in her feeble hands. Apparently, the box held more than photos. "I didn't want to kill you, Vera. I still don't. But you started putting your nose where it didn't belong, and I was afraid you'd figure it out."

Dread pooled in the pit of Vera's stomach. And she'd thought Mrs. Dorotea wouldn't shoot her with Buddy in her hands. "You… you don't have to do this."

"You give me no other choice." The older woman sighed. "Pity, as I like your grandmother. She's fun to talk to, and she bakes great pies. Well, it's time to put the end to this."

Vera ducked as the shot rang out.

CHAPTER TWENTY-FOUR

Later, Vera tossed and turned most of the night in her room at her grandmother's house.

Once she'd revealed her plan to Maverick during their trip, talking him into it hadn't been easy. Of course, they'd gotten the police involved and she'd been wearing a wire and carrying a weapon in her purse, but he'd thought it was too risky. Only when she'd said she'd do it with or without his help had he agreed.

Her primary concern had been Buddy, but Vera didn't think Mrs. Dorotea would hurt the cat she'd loved so much.

Buddy, as if sensing Vera'd thought about him, jumped into bed and snuggled next to her. She stroked his soft fur, then hugged him close. "Sorry I put you in danger. Glad it's over, aren't you?"

Buddy meowed as if complaining that wasn't the welcome home he'd counted on.

Vera sighed. "I know. Me, either. I feel sorry for Mrs. Dorotea. But wanting to stay alive outweighed my empathy."

With the first rays of sunlight, she slipped out of bed and fed Buddy. Then she dressed. Tears burned her eyes as she touched the window Maverick had used to climb into her life. He'd leave soon.

Her heart ached. Losing him a second time was much more painful than the first time.

Downstairs, Buddy stretched on the kitchen floor, likely knowing she needed company, and she made hot tea. The mint-flavored scent, the kitchen interior, raspberry jam… Pretty much everything reminded her how much she missed her grandmother, how desperate she was for human connection, some physical comfort.

Talking over the phone wouldn't be the same as talking in person. She took several sips. Grandma always said a lot of issues could be solved with a hot cup of tea.

Vera placed the cup on the saucer with a rattle as she couldn't pour any more liquid past the lump in her throat. Some issues even tea couldn't solve.

She pulled her shoulders back, a decision forming up in her mind. As much as she loved her hometown, without her grandmother and Maverick, this place felt as empty as her heart.

It wasn't right to leave without saying goodbye to Maverick, but hadn't he done it to her once? Besides, he didn't need her any longer. His fabulous career and fatherhood awaited him.

So she'd wish him the best with a postcard or a phone call later.

Make it easier for him.

She leaned to the cat and scratched behind his ear. "I'm sorry to leave you again. But you understand, right? I'll have someone take care of you while I'm gone." She paused for a moment. "Someone who wouldn't try to murder me. Don't miss me too much, okay?"

Buddy got up and strode away, keeping his head high, unhappy at such a turn of events.

Vera winced. Maybe she should stay.

But her insides were getting emptier by the moment.

"Lord, what should I do?"

The doorbell was a welcome distraction. That might be Gwendolyn or... Could it be Maverick? She rushed to the hall, stumbled over Buddy, who meowed his complaint, righted herself, and looked into the peephole.

Then she froze.

This was the last person she'd expected to see.

Her mother.

Vera gestured for her mother to come in as her own eyebrows shot up at the large designer suitcase. "Are... are you going to stay here?"

Chuckling without mirth, her mother walked inside and put the expensive suitcase on the tiled floor. Her creamy designer coat with large buttons hugged her slim figure, as elegant as ever, her makeup was impeccable, and her short blonde hair was still stylish. But for the first time, guilt settled deep in her blue eyes. "No. Don't worry. I know we've got a lot to repair in our relationship. I *am* so sorry for all the mistakes I've made."

Something shifted inside Vera as she gestured for her to proceed. She took a place at the table, and her mother did the same.

Vera got up to make tea but was stopped with a wave of the hand. "I'm not staying for long."

Her mother never had.

Vera sank onto the chair again. Maybe this was her chance to get some answers. There was only one reason her mother told her father she was a preemie when she wasn't. "Why have you never told me that my dad, well, wasn't my biological dad? You knew you were pregnant with me when you married him, and you didn't tell him *then*."

Her face contorting, her mother wrung her hands, so different from her confident self. "I wanted you to have a father. To be happy."

"Was I..." Vera looked away. "An accident? With someone who ran fast when he found out you were pregnant?" She was

217

finally getting more scraps to piece together for the quilt of her life, but so far, it hadn't brought her warmth or peace.

Her mother's lips trembled. "I loved your father very much. And he loved me. I lost my head. I admit I shouldn't have. But I was young and in love."

"What…" Her throat closed. She struggled to get out the question she had to know. "What happened then?"

"He d–died in an accident a month after we met." Her voice broke.

There was a pause, and this time Vera didn't say anything. She could barely breathe.

"The next day, I found out I was pregnant."

Vera stared at her, trying to process everything. "So you married a different man?"

Her mother's lips thinned. "He knew I didn't love him the way he loved me, but he still wanted to marry me. After some time, I agreed. Things were different at the time. Babies out of wedlock weren't exactly met with open arms. I thought it would be easier for me to give you the future you deserved. And maybe even forget my loss."

Things started making more sense. "But I reminded you about your lost love all the time, right? That's why you threw yourself into your career. Why you spent so little time with me. Why Dad—or whatever the word is I should use now?—started treating me differently when he found out I wasn't his. Why he found a different woman, started a different family."

A miserable sigh seemed to deflate the last of her mother's strength. With it, her chest curved in, and her shoulders slumped. "I finally told him when you were a teen. He felt betrayed, and I couldn't blame him."

"Then you married again." Just like that, she'd started over. All emotions slipped from Vera's body, even anger.

"I couldn't survive being left behind. And I realized I wanted more children. I really did. It was my last chance. I wanted to give them the love I failed to give you." Tears sparkled in her eyes. "Can you ever forgive me?"

Vera got up and hugged her mother, for the first time feeling close to her. "You should've told me a long time ago."

"I didn't want to cause you pain." Her mother hugged her back, droplets of tears dampening the cheek held close to Vera's.

Vera withdrew to look into her eyes, her vision blurring. "Then why are you telling me now?"

"Because I was selfish not to tell you before. It wasn't your fault he died. I should've treasured you as a part of him left to me instead of making myself and you suffer. I'm so sorry I pushed you away. Have been doing it for years. If it's not too late to ask, I want to be in your life. Will you let me?" She dabbed at her eyes with a paper napkin from the table.

Vera concentrated on breathing. This was a lot to take in.

All the family secrets.

All the pain they'd caused.

Her mother got up. "I decided to go to Russia. I need to be closer to my mother, too. I have two tickets for business class. I know it was presumptuous of me, but… Will you go with me?"

Vera finally found her tongue. "Yes and yes."

Her mother hugged her, and for a few moments, they wept for all the things lost, cleansing the dirty secrets with tears.

Buddy walked into the kitchen, and Vera lifted him as tears streaked her face. "Sorry, Buddy, you'll have to survive without us for some time more."

Getting Vera's suitcase ready didn't take much time, especially considering she hadn't unpacked everything yet. Strangely, though she'd packed the same amount of clothes for the previous trip, the suitcase felt much heavier. Her shoulders drooped, her mood so different from when she'd left with Maverick and Grandma.

She called Gwendolyn and asked her to take care of Buddy. Then, after they disconnected, Vera dressed in a sweater and jeans and, despite her queasy stomach, managed to have a snack without really tasting it.

Her phone played a melody, and her heart squeezed when Maverick's name appeared on the screen. She rubbed the tightness in her chest as she stared at the screen.

She couldn't talk to him now.

She was too afraid to stay.

Maverick frowned at his phone. Then he winced. What was he thinking, calling so early? She might still be jet lagged and sleeping in.

But when she didn't return his calls four hours later, he felt ill at ease. Though the case was wrapped up, what if something had happened to her?

Without a second thought, he jumped into the car and drove to her grandmother's place. He rushed to the door, his healing leg moving much faster than before, and rang the doorbell.

Silence.

A shiver ran down his spine over what had happened the previous time she hadn't answered the doorbell. But the curtains were drawn this time.

Could she have left somewhere?

He slapped himself on the forehead. Of course, she must've gone grocery shopping after a long absence.

As he climbed inside his vehicle again, his phone played a rap song. Air whooshed out of his lungs when he saw her name on the screen.

Thankfully, he worried for nothing.

He swiped the phone screen to answer. "I'm so glad you called me."

"Oh, good. I mean, great. I mean…" Her voice sounded distant. Background noise scrambled it. People talking? Well, yes, if she called from a grocery store.

But she didn't need to cook tonight.

He was going to invite her to dinner. His family could help him set up a romantic dinner for two, and he'd do his best to make it special. One day, he'd love to take her on a tour of the fountains in Kansas City she'd mentioned. Maybe even go scuba diving like her grandmother had. Missouri had so much to offer, and while he'd traveled the world for car races, he hadn't explored treasures in his home state.

He'd love to do that with Vera. He wanted to share so much with her. Maybe even a lifetime?

Maybe they could fly to see Izzy together tomorrow. His heartbeat quickened. He couldn't believe two of his dreams—the ones he didn't even know about until now—could come true at the same time.

"How do you feel about—"

She interrupted him. "I'm sorry. I've got to go. I need to go through customs."

His brows shot up. "Customs? Where are you?"

"I'm at the airport." Her words, flat as they sounded, struck him like a slap. "That's the reason I'm calling you."

He started the engine as if that could supply fuel to his brain, too, to comprehend the situation. "What? You decided to fly to see Izzy already? But I thought about doing that together tomorrow."

"No. I… I'm going to stay with Grandma." Her voice dropped so low he had to strain his ears to hear her, especially with other people talking near her.

"But…" Mrs. Tsareva? "But she's on the other side of the world in Moscow!"

"Well, actually, she and Mikhail went back to his town. But yes, still the other side of the world. Listen, our paths intertwined for some time while you needed me. But now you can return to the stellar career you worked so much for. You'll be able to be with your daughter. When you're with Izzy, I've seen a light in your eyes I've never seen before. Not even when you won your first race. You'll make a great father."

"Thank you, but—" His mind whirled. "Hold on. I have something to tell you. I've got a lot of things to tell you."

How could she not understand he needed her more than ever? Though he hadn't realized it himself until now.

How could she leave?

He clenched his grip on the steering wheel as he drove off, remembering that was what he'd done once. Left her at eighteen without even saying goodbye.

But this was different.

His heart dropped to a place somewhere between the accelerator and the brake pedal.

"I really, truly wish you the best. I want you to be happy so much. And now I've got to go." She disconnected.

With a tight band around his lungs, he called her on the hands-free phone as he sped up on the road leading to the nearest international airport. Customs! She was already going through customs! He slammed his foot harder on the gas. He had to make it before she left.

Please pick up. Please pick up!

But she didn't.

Thoughts whirled in his mind as he touched his stubble. His scars didn't bother him much any longer. He could have plastic surgery if he wanted to remove them. And Vera didn't mind his scars at all.

Loving someone didn't make one weak.

And in reality, Maverick should let himself be weak because God was strong. There was nothing wrong with asking God for help.

Vera was right. There was nothing wrong with accepting other people's help. In fact, it had often been necessary, like when they'd rescued the drowning man. Had Maverick tried to do it on his own, he could've gone under the ice, too.

Being manly didn't mean always being the first, always being in charge. Relying on God, relying on the people God had sent him didn't make him any less of a man. But his pride and stubbornness might have.

He made a sharp turn, the road map of his life becoming clearer than ever. He'd concentrated so much on winning that he'd forgotten to humble himself.

Winning was everything. Losing was unacceptable.

But like Vera had said, wins could become losses, and losses could become wins. He'd learned more from his failures than from his wins. But somewhere along the way, he'd lost himself. Now he was finding himself again.

And just as he realized he was about to lose Vera, he realized a simple truth.

He loved her.

CHAPTER TWENTY-FIVE

THE NEXT EVENING, Vera did her best to keep up with the fluent Russian conversation between her grandmother, her mother, and Mikhail at the dinner table that was overflowing with food in his apartment. But her thoughts kept returning to Maverick and Izzy.

By now, he was probably with his daughter. An image of him holding the baby and kissing her soft hair appeared in front of Vera's eyes, and Vera could nearly smell the baby shampoo. Giggles rang in her ears.

A longing to be with them unraveled her strength with an unparalleled force. She knew now, with absolute certainty, what road she wanted to take. She wanted to be a wife and a mother, among other things.

And even if she didn't give birth to Izzy, it was impossible not to fall in love with that precious baby. In some way also because she was part of the man she loved.

Her grandmother touched Vera's elbow, and Vera realized Grandma was asking something. She forced a smile. "What did you say, Grandma?"

"I was asking whether you'd like more bread. But you're not with us right now, are you?" Attentive gray eyes studied her.

"Sorry, I…" A lump clogging her throat prevented her from saying anything else.

She didn't need to.

Grandma patted her hand. "You miss him, don't you?"

It was no use trying to hide anything from Grandma.

Vera sighed as she got up and placed her plate in the sink. Despite the delicious dinner of *kotlety*, fried potatoes, and salad Mikhail had cooked, her appetite seemed to have stayed with her heart, an ocean away. "More than you can imagine. But I'm not what he wants."

"How do you know? Have you asked him?" Her mother handed her an empty plate.

Mikhail polished off his kotlety, and as she picked up his plate, too, sadness settled in his eyes. "Men have difficulty expressing their feelings. But it doesn't mean we don't have them."

Well, whatever feelings Maverick had for her were not enough.

"I'll wash the dishes." Vera cleaned the table. "I know Maverick. He wanted to be a race car driver since he was a boy. It's his passion. It's his dream."

"I understand you don't want to follow him, right?" Grandma tucked leftovers into containers.

"First, he never asked. Second, I don't think I'd fit in that world. Third, Rance's affections change fast. Maverick and Embry might try to build a family together for the baby's sake. They were attracted to each other once, after all. I'm not going to stand in the way of that."

No matter how much staying away was going to hurt.

Her heart ached, but she tipped her chin and filled the yellow sponge with a cleaning solution that smelled like watermelon, then scrubbed the dishes. The mundane task soothed her raw nerves just a tad.

Then she turned around as she realized something.

She'd tried to push the boundaries, to follow her ancestors' footsteps. Her great-grandmother was a pilot and a hero. Her grandmother had been a successful business owner before retiring. Her mother was a doctor.

But maybe Vera didn't need to measure up. She didn't need to prove her worth. Maverick had a point. She needed to do something that brought her—and others—joy.

"I'm sorry if I disappointed you, Mom."

Her mother's eyes widened. "You never disappointed me. I'm proud of who you are. You became a wonderful person despite my lack of parenting." She sent a guilty glance Grandma's way. "Thank you for stepping in and doing what I couldn't."

While Vera's heart warmed, confusion settled in as she rinsed a few more dishes. "I mean you told me so many times I could be anything—an astronaut, a doctor, a pilot—that anything less seemed to be unacceptable. I tried to want to be a doctor to make you proud of me, to make you love me. I really did. But I couldn't."

Her mother's hand flew to her mouth. "Oh no. What I meant was for you to spread your wings. To believe in yourself. To do something that you love like I do. I wanted you to be a doctor because it's something that makes me feel so fulfilled. It's not an easy field to work in, but I could pay for the best universities, pass my knowledge on to you. Maybe even pass on my practice. I could finally help you along the way. Not that it could make up for all the times I failed, but still…"

Vera turned off the water and whirled around. "So if I had a chance to be a stay-at-home mom or work in the kitchen, you wouldn't think less of me?"

"Oh, honey. Of course not. I'm so proud of the amazing person you've become. And I don't know what could be more honorable

than being a mother. The most important thing for me is for you to be happy. To be who you want to be."

Her heart swelling, Vera hugged her mother. When she let her mother go, she stared ahead of herself.

Maybe real heroism was being true to yourself. And she'd found herself in the place she'd least expected.

Something that she should've learned from her great-grandmother's letters.

"Grandma, how do you feel about opening a pastry store again?"

Grandma grinned. "If you want to help, I'd love to."

Her mother's words rang in her ears.

Believe in herself.

After all, her name meant "faith."

Loud cheering of her name made her look toward the window.

Of course, it wasn't *her* name. It was a popular one here, after all.

Guitar chords made her still for a moment. Was someone about to serenade her namesake? Oh, to be young and in love. Hopefully, that girl would appreciate what she had.

Vera did her best not to pay attention to a stab of envy as she set the dishes to dry.

Mikhail got up and walked onto the balcony where glass windows rested in wooden frames. "I think you all should look at this."

Grandma hurried out onto the balcony, giggled like a little girl, and rushed back with surprising agility for her age. "Seriously, come here."

Mikhail got their coats and laid Grandma's over her shoulders, then the same with Vera and her mother. "I don't want you to get cold."

"Thanks." Vera stepped onto the balcony and froze, but not from cold.

Her vision must be playing tricks on her.

Hmm, her ears, too, because the voice singing off-key sounded painfully familiar.

That couldn't be…

She blinked and blinked again, expecting the image to disappear.

But there he was, standing, holding a bouquet of red roses and yelling at the top of his lungs now. One of her favorite songs by the boy band she'd loved in high school.

Windows lit in the large building, and a few male voices shouted for Maverick to shut up in Russian, but female voices hushed them up.

The fisherman whom they'd helped out of the icy water was playing the guitar surprisingly well. And the children from the skating rink were forming some words on the snow from the tree branches. A girl in a pink sweater and a matching knit hat was standing on crutches and giving orders on how to spell it better.

When Vera realized what they were trying to spell, she gasped.

How…

Why…

"He should've asked them to spell it in English. Would've been only two words instead of four," Grandma said from the kitchen.

Thankfully, there was some applause when Maverick finished with the song.

He coughed a little as if gearing up for another song.

But Vera wasn't sure someone wouldn't pour a bucket of water over his head. And okay, she needed to feel his arms around her to know all this was real.

"Get over here!" she yelled.

He said something to the children, who were still only on the second word, and rushed inside.

She took in his dear features. "How did you bribe the children?"

She cringed.

Yes, that was the most important question of the day.

He grinned as he handed her the roses. "I promised them candy." He thought a moment. "Lots and lots of candy."

Then he fished out a box from his coat pocket and dropped on one knee. "All my life I was driving in circles while I should've driven to you. The biggest joy for me is to see the joy in your eyes. You make me want to dream, to strive for the better. You make me feel alive. I love you with all my heart, and I was a fool for not realizing it earlier. Will you marry me? You don't have to answer right now. But I needed to ask the question I should've asked at eighteen."

There was loud cheering behind the window, "Skazhi da! Skazhi da! Skazhi da!"

He smiled nervously. "Your grandma told me it means 'say yes'. I hope I didn't butcher the words."

Vera chuckled and glanced at her grandmother, who fluttered her eyelashes innocently.

Vera's every cell filled with delight. "No."

Everyone froze, and her grandmother gasped. Maverick's shoulders slumped.

She hurried to explain, "No, you shouldn't have asked me at eighteen. We had a lot of maturing to do at the time. Our marriage wouldn't have worked out because we were going in different directions."

His gaze pensive, he nodded. "I needed to be the winner then. In everything. I wouldn't have been an equal partner in marriage to you."

"And I wasn't ready to be a wife and a mother or to combine marriage and career. Now, we learned a lot of lessons we needed to learn. God's timing is always the best. Oh, and the answer is yes."

He lifted her and kissed her while Grandma rushed to the balcony and yelled, "*Ona skazala da!*"

"That means, 'She said yes'," Vera whispered to Maverick.

There was more loud cheering.

When Maverick hugged her again, her heart swelled with more happiness than she thought it could hold.

Three days later, Cowboy Crossing.

Standing in the nursery, Maverick couldn't believe this bliss as he hugged his two favorite girls, the scent of baby shampoo making his heart jump into his throat. "I didn't expect Embry to let us have Izzy. I'm still shocked."

Vera stroked his face, and the simple gesture never failed to make his pulse skyrocket. "She did watch us for a while with Izzy. She probably realized the baby would be better off with us. It's a big sacrifice to make, and I'm grateful to her for that."

A small cloud among the sunshine made him frown. "I hope she'll reconcile with Rance. He's still angry with her for deceiving him and leaving a note saying it was his child."

"We'll pray for them. They both need to learn a lot of lessons. At least Rance is staying sober for now. Oh, and to think that Rance forgot to put Embry on the list of potential mothers. Though they'd dated on and off, they'd only been together that way once, and he was too drunk to remember." She shook her head in disbelief, then stepped aside to pick up Izzy's favorite teddy, making him miss her in her arms. "I wish my grandmother found her soul mate, too. She doesn't think things are going to work out with Mikhail."

He winked at her, wanting to do everything to make her happy. "I'll work on a list of eligible bachelors in our town. Maybe we can play matchmakers."

She chuckled as she handed Izzy the teddy bear, causing immediate giggles. "I'd like that. I love Russia—I really do. But I don't want her to move half the world away. She is ecstatic about Izzy, her first great-grandbaby. She forgot about her motorcycle and gun collection and is happily trading them for rattles and toys. Mom is excited, too, and is buying all the baby clothes in sight."

Gratitude warmed him. "I'm glad." It obviously hadn't mattered to the women of Vera's family whether Izzy was related to them by blood or not.

Vera returned his smile. "Oh, and thank you so much for talking to my half brother." She stumbled. "Well, not half brother, really, as we're not related by blood. But I still care about him. You're probably the only person he'd listen to at this point. I didn't even know he was your fan. His… father is finally talking to me."

A pleasant feeling spread inside him at hope in her blue eyes. "I'm glad I could help. And I'll be praying for him."

"Me, too. By the way, we loved your idea of the Christmas drive for the elderly. Grandma is already baking up a storm. I enjoy helping her. And don't worry, everything is edible."

He laughed. "I'm so proud of you. For being just who you are."

She looked at him then out the window. "I still admire my great-grandmother a lot. But I finally learned it's about doing what makes your heart soar, not your body. Being with you, with Izzy, even cooking and baking for the unsuspecting citizens of our small town makes my heart soar."

"Mine, too. Well, except for the cooking and baking part."

The sound of her laughter was music to his ears. "I learned that stereotypes are never good beacons. First, we were told that women's place is in the kitchen. Then my mother constantly told me I could be anything, a doctor like her, a pilot like my great-grandmother, or even an astronaut. But what if I was scared of heights or didn't care about studying human organs? I should have the right to that choice, too."

He nodded. "The brightest beacon should be our own compass, staying true to ourselves."

Giggling again, Izzy said, "Daa–*dy*."

He froze. He probably misheard her.

But the gentle smile on Vera's beautiful face said otherwise.

He finally found his tongue. "Did she say what I think she did?"

Vera kissed his cheek. "Well, I sure hope so. I've worked so much with her on that one word."

"Dad–dy," Izzy said again with a gap-toothed grin.

Just when he thought his heart couldn't expand any more, it did.

EPILOGUE

Torn, Jenna stilled near the restaurant window where Maverick and Vera's wedding reception was about to start. She'd stayed in the last pew in church during the wedding ceremony, doing her best to be unnoticed.

Tears prickled her eyes while snowflakes whirled around her.

What was she doing?

How many years would she be hiding? This was her favorite brother getting married, after all, the one she'd loved so much.

Vera had even invited her to be her bridesmaid.

And still, Jenna was missing this wedding, an outsider in her own family.

She drew a deep breath of frosty air as the scent of steak and potatoes drifted from the restaurant. While the previous wedding receptions had been in the family mansion's backyard, cold weather forced this one inside.

A shiver went down her spine, but she didn't move and only ran her arms over her coat and drew the hood lower over her head. She couldn't force herself to go in.

Maybe soon.

But not yet.

At least, she'd found out who'd followed her in Moscow and had tied up that loose end well upon return. And she'd been extra careful before coming here, so there shouldn't be any trail.

The one bright thing—Maverick and Vera looked deliriously happy together. It had taken them many years, but they'd realized how right they were for each other. She smiled at an unexpected warmth.

She wished them all the happiness that eluded her during her years of frantic searches in Europe.

Only to yield zero results.

She shuddered, not so much from cold, though it was getting frosty, as from memories.

The sound of a child's laughter jerked her head up. She'd become too distracted. Usually, she was more alert as her life often depended on it.

Often, it did.

At the sight of a man in a coat and a cowboy hat balancing a large white gift box while trying to shepherd a boy out of the street and back onto the sidewalk, Jenna winced.

Well, of all people!

Her oldest brother's best friend she'd once had a crush on. Surely, Riley hadn't noticed the science geek she'd been then, all acne and braces.

The coat couldn't hide his muscular frame, and he was more attractive than ever. Her heart made a strange movement. It'd been ages since she'd been drawn to anyone, unable to let go of the one man she truly loved, unable to accept the bitter truth.

Probably just muscle memory from her adolescence.

So he had a child now. Maybe more than one. Married, of course. There was no reason for disappointment to stab her insides.

None whatsoever.

She turned away to make sure he didn't recognize her. Yes, many years had passed, and she was different now. Besides, she

was wearing a blonde wig with two braids and long bangs falling on her forehead.

The boy, dressed in an eggplant-color coat and a matching knit beanie, barreled into her, and she staggered and leaned forward.

What on earth!

Then the boy tugged on her braid, making her wig slip a little before she had a chance to block it. He giggled.

"I'm so sorry! I still need to teach him manners." Riley rushed to her and stopped in his tracks. "Jenna?"

She cringed. She really needed to retire if a child could destroy her disguise like this. "Um, hi."

"I'm sorry," the boy said.

Riley looked as uncomfortable as she felt. But somehow, he managed to slide his hand over the gift and hold the boy's hand to keep him rooted in one place. "Hi. I mean, it's great to see you again. I mean, glad you came for your brother's wedding."

When she didn't reply, he shifted his weight from one foot to the other. "Um, aren't you going to go inside?"

She still didn't reply. He probably wondered what was wrong with her.

Then she said slowly, "No."

He didn't comment, just told the boy, "This is my friend, Jenna." Then he introduced the kid to her.

She managed to smile, lean to them, and shake the boy's tiny hand as he eyed her with curiosity. "Great to meet you." Then she straightened out and faced him. "I'm glad you're happily married."

Oh great.

If that wasn't fishing for information, she didn't know what was.

A muscle moved in his jaw. "I'm single. This is my nephew. My sister…" He didn't finish as he glanced at the boy.

Something happened to his sister. "I'm sorry. I–I have to leave."

"Will I see you again?" he asked as if it mattered to him.

Maybe it was finally time to return, or try to.

Just in time for Christmas.

THE END

THANK YOU FOR READING

Thank you for reading *Show Me Best Friends*. If you write even several words on Amazon, BookBub, and/or Goodreads, it'll mean a lot to me. You can make a difference! I'm grateful to every person who reads my books, and every review matters to me.

What do you think about the series about single fathers cowboy and curvy heroines? This series has been so much fun to write! If you'd like to read Jenna and Riley's story, that's Book 5, *Show Me my Brother's Best Friend,*

I do love hearing from readers, and if you email me at alexaverde7@gmail.com, or visit me on Goodreads, Facebook, BookBub, or Twitter, you'll make my heart sing. And if you'd like to know about my upcoming releases, please follow me on Amazon. Of course, I'd be thrilled if you looked at my other books, and I pray and hope they'll bring you joy and encouragement.

For giveaways, news, free ebooks, and recipes, please sign up for my newsletter. Subscribers have access to exclusive subscriber-only contests, subscriber free ebooks, and book news. Emails won't arrive more than weekly; your email address will never be passed on to anyone else, and you can unsubscribe at any time. Also, you'll get the download link for a FREE sweet Christian romance ebook, *Season of Mercy*, as soon as you confirm your email address as a thank you gift.

Thank you very much for sharing your time with me and my books, and I hope we'll meet again. God bless you.

With love,
Alexa Verde

ABOUT ALEXA VERDE

ALEXA VERDE writes sweet, wholesome books about faith, love, and murder. She has had 200 short stories, articles, and poems published in the five languages that she speaks. She has bachelor's degrees in English and Spanish, a master's in Russian, and enjoys writing about characters with diverse cultures. She's worn the hats of reporter, teacher, translator, model (even one day counts!), caretaker, and secretary, but thinks that the writer's hat suits her the best.

After traveling the world and living in both hemispheres, she calls a small town in south Texas home. The latter is an inspiration for the fictional setting of her series *Rios Azules Christmas* and *Secrets of Rios Azules.*

Please visit Alexa's website for more of her books and to sign up for her email newsletter: www.alexaverde.com

You can also find Alexa on social media:
Facebook : alexaverdeauthor
Twitter : alexaverde3
Goodreads : 8180452.Alexa_Verde
Bookbub : authors/alexa-verde
Amazon : amazon.com/author/alexaverde

Books by Alexa Verde

Christian Contemporary Romance

COWBOY CROSSING

Show Me A Marriage of Convenience (Book 1) (Kade and Heather

Show Me A Second Chance (Book 2) (Mac and Kimberly)

Show Me The Boss (Book 3) (Liberty and Kansas)

Show Me Best Friends (Book 4) (Maverick and Vera)

Show Me my Brother's Best Friend (Book 5) (Jenna and Riley)

Show Me a Family for Christmas (Book 6) (Conner and Gwendolyn)

Show Me a Mistaken Identity (Book 7) (Cat and Roberto)

Show Me a Fake Fiancé (Book 8) (Nelly and Constanzo)

Show Me a Stand-In Husband (Book 9) (Aurora and Carter)

RIOS AZULES CHRISTMAS SERIES

In Love by Christmas Box Set (Season of Miracles, Season of Joy, Season of Hope)

Season of Miracles (*Book 1*) (Arturo and Lana)

Season of Joy (*Book 2*) (Dylan and Joy)

Season of Hope (*Book 3*) (Brandon and Kelly)

Christmas Love & Joy Box Set (Season of Love, Season of Miracles, Season of Joy)

RIOS AZULES ROMANCES: THE MACALISTERS SERIES

Season of Romance (*Book 1*) (Andrey and Melinda)

Season of Love (*Book 2*) (Petr and Lacy-Jane)

Season of Amor (*Book 3*) (Ray and Sylvia)

CHAPEL COVE ROMANCES SERIES
Love Me
Hold Me
Belong with Me

Christian Multicultural Romantic Suspense
Sweet, wholesome books about faith, love, and murder

SECRETS OF RIOS AZULES SERIES
Welcome to Rios Azules, a small south Texas town, where rivers and emotions run deep and the secrets are deadly.
Dangerous Love Box Set (Color of Danger,
Taste of Danger, Touch of Danger)
River of Danger (*Prequel*) (Jacob and River)
Color of Danger (*Book 1*) (Luke and Mari)
Taste of Danger (*Book 2*) (James and Soledad)
Touch of Danger (*Book 3*) (Ivan and Julia)
Scent of Danger (*Book 4*) (Connor and Maya)

ACKNOWLEDGMENTS

Special thanks go to:

First of all, thank You to God for putting up with me and for all the blessings!

A millions thanks to you, my readers, for reading my books, for sending me encouragement, and for supporting me.

Heartfelt thanks to author Jessie Gussman for coming up with the idea for this series and for helping me so much on the way. Jessie, you make me laugh, you make me smile, and you make the world a better place.

Many thanks to my street team, Alexa's Amazing Readers, and to my beta readers, whom I love to pieces. Kim, Trudy, Paula, Susan, Jean, Deanna, Sarah, and Andrea, you're all amazing. Thank you, Renate and Edwina, for helping me to name several characters in this book. Thanks to Robin and Lisa for helping me name the horses. Special thanks to Helen for suggesting Nehemiah, Miah for short.

I thank you wonderful editor, Deirdre, for coming through for me every time.

Last but in no way the least, thank you, Autumn. You're the best part of me.